SUPER

STORIES OF

HEROES

& VILLAINS

Interior and cover design by Elizabeth Story
Author photo by Marc Tessier

Tachyon Publications
1459 18th Street #139
San Francisco, CA 94107
(415) 285-5615
www.tachyonpublications.com
tachyon@tachyonpublications.com

Series Editor: Jacob Weisman
Project Editor: Jill Roberts

ISBN 13: 978-1-61696-103-9
ISBN 10: 1-61696-103-1

Printed in the United States of America by Worzalla
First Edition: 2013
9 8 7 6 5 4 3 2 1

FOR PHILIP JOSÉ FARMER, STEVE GERBER, AND JACK KIRBY

SUPER STORIES OF HEROES & VILLAINS

EDITED BY CLAUDE LALUMIÈRE!

TACHYON • SAN FRANCISCO

CONTENTS!

INTRODUCTION:
THE RETURN OF THE SUPER STORY

The concept of the superhero may have crystallized in the comics, with the 1938 publication of the first Superman story in *Action Comics* #1, and then evolved and been nurtured and expanded upon for the next few decades in the pages of comic books, with the creation of archetypal characters such as Batman, Captain Marvel, Captain America, Wonder Woman, Plastic Man, Spider-Man, Doctor Strange, the Fantastic Four, the Question, and the Black Panther. But the time for that type of character and storytelling was ripe, and, in the years before Superman burst on the scene with more power than a locomotive, prose fiction proved to be a fertile testing ground for the superhero genre—as even a cursory survey demonstrates.

At the dawn of the twentieth century, Baroness Emma Orczy gave us an early noteworthy example of a masked vigilante: the Scarlet Pimpernel. The idea of a man so driven to fight injustice that he would be willing to let the reputation of his true identity suffer, to appear in public life as a spineless coward, is a trope by now familiar to all superhero readers.

In 1912, Edgar Rice Burroughs laid down solid foundations for the super-human hero with the first appearances of two proto-superheroes: John Carter in the serial *Under the Moons of Mars* (famously retitled *A Princess of Mars* for its book publication) and Tarzan, both in *All-Story Magazine*. John Carter gained superhuman strength under Mars's lighter gravity (not unlike, say, a Krypto-nian on Earth) and Tarzan was the pinnacle of human achievement, a self-made superman whose mind and body operated at peak efficiency (like, for example, Batman).

Johnston McCulley's "The Curse of Capistrano" (1919, from *All-Story Weekly*) improved on the Scarlet Pimpernel formula and got us even closer to Batman by introducing the enduring character of Zorro, whose underground lair, dark horse of exceptional speed, civilian identity of Don Diego de la Vega, and dark caped costume are clear antecedents of the Batcave, the Batmobile, playboy Bruce Wayne, and the Batman's own dark caped costume.

Reviewing the Bison Books reprint of Philip Wylie's groundbreaking 1930 SF novel, *Gladiator*, I wrote:

> Philip Wylie's *Gladiator* is often cited as the inspiration behind Superman. The parallels are obvious: both Hugo Danner and Clark Kent grow up in rural small-town America, possessing powers far beyond the common mortal; both are imbued, from an early age, with a profound sense of fairness and justice; and they hide their respective secrets from the world at large. The resemblance is even more obvious when you consider the original 1930s conception of Superman. Their powers are the same: great strength, skin so tough that it can withstand just about anything short of an explosive artillery shell, and the ability to jump so high and so far that it almost gives the impression of flight. And both, despite their superhuman status, espouse a political philosophy that celebrates the common human being over capitalist elites.
>
> In *Gladiator*, readers will find the roots of other superheroic icons. Hugo Danner's scientific creation and upbringing by a scientist father recall Doc Savage's origins. And rarely mentioned are *Gladiator*'s links to Spider-Man. The prototype for the famous scene in which the fledgling Spider-Man defeats a hulking wrestler to make money is found in Wylie's novel; Hugo's bout in the ring is eerily similar to Spider-Man's as seen in 1962's *Amazing Fantasy* #15 (a scene later filmed by Sam Raimi in 2002's *Spider-Man*). Even Spider-Man's famous motto—"With great power comes great responsibility"—is touched upon during Hugo's many ruminations about his place in the world. At one point, in this novel from the pre-superhero era, Hugo even considers using his powers as a vigilante crimefighter!
>
> (*—Sci Fi Weekly* 2004)

The following year, in 1931, the Shadow jumped from being the host (but not yet protagonist) of a radio series to full-fledged gunslinging, justice-wielding character with the publication of *The Shadow* #1, officially kicking off the era of the hero pulps. By 1933, hero pulps were all the rage, with characters such as the Moon Man, the Phantom Detective, the Spider, and, most notably, Doc Savage.

Proto-superheroes also appeared in other media—for example: the Lone Ranger (1933) and his great-nephew the Green Hornet (1936) on the radio; Lee Falk's two famous characters, Mandrake the Magician (1934) and the Phantom (1936), in newspaper comic strips—but the bulk of the early mythweaving was done in prose fiction.

After decades of being primarily associated with comic books, superheroes are now all over the media landscape. While never altogether disappearing from prose fiction, the genre was marginalized in literary circles for much of the mid-twentieth century. Since the 1980s, superhero fiction has been gradually reclaiming its rightful place as a full-fledged prose genre. The groundswell from dedicated writers and readers has borne fruit, with superhero anthologies and novels now appearing regularly from both mainstream and genre imprints. Here, we present some of the best examples of superhero short fiction by some of today's most exciting writers of imaginative fiction, culled from this thrilling era of resurgence.

Claude Lalumière
Vancouver, BC, January 2013

ÜBERMENSCH!

KIM NEWMAN

Kim Newman is a master of postmodern pulp. The question was never whether he would appear in this anthology but rather which story among his many superb superhero stories I might use. Even when not directly dealing with superheroes, much of his fiction is imbued with the aura of the genre; particularly noteworthy in this regard are the collections *Famous Monsters* and *The Original Dr. Shade and Other Stories*, as well as the Diogenes Club series: *The Man from the Diogenes Club*, *The Secret Files of the Diogenes Club*, and *Mysteries of the Diogenes Club*.

O n the way from the aeroport, the cab driver asked him if he had ever been to Metropolis before.

"I was born here," Avram said, German unfamiliar in his mouth. So many years of English in America, then Hebrew in Israel. In the last forty years, he'd used Portuguese more than his native tongue. He had never been a German in his heart, no more than he was now an Israeli. That was one thing Hitler, and his grandparents, had been right about.

He had been—he was—a Jew.

This was not the Metropolis he remembered. Gleaming skyscrapers still rose to the clouds, aircars flitting awkwardly between them, but on this grey early spring day, their facades were shabby, uncleaned. The robotrix on traffic duty outside the aeroport had been limping, dysfunctional, sparks pouring from her burnished copper thigh. Standing on the tarmac, Avram had realised that the pounding in the ground was stilled. The subterranean factories and power plants had been destroyed or shut down during the War.

"That's where the wall was," the driver said as they passed a hundred yards of wasteland which ran through the city of the future as if one of Mr. Reagan's orbital lasers had accidentally cut a swath across Germany. The satellite weapons were just so much more junk now, Avram supposed. The world that needed the orbital laser was gone.

Just like the world which needed his crusade.

Perhaps, after today, he could spend his remaining years playing chess with a death-diminished circle of old friends, then die from the strain of playing competitive video games with his quick-fingered grandchildren.

"That used to be East Metropolis," the driver said.

Avram tried to superimpose the city of his memory on these faceless streets. So much of Metropolis was post-war construction, now dilapidated. The cafés and gymnasia of his youth were twice forgotten. There wasn't a McDonald's on every corner yet, but that would come. A boarded-up shack near the wall, once a security checkpoint, was covered in graffiti. Amid the anti-Russian, pro-democracy slogans, Avram saw a tiny red swastika. He had been seeing posters for the forthcoming elections, and could not help but remember who had taken office the last time a united Germany held a democratic election.

He thanked the driver, explaining "I just wanted to see where it was."

"Where now, sir?"

Avram got the words out, "Spandau Prison."

The man clammed up, and Avram felt guilty. The driver was a child, born and raised with the now never-to-be-germinated seeds of World War Three. Avram's crusade was just an embarrassing old reminder. When these people talked about the bad old days, they meant when the city was divided by concrete. Not when it was the shining flame of fascism.

The prison was ahead, a black mediaeval castle among plain concrete block buildings. The force field shone faintly emerald. Apparently the effect was more noticeable from outer space. John Glenn had mentioned it, a fog lantern in the cloud cover over Europe.

The cab could go no further than the perimeter, but he was expected. From the main gate, he was escorted by a young officer—an American—from the Allied detachment that had guarded the man in the fortress for forty-five years.

Avram thought of the Allies, FDR embracing Uncle Joe at Yalta. Old allies, and now—thanks to the baldpate with the blotch—allies anew. If old alliances were being resumed, old evils—old enmities—could stir too.

Captain Siegel called himself Jewish, and babbled sincere admiration. "As a child, you were my hero, sir. That's why I'm here. When you caught Eichmann, Mengele, the Red Skull..."

"Don't trust heroes, young man," he said, hating the pomposity in his voice, "that's the lesson of this green lantern."

Siegel was shut up, like the cab driver had been. Avram was instantly sorry, but could not apologise. He wondered when he had turned into his old professor, too scholarly to care for his pupils' feelings, too unbending to see the value of ignorant enthusiasm.

Probably, it had started with the tattoo on his arm. The bland clerk with the bodkin was the face that, more than any other, stayed with him as the image of National Socialism. These days, almost all young men looked like the tattooist to Avram.

The cab driver had, and now so did Captain Siegel. So did most of the guards who patrolled the corridors and grounds of this prison.

Not since Napoleon had a single prisoner warranted such careful attention.

"Jerome," Siegel said, summoning a sergeant. "Show Mr. Blumenthal your rifle."

The soldier held out his weapon for inspection. Avram knew little about guns, but saw this was out of the ordinary, with its bulky breech and surprisingly slender barrel. A green LED in the stock showed it was fully charged.

"The beam-gun is just for him," Siegel said.

"Ahh, the green stuff."

Siegel smiled. "Yes, the green stuff. I'm not a scientist..."

"Neither am I, any more."

"It has something to do with the element's instability. The weapon directs particles. Even a glancing hit would kill him in a flash."

Avram remembered Rotwang—one of "our" Germans in the fifties—toiling over the cyclotron, trying to wrestle free the secrets of the extra-terrestrial element. Rotwang, with his metal hand and shock of hair, was dead of leukaemia, another man of tomorrow raging against his imprisonment in yesterday.

Jerome took the rifle back, and resumed his post.

"There've been no escape attempts," Avram commented.

"There couldn't be."

Avram nearly laughed. "He surrendered, Captain. Green stuff or not, this place couldn't hold him if he wanted to leave."

Siegel—born when the prisoner had already been in his cell twenty years—was shocked. "Mr. Blumenthal, careful..."

Avram realised what it was that frightened the boy in uniform, what made every soldier in this place nervous twenty-four hours a day.

"He can hear us, can't he? Even through the lead shields?"

Siegel nodded minutely, as if he were the prisoner, trying to pass an unseen signal to a comrade in the exercise yard.

"You live with the knowledge all your life," Avram said, tapping his temple, "but you never think what it means. That's science, Captain. Taking knowledge you've always had, and thinking what it means..."

After the War, he had been at Oak Ridge, working with the green stuff. Then the crusade called him away. Others had fathered the K-Bomb. Teller and Rotwang built bigger and better Doomsday Devices—while Oppie went into internal exile and the Rosenbergs to the electric chair—thrusting into a future so bright you could only look at it through protective goggles. Meanwhile, Avram Blumenthal had been cleaning up the last garbage of the past. So many names, so many Nazis. He had spent more time in Paraguay and Brazil than in New York and Tel Aviv.

But it had been worth it. His tattoo would not stop hurting until the last of the monsters was gone. If monsters they were.

"Through here, sir," Siegel said, ushering him into a bare office. There was a desk, with chairs either side of it.

"You have one hour."

"That should be enough. Thank you."

Siegel left the room. Even after so short a time on his legs, Avram felt better sitting down. Nobody lives forever.

Almost nobody.

When they brought him in, he filled the room. His chest was a solid slab under his prison fatigues, and the jaw was an iron horseshoe. Not the faintest trace of grey in his blue-black hair, the kiss-curl still a jaunty comma. The horn-rimmed glasses couldn't disguise him.

Avram did not get up.

"Curt Kessler?" he asked, redundantly.

Grinning, the prisoner sat down. "You thought perhaps they had the wrong man all these years."

"No," he admitted, fussing with the cigarette case, taking out one of his strong roll-ups. "Do you mind if I smoke?"

"Can't hurt me. I used to warn the children against tobacco, though."

Avram lit up, and sucked bitter smoke into his lungs. The habit couldn't hurt him either, not any more.

"Avram the Avenger," Kessler said, not without admiration. "I was wondering when they'd let you get to see me."

"My request has been in for many years, but with the changes..."

The changes did not need to be explained.

"I confess," Kessler said, "I've no idea why you wanted this interview."

Avram had no easy answer. "You consented to it."

"Of course. I talk to so few people these days. The guards are superstitious about me."

Avram could understand that. Across the table, he could feel Kessler's strength. He remembered the old uniform, so familiar in the thirties. The light brown body-stocking, with black trunks, boots and cloak. A black swastika in the red circle on the chest. He'd grinned down from a hundred propaganda posters like an Aryan demi-god, strode through the walkways of Metropolis as Siegfried reborn with X-ray eyes.

He felt he owed Kessler an explanation. "You're the last."

Kessler's mouth flashed amusement, "Am I? What about Ivan the Terrible?"

"A guard. Just a geriatric thug. Barely worth the bullet it'd take to finish him."

"'Barely worth the bullet.' I heard things like that so many times, Avram. And what of the führer? I understand he could be regrown from tissue samples. In '45, Mengele..."

Avram laughed. "There's no tissue left, Kessler. I burned Mengele's jungle paradise. The skin-scraps he had were of dubious provenance."

"I understand genetic patterns can be reproduced exactly. I try to follow science, you know. If you keep an ear out, you pick things up. In Japan, they're doing fascinating work."

"Not my field."

"Of course. You're an atom man. You should have stayed with Rotwang. The Master Engineer needed your input. He could have overcome his distaste with your racial origins if you'd given him a few good suggestions. Without you, the K-Bomb was ultimately a dead end."

"So?"

Kessler laughed. "You are right. So what? It's hard to remember how excited you all were in the fifties about the remains of my home planet. Anything radio-active was highly stimulating to the Americans. To the Russians too."

Avram couldn't believe this man was older than him. But, as a child, he had seen the brown streak in the skies, had watched the newsreels, had read the breathless reports in the *Tages Welt*.

"If things had been otherwise, I might have been Russian," Kessler said. "The Soviet Union is the largest country on the planet. If you threw a dart at a map of the world, you'd most likely hit it. Strange to think what it'd have been like if my little dart had missed Bavaria. Of course, I'd have been superfluous. The USSR already had its "man of steel." Maybe my dart should have struck the wheatfields of Kansas, or the jungles of Africa. I could have done worse than be raised by apes."

"You admit, then, that you are him?"

Kessler took off his glasses, showing clear blue eyes. "Has there ever really been any doubt?"

"Not when you didn't grow old."

"Do you want me to prove myself? You have a lump of coal for me to squeeze?"

It hit Avram that this young-seeming man, conversing in unaccented German, was hardly even human. If Hitler hadn't got in the way, humanity might have found a champion in him. Or learned more of the stars than Willy Ley imagined.

"Why weren't you in the army? In some SS elite division?"

"Curt Kessler was—what is the American expression?—4F. A weakling who wouldn't be accepted, even in the last days when dotards and children were being slapped in uniform and tossed against the juggernaut. I believe I did my best for my führer."

"You were curiously inactive during the war."

Kessler shrugged. "I admit my great days were behind me. The thirties were my time. Then, there seemed to be struggles worth fighting, enemies worth besting."

"Only 'seemed to be'?"

"It was long ago. Do you remember my enemies? Dr Mabuse? His criminal empire was like a spider's web. The führer himself asked me to root it out and destroy it. He poisoned young Germans with drugs and spiritualism. Was I wrong to persecute him? And the others? Graf von Orlok, the nosferatu? Dr Caligari, and his somnambulist killers? The child-slayer they called 'M'? Stephen Orlac, the pianist with the murderer's hands."

Avram remembered, the names bringing back *Tages Welt* headlines. Most of the stories had born the Curt Kessler byline. Everyone had wondered how the reporter knew so many details. Germany's criminals had been symptomatic creatures then, twisted and stunted in soul and body, almost an embodiment of the national sickness. And Kessler, no less than the straight-limbed blonds trotted out as exemplars of National Socialism, made the pop-eyed, needle-fingered, crook-backed fiends seem like walking piles of filth. As a child, Avram's nightmares had been of the whistling "M" and taloned nosferatu, not handsome tattooists and smart-uniformed bureaucrats. It was possible for a whole country to be wrong.

"They're all gone," Kessler said, "but they'll never go away really. I understand Mabuse's nightclub is due to reopen. The Westerners who've been flooding in since the wall came down like to remember the decadent days. They have the order of history wrong, and associate the cabarets with us, forgetting that we were pure in mind and body, that we closed down the pornographic spectacles. They'll have their doomrock rather than jazz, but the rot will creep back. Mabuse was like the hydra. I'd think he was dead or hopelessly mad, but he'd always come back, always with new deviltry. Perhaps he'll return again. They never found the body."

"And if he returns, will others come back?"

Kessler shrugged again, huge shoulders straining his fatigues. "You were right. Adolf Hitler is dead, National Socialism with him. You don't need X-ray vision to see that."

Avram knew Kessler could never get tired as he had got tired, but he wondered whether this man of steel was truly world-weary. Forty-five years of knowing everything and doing nothing could be as brutally ache-making as the infirmities visited upon any other old man.

"Tell me about your childhood."

Kessler was amused by the new tack. "Caligari always used to harp on about that, too. He was a strange kind of medieval Freudian, I suppose, digging into men's minds in search of power. He wanted to get me into his asylum, and pick me apart. We are shaped by our early lives, of course. But there's more to it than that. Believe me, I should know. I have a unique perspective."

"There are no new questions for us, Kessler. We must always turn back to the old ones."

"Very well, it's your hour. You have so few left, and I have so many. If you want old stories, I shall give you them. You know about my real parents. Everybody does. I wish I could say I remember my birthplace but I can't, any more than anyone remembers the first days of their life. The dart was my father's semen, the Earth my mother's womb. I was conceived when the dart ejaculated me into the forest. That is my first memory, the overwhelming of my senses. I could hear, see, smell and taste everything. Birds miles away, blades of grass close to, icy streams running, a wolf's dung attracting flies. I screamed. That was my first reaction to this Earth. My screams brought people to me."

"Your parents?"

"Johann and Marte. They lived in the woods just outside Kleinberg. Berchtesgarten was barely an arrow's-reach away."

"How were you raised?"

"There was a war. Johann and Marte had lost four true sons. So they kept the baby they found."

"When did you realise you were different?"

"When my father beat me and I felt nothing. I knew then I was privileged. Later, when I joined the Party, I felt much the same. Sometimes, I would ask to be beaten, to show I could withstand it. There were those among us too glad to oblige me. I wore out whips with my back."

"You left Kleinberg as a young man?"

"Everyone wanted to go to the big city. Metropolis was the world of the future. We would put a woman on the moon one day soon, and robots would do all our work. There would be floating platforms in the seas for refuelling aeroplanes, a transatlantic tunnel linking continents. It was a glorious vision. We were obsessed not with where we were going, but with how fast we would get there."

"You—I mean, Curt—you became a reporter?"

"Poor, fumbling Curt. What a big oaf he was. I miss him very much. Reporters could be heroes in the thirties. I was on the *Tages Welt* when Per Weiss made it a Party paper. It's hard to remember when it was a struggle, when the Mabuses and the Orloks were in control and we were the revolutionaries. That was when it became exciting, when we knew we could make a difference."

"When did you start..."

"My other career? An accident. Johann always tried to make me ashamed of what I was, insisted I keep myself hidden. That was the reason for the eyeglasses, for the fumbling idiocy. But 'M' was at large, and I knew—knew with my eyes and ears—who he was. I could not catch him as Curt Kessler and the police would not listen to me, so the man inside came out."

The man named "M" had been turned over to the police, eventually. There had been little left of him. He had spent the rest of his life in Caligari's asylum, in the cell next to the often-vacant room they reserved for Dr Mabuse. He never killed again, and he would have been unable to rape even if the opportunity arose.

"Why the uniform?"

Kessler smiled again, teeth gleaming ivory. "We all loved uniforms, then. All Germans did. The cloak might have been excessive, but those were excessive times. Theatre commissionaires looked like Field Marshals. I was at the rallies, flying in with my torch, standing behind the führer, making the speeches Luise wrote for me. All men want to be heroes."

"You were a Party member? A Nazi?"

"Yes. Even before I came to Metropolis. We prided ourselves in Bavaria on seeing the future well before the decadents of the cities."

"They say it was the woman who brought you into the Party?"

"Luise? No, if anything, she followed me. The real me, that is. Not Curt. She always despised Curt Kessler."

"Was that difficult for you?"

"It was impossible," Kessler smiled. "Poor Luise. She was born to be a heroine, Avram. She might not have been blonde, but she had everything else. The eyes, the face, the limbs, the hips. She was born to make babies for the führer. Goebbels was fond of her. She wrote many of his scripts before she began broadcasting herself. She was our Valkyrie then, an inspiration to the nation. She committed suicide in 1945. When the Russians were coming. Like many German women."

"Luise Lang would have faced a War Crimes tribunal."

"True. Her other Aryan quality was that she wasn't very bright. She was too silly to refuse the corruptions that came with privilege. She didn't mean any of the things she did, because she never thought them through."

"Unlike you?"

"By then, I was thinking too much. We stopped speaking during the War. I could foresee thousands of differing futures, and was not inclined to do anything to make any of them come to pass. Goering asked me to forestall the Allies in Normandy, you know."

"Your failure to comply was extensively documented at your own trial."

"I could have done it. I could have changed the course of history. But I didn't."

Avram applauded, slowly.

"You are right to be cynical, Avram. It's easier to do nothing than to change history. You could have given Truman the K-Bomb, but you went ghost-hunting in Paraguay."

"I'm not like you," he said, surprised by his own vehemence.

"No one is."

"Don't be so sure."

Kessler looked surprised. "There've been other visitors? No, of course not. I'd have known. I scan the skies. Sometimes things move, but galaxies away. There were no other darts, no tests with dogs or little girls. Since Professor Ten Brincken passed away, no one has even tried to duplicate me as a homunculus. That, I admit, was a battle. The distorted, bottle-grown image of me wore me out more than any of the others. More than Mackie Messer's green knives, more than Nosferatu's rat hordes, more even than Ten Brincken's artificial whore Alraune."

Ten Brincken had been second only to Rotwang as the premier scientific genius of Metropolis. Either could have been the equal of Einstein if they had had the heart to go with their minds.

"I am reminded more and more of the twenties and thirties," Kessler said. "I understand they want to get the underground factories working again. Microchip technology could revive Rotwang's robots. Vorsprung durch technik, as they say. The future is finally arriving. Fifty years too late."

"You could be released to see it."

The suggestion gave the prisoner pause. "These glowing walls don't keep me in, Avram, they keep you out. I need my shell. I couldn't soar into the air any more. A missile would stop me as an arrow downs a hawk. The little men who rule the world wouldn't like me as competition."

Avram had no doubt this man could make the world his own. If he chose to lead instead of follow.

"I've seen swastikas in this city," Avram said. "I've heard Germans say Hitler was right about the Jewish problem. I've seen Israelis invoke Hitler's holocaust to excuse their own exterminations. The world could be ready for you again."

"Strength, Purity and the Aryan Way?"

"It could happen again."

Kessler shook his head. "No one eats worms twice, Avram. I was at the torchlight processions, and the pogroms. I wrestled the nosferatu beyond the sunrise, and I saw shopkeepers machine-gunned by Stormtroopers. I was at Berchtesgarten, and Auschwitz. I lost my taste for National Socialism when the stench of ovens was all I could smell. Even if I went to China or Saturn, I could still taste the human smoke. I surrendered, remember? To Eisenhower personally. And I've shut myself up here. Buried myself. Even the human race has learned its lesson."

Avram understood how out of date the man of tomorrow's understanding was. "You're an old man, Kessler. Like me. Only old men remember. In America, seventy-five percent of high school children don't know Russia and the United States fought on the same side in the Second World War. The lesson has faded. Germany is whole again, and Germans are grumbling about the Jews, the gypsies, the Japanese even. It's not just Germany. In Hungary, in Russia, in the Moslem countries, in America and Britain, in Israel, I see the same things happening. There's a terrible glamour to it. And you're that glamour. The children who chalk swastikas don't know what the symbol means. They don't remember the swastika from the flag, but from your chest. They make television miniseries about you."

Kessler sat back, still as a steel statue. He could not read minds, but he could understand.

"When I was a boy, a little Jewish boy in Metropolis, I too looked up at the skies. I didn't know you hated me because of my religion, because of the religion my parents practiced no more than I did. I wore a black blanket as a cloak, and wished I could fly, wished I could outrace a streamlined train, wished I could catch Mackie Messer. Do you remember the golem?"

Kessler did. "Your rabbi Judah ben Bezalel raised the creature from clay in Prague, then brought it to Metropolis to kill the führer. I smashed it."

The echo of that blow still sounded in Avram's head.

"I saw you do it. I cheered you, and my playmates beat me. The golem was the monster, and you were the hero. Later, I learned different."

He rolled up his shirtsleeve, to show the tattoo.

"I had already seen that," Kessler said, tapping his eyes. "I can see through clothing. It was always an amusing pastime. It was useful at the cabarets. I saw the singer, Lola..."

"After you killed the golem," Avram continued, "all the children took fragments of the clay. They became our totems. And the brownshirts came into the Jewish quarter and burned us out. They were looking for monsters, and found only us. My parents, my sisters, my friends. They're all dead. You had gone on to Nuremberg, to present Hitler with the scroll you snatched from the monster's chest."

"I won't insult you by apologising."

Avram's heart was beating twice its normal rate. Kessler looked concerned for him. He could look into another's chest, of course.

"There's nothing I could do to make reparation. Your family is dead, but so is my whole planet. I have to live with the guilt. That's why I'm here."

"But you are here, and as long as you remain, you're a living swastika. The fools out there who don't remember raise your image high, venerate you. I know you've been offered freedom by the Allies on six separate occasions. You could have flown out of here if you'd consented to topple Chairman Mao or Saddam Hussein, or become a living weather satellite, flitting here and there to avert floods and hurricanes. Some say the world needs its heroes. I say they're wrong."

Kessler sat still for a long time, then finally admitted, "As do I."

Avram took the heavy metal slug from his cigarette case, and set it on the table between them.

"I've had this since I was at Oak Ridge. You wouldn't believe how much of the stuff Rotwang collected, even before they found a way to synthesise it. The shell is lead."

The prisoner played with his glasses. His face was too open, too honest. His thoughts were never guarded. Sometimes, for all his intelligence, he could seem simple-minded.

"You can bite through lead," Avram said.

"Bullets can't hurt me," Kessler replied, a little of the old spark in his eyes.

"So you have a way out."

Kessler picked up the slug, and rolled it in his hand.

"Without you in the world, maybe the fire won't start again."

"But maybe it will. It started without me last time."

"I admit that. That's why it's your decision, Curt."

Kessler nodded, and popped the slug into his mouth. It distended his cheek like a boiled sweet.

"Was I really your hero?"

Avram nodded. "You were."

"I'm sorry," Kessler said, biting through the lead, swallowing.

He did not fade away to mist like the nosferatu, nor fragment into shards like the golem. He did not even grow old and wither to a skeleton. He just died.

Guards rushed in, confused and concerned. There must have been a monitor in the room. They pointed guns at Avram, even though their beams couldn't hurt him. Doctors were summoned, with enough bizarre machinery to revive a broken doll or resurrect a homunculus from the chemical stew. They could do nothing.

Avram remembered the destruction of the golem. Afterwards, the brown streak had paused to wave at the children before leaping up, up and away into the skies of Metropolis. They had all been young then, and expected to live forever.

Captain Siegel was upset, and couldn't understand. Doubtless, his career would be wrecked because this thing had happened during his watch. The Russians would insist an American take the blame. Siegel kept asking questions.

"How did he die?"

"He died like a man," Avram said. "Which, all considered, was quite an achievement."

A KNIGHT OF GHOSTS AND SHADOWS
CHRIS ROBERSON

In addition to being the brains behind MonkeyBrain—which, in its various incarnations, has published excellent superhero and neopulp prose fiction, nonfiction, and comics—Chris Roberson has recently delved into the raw matter of superhero fiction by writing the comics series *Masked*, which features an assemblage of classic pulp heroes—the Shadow, the Spider, the Green Hornet and Kato, and more—united in one epic adventure.

As the chimes of midnight rang out from the tolling bells above, a hail of argent death rained from the twin silver-plated Colt .45s onto the macabre invaders from the Otherworld, and the cathedral echoed with the eerie laughter of that silver-skulled avenger of the night—THE WRAITH.

FROM THE SECRET JOURNALS OF ALISTAIR FREEMAN
SATURDAY, OCTOBER 31, 1942

I dreamt of that day in the Yucatan again last night. Trees turned the color of bone by drought, skies black with the smoke and ash of swidden burning for cultivation, the forest heavy with the smell of death. Cager was with me, still living, but Jules Bonaventure and his father had already fled, though in waking reality they had still been there when the creatures had claimed Cager's life.

As the camazotz came out of the bone forest towards us, their bat-wings stirring vortices in the smoke, I turned to tell my friend not to worry, and that the daykeepers would come to save us with their silvered blades at any moment. But it was no longer Cager beside me, but my sister Mindel, and in the strange logic of dreams we weren't in Mexico of '25 anymore, but on a street in Manhattan's

Lower East Side more than a dozen years before. And I realized that the smoke and ash were no longer from forest cover being burned for planting, but from the flames of the Triangle Shirtwaist Factory fire that had ended her young life. "Don Javier will never get here from Mexico in time," I told my sister, as though it made perfect sense, but she just smiled and said, "Don't worry, Alter. This is the road to Xibalba." Then the demons had arrived, but instead of claws, they attacked us with the twine-cutting hook-rings of a newsvendor, and we were powerless to stop them.

Charlotte is still out of town visiting her mother, and won't be back until tomorrow. When I awoke alone in the darkened room this morning, it took me a moment to recall when and where I was. In no mood to return to unsettling dreams, I rose early and began my day.

I ate alone, coffee and toast, and skimmed the morning papers. News of the Sarah Pennington murder trial again crowded war-reports from the front page of *The Recondito Clarion*, and above the fold was a grainy photograph of the two young men, Joe Dominguez and Felix Uresti, who have been charged with the girl's abduction and murder. Had it not been an attractive blonde who'd gone missing, I'm forced to wonder whether the papers would devote quite so many column inches to the story. But then again there were nearly as many articles this morning on the Sleepy Lagoon murder case just getting underway down in Los Angeles, where seventeen Mexican youths are being tried for the murder of Jose Diaz. Perhaps the attention is more due to the defendants' zoot-suits and duck-tail-combs, and to Governor Olson's call to stamp out juvenile delinquency. If the governor had the power simply to round up every pachuco in the state and put them in camps, like Roosevelt has done with the Japanese, I think Olson would exercise the right in a heartbeat.

I didn't fail to notice the item buried in the back pages about the third frozen body found in the city's back alleys in as many nights, but I didn't need any reminder of my failure to locate the latest demon.

But this new interloper from the Otherworld has not come alone. Incursions and possessions have been on the rise in Recondito the last few weeks, and I've been running behind on the latest *Wraith* novel as a result. I spent the day typing, and by the time the last page of "The Return of the Goblin King" came off my Underwood's roller it was late afternoon and time for me to get to work. My *real* work.

As the sun sank over the Pacific, the streets of the Oceanview neighborhood were crowded with pint-sized ghosts and witches, pirates and cowboys. With little care for wars and murder trials, much less the otherworldly threats which lurk unseen in the shadows, the young took to their trick-or-treating with a will. But with sugar rationing limiting their potential haul of treats, I imagine it wasn't long before they turned to tricks, and by tomorrow morning I'm sure the neighborhood will be garlanded with soaped windows and egged cars.

I can only hope that dawn doesn't find another frozen victim of the city's latest invader, too. After my failure tonight, any new blood spilled would be on my hands—and perhaps on the hands of my clowned-up imitator, as well.

The dive bars and diners along Almeria Street were in full swing, and on the street corners out front pachucos in their zoot-suits and felt hats strutted like prize cockerels before the girls, as if their pocket chains glinting in the streetlights could lure the ladies to their sides.

On Mission Avenue I passed the theaters and arenas which cater to the city's poorer denizens, plastered with playbills for upcoming touring companies, boxing matches, and musical performances. One poster advertised an exhibition of Mexican wrestling, and featured a crude painting of shirtless behemoths with faces hidden behind leather masks. A few doors down a cinema marquee announced the debut next week of *Road to Morocco*. I remembered my dead sister's words in last night's dream, and entertained the brief fantasy of Hope and Crosby in daykeepers' black robes and silver-skull masks, blustering their way through the five houses of initiation.

The last light of day was fading from the western sky when I reached the cemetery, wreathed in the shadows of Augustus Powell's towering spires atop the Church of the Holy Saint Anthony. A few mourners lingered from the day's funeral services, standing beside freshly filled graves, but otherwise the grounds were empty.

I made my way to the Freeman family crypt, and passing the entrance continued on to the back, where a copse of trees grow a few feet away from the structure's unbroken rear wall.

As Don Javier had taught me a lifetime ago in the Rattling House, I started towards the wall, and an instant before colliding with it turned aside towards an unseen direction, and shadowed my way through to the other side.

Don Mateo was waiting for me within. He'd already changed out of his hearse-driver's uniform, and had dressed in his customary blue serge suit, Western shirt printed with bucking broncos and open at the neck, a red sash of homespun cotton wound around his waist like a cummerbund.

"Little brother," he said, a smile deepening the wrinkles around the corners of his eyes. He raised his shotglass filled to the rim with homemade cane liquor in a kind of salute. "You're just in time."

When Mateo speaks in English it usually means that he's uncertain about something, but when he gets excited—or angry—he lapses back into Yucatan.

Tonight he'd spoken in Spanish, typically a sign his mood was light, and when I greeted him I was happy to do the same.

"To your health," I then added in English, and taking the shotglass from his hands downed the contents in a single gulp, then spat on the floor a libation to the spirits. Don Javier always insisted that there were beneficent dwellers in the Otherworld, and libations in their honor might win their favor. But while I'd learned in the years I spent living with the two daykeepers, either in their cabin in the forest or in the hidden temples of Xibalba, to honor the customs handed down by their Mayan forebears, and knew that the villains and monsters of their beliefs were all-too-real, I still have trouble imagining that there are any intelligences existing beyond reality's veil which have anything but ill intent for mankind.

When I'd finished my shot, Don Mateo poured another for himself, and drank the contents and spat the libation just as ritual demanded. Then, the necessary business of the greeting concluded, he set the glass and bottle aside, and began to shove open the lid of the coffin in which my tools are stored.

"Four nights you've hunted this demon, little brother," he said, lifting out the inky black greatcoat and handing it over. "Perhaps tonight will be the night."

I drew the greatcoat on over my suit. "Three victims already is three too many." Settling the attached short cape over my shoulders, I fastened the buttons. "But what kind of demon freezes its victims to death?"

The old daykeeper treated me to a grin, shrugging. "You are the one with the Sight, not I." His grin began to falter as he handed over the shoulder-holster rig. "Though Don Javier might have known."

I checked the spring releases on both of the silver-plated Colt .45s and then arranged the short cape over my shoulders to conceal them. "Perhaps," I said. But it had been years since the great owl of the old daykeeper had visited us in dreams.

As I slid a half-dozen loaded clips, pouches of salt, a Zippo lighter, and a small collection of crystals into the greatcoat's pockets, Don Mateo held the mask out to me, the light from the bare bulb overhead glinting on the skull's silvered surface.

The metal of the mask cool against my cheeks and forehead always reminds me of the weeks and months I spent in the Rattling House, learning to shadow through solid objects, cold patches left behind as I rotated back into the world. I never did master the art of shifting to other branches of the World Tree, though, much to Don Javier's regret.

The slouch hat was last out of the coffin, and when I settled it on my head Don Mateo regarded me with something like paternal pride. "I should like to see those upstarts in San Francisco and Chicago cut so fine a figure."

The mask hid my scowl, for which I was grateful.

Since beginning my nocturnal activities in Recondito in '31 I've apparently inspired others to follow suit—the Black Hand in San Francisco, the Scarlet Scarab in New York, the Scorpion in Chicago. Perhaps the pulp magazine's ruse works as intended, and like so many here in the city they assume the Wraith to be entirely fictional. There are times when I regret the decision to hide in plain sight, fictionalizing accounts of my activities in the pages of *The Wraith Magazine* so that any reports of a silver-masked figure seen lurking through the streets of Recondito will be written off as an over-imaginative reader with more costuming skill than sense.

But noisome as such crass imitators are, whether inspired by the reality or the fiction, as I tooled up this evening I never imagined that I'd be forced to contend with one here in my own city.

Don Mateo recited a benediction, invoking the names Dark Jaguar and Macaw House, the first mother-father pair of daykeepers, and of White Sparkstriker who had brought the knowledge to our branch of the World Tree. He called upon Ah Puch the Fleshless, the patron deity of Xibalba, to guide our hands and expand my sight. Had we still been in the Yucatan, the old daykeeper would have worn his half-mask of jaguar pelt, and burned incense as offering to his forebears' gods. Since coming to California, though, he's gradually relaxed his observances, and now the curling smoke of a smoldering Lucky Strike usually suffices.

This demon of cold has struck the days previous without pattern or warning, once each in Northside, Hyde Park, and the waterfront. When Don Mateo and I headed out in the hearse, as a result, we proceeded at random, roaming from neighborhood to neighborhood, the old daykeeper on the lookout for any signs of disturbance, me searching not with my eyes but with my Sight for any intrusion from the Otherworld.

I glimpsed some evidence of incursion near the Pinnacle Tower, but quickly determined it was another of Carmody's damnable "experiments." I've warned Rex before that I won't allow his Institute to put the city at risk unnecessarily, but they have proven useful on rare occasion so I haven't yet taken any serious steps to curtail their activities. I know that his wife agrees with me, though, if only for the sake of their son Jacob.

I caught a glimpse of the cold demon in the Financial District, and I shadowed out of the moving hearse and into the dark alley with a Colt in one hand and a fistful of salt in the other, ready to disrupt the invader's tenuous connection to reality. But I'd not even gotten a good look at the demon when it turned in midair and vanished entirely from view.

The body of the demon's fourth and latest victim lay at my feet. It was an older man, looking like a statue that had been toppled off its base. Arms up in a defensive posture, one foot held aloft to take a step the victim never completed. On the victim's face, hoarfrost riming the line of his jaw, was an expression of shock and terror, and eyes that would never see again had shattered in their sockets like glass. But before I'd even had a chance to examine the body further I heard the sounds of screaming from the next street over.

There is a body, I Sent to Don Mateo's thoughts as I raced down the alleyway to investigate. Had the demon retreated from reality only to reemerge a short distance away?

But it was no denizen of the Otherworld menacing the young woman huddled in the wan pool of the streetlamp's light. Her attackers were of a far more mundane variety—or so I believed. I pocketed the salt, and filled both hands with silver-plated steel.

Eleven years writing purple prose for *The Wraith Magazine*, and it creeps even into my private thoughts. Ernest would doubtless consider his point made, if he knew, and that bet made in Paris decades ago finally to be won.

The young woman was Mexican, and from her dress I took her to be a housekeeper, likely returning from a day's work cleaning one of the miniature mansions that lined the avenues of Northside. She was sprawled on the pavement, one shoe off, arms raised to shield her face. Two men stood over her, Caucasians in dungarees, workshirts, and heavy boots. The older of the two had the faded blue of old tattoos shadowing his forearms, suggesting a previous career in the merchant marine, while the younger had the seedy look of a garden-variety hoodlum. With hands clenched in fists and teeth bared, it was unclear whether they wanted to beat the poor girl or take advantage of her—likely both, and in that order.

The hoodlum reached down and grabbed the woman's arm roughly, and as he attempted to yank her to her feet she looked up and her gaze fell on me. Or rather, her gaze fell on the mask, which in the shadows she might have taken to be a disembodied silver skull floating in the darkness. Already terrified by her attackers, the woman's eyes widened on seeing me, and her shouts for help fell into a hushed, awestruck silence.

The prevention of crime, even acts of violence, is not the Wraith's primary mission, nor did the situation seem at first glance to have any bearing on my quest for vengeance, but still I couldn't stand idly by and see an innocent imperiled. But even before springing into action my Sight caught a glimpse of the tendril which rose from the shoulders of the tattooed man, disappearing in an unseen direction. No mere sailor down on his luck, the tattooed man was possessed, being "ridden" by an intelligence from beyond space and time. And protecting the people of Recondito from such incursions *is* the mission of the Wraith—and if the Ridden was in league with those whom I suspected, vengeance might be served, as well.

"*Unhand her,*" I said, stepping out of the shadows and into view. I Sent as I spoke, the reverberation of thought and sound having a disorienting effect on the listener that I often used to my advantage. "*Or answer to me.*"

The two men turned, and while the hoodlum snarled at my interruption, there glinted in the eyes of the Ridden a dark glimmer of recognition.

The possessed, or Ridden, can be deterred by running water and by fire, both of which tend to disorient them, but neither is capable of stopping them altogether. Even killing the Ridden's body is not a permanent solution, since the Otherworldly parasite will continue to move and operate the body even in death. The only way to put a Ridden down is to introduce pure silver into the body, by bullet or by blade, which serves to sever the connection between the parasite and host.

That's where my twin Colts come in.

The hoodlum released his hold on the woman's arm, letting her slump back onto the pavement, as the Ridden turned to face me, his eyes darting to the silver-plated .45s in my fists. I wondered whether the hoodlum knew that his companion was more than he seemed to the naked eye.

Typically the Ridden I encounter in Recondito are lackeys of the Guildhall, working as muscle for a political machine whose methods and reach would have eclipsed Tammany Hall in its heyday; the demon parasites from beyond are offered the chance to experience the sensual joys of reality in exchange for their services, while the hosts are most often thugs-for-hire who have disappointed their employers once too often. That one of the two attackers was Ridden suggested strongly that these two were Guildhall bruisers enjoying a night away from roughing up the machine's political enemies.

"*Now step away,*" I ordered, aiming a pistol at each of them.

After I recovered Cager's body from the jungle, I took his Colt M1911 and my own and plated them with silver from the daykeeper's secret mine, and cast silver bullets to match. I usually carry a pistol in either hand, but make it a habit never to fire more than one at a time. Despite what the pulp magazines would have readers believe, no one can hit the broadside of a barn firing two guns at once. The first time I tried it, honing my skills in the forest above Xibalba, the recoil drove the pistol in my left hand crashing into the one in my right, with my thumb caught in-between, the skin scraped off like cheese through a grater. And though the gloves I wear as the Wraith would save me from another such injury, I've found that the second Colt is much more useful as a ward against attack—the silver serving to keep any Ridden from venturing too close—and then ready with a full magazine to fire if the seven rounds in the other pistol run out before the job is done.

The silver of the Colt in my right hand was enough to make the Ridden think twice about rushing me, while the bullets in the Colt in my left were sufficient to give the hoodlum pause—I wouldn't fire on a man who wasn't possessed unless it was absolutely necessary, but it was clear that *he* didn't know that.

"*Por favor...*" the woman said in pleading tones, scuttling back across the pavement from me, seeming as frightened of the Wraith's silver mask as she'd been of her two attackers' fists only moments before. "*Ayuda me...*" I knew it wasn't me she was asking for help. But then, who? The shadows?

I intended to end the suffering of the Ridden's host-body, a single silver bullet driving the parasite back to its home beyond the sky, and to chase the hoodlum into the night with enough fear instilled in him that he wouldn't soon menace another girl walking alone by night.

"*Now,*" I said and Sent, gesturing towards the hoodlum with the Colt in my left hand, "*one of you I shall send back to your Guildhall masters with a message...*"

The hoodlum began to turn away, shifting his weight as he prepared to take to his heels and flee.

I smiled behind my mask, raising the pistol in my right hand and training it between the eyes of the Ridden. "*...and the other shall* be *that message...*"

And then, the arrival of my clowned-up imitator made a hash of all my plans.

"No, *malvado*," came a somewhat muffled voice shouting from the shadows, "you're not going anywhere!"

Before the hoodlum knew what had hit him, a blur of silver and black came rushing out of the shadows, tackling him to the ground. Raining a welter of blows down on the hoodlum's head and shoulders, the newcomer kept his opponent pinned to the ground like a wrestler on a mat. And the impression of a wrestler was only strengthened when he looked up in my direction and I saw the black leather mask he wore—it was of the same type as those worn by the Mexican wrestlers, but this one had a stylized white skull stitched over the face.

The young woman still huddled at the edge of the streetlamp's light, looking in wide-eyed shock at the strange figure dispensing a beating on her erstwhile attacker. She whispered, "*Sepultura,*" and I wondered why she spoke of the grave.

"Don't worry, *señorita,*" the masked man said, leaping to his feet and striking a faintly ridiculous pose, hands on his hips and arms akimbo. "Sepultura is here to help!"

The masked man—this *Sepultura*—wore a grey boilersuit, black leather para-trooper boots, and black leather gloves, with an Army officer's web belt cinched at his waist with pouches all around. He stood perhaps a few inches shorter than me, and while he was clearly in fighting trim—the moaning hoodlum on the pavement a testament to the strength of his blows—the ill-fitting boilersuit made him look somewhat paunchy.

"*Depart, interloper!*" I took a half-step forward and waved him away with the barrel of the Colt in my left fist. "*This is none of your concern...*"

In the confusion created by the arrival of this so-called Sepultura, the Ridden saw the opportunity to escape. And while I warned the masked fool away, the tattooed Ridden spun on his heel and started to run away in the opposite direction.

"Don't worry, *Señor* Wraith," Sepultura said with a jaunty wave, lunging after the fleeing Ridden. "I'll stop him..."

The Ridden looked back and glared at the pursuing Sepultura, and the phantasm which clung to the Ridden's shoulders flared bright with hatred, feeding off the emotions of its host body.

At that precise moment Sepultura stumbled, throwing his hands up before him protectively, his eyes widening in surprise visibly behind the eye-slits of his mask.

The Ridden was already several strides away, and increasing the distance between us with every footfall. But Sepultura was now directly in my way, and any shot fired might strike him by mistake. Fool that he clearly was, I wasn't about to shoot him down, but at the same time I wasn't going to let the Ridden escape back into the city.

"*Fiend!*" I shouted, Sending out waves of anger to disorient the parasite's senses. I took two steps forward and before colliding with Sepultura I shadowed, ghosting right through him and only returning fully to reality when I was clear on the other side. "*Give my regards to hell!*"

I fired a single round from the .45 in my right fist, the silver slug catching the Ridden just above his left shoulder-blade, driving through his heart, and exiting out the front. As the host body shouted a quick bark of pain, I could See the parasite's tendrils recoiling in aversion to the silver, retreating back beyond the walls of reality. By the time the tattooed form collapsed to the pavement, life slipping away, the parasite was already gone.

I turned, ready to render aid to the young woman and to Sepultura an admonishment to keep out of my business. But there was no sign of either of them, the moaning form of the hoodlum all that remained in the streetlamp's pool of light.

I rejoined Don Mateo in the hearse and we resumed our rounds of the city's streets, though I didn't catch the slightest glimpse of the cold demon again tonight. It was not until relating to Don Mateo the encounter with the young woman, her attackers, and the masked meddler that I realized that the white skull emblazoned on Sepultura's leather mask must have been inspired by my own silver skull.

Bad enough that I have imitators in San Francisco, Chicago, and New York, but *now* I have to contend with one right here in Recondito?

> *The crooked police officer turned, a still-smoking revolver in his hands, and froze at the sight of a black-shrouded silver skull emerging from the darkness. "The last innocent has suffered at your hands, recreant," grimly intoned THE WRAITH.*

SUNDAY, NOVEMBER 1, 1942

I awoke well before dawn this morning, my shuttered bedroom drenched in inky darkness. As so often happens when I find myself in dark silence so complete, I fancied that I was still an initiate in the Dark House, learning to expand my senses beyond the mundane five. Could the dozen years since have been one long dream, and at any moment Don Javier might bring a lantern and lead me out into the daylight once more? Or perhaps even Xibalba was a dream, and I am still a child in the Lower East Side, racked with fever and lying in my parents' bed, all alone in our rooms as mother, father, and sister are away at work. If my whole life since then *were* a fever dream it would explain a great deal. Wartime adventures, European wandering, jungle expeditions, hidden temples, secret orders, invaders from beyond—easily the stuff of a child's fevered imagination.

I sometimes wonder whether the situation isn't even more prosaic than that. How easy it would be to believe that I, a Jew posing as a Gentile, became dissatisfied with too ordinary a life and simply created one more worth the living. Rather than a masked avenger who passes his activities off as fiction, I could be a writer of cheap fictions who imagines himself the heroic figure about whom he writes.

But all too quickly my idle musings in the night can turn darker. I remembered the chill of the Rattling House, and Don Javier's lessons about shadowing and shifting. And though I mastered the art of shadowing through solid objects, my one attempt to shift away from reality entirely ended in disaster, with only the beacon of Don Javier's Sent thoughts to guide me back to the here and now. But for a brief instant I was lost in the Unreal, adrift in that space that is no space, a realm which the mundane senses are completely incapable of perceiving—the only impression I have of unreality is that of unending cold and darkness.

Don Javier had taught me about those who get lost in the midst of shifting, unable ever to return. Some are initiates like I had been, trained in the use of their Talents, but others are merely ordinary men and women who don't realize the skills they possess until it is too late. Most who have the Sight but not the training are driven mad by the voices in the end, and those who shadow without first learning the art can return to the Real with their hearts on the wrong sides of their bodies, or with their internal organs on the outside and their skin and hair buried within.

All over Mexico the story is told of *La Llorona*, the Wailing Woman, but only in Xibalba is it understood that she was an untrained shifter unable to realign with reality, stuck forever between the Real and the Unreal, invisible to all except for those who possess the Sight.

When I refused to continue studying the art of shifting, I never admitted that it was because I feared following in the ghostly footsteps of *La Llorona*, feared becoming an insubstantial figure belonging neither to this world or the next. But considering that Don Javier could peer right into my thoughts, I imagine I didn't have to say a thing.

The latest *Wraith* novel complete, and Charlotte not due to return until later in the day, I rose early, shaved and bathed, and having dressed in a freshly laundered suit made my way to the cemetery. Even at that early hour, there were any number of Mexican families already gathering at the gravesides of their loved ones, preparing for *Dia de los Muertos*.

When I shadowed unseen through the rear wall of the crypt, Don Mateo had breakfast waiting for me—hot coffee laced with cinnamon, fresh thick corn tortillas, and meat jerky broiled on an open flame.

The old daykeeper was in a sentimental mood, perhaps inspired by the Day of the Dead celebrations only now getting underway outside, and fell to talking about the Yucatan jungle as we sipped our steaming cups of coffee.

I asked him if he ever regrets coming with me to Recondito, leaving behind the only life and home he'd ever known.

Don Mateo was philosophical about the whole matter. "When the doors to the Unreal began to close in Mexico, the daykeepers gradually lost their purpose. Recondito is now the most active of the true places. Where else should my duty take me than here?"

I realized today that I am now almost as old as Mateo was when he and Don Javier first found me in the jungle, close to death after the attack of the camazotz. Don Mateo had already seemed so old, to be only in his middle forties. But then, when my father was forty-three years old, he'd already been an old man, as well, or had seemed like one in the eyes of his young son. I don't *feel* old—at least, not until a full night's patrol, when my joints ache from the chill of shadowing and my muscles grow as taut as steel knots—but there are lines around the eyes that stare back from my mirror, and the streak of white that's been in my hair since Cager's death is growing steadily larger. I'll eventually have a full head of white hair with a single streak of black, assuming I should live so long.

I stayed and chatted idly with Don Mateo as the morning wore on, as we serviced my tools, casting new bullets out of the lumps of silver ore we'd brought from Xibalba, honing the edges on the silver blades I carry up my sleeves.

When a glance at my wristwatch showed me that noon was approaching, I made my farewells to Don Mateo and arranged to meet him back at the crypt that evening for another patrol. For the moment, though, I intended to head over to Charlotte's place and welcome her home in style.

By the time I left the crypt Mass had ended at Saint Anthony's, and the Mexican families who'd been just beginning to gather in the early morning were now settling in, decorating the graves of their loved ones with *ofrendas*—golden marigolds to attract the souls of the dead, toys atop the tiny graves of the dearly departed *los angelitos,* and bottles of tequila or mezcal for their full-grown relations. Everywhere could be seen *confite, calvera, pan de muerto,* and *calacas*—or candy, sugar skulls, "bread of the dead," and miniature figurines of skeletons dressed in the clothes of the living.

In the stories Cager told me of Recondito, the Oceanview neighborhood was described as the home of Irish sailors and seamstresses who worked hard, drank their fill, and prayed for forgiveness come Sunday morning. When I first moved to the city, having taken my friend's name and identity as my own, I quickly settled on a townhouse in Oceanview, close by the cemetery where Don Mateo had found employment. But while my new Irish neighbors were always quick to complain about the growing number of Mexicans moving into the area, I found that the oldest headstones in the cemetery were inscribed with Spanish surnames, dating back to the time when a Franciscan mission had stood on the ground Saint Anthony's now occupied, back when this part of Recondito was little more than a collection of rude huts housing the new city's principle workforce. Though there are increasing numbers of newcomers immigrating from Mexico to Recondito every day—bringing the zoot-suiter gangs and their violence with them—the Irish didn't make their way to the Hidden City until the turn of the current century, after generations of their Hispanic neighbors had been born, christened in the Church of the Holy Saint Anthony, and buried in old age in the adjacent cemetery.

As I made my way out of the cemetery this morning, I passed a heated argument underway in the shadow of one of the largest and oldest of the headstones, a family marker inscribed simply with the name "AGUILAR," with smaller stones placed in front marking individual burial plots. The two men shouting at one another might have been father and son. The older was dressed soberly, having likely just walked out of the morning's church service, but the younger was a pachuco in high-waisted baggy pants held up by suspenders, the legs cuffed over double-soled Florsheim shoes, his hair slicked back with pomade in a duck-tail-comb.

In a mix of Spanish and English, switching back and forth sometimes in the span of a single sentence, the two men were heatedly discussing the Sarah Pennington murder trial, the young man apparently taking the position that the defendants had been unfairly accused, the older arguing that the two simply *had* to be mixed up with gangs and violence, or else why would they dress as they did. This lead to the young man demanding to know whether the older man was accusing *him* of being in a gang, simply because of his manner of dress, and the older man replying that if the double-soled shoe fit...

All of this shot back and forth between the pair before I'd taken six steps past them, when the older man suddenly ended the discussion and my forward motion with a single word: "*Sepultura.*"

I was brought up short, and glanced back over my shoulder at them. It took me a moment to parse out the last sentence I'd heard. The older man had said something like, "Why can't you be more like that Sepultura?"

I wondered for a moment if the older man had simply switched from English to Spanish in mid-sentence again, and had been referring to a "grave" instead of saying the *nom de guerre* of my latest imitator.

But then he went on, saying, "*Sepultura* saved your cousin last night from *violadores*. He is a hero to our people. What are you but *un delincuente juvenil*?"

The young man seemed to deflate, like the fight had gone out of him, and instead of shouting back he covered his mouth, as if concealing his expression. I noted a cross tattooed inexpertly on the fleshy part of his right hand between thumb and forefinger. Most likely a gang sign of some kind, I reasoned.

The older man noticed me looking their way, no doubt seeing the expression of annoyance on my face, and I hastened to look away, continuing out of the cemetery and onto the street. It was several blocks before my fists unclenched at my sides.

How long *has* this Sepultura clown been skulking about the shadows of Recondito without me noticing? Or has he, like the zoot-suiters, come to my city from elsewhere, perhaps arriving from Mexico with the wrestling exhibition? It would explain the leather mask, if so.

I'd forgotten to bring the present I picked up last week for Charlotte, so stopped by my place to get it before heading over to her apartment. But when I got home, I found Charlotte waiting for me there, brewing a fresh pot of coffee and idly paging through a book bound in green leather. In gilt letters on the front cover was the title, *Myths and Legends of Varadeaux*.

"I thought you despised this translation," Charlotte said, without looking up from the pages.

"I do," I answered, draping my suitcoat over a chair and coming to stand beside her. "But I knew you'd love the Xenophon Brade illustrations. Besides, once you take it home I won't have to look at Lovelock's execrable translation anymore, so it hardly matters."

Snapping the book shut, Charlotte looked up at me with eyes widening. "This is for *me*? But Alter, it must have cost a *fortune*."

Charlotte is the only person who calls me Alter. But then, she's only one of two people still living who know that it was Alistair Micjah "Cager" Freeman who died in the Yucatan back in '25 and not his former squadmate and traveling companion, Alter Friedman. But then, "Alter" wasn't my name either, not really. My parents had already lost two previous babies when I was born on the ship en route from Romania, with my sister Mindel being their only child to survive to that point. I was sickly and small, and my mother insisted that my given name never be spoken aloud for fear that it would alert the *nit-gute* to my presence. Instead, they'd call me Alter, as if calling me "old man" would foil whatever plans the *malekhamoves* had for me. How surprised my mother would have been, to learn that her little baby had grown up to be the Angel of Death himself, in a sense.

"It wasn't cheap," I answered, putting my arm around her shoulders, "but my girl is worth it."

Charlotte leapt to her feet and planted a kiss on my lips, and then spun away with a laugh. "Wait right here, I've got something for you, too."

"What, did Mother McKee knit me another pair of socks?"

She came back with an oversized portfolio in hand, and slugged me playfully in the shoulder. "You should be so lucky. It took Ma *years* to knit that last pair."

Untying the stays on the portfolio, Charlotte slid onto the table's surface a canvas mounted on wooden stretchers, twenty-two inches by thirty, and covered in oils.

"It's the cover for *The Hydra Falls*," she said, eyes searching my expression for approval. "What do you think?"

The painting depicts the Wraith on a rooftop with a crescent moon high overhead, muzzle-flare lighting up the barrels of both Colt .45s as he fires on a massive nine-headed dragon that is rearing up over the skyline of Recondito.

"It's perfect, Red." And it was...even though the real Mr. Hydra stood no taller than six foot three and looked more like George Raft than St. George's Dragon. But the reading public didn't need to know the reality. What mattered to them was the illusion. "And I know that Julie will be glad to have it. Another day and he was going to have to run a stock image, instead."

"Oh, phooey," Charlotte said, waving a hand dismissively. "Bernhardt can go hang. I *told* him I'd finish it when I was away, didn't I?"

I wasn't in any mood to argue about our mutual editor, and let the matter lie, ending the discussion with another kiss.

As Charlotte carefully packaged back up the painting, I poured us a pair of coffees. Do any of the faithful readers of *The Wraith Magazine* suspect that the "Chas. A. McKee" who provides the macabre and otherworldly covers and illustrations for the magazine is "Charlotte McKee"? Would they enjoy her work any less if they did?

But if they don't suspect that the illustrator is a Vassar grad and knockout, they don't even *dream* that the Wraith of the stories might be anything other than a nameless spirit of vengeance, or that there is a living man behind that skull of silver steel.

"I made dinner reservations at that place in Little Canton," I called from the kitchen, and Charlotte replied with a short yelp of delight. Never come between a woman and her dumplings, I have found.

I glanced at a recent issue of *The Wraith* lying on the side table, showing my silver-skulled alter ego in close combat with a brace of demons. Like so many of the other paintings Charlotte had done over the years, this one was drawn from life. She was one of those rare people born with the Sight, able to peer beyond the everyday and see the things that lurk unnoticed in the shadows. That's what brought us together in the first place, years ago, and it's what makes her perfect to illustrate my stories. Even when she exercises a bit of artistic license, as when she imagines Jacob Hydra as an oversized dragon, she draws on her own experiences with invaders from the Otherworld as a model.

"I missed you, Red," I told her as I carried the coffees from the kitchen. She'd only been gone a week, and it had felt like an eternity.

"Come here," she said, taking the cups and setting them on the table next to the book and portfolio, careful not to spill. Then, with the coffee safely out of the way, she grabbed hold of my shirt front and pulled me close, her breath hot on my neck. "*Here's* what you missed, I'll bet."

I'll draw a curtain across the remainder of the day, but suffice it to say that the coffee cooled untouched on the table, and we never did make it to the restaurant for dinner.

Charlotte's asleep now across my bed, and her slight snores are like music to me—will we ever give up the pretense and move her out of her apartment altogether? The moon is rising over the city, and Don Mateo is waiting for me at the crypt. I'll let her sleep. Perhaps tomorrow she and I can discuss our future together for once, instead of always fleeing headlong from our pasts.

> *"You've worked your employees to their deaths," hissed THE WRAITH, looming over the factory owner who quavered in flickering firelight. The ring of salt the masked avenger had cast on the floor would keep at bay any of the villain's unearthly minions who had not already been driven beyond reality's veil by the flames, leaving their corpulent master defenseless. Black-gloved hands reached out in claws towards the wretch's plump neck. "Now you shall sample a taste of their pain..."*

MONDAY, NOVEMBER 2, 1942

Don Mateo and I found another frozen victim last night, a woman of middle age, this time closer to home at the boundary between the Oceanview and the Ross Village. But we weren't rewarded with another glimpse of the cold demon itself. Five victims so far, at least, and we're no closer to driving the fiend back to the Otherworld.

I slept little after returning home, but well, wrapped in Charlotte's arms, and dozed long after she'd risen in the morning to go deliver the cover painting to Julie. When I finally came to full wakefulness I remembered that I owed him a delivery, too, and dressing quickly set out with the latest *Wraith* manuscript bound up in brown twine under my arm.

Julius Bernhardt looked like a cartoon sitting across the desk, chewing on an unlit cigar with his shirtsleeves rolled up over hairy forearms, already sweating despite the cool November morning. He thumbed through the top few pages of the manuscript, his bushy brows knitted.

"It's another winner, Freeman," he said, slamming his open palm down on the stack of paper. "As soon as that dizzy girlfriend of yours comes through with the next cover, we're set to go. God forbid we have another delay."

I failed to mention that my "dizzy" girl hadn't missed a deadline yet, and that the only delays in *The Wraith*'s publication schedule in years had been when Julie had mismanaged the accounts and left us without the funds to cover the printing costs. If I hadn't stepped in and become a silent partner, Bernhardt would probably have given up shares of the company to the printer and distributor to cover the debts, and the outfit would have ended up a "captive publisher," never able to earn its way out.

There's hardly enough Xibalba silver left to cast bullets these days, though, so I won't be investing in any new publishing schemes anytime soon—not that Julie ever guessed where my funds came from. He's always taken at face value that I'm the heir to the Freeman fortune—and that there *is* a Freeman fortune left to speak of, come to that. When I met Cager, he scarcely had a pot to piss in. The scion of the Freemans, son of one of the oldest and most well-established families in Recondito society, he'd been as dirt poor as me. But while my family never had any fortune to lose, Cager Freeman's fortune in shipping and mining concerns had all been lost after the Guildhall had ruined his father's name and seized his family assets.

"But there's just one thing," Julie said, pulling the soggy stogie from his mouth and gesturing punctuation in the air. "Do you *have* to keep writing stories with crooked cops and politicians as the black hats? Can't you truck out everyday *gangsters* now and again?"

In the trenches of France, Cager had confided to me the strange truth about his father's death, and the unearthly creatures he'd glimpsed that night. It was only later that we made the connection, and realized that a secret cabal in Recondito was in league with dark powers, but of course by then it was all too late. Too late for Cager and his family, at least, but not too late for vengeance. That was half the reason I came to Recondito, and my motivation for taking my friend's identity, to knock the Guildhall off their pins with the thought that the son of their rival had returned from exile to haunt them. The fact that the Guildhall was mixed up in so much of the Otherworldly incursion in the city, in one way or another, just meant that my sacred mission as a daykeeper of Xibalba and my quest to avenge the Freeman family could march together hand-in-hand.

"I'll do what I can," I told Julie, lying through my smile.

Pass up the chance to cast as fictional villains the kind of fiends who are really behind so much of the city's evil? Not on your life.

Promising to turn in the next *Wraith* novel in a fortnight, and not a moment later, I left Julie's office and headed up to Little Canton to meet Charlotte for lunch. The dumplings were every bit as good as she'd promised. Leaving the restaurant, we ambled back through the city in no particular hurry rather than hailing a cab; stopping in at the antiquarian bookstore in the Ross Village to rummage for treasures; getting ice cream at the soda fountain in the drugstore on Odessa Avenue, ignoring the youngsters flapping their garishly colored comic books at one another while arguing the relative merits of one tights-wearing buffoon over another. The newsstands are filled with such poorly written and wretchedly illustrated tripe, crowding out the respectable pulps, and seeing the crude cover illustration of a figure in hood and tights swinging on a rope high over a skyline— and swinging from *what*?—I couldn't help but be reminded of my copycat.

But all in all it was a lazy Monday afternoon and a perfect stroll, marred only by a scuffle we encountered outside the bars on Hauser, a fight having broken out between zoot-suiters and a group of servicemen on leave. Charlotte gripped my arm, whispering that I shouldn't get involved, but the police had already arrived to arrest the pachucos, so there wasn't any reason for me to interfere. For a stretch of a few blocks, with the soldiers and policemen out in full force, rounding up the delinquents, it felt for a moment like Recondito was a city under siege, invaded from outside forces. And considering the demons and the zoot-suiters I suppose it is, in a way.

When we got back to my place, Charlotte couldn't stay, having plans to meet her girlfriends for bridge this afternoon. I'm alone for the moment, the sunlight streaming in through the open window. It's days like this when I wish that my life *was* simply a daydream, and that I was no more and no less than what I pretend to be. A lazy afternoon of dumplings and bookstores and ice-cream sundaes with a pretty girl on my arm? Who *wouldn't* want that life?

Later.

It's late night—or perhaps already early morning—and I've barely the strength to lift my pen, but I feel it necessary to record my thoughts on the evening's events while they're still fresh in my mind.

I have been wrong about so many things.

The cemetery was crowded with families concluding the *Dia de los Muertos* celebrations, and I was forced to Send distractions into the minds of more than a few to cover my approach to the crypt. No one took any notice of the hearse as Don Mateo steered out of the garage and onto the thoroughfare, though I sat back in the shadows of the passenger seat and tilted down the brim of my slouch hat to conceal the glinting silver of my mask.

Down on Bayfront Drive, Don Mateo noticed the metallic taste and buzzing sound of a demon incarnating before my Sight even caught a glimpse, the foul impression left on mundane senses when a tiny portion of the Otherworld's alien physics intrudes on our world. As I shadowed out of the moving hearse, one hand filled with salt crystals and the other with a loaded .45, I thought for certain that we'd located the elusive cold demon at last. But the creature I found on the dock was only a minor shade, a mindless moving patch of darkness, nothing at all like the demon I'd briefly glimpsed on Saturday night.

I pinned the shade in a ring of salt, the bare handful I carried more than enough for the task. And though Don Mateo had the acetylene torch ready in the hearse, the flame of my Zippo lighter was sufficient to drive the creature back to the Otherworld.

There was no chance that so insignificant a demon could have been responsible for the gruesome freezing deaths of recent days. It was only as we pulled away from the docks, and the foul impressions of the incursion faded, that I recalled that my previous brief encounter with the cold demon had not been accompanied by any such sensations.

We headed down Prospect Avenue, past the Guildhall that looms like a medieval fortress over the surrounding buildings, and I could sense the lingering etheric disturbance of every summoning and incarnation, every binding and compact, that the grim masters of the political machine have performed over the years. Generations of Guildhall leaders have made deals with devils, literally and figuratively, to maintain their grip on Recondito, and so far as I'm concerned everyone in the organization has blood on their hands. And while I've been able to curtail their activities to a large extent since taking up the mantle of the Wraith, I am only one man, and have yet to put an end to their dark deeds altogether. Some day, I know, I'll lose my patience, tire of the long game, and storm that castle with guns blazing—and though such an open assault would doubtless mean my life, I'd at least be able to take with me as many of those overfed bastards as possible. But that would leave Recondito unprotected in my absence, and so I marshal my reserves of patience, and continue to take the Guildhall's pieces off the board one pawn at a time.

We made our way through the Financial District, up through Northside, and down through Hyde Park and Ross Village, all without any sign of the cold demon. We skirted Ross University and turned onto Mission Avenue to cut through Oceanview on our way south, and that's when I saw him. Not the demon of cold we'd been seeking, but that imitator who calls himself Sepultura.

He was lurking in an alleyway, his grey boilersuit and black gloves and boots rendering him almost invisible in the shadows, but the stark white skull sewn onto his mask shone in the dim light like the full moon.

Perhaps it was my mounting frustration over my inability to locate the cold demon, or perhaps I was simply annoyed to be reminded that a copycat was skulking around the streets of *my* city, but as soon as I saw Sepultura in the alley I shadowed through the side of the hearse and dove for him, hands out and grasping. Did I intend to throttle him? To knock some sense into his masked head and drive him out of Recondito? I'm not sure, in retrospect, and now I'll never know.

I regained solidity as soon as I passed through the closed door of the hearse, and was less than an eyeblink away from tackling Sepultura to the ground. But to my astonishment he reacted immediately to my sudden appearance before him, diving to one side as I approached. I sailed past, only narrowly avoiding crashing to the rough pavement of the alleyway, and tucked and rolled my way into a crouch. When I spun around, I saw that Sepultura had dropped into a defensive posture, shoulder to me and hands held loosely before him like a wrestler waiting for his opponent to make the next move.

"You've trained," I said in faint admiration. "Not bad." Then I added an undertone of Sent thought to my spoken words, *"But you're no match for the Wraith."*

I surged forward, my greatcoat swirling around me to conceal my arm motions, and my right fist lashed out like a striking cobra at his head.

Sepultura managed to duck to the side and block the blow with his forearm, but just barely, and the force of the impact sent him side-stepping to retain his balance.

"*Órale!*" he said, and I could almost hear him grinning behind his mask. "You're fast." Lightning quick he jabbed straight at my neck with his left. "Always talk about yourself in the third person, though?"

I snapped back in time to avoid the jab, and then swept a leg out in a sidekick, catching him with a glancing blow to the hip. "I've heard you do the same, 'Sepultura.'"

He staggered back, gripping his hip and hissing in pain through the mouth-slit of his mask. But he kept on his feet, and after a split second was back in a defensive posture. "Touché."

He'd managed to shrug off the disorienting effects of my Sending, and was holding his own in hand-to-hand. It was clear that my copycat was not to be dismissed lightly.

"Why did you come to my city?" I demanded.

"*Come* here?" Sepultura snarled. "*Pendejo*, I was *born* here."

I was wearying of this game, and eager to get back to the hunt. Bracing myself, I readied to leap forward and shadow straight through Sepultura, intending to solidify as soon as I was past him and then strike a blow from behind before he knew what had happened. But before I could move he suddenly straightened, his gaze trained past my shoulder at something further up the alleyway.

"Sarah?" he said, arms falling to his sides and shoulders slumping.

I turned, and there before me hovered the demon of cold.

Only it wasn't any demon, whether of cold or any other sort. It was a girl, or rather the ethereal and not-entirely-present specter of a girl. I recognized the murder victim from the front pages of the *Clarion*—Sarah Pennington.

I could feel the waves of cold radiating from her, and my breath fogged in the frigid air as it passed through my skull-mask.

"F-Felix…?" the specter said, in a voice that reverberated strangely with distant echoes.

"No," Sepultura said, and stepped past me, tugging the leather mask from his head. He turned his bare face to the specter above. "It's Beto." He paused, and then said, "Roberto. Roberto Aguilar."

The specter wailed in dismay, and seemed to flicker from view for the briefest of instants.

"Where…where is Felix…?" her echoing voice called out.

The unmasked Sepultura was revealed to be a young Mexican man, no more than twenty years old. He was looking right at the apparition of the girl, though mundane vision would see only an empty alley in front of him. That meant that he had the Sight, though he might never have realized it until now.

But though we live in a demon-haunted world, the spirits of the dead never return to visit the living. There is only one way I know for a live person to become a specter such as floated before us.

The echoing voice of Sarah Pennington howled in sorrow and fear once more, and muttering beneath my breath I named her. "*La Llorona*." Wailing Woman.

I stepped forward and placed my hand on Sepultura's shoulder. "You know this girl?"

He turned to me with wide eyes, looking as though he'd forgotten I was ever standing there. "I didn't think…Felix *couldn't* have hurt her…killed her…"

"Felix!" the specter of Sarah Pennington wailed.

"No one hurt her, son," I said. "And she isn't dead. She is simply…lost."

It was likely the girl hadn't ever imagined that she could shift away from reality. Not until she did it for the first time, and found she couldn't get back.

"She's been seeing my friend Felix," Sepultura finally said. "Felix Uresti. But her dad, he wasn't happy about her dating a Mexican. Said he was going to put an end to it. Joe Dominguez went with Felix to her house, to help her get away from the old man, but Pennington came out with a shotgun. Started shooting in the air like it was the Fourth of July. The way Felix tells it, things went crazy, Sarah came running towards him, then she just…vanished."

Typically the untrained shift instinctively in states of agitation and trauma, often fleeing some perceived danger. The poor girl running away from a shotgun-wielding parent would definitely qualify.

"Felix and Joe took off running," Sepultura continued, "and the next day the police came and carted them away, charged with kidnapping and murder."

"Felix!" the specter wailed, perhaps in response. "Where are you?"

The specter drifted a few feet nearer, and waves of freezing cold lapped over us. I thought back to the Rattling House, and the brief moment I'd spent in the Unreal, that unending realm of darkness and cold. I knew now how the victims had come to be frozen; she'd been searching for a way back, and grabbed hold of anyone she could. How was she to know that her very touch would bring cold death?

Was she too far gone now to attempt to grab onto either of us? Or was the reminder of her lost "Felix" enough to stop her in her tracks, ignoring us because neither of us were the one she sought? I couldn't say, but knew that we would have to put an end to the danger she presented, and soon.

"But you knew your friends were innocent," I said, looking from the specter to the young man beside me. I recognized him now as the young man from the argument I'd overheard in the cemetery.

He nodded. "That's why...well..." He paused, and gestured with the skull-faced mask in his hand. "Sepultura."

"You were trying to clear your friends' names."

The young man drew himself up straighter, lifting his chin. "I'd read all about you in the magazines. I figured, if *he* can do it, then why can't I?" He looked back to the specter. "I never believed that Felix killed the girl, but she *couldn't* have just vanished. I figured that she had slipped away in the confusion, and that someone *else* had nabbed her before she could rejoin Felix. So I put on the mask and started searching the streets, looking for the kind of *cabrón* who would snatch pretty girls. But now that we've found her, we can *prove* Felix and Joe didn't kill her." He glanced over to me, his expression hopeful. "Right?"

I tightened my hand on his shoulder, sympathetically. "I'm afraid it won't be so simple."

I released my hold on his shoulder, and pulled pouches of salt out of my greatcoat's pockets in either hand. I passed one of them to the young man, who accepted it with a questioning look.

"We'll do what we can about your friends," I told him, tugging open the drawstring on the pouch. "But there's something we must do, first."

Though one is a lost human being and the other is a fiend of the Otherworld, there was much in common between the specter before us and the shade that I had banished on the dock earlier tonight. Neither of them can abide crystalline structures of any kind, and the perfectly cubed molecules of everyday salt are particularly anathema. And running water and flames are capable of discomfiting both, and of driving them away from reality.

I motioned the young man to mirror my actions, and began laying down a wide ring of salt on the ground beneath the specter's hovering form.

"I will explain later," I said, not unkindly, when I saw his confused expression.

There is simply no way to end Sarah Pennington's suffering, at least no way that Xibalba ever knew. But it *is* possible to drive her away from reality, pushing her further into the Unreal where she will pose no further risk to the world she's left behind. And god forgive me, I had to do it.

"*Don Mateo*," I Sent to the old daykeeper in the hearse idling a short distance away. "*I'm afraid we will need the acetylene torch.*"

Already the sky outside has begun to lighten, and dawn is not far off. I'm reluctant to sleep, worried that the image of that poor girl will revisit me in my dreams, but I can't keep my eyes open any longer.

> *The city was safe...for now. It was only a matter of time before evil once more imperiled her innocent citizens. But whatever the threat, whether man or monster, from earth or beyond, they would have to contend with the city's ever-vigilant silver-skulled sentinel—THE WRAITH.*

TUESDAY, NOVEMBER 3, 1942

The papers this morning carried the story of how Joe Dominguez and Felix Uresti escaped from jail in the night. The *Clarion* quoted the Recondito Chief of Police as insisting that the two young men could not have broken out of their cells on their own, and must have had outside assistance. The *Telegraph*, never shrinking from sensationalism, quoted an unnamed jailer as saying that "only a *ghost* could get through those walls."

Or a Wraith, I'm tempted to point out.

Without a body to produce, living or dead, there was simply no way of proving the innocence of the two men. Even if I *had* been willing to step forward, reveal myself, and testify in court, the account would simply be too fantastic for a jury to accept. But I could not allow two innocent men to go to the gas chamber, not if I had the power to see justice done.

The two were startled when I shadowed through the wall of their cell, to say the least. But when I explained why I had come, and what awaited them if they remained, they were all too eager to leave with me. Shadowing with even one full-grown man taxes my abilities to their limits, so Uresti had to hide in the darkened alley behind police headquarters while I shadowed back through the brick wall for Dominguez, but by the time I had both of them free Aguilar had arrived with changes of clothes and bus fare for his friends.

They are already on their way south to Mexico, where new lives and new names wait for them. Like my new associate in the boiler-suit and wrestling mask, Dominguez and Uresti were both born in California, and neither have left the country before. But I know they will adapt. They are hardly the first to have to leave the land of their births and adopt new names in order to survive.

A dozen years behind the mask of the Wraith, and I've become too quick to make assumptions. Have I learned so much since the day Don Javier found me in the jungle that there is nothing left for me to be taught? Not hardly.

I had assumed the deaths by freezing to be the work of a demon of cold, though neither Don Mateo nor I had ever heard of any such creature before. Had I stopped and thought a bit more, might I have recognized the telltale signs of an untrained-shifter-turned-specter, one whose touch bled heat away into the Unreal? And if I *had* recognized the signs, might some of those who died at the specter's touch still be alive today? Perhaps.

Too, I was all too quick to assume that a pachuco in zoot-suit was naturally guilty of any accusation. Like the "cold demon" I sought, the young delinquents were an invasion from without, a threat to the security of my city. But like poor Sarah Pennington, boys like Dominguez and Uresti were no invasion, but had been here all along.

I won't be around forever. And one day my patience may wear thin enough for me to storm the gates of the Guildhall and bring that monstrous building crashing down on the fat-cats' heads. When I am gone, there needs to be someone who can pick up where I left off. There must be a successor with the Sight capable of protecting this city against all threats, from without *and* from within.

Last night, Sepultura tangled with the Wraith. (Damn, I *do* refer to myself in third person, don't I?)

Today, assuming he makes our scheduled meeting at the cemetery, Roberto Aguilar will be properly introduced to Alistair Freeman.

And tonight, my successor's training will begin.

I may not be the daykeeper that Don Javier was, but with Don Mateo's help—and assuming that Aguilar is an apt pupil—I will make sure that the legacy of Xibalba does not end with me.

Charlotte will be here soon. I've not seen her since yesterday afternoon, and all she knows about the events of the night is what she might have gleaned from the morning papers. I will have to tell her that I banished an innocent girl to endless exile in unreality, all to safeguard a thankless city—but perhaps not right away. Let me pretend for a moment to be a simple writer of cheap fiction, an old man in fact as well as name, who can turn away from the night's horrors as simply as lifting his hands from his typewriter's keys. I know night will fall, and with it the need to take up the silver mask once more, but give me this one bright moment of sunshine for my own.

Can't I turn away for just an instant, just this once?

And somewhere past the edge of hearing the wailing voice of Sarah Pennington calls out for help that will never arrive, joining the echoes of Cager Freeman's dying cries, and his father's pleas for mercy, and my sister Mindel shouting above the crackling flame, and all of the other countless voices crying out to be avenged...

...and I know that I have my answer.

TRICKSTER
STEVEN BARNES & TANANARIVE DUE

Bestselling authors Steven Barnes and Tananarive Due are best known, respectively, for writing hard SF and horror. In this remarkable and insightful collaboration, from the superhero anthology *The Darker Mask*, they explore some of the stranger—yet subtly persistent—mythic archetypes of the superhero genre.

*T*he American came during the time when the rains shunned us; when the grass withered, the drinking pools grew shallow and the earth revealed its age.

He came in one of the fleet, five-footed Spiders that gleam in the sun. I have painted the day of his arrival on the wall of our sacred cave, where we return once a year to sing new songs to our ancestors. Like my father and his father, I visit Shadow Cave whenever our roaming takes us back to the southwest. There, beneath its vast ceiling and beneath the eyes of my dead fathers, I paint the cave walls with pigments of ground clay with eland fat.

My name is Qutb, which means "protects the people." I am an old man now, and I know many things. My head holds my people's story, which I paint on the cave walls. I draw natural things: animals hunted, raindrops upon my face, the eternal walking circle of giraffe and antelope and lion north through what the white men call the Great Rift Valley, and we of the People call home.

It is difficult to draw the Spiders, because these are not of nature: rounded backs like silver tortoises, yet as big as a hut where even six people could sleep without touching. Five legs racing across the plain faster than a cheetah. White men use Spiders in place of their legs, or the boxes with wheels men rode when I was a boy. It is rare to see a white man walking.

But this stranger was not a white man. Or a black man. His skin was very like mine, but he had orange-red dusk fire hidden underneath his night. He stood a full head taller than me, with a runner's body, although our children could out-run him. He wore pieces of glass held by wire over his eyes, and a white shirt beneath a tan jacket.

He said his name was Cagen. It sounds like Kaggen, the trickster mantis of our stories, he who loves eland well. It is in Kaggen's honor that I use the fat of his best beloved in Shadow Cave.

Like a white man, Cagen had never been taught which roots heal and which kill. He did not know how to dance to please the gods or amuse the ancestors. Any mother would have been ashamed to raise a small child who knew as little as Cagen.

He did not speak the People's tongue, a proper language. But he did speak the Swahili, so we were able to understand each other after a fashion. His skin was too pale for the sun, his head filled with a place called America. He called us his "brothers" because of the night in his skin, but to us he was just another white man who wanted to learn our ways. Our children laughed at him and with him.

He offered our children trinkets and sweets, offered the men tobacco and knife metal, gave my second wife Jappa cloth for a dress. He asked me if I had sons and I said that once I had, but they had gone to the great villages, and I had never seen them again. He said he wanted to learn our stories and knowledge of the plant people. He said his head was empty and he wished knowledge. Empty head! Our children called him Empty Head for a moon.

I laughed and he laughed, as if we had made an agreement. He wished knowledge. I wanted to paint Cagen's story, so I said I would teach him.

I watched Cagen for many days from the corner of my eye; and he never sought a quarrel with our men or a bed with our women, so at last I trusted him. After I knew him for a time, I took him to Shadow Cave to see the paintings my fathers and grandfathers had made. Some I watched my father make, when I was but a boy.

Shadow Cave is at the center of a wheel. My people walk the wheel every few years, moving from place to place for water and game. But the sacred cave is never more than a few days' walk away.

Although the entrance is taller than a man, and wide, we crawl when we enter the cave, a sign of respect. We are all children in the sight of the gods.

Once in, light a torch to watch shadows leap to the spiked ceiling. My heart always leaps to see the smooth stones, the empty rock stream-bed, and most of all the walls covered with endless paintings, some made when men still had tails.

"Ah, you have drawn the war," Cagen said, pointing to my paintings of clouds and lights above a burnt horizon. Some visitors to the sacred cave stared straight at a thing and could not hear what their eyes said. His words gave me hope he might have a mind after all.

I told him we did not call it "war" when I was a boy, fifty summers ago. We called it the time of silent thunder. Thunder you hear with your body, not your ears.

"Not silent!" Cagen said. "Far from silent."

Cagen said that men from another sun came to this world, with strange, strong machines that made the white man's knowledge useless. The machines destroyed the great villages of the world, some even larger than Dar Es Salaam!

I had a hard time believing this, because once I traveled to the markets of Dar Es Salaam, and it must be the largest village in the world. But Cagen told me this, and I tell you what he said. I have inscribed the words he spoke to me in my head and on the cave walls the way my father taught me.

Five rains before, I had heard another story like Cagen's. Then, a white man had come to us, and he knew some of our tongue. He said he was called *Pro-fes-sor*, and his face was half burned away by fire. He must have wandered in the desert for days before finding us, and his mind was gone.

He spent his days digging in the earth for rocks. He told us that when he was a boy in the year he called 1954, a machine fell from the sky, glowing like white gold and spitting fire. He said his mother, his father, his brothers and sisters and everyone he knew died during its rage, and he was lucky to escape with his life. He said he had spent his life searching for ancient treasures of forgotten peoples, that one day he planned to return to his demolished village to collect his own people's treasures so that they, too, would not be forgotten. This was what he said.

"Now men have the machines," he said, weeping from his one eye. It was the last thing he said to us. He dug a few days more, then fell into a fever, and died.

Cagen had not lived as long, but his story was much the same. Once two men have told you the same tale, you must consider that they are telling the truth, no matter how much like a dream the story sounds.

"And what stopped them?" I said. "Did the whites build some great machine to fight for them?"

"No one knows," Cagen said, and shrugged his shoulders. "Lots of guesses, but no answers. Some say disease, some that they fought among themselves. We crawled out from under our rocks, and there were these big metal *things* everywhere. All dead. We pried them open, and studied the machines. We learned from them. The machines changed everything."

"Then they were offerings from the gods," I said. Too often, humans do not give praise to the beings who watch over us.

"That's as good an answer as any," he said.

He told me that the world's chiefs, who ruled the people with what he called *governments*, promised to protect their people from the machines and the sky men who built them. The *governments* traveled as far as the moon to build a great walled village with many guns. Such things are beyond my simple mind. I look up at the moon and see no village, so perhaps this is a lie.

"But we've lost our freedom," Cagen said, gazing at the walls of Shadow Cave. His sigh was as heavy as an old man's. "Everything is so peaceful here. Not like out there."

"Are there not sunsets in your land?"

He laughed, but the sound was not happy. "Yes. But things are…different now. That's what the history books say." He paused. "When you can find a history book. My father was a history teacher."

"Ah. He held your people's stories?"

Cagen smiled. "Yes. But by the end of his life, men like him had a hard time finding work. Where I come from, too many believe it's better to forget the past."

What would become of a people who forget their stories? Surely even white men have grandfathers and grandmothers who must be remembered.

"I think you tease me," I said to him. "You are a trickster, like Kaggen, your name."

"The Mantis," he said. We had spoken of this before.

I took the torch and moved him down to the other side of the cave, and found an image I knew he would like. It may have been painted by my grandfather's grandfather. It was a half-circle of men driving a giraffe over a cliff. Behind them was Kaggen, the Mantis, mighty arms spread wide.

"The Trickster."

"Yes," I said. "The hunters tricked the giraffe into killing itself. They ate well." I paused. "The men from the stars…were they hunters?"

"They killed us. But did they eat? I don't know. I don't think so. We never found out why they killed us. Never."

He stared at the painting of the men, and the giraffe, and the trickster god, as if his heart was close to an understanding too great, or too heavy, for his head. Then we left the cave.

Cagen and I spoke for many days, hours, and then moons. In times of drought, the hunters, even my own sons, have less time to sit at an old man's feet, so I enjoyed Cagen's eager eyes, full of wondering. Not stupid, I learned—he had never been taught. Cagen learned quickly, as if our grandmothers whispered in his ear. Tell him a thing but once, and he could recite it back to you even if you roused him from sleep in the middle of the night.

Among the possessions he brought with him was a small box, a listening machine he called a *radio*. He would play it at night, strange talk and strange music from far away. Our children would try to dance to the music, but they always laughed too hard to dance long.

One afternoon, Cagen toyed with a scraggly red plant with white veins, growing at his feet. Like all things that lived in the earth during that time, the plant thirsted for water during those days. "Is this bloodweed?" he asked.

"Your eyes have grown wiser," I said. "I did not know if you would see it. Tell me what you would do with this."

"Strip off the bark," he said. "Boil to make a paste."

"And?"

"And...spread on wounds to stop the blood."

"After the wounds have been washed. After."

We paused when we heard a whistling sound. Something glided through the sky. It looked like a wheel made of silver-blue metal. As it flew in front of a cloud, it turned white. Against the blue sky a moment later, it turned blue again. Faintly, I could see snake-like tendrils trailing behind it.

Cagen flinched.

"Why should you fear?" I said. "Rejoice. Now they are the white man's machines."

"I'm not a white man," he said.

"You are white on the inside," I said, sorry to insult him so.

"They were left behind after the war," Cagen said quietly. "They could make their own spare parts, and we used those parts to change our world. We started out using them. Now, I think, they're using us."

"What do you mean?" I asked, hoping to learn something new for my cave from this strange young man.

He scratched his head. "Hell, I don't know. No one knows why they came. They just arrived, and started killing. Maybe they were just thinning the herd. Trying to do us a favor. Hell, I don't know. Sometimes I think that our own government is turning into a bigger threat than the aliens ever were."

"Why don't you go to your elders and tell them that they are wrong?"

"I don't even know who our leaders *are* any more. And I don't know anyone who does."

"Your villages are so large that you don't know your grandmothers and fathers?"

Cagen did not answer. He seemed terribly tired.

"You go home soon," I said to him one night as we watched the moon. It was almost full. "I think you don't want to go."

Cagen sighed. Then his eyes brightened. "Can we go to Modimo's Hand before I leave?"

Modimo is the Big God, the one who made all the others, who in turn made the mountains and clouds and animals and men. The place we call Modimo's Hand is a clearing surrounded by four oblong stones jutting from the ground, two days walk south from where our people camped. It is sacred to all the People, and every two years all of the families scattered across the savannah meet there to trade and make marriages. It is a place of power.

I had spoken to him of Modimo's Hand, how my own father had there given me my secret name, how I had met my first wife there, Nela of the bright eyes, who gave me two sons and a daughter before the fever took her.

Many times Cagen had asked me to take him. Always I had said "some other time." We had no more time. I said yes.

"We pack food for four days," I said. "It will be good to have this last time together."

So we walked, out south across the grasslands. We would have seemed a strange sight, this black white man with his rifle, and an old man half his size, carrying the spear of his fathers. My bones groaned much of the time, as they often do now, but Cagen's spirited walking carried my heart with him. We walked and talked, and at night, watched the stars.

"You say they are flaming gas," I said, poking at the fire. I watched as the sparks fly up into the sky. Could they go high enough, far enough, to become stars? "My grandfather said they were the eyes of the dead and the unborn."

He chuckled. "I think I like your story better."

"Mine does not explain all things."

"Neither does mine."

Far up in the clouds, another of those odd metal machines moved silently across the sky.

They flew. They walked. They changed color and shape like chameleon lizards. I wondered who the star men had been, and what bad thing had happened to them to make them worship death.

On the second day, when I could no longer quiet the ache in my bones with ginger bark, I chose a path that would tax me more at the start, but give more relief at the finish because it would save us a half day's travel. We climbed over rocks unseen since my boyhood, long forgotten now. Here, the grass thinned, brown sand and rock pushed through the earth's skin. I stopped, seeking direction: Modimo's Hand was no more than half a day from this spot, but because this path was new to me, I was uncertain which way to go.

I squinted my eyes against a sudden flash of light.

"What is it?" he asked.

Not ten steps away, behind a fever bush, the light sparked again, and then died away.

"I do not know," I said.

The light was *wrong*. Too much brightness where an overhang should have left only shadow. From this odd angle I saw the glimmer again, more brightly.

The rocks shimmered as they might in great heat. This, at a time of day when the sun was too young to be so boastful.

"What in the hell...?" Cagen asked.

I do not believe in Cagen's hell, but in other times I might have scolded him for speaking of devils so close to our sacred grounds.

We moved rocks away, revealing metal, unblemished but dull with dirt. Limp metal snakes, as long as two men were tall and as thick as my body, coiled at its side.

This was a sky machine. One that had come from above, not one built by white men from odd parts. Begging my grandfather for protection I backed away, making the secret signs he taught me to banish demons. This metal thing was not of my world. Not of any world of men. For how long had it crouched here in the earth, so near our sacred grounds?

When I backed away, the thing appeared to be *gone*, hiding itself among the rocks with nothing but the shimmering to show where it lay. Two steps to the right...and it became whole, sitting as if it had been planted there by the gods at the dawn of time. A man could have stood right next to it, and if the sun was not just *so*, and your eyes attuned just *so*, it would not be seen.

I backed away. An evil smell hung in the air. Burnt, choking, sudden and strange. It caught in my throat and made me cough.

"This is a bad thing," I said.

Fire seemed to dance on Cagen's face. Instead of stepping away from the thing, he moved toward it like a man walking in sleep. Instead of preparing himself for struggle, his arms lay limp at his sides.

"I've seen them in museums, but never been this close..." he said. "Jesus Christ, this must have been buried half a century, since the War."

He took another step toward the metal tortoise.

Most of it was buried, but what gleamed in the sun was a curve like the roof of a large family's hut. The machine was tilted, like a silver tortoise shell laying half against a rock wall. Had it contained something alive, and somehow wounded? Had its own metal arms tunneled into the earth to hide from its enemies, or to find a place to die at peace? My mind spun. Cagen thrust himself against one of the largest rocks. He grunted, strained, and sweat burst out on his forehead. The rock groaned, then slid down the silvery metal and was still.

The machine made a sound like angry bees. Then, a door as high as my shoulder slid up with speed I had never seen, as if the open space it revealed had always been. Inside, blackness stared back at us.

I took at least six steps away, crouching behind a rock in case the machine spit fire at us.

"Hide yourself!" I said to Cagen, but he seemed not to hear me. "Is something still...alive?"

"I don't know," he said. "Fifty years? No, it's dead."

We watched the open doorway for several minutes, and no sky creature moved inside the machine, nor any man. The smell from inside was an old smell, like dirt and dust and old dead flesh. The burnt smell had faded. The door seemed to invite us closer, like a sweet voice in our ears, although it was silent.

"I'm going to look inside," Cagen said.

I meant to tell him he was being foolish, but I said nothing. Instead, my feet surprised me and trailed behind his on the rocky soil.

Cagen's arm clung to the thing's doorway, perhaps so he could pull away if a sky-beast tried to yank him inside. I stooped beneath his raised arm to see what his eyes beheld, telling myself that even if the machine roasted me, or somehow stole my breath, it would make a worthy last sight to bring my grandfather.

In the next breath, my courage was rewarded.

There, on the floor just inside the doorway, lay something dead. It was not human or animal. Although it was curled like an infant, the creature had once been as tall as a man, or taller. The bones made me think of a wasp mated to a crocodile.

Cagen grabbed my hand, squeezing my tender bones hard. I knew why: We were men of two legs, born beneath the same sky, who had seen a creature from beyond the sun. It looked like a cousin of our world; a creature that might walk here, or could have walked here long ago, in the old days when gods and giant beasts ruled the earth.

It was the only time in my many rains that I felt my body root itself like a tree, unable to move. If Cagen had not been struck in the same state, I might have blamed the weak heart of an old man who can no longer run or climb. It is too easy to make old men fearful, and I vowed from the time I was a boy that I would never be made weak.

But as I stared at that thing in the ship, Cagen's stories became real in my mind. Now I could see the horror of the flying machines. Now I could see that the people who attacked the villages of the world were not people at all. I had imagined that men could come with skin as red as clay, or wearing animal stripes. A white man is a shocking sight the first time: Bleached of color, and hair that flies helplessly in the wind, unbound to the head. I had imagined that this creature was some strange form of white man. Compared with this thing, the oddest white man and I were brothers.

"We must leave here," I said.

Cagen held his hand up in a gesture to silence me. This is a great insult to an elder, but I knew his intent.

We waited in a long silence, and no army of demons swarmed from within the machine's belly. Perhaps we would not be killed after all.

Cagen was now teacher, not student. He knew the ways of white men who could salvage broken machines and learn to make them fly in the air. The lands I knew were behind me; and in front of me was Cagen's world.

One at a time, we bent and entered the door. It remained open behind us, but the walls themselves began to glow, enough pale red light to see everything within.

Whatever had once lived inside the machine was now dead. It was good to know these creatures were mortal, not gods. Its bones were splintered just like mine would have been. Its black eyes, hollowed with dust, were larger than a man's, almost half its face. The skin on its face was withered, but seemed like a reptile's.

Although its head was about the size of a man's, its body was smaller, almost stunted. It seemed to have five arms and legs, and they had many joints, like the neck of an ostrich.

Walking further in was like entering an animal's stomach, all dark red walls, cords and membranes. The floor of the machine held three nests of woven vine-like cables, each nest large enough for a small man.

Cagen stared at the nests. I could hear his mind telling him to lay down. I saw it in his eyes.

"Do not do it," I begged him.

He did not listen to me, and lowered himself into the vine net.

The moment he touched them, the vines *moved.* Fifty years may have been enough to kill men from the stars, but the machine itself still lived. Cagen screamed and struggled, but the vines snatched him backward like a mother might an infant. Cagen's arms were pinned. Metal snakes darted from the ceiling, burrowing into his flesh as he howled and bled. First his arms. Then his legs. His head. He writhed, screaming an English curse. Afraid, we always speak our first tongue.

But the next language he spoke was not English. I had never heard it before. His words no longer sounded as if they came from a human throat.

I grasped Cagen's wrist, and the chair swallowed me too—but not in the way it swallowed Cagen, with tiny spears. The machine swallowed my mind. My thoughts were no longer my own. I felt as if I was drowning in someone else.

All the world shattered into pieces. Great villages burning. The shadows of flying and walking machines plagued the land, as the metal tortoises slaughtered the fleeing. Rivers boiled with blood. Screams and running and endless death.

And above, the pitiless stars.

I screamed prayers, and quickly reached for my medicine pouch. I shook powdered frog skin on Cagen three times, begging the gods to help him. Still, his body convulsed, eyes bulged, hands clutched at the vines. He screamed again.

And bucked.

Then...

The machine *rocked*. I lurched and caught myself...then realized that the tortoise-shell had heaved in time with Cagen's motion, just a beat late.

I understood: *Cagen* had made the machine move.

I did not know how that could be so, but I had felt the humming beneath my feet from the instant Cagen was trapped in the chair. When he moved, the vibration grew stronger.

The machine was feeding on him. The machine was a hunter, too, like its long-dead master. A dog will hunt with a man, will follow his orders. This thing obeyed like a dog...

But it was no dog.

I pulled at the cords binding Cagen. One came loose from the back of his head, and the others dislodged as well. I pulled him from the chair. He was babbling as I pulled him from the ship.

The door closed behind us.

I pulled him back only a few steps, but the machine was gone when I glanced behind me. A chameleon. Unless you were very lucky—or unlucky—or the machine wanted you to see it—you would pass by and not see where it lay. The machine might have been there when I was a boy, but spared me.

No wonder the white men feared.

This was a thing of the gods.

I pulled Cagen as far as I could, but the rocks made our journey difficult. He was gasping for breath, eyes wide and staring wildly. I understood: The machine might be chasing us, hiding in the wind.

"Ohhh..." he finally groaned. "My head. Christ."

"What happened to you?" I said to Cagen.

"I don't know," he said, and cursed in English again. He brought his knees to his chest and rocked, mumbling to himself. More curses? Prayers?

The vines had entered his arms, but the wounds had already stopped bleeding, as if someone had held fire to them. Strange.

I could not leave him. If the machine came for us, we would die together.

But darkness took mercy on us, and when the dawn sun awakened we breathed still.

The next day we began our trip back to our camp.

"I think it might be best if we didn't tell anyone about it," Cagen said, limping as he walked. "I can't think of any good that would come of it."

He spoke first, but the words could have been from my own mind.

"The people will not understand," I said, although it was my duty to report the discovery to the elders. "It will make them afraid. Fear and drought are too heavy on us to carry at once."

By the time we returned to the camp, we had agreed never to tell anyone what we had found. Cagen, returning to the white man's world, would say nothing. I would not offer it even to my ancestors on the wall. I am ashamed to admit I was afraid.

A day after we returned, a Spider came from the sky for Cagen, driven by a soldier. Air *shooshed* from each of its five legs, sending dust over everything. Most of my people had only seen a Spider once. Now, it was twice. But despite their curiosity, they turned their faces away from the thing, pretending not to see him as they left.

It is a great sign of affection—as we say, *My eyes would hurt too much at the sight.* The People live and die together, so we do not have practice with saying goodbye.

Cagen came to me, and gave me his listening device. His radio. He shrugged. "Not like there's anything out there for you, but..."

I took the gift with tears of gratitude. "You are my friend," I said.

I was brave enough to watch him leave; my eyes were stronger because of what Cagen had seen with me on the rocks. He alone had shared the sight, so I could not turn away as he left.

The machine had won a battle with Cagen. He had not been the same man when he returned, barely speaking to anyone. I told everyone who asked about him that he was sick with the sand fever, because the true illness could not be explained. Even as the soldier helped him climb into the Spider, Cagen looked around him as if he was lost, as if he was a frightened old man, the kind I fight never to be. Cagen gave a final wave, and seemed more alive when he saw my face alone staring back at him. He tried to smile at me, but his face was a sad, broken thing.

As the Spider flew into the sky, two old women wailed funeral songs. The youngest children cried, chasing behind the Spider's shadow as it glided through the dying grasses.

"Bring him back!" the youngest children screamed to the metal beast, throwing rocks. "Bring our friend Cagen back!"

Their mothers called to them, clucking. Their fathers laughed and tried to explain that the Spider wasn't going to eat Cagen for dinner.

They were right, and they were wrong.

I do not know much of these man-made Spiders. But the other machine, the one from the stars, in the rocks, had eaten Cagen already.

Warm water from the clouds meant that the drought had finally ended, but the rain gods were no happier with us than the sun gods. The pools stayed muddy. For days, hunger pinched our bellies. The hunters traveled long distances for small game.

Times were bad in the big villages too.

At night, lying beside Jappa I saw bright lights on the western horizon, like the times I remember from childhood. Silent thunder, thunder you heard with your body, not your ears. But my inner eyes, this time, were wiser: I imagined the flying machines swooping in the air, trailing their metal snake-legs behind them. I saw fire shooting from their mouths. When the wind shifted, I thought I could smell burnt flesh.

Had another Great War been waged by the sky lizards? Or had men turned themselves into sky lizards the way the machine turned into a chameleon against the rocks?

My teeth chattered, although it was not cold. I feared for my people. The death that had killed the cities could come for us, and there was nothing we could do.

I feared for my sons, whom I might never see again. For my daughter, with her husband and family a moon's walk to the north.

I feared for my friend. If he was not dead, I knew he would come to us again, to tell his tales. He would come to paint his wall.

If he was not dead.

I heard the shouting before I saw him. It was nearing dusk, four moons after Cagen left us. Four of the young herders ran in to us, calling for the men. They went out, were gone until the sun set, and then returned carrying Cagen.

He was half-dead with starvation and thirst, and there were cruel wounds on his back and legs, like healed burns. He wore tattered grey pants and shirt, painted with black numbers.

Always had I hoped he would return, but never thought that it would be in such a manner. We gave him water, meat, and herbs, and heard his story:

He told us he returned to the greatest city in the world, Dar Es Salaam, to the *un-i-ver-si-ty*, a great school run by many elders. (Cagen had mentioned this *un-i-ver-si-ty* before, but as he seemed to know little of value, I am not certain what these elders taught.)

This land around you is a nation, and that nation is called Tanzania. Because past relations have been so poor between black nations and white, Tanzania and several other nations in this continent called Africa wish to break free of a gov-ern-ment called "United Nations of Earth."

The white nations did not want this to happen, because much of Africa, while poor, is rich with treasures the white nations hold dear. When their petition to separate was brought to court, the UNE retaliated with force. Alien war machines rained from the skies, flown by men who had learned to master them. Dar Es Salaam was driven to rubble. Untold thousands of people died in the fires, and thousands more were taken to camps.

The camps were shanty towns surrounded by barbed wire and vicious dogs. I was in one of those camps, but I escaped, came here.

I did not know where else to go.

It was customary for Cagen to sleep in the hut for boys, the unmarried hunters who had not yet earned their brides. This hut was where Cagen had always made his bed.

But when he returned, I took him to my hut, and he slept where my children slept before they were grown. My wife Jappa served him hedgehog and the ant larvae he called "Bushman Rice." Cagen had walked to us out of a bad dream. A man who has walked away from a dream should be an honored guest. Most men who live too long in the dream never return.

But Cagen was not as other men. Cagen returned.

Over the next days, as Cagen healed, he told me more of his time in the world of dreams and machines.

I'm an American citizen, which used to mean something. Not anymore. Because I was a student at the university, I was arrested as an "unaffiliated intellectual" and thrown into a camp. It was a place of hunger and fear...and pain. Men and women were beaten and tortured if our captors believed they were lying, or thought we could give them information about Africa's leaders. We lost everything—even the clothes from our backs. We were clothed in prison grey. Criminals, accused of no crime.

And it was in that terrible place where, for the first time in my life...I fell in love.

As he spoke of love, Cagen gazed toward my wife, who was listening from the folds of the hut so she would not appear to intrude on the talk of men. All women listen—but Jappa is the queen of hiding herself.

Fat, laughing Jappa is the queen of all.

I married my second wife when she was sixteen rains and had the most perfect face ever created. I was twenty-five rains then, and my first wife had died two years before. Now I have many more than twenty-five rains, and Jappa still has the most beautiful face. She is my second wife, but unlike some of the other men, I have had but one wife at a time.

Cagen looked at my wife as if he knew stories that had never been spoken between us. He smiled, and sunlight glowed from his face.

Yes, I found the woman I want. A medical student from Kenya—Chanya. Even her name is music. She is everything to me.

She is the only reason I remember how to smile.

She alone gives me hope there is a God.

Many gods, I corrected him with a laugh. Love for a woman has made many men forget much more than how to count, or to thank the gods. There are men who grow insane from a woman. But Cagen was not that kind. She did not bring war to his heart; the woman he had found brought him peace.

We comforted each other as people have since the beginning of time. Without her, I wouldn't have survived. I saw people sit in the corner and will themselves to die. Their families were lost to them, and we had no way to contact them. We knew people were dying when the beatings went too far, and that troops could pull anyone from their beds any time of the day or night. I wanted to die, too.

But Chanya kept my soul alive.

It is dangerous to find love in such a dark place.

"Your heart is strong as well," I said. "Seeds do not grow without fertile soil."

"The mustard seed..." he began, like a prayer.

"All seeds need soil. And rain."

We had plenty of rain.

Just not enough shelter, except for each other. But it was all right for a while. All we needed was to clasp each other's hands to get through the day.

But I knew our time together would not last.

Foreigners who were not from Africa were being taken for "questioning," but did not return to relate the questions. Whispers began: Foreigners were being sent home, or they were being killed. No one knew which.

I was a foreigner, so I knew that soon, this question would be answered.

Someone who worked with the guards, who had been taunted as a traitor to his people, whispered to me that they would come for me at dawn. I saw in his eyes then that he was only a desperate young man trying to live, and to protect his family, but he wanted to do good. He did not give me a gun to escape, but he gave me the kindness of knowing I had only one more night with my love.

I found Chanya, of course. Had the guard not told me, I would not have risked sneaking out of the men's barracks to find her in the women's tent. Any of the women there would have told what I did for extra bread and rice for their children.

That night, I held my beautiful Chanya's hands, looked into her eyes, and told her to find a way to survive.

Any way at all.

At first, she did not understand my meaning. I reminded her that she had brushed aside the attention of the guards. This was foolish. Beauty is a gift, I told her. Some of the guards were good men in bad circumstances.

Find kindness, I told her.

Find mercy.

Give whatever you must.

I made Chanya cry.

And then Cagen wailed like a woman. The children stared: They had never seen a man cry so.

So that Cagen would not shame himself, my wife and I took him back into our hut and gave him a bed.

"He has lost his wife," I explained to the children who waited outside.

But they did not understand. How could they?

Children have yet to lose anything.

Children have not seen the world's end.

One night, Cagen and I sat together and watched the pale yellow fire from the eastern horizon.

Not flashes. Fire.

"Dar Es Salaam is burning," Cagen said. And cried.

"You are not thinking of a city," I said.

"No."

"The woman," I said. "Chanya."

The sound of her name seemed to lance him like a spear-tip. "Yes." His answer was a whisper.

Something changed in me when I knew I would die.

I came to the end of myself. I cried and trembled and tried to talk to God even though I doubted Him again when I needed Him most. I did not sleep.

By dawn, my fear was no more. Maybe God took it from me, or I didn't have room to carry it.

When they came for me, I was on my feet. Waiting.

Because I had no fear, I noticed everything:

Many of the soldiers were boy children. They were hopped up on drugs, full of childlike glee as they beat us or took women to be raped. These boys had chosen to be called Executioners, and they enjoyed their work.

They stood me up in a line of other men and women waiting to die, standing atop a trench that was already lined with corpses. We were that morning's chosen. Up until that instant, a few of those in line had believed they one day would be able to phone home to Canada, the United States, Saudi Arabia or wherever home was to them, believing our captor's lies about ambassadors and ransoms and high-level meetings.

Once we were in the line, no illusions remained. Those who were not crying did not meet each other's eyes. We were all lost inside ourselves. Even when you die together, you die alone.

The boys had made a counting game of the executions. One boy wearing a general's cap too big for his head raised a baton and counted "Moja, mbili, tatu!" One, two, three. Three machine guns chattered, and ten men crumpled back into the ditch.

They brought the next ten of us forward. I stood there in front of the ditch, smelling the blood and stink behind me, and knew that these men and boys, the ragged line of distant mountains, the smell of dead men's shit in the air...that this was what my senses would hold in the last moments of my life.

When I heard the boy count "Moja" I began a prayer I knew I would never finish. I heard "mbili."

There was no "tatu." Before he could speak that word, gunfire exploded all around me. I watched the guards, my executioners, flinch in horror to realize that they were the targets. From around us, hidden behind rocks and in pits covered with cloth and sand, leapt a dozen desperate men and women, all armed, all firing at the guards. Rebels, who had laid in wait at the execution spot, probably avenging loved ones.

The children screamed and ran, dropping their guns.

If the rebels had arrived a breath sooner, the previous ten would not have died.

If the rebels had arrived a breath later, one of the older boys might have inspected the bodies and put a bullet in my head. My nightmare would be over.

The rebels came too late.

The rebels came too soon.

Only six of us remained when the ambush began. I do not know why they waited. I remember thinking that as I ran out into the tall grass. Why had they waited? I will never know. What I did know was that I was still alive, and although my mind was confused my legs wanted desperately to remain that way.

The other five ran roughly west, toward Dar Es Salaam. I ran east. I had no family or friends to hide me.

But I knew where I could find the People, and I came to you.

I was blessed again. I met Sinas, a goatherd whose family camps two days' walk from here. He knew your people, Qutb.

He knew how to bring me home.

A moon after Cagen came to us, white and black soldiers arrived in three Spiders and asked questions about him. They showed us his face on paper; a *pho-to-graph.*

Cagen hid in my hut, a blanket over his head, but even if they caught a glimpse of him, they might not have known who he was. He did not look like the black-skinned white man in the photograph. His hair grew longer, a regal mane. He was learning our ways and language, was dressed as one of us, and he had lost the disgusting fat that whites wear like a second and third skin.

Even the children knew how to shrug their shoulders and shake their heads when they saw Cagen's photograph. We laughed when the soldiers were gone.

Cagen was safe.

But were we?

Soon Cagen built his own hut, but with no wife to share it, it must have been a lonely place. Marriageable girls tried to catch his eyes and gave him secret smiles, but Cagen rejected them with kindness and kept his own company.

He did not want to be a burden to us, so he kept goats and helped with cooking, which made the small boys laugh. I did not understand why the girls smiled at him so, since he would starve before he could catch a rabbit. But maybe the girls smiled because they saw in Cagen what I saw: His talent was for other things.

Cagen's talent was in his head. In his heart.

I began to teach him again, and his sadness touched me. I taught him things I had withheld from the other men who had come to me, because it would be too much knowledge for an ordinary man to keep.

This is how Cagen, an outsider, became my apprentice. He was more interested in the old stories than my own sons. This went on for moons, and then one night when four of our boys had reached manhood, I performed the Starlight ceremony for them all. I invited Cagen to join.

We walked out into the tall grass, where each man created a circular clearing for himself in the stalks. The boys, and Cagen, each took their *Go*: a handful of cactus and nettle grindings, chewed until it was mush in their mouths, then spit out. This has been the Way for all of time.

Then, they all lay on the ground, in the midst of their circles. The first time passes in silence. Then, they all thrashed and made animal sounds, barking up at the moon and speaking in the unknown language. The *Go* plants take away the human, awakens the animal self. The man who returns from this journey knows his totem animal, and thereby earns a name.

When dawn was nearly upon us, and I knew that each of them had seen their animal selves I gave them *Return*: a ball of cactus root and a moss that grows only beneath the poison grub plant. I pushed one thumb-sized ball into each of their mouths, so that they would come back to the world.

Cagen rolled over, vomited, and then sprang to his feet. His eyes were alight while the other boys still moaned. Only the strongest warriors wake with fire.

"I saw," Cagen said, an excitement in his voice that I had not heard since his first days among us. "I know what I have to do. We have to go back."

"Go back?"

His fingers dug into my shoulders so strongly that I thought that the cactus was still upon him. "The world came apart. I was gone. Just...gone." He took off the wire-rimmed pieces of glass, rubbed at them with shaking hands. "Everything that was the man I am, stripped down to just raw function: hunger for food and an urge to mate. Then you gave me *Return*, and I felt my mind come back together. What *Go* did to me..." His fingers dug into my arms. "Was what the *machine* did to me. Qutb. You've shown me how to hook in and stay sane."

I stared. "Your mind is still sleeping."

"No," he said. "My mind is awake, for the first time in my life. My heart. I'm going back, whether you help me or not. But if you love me. If you'll help me..." He paused, tongue flickering across cracked lips. "Give me *Return*."

We two stared at each other. I knew what he wanted, and why.

At long last, I nodded.

I would take him to Modimo's Hand again.

And so we walked again out into the grass, then to the jagged place where if the sun is just so high and you stand with your body facing north, you could see a strange thing. A thing not of this world.

Although the machine hid from us, we knew where it rested. We would never forget the place; not until our sleep at life's end, when everything is forgotten unless your grandchildren call your name and sing you stories.

We stood just outside the metal tortoise shell, and I reached into my medicine bag to pull out a ball of mushrooms and moss for Cagen. *Return*, we had always called it. *Return*, from the place where given names are forgotten, and true essence discovered.

"I give you this, and you take it of your own free will," I said. I did not want to give him false promises. "I cannot protect you, but perhaps our gods can."

Cagen took the ball. As he chewed, we sat outside the machine, in its wavering shadow. Within minutes, Cagen began to sway. When he stood and walked, his step was unsteady. I almost reached to help stand him upright, but I did not move. Like all men, Cagen had to learn to walk by himself.

Cagen did not look at me. Instead, his eyes saw only the ship's open door. He crawled inside.

I thought of my wife waiting. My cave, and the unfinished pictures.

Cursing myself for a fool, I climbed into the machine behind Cagen. The door closed as soon as my foot was inside, leaving no time to consult the gods. No time for wiser thinking. I had done this thing.

I stared at the floor beneath my weathered, cracked, sandaled feet as I stood in that machine, to be certain I was really there.

Long ago, all people could flap their arms and fly in the skies and visit their ancestors. But when people flew, the skies grew crowded, and they fought over the open air. That is why the gods condemned us to forever walk the ground, staring up at what we could no longer touch.

The sky separates the living from the dead.

This day, we would visit the dead.

My heart drummed loudly enough for my grandfather to hear.

I have never raised a spear against another man, because my people have been at peace for generations. Never had I, a man of herbs and drawings, expected to find myself in battle. And certainly not in a machine from the sky.

Cagen did not hesitate before he lay in the net. He flinched, but did not scream when the metal snakes chewed into his flesh, into the back of his skull.

He closed his eyes and cried out, his lips curled.

And he waited.

Cagen jerked his body forward slightly, and the machine lurched like a waking snail. Cagen's eyes remained closed, as if he were sleeping, but his lips curled in the coldest smile I have ever seen.

A great humming sound surrounded us, like a swarm of bees large enough to cover the clouds.

Lurching again. I heard rocks slide off the outside of the metal shell. Felt the machine rise up beneath me. I sat on the floor between coils—I would not lay in a net, no!

The machine tilted left and then right. Then leveled.

Then the floor of the machine vanished from sight. I saw the rocks shadowed beneath us. The humming quieted. The rocks fell away from our feet. We rose up.

I stood on the sky.

The thing about Cagen is this: He was a fast learner, as I have said, in everything except hunting. When he did tumbling tricks for the delight of our children, his body was clever. But that body failed him when it came to learning the things a hunter must know: when to pull the net, when and how to throw the spear. These things Cagen could not do.

Perhaps he had never been hungry enough in America. He could not find his way to the killing place in his heart. He did not know the prayers to offer the gods in thanks, and so taking life was a great theft in his mind. This is what I believe.

But the Cagen who lay in the machine's innards was a hunter in his heart. The vines in his arms and head joined him to the machine, but the other, newer part of Cagen had been born in the camp, at the hands of his tormentors, and in the arms of his love.

Now he would fight. He was hungry. Hungry for the thing that feeds all men but has no taste or smell. The machine would give him what he hungered for.

Cagen hungered for love. And death.

As the machine flew, I am not ashamed to say that I was afraid. I could feel the floor but not see it. I was looking down on the ground far below us, as high as birds fly, my stomach flipping all the while because it thought I was falling from a great height. It took all my strength not to spit up like an infant.

I sat on the floor between the coils, and chanted.

The machine flew and flew. We entered a cloud, and all about us was whiteness.

I had walked in a cloud! This was a story my grandfather would love to hear.

Cagen's eyes were wide, and filled with blood and fear, but the machine flew on.

And then it came down near a great nest of barbed fences. The machine brought us to rest softly; this time, I did not sway from side to side.

The door suddenly opened, and I knew it was my time to get out. I tried to hold Cagen's gaze, but his eyes were sightless as they stared out from the head-piece of twisted metal vines.

I left the machine, and the door sealed Cagen inside.

Outside, for the first time, I saw the machine standing, alive and terrible. Standing high on three unfolded legs, with two snakes reared up to make arms, the machine looked less like the Spiders and more like a Mantis. Like the Trickster, Kaggen.

The Mantis took long steps toward the webs of fences.

Behind the fences, enough people to fill many villages stared and screamed. When they ran in a frenzy, I could almost hear the bones breaking as the weak and small were trampled by those who were quicker, and more able. Such is always the way.

Soldiers screamed as well, but with better cause: A river of fire shot from the Mantis's mouth, and snakes of fire wove themselves through the lines of soldiers, touching one and then the next. In an instant, a dozen armed men died. As they did, the machine's skin rippled. Cagen's face appeared there, twisted with pain and thoughts I could never dream. It was a horror, but still the face of my friend.

The eyes were vast and empty. His mind was gone. Cagen's insane face howled, and the metal disk belched fire once again.

The scream of an alarm filled the air. Cagen slaughtered those men, so that I had to turn my eyes. With the guards dead or fleeing, the prisoners tore the fences and fled in every direction.

I think I saw the woman at the same moment Cagen did.

How did I know she was the one?

Because where so many others were running away, this woman stood watching the machine despite her fear. It towered above her like a walking god, but she did not waver. She looked up into the face, and knew what he was.

She jumped as if waking from a dream and screamed. She stood in a corner against walls made of brick, afraid to run. Suddenly, a soldier ran to the woman. He was a young man, with a hunter's strong body, and a good face. Screaming in Kikuyu, he howled up at the machine, putting his own body between it and the woman.

All the while he screamed at the machine, tears watered his face. He believed he would die for this woman.

The machine paused, and Cagen's eyes, the things that looked like Cagen's eyes, blinked. Its legs folded, so that its face came closer to the woman.

She pushed the soldier back, came to stand between the soldier and Cagen. She spoke up to him, but I could not hear her words. She seemed strong and beautiful.

I finally made out one word. "No," she kept saying. But instead of screaming like the soldier, she spoke as gently as if he were standing against her ear. "No." And then I made out another word. "Cagen. No. No. No."

She knew Cagen. And she loved another.

The machine sank to its knees. He saw what I saw: His woman had survived, as he had begged her to. But in doing so, she had lost her heart. The heart is strange. The heart is the one part of us we never learn to understand. Great men, smart men, are as weak and stupid as any others.

Cagen did not have time to grieve his woman.

A second machine approached. This one was like Cagen's, not like the little Spiders that carry men across the grass and through the sky. It was a metal disk, and then a white man's face appeared across the curve of the shell. The white man looked...twisted. The muscles in his face strained. The eyes inhuman with blood-lust. Whatever the machine had done to this man, I prayed that Cagen could resist.

The two machines circled like angry baboons. Guards and prisoners alike fled as the two machines came to grips, like our men's dances when they are inviting one another to wrestle.

As their snake-arms entwined, their metal skin glowed, and the air around them sizzled with their energies. I fled, knowing that this sight was not for mortal eyes. It was the battle of gods, something that no man should witness.

Before I ran, I saw Cagen's woman and the guard flee together.

It took me ten days to return to my people. After a time, when I was ready to see that day again in my memories, I told my people what I had done, and seen.

We were in danger, and we knew we must move on and find a lonelier place to camp. We could afford talk of nothing else. The days were long and hard.

Time passed. Some nights, I heard distant explosions, or the sounds of gunfire. Sometimes, screams drifted in the wind.

Two moons passed.

And then one day, the Mantis appeared.

It walked like a Spider, but stumbled as it did. At first, I believed I had not yet shaken sleep from my eyes. Many nights, I had dreamed of Cagen's return. Sometimes, in my dreams, he was a friend. In others, he brought death to my people.

The machine I saw that day was not like the one that came in my dreams. It moved as if it was confused.

The machine rocked, stopping. Suddenly, liquid fire spat out. A goat bleated, eaten by flames. Boiling blood and steam filled the air. My people hid themselves, terrified. Even if I had not told them my story, a child would have known that we had reached the time of dying.

It was Cagen. I could not see his face on the machine the way I once had, but I knew. So afraid I could barely walk, I went out to the machine.

The metal curve of the machine shifted, and finally Cagen showed himself to me. And then it looked like me, Qutb. He made me look older than I think of myself, but it was me.

Then it was a metal disk again. It sank to the sand. And opened.

The American crawled out, his naked body covered with fresh scars. He looked thinner than the frailest of us, as if he had not eaten in at least a moon.

He crawled to me, and rested his cheek upon my sandaled foot.

We dragged the machine to Shadow Cave. You should have seen us! Ropes and men and boys pulling for three days. There, deep within the rocks, it will never be found. The ancestors stand watch over it for us.

The American is healing in my hut now. My wife Jappa feeds him soup made of spring hare and yellow grass, her grandmother's medicine for all ailments. He is not Cagen again yet, but he will be very soon. From time to time I see my friend in his eyes once again.

The world beyond our sight is strange, and violent. We use Cagen's listening machine, and I hear men talking in Swahili about the strange events.

They say the slaughter in Dar Es Salaam was stopped by a machine. Was it a rebel? An alien? A soldier of conscience? A war between the shadowy rulers? Or something else...? Some, it was said, believed he was Modimo himself, protecting his children.

The machine is talked about again and again. It did not rest after Dar Es Salaam, fighting in other places whose names I had never heard. Again and again, I hear them give thanks to the unknown hero.

I smile as I listen. And I cry an old man's tears of gratitude.

After the first nights, we moved Cagen to a hut outside the camp, so that he will not frighten the children with his screams. I do not know what he sees and hears. I think that he dreams of the spaces between the stars.

I never fully understand the American with brown skin, and now he does not understand himself. He stares into the night with sightless eyes. He cannot feed himself. But we drum for him, and feed him herbs, and walk with him, and slowly, he returns. And I know that if the soldiers ever come to hurt us, he will remember who he is. What the gods made him. Why they gave him to us. I remember praying that we could stay away from the madness that came from beyond the sun. Or that if it came to us, as it had to Dar Es Salaam, there would be a way to survive.

The gods heard. They sent us Kaggen, the trickster. And as a trickster, he came masked as a student, that he might reveal himself as teacher. He is Cagen, my friend. When he is healed, I may ask him if he will take my name. He has no father. I have no son. It would be good. My name is Qutb, which means "Protector of the People." For Cagen, it would be truth.

He stands between the People and the sky.

THEY FIGHT CRIME!

LEAH BOBET

Leah Bobet's debut novel, *Above*, was released in 2012. In this energetic story she playfully defines what it is that superheroes do.

THEY FIGHT CRIME!

Jack and Terri spend their nights off in the back of a '75 Caddy, fighting crime.

They've only been together for five months, sleeping together for two. It's long enough that she's more than happy to sleep with him, but they're still in that grey area of euphemism and subterfuge: they don't do it in her apartment 'cause her roommate might hear, they don't do it at his place 'cause his wife might hear (separation pending, he promises), and they don't talk about it in the naked terms that'd make the whole thing real. *Fighting crime* was something Terri read in a book in college, the title something involving shampoo and the plot consistently escaping her.

It sounds much more glamorous than this: the seatbelt digging into her shoulder, the leftover gym smell and the smell of a beer they still stop for beforehand, the equivalent of setting up an alibi. *She's the psychic queen of the dead with an MBA from Harvard,* he murmurs in her ear when he undoes her blouse. *He's a...Nobel prize-winning astronaut with a past,* she replies, and they giggle, but not too loud. Terri privately thinks the lives Jack spins for her are always better than the vice versa, though she knows if she said it he'd disagree.

Tonight she packs a surprise in her bag, along with the shoes and tennis racket and triple-sealed water canteen. She's not much for sewing, but was forced through enough years of Home Ec to make a Halloween costume that lasts—and surprisingly, still fits. She puts it on under the jeans and T-shirt once they meet by chance at the gym, have a chance beer, go through all the other steps of the ritual they know so well. Spandex ought to make him hot. Spandex always makes guys hot.

The fabric keeps heat in, makes her sweaty, pulls at her thighs in a kind of scratchy way, but the look on his face when he takes off her clothes is worth a thousand years of torment. Terri and Jack fight crime with a surprising thoroughness.

What is not surprising is that their car should attract some attention.

He's just about found the right rhythm when: "Hey, fuck," a voice yells, and there's a loud rap on the window. "It's superheroes! Superheroes fucking!"

"Shit," Jack says, and falls right out of her.

Hands push the car, rocking it back and forth on its axles. "Superheroes, man!" says the voice, high-pitched and malicious. Terri can't see much from where she is: a flash of jacket, silver under the faraway streetlights, pale, pale hands on the windows.

The door opens and Jack's yanked out from on top of her, half-naked and torn between shouting his lungs out and being quiet as he can. The one who yelled starts laughing, pokes the slight potbelly, pulls a knife.

She doesn't know what to do; all she wants to do is get them as far away from her as she can, give herself some time to think—

Something builds up inside of her, and there's a *push*—

The nearest thug catapults off of nothing, yelping, and arcs smoothly into the horizon.

Jack's eyes are flaming. Literally. Once he remembers his tae kwon do (which he abandoned for a corner office and a growing waistline), three more flee stumbling and burning. He throws a fireball after them for good measure.

Panting, half-naked, they stare at each other. He pulls up his pants.

"She's an archaeologist with the power to bend men's minds," he says wonderingly.

"He's a fire-wielding accountant on a mission from God," she replies.

They look at each other for a moment, and at the leather jackets smouldering on the ground. There's the sound of a siren in the distance, dopplering its way towards the deserted parking lot.

"Why not?" she tells him, and perches on the trunk to wait for the cops.

CRIMES AGAINST HUMANITY

Jack is working late. Or working out late, or whichever he says this time. Again.

Rosie's had it with his bullshit. Yes, the doctor said he had to cut down his weight or the cholesterol would get him by forty-five (not too far away, now). Yes, he is looking in better shape than he was before, and the Christmas bonus went a long way to paying off the last of the mortgage, and she really shouldn't complain. But he went from coming home late twice a week to three times, to four times, and now she barely sees him at all. There's a vague look in his eyes these days.

He has to be seeing someone.

She's already sent the girls to her mother's—for a sleepover, she told them all—and the last touches are about to fall into place. The bag's packed. The note—which she agonized over a bit, trying to choose the right words to convey her pain, her anger, the right amount of vitriol to wound and not cause retaliation but penance—is on the table. After six drafts, she concluded that all Dear John letters will inevitably sound the same, and scribbled whatever on the back of an old bank statement. Anything that's valuable to her, she's taking with. Anything she can carry, that is. The rest will see her in court.

There's a rattle at the door. She zips up the bag and swings on her coat. It's probably him right now, and then there'll be a scene, and he'll promise all sorts of things like he has before (and like every cheating husband on film and small screen does) and it'll just go back to usual.

No. It's better this way. She'll go out the back.

She opens the back door and runs smack into a man all in black, a balaclava covering his face even though it's summer. He probably squeals louder than she does when he pulls the gun. "This is...this is a stickup!" he says.

She puts down the bag and tries to take slow, calming breaths.

There are three of them in all. They drag out a kitchen chair, and after a quick conference in the other room (leaving her with the man with the gun), they tie her to a chair with a freshly laundered bedsheet.

Rosie sighs. "You don't have to tie me up. I'm leaving, and you can take whatever you want of my ex-husband's shit." She puts the emphasis on *ex*.

He squints. "Gotta say, you talk a good line, lady," and shoves a pillowcase gag into her mouth.

Her nose tingles; the fabric softener smells sickly sweet at this distance, and she wants to sneeze. Of course this would happen tonight.

The thieves, from where she's watching, are at least thorough. They take out the stained-glass window in the bar expertly and slip it into a waiting case. They appraise the paintings on the walls, select a few, leave others behind. They don't bother with the small things—the crystal, the electronics, or the books—and they don't bother with her bag, which is fine by her. She watches them with a strange sense of peace, the kind you get when you know all those best-laid plans have just been swept away. He'll pay attention now when she sends the kids to Mom's. He'll notice these things. The Great Escape is over.

There's a clunk behind her, in the living room. She squints; a line of orange is snaking across the floor. And she smells smoke.

The masked man staggers back under a flurry of invisible blows; the painting in his hands doesn't fall to the floor, but is lifted by some force and set on the dining room table. Fire explodes on the chest of the second and he drops his case, starts batting frantically at his shirt. Sirens ring outside, and the thieves panic, drop everything, start to run.

Hands loose the sheets binding her to the chair, the fabric in her mouth. And there they are, in her own house, the mysterious InvisiGirl and Fireman, the greatest superheroes the city's ever seen. Or at least in the past few months.

Rosie gets out the fire extinguisher and puts out the carpet.

InvisiGirl starts tidying up a bit, asking her questions about the thieves— where did they come in, what did they look at, could she maybe recognize the voices in a lineup?—but Fireman's standing off to the side, uncomfortable, shy-seeming. He won't look at her at all.

Rosie's no fool. It takes more than a bit of spandex and a movie-announcer voice to make her not recognize her own damn (ex-)husband. "About time you came home," she says to him.

InvisiGirl nearly drops the vase they got for their anniversary on the floor.

Jack looks at the debris of the bedsheet and pillowcase, at the note on the table, at the bag by the door.

"Aw, shit," Jack says, and gets himself a beer.

FASHION CRIMES

Terri doesn't like being InvisiGirl.

For one, she is not invisi, more telekinetic. If people don't know how to look in the right direction, that's their problem. For two, she spent a lot of time and money to stop being a girl in the eyes of the world at large, and she's not about to go back now. For three, Jack's been on edge ever since the foiled robbery at his place, and it's a strain on the relationship. It's not like Rose knows that they're anything but partners, after all, even though Terri is sure the woman has her suspicions. Anyone would have their suspicions.

Jack and Terri play racquetball together every day now in the gym where they met, in the building that houses both their companies. It's more important these days to stay in shape.

"Jack," she says, "you're getting paranoid. It's not like it's painted on your chest that we slept together." Slept, past tense. Fighting crime leaves very little time these days for...well, fighting crime.

He shakes his head again, slams the ball against the wall so hard she doesn't dare intercept it.

"You said you were gonna leave her," Terri says softly, and he doesn't answer.

He avoids talking about them these days. Now that they're front-page news, everyone's on the lookout for a flash of red cape. The police officers they worked with are interviewed, every detail of the interactions dissected on websites, in magazines, on the news. They're stalked, profiled, patterned and analyzed.

"We can't be seen together like this," he says again once they hit the bar, putting all those calories back on with a pint of cold whatever. Her own weight hasn't changed; maybe she's replacing fat with muscle or whatever. Maybe it's doing nothing at all for her. Maybe she's running in place. "God help us if the press connects it up."

They stop meeting at the bar.

Terri starts seeing someone else. She doesn't tell either of them about the other. There's no point. The relationship ends after three months. The new guy isn't a fiendish flyboy sorcerer for the twenty-first century.

On weeknights, Terri and Jack fight crime.

HATE CRIMES

Rosie finds lipstick on a collar that's five months old, shoved in the back of his gym bag, in the middle of a fit of spring cleaning. She breaks the vase she got for their anniversary on the paintings that were recovered from art thieves, thanks to Fireman and InvisiGirl.

Terri deletes every single e-mail that Jack ever sent her, rooting them out of their special hidden folder and consigning them to the bit bucket. He gave her nothing, afraid of it being tracked, so she has nothing else to destroy. After an hour of flailing and wanting to scream and feeling too scared to scream because someone might hear her, she burns the costume. It doesn't burn well, and what she's left with after half an hour is a pile of reeking, plasticky shreds. *Even the gesture of it doesn't work out right*, she thinks to herself, and goes home to cry for three hours.

Jack takes a business trip to Boston. He knows none of this.

LOVE CRIMES

Jack comes home to the second Dear John note this year and an empty house, and drops his suitcase on the bed. The girls are probably at her mother's. The paintings are off the walls. It looks like art thieves have hit the place, except Rosie does a better, cleaner job.

She's his wife. He loves her, despite all the rough shit they've been through the past year. He calls her at her mother's house, and leaves a message on the machine: *Babe...I'm wrong. I've been looking for fulfillment in the wrong places. It's been over for a while now.*

Let me make it up to you. Please.

He goes to the office the next day, and Terri's resignation is in her e-mail. She doesn't sign it InvisiGirl like she had been.

She's his partner. This has gotten bigger than the two of them; maybe the city doesn't need or depend on them, but they do good things. They help. He doesn't want her for her body anymore. They're a team. He cares about her.

He e-mails Terri back: *Baby...let me make it up to you. Please.*

CRIMES OF OMISSION

She meets him at the parking lot where they made love in his Caddy, and he doesn't kiss her cheek like he used to.

He never said he wanted out.

CRIMES OF OMISSION II

He meets her at the parking lot where they made love in his Caddy, and she doesn't have her costume anymore.

She never said she wanted out.

CRIMES OF NECESSITY

There is nobody else in the parking lot tonight. Not even superheroes.

"She's a lovesick idiot who set herself up for a fall," Terri says thickly, when she can speak.

"He's an insensitive shit who doesn't know what he wants," Jack replies.

They know they're hurting each other, and they're not about hurting people. It's not what crimefighters do. At least not what they mean to.

They know they're not about to see each other again.

In the months to come, Fireman goes out in a very public blaze of glory. InvisiGirl isn't seen or heard from again after that.

Terri moves to New York and takes a job with a museum. On the weekends she haunts secondhand bookstores, trying to track down that book she read in college. She never does. Several professional attempts to steal visiting artifacts from her place of employment are quietly and anonymously foiled in the years to come.

Jack and Rosie do not stay married. All she says is: *I know there's someone else. Maybe not in your pants anymore, but there's still someone else.* Jack dies when someone sets fire to his office building, immolating the gym and the bar at its base. He is the only casualty, and Rosie and the girls are given a generous life insurance settlement. None of them attend his funeral.

One day a masked man knocks on Terri's door and lets himself in. Fighting crime is big business now; Terri and Jack were hardly the first, but their methods and budgets pale in comparison to modern standards. The masked man sits in her chair and shakes her hand. "You're InvisiGirl," he says.

"Not anymore," she tells him, without looking up. And she isn't anymore.

"You know it can be good," the masked man says. "You make people happy, and that's what's important. You keep people safe. It can be good if you do it right."

"No," she says. "I don't think so."

She goes back to cataloguing bones. After a while the masked man leaves.

That night Terri takes out her old scrapbook. She couldn't bear to burn everything of the old days. It was as much a part of her life as it was his.

She won't go back. She knows she won't. But at least she has the option.

After all, it's not like they'll ever run out of crime.

THE REMEMBERER

J. ROBERT LENNON

One of my favourite anthologies ever, in or out of the superhero genre, is *Who Can Save Us Now? Brand-New Superheroes and Their Amazing (Short) Stories*, edited by Owen King and John McNally. For *Super Stories of Heroes & Villains*, I've culled three stories from it: Will Clarke's "The Pentecostal Home for Flying Children," George Singleton's "Man Oh Man—It's Manna Man," and this story, J. Robert Lennon's "The Rememberer." Lennon reminds us that superheroism is an ideal fuelled by the utopian and egocentric dreams of childhood.

The Rememberer is born to middle-class parents in a small town in the upper Midwest, and appears, in all particulars, to be a normal and healthy child. She is given a name and introduced into a family of good-natured, self-satisfied people who aspire to, if anything, a kind of strident ordinariness. They are kind, decent, of above-average intelligence, but suspicious of any ostentation or personal peculiarity. They are generous in their deeds, but conservative in their politics and social habits.

The Rememberer develops normally, giving no one in her family any grounds for concern. Certain traits, however, are noted by her mother and father. As an infant, she has an unusually steady, determined gaze. While reclining in her little padded plastic seat, she often cranes her neck, appearing to be looking for something. She is able to sit up straight at a young age, and attempts to crawl long before her body is strong or agile enough to accomplish it. She betrays no obvious frustration, however, at her incapacity to achieve this goal. Rather, she practices until she gets it right. The same dynamic applies to standing up, and walking. The result is a child whom people are impressed by. The Rememberer, however, receives their expressions of delighted surprise with calm impassivity.

Her intellectual development also appears accelerated. She begins to speak at the usual age, but very quickly accumulates an enormous vocabulary. Unlike her brother and sister, she never seems to lose a toy. She calls everyone, even adults, by name. At her play group, she is watchful and alert. She is, by any standard, a distinctive, highly appealing-looking child; nevertheless nobody ever seems to try picking her up or engaging her in play.

One night, while her parents are lying in bed, discussing their day, her father refers to her as "odd." Her mother sighs, but does not disagree.

The Rememberer fares well in school. Uncannily so, in fact. She never seems to do anything wrong. At a conference, her teacher remarks upon this, ostensibly with considerable enthusiasm. But her parents correctly detect a note of distaste in the woman's voice. They discuss the possibility of sending The Rememberer to a special school, for gifted children, but after some thought decide against it. They prefer that she lead a normal life. For her part, The Rememberer soon realizes that her perfect test scores are making those around her uncomfortable, so she begins to make the occasional mistake. Afterward, everyone seems to relax.

The fact is, though she is thought to be the smartest child in the school, there is a consensus among a small group of teachers that this is not the case. The Rememberer seems uncomfortable judging novel social situations, and often offends or irritates other children. However, she soon makes it up to them by recalling their birthdays, or their pets' names, or that they like certain snacks, which she then gives to them. This is learned behavior, the doubting teachers believe, not instinct. They are kind to her, but resent her, in some obscure, unexamined way.

The first real crisis in The Rememberer's life comes when her beloved cat, Louie, is hit by a car and dies. The family is devastated, and is too sad to do much of anything for several days. After that, however, The Rememberer's parents and siblings begin to cheer up, and resume their usual activities; within a few weeks, life is almost back to normal.

But The Rememberer cannot be consoled. She cries constantly, even at school. The pain of loss refuses to dull. Worse, she feels compelled to bring up, during family meals, obscure events from the cat's life, such as the time he was chasing one particular chickadee, the one that lived under the garage eaves, not the one from the birdhouse at the edge of the yard; or the time he was sitting on the porch steps, and then moved over to the far edge of the porch, and then hopped down and sniffed in the grass, and then returned to the steps again; or the time he went outside and sat on the woodpile, then licked himself, then hid underneath the wheelbarrow when it started to rain, then came inside when the rain stopped. The stories seem pointless, but at first the family indulges them, joining The Rememberer in her sadness. After a while, however, they ignore the stories, and finally they tell The Remember to please just stop it, to get over it for goodness' sake, it was just a cat.

Her parents decide that a new cat will cheer her up, so they all go to the pound to pick one out. The Rememberer is indeed temporarily distracted from her grief, and chooses a black shorthair with white paws. And though she appears to like the new cat a great deal, she doesn't stop crying about Louie.

One night she overhears her parents discussing the possibility of bringing her to a psychiatrist. She resolves then to stop crying, and succeeds. However, she remains miserable. From here on in, it will be said of her that she was never the same again.

When she enters junior high, The Rememberer finds herself developing romantic longings for a boy named Nathan. The two sit beside one another at a school football game, and afterward, beneath the bleachers, share a kiss. It isn't long before the two are an inseparable "item," and are seen everywhere together, at the burger joint, the shopping mall, the park. Their relationship lasts until, at a party The Rememberer is unwilling to attend (by this time she has begun to find large social gatherings wearying), her boyfriend "hooks up" with her best friend, and The Rememberer instantly loses the two people closest to her.

Her grief and anger seem inexhaustible, and she stays home from school for several days, wailing in her bedroom. Through her tears she manages to write a pair of letters to her former boyfriend and best friend, listing every single thing either one of them ever said or did that they might be embarrassed for the other to learn. Each letter runs to nearly twenty pages. She manages to choke back sobs long enough to walk to the post office and mail them, and resumes her mourning the moment she exits the building. She mourns not only her cruel friends, but Louie the cat, and every other thing she has ever lost in her life—a beloved Barbie makeup kit stolen by another child on the beach during a family trip to Florida, a glittery tiara that fell off her head during a ferry ride across a Great Lake, an encyclopedia of trees that she left on the bathroom floor and that was ruined when the toilet overflowed, a stolen bicycle, a portrait of her second-grade teacher she drew that her mother inadvertently threw out. Over the years she has managed to pile these things at the edges of her mind, where they would least get in the way. But now they were back at the fore, lying in plain sight, and she is utterly crushed by them.

This time, her parents really do bring her to a psychiatrist. She is prescribed an antidepressant. It succeeds in dulling her pain, but she forgets nothing.

In the years leading up to adulthood, The Rememberer hardens. She keeps to herself, and makes no close friends. Her former best friend eventually breaks up with the boy, and both of them try to win her back. And though her desire to be with them again is great, she resists their overtures. She throws away all her clothes, even her favorites, and uses her allowance, saved over many years, to buy herself an entirely new wardrobe of identical black stretch jeans, black cotton blouses, and black turtleneck sweaters. This becomes her uniform. She wears no makeup. At first she ties her hair back in a tight ponytail; later, she simply has it cut off. She schedules a haircut once a month, in fact, and appears never to change. She eliminates from her life anything that could remotely be construed as evocative. She graduates at the top of her high-school class, but declines to give a speech or even to attend the ceremony. No one bothers to try to convince her otherwise—she is too strange to speak to.

In college, The Rememberer puts in a request to live alone, in a single dormitory room. Instead, she is assigned a roommate. The girl destined to room with her seems nice enough, but The Rememberer goes to the residence office and demands, once again, a single. When her request is denied, she brings her complaint up the ladder of authority, until she finds herself staging a sit-in at the office of the dean of students. When the dean calls her parents, they urge him to just give in, warning that he would likely regret doing otherwise. The semester has only just begun, and the dean has other things to worry about. He capitulates. The Rememberer remains alone for her four years of college.

While there, she takes a class in criminal psychology, and this leads her to major in criminology. She achieves perfect scores on every exam she takes, and is recruited by the FBI to take part in their Special Agent training program. She rises quickly through the ranks, and soon develops a reputation as one of the most promising new agents in institutional memory. Pieces of evidence or information that other agents must review thousands of pages of documents in order to recall, The Rememberer can bring immediately to mind. She memorizes crime scenes with eidetic precision, and can remember within the inch the exact position of cigarette butts, loose change, broken branches, or footprints. Important scraps of a suspect's personal history, which most investigators might dismiss as meaningless and forget immediately, The Rememberer retains. Addresses, telephone numbers, email addresses; notes scribbled on matchbook covers or the backs of envelopes—there is nothing that she sees that is not immediately accessible to her, however much time has passed.

Her colleagues regard her as superhuman. She is respected and feared and has no friends whatsoever.

Throughout the years of her meteoric rise, The Rememberer indulges, from time to time, in acts of shallow pleasure. She experiments with illegal drugs and engages in risky sexual encounters. Once she is established at the Bureau, she quits the drugs; they don't agree with her, in any event, and do little to relieve her pain. She continues, however, to seek out sexual release. At first, she dates men she likes. But inevitably she grows attached to them and, anticipating a sorrowful end, withdraws. Better is a quick, almost violent encounter with a man she does not find especially appealing. She is able to enjoy the thin gruel of carnal relations without the more complex pleasures of commitment. Coupled, however, with her tense associations at work, these experiences cause her to loathe her fellow man.

It takes several years, however, for these tensions to come to the fore. There is one particular agent with whom she once spent the night at the beginning of her training, and who later married another woman, and had a child. Perhaps this life has failed to please the agent; perhaps he has other troubles The Rememberer is not privy to. In any event, he begins to drink, and to become unreliable on the job, and for whatever reason, it is The Rememberer he chooses to bear the brunt of his disappointment. He treats her harshly when they are forced to work together and begins to spread the information, entirely false, that The Rememberer broke up his marriage. When The Rememberer brings her complaints to her superiors, she is told that she made her bed, and now must sleep in it.

Livid with anger, The Rememberer resigns from the Agency. She has saved up a considerable amount of money, having lived these years in solitude and without any desire for costly entertainments, so she can do without the income. But the insult remains fresh in her mind, and her anger does not cool. She recalls all of her life's slights and humiliations, and in her mind they fuse and begin to grow, into one tremendous, terrifying bonfire of rage.

It is at this point that The Rememberer decides to embark upon a life of crime. Her skills make her an ideal blackmailer and planner of robberies. Over the following week, she makes plans—her targets, her techniques, the underworld contacts on whose expertise she will draw. But then, just when she feels ready to take action, she realizes that there is no point. She has no need for money. There is no thrill in harming others, even for revenge. None of it will alleviate her own suffering. With exhausting, forceful effort, she douses the flames of anger. She is left weak and insensible from this labor, and lies in bed for days, her mind and body numb.

And then, one morning, she wakes, and removes from her closet the sewing machine her mother gave her when she was nine years old, back when her parents still held out hope that she might become a "normal" girl. She also finds a dress—a red prom dress, another hopeful gift from Mother—and out of it she cuts an elegant and distinctive shape, a script letter R. She sews the R onto one of her turtlenecks, and examines herself in the bathroom mirror. It would be a peculiar fashion choice for anyone, but for her it is a bizarre ostentation, and the sight of it gives her the first smile she has shown in months. Over the next few days, she cuts dozens of Rs out of the prom dress and stitches them onto her sweaters and blouses. It isn't long before she has no clothes that do not bear the R. She will wear them as a badge of honor. She will no longer deny her deepest nature. She is, once and for all, The Rememberer.

If she is aware that this noble decision will lead inexorably to her own destruction, she gives no sign. All evidence implies that she has found her true calling. She begins by visiting nursing homes and hospitals, interviewing the elderly and infirm, plumbing the depths of their memory. There is something about her—her quiet, impassive, yet kind demeanor—that stirs up the past in these needy people and brings their memories forward. Some are painful, but The Rememberer accepts them, accepts the pain. She listens in receptive silence as the memories pour forth, and while many of them recede into the dark recesses of their bearers' minds mere moments after they emerge, The Rememberer does not forget. She cannot forget. She interviews her subjects' friends and families, tours their homes, turns over their possessions in her pale narrow hands, and soon she is able to tell the story of their lives, unadulterated by the passage of time, as though it were her own. The tellings last for hours and hours, and as she presents her findings, no one becomes tired or distracted, no one asks to take a break. They are mesmerized by The Remember, as if by an impossibly absorbing novel, or an impossibly beautiful song. The lives of the famous and the obscure; lives of loneliness and pain, or of experience and delight—no matter, The Rememberer makes them whole. The dead and dying live as perhaps they never did when their lives were vital. She is an artist and a hero.

But this period of fame is to be brief. No one notices how The Rememberer suffers; she hides her suffering well. When she is through presenting her findings to her subjects' families, she strides from their homes with strength and dignity; but when she reaches her own quarters deep within the warrens of the city, she collapses to the floor and lies unconscious for hours, even days. She must force herself to stand, to eat, to wash. The weight of memory—her own, and others'—is brutally huge.

And then, one day, she cannot even make it home. She collapses on the street, a frail black bundle. She is recognized, carried by a band of concerned passersby to the city hospital. She has fallen into a coma; her vitals are frighteningly out of kilter, but her brain is like a hurricane of electricity, the neurons firing at an astounding rate. Her doctors are stunned when she wakes. Her face is drawn and waxy; she says only one thing: Take me home.

They are still there, The Rememberer's family, living where they always have, in the small town where she grew up. Long estranged, they have not seen The Rememberer in years, though they have followed her exploits in the papers and on TV with pride and shame. She arrives in a magnificent, spontaneous procession, a city ambulance followed by thousands of cars, bicycles, people on foot. The Rememberer's parents tearfully accept her back into her home, carry her to her room, lay her down on the bed. There is so little of her left—yet she lies there for days, her lips moving in a blur of silent reminiscence, all her stored memory leaving her at last. As she withers away, her eyes grow sharper. Her brother, her sister, her parents believe they see happiness in them, for the first time. At last there is nothing left of her: she is merely a shell. The Rememberer is dead.

The funeral is attended by teeming, wailing crowds. There are speeches, but they disappoint: nobody was close to her, nobody could recall what she was really like. When at last she is laid to rest, in the family plot at the edge of town, near the highway, there is much discussion of the memories she contained— how could she have held so many in her mind? And where did they go as they left her? Did they have some substance, did they still linger in the air around the town? Or were they purely ephemeral? And if so, how could something so insubstantial cause such pain?

The questions are never answered, not to anyone's satisfaction, and as the years go by, people begin to wonder if perhaps the tales of The Rememberer's skills have been exaggerated. Those who benefited from her talents remain grateful, but they can't seem to recall half of what she said.

It is not long, in fact, before The Rememberer is almost entirely forgotten. Among the few who do remember, however, is commonly held the conviction that this outcome would ultimately have pleased her.

THE NUCKELAVEE: A HELLBOY STORY
CHRISTOPHER GOLDEN & MIKE MIGNOLA

Mike Mignola has been plunging eager comics readers into the endlessly fascinating pulp- and myth-fuelled world of Hellboy since 1993. Mignola's signature character has also appeared in animated cartoons, live-action films, novels, and a series of *Odd Jobs* anthologies, from which this story is taken. Christopher Golden wrote the first two Hellboy prose novels, the Doc Savage-flavoured *The Lost Army* and the Jack Kirby-infused *The Bones of Giants*—both of which are exciting and evocative neopulp adventures.

The old man had a shuddery way about him, a fidgety, near-to-tears aspect to every glance and gesture that said he'd jump at every shadow, if only he had the strength. If only he weren't so damned old. But his eyes weren't old. His eyes were wild with terror.

It was a cold, clear evening in the north of Scotland, and the sky was striped with colors, from a bruised blue on one horizon to the pink of sorrow or humiliation on the other. The rolling hills that surrounded the crumbling stone estate had no name save for that of the family which had resided there for more than five hundred years: MacCrimmon.

"That's it, then. Just as I said. It's dry as kindling, now, and ne'er will run again," said the old man, whose name was Andrew MacCrimmon.

He was the last of them.

MacCrimmon's wild eyes darted about like those of a skittish horse, as though he waited for some shade to steal upon him. Night had not quite fallen, and already, it seemed the man might die of fright, heart stilled in his chest so as not to be heard by whatever he feared might be hunting him.

Whatever it was, it had to be horrible, for the old man stood on the slope of the hill beside a creature whose countenance would give a hardened killer a week of restless nights and ugly dreams. Hellboy carried himself like a man, but his hooves and tail, his sawed-off horn-stumps, and his sheer size spoke another truth.

There were those who thought him a devil. But Andrew MacCrimmon would have sought help of the devil himself if he thought it would have done him any good.

"You'll stay, then, won't you?" the old man asked. "You must."

Hellboy grunted. He stared at the dry river bed, gazing along its path in both directions. It didn't make any sense at all to him, but he hadn't been there more than fifteen minutes. Just a short way up the bank of the dry river was a small stone building. When the water had still run through there, it would have stood half in, half out of the river.

"What's that?" Hellboy started off toward the stone structure.

"Ye don't understand," the old man whimpered. "Ye've got to help me. I was given to understand that ye do that sort of thing."

As he approached the small building, Hellboy narrowed his eyes. The thing was ancient. Older, even, than the MacCrimmon place, which stood on the hill behind them. It wouldn't have been called a castle. Too small for that. But it was too big to be just a house, and too dilapidated to be called a mansion.

But this other thing...

"What is this?" he asked again.

"It's as old as the family," the old man told him. "Been there from the start. My grandfather told me he thought it was the reason the MacCrimmons settled here."

Hellboy studied the structure, the ancient stone was plain, but overgrown with ivy save for where the water would have washed across it before the river had gone dry. Centuries of water erosion had smoothed the stone, but Hellboy could still make out the faintest impression of carving. Once upon a time, there had been something drawn or written on that stone surface, but it was gone now.

Curiously, he clumped down into the dry river bed and around the other side of the edifice. His hooves sank in the still damp soil. There was something else on the river side of the building. Set into the stone, there was what appeared to be a door.

"How do you get in there?" he asked.

The old man whimpered.

There were no handles of any kind, nor any edges upon which he might get a significant grip. Still, Hellboy tried to open the door, to no avail.

"Please, sir, ye must listen to me," MacCrimmon begged.

Hellboy paused to regard him. The man's long hair and thick, bristly beard were white, and his face was deeply lined. He might have been a hermit, a squatter on this land, rather than its lord. Of course, "lord" was a dubious title when it referred to the crumbling family home, and a clan which no longer existed.

"Go on."

"The river was here before us, but the legend around the doom of Clan Mac-Crimmon was born right here on this hill. When the river goes dry, the legend says, it'll mean the end of Clan MacCrimmon. I've no children, ye see. I'm the last of the clan. Now that the river is dry, death will be coming for me."

"I knew it right off," the old man said, becoming more and more agitated. "Took three days for the river to run dry. Three days, you understand?"

Hellboy grunted. "Not really."

It was then that he noticed that the river wasn't completely dry. A tiny trickle of water ran past the door, past the building. It wasn't more than three inches wide, and barely deep enough to dampen the earth, but it was there. Hellboy reached down to put his finger into the water, and MacCrimmon cried out as if in pain.

"No, you mustn't! It's the doom of the MacCrimmons, don't you see? When the water stops running, the doom of my clan will be released."

"That's...interesting." With a shrug, Hellboy stepped up onto the slope again. "So what do you expect me to do?" he asked, massively confused by the old man's babbling. "Some legend says you're gonna die, I don't know how I'm supposed to deal with that."

The old man clutched at Hellboy's arm with both hands, eyes flicking back and forth in that disturbing, desperate twitch.

"You'll stay for dinner," he said, but it wasn't really a question. "You'll stay, and you'll see."

It was a very long drive back to anywhere Hellboy might stay that he wouldn't be shot at by local farmers or constabulary, so when Andrew MacCrimmon urged him on, he trekked up the hill to the crumbling manse alongside the old man. It was a gloomy place, a testament to entropy, with barely a whisper of the grandeur it must once have had.

Once they had entered, Hellboy saw that he had not been entirely correct about its origins based on his initial observations. While the manse itself was no more than three hundred years old, it was built around an older structure, a cruder, more fundamental tower or battlement, that must once have served as home and fortress for whomever had built it.

MacCrimmon Keep, someone at the BPRD had called it. Hellboy hadn't understood before, but now he saw it. This was the keep, and the rest of the place had been built up around it.

When they had settled inside, the old man brought out cold pork roast and slightly stale bread. There was haggis as well, but it looked like it might have gone over somewhat. Not that Hellboy was the world's greatest expert on haggis, but there was a greenish tint to it that made him even less likely to eat it than if he'd been trapped for a week on Everest with nothing to gnaw on but coffee grounds and it was a choice between haggis or his fellow climbers—which was pretty much the only way he would've eaten haggis even if it were fresh.

"Sorry I don't have more to offer," MacCrimmon muttered, a mouthful of questionable haggis visible between what was left of his teeth as he spoke. "The cook and t'other servants left three days ago, when the river started to slow. They *know*, y'see. They know."

When the meal was done, MacCrimmon seemed twitchier than ever. The manse was filled with sounds, as every old building is—a sign of age like the rings in a tree stump. The old man must have been familiar with most of those sounds, but now they frightened him, each and every one. He seemed to draw into himself, collapsing down upon his own body, becoming smaller. Decaying already, perhaps, at the thought of death's imminent arrival. Or imagined arrival.

"Cigar?" he asked suddenly, as if it were an accusation.

Hellboy flinched, startled. "Sure."

MacCrimmon led him to the library, which was larger than the enormous dining room they'd just left. Two walls were lined floor to ceiling with old, desiccated books, but Hellboy's eyes were drawn immediately to the other walls. To the paintings there, above and around the fireplace—where the old man now built a roaring blaze—and around the windows on the outer wall. Clan MacCrimmon came to life on those walls, in the deep hues and swirls of each portrait, but none of them was more vibrantly powerful than the one at the center of the outer wall. It hung between two enormous, drafty, rattling windows, and seemed, almost, a window itself. A window onto another time, and another shade of humanity. For the figure in the portrait was a warrior, that much was clear.

"Clan MacCrimmon?" Hellboy asked, glancing at the other portraits on the wall.

The old man seemed reluctant even to look at the portraits, but he nodded his assent as he handed Hellboy a cigar. With wooden matches, they lit the sweet-smelling things and began to smoke. After a short while in which nothing was spoken between them, the old man looked up at the portrait of the warrior that hung between the windows.

"That'd be William MacCrimmon. A warrior, he was, and fierce enough to survive that calling. Old William lost his closest friend in battle in 1453, and promised to care for the other warrior's daughter, Margaret."

Hellboy took a long puff on the cigar, then let the smoke out in a huff as he studied the old man. MacCrimmon was warming to the story of his ancestor, clinging to it as though it were a life preserver. It might only have been a way to pass the time, but Hellboy wondered if, in some way, it was the old man's way to keep his fears at bay, just for a while.

"Though already quite old for his time, William fell in love with Margaret, and married her. It was a sensible thing, perhaps the best way to care for the girl. Trouble was, Margaret was a Christian. William had to make some changes. He wasn't from the mainland, ye see. But from the Isle of Malleen. Margaret wouldn't hear of living on the island, for there were stories, even then, of the things which thrived on Malleen."

Hellboy raised an eyebrow and scratched the stubble on his chin. "Things?"

For the first time since he began the story, MacCrimmon looked at him. The old man grinned madly.

"Why, the fuathan, o' course. Ye've never heard of them?"

Hellboy didn't respond. Considering the job, he didn't study nearly as much as he should. The old man didn't seem to notice, his attention drawn back to the portrait of his warrior ancestor.

"Old William had known the people, the fuathan, since he was a bairn, ye ken. Shaggy little beasts that might be men if not for the way nature twisted their bodies. The legends say they hated men, but not so, not so. They were the servants and allies of the islanders, and held malice only for those from the mainland.

"Still, when William married Margaret, and chose to remain here in the north country, rather than return to the island, the fuathan had no choice. They came along. It were they who built the original keep, and that pile out in the river bed. It were they who made the river run, so the legend goes, for the fuathan were ever in control of the water.

"What it was built to house, the legends dinna say, but the story has it that they raised it in a day, and the keep itself in a week, all the while, making certain Margaret MacCrimmon would never see them. There's a circle of stones in the wood over the hill that were used for worship. The fuathan lived there, in the wood around the circle, and the clan grew with both the new religion and the old faith."

Hellboy shivered. He'd heard similar stories dozens of times, about the encroachment of Christianity into pagan territories, one family at a time. But in this case, with the results crumbling and gloomy around him, it seemed far more tangible. Honestly, it gave him the creeps. The clash of old and new faiths could not have been a healthy one. He had to wonder what it had done to the offspring of that union, down across the centuries.

The old man seemed to have run out of steam, though he still stared at the portrait of the warrior. And there was something odd about that portrait, something that held the eye. Hellboy tore his gaze away, took a puff of his cigar, and turned his attention on the old man again.

"So you live here alone, now? I mean, except for the servants who ran off?"

"Last of the clan," MacCrimmon agreed, apparently forgetting that he'd told Hellboy that already. "Alone here since my brother died."

With the fat cigar clenched in his teeth, the old man moved to the stone fireplace, the blazing light flickering over his features. There were faded photographs in silver frames on the mantel, and MacCrimmon pulled one of them down and handed it to Hellboy. In the corner, a dusty grandfather clock ticked the seconds by, its pendulum glinting with the light of the fire as it swung back and forth.

In the photograph, two young men flanked a beautiful girl, whose raven hair and fine china features reminded Hellboy of a woman he had once known. He pushed the thought away. The two men were obviously MacCrimmon and his brother. Though Andrew had grown old now, though his face was wrinkled and bearded, the eyes staring out of that photograph were the same.

Wild, even then. And Hellboy had to wonder if the man had ever been sane.

He handed the photograph back to the old man. "Who's the girl?"

MacCrimmon set his cigar on the stone mantel, and stared at the photo, a dreamy look relaxing his features for the first time since Hellboy had arrived.

"That'd be Sarah Kirkwall. She was here all that long summer. This photo was taken the day before me brother Robert announced that they were to be engaged." The old man frowned, and rubbed distractedly at his forehead. When he spoke again, his voice was lost and far away. "They lived here, with me, until Robert...died. I told Sarah she could stay, that I'd care for her, just as Old William MacCrimmon had taken care of Margaret five hundred years ago. That she could...marry me."

The anguish in the old man's voice was horrible to hear, and Hellboy felt the sadness in that old stone dwelling creeping into his bones.

"So you married?"

The old man shook his head, still staring at the photo. "It were Robert she loved. When he died, she...went away. I never did marry. Sarah was the girl for me. There never were anyone else."

MacCrimmon looked even older now, shrunken, staring down at the photograph as though trapped, now, in that other time, back when. Hellboy thought again of the portrait of the warrior on the wall, how it looked almost like a window on another time, and seemed to draw you in. The photograph in the silver frame had the same effect on the old man.

Hellboy scratched the back of his neck, where what hair he had was tied back in a knot. "How did Robert die?" he asked.

The frame tumbled from the old man's hands and shattered on the stone in front of the fireplace. Hellboy prepared to catch MacCrimmon, thinking he must be about to collapse, but the old man just stared at his hands, the spot where the frame had been. Slowly, he reached out and took his cigar from the mantel, and pulled a long puff on it.

"Ten years ago, this very night," MacCrimmon said.

He seemed almost calm, and then a shudder ran through him and he turned and looked at the grandfather clock. When he spoke again, his voice cracked with a panic he could no longer hide.

"Ten years ago tonight," he repeated. "He died at three minutes past nine."

Hellboy glanced at the clock. It was only a few minutes before nine then, half a dozen minutes to go before the dreadful anniversary.

With that edge of panic still in his voice, the old man continued. "He was three days sick, dying, before he went at last. Just as the river was three days, drying up. Now it's almost time. The last trickle will run through the dry bed out there, and he'll come for me."

Minutes ticked by, and Hellboy just watched the old man in silence. The cigar burned in MacCrimmon's hand, but he made no effort to smoke it. Then, suddenly, the old man glanced at the burning weed in his hand, and he narrowed his gaze, as if seeing it for the first time. With a tremor of disgust, he threw the cigar into the fire, which now had begun to burn low. The flames flared up inexplicably, tendrils of fire lashing out at the stone masonry, then dying down again.

The grandfather clock chimed nine.

Andrew MacCrimmon dropped to his knees before Hellboy, tears beginning to slip down his craggy features.

"Save me!" he pleaded.

Hellboy only looked at him dubiously.

The clock continued to chime.

As if he'd been startled by some sudden noise, the old man turned his head and glanced about, eyes more wild than ever, hands on his head as though he might hide himself away.

"Did ye not hear that? It's the doom of the MacCrimmons!"

"It's just the clock," Hellboy told him.

The old man rushed to one of the wind-rattled windows and threw it open. He leaned out, but Hellboy knew that from that angle, there was no way MacCrimmon could see what he was looking for. The river bed, of course, and that little stone building the man had insisted was built by horrid little fairy creatures.

"Not the clock! Don't you see? It's him. It's *it*. The stream's gone dry, and it's coming out. Battering down that door. It's coming up the lawn now, coming for me!"

The old man turned from the window and fell again at Hellboy's feet. He clutched the bottom of Hellboy's duster and buried his face in it, whimpering, muttering.

Hellboy frowned. "Did you bury your brother in that little building out there?"

"You saw that place," the old man stammered. "There's no way to open it from the outside, but...from the inside...no. Robert's cremated and his ashes are in a niche at St. Brendan's, where they ought to be. But..."

MacCrimmon gripped his jacket even more tightly, his voice barely a whisper. "There, you *must* hear it. It's coming for me. His ghost has set it free. There! It's broken down the door. Can't you hear it on the stairs?"

Hellboy heard nothing. He looked down at the old man and felt a little sorry for him, though he had a strong suspicion what had driven him so completely mad.

"You killed him."

The old man wailed. "Robert has loosed the doom of the MacCrimmons on me for murderin' him. I fed him poison and sat by those three days while it killed him. I did it for her, I did it for the girl, and it wasn't ever me that she wanted..."

His voice trailed off after that. He fell quiet, listening. Then the old man jerked, suddenly, as if he'd been pinched.

"It's there now!" he screamed, voice raspy and hoarse. "In the hall, just outside the door. Please, help me. Take me with you. Kill me! Anything. Just don't let that thing take me!"

Despite the old man's mad cries, however, the room was silent save for his blubbering and the ticking of the clock. On the face of that antique timekeeper, the long hand had moved inexorably along so that it was now four or five minutes after nine o'clock. The anniversary of Robert MacCrimmon's death had come and gone.

"Don't have a heart attack or anything," Hellboy said. "Look, I'll show you."

He reached for the door knob, shaking his head ruefully. But just as his fingers touched it, the door came crashing down at him, tearing off its hinges and slamming Hellboy to the floor.

"Jeez!" he shouted in surprise.

As he tried to get out from under the heavy door, a sudden and tremendous weight was put on it from above, pinning him there. Hellboy grunted in pain, struggled to move, and could not. There was a horrid stench, like nothing he had ever smelled before, death and rot and fecal matter, blood and sweat and urine, matted horse hair and putrefying fish, and something else, something worse than all of those disgusting odors combined.

Then, without warning, the weight was removed. Something stepped off the door and into the room. Hellboy summoned his strength and his anger, and tossed the shattered door off him. He glanced around, and then he saw it, one of the most horrifying monstrosities he had ever laid eyes on. It was like a huge, equine creature that might have been a horse if it had any skin. Instead, there was only naked purple muscle and white tendons and swollen black veins. Growing out of its back was a human torso, also stripped of skin, with a head that swung about wildly as if there were no bones in its neck. Its huge mouths, both human and horse, gaped open and that stink poured out, almost visible, like breath in winter.

Its long arms snaked out and grabbed hold of old man MacCrimmon, and hauled him up onto the back of its horse segment. Hellboy started to roar, started to lunge for it, but a hoof lashed out and cracked against his skull, and he went down hard on the floor of the library, not far from the blazing fire.

By the time he shook off the blow, the creature was gone, the old man's screams echoing through the house and down the hillside. Hellboy rose, ready to give chase, but the fire flared again, and he turned to see that it was blue now. Tendrils of blue flame shot out of the blaze and seemed to touch each of the portraits in turn, ending with that of William MacCrimmon, founder of the clan.

Blue fire seemed to seep into the portrait, becoming paint, becoming one with the history in that window on that past. It truly was a window now, and through it, Hellboy could see the old warrior moving, turning to glare into the library with a stern countenance, cold and cruel in judgement. Tendrils of blue flame jumped from portrait to portrait, and the painted images of the warrior's descendants were somehow erased from their own frames, to appear behind the original, the founder. That portrait seemed to grow, with all of them standing therein, arms crossed before them, glaring down like inquisitors.

Then the portrait burst into flame, and Hellboy heard an enormous crack. The keep, the part of the MacCrimmon homestead that had been built so long ago by the fuathan, began to fall, to collapse down into the remainder of the house. The shelves and books in the library were set aflame, but the flame was nearly snuffed out as the walls collapsed, tumbling toward Hellboy.

He ran for one of the huge windows, not daring to look at the burning, living painting, at the ghosts of the clan MacCrimmon, for fear he might be sucked into that collective past. Hellboy crashed out through the window and fell twenty feet to the hillside below. The walls were crumbling in on themselves, but several stones came falling after him, and he rushed to avoid being crushed or buried.

He could hear Andrew MacCrimmon screaming, down the hill, where the river bed was now completely dry. Hooves pounding the grass, Hellboy gave chase.

Where the river had run, he saw hoof prints from the beast in the soft, damp earth. As he passed the structure that stood on the river's edge, he saw that the stone door he had found impossible to open now hung wide. Seconds after he crossed the dry river bed, he heard a kind of explosion, and turned to see that even that stone structure had been part of the chain reaction. It was nothing but rubble now.

The doom of the MacCrimmons had come, all right.

There came another scream. Hellboy glanced up the opposite hill and saw the beast disappearing over its crest, looking like nothing more than a large horse bearing two riders. But the way its raw, skinless form glistened wetly in the moonlight...it was no horse.

When he reached the top of the hill, however, neither beast nor man were anywhere in sight. Hellboy crouched in the spot he had last seen them, and found a trail. It was relatively easy to track; the beast was so heavy that its hooves left prints in the hardest, driest ground.

Hellboy followed.

Hours passed, and he made his way across farms and estates, through groves and over hills, and finally he came to a town on the north coast, the tang of the ocean in the air, the sound of the tides carrying through the streets. It was after midnight, and most of the residents had long since retired for the evening. In the midst of the town, on a paved road, he lost the trail. Hopelessly, he looked around for someone who might have seen something. After a minute or two, he spotted a portly man slumped in a heavy, old chair on the porch of what appeared to be some kind of mercantile.

"Hey, wake up," Hellboy said, nudging the portly man with the weight of his stone hand.

The man snorted, blinked his eyes open, and let out a yell of surprise and fear. The odor of whiskey came off him in waves.

"Quiet," Hellboy snapped. "I'm just passing through."

"Thank the Lord for that," the man said in a frightened whisper.

"You see anything strange go through here?"

The man stared at him as if he were insane.

"Anything *worse*?" Hellboy elaborated.

"Depends on your definition of strange, I suppose," the man said. "Two men came through, not long ago. Two men riding the same horse. Only one of them wasn't riding. He *was* the horse. That's pretty strange."

"You see where it went?" Hellboy demanded.

"Down to the rocks," the man replied. "Down to the sea. And that old one screaming all the way. Weren't a surprise, though. I'd scream too, that horse, and the whole thing smelling like a fisherman's toilet."

His voice trailed off and he moaned a bit, and fell back to sleep, or into unconsciousness. The whiskey had claimed him again.

Hellboy scratched his chin and looked along the paved road to the rocks and the ocean beyond. He could hear the waves crashing, and he started to walk toward them. At the end of the road, he stopped where the rocks began. There was a cough off to his left, and he turned to see an old woman standing on the front stoop of her home in a robe that was insufficient for the chill ocean breeze.

"It was a Nuckelavee," she told him.

Hellboy looked at her oddly, but she didn't even turn her face to him. She just stared out at the ocean.

"When I was but a wee girl in the Hebrides, my father told me a story. He were coming home late one night, and a Nuckelavee come up out of the ocean and chased him. He only escaped by jumping over a little stream of fresh water. The monster roared and spit and with one long arm snatched off me father's hat, but he got away clean save for a pair of claw marks to show off to prove the truth of it."

Now she looked straight at Hellboy for the first time.

"He was luckier than that old man tonight. That's certain."

Hellboy nodded and looked out across the waves again. He could see a dark hump in the distance, out on the ocean.

"What's that?"

The old woman hesitated. At length, she spoke, her voice low and haunted. "'Tis the Isle of Malleen. But don't ye think about goin' out there. It's not a place fit for man, nor e'en a thing such as yourself. There's only evil out there, dark and cruel. If that's where the Nuckelavee was headed, no wonder the old man were screaming so."

Hellboy considered her words, staring at the island in the distance.

"I guess maybe he deserved it," he said after a bit. "I'm starting to wonder if maybe all it did was take that old man home. And I think there'll be hell to pay when he gets there."

The wind shifted, then, and for a moment, it seemed as though he could hear a distant scream, high and shrill and inhuman. But then the waves crashed down again on the rocks, and it was gone.

FACES OF GEMINI
A. M. DELLAMONICA

From A. M. Dellamonica, author of the Astrid Lethewood novels and, for Tor.com, of a series of articles—Buffy Rewatch—about Joss Whedon's celebrated vampire-slaying superhero, here's a tale that first appeared in *Girls Who Bite Back: Witches, Mutants, Slayers and Freaks*.

Gemini found her twin sister Leela crashed on the couch in her ratty apartment, snoring raspily with a melted bottle of champagne clutched to her breast and teary lines of mascara on her cheeks. The dregs of the alcohol had spilled when the bottle liquefied, and the room smelled of booze and farts.

Eau de fraternity, Gemini thought. *This isn't going to work.* Despite the urge to flee she remained in place, helmet in hand, looming over the couch wearing the ill-fitting battlesuit she'd put on an hour before.

As she woke, Leela said Gemini's given name with a snort and a quiet belch: "Chelsea?"

"Yeah, it's me."

"What are you doing in that get-up?"

"There's an emergency," said Gemini. "Are you drunk?"

"Could be," Leela said.

"Meaning yes, I suppose, or you'd take my head off for even asking."

"Have it your way." Leela flashed an uncharacteristic grin. "I saw you on the news today. Amazing footage. Is it always like that?"

"It's a blur," Gemini said. The words were out before she realized they were true.

Leela stretched, curling her toes. "Mom already has a nice glossy photo of you saving that baby—for her scrapbook."

"Baby..." she said, just barely remembering.

"You drippified the guy's sword before he could decapitate the kid, and then took out his reins. Bastard fell right off his horse."

"I vapourized a lot of tack today," Gemini said, thinking of the dozens of horses still running loose downtown.

"No surprise you forgot. It looked pretty intense."

"Intense," she echoed sarcastically. "Five thousand barbarian warriors—"

"Relax, Chelsea, I'm not trying to minimize. It must have been terrible."

Gemini nodded, not trusting herself to speak. The horde had thundered into Stanley Park at dawn, killing everyone they found. The barbarians' weapons had been primitive, but pitted against a scattering of unarmed joggers, tourists and kids, they had done plenty of damage. Dozens of civilians had been murdered before Crucible had arrived to contain the threat.

"So..." Leela said. "Bad guys gone now?"

"No. The army's taken over. Did you say you were at Mom's? Was there—" She bit back the tactless question—was there some kind of crisis? "I mean..."

A muscle in Leela's cheek jumped. "Dodd's moving."

"Where?"

"Back to London."

Of course. The tears, the boozing—it made sense now. The ex-husband was hauling Leela's son—Gemini's nephew—across the Atlantic. "What are you doing about this, Leela? Sitting back and letting him take your kid without a fight?"

"No, I—"

"You had to drive him away, didn't you?"

Leela squinted up at her. "If you came here to abuse me, you'll have to get out."

Gemini reined her feelings in with difficulty. "Sorry."

"Thanks. You want coffee?"

"Uh..." The offer caught her off-guard—Leela was rarely so quick to let bygones be bygones.

Getting up, Leela finally noticed the now-hardened glass lump of bottle fused to her tank top. Her mouth bunched. "Jeez, Chelsea, did you have to?"

"No, it was you who—" Gemini protested, but Leela had peeled off the shirt. She let it fall to the floor as she vanished into the kitchen.

"Leela, stop a sec. You'd better—"

"I better what?" The warning came too late—a kitchen cupboard melted away, dribbling like hot mozzarella. The jars inside the cabinet came cascading down, shattering on the counter. By the time Gemini got there, her sister was covered in bits of broken glass, coffee grounds and flour.

My reaction time is down, she realized. *Am I still in shock?*

"Shit." Leela eyed the mess with mild surprise. "Why didn't you tell me I had your superpowers again?"

"They're our powers."

"Bull." Leela clamped flour-covered fingers over her mouth before her breath could melt anything else. Then, brow furrowed in concentration, she sighed loudly. The flour on her hand became little beads, dribbling and then evaporating so that the flesh beneath was left clean.

Gemini's spirits lifted. If Leela had that much control over the most destructive of their handful of powers, her plan might work after all. "I need a favour. Can you help? With you in possession of our abilities—"

"It all depends on what the favour is, Chelsea."

"I need you to go on a mission," Gemini said. "As me."

"Forget it."

"But—"

"Don't piss me off, Chelsea. I can't afford to melt this apartment to slag."

"Remain calm, breathe slowly—"

"Don't you give me orders." Leela's voice finally had an edge. The kitchen wall thinned and dribbled, like wax near an open flame.

"Look," Gemini said. "All I need—"

"No." Leela put up a hand, silencing her. "We'll switch the powers back to you."

"That won't work. I'm in a terrible mood, Leela."

"As if I hadn't noticed. You'll have to sort yourself out, Chelsea."

"It's not that simple."

"Funny, it's what you always say to me."

Gemini felt her hands balling into fists. She sucked her lips over her teeth and clamped her jaw shut over the skin until it hurt.

Leela was unmoved. "Take that stupid suit off."

Surrendering, Chelsea unhinged the battlesuit so that its torso fell open. Her breasts, relieved of the armour's compression, immediately started to ache. She levered herself up out of the suit's legs, setting one bare foot on the floor.

"Watch the wreckage," said Leela, but the warning came too late—Gemini's heel crunched down onto glass with an intense, shocking sting.

"Over here." Leela headed back to the dingy dining room, already stripping off her clothes. Gemini hopped in pursuit, leaning one-legged against the plastic table as she tugged the shard of glass from her foot. She wriggled out of her shirt and bra, one-handed, then paused—if she let go of her punctured foot, it would drip blood on the faded carpet.

Leela retrieved her ruined, bottle-smeared tank top and nudged it towards Gemini. "Stand on this."

"Thanks." She put her foot down and then peeled the rest of her clothes, folding them nervously.

"You ready?"

"Ready," Gemini said, suddenly breathless.

Nude, they hugged each other tightly. There was an instant where the embrace seemed normal, even comforting. Then they began to fuse, flesh melting together until they were once again as they had been at birth: twins, identical and conjoined, they now had one wide body between them. Leela controlled the left leg and arm, Gemini the right. To all outward appearances, they were a two-headed woman.

Gemini stared at their reflection in the glass of the dining room window. They had learned to walk like this, to ride a bicycle together, sleep, to swim. For seven years they had been together constantly. Everything had been a negotiation: where to go, when to sit or stand, who would hold which lace as they tied their shoes.

Then Dad had found an old sorcerer, one willing to reshape them, to melt them apart as if their flesh was wax. He'd "drippified" their body—to use Leela's term—remaking them into two. They'd had to learn to walk again, to swim, write and eat separately.

They had to learn to be alone.

The solitude had been terrifying. But Leela and Gemini had their own separate hearts now, their own lungs and wombs and control of two hands each. The superpowers they'd gotten during that mystic separation, though, were throwbacks—abilities shared by them both.

"Okay," Leela's breath warmed her ear. Their faces were canted away from each other; they had never quite been able to look each other in the eye when joined. "I had the powers, we've merged, you should have them when we separate."

"One, two, three, go," Gemini said.

They pulled apart, flesh stretching between them. As her inner hand and foot took shape, seeming to grow out of the wet tissue of Leela's innards, Gemini sensed that the switch had worked. Her skin no longer felt raw and oversensitive. Her cuts and bruises did not ache. They separated, and Gemini's vision sharpened. Her fatigue vanished and her mind started to clear...

She reached for the duffel gratefully, hand closing around the fabric of her Gemini uniform. But as her gaze took in the familiar black bodysuit, with its pattern of white stars, everything snapped back. The tiredness and pain returned, hitting like bricks or fists.

"Shit," Leela said. "Okay, new plan. I'll think of the most depressing thing I can until the powers go back to you."

"Leela, it won't work."

"Come on. You're the perky one."

"It's not about perk."

"Right. It's psychic strength, well-being, self-esteem. You have your shit to-gether and I don't. You're the one everyone's proud of, I've made all the mistakes..."

"I never said that..."

"I know, but I'm trying to bring myself down, okay?"

"Oh. Right. You're a mess."

Leela laughed. "Get your happy back and get the hell out of here, okay?"

Closing her eyes, Gemini dug into her cache of pleasant memories. She evoked her first encounters with the others—Balm, Serpentine, Crimson and Mortar. They'd all been working solo back then, Little League vigilantes busting crime lords and small-time supervillains. Over time they'd clustered into a group, one that eventually received an official law-enforcement mandate from the Province. Shortly afterward they became Crucible, then Looking Glass—Powell—had joined the group. The team had saved the world that day, and Gemini had fallen in love.

It was no good. Her past seemed tainted, and her mind was drawn instead to this morning's battle. She heard the screams again, saw the pile of severed heads, remembered a horse tangled and panicked, caught in the chains of a swing-set. There'd been a body beside the animal, a bike courier punctured by arrows...

"Dammit," Leela hissed. "We used to do this on the phone. Are you trying?"

Gemini nodded.

"So what's wrong? Would it help if you talked about it or something?"

"No. It's—" She fought back the tears, the panic-inducing sense of shock. "It's been an unspeakable day."

"I'm sorry, Chelsea. Really. But I'm no superhero."

"I just need you to—"

"No! Fuck, isn't this why you have a team?"

"They're—" Gemini slumped against a chilly wall; without the battlesuit holding her upright, she could barely stand. "Purgatoire has them."

Leela's eyes widened. "All of them?"

Gemini nodded, gaze lowered. The room seemed to get quieter and quieter, and it sank in that she was still undressed. She scooped her panties off the table and stepped into them. Fingering her bra, she sighed, dreading the idea of strapping up her aching breasts again. Then she made herself do it.

When she risked a peek up, Leela was dusting flour off her skin and eyeing Gemini warily. "You want me to dress up as you and take on a big-name super-villain," she said. "With no experience, backup, and imperfect control over your powers—"

"*Our* powers, Leela—"

"Plus he has hostages?"

"It's Purgatoire. There are always hostages."

"These are your friends, Chelsea. What if I screw up? Six months ago we were barely speaking. If I get your team killed..."

"They'll die if you don't help. Please, I need one small assist—and it's entirely nonviolent."

Leela's eyes narrowed. "No combat?"

"No fighting, I swear. Help with one thing and I'll take over."

"How? In that?" Leela gestured at the empty battlesuit, standing like an eggshell abandoned by a newly hatched chick, at the edge of the kitchen.

"Yes," Gemini said.

Leela grunted, examining the suit. Nine feet tall, it was emphatically male, albeit with skewed proportions. Its limbs were elongated, its hands and feet massive, its groin robust. The whole of its musculature was exaggerated and lumpy. They could have been pleasing dimensions, maybe, but the helmet was just a shade too small. Overall, it made the wearer seem bulky and pinheaded.

That helmet stared at Gemini from the tabletop now. She had melted its front to waxy lumps in a battle long ago. Faceless, it was topped with sculpted curls of hair.

Gemini had put the suit on for the first time only an hour before, after she'd finally made it back to Base Pacific. With her teammates abducted and her powers gone, getting home had been an ordeal, one that took hours her friends might not have.

She had crawled down to the base Vault and found the suit. It had seemed hideous, a totem lying under layers of dust.

Moving in it felt like being joined to Leela again: everything was slow, each movement a bit delayed.

Leela touched the suit's metal skin lightly, with just her fingertips. "Is this the outfit from the guy who almost killed Powell?"

"Yes, a villain named Sliver. His suit was in our evidence vault."

"Won't he want it back?"

"I killed him," Gemini said shortly. "Leela, we're wasting time."

"Strategize this, Chelsea. If you can just go and borrow some suit full of superpowers anytime you want to, what do you need me for?"

"To free one of my teammates, that's all. You won't be involved in the fighting, Leela. I promise."

"Shit." It was a long exhalation. "I am officially unhappy about this, okay?"

"Apparently you're happier than me," Gemini said morosely.

Dimples ghosted on and off of Leela's cheeks, and Gemini's suspicion that her sister was drunk resurfaced. But she couldn't be, could she? She had the super-metabolism now.

"It had to happen sometime," Leela said.

Within the hour, they were flying low over the Burrard Inlet in the Crucible Orb, the team's primary vehicle. Leela was slouched on a passenger couch, wearing Gemini's black suit. Picking at the fabric, she twisted in her seat.

"Are you okay?" Gemini finally asked.

"I guess. Being you is a little weird."

"Imagine doing it full-time."

"Well, there's the fame, the public service medals, the fans, the perfect boyfriend..."

"The secret identities and the terrible hours," Gemini rejoined, stung. "Not to mention the fighting and the injuries."

"Yeah. I'm glad you guys have that healer..."

"Balm," Gemini said.

"Though I guess he can't fix everything."

"No," she said. The Orb controls shimmered briefly, obscured by tears.

"I'm glad you have Balm," Leela repeated. "You know we worry sometimes. Mom and I."

Gemini didn't answer that. *Am I supposed to apologize?*

"Speaking of fighting, can you actually operate that old battlesuit?"

"It's fine," Gemini said. In fact, Sliver's suit was tight around her hips, its outward appearance of roominess compromised by the power packs and equipment housed inside. Its manly form-fitted chest was mashing her breasts again; they were practically bumping her chin. "The controls are well-designed; a kid could fly it."

"Controls for what?"

"Oh—flight maneuvers, guns."

"Guns?"

Gemini triggered a sequence and tiny silver needles erupted from the battlesuit's enlarged fingertips, homing in on one of the Orb's couches and puncturing the upholstery. "Guns."

"Gross." Leela arched her back, still tugging at Gemini's unitard. "I'm never gonna pass for you."

Privately, Gemini agreed. "Remember you aren't wearing clothes: the costume is more of a skin. There are no pockets, you can't fuss with your hair because of the mask, and don't scratch yourself. If you stand still you'll look aloof, otherworldly."

"Riiiight," Leela said dubiously. "That reminds me, I wanted to ask. We were born in Regina. But you're always telling the press you come from some planet orbiting Castor..."

"Pollux."

"Whatever. Why the lie?"

"You want people to know my powers are linked to a twin sister with a vulnerable little boy? What if my enemies found out I had a sweet old mom?"

"Oh. Have I mentioned lately I hate your life?"

"Every time you see me," Gemini said. She'd meant to sound lighthearted; instead her voice came out brittle, and Leela's head whipped around.

Gemini tensed, in the silence that followed, for the inevitable fight.

"Ah," Leela said at last. "Well, I'm sorry about that."

"Are you joking?" With Leela's face hidden behind the Gemini mask, she honestly couldn't tell.

"No. Actually, I'm pretty proud of you. Not scrapbook proud or anything. But...what you do. It's important. And you're good at it." She laughed, sounding embarrassed. "I'll shut up—I can't tell what you're thinking in that getup."

"I was just thinking that about you," Gemini said. Praise from Leela—a watery sense of pleasure suffused her, warring with a suspicion that this was a trick, some tactic that would blow up on her the next time the two of them argued.

It's the kid going away, she concluded—*it's shaken Leela up. She's apologizing, cleaning house emotionally. Please,* she prayed suddenly, *don't let her be suicidal.*

Leela folded her hands in her lap—a visible effort to keep still. "So, what's the deal? Tunnels? Booby-trap-a-minute electronics, idiot henchmen posted at every door?"

Gemini shook her head. "Purgatoire doesn't go for underground warrens. He likes to have lots of civilians handy."

"Hostages, right," Leela murmured.

Gemini pushed away a memory from this afternoon—herself, bobbing powerlessly in the Pacific while mind-controlled civilians dragged her teammates into Purgatoire's lair. "He charms people—that's what he calls it: 'charm'—into becoming his captives."

"And you know where he is now?"

"Canada Place. We were on our way to apprehend him when they brought in the horsemen to distract us. Here, I've got the target on-screen."

"Target," Leela grumbled. The Crucible Orb brought up a high-resolution image of the terminal. The cruise ships had been pulled away from the dock, and the walkways were eerily devoid of tourists. Yellow police tape formed a perimeter around the building. "Aren't the cops going to do *anything*?"

"No point," Gemini said. "He'd charm them once they got within range...and then he'd have puppets with guns."

"Great. So what's our plan?"

"We take the Orb underwater, like so." Making the vehicle's bulkheads transparent, she brought the ship out of flight, entering the water silently. "With luck, we can get in from below."

"And what exactly is this teeny tiny thing I have to do?"

The colour of the water deepened to green as they moved into the Inlet. Gemini turned on the Orb's running lights. "Help me free Evangeline."

"Which one is Evangeline?"

"Jesus, Leela, she's Crimson."

"Don't snap." Leela's voice was maddeningly calm. "You told me everyone's real name once...what? Five years ago?"

"Sorry." Fighting a tremble in her hands—probably fatigue or low blood sugar, things that didn't worry her when she had powers—Gemini brought up a team photo on Orb's main screen. "Reading left to right: Crimson is Evangeline. Serpentine is Maria. Mortar and Balm are Rufus and Cray, respectively..."

"And Looking Glass is your dear sweet Powell. Okay, got it. Thanks for the review." Leela fiddled with her mask. "Hey, shouldn't you have back-up plans for everyone getting captured?"

"This is a contingency plan, sort of. It's one they won't think of." Gemini shifted inside the battlesuit, trying to get comfortable. It had been so long since she'd lost her powers that she had forgotten how sensitive her skin could be, how every touch could set off a parade of sensations. The unyielding press of the battlesuit's interior mouldings was creating bruises, unfamiliar, hard-to-ignore aches. The only thing the increased sensitivity that came with being powerless made better was sex. Her loins burned dully at the thought, a quick surge of rote horniness that rose and then dropped away.

She focused on Leela, who was staring out at the sea. In the pale glow cast by the Orb, even the polluted and litter-strewn underworld of Burrard Inlet seemed romantic. Lank plaits of seaweed caressed the hull, and schools of fish—probably toxic and inedible—swam past, their every move a whipsaw mystery. A seal nosed over to investigate them.

"The things you get to do," Leela murmured, voice full of wonder. "Miracles for breakfast."

Gemini surprised herself by speaking: "What was it like when Dodd said he was going to England? I mean—how did it feel?"

"I dunno," Leela said. She was still watching the seal. "He's been homesick."

"Yeah, but—"

"He's not leaving to punish me, Chelsea."

"Do you still love him?"

"Maybe. When he first left, I was...a million mood changes a day. Stormy."

"It came out of nowhere," Gemini remembered.

"Yeah." The black and white costume with its star-field pattern radiated cool competence. Leela's voice was soft, thoughtful. "One second I feel sucker-punched, the next I'm celebrating the things I don't have to put up with anymore. The petty irritations, you know? Two seconds later I'm forgiving, then I'm mad, then I'm crying..."

Gemini felt her mouth working, but no sound came.

"Are we here?" Leela asked. They had come under a scroll of shadow, moving into blackness.

"We're under the pier. I'll scan for warm bodies." Leela leaned close to watch as Gemini scanned the structure above them. "There—that'll be Purgatoire, and there's my team..."

"They're the green lights? So what are those pale pink dots?"

"Puds—I mean, civilians. People without powers."

"Other hostages."

Blushing inside the clunky helmet, Gemini nodded. "He's got them scattered around the building to make it harder to assault the place."

"You think there's a route in from below?"

"Yes." She tapped the screen, highlighting it. "You melt a corridor straight upward from this point."

"And then?" Leela asked.

Gemini circled the brightest of the green lights on the display. "Crimson is immune to our powers. You'll poke your head into the conference room and vapourize whatever restraints they're using to hold her. She'll get loose, I'll fly in. She and I will mop up Purgatoire. Meanwhile you'll get back into Orb and wait for us."

"What if I free Crimson and he just zaps her again, or she's knocked out..."

"It doesn't work that way. Evangeline can't lose consciousness; it's one of her abilities. And she'll have been thinking about counter-tactics ever since they captured her. Believe me, nobody takes out Crimson twice in a row."

"I need to know this plan of yours will work, Chelsea."

"It will," Gemini said. She suddenly realized the voice coming through her mask was Sliver's, high, crystalline and sexless. It was almost a child's voice, and to her ear it sounded vulnerable, full of doubt.

"Okay," Leela said. "Let's go."

They surfaced and Leela clambered out of the Orb, arms flailing until she got her footing and exhaled upward, melting them a tunnel. Everything thinned, dribbled, and then vanished, leaving a lumpy-edged corridor that led upward through the deck, and various building materials. Gemini couldn't have done a better job herself. She felt hollow suddenly—redundant, unnecessary.

The team needs me, she reminded herself.

"The drips can be used as handholds as they harden," she said. But Leela was already climbing up through the tunnel she had made, her spandexed ass swaying as she switched from grip to grip, moving upward.

Thumbing the battlesuit controls, Gemini flew up in pursuit of her sister. They ascended in silence, reaching the concrete floor just below the conference room.

"I'm not ready for this," Leela said, voicing Gemini's own thought.

"Melt the cement and soften the carpet just a bit, then push up and take a peek. We're in the corner of the room...it should be nice and unobtrusive."

"Should." Leela sighed and the cement vanished. The carpet got stringy and thin. She poked upward, peered out...and did nothing.

"Free Crimson," Gemini reminded her in a whisper. But Leela was gesturing for them both to descend, making choppy gestures and then climbing down so rapidly she almost fell into the water.

"Problem?" Gemini hissed at the bottom as Leela fell to her hands and knees, heaving. "You're not going to barf in my costume, are you?" She tried to chuckle, to break the tension. Instead the sound came out forced, hiding nothing.

"No. Probably no. Um...Chelsea. Crimson can't be killed?"

"She's completely immortal. Why?"

"Just that...he's cut her into pieces."

Inside the battlesuit, all Gemini's limbs went slack. The suit itself did not react; she remained in place, hovering before her sister.

"Oh." The Sliver voice was definitely childish this time, almost a quaver.

"And Powell—"

"No civilian names," Gemini said automatically.

"Looking Glass is up there, walking around loose. He can open dimensional gates, can't he? Could he have brought in the horsemen? I'm not saying it's his fault. Purgatoire must be...what did you call it? Charming him."

The words sounded dim, like they were being drowned out by the babble of a crowd. All the louder voices were inside Gemini's head: her own doubts and fears shouting recriminations and denials.

"Chelsea?" asked Leela, impatiently.

"We've been fighting," Gemini said finally.

The mask—her mask, Gemini's face—came up sharply. Then Leela pulled it off, revealing her pale face and wide, stunned eyes. "What?"

"Fighting. Over little stuff. For a couple years. Nothing important. He got remote, I stopped trusting him as much. We'd been trying to work it out."

"But?" Leela asked.

"We...I had to leave him in the middle of a battle. It was about a week ago. I thought he'd just take a portal to safety, like always. But the perps we were fighting had neutralized his powers."

"You abandoned him?"

"No—we rescued him as soon as we realized."

"Was he hurt?"

"Hurt and angry," Gemini said. "But we couldn't have done anything differently. The Legislature was in session—government types were in danger, you know? Balm healed Powell up, but he was upset, and we...*I* might not have been all that sympathetic."

"I bet. You need to work on your empathy skills," Leela said, but her eyes were kind, her voice gentle.

What I need is to get back on task, Gemini thought. The others were suffering, just above them. But she kept talking: "The next thing I knew barbarians were all over Stanley Park. I thought I saw one of Powell's portals, but I told myself I had to be wrong."

"So...you're saying Looking Glass is working with Purgatoire?" Leela said. "Of his own free will."

Gemini nodded miserably.

"I should've thought about where your happy went." Leela patted her absently, her palm making an almost-silent bong against the metal of the armour. "Chelsea, I'm so sorry."

"Don't sympathize. I'll cry and my tactical display will mist up. Is Crimson really in pieces?"

"Yes. Sorry."

Only discipline and long habit kept Gemini from trying to rub her throbbing eyes. "What am I going to do?"

"Strategize anew, I guess," Leela said. "Will the guns in that suit do any good at all against Purgatoire?"

"Sure," Gemini said. "But what about Looking Glass?"

Leela scratched her nose. "How would you take him out?"

"What?"

"Come on, tell me you haven't been thinking about it."

With a stab, Gemini realized she had. "He'll be expecting me to try something non-lethal. To entangle him in the floor, or a partially melted chair."

"You can't do what he's expecting though, can you?" Leela asked.

"No. So I'd have to burn him—hit him hard and..." As Gemini spoke, her voice thinned and got higher, but she pushed on through the sob. "...hope Balm can heal him after."

Leela nodded. "'Kay. That's what I'll do."

"I can't ask—you hate violence."

"I'll hate it more if he's loose killing people. Besides, he knows the truth about me and Mom, doesn't he?"

Gemini nodded. "We never had secrets."

"Okay. You bust in there and put a hole in Purgatoire. I'll climb up behind you and get Looking Glass."

"You're sure?"

"I'll be right behind you," Leela promised.

"All right." Gemini toggled the suit controls, flew upward at low speed and broke through the softened carpet. Even after the darkness below the pier, the room seemed murky, lit only by computer screens and a single dim chandelier. Crimson was hacked into seeping, scattered pieces. Balm was dangling from the ceiling, chained with his eyes gouged out and his fingers broken, while Mortar slowly dissolved in a tank of antifreeze-pink liquid. As for Serpentine...the lower half of her body was simply gone. Her torso issued from midair, her body bisected by a blue-white ring that could only be one of Powell's dimension portals. Her upper body jittered in a wild and grotesque dance; as she flailed she was trying to scream, but her voice was gone.

The room was filled with machines, and neither of the villains was in sight.

Somewhere in the midst of all this gadgetry had to be a device that was keeping Crimson from shifting to her energy state and reintegrating herself, Gemini reasoned. Turning her back on her friends, she began destroying Purgatoire's equipment, driving a stream of needles into each unit of hardware, into every cable.

Battlecalm descended and her mind was suddenly clear. She noted that Purgatoire had found himself a new army. No low-tech rampaging hoard this time, either—an inter-dimensional viewer showed row upon row of German infantry, soldiers with bayonets and tanks and blank charmed eyes.

That's where he and Powell are, then, Gemini thought—recruiting. Hopefully the destruction of their equipment would bring them back.

It was the work of an instant to destroy every machine in the room. And it worked. Crimson's scattered pieces were already glowing a deep red when Purgatoire darted out of a blue-white portal, brandishing his Pandemonium Globe, a device that would subject every pud within its range to lethally terrifying visions.

Gemini was ready. She shot a score of spikes through the villain's wizened hand. His fingers dropped open and the globe bounced to the floor.

They dove for it, Purgatoire with his uninjured hand extended, Gemini with her suit's massive fingers splayed. The battlesuit fought the dive, though, pushing her away from the floor. She skimmed over her target, fumbling what should have been a perfect grab.

As the suit rigorously brought itself upright she watched, helpless, as the villain regained possession of his globe.

"Haha," he squeaked. Beyond the door, people began to shriek. Purgatoire crawled upright, yanking needles out of his impaled hand with his teeth. "Not so fast, Mr. Giant."

"Easy," she said. His nose came only as high as her chest, but he seemed unafraid. "Don't hurt anyone. You've got me."

"Oh, I don't got you yet, Giant."

"This suit is impervious to your charms."

"Then take it off," said a new voice, behind her.

Powell.

She let her gaze flick left, shocked at how hard it was even to look at Powell as he stepped through the blue-white portal. He'd gone from being her lover and confidante; he had become her foe. It was inconceivable.

"It is you, isn't it, Gem? Come to bring me to justice?"

"I've killed for you," she said softly. "I've all but died for you."

"You abandoned me when it counted."

"You knew the stakes—"

"There's always something more important than me, isn't there?" His mask was more mobile than hers—she could see pain in his face. For an instant she could forgive him anything, even this.

"Switch sides," she told him breathlessly. "Glass, switch back. I'm begging."

"Take off the helmet, Gem, or I'll cut Serpentine in half. Do you remember... she was laughing when you guys came to rescue me? 'Poor hapless Looking Glass, can't get himself out of a simple jam'—"

"Glass..." She was stalling him now...but for what? Leela was nowhere in sight.

"I'm a joke to you all. You weren't even worried."

Leela can't do it, Gemini thought, she just can't hack the violence. Even now, at risk of becoming Purgatoire's puppet, she found she almost admired her sister for that.

"Stormy," she murmured. "One minute scared, one minute mad..."

"Helmet. Now," commanded Powell, resolution settling into the features of his mask. He pulled the dimension portal taut around their friend, cutting a bloody line into her torso. Serpentine's face wrenched; her forked tongue flicked out, and Gemini saw punctures in its spotted black and white tissue—in her distress, Maria had bitten herself. "Not laughing now, is she?"

"I give up, okay?" Gemini reached for the catch on her battlesuit's helmet.

"You'll feel better in a minute, Mr. Giant," Purgatoire crooned, shoving the Pandemonium Globe up against her face as Gemini unlatched. She lifted the helmet, slowly surrendering...

And then Looking Glass was gone.

The carpet vanished from beneath his feet and Gemini heard him cry out as he fell, then splashed. Instinct took over: she backhanded Purgatoire with all the suit's considerable strength, sending him across the room. The globe fell and she dropped a heavy desk on it, crushing it casually as she ran to the edge of the wide pit yawning in the centre of the conference room. Forty feet below, her sister was wrestling with Powell in the ocean, their distant thrashing forms illuminated by the greenish-white light of the Crucible Orb's running lights.

"Hang on," Gemini bellowed. "I'm coming."

"No—save the team," her sister's voice echoed up amid splashes.

It wasn't fair to leave Leela down there, but she was right. Gemini turned, driving a fist into the tank holding Mortar prisoner and leaving it to drain as she flew to Serpentine. Grasping her friend under one sinuous, scaly arm, she eased her up through the narrow bottleneck of the dimension portal. She nearly gagged then, as she saw the burgered flesh of her teammate's legs. Something had been eating her.

She went to Balm, crushing the chains that held him with her armoured hands. The metal crumbled and it was oddly satisfying, more messily destructive than sighing things into sterile nothingness.

"Cray?" She whispered his real name, lowering him to the floor. "Cray, it's me."

"Gem?" He blinked bloodied sockets at her.

"Yeah. Can you walk?"

"Legs are busted," he said. "Glass?"

"Taken care of," she said, hoping it was true. "I know you're injured, but Serpentine's pretty bad. Mortar too."

His jaw firmed, all business. "Crimson?"

She checked the red glow, finding it brighter and less diffuse. "Reassembling."

He shivered slightly.

"Can you help the others if you can't see?"

"Take me to whoever's worst."

She carried Balm to Serpentine's side and moved his broken hands to their teammate's heart, watching as he summoned a crackling halo of healer's energy and directed it into her body.

As Gemini stepped back his blind face followed her. "Feels like war today, doesn't it?"

"Sometimes that's what it is." It was a mantra for their bad days. It had never felt so true.

Damn. Leela.

She whirled back to the pit just in time to see her sister climbing back up into the ballroom. She had Looking Glass over her shoulder, slung in a fireman's carry.

"Are you okay?" Gemini asked.

"No," Leela said, letting Powell fall to the floor with a thud. "I'm going to throw up after all. Getting hit is exactly as rotten as I remembered."

"I'm sorry."

"Thanks. It turns out hitting back doesn't suck though."

"I think I said as much when you were dating that abusive psychopath..."

"You could work on being less smug, you know." Shaking water off her costume, Leela nudged Powell with a toe.

"How did you take him out?" Gemini asked.

"Surprised?"

"Maybe a little."

"I put my hands around his throat, thought about the way he'd screwed you over, and just...squeezed. Eventually he went limp." Leela said. Her voice was colder—scarier—than Gemini had ever heard it, despite their years of fighting. Then she sighed. "I guess you have to jail him, huh?"

"He brought the barbarians here," Gemini said. "Even if we could overlook what he did to all of us..."

"People died. Yeah. Well, you want my opinion, he deserves it."

Misting up again, Gemini looked at her lover's sea-soaked form. "So that's it. Fifteen years of history. Broken."

"Oh, I don't know." Leela bent to bind his hands. "There was a time when I thought you and I would never speak again. People do surprise you."

"This from the woman whose kid is going to be living on Greenwich Mean Time." Still looking at Powell, she tried to draw breath. It felt as though something was lodged between her lungs.

Was that a chuckle?

Gemini examined her sister, suddenly suspicious. The mask hid every hint of an expression, but...

"You don't drink champagne when you're *un*happy," Gemini said at last, thinking back to her sister's earlier intoxicated state.

"I only said you-know-who was moving to London," Leela said.

"But when I asked—"

"You mean when you totally assumed that if he wanted to take my son to Europe I'd just let him?"

Gemini frowned. "You misled me."

"You need to quit thinking I'm spineless," Leela said.

"So...the kid's staying with you?"

Leela gave her a goofy thumbs-up. "Seven days a week, twelve months a year. He moves in Monday after school."

Gemini grabbed her with Sliver's powerful hands then, pulling her sister in for a hug they could never have shared in civilian gear, for fear of gluing themselves together.

"You could kill a girl doing that," Leela said when Gemini finally released her.

"Only a civilian."

"You mean a pud?"

"You were never a pud."

Leela laughed. "I'm a textbook case."

"No," Gemini said. "You're extraordinary."

A squeak interrupted them, and then a tentacle edged under the door. Leela tilted forward, mouth open, ready to attack.

"Don't kill it—it's just a police probe," Gemini murmured. "They must have heard the battle."

"Right." She struck an overly heroic pose. "This is Gemini. The situation is under control. Send a containment thingie..."

"Unit," Gemini whispered.

"Right, a unit to take the, um, the perpetrators into custody."

As the probe withdrew, she turned back to Gemini. "You better plan on wearing that battlesuit for a while, huh?"

"Oh, I'll bounce back..." Then it sank in again: Powell a villain, Powell going to trial. The media coverage. And Powell just being gone, when he'd been there day in and day out for all these years. She thought fleetingly of their bed, his clothes hanging in their shared closet, all the things in Base Pacific that were his. Team equipment the two of them had built together, items they wouldn't be able to get rid of. All those things, like ghosts, bringing up memories...

"Maybe we better melt-proof your apartment," she said to Leela.

"Fuck. I guess so."

"You know what?"

"Yes?"

"I'm glad you get to be a full-time mom again." Another mood switch now, as the containment team bustled in to whisk Purgatoire away and Leela had to explain that Looking Glass was going into custody too.

As the police carried Powell away, Gemini's heartbreak dimmed to something like numbness. In its absence she saw, to her surprise, that Leela was standing up straight, that she wasn't plucking at her uniform.

"Hey," she said, "Can I get one more favour?"

"Sure."

"Don't you want to know what?"

"No, actually. I trust you."

She led Leela up a staircase, heading for the roof. "I've been thinking I may need to make a more expressive mask for my costume."

"Gemini's?" Leela asked. "Or this big metal shell?"

"Both, I guess. If my emotions are up and down for a while, I'll probably be using both costumes."

"Will you tell the press it's you in the statue suit?"

"No. I don't want word getting out that my powers come and go. I'll pretend there are two different heroes. Gemini and...I'll need a second name for when I'm wearing this." *So much work*, she thought. *So many changes. Powell gone.*

"Being you is pretty complicated, huh?" Leela said.

"Usually I don't notice," she said, feeling heavy, weighted down.

"Well, softening the masks isn't a bad idea," Leela offered. "Being inscrutable gets old."

"Yes," Gemini agreed, opening a fire door and bowing Leela outside. "I don't know what I was thinking."

Beyond the doorway was the city, its sky, above the office towers, full of police helicopters that chattered and vied for room with the news service birds. It was just dusk, and the streetlights were coming on in irregular patches, street by street. The air, warm and barely humid, smelled of the sea.

A familiar layer of sound—camera shutters clicking like locusts—rolled toward them as Leela stepped out into view. Wearing Gemini's costume, she looked every inch the hero.

"Hey," Leela took an uncertain half-step back from the cameras but her sister caught her before she could backpedal fully, nudging her out into sight. "Why am I out here?"

"For Momma's scrapbook." Chelsea said. "Wave, Leela."

ORIGIN STORY
KELLY LINK

Many of the stories in Kelly Link's collections *Stranger Things Happen* and *Magic for Beginners*—with their young women embroiled in weird adventures that defy easy explanation or categorization—have a subtle whiff of the superheroic to them. Since then, she has delved more explicitly into the genre, such as in this tale, which, among other things, suggests a link between Superman and Dorothy Gale. Think about it: one comes from a faraway land and crashes in rural Kansas, while the other comes from rural Kansas and crashes in a faraway land.

"Dorothy Gale," she said.

"I guess so." He said it grudgingly. Maybe he wished that he'd thought of it first. Maybe he didn't think going home again was all that heroic.

They were sitting on the side of a mountain. Above them, visitors to the Land of Oz theme park had once sailed, in molded plastic gondola balloons, over the Yellow Brick Road. Some of the support pylons tilted or tipped back against scrawny little opportunistic pines. There was something majestic about the felled pylons now that their work was done. They looked like fallen giants. Moth-eaten blue ferns grew over the peeling yellow bricks.

The house of Dorothy Gale's aunt and uncle had been cunningly designed. You came up the path, went into the front parlor and looked around. You were led through the kitchen. There were dishes in the kitchen cabinets. Daisies in a vase. Pictures on the wall. Follow your Dorothy down into the cellar with the other families, watch the tornado swirl around on the dirty dark wall, and when everyone tramped up the other, identical set of steps through the other, identical cellar door, it was the same house, same rooms, but tornado-tipped. The parlor floor now slanted and when you went out through the (back) front door, there was a pair of stockinged plaster legs sticking out from under the house. A pair of ruby slippers. A yellow brick road. You weren't in North Carolina anymore.

The whole house was a ruin now. None of the pictures hung straight. There were salamanders in the walls, and poison ivy coming up in the kitchen sink. Mushrooms in the cellar, and an old mattress that someone had dragged down the stairs. You had to hope Dorothy Gale had moved on.

It was four in the afternoon and they were both slightly drunk. Her name was Bunnatine Powderfinger. She called him Biscuit.

She said, "Come on, of course she is. The ruby slippers, those are like her special power. It's all about how she was a superhero the whole time, only she didn't know it. And she comes to Oz from another world. Like Superman in reverse. And she has lots of sidekicks." She pictured them skipping down the road, arm in arm. Facing down evil. Dropping houses on it, throwing buckets of water at it. Singing stupid songs and not even caring if anyone was listening.

He grunted. She knew what he thought. Sidekicks were for people who were too lazy to write personal ads. "The Wizard of Oz. He even has a secret identity. And he wants everything to be green, all of his stuff is green, just like Green Lantern."

The thing about green was true, but so beside the point that she could hardly stand it. The Wizard of Oz was a humbug. She said, "But he's *not* great and powerful. He just pretends to be great and powerful. The Wicked Witch of the West is greater and more powerfuller. She's got flying monkeys. She's like a mad scientist. She even has a secret weakness. Water is like kryptonite to her." She'd always thought the actress Margaret Hamilton was damn sexy. The way she rode that bicycle and the wind that picked her up and carried her off like an invisible lover; that funny, mocking, shrill little piece of music coming out of nowhere. That nose.

When she looked over, she saw that he'd put his silly outfit back on inside out. How often did that happen? She decided not to say anything. There was an ant in her underwear. She made the decision to find this erotic, and then realized it might be a tick. No, it was an ant. "Margaret Hamilton, baby," she said. "I'd do her."

He was watching her wriggle, of course. Too drunk at the moment to do anything. That was fine with her. And she was too drunk to feel embarrassed about having ants in her pants. Just like that Ella Fitzgerald song. Finis, finis.

The big lunk, her old chum, said, "I'd watch. But what do you think about her turning into a big witchy puddle when she gets a bucketful of water in the face? When it rains does she say, Oops, sorry, can't fight crime today? Interesting sexual subtext here, by the way. Very girl on girl. Girl meets nemesis, gets her wet, she just melts. Screeches orgasmically while she does it, too."

How could he be drunk and talk like that? There were more ants. Had she been lying on an antpile while they did it? Poor ants. Poor Bunnatine. She stood up and took her dress and her underwear off—no silly outfits for her—and shook them vigorously. Come out with your little legs up, you ants. She pretended she was shaking some sense into him. Or maybe what she wanted was to shake some sense out of him. Who knew? Not her.

She said, "Margaret Hamilton wouldn't fight crime, baby. She'd try to conquer the world. She just needs a wetsuit. A sexy wetsuit." She put her clothes back on again. Maybe that's what she needed. A wetsuit. A prophylactic to keep her from melting. The booze didn't work at all. What did they call it? A social lubricant. And it helped her not to care so much. Anesthetic. It helped hold her together afterward, when he left town again. Super Glue.

She'd like to throw a bucket of Super-Be-Gone at him. Except that Super-Be-Gone was expensive, even the no-brand stuff. And it didn't really work on him. Just made him sneeze. She could throw the rest of her beer, but he would just look at her and say, Why did you do that, Bunnatine? It would hurt his feelings. The big lump.

He said, "Why are you looking at me like that, Bunnatine?"

"Here. Have another Little-Boy Wide Mouth," she said, giving up. Yes, she was sitting on an anthill. It was definitely an anthill. Tiny superheroic ants were swarming out to defend their hill, chase off the enormous and evil although infinitely desirable doom of Bunnatine's ass. "It'll put radioactive hair on your chest and then make it fall out again."

"Enjoy the parade?" Every year, the same thing. Balloons going up and up like they couldn't wait to leave town and pudding-faced cloggers on pickup trucks and on the curbs teenage girls holding signs. We Love You. I Love You More. I Want To Have Your Super Baby. Teenage girls not wearing bras. Poor little sluts. The big lump never even noticed and too bad for them if he did. She could tell them stories.

He said, "Yeah. It was great. Best parade ever."

Anyone else would've thought he was being one hundred percent sincere. Nobody else knew him like she did. He looked like a sweetheart, but even when he tried to be gentle, he left bruises.

She said, "I liked when they read all the poetry. Big bouncy guy / way up in the lonely sky."

"Yeah. So whose idea was that?"

She said, "*The Daily Catastrophe* sponsored it. Mrs. Dooley over at the high school got all her students to write the poems. I saved a copy of the paper. I figured you'd want it for your scrapbook."

"That's the best part about saving the world. The poetry. That's why I do it." He was throwing rocks at an owl that was hanging out on a tree branch for some reason. It was probably sick. Owls didn't usually do that. A rock knocked off some leaves. Blam! Took off some bark. Pow! The owl just sat there.

She said, "Don't be a jerk."

"Sorry."

She said, "You look tired."

"Yeah."

"Still not sleeping great?"

"Not great."

"Little Red Riding Hood."

"No way." His tone was dismissive. *As if*, Bunnatine, you dumb bunny. "Sure, she's got a costume, but she gets eaten. She doesn't have any superpowers. Baked goods don't count as superpowers."

"Sleeping Beauty?" She thought of a girl in a moldy old tower, asleep for a hundred years. Ants crawling over her. Mice. Some guy's lips. That girl must have had the world's worst morning breath. Amazing to think that someone would kiss her. And kissing people when they're asleep? She didn't approve. "Or does she not count, because some guy had to come along and save her?"

He had a faraway look in his eyes. As if he were thinking of someone, some girl he'd watched sleeping. She knew he slept around. Grateful women saved from evildoers or their obnoxious blind dates. Models and movie stars and transit workers and trapeze artists, too, probably. She read about it in the tabloids. Or maybe he was thinking about being able to sleep in for a hundred years. Even when they were kids, he'd always been too jumpy to sleep through the night. Always coming over to her house and throwing rocks at the window. His face at her window. Wake up, Bunnatine. Wake up. Let's go fight crime. You can be my sidekick, Bunnatine. Let's go fight crime.

He said, "Her superpower is the ability to sleep through anything. Lazy bitch. Her origin story: she tragically pricks her finger on a spinning wheel. What's with the fairy tales and kids' books, Bunnatine? Rapunzel's got lots of hair that she can turn into a hairy ladder. Not so hot. Who else? The girl in Rumpelstiltskin who can spin straw into gold."

She missed these conversations when he wasn't around. Nobody else in town talked like this. The mutants were sweet, but they were more into music. They didn't talk much. It wasn't like talking with him. He always had a comeback, a wisecrack, a double entendre, some cheesy sleazy pickup line that cracked her up, that she fell for every time. It was probably all that witty banter during the big fights. She'd probably get confused. Banter when she was supposed to *POW! POW!* when she was meant to banter.

She said, "Wrong. Rumpelstiltskin spins the straw into gold. She just uses the poor freak and then she hires somebody else to go spy on him to find out his name."

"Cool."

She said, "No, it's not cool. She cheats."

"So what? Was she supposed to give up her kid to some little guy who spins gold?"

"Why not? I mean, she probably wasn't the world's best parent or anything. Her kid didn't grow up to be anyone special. There aren't any fairy tales about Rapunzel II."

"Your mom."

She said, "What?"

"Your mom! C'mon, Bunnatine. She was a superhero."

"My mom? Ha *ha*."

He said, "I'm not joking. I've been thinking about this for a few years. Being a waitress? Just her disguise."

She made a face and then unmade it. It was what she'd always thought: he'd had a crush on her mom. "So what's her superpower?"

He gnawed on a fingernail with those big square teeth. "I don't know. I don't know her secret identity. It's secret. So you don't pry. It's bad form, even if you're arch-enemies. But I was at the restaurant once when we were in high school and she was carrying eight plates at once. One was a bowl of soup, I think. Three on each arm, one between her teeth, and one on top of her head. Because somebody at the restaurant bet her she couldn't."

"Yeah, I remember that. She dropped everything. And she chipped a tooth."

"Only because that fuckhead Robert Potter tripped her," he pointed out.

"He didn't mean to."

He picked up her hand. Was he going to bite her fingernail now? No, he was studying the palm. Like he was going to read it or something. It wasn't hard reading a waitress's palm. You'll spend the rest of your life getting into hot water. He said gently, "No, he did. I saw the whole thing. He knew what he was doing."

It embarrassed her to see how small her hand was in his. As if he'd grown up and she just hadn't bothered. She still remembered when she'd been taller. "Really?"

"Really. Robert Potter is your mother's nemesis."

She took her hand back. Slapped a beer in his. "Stop making fun of my mom. She doesn't have a nemesis. And why does that word always sound like someone's got a disease? Robert Potter's just a fuckhead."

"Once Potter said he'd pay me ten dollars if I gave him a pair of Mom's underwear. It was when Mom and I weren't getting along. I was like fourteen. We were at the grocery store and she slapped me for some reason. So I guess he thought I'd do it. Everybody saw her slap me. I think it was because I told her Rice Krispies were full of sugar and she should stop trying to poison me. So he came up to me afterward in the parking lot."

Beer made you talk too much. Add that to the list. It wasn't her favorite thing about beer. Next thing she knew, she'd be crying about some dumb thing or begging him to stay.

He was grinning. "Did you do it?"

"No. I told him I'd do it for twenty bucks. So he gave me twenty bucks and I just kept it. I mean, it wasn't like he was going to tell anyone."

"Cool."

"Yeah. Then I made him give me twenty more dollars. I said if he didn't, I'd tell my mom the whole story."

That wasn't the whole story either, of course. She didn't imagine she'd ever tell him the whole story. But the result of the story was that she had enough money for beer and some weed. She paid some guy to buy beer for her. That was the night she'd brought Biscuit up here.

They'd done it on the mattress in the basement of the wrecked farmhouse, and later on they'd done it in the theater, on the pokey little stage where girls in blue dresses and flammable wigs used to sing and tap-dance. Leaves everywhere. The smell of smoke, someone further up on the mountain, checking on their still, maybe, chain-smoking. Reading girly magazines. Biscuit saying, Did I hurt you? Is this okay? Do you want another beer? She'd wanted to kick him, make him stop trying to take care of her, and also to go on kissing him. She always felt that way around Biscuit. Or maybe she always felt that way and Biscuit had nothing to do with it.

He said, "So did you ever tell her?"

"No. I was afraid that she'd go after him with a ball-peen hammer and end up in jail."

When she got home that night. Her mother looking at Bunnatine like she knew everything, but she didn't, she didn't. She'd said: "I know what you've been up to, Bunnatine. Your body is a temple and you treat it like dirt."

So Bunnatine said: "I don't care." She'd meant it too.

"I always liked your mom."

"She always liked you." Liked Biscuit better than she liked Bunnatine. Well, they both liked him better. Thank God her mother had never slept with Biscuit. She imagined a parallel universe in which her mother fell in love with Biscuit. They went off together to fight crime. Invited Bunnatine up to their secret hideaway/love nest for Thanksgiving. She showed up and wrecked the place. They went on *Oprah*. While they were in the studio some supervillain—sure, okay, that fuckhead Robert Potter—implemented his dreadful, unstoppable, terrible plan. That parallel universe was his to loot, pillage, and discard like a half-eaten grapefruit, and it was all her fault.

The thing was, there *were* parallel universes. She pictured poor parallel Bunnatine, sent a warning through the mystic veil that separates the universes. Go on *Oprah* or save the world? Do whatever you have to do, baby.

The Biscuit in this universe said, "Is she at the restaurant tonight?"

"Her night off," Bunnatine said. "She's got a poker night with some friends. She'll come home with more money than she makes in tips and lecture me about the evils of gambling."

"I'm pretty pooped anyway," he said. "All that poetry wore me out."

"So where are you staying?"

He didn't say anything. She hated when he did this.

She said, "You don't trust me, baby?"

"Remember Volan Crowe?"

"What? That kid from high school?"

"Yeah. He used to draw comics about this superhero he came up with. Mann Man. A superhero with all the powers of Thomas Mann."

"You can't go home again."

"That's the other Thomas. Thomas Wolfe."

"Thomas Wolfman. A hairy superhero who gets lost driving home."

"Thomas Thomas Virginia Woolfman Woman."

"Now with extra extra superpowers."

"Whatever happened to him?"

"Didn't he die of tuberculosis?"

"Not him. I mean that kid."

"Didn't he turn out to have a superpower?"

"Yeah. He could hang pictures perfectly straight on any wall. He never needed a level."

"I thought he tried to destroy the world."

"Yeah, that's right. He was calling himself something weird. Fast Kid with Secret Money. Something like that. Got kidnapped by a nemesis. The nemesis used these alien brain-washing techniques to convince him he had to destroy the world in order to save the world."

"That's really lame. I wouldn't fall for that."

She said, "Shut up. I hear you fall for it every time."

"What about you?"

She said, "Me?"

"Yeah."

"Keeping an eye on this place. They don't pay much, but it's easy money. I had another job, but it didn't work out. A place down off I-40. They had a stage, put on shows. Nothing too gross. So me and Kath, remember how she could make herself glow, we were making some extra cash two nights a week. They'd turn down the lights and she'd come out on stage with no clothes on and she'd be all lit up from inside. It was real pretty. And when it was my turn, guys could pay extra money to come and lie on the stage. Do you remember that hat, my favorite hat? The oatmeal-colored one with the pompoms and the knitted ears?"

"Yeah."

"Well, they kept it cold in there. I think so that we'd have perky tits when we came out on stage. So we'd move around with a bit more rah-rah. But I wore the hat. I got management to let me wear the hat, because I don't float real well when I'm real cold."

"I gave you that hat," he said.

"Yeah. At Christmas. I loved that hat. So I'd be wearing the hat and this dress—nothing really revealing or cheap-looking—and come out on stage and hover a foot above their faces. So they could see I wasn't wearing any underwear."

He was smiling. "Saving the world by taking off your underwear, Bunnatine?"

"Shut up. I'd look down and see them lying there on the stage like I'd frozen them. Zap. They weren't supposed to touch me. Just look. I always felt a million miles above them. Like I was a bird." *A plane.* "All I had to do was scissor my legs, kick a little, just lift up my hem a little. Do twirls. Smile. They'd just lie there and breathe hard like they were doing all the work. And when the music stopped, I'd float offstage again. But then Kath left for Atlantic City, to go sing in a cabaret show. And then some asshole got frisky. Some college kid. He grabbed my ankle and I kicked him in the head. So now I'm back at the restaurant with Mom."

He said, "How come you never did that for me, Bunnatine? Float like that?"

She shrugged. "It's different with you," she said, as if it were. But of course it wasn't. Why should it be?

"Come on, Bunnatine," he said. "Show me your stuff."

She stood up, shimmied her underwear down to her ankles with an expert wriggle. All part of the show. "Close your eyes for a sec."

"No way."

"Close your eyes. I'll tell you when to open them."

He closed his eyes and she took a breath, let herself float up. She could only get about two feet off the ground before that old invisible hand yanked her down again, held her tethered just above the ground. She used to cry about that. Now she just thought it was funny. She let her underwear dangle off her big toe. Dropped it on his face. "Okay, baby. You can open your eyes."

His eyes were open. She ignored him, hummed a bit. Why oh why oh why can't I. Held out her dress at the hem so that she could look down the neckline and see the ground, see him looking back up.

"Shit, Bunnatine," he said. "Wish I'd brought a camera."

She thought of all those girls on the sidewalks. "No touching," she said, and touched herself.

He grabbed her ankle and yanked. Yanked her all the way down. Stuck his head up inside her dress, and his other hand. Grabbed a breast and then her shoulder so that she fell down on top of him, knocked the wind out of her. His mouth propping her up, her knees just above the ground, cheek banged down on the bone of his hip. It was like a game of Twister, there was something Parker Brothers about his new outfit. There was a gusset in his outfit, so he could stop and use the bathroom, she guessed, when he was out fighting crime. Not get caught with his pants down. His busy, busy hand was down there, undoing the Velcro. The other hand was still wrapped around her ankle. His face was scratchy. Bam, pow. Her toes curled. He's got you now, Bunnatine.

He said up into her dress, "Bunnatine. Bunnatine."

"Don't talk with your mouth full, Biscuit," she said.

She said, "There was a tabloid reporter around today, wanting to hear stories."

He said, "If I ever read about you and me, Bunnatine, I'll come back and make you sorry. I'm saying that for your own good. Do something like that, and they'll come after you. They'll use you against me."

"So how do you know they don't know already? Whoever *they* are?"

"I'd know," he said. "I can smell those creeps from a mile away."

She got up to pee. She said, "I wouldn't do anything like that anyway." She thought about his parents and felt bad. She shouldn't have said anything about the reporter. Weasely guy. Staring at her tits when she brought him coffee.

She was squatting behind a tree when she saw the pair of yearlings. They were trying so hard to be invisible. Just dappled spots hanging in the air. They were watching her like they'd never seen anything so fucked up. Like the end of the world. They took off when she stood up. "That's right," she said. "Get the hell away. Tell anybody about this and I'll kick your sorry Bambi asses."

She said, "Okay. So I've been wondering about this whole costume thing. Your new outfit. I wasn't going to say anything, but it's driving me crazy. What's with all these crazy stripes and the embroidery?"

"You don't like it?"

"I like the lightning bolt. And the tower. And the frogs. It's psychedelic, Biscuit. Can you please explain why y'all wear such stupid outfits? I promise I won't tell anyone."

"They aren't stupid."

"Yes they are. Tights are stupid. It's like you're showing off. Look how big my dick is."

"Tights are comfortable. They allow freedom of movement. They're machine washable." He began to say something else, then stopped. Grinned. Said, almost reluctantly, "Sometimes you hear stories about some asshole stuffing his tights."

She started to giggle. Giggling gave her the hiccups. He whacked her on the back.

She said, "Ever forget to run a load of laundry? Have to fight crime when you ought to be doing your laundry instead?"

He said, "Better than a suit and tie, Bunnatine. You can get a sewing machine and go to town, dee eye why, but who has the time? It's all about advertising. Looking big and bold. But you don't want to be too designer. Too Nike or Adidas. So last year I needed a new outfit, asked around, and found this women's cooperative down on a remote beach in Costa Rica. They've got an arrangement with a charity here in the states. They've got collection points in forty major cities where you drop off bathing suits and leotards and bike shorts, and then everything goes down to Costa Rica. They've got this beach house that some big-shot rock star donated to them. It's this big glass and concrete slab and the tide goes in and out right under the glass floor. I went for a personal fitting. These women are real artists, talented people, super creative, and they're all unwed mothers, too. They bring their kids to work and the kids are running around everywhere and the kids are all wearing these really great superhero costumes. They do work for anybody. Even pro wrestlers. Villains. Crime lords, politicians. Good guys and bad guys. Sometimes you'll be fighting somebody, this real asshole, and you'll both be getting winded, and then you start noticing his outfit and he's looking too and then you're both wondering if you got your outfits at this same place. And you feel like you ought to stop and say something nice about what they're wearing. How you both think it's so great that these women can support their families like this."

"I still think tights look stupid." She thought of those kids wearing their superhero outfits. Probably grew up and became drug dealers and maids and organ donors.

"What? What's so funny?"

He said, "I can't stop thinking about Robert Potter and your mother. Did he want clean underwear? Or did he want dirty underwear?"

She said, "What do you think?"

"I think twenty bucks wasn't enough money."

"He's a creep."

"So you think he's been in love with her for a long time?"

She said, "What?"

"Like maybe they had an affair once a long time ago."

"No way!" It made her want to puke.

"No, seriously, what if he was your father or something?"

"Fuck you!"

"Well, come on. Haven't you wondered? I mean, he could be your father. It's always been obvious that he and your mom have unfinished business. And he's always trying to talk to you."

"Stop talking! Right now!"

"Or what, you'll kick my ass? I'd like to see you try." He sounded amused.

She wrapped her arms around herself. Ignore him, Bunnatine. Wait until he's had more to drink. *Then* kick his ass.

He said, "Come on. You used to wait until your mom got home from work and fell asleep. You said you'd sneak into her bedroom and ask her questions while she was sleeping. Just to see if she would tell you who your dad was."

"I haven't done that for a while. She finally woke up and caught me. She was really pissed off. I've never seen her get mad like that. I never told you about it. I was too embarrassed."

He didn't say anything.

"So I kept begging and finally she made up some story about this guy from another planet. Some *tourist*. Some tourist with wings and stuff. She said that he's going to come back someday. That's why she never shacked up or got married. She's still waiting for him to come back."

"Don't look at me like that. I know it's bullshit. I mean, if he had wings, why don't I have wings? That would be so cool. To fly. Really fly. Even when I used to practice every day, I never got more than two feet off the ground. Two fucking feet. What is it good for? Waiting tables. I float sometimes, so I don't get varicose veins like Mom."

"You could probably go a little higher if you really tried."

"You want to see me try? Here, hold this. Okay. One, two, three. Up, up, and a little bit more up. Impressed?"

He frowned, looked off into the trees as if he were thinking about it. Trying not to laugh.

"What? Are you impressed or not?"

"Can I be honest? Yes and no. You could work on your technique. You're a bit wobbly. And I don't understand why all your hair went straight up and started waving around. Do you know that it's doing that?"

"Static electricity?" she said. "Why are you so mean?"

"Hey," he said. "I'm just trying to be honest. I'm just wondering why you never told me any of that stuff about your dad. I could ask around, see if anybody knows him."

"It's not any of your business," she said. "But thanks."

"I thought we were better friends than this, Bunnatine."

He was looking hurt.

"You're still my best friend in the whole world," she said. "I promise."

"I love this place," he said.

"Yeah. Me too." Only if he loved it so much, then why didn't he ever stay? So busy saving the world, he couldn't save the Land of Oz. Those poor Munchkins. Poor Bunnatine. They were almost out of beer.

He said, "So what are they up to? The developers? What are they plotting?"

"The usual. Tear everything down. Build condos."

"And you don't mind?"

"Of course I mind!" she said.

He said, "I always think it looks a lot more real now. The way it's falling all to pieces. The way the Yellow Brick Road is disappearing. It makes it feel like Oz was a real place. Being abandoned makes you more real, you know?"

Beer turned him into Biscuit the philosopher-king. Another thing about beer. She had another beer to help with the philosophy. He had one too.

She said, "Sometimes there are coyotes up here. Bears, too. The mutants. Once I saw a sasquatch and two tiny sasquatch babies."

"No way."

"And lots and lots of deer. Guys come up here in hunting season. When I catch 'em, they always make jokes about hunting Munchkins. I think they're idiots to come up here with guns. Mutants don't like guns."

"Who does?" he said.

She said, "Remember Tweetsie Railroad? That rickety rollercoaster? Looked like a bunch of Webelos built it out of Tinkertoys? Remember how people dressed like toy-store Indians used to come onto the train? I was always hoping I was gonna see them scalp someone this time."

He said, "Fudge. Your mom would buy us fudge. Remember how we sat in the front row and there was that one showgirl? The one with the three-inch ruff of pubic hair sticking out the legs of her underwear? During the can-can?"

She said, "I don't remember that!"

He leaned over her, nibbled on her neck. People were going to think she'd been attacked by squids. Little red sucker marks everywhere. She yawned.

He said, "Oh, come on! You remember! Your mom started laughing and couldn't stop. There was a guy sitting right next to us and he kept taking pictures."

She said, "Why do you remember all this stuff? I kept a diary all through school, and I still don't remember everything that you remember. Like, what I remember is how you wouldn't speak to me for a week because I said I thought *Atlas Shrugged* was boring. How you told me the ending of *The Empire Strikes Back* before I saw it. 'Hey, guess what? Darth Vader is Luke's father!' When I had the flu and you went without me?"

He said, "You didn't believe me."

"That's not the point!"

"Yeah. I guess not. Sorry about that."

"I miss that hat. The one with the pompoms. Some drunk stole it out of my car."

"I'll buy you another one."

"Don't bother. It's just I could fly better when I was wearing it."

He said, "It's not really flying. It's more like hovering."

"What, like leaping around like a pogo stick makes you special? Okay, so apparently it does. But you look like an idiot. Those enormous legs. That outfit. Anyone ever tell you that?"

"Why are you such a pain in the ass?"

"Why are you so mean? Why do you have to win every fight?"

"Why do you, Bunnatine? I have to win because I have to. I have to win. That's my job. Everybody always wants me to be a nice guy. But I'm a good guy."

"What's the difference again?"

"A nice guy wouldn't do this, Bunnatine. Or this."

"Say you're trapped in an apartment building. It's on fire. You're on the sixth floor. No, the tenth floor."

She was still kind of stupid from the first demonstration. She said, "Hey! Put me down! You asshole! Come back! Where are you going? Are you going to leave me up here?"

"Hold on, Bunnatine. I'm coming back. I'm coming to save you. There. You can let go now."

She held onto the branch like anything. The view was so beautiful she couldn't stand it. You could almost ignore him, pretend that you'd gotten up here all by yourself.

He kept jumping up. "Bunnatine. Let go." He grabbed her wrist and yanked her off. She made herself as heavy and still as possible. The ground rushed up at them and she twisted, hard. Fell out of his arms.

"Bunnatine!" he said.

She caught herself a foot before she smacked into the ruins of the Yellow Brick Road.

"I'm fine," she said, hovering. But she was better than fine! How beautiful it was from down here, too. Holy Yellow Brick Road, Bunnatine!

He looked so anxious. "God, Bunnatine, I'm sorry." It made her want to laugh to see him so worried. She put her feet down gently. The whole world was made of glass, and the glass was full of champagne, and Bunnatine was a bubble, just flicking up and up and up.

She said, "Stop apologizing, okay? It was great! The look on your face. Being in the air like that. Come on, Biscuit, again! Do it again! I'll let you do whatever you want this time."

"You want me to do it again?" he said.

She felt just like a little kid. She said, "Do it again! Do it again!"

She shouldn't have gotten in the car with him, of course. But he was just old pervy Potter and she had the upper hand. She explained how he was going to give her more money. He just sat there listening. He said they'd have to go to the bank. He drove her right through town, parked the car behind Food Lion.

She wasn't worried. She had the upper hand. She said, "What's up, pervert? Gonna do a little dumpster diving?"

He was looking at her. He said, "How old are you?"

She said, "Fourteen."

He said, "Old enough."

"How come you left after high school? How come you always leave?"

He said, "How come you broke up with me in eleventh grade?"

"Don't answer a question with a question. No one likes it when you do that."

"Well maybe that's why I left. Because you're always yelling at me."

"You ignored me in high school. Like you were ashamed of me. I'll see you later, Bunnatine. Quit it, Bunnatine. I'm busy. Didn't you think I was cute? There were plenty of guys at school who thought I was cute."

"They were all idiots."

"I didn't mean it like that. I just meant that they were really idiots. Come on, you know you thought so too."

"Can we change the subject?"

"Okay."

"It wasn't that I was ashamed of you, Bunnatine. You were distracting. I was trying to keep my average up. Trying to learn something. Remember that time we were studying and you tore up all my notes and ate them?"

"I saw they still haven't found that guy. That nutcase. The one who killed your parents."

"No. They won't." He threw rocks at where the owl had been. Nailed that sorry, invisible, absent owl.

"Yeah?" she said, "Why not?"

"I took care of it. He wanted me to find him, you know? He just wanted to get my attention. That's why you gotta be careful, Bunnatine. There are people out there who really don't like me."

"Your dad was a sweetheart. Always tipped twenty percent. A whole dollar if he was just getting coffee."

"Yeah. I don't want to talk about him, Bunnatine. Still hurts. You know?"

"Yeah. Sorry. So how's your sister doing?"

"Okay. Still in Chicago. They've got a kid now. A little girl."

"Yeah. I thought I heard that. Cute kid?"

"She looks like me, can you imagine? She seems okay, though. Normal."

"Are we sitting in poison ivy?"

"No. Look. There's a deer over there. Watching us."

"When do you have to be at work?"

"Not until 6 A.M. I just need to go home first and take a shower."

"Cool. Is there any beer left?"

"No. Sorry," she said. "Should've brought more."

"That's okay. I've got this. Want some?"

"I need a new job."

"You've already got like a hundred jobs, Bunnatine."

"Ski instructor, Sugar Mountain. Security guard, Beech Mountain. Lifeguard at the beach on Grandfather Mountain. Just applied for She-Devil of Mountain Mountain. Do you think that pays well? Lifeguarding was okay. I saved this eight-year-old's life last summer. His sister was trying to drown him. But I always end up back at the restaurant. Waitressing. Waitressing is my destiny."

"Why don't you leave?"

"Why go wait tables in some other place? I like it here. This is where I grew up. It was a good place to grow up. I like all the trees. I like the people. I even like how the tourists drive real slow between here and Boone. I just need to find a new job or Mom and I are going to end up killing each other."

"I thought you were getting along."

"Yeah. As long as I do exactly what she says."

"I saw your mom at the parade. With some little kid."

"Yeah. She's been babysitting for a friend at the restaurant. Mom's into it. She's been reading the kid all these fairy tales. She can't stand the Disney stuff, which is all the kid wants. Now they're reading *The Wizard of Oz*. I'm supposed to get your autograph, by the way. For the kid."

"Sure thing! You got a pen?"

"Oh shit. It doesn't matter. Maybe next time."

It got dark slow and then real fast at the end, the way it always did, even in the summer, like daylight realized it had to be somewhere right away. Somewhere else. On weekends she came up here and read mystery novels in her car. Moths beating at the windows. Got out every once in a while to take a walk and look for kids getting into trouble. She knew all the places they liked to go. Sometimes the mutants were down where the stage used to be, practicing. They'd started a band. They were always asking if she was sure she couldn't sing. She really, really couldn't sing. That's okay, the mutants always said. You can just howl. Scream. We're into that. They traded her 'shine for cigarettes. Told her long, meandering mutant jokes with lots of hand gestures and incomprehensible punchlines. Dark was her favorite time. In the dark she could imagine that this really was the Land of Oz, that when the sun couldn't stay away any longer, when the sun finally came back up, she'd still be there. In Oz. Not here. Click your heels, Bunnatine. There's no home like a summer place.

She said, "Still having nightmares?"

"Yeah."

"The ones about the end of the world."

"Yeah, you nosy bitch. Those ones."

"Still ends in the big fire?"

"No. A flood."

"I keep thinking about that television show."

"Which one?"

"You know. *Buffy the Vampire Slayer*. Even Mom liked it."

"I saw it a few times."

"I keep thinking about how that vampire, Angel, whenever he got evil, you knew he was evil because he starting wearing black leather pants."

"Why are you obsessed with what people wear? Shit, Bunnatine. It was just a TV show."

"Yeah, I know. But those black leather pants that he'd wear, they must have been his *evil* pants. Like fat pants."

"What?"

"Fat pants. The kind of pants that people who get thin keep in their closet. Just in case they get fat again."

He just looked at her. His big ugly face was all red and blotchy from drinking.

She said, "So my question is this. Does the vampire keep a pair of black leather pants in his closet? Just in case? Like fat pants? Do vampires have closets? Or does he donate them to Goodwill when he's good again? Because if so then every time he turns evil, he has to go buy new evil pants."

He said, "It's just television, Bunnatine."

"You keep yawning."

He smiled at her. Such a nice smile. Drove girls of all ages crazy. He said, "I'm just tired."

"Parades can really take it out of you."

"Fuck you."

She said, "Go on. Take a nap. I'll stay awake and keep lookout out for mutants and nemesissies and autograph hounds."

"Maybe just for a minute or two. You'd really like him."

"Who?"

"The nemesis I'm seeing right now. He's got a great sense of humor. Sent me a piano crate full of albino kittens last week. Some project he's working on. They pissed everywhere. Had to find homes for them all. Of course first we checked to make sure that they weren't little bombs or possessed by demons or programmed to hypnotize small children with their swirly red kitten eyes. Give them bad dreams. That would have been a real PR nightmare."

"So what's up with this one? Why does he want to destroy the world?"

"He won't say. I don't think his heart's really in it. He keeps doing all these crazy stunts, like with the kittens. There was a thing with a machine to turn everything into tomato juice. But somebody who used to hang out with him says he doesn't even like tomato juice. If he ever tries to kidnap you, Bunnatine, whatever you do, don't say yes if he offers you a game of chess. Try to stay off the subject of chess. He's one of those guys who think all master criminals ought to be chess players, but he's terrible. He gets sulky."

"I'll try to remember that. Are you comfortable? Put your head here. Are you cold? That outfit doesn't look very warm. Do you want my jacket?"

"Stop fussing, Bunnatine. Am I too heavy?"

"Go to sleep, Biscuit."

His head was so heavy she couldn't figure out how he carried it around on his neck all day. He wasn't asleep. She could hear him thinking.

He said, "You know, some day I'm going to fuck up. Some day I'll fuck up and the world won't get saved."

"Yeah. I know. A big flood. That's okay. You just take care of yourself, okay? And I'll take care of myself and the world will take care of itself, too."

Her leg felt wet. Gross. He was drooling on her leg. He said, "I dream about you, Bunnatine. I dream that you're drowning too. And I can't do anything about it. I can't save you."

She said, "You don't have to save me, baby. Remember? I float. Let everything turn into water. Just turn into water. Let it turn into beer. Clam chowder. Let the Land of Oz become an exciting new investment opportunity in underwater attractions. Little happy mutant Dorothy mermaids. Let all those mountain houses and ski condos sink down into the water, and the deer and the bricks and the high school girls and the people who never tip. It isn't all that great a world anyway, you know? Biscuit? Maybe it doesn't want to be saved. So stop worrying so much. I'll float like a bar of Ivory soap. Even better. Won't even get my toes wet until you come and find me."

"Oh good, Bunnatine," he said, drooling, "that's a weight off my mind"—and fell asleep. She sat beneath his heavy head and listened to the air rushing around up there in the invisible leaves. It sounded like water moving fast. Waterfalls and lakes of water rushing up the side of the mountain. Biscuit's flood. But that was some other parallel universe. Here it was only night and wind and trees and the stars were coming out. Hey, Dad, you fuckhead.

Her legs fell asleep and she needed to pee again, but she didn't want to wake Biscuit up. She bent over and kissed him on the top of his head. He didn't wake up. He just mumbled, quit it, Bunnatine. Love me alone. Or something like that.

She remembered being a kid. Nine or ten. Sneaking back into the house at four in the morning. Her best friend Biscuit has gone home too, to lie in his bed and not sleep. She had to beg him to let her go home. They have school tomorrow. She's tired and she's so hungry. Fighting crime is hard work. Her mother is in the kitchen, making pancakes. There's something about the way she looks that tells Bunnatine she's been out all night, too. Maybe she's been out fighting crime, too. Bunnatine knows her mother is a superhero. She isn't just a waitress. That's just her cover story.

She stands in the door of the kitchen and watches her mother. She practices her hovering. She practices all the time.

Her mother says, "Want some pancakes, Bunnatine?"

She waited as long as she could, and then she heaved his head up and put it down on the ground. She covered his shoulders with her jacket. Like setting a table with a handkerchief. Look at the big guy, lying there so peacefully. Maybe he'll sleep for a hundred years. But more likely the mutants will wake him, eventually, with their barbaric yawps. They're into kazoos right now, and heavy-metal hooting. She can hear them warming up. Biscuit hung out with some of the mutants at school, years and years ago. They'll get a real kick out of his new outfit. There's a ten-year high-school reunion coming up, and Biscuit will come home for that. He gets all sentimental and soft about things. Mutants, on the other hand, don't do things like parades or reunions. They were good at keeping secrets, though. They made great babysitters when her mom couldn't take care of the kid.

She keeps her headlights off, all the way down the mountain. Turns the engine off too. Just sails down the mountain like a black wing.

When she gets home, she's mostly sober and of course the kid is still asleep. Her mom doesn't say anything, although Bunnatine knows she doesn't approve. She thinks Bunnatine ought to tell Biscuit about the kid. But it's a little late for that, and who knows? Maybe she isn't his kid anyway.

The kid has fudge smeared all over her face and her pillow. Leftover fudge from the parade, probably. Bunnatine's mom has a real sweet tooth. Kid probably sat up eating it in the dark, after Bunnatine's mom put her to bed. Bunnatine kisses the kid on the forehead. Goes and gets a washcloth, comes back and wipes off some of the fudge. Kid still doesn't wake up. She's going to be real disappointed about the autograph. Maybe Bunnatine will just forge Biscuit's handwriting. Write something real nice. It's not like Biscuit will care. Bunnatine would like to crawl into the kid's bed, just curl up around the kid and get warm again, but she's already missed two shifts this week. So she takes a hot shower and goes to sit with her mom in the kitchen until she has to leave for work. Neither of them have much to say to each other, which is normal, but her mom makes Bunnatine some eggs and toast. If Biscuit were here, she'd make him breakfast, too, and Bunnatine imagines that, eating breakfast with Biscuit and her mom, waiting for the sun to come up so that the day can start all over again. Then the kid comes in the kitchen, crying and holding out her arms for Bunnatine. "Mommy," she says. "Mommy, I had a really bad dream."

Bunnatine picks her up. Such a heavy little kid. Her nose is running and she still smells like fudge. No wonder she had a bad dream. Bunnatine says, "Shhh. It's okay, baby. It was just a bad dream. Just a dream. Tell me about the dream."

BURNING SKY
RACHEL POLLACK

Rachel Pollack, author of the phenomenal novel *Unquenchable Fire*, delves into the psychosexual mythology of the Amazon archetype. I don't think anyone's done Wonder Woman right since her creator, William Moulton Marston (AKA Charles Moulton). If DC were ever to give Pollack (who has also written comics) free reign on the character, I suspect the results would be sensational and provocative.

Sometimes I think of my clitoris as a magnet, pulling me along to uncover new deposits of ore in the fantasy mines. Or maybe a compass, like the kind kids used to get in Woolworth's, with a blue-black needle in a plastic case, and flowery letters marking the directions.

Two years ago, more by accident than design, I left the City of Civilized Sex. I still remember its grand traditions: orgasms in the service of loving relationships, healthy recreation with knowledgeable partners, a pinch of perversion to bring out the flavor. I remember them with a curious nostalgia. I think of them as I march through the wilderness, with only my compass to guide me.

Julia. Tall, with fingers that snake round the knobs and levers of her camera. Julia's skin is creamy, her neck is long and smooth, her eyebrows arch almost to a point. There was once a woman who drowned at sea, dreaming of Julia's eyes. Sometimes her hair is short and spiky, sometimes long and straight, streaming out to one side in the wind off Second Avenue. Sometimes her hair is red, with thick curls. Once a month she goes to a woman who dyes her eyelashes black. They darken further with each treatment.

Julia's camera is covered in black rubber. The shutter is a soft rubber button.

The Free Women. Bands of women who roam the world's cities at night, protecting women from rapists, social security investigators, police, and other forms of men. Suits of supple blue plastic cover their bodies from head to toe.

Only the faces remain bare. Free Skin, they call it. The thin plastic coats the body like dark glistening nail polish.

Julia discovers the Free Women late one summer night when she can't sleep. She has broken up with a lover and can't sleep, so she goes out walking, wearing jeans and a white silk shirt and high red boots, and carrying her camera over one shoulder. On a wide street, by a locked park, with a drunk curled asleep before the gate, a man with a scarred face has cornered a girl, about fourteen. He flicks his knife at her, back and forth, like a lizard tongue. Suddenly they are there, yanking him away from the girl, surrounding him, crouched down with moon and street-lights running like water over their blue muscles. The man jerks forward. Spread fingers slide sideways. The attacker drops his knife to put his hand over his throat. Blood runs through the fingers. He falls against the gate. The women walk away. Julia follows.

Julia discovers the Free Women one night on the way home from an assignment. Tired as she is, she walks rather than take a taxi home to an empty apartment. She has just broken up with a lover, the third in less than two years. Julia doesn't understand what happens in these relationships. She begins them with such hopes, and then a month, two months, and she's lost interest, faking excitement when her girlfriend plans for the future. Recklessly, Julia walks down the West Side, a woman alone with an expensive camera. She sees them across the street, three women walking shoulder to shoulder, their blue boots (she thinks) gliding in step, their blue gloves (she thinks) swinging in rhythm, their blue hoods (she thinks) washed in light. Julia takes the cap off her lens and follows them, conscious of the jerkiness in her stride, the hardness in her hips.

She follows them to a grimy factory building on West 21st Street. As they press buttons on an electronic light Julia memorizes the combination. For hours she waits, in a doorway smelling of piss, thinking now and then that the women are watching her, that they have arranged for her to stand there in that filth, a punishment for following them. Finally they leave and Julia lets herself inside. She discovers a single huge room, with lacquered posts hanging with manacles, racks of black-handled daggers along the walls, and in the middle of the floor a mosaic maze, coils of deep blue, with the center, the prize, a four-pronged spiral made of pure gold. On the wall opposite the knives hang rows of blue suits, so thin they flutter slightly in the breeze from the closing door.

Over the next weeks Julia rushes through her assignments to get back to the hall of the Free Women. She spends days crouched across the street, waiting for the thirty seconds when she can photograph them entering or leaving. She spends more and more time inside, taking the suits in her hands, walking the maze. In the center she hears a loud fluttering of wings.

She tells herself she will write an exposé, an article for the Sunday *Times*. But she puts off calling the paper or her agent. She puts off writing any notes. Instead she enlarges her photos more than lifesize, covering the walls of her apartment, until she can almost imagine the women are there with her, or that the maze fills the floor of her kitchen.

And then one day Julia comes home—she's gone out for food, she's forgotten to keep any food in the house—and she finds the photos slashed, the negatives ruined, and all the lenses gone from her cameras.

Julia runs. She leaves her clothes, her cameras, her portfolios. She takes whatever cash lies in the house and heads into the street. Downtown she takes a room above a condemned bank and blacks out all the windows.

Let me tell you how I came to leave the City-state of Civilized Sex. It happened at the shore. Not the ocean, but the other side of Long Island, the Sound connecting New York and Connecticut. I'd gone there with my girlfriend Louise, who at nineteen had seduced more women than I had ever known.

Louise and I had gotten together a few months after my husband Ralph had left me. On our last day as a couple Ralph informed me how lucky I was not to have birthed any children. The judge, he said, would certainly have awarded them to him. He went on to explain that it was no coincidence, our lack of children, since any heroic sperm that attempted to mount an expedition in search of my hidden eggs (*Raiders of the Lost Ovum*) would have frozen in "that refrigerator cunt of yours." Ralph liked to mix metaphors. When he got angry his speech reminded me of elaborate cocktails, like Singapore Slings.

I can't really blame Ralph. Not only did I never learn to fake orgasms properly (I would start thrusting and moaning and then think of something and forget the gasps and shrieks) but even in fights I tended to get distracted when I should have wept or screamed or thrown things.

Like the day Ralph left. I'm sure I should have cried or stared numbly at the wall. Instead I made myself a tuna sandwich and thought of sperms in fur coats, shivering on tiny wooden rafts as they tried to maneuver round the icebergs that blocked their way to the frozen eggs. I don't blame Ralph for leaving.

Anyway, he went, and I met Louise window-shopping in a pet store. That same night we went to bed and I expected to discover that my sexual indifference had indicated a need for female flesh. Nothing happened. Louise cast her best spells, she swirled her magician's cloak in more and more elaborate passes, but the rabbit stayed hidden in the hat.

I became depressed, and Louise, exhausted, assured me that in all her varied experiences (she began to recite the range of ages and nationalities of women she'd converted) she'd never failed to find the proper button. It would just take time. I didn't tell her Ralph had said much the same thing. I wondered if I'd have to move to my parents' house upstate to avoid safaris searching for my orgasms like Tarzan on his way to the elephants' graveyard.

Julia runs out of money. She disguises herself in clothes bought from a uniform store on Canal St. and goes uptown to an editor who owes her a check. As she leaves the building she sees, across the street, in the doorway of a church, a black raincoat over blue skin. Julia jumps in a taxi. She goes to Penn Station, turning around constantly in her taxi to make sure no blue-hooded women sit in the cars behind her. At the station she runs down the stairs, pushing past commuters to the Long Island Railroad where she searches the computer screens for the train to East Hampton.

On track 20 she hears a fluttering of wings and she smells the sea, and for a moment she thinks she's already arrived. And then she sees a trenchcoat lying on the floor. Another is falling beside her. A flash of light bounces off the train, as if the sun has found a crack through Penn Station and the roof of the tunnel. She tries running for the doors. Blue hands grab her wrists. Blueness covers her face.

No. No, it happens along Sixth Avenue. Sixth Avenue at lunchtime, among the push carts selling souvlaki and sushi, egg rolls and yoghurt, tofu and pretzels. Julia's pants are torn, the wind dries the sweat on her chest, she's been running for hours, her toes are bleeding, no cabs will stop for her. She turns a corner and tumbles into a class of twelve-year-old girls. The girls are eating hot dogs and drinking Pepsi-Cola. They wear uniforms, pleated skirts and lace-up shoes, brown jackets and narrow ties. The girls surround Julia. They push her down when she tries to stand up. Somewhere up the street a radio plays a woman singing "Are you lonesome tonight?" The girls tear off Julia's clothes. They pinch and slap her face, her breasts. Grease streaks her thighs. The girls are whistling, yelping, stamping their feet. Now come the wings, the smell of the sea. The girls step back, their uniforms crisp, their ties straight. They part like drapes opening to the morning. A woman in blue steps into the circle, bright shining as the sun. Spread fingertips slide down Julia's body, from the mouth down the neck and along the breasts, the belly, the thighs. Wherever the woman touches, the welts disappear. She lifts Julia in her arms. Slowly she walks down the street, while the crowd moves aside and the whole city falls silent, even the horns. Julia hears the cry of gulls searching for food.

Over the weeks Louise changed from bluff to hearty to understanding to peevish as her first failure became more and more imminent. She suggested I see a doctor. I told her I'd been and she got me to admit the doctor had been a man. She lugged me to a woman's clinic where the whole staff consisted of former lovers of hers. While Louise went in to consult the healer on duty I sat in the waiting room.

I got into a conversation with a tall skinny woman wearing a buckskin jacket, a gold shirt, and motorcycle boots. She showed me the French bayonet she carried in a sheath in her hip pocket, explaining it would "gut the next prick" that laid a hand on her or one of her sisters. I asked her if she'd undergone any training in knifeware. Not necessary, she told me. Pricks train. The Goddess would direct her aim. The Goddess, she said, lived in the right side of the brain. That's why the government (99% pricks) wanted to burn left-handed women.

"Janie's a little strong-minded" Louise told me as she led me down a corridor to see Doctor Catherine. The corridor's yellow-striped wallpaper had started to peel in several places, revealing a layer of newspaper underneath.

"Did you sleep with her?" I asked.

"Only a couple of times. Did she show you her bayonet?" I nodded. "She kept it under the pillow in case the police broke in to arrest us for Goddessworship. That's what she calls women screwing."

I didn't listen very closely to Catherine, who didn't like the name "Doctor." I wanted to think about pricks training for their life's work. They probably do it in gym class, I decided. While the girls try backward somersaults and leap sideways over wooden horses the boys practice erections, and later, in advanced classes, learn to charge rubber simulations of female genitals. At the end of each lesson the instructor reminds them not to speak of this in front of their girlfriends.

Catherine didn't find my G spot or raise my *Mary Rose* (I strongly identified with Henry VIII's sunken flagship and all its chests of gold. I cried when they raised it, all crusted in barnacles and brine. That left only one of us hidden in the murk.). She did give me some crushed herbs for tea and a bag of tree bark to chew on while I lay in the bathtub. Louise raged at me whenever I neglected my treatment. "You can't let yourself get negative," she shouted. "You've got to believe."

In the ritual hall Julia spends days hanging from copper, then brass, then silver manacles. Six, no, nine of the women weave in and out of sight, sometimes whispering to each other, sometimes laughing, sometimes standing before Julia and silently mouthing words in a foreign language. Across from her the blue suits rustle against each other.

Julia learns to catch bits of food thrown at her from across the room. Twice, no, three times a day one of the women brings her water in a stone bowl. A gold snake coils at the bottom. Sometimes the woman holds the bowl in front of her, and Julia has to bow her head and lap up as much as she can. Or the woman moves the bowl away just as Julia begins to drink. Or throws the water in her face. At other times she gently tilts the bowl for Julia. Once, as Julia drinks, she discovers that a live snake has replaced the metal one. The head rises above the water and Julia's own head snaps back so hard she would bang it against the wall if a blue hand wasn't there to cushion her.

They shave her head. No, they comb and perfume her hair. They rub her with oils and smooth the lines in her face and neck, slapping her only when she tries to bite or lick the cool fingertips sliding down her face.

Once or several times a day they take her down from the wall and force her to run the maze. The women surround the tiled circle, hitting the floor with sticks and trilling louder and louder until Julia misses a step or even falls, just outside the gold spiral. When she's failed they yank her out of the maze and hold her arms out like wings as they press the tips of her breasts into champagne glasses filled with tiny sharp emeralds.

On the day Julia completes the maze the women dress her in shapeless black overalls and heavy boots. They smuggle her out of the country to an island where a house of white stone stands on top of a hill covered in pine trees. The women strip Julia. With their sticks they drive her up a rock path. The door opens and a cool wind flows from the darkness.

A woman steps out. Instead of blue her suit gleams a deep red. It covers the whole body, including the face, except for the eyes, the nostrils, the mouth. Her muscles move like a river running over stone. Her name is Burning Sky, and she was born in Crete six thousand years ago. When she walks the air flows behind her like the sundered halves of a very thin veil.

One night, after a fight, Louise kicked the wall and ran from the house. The next morning, the doorbell woke me at 6:00. Frightened, I looked out the window before I would open the door. There stood Louise in a rough zipper jacket and black turtleneck sweater. She saw me and waved a pair of rubber boots. Afraid she planned to kick me I didn't want to let her in but I couldn't think of how to disconnect the doorbell. She'd begun to shout, too. "For heaven's sake, Maggie, open the fucking door." Any moment the police would show up.

While I buttered toast and boiled water Louise announced our plans for the morning. We were going fishing. Dress warm, she said, and gave me the spare boots she'd brought for me. I had to wear two pairs of socks, and my feet still slid around.

In her pickup truck I tried to sleep, despite Louise's cheerful whistle. But when we got all our gear and bodies in a rowboat out in the Sound, it turned out that Louise didn't plan to fish at all. "Now, goddamnit," she said, "you can't whine and get away from me. I'm not taking this boat back to shore until you come and I can feel it all over my fingers."

"What?" I said, ruining her powerful speech. Her meaning became clearer as she began to crawl towards me. She scared me but she made me want to laugh too. It reminded me of the time Ralph had locked us in a motel room with a bottle of wine, a bag of marijuana, and a pink nightgown. At least motel rooms are comfortable. Maybe Louise considered rowboats romantic.

I decided I better hold my face straight. "You rapist prick!" I shouted, and tried to grab an oar to threaten her but couldn't work it loose from the lock. I snatched the fish knife and held it with both hands in front of my belly. "Keep away from me," I warned.

"Put that down." Louise said. "You'll hurt yourself."

"I'll hurt you, you prick."

"Don't call me that. You don't know how to use that."

"The Goddess will show me."

Apparently this all became too much for her. "Shit," she said, and turned around to grasp the oars for the pull to shore. I sat slumped over and shivering. My hands clenched around the knife.

In a ceremonial hall hung with purple silk and gold shields the women tattoo a four-pronged spiral in the hollow of Julia's neck. They present her with a blue suit. With four others she returns to New York on a cruise ship secretly owned by the Free Women. They wear disguises, like the Phantom, when he would venture out as Mister Walker, wrapped in a trench coat and slouch hat, to rescue his beloved Diana from Nazi kidnappers.

Despite the women's clever tricks someone on the boat recognizes them. A television anchorwoman, or maybe a right-wing politician. This woman once served Burning Sky, but disobeyed her leader on some assignment. Now she comes to their suite of cabins and begs the Free Women to readmit her. They play with her, attaching small intricately carved stone clips all over her skin. She suffers silently, only to have them announce she has forgotten how to break through the wall. They can do nothing for her. She goes away, later becomes Prime Minister.

When we got back to the rental dock Louise began to lug the boat onto the wooden platform. "If you want to go home," she said, "give me a hand." I took hold of the rope to tie it to the iron post that would hold it fast when the hurricane came.

At that moment a woman came out of the water. Dressed in a black wet suit with long shiny flippers and a dark mask that completely hid her face, she stood for a moment rotating her shoulders and tilting her head up to the sun. Her spear gun pointed at the ground.

My heart began throwing blood wildly around my body: my vagina contracted like someone running for her life. "Will you come on?" Louise said.

I stammered something at her. Louise had never heard me stammer before. "What the hell is the matter with you?" she said. Then her eyes followed the invisible cable connecting me and my beautiful skindiver. She looked back and forth between us a couple of times while a wolfgrin took over her face. "Sonofabitch," she said, and laughed. "Why didn't you tell me?"

"I didn't know," I said, and Louise got to see another first. I blushed.

It was certainly a day for firsts. That evening, in the sloppy cavernous apartment Louise had inherited from her grandfather, she took out her collection of "toys": whips, handcuffs, masks, chains, nipple clips, leather capes, rubber gloves, and one whalebone corset, c. 1835. No wetsuits, but it didn't really matter. I hope none of Ralph's sperm remained camped inside me anymore. The spring thaw came that night, and the flood would have washed the courageous little creatures away forever.

The Free Women order Julia to go alone to her apartment and renew her professional contacts. At first she finds it hard to function without her instructors. She hates going out "naked," as she thinks of her ordinary clothes. With no one to command her she forgets to eat and one day passes out while photographing a police parade in the South Bronx.

Gradually the dream fades. Julia stops dressing up in her Free Skin at night, she goes on holiday with a woman reporter who asks about the tattoo on Julia's neck. Julia tells her she got it to infiltrate a group of terrorists. When the woman falls asleep Julia cries in the shower and thanks the Virgin Mary for her deliverance. She wonders how she ever could have submitted to such strange and wretched slavery.

An order comes. Something simple, maybe embarrassing a judge who suspended the sentence of a man who raped his five-year-old daughter. Something with a clear moral imperative.

Julia takes off from work to decide what to do. In a cabin in the woods she tries on her Free Skin and lies in bed, remembering Burning Sky's face, and the way her fingers looked extended into the air. She remembers lying with the other women in a huge bed, how they slid in and out of each other, while their bodies melted inside their blue suits. She remembers hanging from silver manacles, remembers dancing to the heart of the labyrinth.

Julia returns to the city and locks the blue suit in a metal cabinet. The day of her assignment passes. She falls into a fever, attended by her reporter friend. When she recovers and the woman has left, Julia opens the cabinet. Her Free Skin has vanished. In its place lies a Chinese woman's dagger, five hundred years old, with an ivory handle bearing the same spiral sign that marks Julia's neck. Terrified, she waits for retribution. Weeks pass.

And so I left the City of Civilized Sex in one great rush on the back of a skindiver. Now that she'd preserved her record Louise lost interest very quickly, but at least she gave me some leads to "your kind of trick," as she delicately put it. I didn't know whether she meant the lovers or the activities.

I discovered not only a large reservoir of women devoted to farfetched sexual practices, but several organizations, complete with buttons, slogans, jackets, and conflicting manifestoes. After a while they all began to strike me as rather odd, not just for their missionary zeal, but their hunger for community. Had I left the City only to emigrate to another nation-state?

It wasn't so much the social as the sexual conformity that disturbed me.

Everyone seemed to agree ahead of time on what would excite them. I began to wonder if all those people in the Land of Leather really liked the same sort of collar (black with silver studs) or if each new arrival, thrilled at finding a town where she'd expected only a swamp, confused gratitude with eroticism, and gave up her dreams of finding leather clothes and objects of exactly the right color, cut and texture.

As my imagination began to show me its tastes I became more and more specific with the women who tried to satisfy me. That first night with Louise she could have tied me up with a piece of filthy clothesline and I wouldn't have complained. A few months later I was demanding the right ropes (green and gold curtain pulls with the tassel removed) tied only in particular knots taken from the *Boy Scout Handbook*.

And even that phase didn't last. For, in fact, it's not actions that I'm hunting. No matter how well you do them they can only approximate reality. City dwellers believe that fantasies exist to intensify arousal. Out here in the Territories the exiles should know better. I want to stand on a tree stump and yell through the forest, "Stop trying to build new settlements. Stop trying to clear the trees and put up walls and lay down sewers." I want them to understand. Sex exists to lay traps for fantasies.

Julia's life becomes as pale and blank as cheap paper. She goes to bars and picks up women. They all go away angry when they get back to Julia's apartment and Julia just sits on the bed, or else goes to the darkroom and doesn't come out. Julia returns to the ritual hall. She finds it replaced by a button factory.

She drives out to the beach on a hard sunny day in December. Ignoring the cold wind she strips naked and walks toward the water, both hands gripping the Chinese dagger. She raises it to the sun to watch the light glint off the blade. But then she notices flashes beyond the knife. Small spots on the horizon. As she watches, they grow larger, become blue sails, then a row of boats coming out of the deep. Each one contains a single woman. The sails rise out of their shoulders like wings. They call to each other like birds, their voices piercing the wind. When they land they detach their skins from the boat masts and the plastic snaps back against their bodies.

Julia falls down in the wet sand. A wild roaring in the Earth drowns out the sea as the six women lift her to her feet (six is the number of love, with Julia they become seven, the number of victory). They wash the mud and loneliness from her and dress her in the Free Skin she abandoned for an illusion of freedom.

"The only real happiness for anybody is to be found in obedience to loving authority."
—Charles Moulton, speaking as Queen Hippolyte of Paradise Island to her daughter, Princess Di, *Wonder Woman Comics*, 1948

THE NIGHT CHICAGO DIED

JAMES LOWDER

James Lowder has edited numerous anthologies, spanning genres such as pulp action (*Astounding Hero Tales: Thrilling Stories of Pulp Adventure*), superheroes (*Path of the Just*), and zombies (the *All Flesh Must Be Eaten* series). In this thrillingly boisterous tale, he combines all three of those genres.

Chicago's most vicious criminals fear but one man: Tristram Holt, known throughout the underworld as the Corpse. But when his most powerful enemies band together to throw wide the gates of Hell, can even the Scourge of Evil turn back an army of the walking dead?

CHAPTER ONE
THE CORPSE STRIKES

Johnny "Gat" Garrison was a man of few words. In fact, he usually let his twin .38s do his talking for him—and those lethal surrogates were about to speak now.

"Honest, Gat, I didn't mean nothing by it," stammered Eddie O'Rourke as he stared, quaking, into the black barrels of Garrison's guns. They gaped at him like a skull's empty eye sockets, the face of Death itself. "I'm sure the boss will take care of anyone who gets in our way. Even...*him*. I wasn't doubtin' what ya said. Besides, I'm yer pal, right?"

The .38s barked their reply. O'Rourke was not a little man, but the blast still sent him staggering back a half-dozen steps before he collapsed in a bloody, lifeless heap. Garrison didn't spare his victim another look, so accustomed was he to seeing corpses sprawled before him. Instead, he turned his murderer's gaze on the other eight men gathered around him.

"Well?" he rumbled.

The challenge lingered in the bitter February air. By way of a reply, the bootleggers and hit men and racketeers studied the tips of their perfectly polished shoes or puttered with the tools and boards stacked around them in the gutted barn, which was in the process of being turned into a road house. More than one of the gangsters wished he could slip away into the shadows that hung thick in the corners. But the only warmth in the place came from the trash fire burning in an empty oil drum positioned at the room's center. Get too far from that and the winter night tore into you like a bitter old man with a shiv. Besides, Garrison would cut down anyone who stepped out of the glare created by the trio of work lights set up to illuminate the meeting place. So the men stuck close together, even though distrust hung as thick around them as the dark, curling smoke from the oil drum.

Suspicion was to be expected with a meeting as unprecedented as this. Half the criminals in attendance were veterans of Al Capone's South Side gang, the other half supposedly loyal to "Bugs" Moran, who ran the rackets on the North Side. Warfare between the two Chicago mobs had been constant for the past decade. Capone's predecessors had either been murdered, like "Big Jim" Colosimo, or frightened into retirement, like Johnny Torrio. On the North Side, Moran had been one of a triumvirate of ambitious men to take over after Dion O'Banion was gunned down in the florist shop he ran. Two of O'Banion's would-be successors soon followed him to an early grave. First George "Hymie" Weiss, riddled with machine gun bullets in front of that same fatal florist shop. Then "Schemer" Drucci, on election day in 1927, killed in a bizarre scuffle with police after being picked up for the attempted kidnapping of a rival to his candidate for mayor. That left the North Side under the control of Moran, who made it his mission in life to wipe out Capone. The South Side mob accepted the threat and returned it in kind, bullet for bullet, until the streets of the Windy City ran red.

If the mobsters gathered on that winter-wracked midnight had anything to say about it, the gang war would end soon. And Gat Garrison was going to make certain his boss was the one to be declared the new crime king of Chicago. The same fatal hand he'd dealt O'Rourke awaited anyone who questioned that inevitability.

"Well?" prompted the killer, guns still leveled before him.

It was Dario Fulci who finally spoke. "You'll get no back talk from us," the Italian said in his rasping, almost inhuman voice—a voice horribly familiar to the families of kidnap victims in a dozen states east of the Mississippi. "You done right in shutting up O'Rourke. If he doubted the plan, he would've turned rat on us sooner or later."

"And we don't stand a chance of getting rid of Capone and Moran if someone spills his guts," chimed in a stunted Northsider by the name of Ulysses Flynn. He glanced from under his bowler hat at the gory corpse of his fallen fellow Irishman, then laughed rather idiotically at the unintended joke. "I mean—uh, if somebody *tips off* the other bosses to what Bruiser Bill has planned for this burg."

When the rest nodded in agreement, Garrison finally lowered his guns. But the murderer didn't holster the .38s. He simply let them drop to his sides as if they were extensions of his arms.

Flynn's foolish laughter chased away the silence. "I can't wait 'til we're all one gang, with one boss," he said cheerfully, stepping forward to warm his hands over the trash fire. He flashed an impish smile that belied his status as a white slaver. "After Bill Sullivan becomes top dog, nobody will be strong enough to stand against us—not the cops, not the Secret Six, not even the Corpse."

For a few moments more, Flynn rambled on about the plan, lingering over certain details he found particularly clever. The others joined in, grateful to have something to take their minds off their boss's absence. That absence made them more uncomfortable than the bitter cold or even Gat Garrison's fury. "Bruiser" Bill Sullivan was never late. Eventually, even Garrison had to admit that something wasn't right. He glared at his watch with a look almost mean enough to make the hands run backward, and said simply, "Trouble."

"Yeah," Fulci rasped, "this ain't good. The boss is always early to meetings."

"Speaking of early birds," Flynn said, "there was this old yegg working for—" He paused when something small dropped onto the brim of his hat. Had it not been so cold, he might have mistaken it for a raindrop. A second and a third little impact quickly followed the first, then several more. "Hey," Flynn said, pulling off his hat, "what gives?"

Fat yellow-white maggots wriggled on the brown bowler. Flynn dropped his hat and crossed himself. "Christ almighty," the Irishman gasped. "He's here...."

As one, the gathered criminals drew their guns. Flynn scrambled forward and redirected a work light so that it pointed up. The bright white beam cut through the smoke and darkness to reveal two men perched in the rafters. Then one of the figures dropped.

"It's the boss!" Garrison cried when he saw the raccoon coat and wide-brimmed gray hat on the figure plummeting toward them. "Catch him, somebody!"

Though none of the gangsters moved quickly enough to act on that order, the body never hit the floor. A rope around the man's neck snapped taut and he jerked to a stop, three feet of air still beneath his heels. He danced for a moment on the rope's end, shudders wracking the thin form beneath the heavy coat. Bruiser Bill Sullivan was not, as his name might suggest, a big, burly fellow. He'd gained his moniker from his expertise with a machine gun, the use of which often bruised the gunman's arms and shoulders. An instant after the last traces of life appeared to flee the dangling body, Sullivan's own trademark trench sweeper dropped from above and hit the floorboards with a startling clatter.

All eyes moved from the fallen Tommy gun to the unfortunate mobster dangling above them, then up the hangman's rope to the rafters, where the second man still slouched against a vertical beam. The Corpse! The gangsters, like all the denizens of Chicago's underworld, recognized him on sight. And if they could not see the figure clearly enough to make out the details of his bloody, bullet-torn clothing and his gaunt features, the maggots that had rained down upon Ulysses Flynn announced the Corpse's presence. The vermin were his calling card, the things with which the Scourge of Evil marked his victims....

The boom of a dozen guns going off at once echoed in the barn. The figure in the rafters danced a moment in the crossfire, then toppled forward. No rope impeded his fall. He crashed, face down, to the ground. A second roar of gunfire masked the impact's sickening thud and the sound of bones breaking. The gangsters kept up the hail of bullets until their guns clicked empty.

His twin .38s smoking at his sides, Gat Garrison approached the body cautiously. He dug his toe under the bullet-riddled body and kicked it over, so that it lay on its back. The face was horrible to see, but it was not the Corpse's grim visage staring up at the gangsters. The face belonged to the would-be crime king of Chicago, Bill Sullivan.

Garrison figured it out an instant before the others. He turned, guns pointed at the body dangling on the rope, even as the hanged man raised his head. Garrison smirked and squeezed both triggers at once. The empty guns clacked hollowly.

A horrible smile spread across the pale face of the Corpse. It sliced his blue-white flesh like a razor's cut. There were guns in his hands now, too, and when his shriveled fingers curled, those gleaming black automatics shouted their owner's hatred of the corrupt and the conniving.

Garrison tried to run for cover, but the body of Eddie O'Rourke tripped him up. Had he any say in the matter, O'Rourke would have kept out of it; he had no interest in helping out his murderer. But the fall saved Garrison from the scythe of bullets that slashed through the barn. Their guns empty, the gangsters faced the Corpse's assault armed only with their courage, which meant that many of them took a bullet in the back as they scrambled for the exit.

Soon the Corpse's ammunition was spent, too. Unlike the gangsters' frantic barrage, though, every one of his shots had found its mark. There were no agonized moans, no cries for help. The Corpse left no man wounded. His aim was much too sure for that. The mobsters were all dead—save one.

From his hiding place behind Eddie O'Rourke's body, Gat Garrison watched in silence as the Corpse casually slipped the empty automatics back into his pockets, seemingly unaware of the danger still lurking in the room. The fall had sent Garrison's twin .38s spinning from his hands. They lay on the dirty floor between him and the Corpse. With his eyes, the murderer measured the distance to them. He could reach the guns before the vigilante could react, but they were still empty. What he needed was a loaded weapon, even one he had to make a grab for....

Bruiser Bill's machine gun.

The discarded Tommy gun rested nearby in a pile of sawdust. It still had a drum loaded, Garrison could see, and seemed to have survived the drop from the rafters intact. The murderer's gaze lingered on the oiled black metal of the machine gun as he weighed his chances of retrieving it. Then his gaze moved upward to his adversary. The horrible smile still split the Corpse's face, and his dark eyes glittered red with the reflected light of the trash fire. And those dark eyes, Garrison saw to his horror, were fixed squarely upon him.

Gat Garrison sprang up with a grace unexpected from someone of his considerable bulk, but he had barely covered half the distance to his goal before the Corpse swung forward on the rope, yanked a release on the harness hidden beneath the heavy coat, and dropped to the floor directly over the machine gun. The weapon was in the crimefighter's hands, the bolt set and the muzzle aimed, even as Garrison skidded to a halt.

The murderer's face displayed no fear. He stood his ground, his barrel chest thrown out as if to present the Corpse a better target. "Get it over with," Garrison rumbled.

The Corpse obliged.

CHAPTER TWO
VOICES OF THE DAMNED

The terrific clatter from the burst of machine gun fire had just died away in the barn when a screech of truck tires sounded outside. The Corpse barely had time to escape into the shadows before the door burst open. Three men, each with a machine gun leveled before him, stepped in from the darkness. They had entered ready to fire, but hesitated when they saw the carnage. "Somebody beat us to it," one of them said.

"You think Capone did it, or Moran?" another asked.

"Neither," came the reply from outside the barn, and the trio of gunmen parted to allow a short, stocky man to enter. "They are both equally ignorant of Comrade Sullivan's plans, just as they know nothing of ours." He sighed and brushed some lint from his Western-style overcoat. "The Corpse, I think."

The name of the Corpse was rarely uttered in Chicago without an edge of fear, but the little Bolshevik spoke it only with exasperation. The Corpse knew why. He had tangled before with Nikodim Fomitch Zametov, known to the United States Secret Service as the Red Death, and their battles had always gone against the madman.

The vigilante was tempted to step out of the concealing darkness and once again teach the Red Death the error of his ways, but there was too much to be gained by listening—for the moment, anyway.

"The Corpse has done our work for us," Zametov said in his labored English, even as he scanned the barn for some trace of the man. "But his involvement so soon in this business is...*unfortunate.*"

The three gangsters would have chosen other, harsher words for this unexpected turn of events. The little Bolshevik noted their nervous glances, the way they gripped their machine guns tightly. "Unfortunate," he concluded, "but nothing to concern us overly. Please, comrades, unload the prototype from the truck."

The three went out. Zametov drew a pistol and kept careful watch on the barn's shadowy corners. The Red Death was a crack shot with any gun. Years of government training and his own secret program of muscle- and speed-building exercises had honed his reflexes. Though small in stature, Zametov easily overmatched all but the most monstrously strong opponents or those highly skilled in the martial arts. The Corpse was neither of those. In fact, the twist of fate that had given him his hideous appearance had left him physically weaker than most men. Yet he had managed, almost through will alone, to defeat the Bolshevik twice before, just as he had smashed many of the gangs infesting the Windy City during his self-proclaimed war on crime. And as soon as the opportunity presented itself, he would make certain this third meeting with Zametov would be the last. The Red Death would foster anarchy in America no more.

The mechanism the three gangsters wheeled into the doorway a short time later resembled something out of *Metropolis*—a small cannon covered in blinking lights and wires pulsing with power. Strange symbols patterned its surface. Cables connected the thing to a portable generator on the truck; the Corpse could hear it humming even through the barn wall.

"Remember, comrades, do not station yourself before the harrowing device once it is operational," Zametov warned as the three thugs moved the cannon through the barn door. "The effect of the beam on the living is quite unpleasant."

The Corpse did not have time to wonder at the meaning of those words before

Zametov threw the main switch. The pattern of the blinking lights became more insistent. The rattle of the portable generator increased to a strained whine. The Corpse braced himself for some sort of explosion, but no volley erupted from the weird device. Instead, a wave of blast furnace-hot air washed over the barn. Another followed, and another, each coming more rapidly than its predecessor. And each wave carried a sound unlike any the Corpse had heard before: a distant wailing, soft at first, but composed of so many different voices it seemed to be the entire city calling out.

The waves came faster now, one after another, until they blurred together. The air within the barn became stifling, and a thick fog filled the air. The soft wail rose into an ear-splitting shriek. Louder and louder the sound grew, until the Corpse slammed his hands over his ears to hold it out. He could still hear them, though, the voices of a million people and more, all crying out in agony. The sound drove all thoughts from his head, threatened to shake his very soul loose from his body. Dimly, distantly, he felt rather than knew what this sound must be.

Hell's cacophony. The voices of the damned.

His back against a thick support column, which hid him from the men in the doorway, the Corpse slid to the ground. The sound was a physical thing now. It hammered at him, pressing down with so much force he could barely draw a breath. With superhuman effort he turned his head and peered around the wooden post. The fog had lifted, though the air shimmered from the heat in the room. Zametov and his assistants still waited behind the sinister cannon. It looked as if they could not hear the Hell-drawn sounds or feel the scorching air, but something was terrifying the three gangsters. Even the Bolshevik's eyes were focused on something in the barn.

The Corpse followed his gaze to the bodies of the men he had killed. They were moving. Bloody fingers clawed the air. Bullet-bitten arms and legs flexed. Bruiser Bill Sullivan and Dario Fulci and Ulysses Flynn all pushed themselves to their feet and moved with shuffling steps toward Zametov. Even Eddie O'Rourke rose up.

Only O'Rourke's murderer, the brutish Gat Garrison, seemed reluctant to heed the call of the Bolshevik's device. The machine gun burst with which the Corpse killed Garrison had all but cut him in half, and his body now proved too unstable to walk. Finally, though, he flopped forward and propelled himself across the wooden floor with his arms alone. His legs twitched and shuddered as he dragged them behind him. A trail of blood and gore marked his wake.

The Corpse fell back against the post. The unbearable heat choked him, and the unbelievable sight of the living dead men battered his thoughts. He, Tristram Holt, had the appearance of a walking corpse, but he played up his now-ghastly features to frighten his enemies. Sullivan and Garrison and the rest had been dead, and yet they lived again! They were in truth what he only pretended to be.

Even as he struggled to comprehend what he had witnessed, the Hell-born cries tore at his sanity. The torture continued for what seemed hours. Finally, the Corpse felt a desperate scream building in his own throat. It tore free, and he shrieked and shrieked, until at last his voice gave out. Only then did he notice the silence in the barn, and the cold.

The howling of the damned had been silenced. The bitter chill of the February night had reclaimed the cavernous room. The Corpse crawled across the floor to the open door, moving in the gory trail left by Garrison. Zametov, his henchmen, and the living dead men were all gone. They had taken the truck and departed— several hours ago, from the first hints of dawn now coloring the sky to the east. Were it not for the blood still staining the wooden floor, the rope still hanging from the rafters, the detritus of his battle with the mobsters scattered everywhere, the Corpse might have dismissed it all as some terrible hallucination. A waking nightmare.

But this was no bad dream. Somehow, the Red Death had discovered a way to reach into Hell and resurrect the dead. He called to them and they came, slaves to his formidable will.

Well, Tristram Holt knew something of will, too. On unsteady legs he crossed the field behind the barn to the concealing darkness of the woods. As he did, he reloaded his gleaming black automatics.

It was up to him now to stop the mad Bolshevik, to bring him at last to justice. And if he had to kill Garrison and Bruiser Bill and the rest all over again to do it, he'd be certain to bring enough ammunition to do the job right this time.

CHAPTER THREE

REX MORTURA

"Gee, Rex, you look like Hell. Rough one last night?"

Rex Mortura, private investigator, continued to stare at the cup of cold coffee sitting on the greasy table between him and Sam Ryan. He knew how he looked— skin the color and texture of dirty clay, eyes bloodshot and rimmed with red, a scowl nastier than the last race for mayor.

Yeah, *Hell* was a pretty good word for it. And more appropriate than the clean-faced cop ever could have guessed.

"The last couple of days have been rougher than some," Mortura admitted. "But I'm still breathing, so I guess other people got it worse. Like Bruiser Bill Sullivan."

"Yeah, he's gone missing alright," Ryan said. "About three days back, as best we can figure." He drummed his fingers lightly on his fat, freckled cheek. He'd been a detective a lot longer than his boyish looks suggested, though he always felt like a rookie around the grizzled investigator. "How'd you know?"

"I read his horoscope," was all Mortura would say. He reached out with a hand gloved in night-black leather and picked up his coffee.

Ryan didn't ask about the gloves, even though it was warm enough in the diner to make them worthy of comment. Everyone knew the story of how Al Capone himself had held Mortura's hands in a washtub of acid to pay the P.I. back for pinning a murder rap on one of his favorite girls. But Ryan had never seen his friend's hands tremble like they were trembling now. He was either exhausted or terrified. Maybe a little of both.

"So you've got nothing on Sullivan's disappearing act?" Mortura prompted.

"It was the Corpse. He killed Sullivan and about a dozen others at some dump outside of town. The mobsters' cars are still parked out there. The inside of the place is painted with blood, and there are enough bullet holes in the walls the building whistles when the wind blows. We even found some of those maggots he leaves as a calling card."

"But no bodies."

"No bodies," Ryan said. "That's the queer thing. The Corpse usually leaves the bodies around as a warning. But if he's decided to add burying the guys he plugs to the other free services he provides the city, that's all right by me." He brayed a laugh. "I just hope Sullivan and the rest have the good sense to stay at the bottom of the river or wherever else they've been dumped."

"They won't," Mortura noted flatly.

"This is kind of an odd case for you," Ryan said, as if he hadn't heard the reply. "One of their girlfriends looking for them? Can't be their wives."

Mortura sighed raggedly and grabbed his hat. "If anyone spots Sullivan or the others—and they will—let me know. I'd appreciate it."

"Sure thing. Hey, go get some rest."

Mortura shrugged. "There'll be time enough for that when I'm dead." He dug into his pocket and dropped a crumpled bill onto the table. "This will cover my coffee and then some. Keep the change for yourself and drop by a juice joint later later. If things play out the way I suspect, you're going to need a drink."

The cop's face went serious. "You know I never touch the stuff when I'm on duty."

"It's almost midnight. You're not on duty."

Ryan slid out of his seat and stood, a solemn look on his boyish face. "I'm *always* on duty." He clapped a hand on Mortura's shoulder. "I know there's no point grilling you about what's going on, Rex. Just let me in on it when you can—and be careful."

"Sure, Sam. You, too."

Mortura felt Ryan's eyes on him as he slouched across the empty diner and out into the night. *To be an honest man in Chicago is to be alone*, someone had once told him. He knew that wasn't true, so long as there were still cops like Sam Ryan in town. But that only made him feel all the worse for the deception he perpetrated on the detective every time they met. For there was no Rex Mortura. The P.I. was only one more false identity for Tristram Holt, alias the Corpse.

Hiding himself beneath the make-up was simple enough. Holt had been an actor in his college days—talented enough to tread the boards on Broadway or even London, some said, and possessor of the looks and charm of a Hollywood leading man. Now, his true face was so gaunt that he had to build up a more normal one, like Mortura's, with prosthetics and greasepaint. Hands were harder to disguise, but the story he'd invented about Capone and the acid provided all the excuse he needed to wear gloves everywhere.

He hadn't always lived life in the shadows. Four years ago, he had simply been Tristram Holt, assistant district attorney, a crusader even then, a foe of the racketeers who had claimed Chicago for their own. Holt took up the war against crime with the same cold resolve with which he'd battled the Kaiser's troops in the trenches of the Great War. Before long, his dedication gained him the welcome attention of the Crime Commission. "The Secret Six," as the commissioners were known, inducted Holt into their hand-chosen brigade of crime-busters and even appointed him their public spokesman.

Others were watching Holt, too, and none so carefully as Schemer Drucci. In one of the bizarre flights of fancy that had earned the gangster his nickname, Drucci had decided that Holt was the key to ridding Chicago of the Secret Six. The wealthy businessmen who formed the Crime Commission kept their identities well hidden. The young assistant D.A., though, was an easy target. The only question was how to turn the firebrand against his patrons.

Drucci concocted a wild plan to transform Holt into a living bomb, a walking powder keg of surgically implanted chemicals and tiny electronic devices wired to explode at the sending of a certain radio signal. He got as far as kidnapping Holt and beginning the chemical injections before the young man escaped. Drucci's thugs chased him to the riverfront. A dozen bullets ripped into Holt and he disappeared into the cold, dirty water. His body was never found. When weeks and then months passed without his return, everyone assumed the mobsters had made him pay the ultimate price for his dedication to the law and order.

More than once after his escape, Holt himself wished they had done just that. But the chemicals intended to make him a human bomb had saved him. They dulled his ability to feel pain and slowed his metabolism enough that he survived his ordeal. They also left him disfigured. Instead of his movie star good looks, he possessed the frightful visage of a drowned man. His athletic frame had been reduced to the withered body of a cadaver.

For much of the following year, Holt kept to the darkest alleys and cellars of the Levee. He was worried Drucci and his gang might try to use him again to get at the Secret Six. Their experiment might have made him dangerous in ways he did not understand. So he hid himself among the Levee's brothels and dope joints. To the denizens of that crime-ridden district he was just another shuffling, rag-wrapped derelict. A hophead, maybe, or a drunk. In fact, he was a student, and the city's meanest streets were his classroom. And after he'd learned enough of the hard lessons those streets taught so well, he struck from the shadows at Chicago's underworld.

By the time the last of Drucci's "doctors"—or at least select parts of them—were found floating in the river, rumors of the weird assassin filled the headlines of every newspaper in the city. "The Scourge of Evil," the *Cicero Tribune* dubbed him, even as they lauded his thorough smashing of a local gambling house. The mobsters of the Windy City referred to him only as "the Corpse." Before long Holt was playing to that name. The actor once more, he carefully staged his entrances and exits. Like the harness that allowed him to appear as the hanged man in the barn, his gimmicks and stunts made it seem as if he really were some supernatural avenger returned from the grave. And maybe he was.

Certainly Tristram Holt seemed to die a little more with each passing day.

As the Corpse, Holt worked outside the system he had once fought to protect. He waged war all across Chicago and fought the gangsters with their own brutal methods—and many far more ruthless than they could imagine. The Crime Commission soon renounced his activities. The police established rewards for his arrest. It didn't matter. He was not proud of what he did, but his time in the Levee had shown him how foolish he'd been to think courts and prisons could prevent the spread of crime. If he was damned for putting that belief into action, that was a price he was willing to pay. He recognized his duty, just as he had recognized it in the trenches of France a decade earlier.

Dark thoughts of those days of mud and endless slaughter filled the head of Tristram Holt—or, rather, Rex Mortura—as the private eye made his way along the midnight streets of Chicago toward his office. He'd taken what amounted to the least direct route possible from the diner. It wasn't that he felt like a stroll through the frigid night air. He simply wanted to pass by one particular building on his way to what he hoped would be a few hours rest.

The doorman at the Garden Arms tried unsuccessfully to hide a sneer of disdain as Mortura, in his cheap suit and rumpled overcoat, walked slowly past. The P.I. fought back a bitter laugh. The same man had never failed to snap to attention when he had visited the ritzy apartment tower as Tristram Holt. He'd been eager enough then to compliment the young man, to tip his hat to Holt's fiancée, the lovely Angela Burton. The doorman still had the privilege of greeting Miss Burton. To Holt she was lost forever.

Midnight had passed. It was now Valentine's Day in Chicago. He'd met Angela a little over a decade ago on that most romantic of holidays, so he indulged himself just a little by taking this road home tonight, to pass as close as he dared to the woman he still loved. She, more than anything, provided the reason for Holt to keep his survival a secret. So long as he remained dead, Angela Burton held no interest for the mobsters and madmen he had thwarted.

A block or two from the Garden Arms, thoughts of the walking dead men crowded out more pleasant memories of Holt's time with his ladylove. Unhappily he pondered what he had witnessed in the barn. Then he catalogued other, more sane possibilities for the gangsters returning to life. Perhaps Zametov's ray induced some sort of temporary psychosis. Under its influence he'd only imagined Sullivan and the other gangsters rising up. That might explain the sounds, too, and the terrible heat. Nothing in the barn had caught fire. And Zametov's men simply carrying the bodies out might account for their disappearance.

Perhaps it really was just an illusion....

That comforting possibility soon shattered like a plate glass window in a hail of gunfire. As Mortura plodded up the steps of his office building, a terrified shriek rang out. Guns drawn, he sprinted the remaining three flights of stairs and emerged into the wide hallway of the fifth floor. The body of a cleaning woman sprawled before the open office door of Mortura Investigations. Blood spurted from her savaged throat and spread across the worn and warped floorboards in an ever-widening pool. More blood stained her clothes and the walls—

And the black-nailed fingers and gaping mouth of Eddie O'Rourke, who stood over the unfortunate old woman and stared down at his gruesome handiwork with dead man's eyes.

CHAPTER FOUR
NIGHTMARES AND ALLIES

With his first shot, Rex Mortura split Eddie O'Rourke's unbeating heart. His second took off the top of the gangster's head. O'Rourke fell back against the door, slamming it shut. The square of frosted glass shattered. For a moment the gangster lay still, impaled upon the jagged edges of the broken pane. Then O'Rourke slowly stood and advanced on Mortura.

Without a moment's hesitation, the investigator took aim and fired again. Three bullets bit into O'Rourke right shin, one after the other in quick succession. The dead man staggered forward another half-step before the damaged leg gave out. He toppled like a felled tree.

Bullets might not stop the things, Mortura told himself grimly, *but they can slow the monsters down....*

The investigator leaped over O'Rourke and threw open his office door. As he stepped inside, he came face to face with the hulking form of Gat Garrison.

The murderer's eyes were black beads of hate. His lips were pulled back in a snarl. The crippling damage the Corpse had done to Garrison with the machine gun had been repaired. He stood stiffly upright. In fact, he was taller now than he had been in life.

Mortura saw the reason for that when Garrison pulled open the long, filthy coat he wore. Four steel rods ran from the dead man's ribs down to his pelvis, anchored to the bones with silver bolts. His stomach and organs had been removed, and in their place curled a tangled mass of yellow tubing. Finely meshed wire enwrapped Garrison's new guts. A cage, Mortura realized. Garrison resembled nothing so much as a walking cage.

That realization saved his life.

Even as the investigator dove past Garrison toward his desk, the dead man gripped the wire with his rotting fingers and tore it open. The mustard-yellow tubing spilled from the rent. It uncoiled as it fell, hitting the floor in thick loops. And when it struck the cheap carpeting, the mustard-yellow mass broke apart into dozens of skittering centipedes. Each of the myriapods was as long as a big man's forearm, from fingertips to elbow. Their heads held poisoned fangs as sharp and deadly as a tong enforcer's silver hatchet.

The centipedes swarmed over Garrison and over Eddie O'Rourke, who had by then crawled into the office. But sensing no living flesh there, they moved on. A few vanished into the hallway. The rest spread across the room.

Rex Mortura watched the saffron assassins from the vantage of the padded, high-backed chair behind his desk. He gripped a bottle of whiskey in one gloved hand, a lit match in the other. Even as the dead men turned to him and the first of the centipedes reached the desk's thick legs, he brought the bottle down, hard. The sound of breaking glass hadn't even died away before he dropped the match onto the spreading alcohol. With a hollow *whoosh*, flame exploded across the scarred and scuffed wooden desktop. The centipedes reared back, retreating for an instant from the fire. The dead men, too, turned away, something akin to human fear flickering across their gruesome features. Mortura just had time to note this before the trap door opened beneath him and his chair disappeared from the room.

Secret passages and hidden rooms honeycombed the entire office building. Holt had installed them soon after buying the place, a purchase financed with money he had stolen from the gangs. The building not only housed the office of Rex Mortura, but some of the Corpse's labs and file rooms. The front had been compromised, though. The presence of the killer centipedes explained how.

The creatures were the creation of Kang Hai, the criminal mastermind known throughout the world of crime as the Celestial Executioner. That genius was the only man who had ever discovered the Corpse's true identity, through the use of a hypno-ray developed by his scientist-sorcerers in fabled Tibet. Under the ray's influence, the Corpse had served the crimelord. For nearly a month, before he finally broke free of Kang Hai's control, the Corpse had terrorized Kang's enemies and the innocent citizens of Chicago, much as he had terrorized the lawless underworld for the rest of his career. He had also revealed to the Celestial Executioner many of his most closely held secrets.

But Kang Hai was dead. The Corpse had beheaded the Celestial Executioner with his own hands.

As his chair moved past the final curve of the escape slide and came to a gentle stop on the building's lowest floor, Mortura noted to himself that the grave seemed to present no real challenge to his enemies. If Zametov could resurrect Garrison and O'Rourke, make them do his bidding, why not Kang Hai, too? In any case, the dead men's presence made it clear that the Bolshevik had also cracked the secret of Mortura's identity. So that charade had lost its usefulness. Rex Mortura was finished.

Holt hesitated only a moment standing at the double switches next to the exit. Through a shell company, he rented out a certain number of small offices in order to conceal the building's true purpose. Some of those tenants, or building staff like the unfortunate cleaning woman on the fifth floor, might still be inside. It was possible they could escape the dead men and the centipedes, but he could not risk Kang Hai's monstrosities escaping into the city at large. The centipedes could kill thousands, trained as they were to sting any living creature they encountered.

Holt gritted his teeth and threw the switches. Then he grabbed a canvas bag hanging by the door and dashed out through the exit.

He was already across the street, watching from a concealed spot on the roof, when the explosive charges brought down the office building. Windows shattered all along the block. A car horn screamed in protest at the cinder block that had crushed the sedan's roof. A dozen small fires in the mountain of debris curled black smoke into the cloud-choked night sky.

Turning away from the wreckage, Holt proceeded to strip away his make-up and shrug off the clothes that had been Mortura's. From the canvas bag he withdrew the tattered, bloody shirt, the threadbare cloak splotched with grave rot, and the weather-stained fedora that served as a uniform of sorts for the Corpse. He had no need of heavier clothes; the biting cold could not penetrate his dulled senses. Finally, with shriveled fingers, he emptied the bag of its remaining contents: a pair of gleaming black automatics and a silver tube filled with maggots.

If the Red Death and the Celestial Executioner had joined forces, they threatened not just the city, but the whole of the United States. Perhaps even the world.

Though he was loath to admit it, Holt understood that this was a danger he might not be able to face alone.

The sanctum sanctorum of millionaire Edward Janus stood high atop the most exclusive building on the most exclusive stretch of Lake Shore Drive. The rooms were a study in taste. Priceless paintings adorned the walls. Atop table and mantle rested artifacts recovered by Janus himself from the most remote corners of the globe. Any museum would offer a king's ransom for just one of these remarkable treasures, had the curators known of their existence outside of legend.

Janus was carefully wrapping one of these—a deceptively plain figure of a falcon, its fabulous worth disguised by a layer of black enamel—when the Corpse crept in from the balcony.

"I'm afraid I can't offer you a seat," Janus said without turning to face his uninvited guest. "The chairs have already been carted off."

Like the Corpse, Edward Janus had a long and strange history, one that set him apart from other men. He was an adventurer, a thief, and a devotee of the occult. The scars that marred his throat and ran along his jawline spoke of perils faced and survived. The faint crimson light that bled from around the battered leather patch covering his left eye provided evidence of more startling mysteries encountered. He possessed the agility and speed of a cheetah, the reflexes of a mongoose. At times he had met the Corpse as an adversary, at times as an ally. No matter which, there was always a tension between the two unprecedented men, for each knew the other was his match.

Janus finally set the falcon in a specially constructed case. With a sigh, he turned to the Corpse. "If you would care to be of some use, you can crate up the artwork. Start with the Bosch, I think. Visions of Hell suit you."

"They're going to be pretty commonplace around Chicago soon." The Corpse looked around the room. Most of the contents had been readied for shipping. "Forget to pay the rent?" he sneered.

"I've heard some distressing things about the new neighbors," Janus replied, moving to a pair of swords hung on the wall. The keen but scarred edges on the blades—one of peerless gray steel, the other of amber-tinted glass—made it clear that these weapons were far from decorative. "I understand you've had the pleasure of meeting some of them already."

"Yes, real charmers. If you know about what's happening, you must know why I'm here," said the Corpse. He took a step forward. "If we work together, we—"

With a quick, fluid motion, Janus drew down one of the swords and spun about to face the vigilante. The tip of the glass blade was pointed directly at the Corpse's heart. The odd weapon hummed softly, menacingly, in the millionaire's hand. "Not too close," he said, smiling.

The Corpse returned the smile, though on his face the expression was ghastly. Janus had the extraordinary ability to make people see the things they most feared. It happened when they stood near him for more than a moment. He'd said once that the phenomenon, which he could not control, was the unwelcome aftereffect of an experiment gone very wrong. The Corpse could sympathize. Though not everyone was susceptible to this weird power, and it had never affected the crimefighter, Janus always kept people at a distance.

"I've already seen my nightmares come true," the Corpse said grimly.

"Not all of them." Janus lowered the blade. "Not yet."

"Are you going to be here when the rest of them play out?"

"No."

"I could use your help."

Janus smirked. "I know. But I'm no fool. I'm not even a hero."

"What can I offer you to stay and fight on my side?"

"It's a losing battle. They've planned too well for *anyone* to stop them. Besides, Zametov's bid was the West Coast. If that wasn't enough to get me involved, I doubt you—"

The Corpse barreled into Janus, pushing him back and slamming him hard against the wall. He had the millionaire by the throat with his left hand, a pistol pressed against the man's temple with his right. Before he could utter the threat burning on his tongue, a sharp jab under his chin brought him up short. Somehow, Janus had managed to get his sword raised in time. It lay pressed between them.

"You can shoot," Janus said, far more calmly than he had any right to be, "but I'll drive the blade through your skull as I go down." The Corpse tightened his grip on the automatic. His finger twitched on the trigger. The millionaire scowled. "You won't be able to do anything to stop them if you're a real corpse— though death *is* less of a liability now than it was last week."

A curse on his lips, the Corpse shoved Janus away. "Did Zametov tell you what he had planned?"

"Enough to entice me to join. Not enough to make me a liability. He dropped by earlier this evening with a few of his soldiers. Seemed quite cheerful, in fact. Claimed that he'd gotten rid of you for good. Anyway, after demonstrating the prototype of the harrowing device and explaining that the working model was now operational, he offered me a position of authority in his new order."

"The West Coast. I'm surprised Kang Hai let him offer you such a plum."

"Kang Hai?" The red glow limning the millionaire's eye patch dimmed, and his lips curled in disgust. "But you and I killed—no, never mind. If he's involved, it's one more reason for me to be glad I declined. And since I've made it clear to Zametov that I have no interest in interfering with his plans, he should be happy if I take my leave of Chicago before the shooting starts."

"Shooting?"

"Lots of shooting. The gang war to end all gang wars."

The Corpse nodded. "And every casualty a new recruit for his undead army. That explains what Zametov was doing when I saw him the other night. He was planning on hitting Sullivan himself. The Bruiser's boys might have touched things off between Capone and Moran before Zametov was ready."

"He's ready now," Janus said darkly, and went back to packing away his swords. When he spoke again, his tone was casual once more, as if the subject were of no more significance than a trade the White Sox had staged. "He's hired McGurn and some of the Purple Gang out from under Capone. They're going to hit Moran later this morning, make it look like Scarface ordered it. I don't know where it'll happen, but if you follow Moran, you're bound to find out."

The Corpse turned toward the window. As he did, he placed the key to a safety deposit box on a table. "I was going to offer what I've got stashed in the box if you'd stay and fight," he said. "Diamonds—a lot of them. I stole them from Capone's couriers over the years. They're not much to a man like you, but they should make it worth your while to take someone with you when you go. Her name is Angela Burton. You'll find her at the Garden Arms."

"Ah, the woman in the case," Janus quipped. "I was married once, you know." He held up his left hand. The ring finger was missing. Barely a stub of the digit remained. "Not a good match."

Then the careless facade fell away, and the millionaire's handsome face took on a serious cast. "It's not too late for you to ask her yourself."

For an instant the Corpse stood framed by the balcony doors, his shape dark and ominous against the bleak dawn sky. "Of course it is," he said bitterly. And then he was gone.

CHAPTER FIVE
THE GATES OF HELL

Valentine's Day did not start well for Bugs Moran. Nightmares woke the leader of the North Side mob shortly after sunrise. The terrifying dream-images of Hell faded quickly, but the sounds of the damned burning in the Pit lingered in his ears all morning. It wasn't a shriek or even a drone. More like an annoying buzz at the back of his consciousness. The annoyance left Moran even edgier than normal, which was no mean feat for a man renowned for his instability. He demonstrated his foul mood shortly after rising, when he beat one of his lieutenants unconscious with a poker just for letting the phone ring one too many times before answering.

Moran might have been more concerned by the phantom sounds had he not typically teetered on the brink of insanity. Everyone around him was acting a bit odd, too. More fights than usual were breaking out among the boys. Even the locals seemed to be down with a case of the crazies. Though the cold and the wind had kept most pedestrians off the streets, preachers huddled on every other corner, shouting at the top of their lungs about the Apocalypse. The king of the North Side chalked it all up to bad booze. Such were the risks of bathtub hooch.

By way of a solution, Moran was headed now toward a rendezvous with a hijacker who had promised him a truckload of Old Log Cabin. This was the real stuff, whiskey swiped right off the river between Detroit and Canada, and not some swill cooked up in a South Side basement. A glass or two of that and you'd be seeing Heaven, not Hell.

Traffic was snarled along North Clark Street, thanks to a three-car accident that had sparked off a brawl, so Moran was on foot. He didn't like to travel without his bodyguards, but he was already late for the meeting and the garage was only four blocks away. Still, he took precautions. His hand was tight on the gun hidden in the pocket of his overcoat, and his eyes raked the empty sidewalks and abandoned storefronts between him and S. M. C. Cartage, alert for any signs of trouble.

"It's a surprise you've lived this long," a voice said from Moran's shoulder, an instant before the snout of an automatic pressed into his back.

"What's this—a stick up?" The mob boss smirked. "You've got no idea who you're messing with, pal."

"I know exactly who I'm messing with. Turn around."

Bugs Moran gasped when he saw that it was the Corpse who held the gun pointed at his heart, and his hand went slack on his own pistol. "Oh, God," the mobster moaned.

"Shut up and listen," the Corpse said. "Your men at the garage are already dead. You're going to hear that Capone did it, but that's a lie. It was me. I killed them, understand?" He waited for Moran to nod. "Good. So don't bother hitting Scarface for this. The only enemy you've got to worry about in this town is the Corpse. I wanted you to know, Bugs. I wanted you to know who your boys should be gunning for. Not the Southsiders. Me."

The Scourge of Evil stepped aside, but kept his gun leveled at Moran's chest. The mob boss was facing back down North Clark. He could see his driver running along the street toward him.

"I'm done with you...for now," the Corpse said. With one grimy shoe he kicked the mobster in the seat of the pants. "Go on. Scurry back to your rat's nest."

Moran staggered a few steps forward, then whirled about. The initial shock of seeing the hideous features of the Corpse had worn off, and the sight of his driver coming to his aid had bolstered the mobster's spirits. He drew his gun, ready to fight. But the Corpse was gone.

Panting, Moran's driver stumbled to a stop at his side. "Jeez, boss. Where'd he go?"

"Weren't you watching him?"

"I was, but I was watching you, too," the driver replied lamely. "When you come forward, I took my eyes off him, but only for a second. I was making sure you was okay."

Moran jammed his pistol into his lackey's stomach and pulled the trigger. The big man went down like a felled oak. "That's for making me drive myself home in this traffic," Moran said coldly. "If you survive, you can have your job back."

Not long after Moran had departed, the Corpse slipped from his hiding place in the abandoned store. He pushed aside the panel of wood that had replaced the broken glass on the door and walked slowly to the gangster writhing in pain on the sidewalk. Pleadingly, the big man reached a hand up to him. Gut-shot as he was, he might last for hours. The freezing cold would only make it worse by slowing his bleeding. The Corpse wasn't certain what the mobster wanted from him—help or the mercy of a bullet through the heart. He gave him neither. There was no time to render aid, and a danger in killing the man. From the buzz of hellish voices in the air, the Corpse understood that Zametov had found a way to turn his harrowing device over the entire city. To kill the mobster now would be to add one more soldier to the Red Death's army, and the Corpse already knew that he would be adding enough men to those ranks in just a few moments.

Without another thought for the wounded criminal, the Corpse made his way down North Clark to the garage and office of S. M. C. Cartage, where seven men unwittingly wasted the last moments of their lives.

"They were dead when we got there." Jack McGurn grumbled. His disappointment at having missed out on the chance to butcher a few of Moran's boys made his voice little more than a mad dog's growl. "Seven of 'em. Shot up real good."

"The work of the Corpse, of course." Nikodim Fomitch Zametov continued to examine the living dead men lined up before him. He studied each man's face carefully, then his hands, and then moved on to the next one in line. Jack McGurn stood behind Zametov, his machine gun trained on the newest recruits for the Red Death's undead army. He didn't trust the walking stiffs, no matter how many times Zametov told him they could not turn against their master.

When the Bolshevik reached the last man, he turned. "There are six here. The seventh?"

"He just didn't get up," McGurn said. "The rest were already on their feet when we got there, but the last guy never even moved a muscle."

"Another beyond our reach." Zametov scowled and clasped his hands behind his back. Muttering, he paced to a writing desk, made a note, then abruptly asked, "Was the body particularly damaged? More so than the others?"

McGurn gestured with the muzzle of his machine gun toward the bullet-riddled bodies standing before him. "Just like them. Hit in the back more times, maybe. Probably tried to run." He thought about it for a moment more. "I never seen him before, so he probably wasn't one of the gang. A leech, maybe. Somebody what liked to hang around, to be near all the money."

Zametov made another note. Then, very methodically, he put down his pen, drew his revolver from his pocket, and slowly scanned the room.

It was like many basements in Chicago's Chinatown—large and low-ceilinged, with a floor of packed earth. Crates were stacked high around the edges. The tang of exotic spices and opium smoke hung in the air. Thick wooden pillars held up the sagging floor above. A few bare lightbulbs lit the expanse, but darkness still claimed the corners. Dozens of rooms very much like it could be found all throughout the eight-block square section that housed the city's Chinese immigrants.

But at the center of this basement stood something quite unique in all the world.

The device resembled a wide door frame constructed out of elaborately decorated silver. The metal itself was twisted into grotesque designs, with insets of gold and jade forming strange slashes and swirls. The designs consisted of an odd mixture of obscure scientific symbols and even more obscure occult glyphs. The silver frame opened onto a pulsing sea of darkness. This endless expanse of shadow roiled and heaved. With each swell of darkness, the buzz of tortured voices swelled, too. The cries of the damned never rose above a soft groan, though, as if the sounds were being bled off by the cables and wires leading from the gate to the control panel at the rear of the room.

Zametov moved close to the harrowing device, gun held before him. "You can come out, Comrade Corpse," he called.

Jack McGurn threw the bolt on his machine gun and whirled around. "Where?" he shouted. "I don't see him!"

"Of course not," Zametov sneered. "Just as you did not see him ride upon the truck from the cartage company, or creep into this building on your heels." He turned to the shadows again. "It is no wonder you have bested these imbeciles time and again, Comrade Corpse."

A jar sailed out of one corner, toward McGurn and the assembled dead men. The gangster aimed his machine gun at it and pulled the trigger, just as Zametov screamed, "No!"

McGurn's aim was perfect, striking the jar with four bullets. The first was enough, though. At its impact, the jar shattered and its contents ignited. The flaming liquid splashed across the risen dead and McGurn, too. A second jar followed the first. Soon, all six dead men were burning.

The Corpse had seen how Garrison and O'Rourke had turned away from the flames in Rex Mortura's office. They feared fire, and that was a weakness he could exploit. His plan seemed to be working perfectly, too. The dead men opened their mouths in silent screams, waved their arms, and dropped to the dirt floor in futile attempts to put out the flames. McGurn wasn't so quiet. His shrieks nearly drowned out Zametov's shouted curses in Russian.

"A miscalculation!" the mad Bolshevik cried. "You cannot kill me until you know how to disable the harrowing device!"

A single shot rang out. Zametov gasped, and the pistol slipped from his grasp. He raised his fingers to touch the dark circle in the exact center of his forehead, but they never reached it. A look of astonishment frozen on his face, the Red Death collapsed and died.

The Corpse emerged from the shadows. "A miscalculation if I believe you are the only one who knows how to shut it off...."

He glanced at the dead men, all fallen now and burning. So, too, Jack McGurn. And the fire was spreading. It had already cut the Corpse off from the exit. That didn't matter, so long as he still could reach the device. Even if they wouldn't tell him how to turn it off, he still had one last option.

"I know you're here, Kang Hai. Come out and finish this."

A figure emerged from behind the control panel at the far end of the room. But it was not Kang Hai, the Celestial Executioner. Instead, a slender woman wrapped in exquisite red silk glided into the light. Blood Lotus, the daughter of Kang Hai. Her eyes were the green of the fathomless ocean, her hair as black as her father's corrupt deeds. An albino monkey crouched on her shoulder. The tiny beast's fingers were tipped with knives.

"You had assumed that the Bolshevik resurrected my father," she said. "My apologies. Such indignity is acceptable for Western devils, not for one of such exalted status as my sire."

"Did you actually say 'Western devils'? Your father always hated when you played to type like this."

"The facade has its uses, as you well know, and my father is dead. I am now the Hand of a Thousand Rings, possessor of all my father's secrets—including yours, Tristram Holt."

The monkey on Blood Lotus's shoulder leaned forward and hissed as she spoke the name. The knives on its fingers jangled. The Corpse raised his gun. The automatic spat lead, and the beast tumbled to the ground.

Blood Lotus wiped a spatter of gore from her golden cheek. "My pet would have killed you, given the chance, so I will forgive you that unkind act. Tell me, how did you know about our plan to assassinate Mr. Moran?"

"A tip from an old friend," the Corpse said, moving closer. The earthen floor kept the fire from getting out of control quickly, but flames had begun to climb the support beams and smoke was spreading along the ceiling. Time was running out. The Corpse knew there was no point in trying to wrench the secret of the device from Lotus. The few times he had crossed paths with her, she had proved herself possessed of an iron will and a devotion to crime even more unshakable than her father's. No, he would have to do this the hard way.

"I've got a tap on Moran's phone," the Corpse said. "Once I heard about the meeting at the garage, it wasn't hard to figure out where you planned to strike."

"No doubt you frightened Mr. Moran away and made certain that he blamed you for the slaughter," Lotus offered, all the while watching the Corpse. Even as she spoke, she stepped daintily over the dead monkey and cut off the vigilante's approach to the harrowing device. "A clever effort to avert the war between the gangs, but a pointless one."

The Corpse gestured to Zametov's still form. "Not entirely."

"He is dead for the moment only." Lotus spoke as if the fire and death surrounding her were only the most minor of inconveniences. The confrontation, it seemed, held no surprises for her. "Besides, his primary missions are now complete."

She ran one perfectly manicured nail along the edge of the harrowing device. The gesture was sensual, a woman caressing a lover's body. "I needed him because his knowledge of science sped the transition of the gate from its prototype form, helped eliminate the problems with heat and its paralyzing effects on the living. And the criminals in this city would not serve a woman, let alone one of my race, long enough for me to set the gang war in motion. That war *will* begin shortly, Tristram Holt, despite your actions today. Feh, you have not even robbed me of the Bolshevik's services for very long."

A cruel smile played across her lips.

"Perhaps Marx and Lenin are there in the Inferno to apologize to Comrade Zametov for their mistakes about religion." She gave a little laugh, though there was no joy in the sound. "He never could believe that the device harrowed the dead from Hell. That's why the ones who refused to rise troubled him so—he could not accept that Heaven was closed to us. Ah, see—he rises. But it is no surprise to us where his soul was bound, eh?"

The Red Death pushed himself unsteadily to his feet. Blood seeped from the hole in his forehead and thick drool slipped from his slack mouth. The Corpse could see the fury of the Pit in the dead thing's eyes. They churned like the darkness in the gateway.

Sounds of the human minions serving Blood Lotus could be heard now over the fire's roar. They called out in panic as they fought the blaze from the entryway to the basement. Water dripped through the ceiling as they doused the floor above to keep the flames from spreading. There were other, more terrible noises in the basement, too: the hiss of charred bones scraping along the packed earth.

The dead men were gathering themselves together—McGurn and the Northsiders from the garage. The fire had not destroyed them. It had only stripped the remainder of the flesh from their bones or baked it hard as steel.

Blood Lotus turned to watch them coming toward her, slaves to her dominating will. In that instant, the Corpse pulled the third of his four homemade bombs from where he had them strapped low on his back, beneath his cloak. His movement toward the gateway had been a feint. His real destination had been the control panel.

He tossed the bomb into the air above the bank of dials and fired. As the flaming liquid spattered the metal casing, seeped into the gauges and scorched the switches, sparks shot into the air.

The wavering light from the fire gave the Corpse's face a demonic cast. He turned and took aim at Blood Lotus, but Zametov grabbed his arm. The shot went wide. The vigilante put a second hole in the Red Death's forehead, and a third. The impacts only made him stagger back a step or two. Before the Corpse could fire again, he found himself surrounded. Dead hands pinned his arms to his sides. They gripped his legs and banded his throat.

"I must thank Zametov doubly," he heard the lovely voice of Blood Lotus say close behind him. "For spoiling your aim and for insisting we install a second, hidden control panel as a failsafe. You could not have stopped us with a hundred bombs. And the price for that failure will be especially steep for you, Tristram Holt, unless you are certain you end your life with only the blood of the guilty on your hands." She laughed again, the sound edged like a thousand daggers.

The hands around his throat tightened. Through the pounding of blood in his ears and the incessant murmur of the damned, the Corpse could hear the laughter of Blood Lotus. She stood close, almost touching his back. He struggled to lift his arms, to turn his automatics just enough to shoot behind him. But the grip of the dead things, urged on by Lotus's will, was relentless. His arms were pinned. He could only turn his wrists inward.

So the Corpse directed the pistol in his right hand toward his own stomach. Even as oblivion threatened to overwhelm his thoughts, and the pounding of his own hammering pulse thundered in his ears, he willed himself to angle the barrel so that the shot would strike its target. And then he pulled the trigger.

The Corpse did not scream as the bullet sliced through his guts and pierced the casing of the last bomb strapped low on his back. He did not even cry out as the incendiary exploded. He did not because he wanted to hear the startled cry of Blood Lotus as the flames took her and she realized that his will was greater than hers. That gasp of horrible surprise was the sound that lingered in his ears as he went tumbling down to Hell.

It was an instant or an eternity. He could not tell which, though it really didn't matter. His sins spread out before him, each one a thick shroud. The deaths of innocents. The ceaseless, unquenchable wrath. The terrible things he had done in the name of Justice. He claimed them all and they enwrapped him, one by one, cutting him off from the light of Heaven. And when that light was gone, so, too, was the last of his humanity. All that had been Tristram Holt fell away into the Pit, while the rest heeded the call of the harrowing device and rose up.

In a smoke-clouded basement in Chinatown, the Corpse opened his eyes. Lotus's human minions had abandoned the depths. The last explosion had driven them away, so that they fought the fire now on the upper floor. Only the living dead remained. Robbed of Lotus's will, they milled and awaited direction. As the Corpse got to his feet, his pistols still clutched in his hands, the men he had slaughtered at the garage turned to him and bowed down. So, too, did McGurn and Zametov—and the resurrected Blood Lotus, though she hesitated a moment before showing her respect to the newly risen king of the dead.

The Corpse willed his hands to reload his pistols. He was uncertain of the reason he needed to do so; he only knew that it was important to be ready. The still-clumsy fingers dug in his pockets until a silver tube spilled out and clattered to the dirt floor. He picked it up and emptied the maggots it contained into his palm. He stared at them for a time, and when their meaning finally came clear to him, he pressed them gently, with suddenly steady hands, into his wounds. He would need the maggots again, just as he would need his gleaming black automatics.

For the Corpse was not done with his war against crime.

But now, the only crime was to be alive.

NOVAHEADS

ERNEST HOGAN

From Ernest Hogan, author of the exuberantly entertaining novels *Cortez on Jupiter*, *High Aztech*, and *Smoking Mirror Blues*, comes this piece of cyberpunk lucha noir. Because no superhero anthology is complete without luchadores.

*H*orst wasn't supposed to explode into flames—he was just supposed to feel like it. He looked so happy as he pressed the bright red nova capsule into his left nostril, squeezed his right nostril shut with his thumb, and inhaled. That beatific smile beamed as he broke into beads of sweet nova sweat and the burn roared through his nervous system, which ached in anticipation of the endorphin-rush nova high.

Then something went wrong.

His eyes opened wide. He grinned, and his body exploded from deep inside like a humanoid soap-bubble, his skin being the last thing to be consumed. A white-hot flash left a Horst-shaped afterimage on Irma Mao's retinas while a fallout of white ashes settled on the sterile hotel sheets.

The air-conditioner blew some ashes onto her small, naked body. She squeaked a breathless scream.

Opening her mouth, she inhaled and gagged on the disgusting stench—plugged her right nostril with her thumb and blew the nova capsule out of the left. It bounced onto the sheets and was soon covered with Horst's ashes.

She sprang off the bed, shaking and whimpering, trying to remove the ashes from her skin. A string of rapid-fire Cuban-Chinese-Americano curses streamed out of her. "Oh God! Oh Horst! Damn! We should have never bought nova from a Bulgarian! Not in Phoenix! Not these days!"

The ashes stuck to her skin wouldn't rub off. The smell nauseated her. She wobbled her way to the shower, turned on the cold water, and collapsed into fetal position. Goosebumps rose as ashes flowed down the drain.

Eventually she felt clean, but all her nerves cried out their lust for a nova high.

The room still stank. All the capsules in the room were from that Bulgarian—she couldn't trust them.

Naked and dripping wet, she rushed to her suitcase, popped it open, and threw its contents all over the room, looking for the bottle of Ultra-Hot Tejano sauce that she kept for emergencies like this. She broke a nail tearing open the freshness seal, then chug-a-lugged over two-thirds of its glowing, red contents.

Her mouth burned that delicious burn. Her inner ears and sinuses tingled. Her forehead sweated and her nose ran. The non-enhanced capsaicin was doing its ordinary molecular magic. Her brain was coaxed into dumping endorphins. Not enough for the magnificent nova high—this was like chewing raw coca leaves as opposed to smoking good old-fashioned crack cocaine, but it was enough to keep her from suffering withdrawals. For a while.

With dainty sips, she drained the rest of the bottle.

She was in real trouble now. As much as she dreaded it, she needed help. Trying not to look at the bed, she went to the nightstand, picked up her phone, and quickdialed Steelsnake.

He appeared on the tiny screen, his head sealed in a metallic wrestler's mask textured to look like chromed scales. From within the mask's mouth-hole, he smiled with stainless steel teeth.

"Irma!" His voice was a deep growl. "You want me?" He moved his phone back to show that he was naked, in bed.

"Who's that?" A woman shared the bed with him. Large as he was, her body was as soft as his was hard. Her folds of flesh moved with a will of their own.

"Somebody from Neurotrolix." He leaned over and kissed what looked like a fat, Caucasian-colored tentacle.

"You're off duty." A thick-fingered hand with emerald-green nails grabbed the phone, blocking the view.

"Hey, it might be personal, or something." He yanked back the phone.

"You said you'd give me a second chance." It was the woman's voice, but Steelsnake's face filled the screen. His smile sickened Irma.

"Well?" His mask amplified the leer.

Irma picked up her remote and pressed a button. His face went offscreen, then swung back. His head shook.

"Okay," he said. "I'll be right over. You in your room in the downtown Columbia?"

"Yes."

Steelsnake's bedmate made a squeal of feminine disapproval as the screen went blank.

Irma gathered the remaining nova capsules. It would probably make sense to keep some so they could be analyzed later, but she couldn't trust herself—her addiction was too strong. She almost stuffed one into her nose as she flushed them down the toilet. A few tears followed the capsules into the plumbing.

Then her phone rang.

She hoped they wouldn't think anything of her calling Steelsnake. But they did.

Neurotrolix's AI logo, Neurotroli, appeared on her phone. It was a simple cartoon character—an exposed brain with Frankensteinian bolts sticking out of each hemisphere; on the frontal lobes perched black-dot eyes magnified by old-fashioned Coke-bottle glasses, under which hung a smiling, have-a-nice-day mouth line. The brainstem wagged like a puppy-dog's tail, brushing the NEUROTROLIX—BETTER LIVING THROUGH MIND-CONTROL slogan at the bottom of the screen.

The eyes blinked. A lightning arc danced between the bolts. The mouth moved as it spoke in a cute AI voice calibrated to be authoritative, yet non-threatening:

"Irma Mao. We have detected that you contacted test vector Steelsnake during a designated off-duty period. Why did you do this?"

Irma knew that Neurotroli couldn't read facial expressions, but tried to look calm. "Uh, it's a personal matter."

"You aren't indulging in fraternization? Have you been taking your pheromone-blockers?"

She tried not to let her eyes get big as she lied. "Why yes, of course. You know I'm not attracted to him." She hadn't taken the blockers that evening—she didn't want them to interfere with her sex with Horst.

"Make sure you don't miss a dose. The experimental enhanced testosterone he's on will give him an extra-powerful pheromone-signature. Most women will find him irresistible."

"Believe me. I take them religiously." She looked around the room. Where could they be?

"Very well. Have a nice night." The smile-line grew teeth, and Neurotroli vanished.

Irma scrambled through the scattered suitcase contents for the pheromone-blockers.

In less than a half hour he was at the door: a massive figure with muscles bulging out of his rumpled, pale yellow, tropical-weight suit. Steelsnake frowned under the unmoving, screaming-serpent mask. "What stinks? Something die in here?"

Irma could barely smell it anymore. Was it dissipating, or was she getting used to it? That idea disgusted her. Another chunk of her humanity was being stripped away. Then she remembered Steelsnake's enhanced senses, but it didn't make her feel any better.

"So what is it, Irma?" His voice boomed as he grabbed the huge bulge at his crotch with a gigantic brown hand. "Finally decide to get your taste of 'Snake? The eurozi prove not to be enough of a man for you?" He unzipped his fly.

Irma threw an empty pheromone-blocker packet at him. "I'm protected from your unfortunate side-effects."

Steelsnake left his fly halfway open, kept walking toward the bed. "Hey, you made them. Sooner or later, you're gonna want to try 'Snakesex out."

"I've been working on a way to increase your aggressiveness without affecting your sex drive." She straightened her tie. She had had enough time to get into a business suit.

He sat on the bed. "That couldn't be why you asked me here. After the match, that eurozi—what was his name? Horst—was all over you. And you were all over him. I figured you and him'd be burning up the sheets by now."

Irma gasped.

"So," he stretched out on the bed, sending up a subtle cloud of ash. "What happened to him? This better be good. I was in the new Rancho Ganesha casino resort, with the Toyota nusumo girl I thrashed earlier. We were having a sort of informal follow match, and those smart implants of hers..."

Irma was glad that all plus-wrestlers were institutionally made sterile as part of their primary alterations.

"She really liked the hot-snake treatment," he went on, making his tiny brown eyes go narrow. "She's waiting for me in a luxury honeymoon suite bed right now, eager for seconds." He leaned back against the pillows and unzipped his fly the rest of the way. "That is, unless you'd like to go a round."

"The reason I called you—" Irma said, averting her eyes.

"You want me. I know it."

"It's about Horst—"

"The eurozi? What about him? He want me, too?"

"You're lying on what's left of him."

Steelsnake looked confused, scanned the bed, frowned. Then he picked up a pinch of the ash and crushed it between a heavy thumb and forefinger. He grinned. "I always figured you were a hot one, Irma Mao, but wow! What were you doing, trying out some new love drug you cooked up?"

She brought her tiny feet together and stood as tall as she could, which made her about five-four. Not much of a match against his eight-foot mass, but with him on the bed, it did the trick. She crossed her arms, frowned like a Brazilian soap opera bitch, and said, "Look—it was nova. Horst and I got hold of some bad stuff. I need your help."

He sat up and said, "You know I am always at your service." No emotion leaked out of his mask.

"But first..." She held up a thumbnail-sized card with a magnetic strip at one end.

"Of course." He sat up, turning to give her access to the back of his mask. "You wouldn't want me to go out of control, would you?"

"Heaven help us if you were ever allowed to do whatever you wanted." She slid the card through the slot, the seam down the back of the mask unlocked, relaxed and fell open.

He reached up, peeled off the mask, and held it tight.

She was glad that his control panel was on the back of his head. She didn't like looking at his face. Jesus ("Don't call me Hayzoos, I'm from L.A., and don't even speak Spanish, dammit!") Guerrero had been an attractive man before he signed the contract that allowed Neurotrolix to make him Steelsnake, one of their plus-wrestler/human guinea pigs. No one would call him handsome now, though some might find scar tissue and cranial and facial implants attractive.

"You know you shouldn't fool around with drugs," he said.

"You idiot!" She made a mistake and had to cancel what she was keying in. "You're nothing but a mass of drugs, experimental steroids, testosterone boosters, reflex-enhancers..."

"You know what I mean. Those are good drugs—sports medicine."

"Yeah." She got back to her keying. "But once you start messing with a natural system, there's no turning back..."

He blinked. Shook his head. "You messed with the lethal force monitor."

"Yes," she waved the card, then snapped it into the remote on her phone wristband, "but I control when you kill."

"So what's new?" He sneered, and turned around to look at her.

She turned so she didn't have to look at his bare face.

He put the mask back on. It locked and sealed itself.

"Do you realize that the address you gave me is outside the Downtown Phoenix smog dome?" asked the rental car.

"Yes," said Irma, distressed that there wasn't enough room in the Ford Gaucho for her to sit comfortably without touching Steelsnake.

"Do you realize that the address you gave me is in Paradise Valley?"

"Yes."

"Do you realize that Paradise Valley has been designated by the Metro Phoenix Crime Net as a high crime area?"

"Yes."

"Do you agree to an insurance waiver of all claims against the Saguaro Urban Transport Company once we are in said high crime area?"

"Yes."

"Very well." The car pulled out of the hotel's covered parking structure. Blinking lights indicated unheard communication between the car and the security kiosk before the barrier rose and they drifted out with an electric purr into lackadaisical night traffic under the neon grid of the dome.

The car slid around a sidewalk incident that was spilling onto the northbound lane of Central: Three sheriff's posse members on horseback with plasma tasers were zapping a homeless man. A group of tourists who had gathered to watch applauded.

"Stop!" Steelsnake said, leaning toward the car's control panel. "I gotta get in on this head-bashing!"

The car screeched to a halt.

"No! Keep going!" said Irma, rubbing her temples. A nova-withdrawal headache was starting.

"I gotta kick ass!" Steelsnake shoved his masked face—eyes bugging, teeth bared, saliva flying—into hers.

Irma fumbled for her remote, and hit the emergency override button.

Steelsnake's pupils instantly shrank to pinhole size. His lips, then the rest of his muscles, relaxed. His face went blank—his eyelids fluttered—then he shook his head.

"I hate it when you do that," he said.

"I have the authority," she said. "It's in your contract."

"Sometimes I hate you and Neurotrolix." He pouted like a monstrous, over-grown boy.

"If it wasn't for us, you'd still be a pathetic little guy always getting your ass kicked."

"You never let me forget it." He clenched his fists, and stared at them.

"Please clarify," said the car. "Am I to let you off here, or continue on the previously selected course?"

Irma pinched the bridge of her nose. "We need to get to that address."

The car eased forward.

Irma rubbed her face, as if she were going to pull it off her skull. "I don't feel well. I need..."

When she lapsed into silence the car said, "I have a supply of onboard pharmaceuticals." A panel slid open, revealing racks of over-the-counter medicines.

"No," she said. "I need something else. Capsaicin...chili..."

"There are many Thai and Mexican restaurants on the way to your selected destination." It was trying so damn hard to help. Irma could have slapped whoever wrote its programming.

"Get us to a convenience store." She didn't know if the car's conversations were monitored. She couldn't risk mentioning being a novahead.

"We have just left the downtown smog dome, and are entering the Sunnyslope area, which has been designated a moderate crime area by the Metro Phoenix Crime Net. Would you like me to turn around and find a convenience store in a safer area?"

The violet black sky was crisscrossed with wispy clouds and space-hopper vapor trails glowing bright pink in the afterglow of the sunset over the Aztlán Global Hub. Through her pain and depression, Irma thought it was pretty. She smiled.

"Keep going in this direction." She elbowed Steelsnake in the arm. "My friend will protect me."

Steelsnake's eyes radiated pure hatred.

The car pulled into a Circle N—owned by Neurotrolix, so she could use her company card. All she had to do was play it cool, act like she was just on a random snack stuff run—grab a couple of squeezable bottles of the hottest sauce on the shelves and some other stuff while not looking like a desperate novahead trying to cop a barely adequate chili-high.

She had grabbed four bottles of extra-hot Mamí Hotcha (which was made in Nueva York and was not as hot as she needed) and was reaching for some Mondo Crunchitos, when three young men whose heads were just under the six-foot mark on the door burst in. They were neomestizos with an Afro-Asian-Hispanic look.

The big Samoan behind the counter reached for something.

The neomestizos reached under their nite-capes, then their eyes and mouths opened wide. They didn't move after that.

Steelsnake was standing in front of them.

Finally one grinned with teeth sheathed in faux jade and said, "Hey, man, you're Steelsnake!"

"Yeah," said Steelsnake. "What about it?"

The other two neomestizos broke out in faux jade smiles.

"Hey, we saw ya splatter that nusumo sweetie!"

"Yeah!"

Irma and the Samoan breathed a sigh of relief. She grabbed a bag of Mondo Crunchitos. He put back the Argentine six-barreled shotgun.

"You should have seen what I did to her in my hotel room a little while ago." Steelsnake leered.

The neomestizos hooted, and looked around.

"Is she here?"

Steelsnake pointed a gigantic thumb at Irma. "Naw, I'm with her right now."

"Hey, not bad! Two in a night!"

"You're the man, 'Snake!"

And what are you guys up to?" Steelsnake smiled and punched his palm.

"Uh, nothing."

"Yeah, just hanging out."

One grabbed a pack of Kawasaki barbecue-flavored squid-sticks. "We're hungry."

As they paid for the squid-sticks, Irma grabbed a two-liter of Pepsi X-tra Caf. Sweat beaded on her forehead. Nausea was churning her insides.

Steelsnake strutted up and said, "Too bad they chickened out. I'd've loved grabbing them and taking this place apart."

She grabbed a chili spray gun off the rack next to the register. It looked like a neon red snub-nosed .38 like the ones private eyes used in old movies.

"Good idea," said the Samoan, "could come in handy tonight."

All she could think about was how good it would feel to have the contents of that weapon flowing inside her bloodstream.

She managed not to collapse until she paid for the stuff and they were back in the car.

Her hands shook too hard for her to break the seal on a Mamí Hotcha bottle. She pointed it at Steelsnake. "Help me, please."

With a smirk, he grabbed the bottle—and her hands—cracking the seal while cutting off the circulation to her fingers. Then his lips curled and his nostrils clamped shut.

"Chili." He shook his head. "Can't stand the stuff."

Irma jerked the bottle away from him. Red drops stained her lapels. Fitting her lips to the bottle, she closed her eyes, leaned back, and sucked it dry.

"Oh baby," said Steelsnake.

She was too caught up in waiting for the burn to kick in. The chemical fire seared her lips and tongue, blazed down her throat, melted away...there was that usual delay, that seemed like hours...then...there...the insides of her ears tingled with the blessed heat. The sweat pouring off her face switched from ice-cold to scalding hot...

She sighed, salsa dribbling down her chin. Still shaking, weak, nausea held her digestive tract—not in a death grip, but an embrace that promised things she didn't want.

"I need another one," she said, not looking at Steelsnake, or anything else.

He rolled his eyes, held his breath, cracked open another bottle.

"More," she soon said.

She wasn't satisfied until she had consumed all but a third of the final bottle. She looked at it, horrified. "I thought this would last me all night!" She held the chili gun to her mouth. "It's going to come to this!"

Steelsnake just look bored.

Irma was spraying herself in the mouth at a stoplight when an Apache prostitute did a double-take that sent her dreadlocks flapping as she honed into Steelsnake's pheromone signals.

The prostitute locked her deadened eye on the car, looking through Irma to Steelsnake, who was looking right back.

Irma was afraid she'd disintegrate in the visual crossfire. She reminded herself to take more of her pheromone suppressors.

Suddenly the prostitute fished something out of her purse—a nova capsule! Irma seethed with jealousy as she watched the capsule slide up a moist nostril. The prostitute's eyes closed, she pinched her nose shut, and—her mouth slack—inhaled. The slack mouth became a weak smile.

"Bitch," whispered jealous Irma.

Then the prostitute exploded just like Horst had.

Irma almost choked. She thanked God that she couldn't smell the charred human flesh and vaporized body fluids.

"Bet she was a hot one, ha-ha," said Steelsnake.

The light turned green. The draft from the traffic sucked the fine, white ashes into the street.

The car said, "We are now entering Paradise Valley. Would you like the additional bulletproof shields deployed?"

Irma wiped her mouth and said, "Yes!"

"Aw," said Steelsnake, "people will think we're wimps!"

"There will be a surcharge of fifty-eight dollars. In addition, you are responsible for any damage."

"Just do it," said Irma.

Bulky slabs of duroplex slid over the windows—and the windshield, since the car's sensors were outboard.

"Now we can't see," complained Steelsnake.

"I've seen this part of town before," said Irma. This area that had once been affluent, full of expensive homes, condos, world-class malls and shopping centers, and was now a deteriorating slum, depressed her. It reminded her of the South Florida sprawl where she had grown up. She had thought that being a neurochemist for a global corporation would take her away from poverty and drugs. She had been naïve.

"I don't like being boxed in like this," said Steelsnake. Enhanced muscles flexed as he squirmed like a caged animal.

"It won't be much longer," said Irma.

"We are just minutes from your destination," said the car.

"Good," he said. "I'm bored and nervous. I need action."

"Don't worry." Irma waved the remote. "You'll get it."

His smile terrified her.

"We are approaching your destination," the car said. "I detect that several security systems are scanning us."

"Good," said Steelsnake. "Maybe we'll get some action."

"Keep heading for our destination. Go evasive if we are attacked."

"Irma Mao, you're no fun," grumbled Steelsnake.

The sound of nearby automatic gunfire pierced the car's shielding.

"I'd rather be safe." Irma clutched the chili gun.

"Safe ain't nothing but boring misspelled," said Steelsnake.

"We are approaching your destination," said the car as it slowed down.

"This is private property! Do not enter!" boomed a voice outside.

"Do you wish to proceed?" asked the car.

Irma glanced at Steelsnake, whose smile was beginning to look manic again. "Yes," she said.

The car lurched up a driveway.

"Identify yourself or be destroyed!"

Irma shook her head, keyed her phone, and said, "Vlad, it's me—remember?"

A pale, bony-faced man with his dark eyes and thin lips outlined in black appeared on the phone screen. He brushed the long, violet hair away from his face, and frowned. "I don't recognize—" Then he smiled. "Ah. Ms. Mao! Last of the red-hot mamacitas! How is that friend of yours...?"

"Horst," said Irma.

"Ah, yes! Horst." Vlad sucked a colorless gas from a long, transparent tube. "How is he?"

"Dead." Irma's eyes were as narrow as they could be without being shut.

Vlad sucked the tube again. "Oh. Really? And he seemed so healthy."

"It was the nova capsules you sold us!" Irma screamed. "You nearly killed me your bile-sucking backstabber!"

"Well." Vlad's brow knitted. "I am not responsible for anything that happens as a result of the use of my products."

The screen went blank.

"Take us in." Irma ordered.

"Oh boy," said Steelsnake.

The car lurched forward.

"You are trespassing!" boomed the voice. "You have been warned! You are targeted! We are firing!"

The car recited: "I must remind you that Saguaro Urban Transport Company is not responsible for any injury or damage, however, you are—" And was interrupted by an explosive blast , causing a crackling noise followed by the smell of fried electronics. Forward motion stopped. All onboard lights went out.

"Car?" Irma asked into the darkness.

"What's going on?" Steelsnake groped for the door control.

"An anti-electronics missile!" Irma held onto the chili gun for dear life. "Fried the car's brains. We're going to have to break out!"

The car shook with thuds of heavy impact. Simultaneously, Steelsnake did comparable damage from the inside.

"These damn shields," he grumbled. Then, with a pop, soft city night light leaked in.

Steelsnake stuck his head out of the hole where the windshield had been, past the smoking missile that clung to the hood like a mechanical leech. Several figures in full combat armor, pointing assault rifles, kicked and smashed their way through the overgrown mesquite and cacti that did as well as barbed-wire in the Southwest. Vlad had unleashed his technicals.

Enhanced sensory and reflex implants helped Steelsnake throw the shield and leap, knocking them all into the vicious desert flora.

Assault rifles fired some useless rounds. Spines from several cactus species pierced Steelsnake's nanosteroid-toughened hide. A few mesquite spikes dug into his hyperdeveloped, mechanofluid-injected muscles. Assorted implants acknowledged the pain signals while not allowing him to feel them, and increased his adrenaline level beyond the fight-or-flight capacity of unaugmented humans.

Irma's finger hovered over the suppressor button. Steelsnake would kill the technicals if she didn't stop him. He could hear heartbeats and the static whisper of brain activity—one by one, they were silenced.

She remembered Horst. And the little prostitute. She put the remote away.

Nova withdrawal hit her with a wave of queasiness. She gave herself a shot in the mouth from the chili gun. Then another. It worked a little less each time. Soon it wouldn't work at all.

"Bravo! Bravo! Viva Steelsnake!" boomed a non-synthesized voice from the loudspeaker.

Steelsnake was in full combat mode. His implants took note of the voice, but put it on standby while the rest of his augmented brain concentrated on further pulverizing the technicals.

Irma hit the remote.

As if he were struck by lightning, Steelsnake stopped in mid-stomp, trembled, then stood upright. He looked around, a bit disoriented, but totally relaxed.

Backlit by the lights from the house, a slim, robed figure carefully made its way through the ruins of the desert landscaping. Long, metallic nails sparkled as thin white hands clapped. Violet hair flew around a skull-like face with a black-rimmed mouth. It was Vlad.

"Bravo! Steelsnake! Bravo!" Unamplified, his voice was higher, with a trace of an Eastern European accent. "That was marvelous! I thought your beating that dreadful nusumo was great, but you rendered my technicals useless. I may sue those Utah mercenaries who said they were giving them the finest military training for my money. I see now that Neurotrolix has developed the cutting edge for today's defense technology. I'm going to order a full set of your augmentations for my new technicals!"

Her hair a tangled rat's nest, Irma stuck her head out of the wreckage. "Honest, Vlad. You sound like a bad commercial."

"My security cameras are running if Neurotrolix is interested in the rights," said Vlad.

"I don't think you can get all my augmentations," said Steelsnake. "Aren't some of 'em secret or something?"

"Experimental and classified," said Irma.

"Help me," said one of the technicals.

"I'm dying," said another.

Still another made a noise like a clogged sink draining.

Irma was struggling to free herself from the car when a wave of nausea hit. She grimaced, and then put the chili gun into her quivering mouth as if she were committing suicide. The blast barely had any effect.

Vlad smiled at her distress, like a happy vampire. "Irma, my dear, aren't you feeling well?"

Her teeth clenched, then chattered.

"Oh, my poor, poor Irma. I think you need something." He reached into his wide sleeve and pulled out a nova capsule that gleamed in the floodlights.

The sight made her drool. To her horror, she found herself running to Vlad, to the nova capsule, like a long-lost lover. Her nose and brain ached for the blazing nova rush.

Then the images of Horst burning alive and the Apache prostitute combusting flashed through her brain.

She stopped just within reach of the capsule.

Vlad held it between his thumb and forefinger, waving it back and forth. "You want it, Irma. You need it."

Her hands clawed toward it, then clenched into fists. Her face convulsed. She fell to her hands and knees, and went into painful dry heaves at Vlad's feet.

The capsule, and Vlad's fingernails, were soon shining inches from her nose.

"This," he said, "can take away your pain."

She cried as she slapped it out of his grip and into a shadowy tangle of broken cacti.

"That wasn't very nice," said Vlad.

She found herself crawling after it.

Suddenly she stopped, turned to Vlad and asked, "Where is it from?"

"Oh." He scanned the sky as if to access his memory. "A secret lab in Chechnya."

"From the same batch as the ones you sold Horst tonight?"

"Yes." He smiled, showing all his teeth.

"You bastard." She tried to get up. "Steelsnake, tear him up!"

There was a loud metallic click as Steelsnake lurched toward Vlad. A technical was aiming a shoulder-fire missile.

Steelsnake froze.

"Bravo," said Vlad. "That armor-piercing warhead would have vaporized you—which would have been a shame. Now, why don't we go into my house and discuss matters like civilized human beings?"

Irma was vaguely aware of being lifted to her feet and pushed around. Her body spasmed. Her nervous system short-circuited. Her vision was out of focus, light splintered into jagged shards that hurt, deeply.

Someone put something in her hand. A small object. A nova capsule.

She brought it to her nose, her arm twitching like a severed frog's leg under an electric current.

"Wait," part of her said. "Is it from the Chechen batch?"

"What's the matter," said Vlad, "don't you trust me?"

She didn't. But, then, she wasn't in control. Her hand brought the capsule to her nose. A ravenous nostril sucked it into position. Her body heat caused an explosion to shoot up her nasal passages and flood her sinus cavities with a heat that canceled the nova sickness. In a nanosecond her traitorous brain soaked up the delicious nova heat. She felt wonderful. She was horrified. A white hot flash blotted out everything...

Tears and sweat poured from her eyes as they fluttered open.

Things weren't in focus yet. She enjoyed the blur.

Unlike the burnt-out bunker look of the outside, the inside of Vlad's house was a complicated, air-conditioned assemblage of spray-on, snap-on, and throwaway luxury: A combination chandelier-ceiling fan rotated in the center of the high ceiling like an upside-down, Arabian Nights UFO. The ceiling dripped soft, glow-foam stalactites. The walls were thickly coated in light-absorbing fungoid flock. The soft, bioform furniture seemed to grow out of the flock. Bodies in various states of semiconsciousness were strewn about like the willing victims of a bloodless massacre—some of them wore the uniforms of law-enforcement agencies.

Steelsnake was sprawled on a thing that looked like a cancerous growth. Two of Vlad's concubines—small women, one thin and copper-colored, the other plump and purple-black, wearing matching harem pants, makeup, and oversized wigs—had fallen victim to Steelsnake's pheromone cloud. They were professionals, and Steelsnake was taking full advantage of their expertise. Irma had to turn away.

"There," said Vlad, "don't you feel better now?"

"Yes." Irma tried not to look at him.

"And you are still alive."

"Sort of." She fumbled for the remote, let her fingers play around the attack button.

"You aren't still mad at me, are you? It was just a silly misunderstanding. Those mad Chechens! Anyway, you know how it is with unauthorized pharmaceuticals." He put his thin, pale hand on her shoulder. "They are dangerous; that's why people like you and I can't resist them." He pushed his fingers onto the exposed skin of her neck. "A woman like you, Irma, understands. You are so full of passion."

Irma shuddered, then said, "Horst."

Vlad put his cold lips on her neck. "He just wasn't man enough for you."

Irma elbowed Vlad in the chest, sending him tumbling into a bowl-shaped coffee table that was brimming over with drugs and paraphernalia.

"Steelsnake!" She screamed. "Kill him! Now!"

Steelsnake was too busy with the concubines to react. So Irma pressed the attack button. Steelsnake sprang to his feet, throwing the concubines aside like a pair of cheap toys. He rushed toward Vlad. Irma left the kill suppressor alone.

Grabbing Vlad by the hair, Steelsnake lifted him off the floor.

"You can't do this!" Vlad shrieked. "I have police on the premises!"

Some uniformed figures stirred, but took no notice.

Irma licked her chapped lips and grinned.

Then her phone rang.

Irma ignored the phone. Her quivering finger hit the attack button again and again. "Kill him!" she whined. "Kill him!"

Steelsnake just stood there, paralyzed, his eyes glazed over.

A voice came from Irma's phone: "Ms. Mao? Ms. Mao? Excuse me, but you are under contract to answer all corporate calls."

It was Neurotroli. Irma didn't have to look to know.

She took a deep breath that ended in a snort, attempted to smooth out her hair, forced a business-like smile, faced the screen, and said, "To what do I owe this pleasure?"

The cartoon brain frown. "You know all my calls are always business."

Irma broke into loud, moist sobs.

"Turn your sound up to max," said Neurotroli. "I need to talk to all of you."

Irma somehow did it.

"First," Neurotroli's voice boomed through the room, "Steelsnake, put Mr. Vlad down."

Steelsnake did, pouting over mayhem interruptus.

Vlad massaged his scalp, and got down on his knees in front of Irma's wrist. "Oh, thank you, sir!"

Irma took a few deep breaths, and said, "I want him dead!"

"That's understandable, but also a personal matter," said Neurotroli. "And this is business."

"I'm a loyal employee, and he killed my...friend."

"Yes." Neurotroli's eyebrows came together. "And you are in violation of the company anti-drug addiction policy."

"You knew?" Blood vessels pulsed at Irma's temples. "How?"

"You are an employee," the logo said. "I know everything about you. I know when you are in violation of regulations, and act on them when it won't interfere with productivity—or in this case, when it will bring in more profits."

"Profits?" Irma's eyes went blank.

"Yes." Neurotroli's face snapped back into his usual smile. "Vlad. Neurotrolix has long been interested in the possibilities of products based on variations of the capsaicin molecule."

"There's nothing like useful molecules." Vlad stood up, swayed on his feet as if he were about to dance.

"How true," the logo said. "So, do you think we can make a deal?"

"Oh, yes, of course," Vlad said, "as I was saying to Steelsnake, I am interested in some of his augmentations for my technicals. I have to keep up with the police. Sometimes paying them off isn't enough."

Neurotroli laughed. "See Irma? It all turned out for the best. Everything is in order. This has been another example of better living through mind control."

Vlad grinned, his body trembled with silent laughter.

Steelsnake's fists shook, his knuckles turned white.

Irma's legs gave out. She sat down.

In the folds of the soft, textured floor, she found a nova capsule. She rolled it in her fingers. With a sigh, she stuck it up her nose. And she didn't die.

This just wasn't her day.

CLASH OF TITANS
(A NEW YORK ROMANCE)

KURT BUSIEK

Kurt Busiek was one of the driving creative voices of the 1990s superhero revival in comics, beginning with his collaboration with Alex Ross, *Marvels*, soon followed by Busiek's iconic, fan-favourite run on *The Avengers*. His greatest contribution to the canon, however, is *Astro City*—launched in 1995—a world of his own creation teeming with keenly realized takes on every superhero archetype imaginable. This 1991 story is from *Newer York: Stories of Science Fiction and Fantasy About the World's Greatest City*; New York is a familiar setting for superhero readers, being the nexus for most superhero activity in the popular Marvel Universe.

*H*e's gone now. They're both gone. But if you've lived in New York for over five years, you remember when the commercials began, and you remember the effect they had. If you moved to New York during that time—and there are a lot of you, too many—the commercials probably had something to do with it. I'm the guy who came up with them.

It all started in a bar. Or, no, it was a few days before that: a hot, humid afternoon, and the air-conditioning was out. We were supposed to be spitballing ideas, but we were just lounging around the big conference table, watching TV, trying not to move around much, and generally crabbing about everything. I work for the Mayor's Commission on Tourism; we do TV spots, print ads, and assorted other stuff, all aimed at getting out-of-staters to come spend their vacation cash here. This was around the time the "I ♥ New York" campaign (Fred's idea) was running out of steam, and we were supposed to have an enhancement or a replacement at least in proposal stage by Monday. We were pretty dry. Sarah suggested getting Ling-Ling and Hsing-Hsing on loan for the Bronx Zoo and featuring them, but that was it for the last half-hour, and nobody even bothered to point out it was a lame idea.

The mayor was on TV, smiling his impenetrable smile and talking about this thing at Lincoln Center and how important it was. You might not remember

Lincoln Center, it was one of her first major targets. Anyway, the mayor was going on and on, and the crowd was visibly wilting, I don't know how anybody can listen to that stuff when the air is warmer and moister than blood, and Fred suggested, "Okay, here we go: We trade Hizzoner for Ling-Ling and Hsing-Hsing and make them mayor. An image change. And a better class of employer."

"Nah," Jeremy said. "You know pandas. They're so cute they'd end up mayor for life, and eight years down the road we'd have the same damn problem."

Then the mayor drowned in a *frzhatsssh* of static, and when the screen cleared, he wasn't there anymore. Instead, it was Demonica. Electric eyebrows, purple beehive, the works. She glared out into the room.

"O-*kay*!" said Fred. "Leona Helmsley's evil twin!" He settled back in his chair and grinned, raising his Orangina to her.

"You stupid, worthless, drooling pigs!" Her voice was like a buzzsaw. I always assumed it was electronically enhanced, until I met her in person. "You unutterably ignorant mouth-breathers! You're all just wasting space on this planet. I could reduce you all to dust—to protoplasm!—and it wouldn't make a single ounce of difference to the world." She paused, sneered, and adjusted her goggles.

"And you know, I just might. It'd be fun. It'd be fresh. It'd be what you deserve. I've got a sweet little protobomb stashed under your miserable island, and when it goes off, it'll trigger the earthquake fault that runs down the East Coast." She laughed, like the gear chain coming off a bicycle. "Does that spell it out in simple enough terms for you? Can you say earthquake? Disaster? Can you say death and mayhem beyond human comprehension? Aw, I knew you could.

"But you can save yourselves," she continued, hitching at her leather jumpsuit. She didn't shave her underarms, and what do you know, that was purple too. "You have that opportunity. You can save your worthless, repugnant lives, and I'll tell you how. You know who I want. You know where that no-good gob of phlegm who calls himself Mister Right is cowering. Deliver him to me. Deliver him to me by midnight tomorrow, or I promise you, New York, you won't live to see..."

She was working herself up into an astonishingly frenetic state, but before she could finish her threat, there was a double flash of static: *frzhatsssh, frzhatsssh*. Between them we caught a glimpse of the mayor blowing on his microphone and looking aggrieved, and then the image of Mister Right filled the screen. Even as early as that, his charisma hit like a physical blow. He stood ramrod straight. His jaw was firm, his eyes were piercing blue, and his blond hair cascaded over his crimson helm.

Sarah pounded the table and whistled. "Hoo hoo, big guy, take it off! Take it all off!"

You have to understand, this was years before Demonica melted the UN. This was before she created those werewolf things that ate Donald Trump. We didn't know how smart—and how deadly—she was, we just thought she was a nut. She hadn't even done much pre-empting of broadcast TV at that point—this was one of the first times. Up till then, she'd mostly just broken in on cable, Channel J and like that. It was just this goofy thing, like Al Sharpton. It was fun to watch.

Mister Right leaned forward on the screen, and his stern, forceful voice filled the air. "The people of New York have nothing to fear from you, Demonica. Truth, justice, and decency will always triumph over your kind of perverted sideshow. Name the place. Name the time. I'll be there—and you'll get taken away in a body bag." His smile was grim, a man who meant business.

Frzhatsssh. Mayor. *Frzhatsssh*. Demonica. "Four o'clock tomorrow, jerk. Tompkins Square Park. Bring your...atomic rod."

Frzhatsssh. Mayor. "As I was saying..."

Frzhatsssh. Mister Right. "I'll be there, you frigid bitch. Count on it. You're going down—and you're going down *hard*!"

There was an extended *frzhatsssh*, but instead of the mayor, what we got when it faded was Yogi Bear extolling the virtues of children's vitamins in Spanish.

"I got it," I said. "It'd be perfect. We get *them* to do an I ♥ New York spot. Mister Right and Demonica, the new fun couple. Better than Garner and Hartley for Polaroid. Better than David and Maddie, may they rest in peace."

"Better than Ling-Ling and Hsing-Hsing?" Sarah asked.

"Oh, c'mon. What says New York better for you? Two panda bears eating eucalyptus leaves, or two emotionally constipated psychotics with heavy weaponry trying to kill each other?"

"The man has a point," said Jeremy.

Fred turned the TV off. "Yeah, Marty, when they check in at Bellevue to pick up their mail, you can take 'em to the Russian Tea Room for blinis and sign 'em up. Any other brilliant ideas? Monday's coming fast."

And that was it. At five o'clock we split up, headed for home (I caught an early train, for once), and we forgot the whole thing. Tompkins Square Park didn't survive the next afternoon, of course. But even then, people were starting to get used to that sort of thing.

That Thursday night I was in the city late. I had to go to that Lincoln Center thing, and it lasted for hours. By the time I could get home and to sleep it'd be time to get up and head in again. So the city was putting me up at the Hyatt.

Actually, the time that matters, I was around the corner from the Hyatt, at a bar on Lexington Avenue, griping to anyone who'd listen. That meant mostly the bartender.

I mean, what would you expect? Here I'd been working for the city—the city itself, mind you—for almost two years, and I couldn't find an apartment. I spent my days sucking people in to New York by whatever means possible, and I had an hour commute. From Connecticut.

There had to be a very special mathematics governing my job and a team of accountants to supervise it. They monitored my performance carefully, and once I got X number of out-of-staters moved to the city permanently, they'd give me a raise so I could look in a new price range. Of course, that was the price range that had just been completely closed off by the new people snapping up the available apartments. So I kept looking, kept commuting, and my next raise would come just when all the places it made affordable were taken. It was a plot, it had to be.

Anyway, I was explaining this to the bartender (who lived on St. Mark's Place, rent-controlled) when I saw him, tucked away in a back booth. I wasn't sure it was him, mind you, I'd only ever seen him on TV and I never thought he was that short. But I got a good look when I went to the men's room, and it was him all right. No mistaking that jawline.

He was drinking boilermakers. I got one and a fourth Scotch for me (those things at Lincoln Center take it out of you) and carried them over. "Mister Right?"

He looked up, a little bleary-eyed. He'd clearly been drinking for a while. With an effort, he focused on the fresh drink. "Did I...?"

"It's on me." I put the drinks down, spilling a little, and slid into the booth. "I wanted to tell you, you were impressive yesterday. You took care of Demonica and kept fatalities and property damage to a minimum. Nice work."

"Huh. She'll be back." His voice was bitter, and he didn't have the commanding presence he'd had before. Of course, he wasn't in his outfit. He was wearing jeans and an ordinary dress shirt, and that might have had something to do with it. Or maybe it was the slurred speech and the defensive slump to his shoulders. "God-damn castrating bitch. Teleported away, but set it up so it looked like she died. That way she can pop up alive and laugh and make me look like a jackass again."

"Demonica's still alive?"

"Always." He knocked back the shot and reached for the beer. "She runs rings around me. I look like King Super Genius with the force field and the atomic cannon and all, but it's her show from top to bottom. She knows the equipment inside out. Me, I'm still doping out basic functions."

"What do you mean, basic functions?" I had a little trouble with the words "basic functions," but I forced them out. The whole conversation was starting to seem a little surreal.

"Well, whaddya think? She built it all, you know."

"You're kidding." I'd assumed Mister Right built the gadgets that let him fly and stuff himself, but no. He told me the whole story. He and Demonica met in college—he was a computer-science geek; she was the filthy-rich shining star of the physics department—and dated for a while. He ran out of money about the time she vaporized several teaching assistants and they asked her to leave, so she hired him as a lab assistant and started doing her own research over in Brooklyn. The area wasn't zoned for atomic research, but she didn't care. He told me she said laws were there to keep stupid people from having any fun. Anyway, he hated working for her. She was demanding, a real top-decibel perfectionist, and the boss/employee thing screwed up the relationship. They stopped sleeping together and the job was hell, but she never paid him much so he couldn't get a stake together to quit and go for something else.

Eventually he got fed up. He stole a truck, filled it up with stuff from the lab, and left. The plan was to sell the stuff and see if he could get a job, but it didn't work out right. She came after him in this stealth chopper she'd whipped up, and started shooting at him. He figured out the controls on the Rebound Ray and bounced her halfway through the New Jersey Palisades. You remember it from the movie, I'm sure. They got the facts wrong, of course—they used what I told them—but it sure made a nice explosion.

Anyway, that's how it all started. They got into the good/evil thing as a sex game back in college, and eventually it—I guess "evolved" is the right word— into this whole elaborate fantasy. He never did know why she kept playing along after they split up. I think there's something about that kind of couple-specific ritual that makes it hard to stop. Either you both stop at the same time, or you don't stop at all. The best part about the whole thing, or at least the part I always liked best, was that the poor schmuck didn't even have a secret identity. His name was Wright. Benjamin Wright. We just heard it on TV and assumed it was a code name.

Her name was Monica, of course. Demonica was what he called her when they got out the whips and the jelly, and the name made a comeback in the early cable days.

He finished up his story and belched plaintively. "And now I'm almost out of plutonium," he said. "I don't have any money to buy more. I don't even know where to find it. A week, ten days max, and all my stuff won't work anymore. Then I'm dead meat." He started drawing circles in the beer on the table.

"Um," I said, not really sure where I was heading, but unwilling to let the moment pass. "What would you say if I said I might be able to get you some plutonium?"

He looked up at me and wiped a drop of beer off his lip. He straightened up and squared his shoulders, going from pathetic drunk to commanding presence in about a second flat. His eyes were blue and bottomless and deadly, but when he spoke, he killed the whole image. "Who...who *are* you, anyway?"

We shot the first commercial a week later. That was when he got the earpieces, the ones with the antennae on them. They didn't do anything, but it helped make him look high-tech.

We had no budget to speak of, so it wasn't like the commercials everyone remembers today. No special effects, no John Williams theme, no action. Just Ben and the American flag. It was a nice piece. He launched into his speech and the camera just loved him. Inside of five words, he owned anyone watching. Just owned them.

What he said didn't matter. It was about justice and safety and freedom, and his guarantee that New York would never fall victim to the encroaching evil Demonica represented, or some such garbage. I've got a copy of it around here, but it just wasn't important. All that was important was that sincerity. It radiated out from him, like he was the sun. A nice piece.

Not long after that, the sidewalk vendors started selling the T-shirts. We had to close 'em down, of course, we had exclusive licensing rights. But we were never able to keep up with the demand, not from the start. It seemed like everyone had a Mister Right T-shirt—or a button, a baseball cap, puffy stickers. About a month after the campaign started, I saw a man on Park Avenue, maybe seventy years old. He had a tweed cap, wool trousers with suspenders, Oxfords, and a walking stick. And a Mister Right T-shirt—the hot-pink one where he's flipping Demonica the bird. That's when I knew it had gone way beyond a fad.

Demonica got really pissy once the commercials started. They had to list her on a separate scale to see what the murder rate would look like under normal circumstances, and it wasn't long before she outdid all other crime in the metropolitan area combined. Still, the ads worked. They worked like crazy. When her side of the murder stats officially doubled everyone else put together, the mayor called me into his office.

"Tourism's at an all-time high, Martin, and it's still accelerating." He beamed at me, and I wondered if I should recommend a good orthodontist. "Better than V-J Day. Better than the World's Fair. It's wonderful."

"Even with the JAL plane blowing up yesterday? That was a pretty ugly mess."

"Pfah!" He waved it away. "They were on their way home, they'd had a great vacation. Besides, isn't that what the big guy's for? To keep us safe from things like that?"

"He didn't stop that one."

"So? So how much worse would it be if he wasn't here at all?" I didn't have an answer. I'd wondered. "Don't be such a Gloomy Gus, Martin. Mister Right souvenirs are selling like there's no tomorrow, and they tell me some knock-off just showed up in LA, calling himself Joe Orange. Atlanta's got something in the works, too, and God knows who's next. Magazines and newspapers are sending reporters to cover the story full-time. Even *Pravda*'s got a guy on the way. And I just got invited to the White House—to the White House!—to talk about special agent status for the big guy. You've done a great thing, Martin. Have a cigar."

A raise came along with the cigar, and I started apartment-hunting again.

I couldn't figure it. New Yorkers were being turned to stone, mutated into big things with tentacles, hurled into orbit and burned up in re-entry, evaporated—all this by the dozen, by the busload. You'd figure there'd be a vacant apartment somewhere nice. But no. The whole world was flooding in to gawk around and get a snapshot of the Big Apple's Sterling Defender of Liberty—and a lot of them must have liked it here, because they moved in in droves. It was harder to find places even to look at than it was before. It was harder to get on waiting lists.

What can you do?

On the other hand, I did find a way around the cosmic accountants who were keeping my salary in the no-available-apartments range. When we cut the deal, I arranged to be listed on the contracts as Ben's agent, and that gave me a cut of everything he made out of it. He did the commercials for free, of course—it was a public service—but all those shirts, dolls, posters, and junk really added up. Most weeks my check from the licensing people was bigger than my paycheck.

That put me in a new class for apartment-hunting, and once we got the merchandise moving good, I managed to find the first place in years that was affordable and didn't outright suck. It was a two-bedroom on the Upper West Side with high ceilings, wood floors, good light, four closets and plenty of electrical outlets. And there was more: the building had a doorman. There was a washer/dryer room in the basement. And the apartment had a balcony. A balcony!

It was a pretty stiff deposit—two and a half months—but it was worth it. I was the first guy to see it, and there were three couples scheduled that evening. So I wrote the check and I signed the form and shook hands with the guy. It was mine, all mine.

I was leaving, heading home to make moving arrangements, smile on face, spring in step, all that, when it happened. I heard a high-pitched whistling and smelled ionized air. There was a dull thump behind me. I turned around and there was a hole in the second and third floors of the building. As I watched, the awning stretched out tight and taut, then started to tear. The doorman bolted.

The base of the building slowly separated from the sidewalk and shrank backward, like a kid stepping into a cold pool. There was a groaning sound. The part of the building above the hole swayed.

People started to boil out of the lobby, but most of them didn't make it. The groan became a roar, the sway became a shiver, and like a cross between a deflating balloon and an avalanche, *kwadathaddathaboom*, the building collapsed, spilling bricks, glass, plaster, furniture, and bodies all over West Eighty-eighth Street.

I didn't know what had happened, not right away. All I knew was my new river-view apartment, my new balcony, both bedrooms, everything, was all Down Here instead of Up There where it belonged.

I stood there, looking at the wreckage, willing it not to have happened, until, *shkvmp*, a shattered bathtub and an overturned bookcase shifted, and he climbed out.

"Ben. Aw, Ben, you dumb shit," I said.

He saw me. "Marty! What a surprise!" Then he got a good look at my face and looked around. "This—this wasn't the place, was it, Marty? The apartment?"

I nodded.

"Well, gee, Marty, I'm sorry. If I'd known I'd have, I don't know, tried to land somewhere else or something." He brushed some plaster dust off his cape. "Uh, Marty, I've got to go. She's up there at the George Washington Bridge, and it's rush hour. You know how it is."

I watched him gather himself for launch. "Ben?"

He stopped.

"You—you wouldn't need a sidekick, would you?"

"Well, I don't know. You're a little old, but we could maybe swing something. Why?"

"Where do you live?"

"Oh," he said, realizing. "Rumson, New Jersey. It's an hour commute, even in the Fusion-Copter. Sorry."

"Well, it was an idea, anyway." I turned to go.

"Hey, Marty, cheer up. Maybe you can get your deposit back." He sprang, and a split second later was airborne and gone.

Yeah, right. The only way you get your deposit back in New York is to skip out on the last month's rent. I headed back toward Grand Central and Connecticut, walking slow. At least I didn't have to drive out of the city. One bridge or tunnel gets tied up, and the others all turn into sheer hell.

One thing you should understand: there was only Demonica, only ever her. The others were all made up, all actors we hired, their powers cobbled together out of Ben's extra stuff or whipped up by the guys at ILM. The Battery Boys, ShBoom, the Sewer Alligator, Mr. Wrong, GEN-11 (Sarah's idea, and kind of tasteless, actually: a techno-genii—hence the name—supposedly created from the reanimated body of a rape victim and seeking vengeance on preppies), the Culture Vultures. All fakes. By the end, we'd even created some for other cities. The Hunchback of UCLA, the Tar Heel, Longhorn—those were ours.

The thing was, Demonica kept winning. Oh, it looked like Ben won a lot, but that was just her being perverse. She faked her own death—publicly, mind you—sixty-seven times, and never repeated a gag once. And every time she did, she was letting Ben know he couldn't touch her. Like the time she turned Columbus Circle into a crater and got "electrocuted" by a falling power cable. Ben got a medal for saving the city, but he knew the truth: she said she was going to wreck Columbus Circle, she did it, and she got away. She was every bit as smart as she thought she was, I'll give her that. But at the same time, she never did her best to kill him, either, never caught him in a death trap she didn't know he could escape.

Still, to keep people from catching on, we had to cook up our own bad guys. That way, Ben had someone he could beat, and beat every time. By then, our budget was huge, and we could really go to town with the special effects. We made sure we got enough footage to use in the ads—that was still the only reason for the whole project—and tried to make sure nobody important got hurt. It worked out well, for the most part. Occasionally one of them went bad for real, but Ben handled those as well as he did the staged battles. And the time ShBoom wanted to "reform" and be Mister Right's partner, and we had to arrange for him to sacrifice himself to save the city. But that's another story.

Looking back on it, I think putting Ben on steroids was a mistake. It made him bigger, and it did wonders for his upper-body development, but he probably could have gotten by on his natural brawn. I don't know for sure it was the drugs, though. It might have been the constant adulation, the groupies, the TV coverage, the money, whatever. But he was losing touch with reality.

This was around the time he was hanging with Diane Brill and Tama Janowitz. All that's in the Ultra Violet diaries, so I won't rehash it here. But one night, when I was in the office late, he came in through the door—I mean, literally through the door.

There were chunks of wood and splinters everywhere, and what was left fell all over Jeremy's desk, burying all the work he'd been doing on the Rainbow Coalition thing for Ben to do at the Koch Memorial the next week. A couple of cinderblocks came out of the wall, too, and we found the doorknob out on the fire escape the next day. I waited for it all to settle, and he waited too, breathing kind of snarly and staring at me.

"What's up, Ben?"

"How could you do it, Marty? I thought you were part of the cause, the crusade. I thought you were fighting for the same principles. I thought we were a team."

I motioned for him to lower his voice. He was in stentorian mode and could be heard for blocks. "What are you talking about?"

"You. You and Demonica!"

"Oh. That."

"'Oh, that'? Is that all you have to say? How could you betray me like that?" He picked up my desk and threw it through the window. I hoped nobody was walking by below. "My best friend and my worst enemy!"

"Easy, Ben. It's not what you think."

"And what is it? Do you deny that you've consorted with the Mistress of Evil? That you—my closest confidant, the keeper of all my secrets—have actually been sleeping with Demonica?" He was starting to breathe heavy again and I didn't like the way his mood was headed.

"Ben, sit down." He glowered at me and clenched his fists, but he sat. "If you promise not to destroy any more city property, I'll tell you what happened. Do we have a deal?"

He made a face, but he nodded.

"Okay. First off, I only slept with her once, and it was months ago. And it was nothing, really." He clutched the arms of the chair, and they started to bend. "Look, I could tell you she took control of my brain, right? And I had no choice, right? But I'm not, I'm being honest with you. Settle down.

"You know I've been in touch with her. She demanded a cut from the Demonica action figures in return for promising hands-off on Gracie Mansion. So every six weeks or so we arrange to courier her a cashier's check." He was relaxing now, bored. Business details always put him to sleep. "So one time I carried the check myself, because there was something I wanted to talk to her about.

"You remember that time it looked like she got run over by the 6 train, only it turned out she had a whole lab-headquarters deal set up in an unfinished subway tunnel, and she just ducked into it? I always thought it was kind of lucky it was so close when you threw the train at her, and I finally asked her. It turns out she has a bunch of them, scattered around the city.

"So I wanted to see if she'd be willing to sublet. She must hardly ever use them, so they're standing empty all the time. Some of 'em are in really prime locations, and you know, with the right kind of decor..."

He nodded. He still felt bad about the balcony building.

"But she didn't go for it. She was nice about it, but she said she never knew when she might need to activate one of them, and I'd get evicted with no notice to speak of. She didn't want to have to do that. Besides, I have a cat.

"And that was it; I gave her the check and we were done. But it was dinnertime and we were both hungry, so we grabbed a pizza and a bottle of wine, and, well, you know how it is. She was wearing that black Spandex outfit with the garters— you know, the one with the skull on the crotch—and we were all alone in this tunnel, and there was all this funky machinery, and the wine—"

"Yeah, Marty, I know." His voice was normal again. "She's always real horny after a couple of drinks. And she's pretty aggressive."

"Tell me about it."

"But, Marty, it can't happen again. It's a lonely crusade I'm on, this war against the evils that would destroy us. I've got to be able to trust the men around me. And you know how devious she is. She'll stop at nothing, and if she ever learned the secrets I've confided in you..." His eyes were glittering, his jaw tight and locked.

"Uh, look, Ben, maybe you need a break. You've been pretty busy lately, haven't had much time out of the suit. It couldn't hurt to go back to being just Ben Wright for a few days." I thought for a second. "How about coming out to Greenwich this weekend? We could catch a movie, maybe go sailing. I can fix us up with a couple of nice girls, you'll like them." A little harmless detox. A reality check.

He stood up and flexed. I always hated that. Looked down at me. "Evil never takes a vacation, Marty. You know that." And he flipped me a salute—a salute, for Pete's sake—as he shot off through the broken window.

I don't know. I think he was starting to believe he really was Mister Right.

The next time Demonica called to arrange for her check, I asked her how he found out. She said she told him. I ask you. The most brilliant woman in the world, sure, but screwed up beyond belief, right?

I found this luxury condo near Central Park. I couldn't afford it, and I knew it. But I could almost afford it, and it had been so long since I'd seen anything I was even close to, it was hard to walk away. So I was up late going over figures. I had projections from the licensing guys (weighted to reflect three new bad guys I didn't know if we could get on line in time), I had papers from the bank estimating what kind of mortgage I could swing, I had my returns for the past five years. And no matter how I punched it in, it added up to no condo.

The phone rang. It was him.

"I did it, Marty." His voice was hollow; I almost didn't recognize it. I hadn't heard him sound like that since the bar, way back at the beginning. "I did it."

"Ben, what do you mean? Did what?"

"She's dead, Marty. She's really dead this time. I've got the body with me."

I had a horrifying mental picture. "You're...not at a public phone, are you?"

"No, no. I'm at home. And she's here. She's dead."

"Yeah, dead. I got it. How did it happen?"

"She called me out again. You know how she does that—whenever she's finished some new gizmo she'll break into the TV channels and challenge me. I have to have the TV monitored all the time, I never know when she's going to break into *Nightline* or *Robin Byrd* or what. One time I missed *Wake Up America*, and—"

"Uh-huh. She called you out. Then what?"

"Well, it was Central Park this time. And as soon as I get there, she shorts out all my stuff. I land, she steps out from behind a tree with this doohickey, and zap, none of my stuff works. And it's heavy. It weighs over 250 pounds and there's no power to keep it up, it's just dragging me down, you—"

"Then what?"

"She starts undressing."

"What?"

"She strips. She's pulling off her clothes, and I'm almost falling over, the damn stuff is so heavy, and she's coming toward me, and she's got this weird grin on her face, and I don't know what she's going to do, I don't know what she's going to do! So I shot her."

"You shot her?"

"I didn't know what she was going to do! Ever since the first time, when I didn't know if the hardware was going to work for five minutes straight, I carried a .45 automatic, just in case. Security, you know."

"So you shot her."

There was a long silence on the other end of the line. For some crazy reason I thought of that sequence in *2001: A Space Odyssey* where the astronaut's tumbling over and over and all of the colors are coming at you. It was that kind of silence.

"She told me she loved me, Marty." Silence again. "Marty?"

"I'm here."

"She was naked, and there was blood all over the place, and I was holding her, and she said she loved me, and—and—and... What am I going to do now, Marty? What am I going to do?"

I couldn't see any way around it. "I don't know, Ben. I don't know how exactly to put this, and I don't want to seem cold, but, well, I think we're going to have to find a new campaign."

"No more Mister Right?"

"Well, there's no more Demonica, Ben. And I don't see how we can justify sending out professional criminals to terrorize New York just so you can fight them. There isn't any more threat."

"You did it before." His voice was low, terrified.

"That was different. That was just to juice things up in between Demonica's attacks. This would be fabricating the whole thing from scratch." I didn't tell him the truth; I'd be happy to send the Vultures after him, or the Battery Boys, but we wouldn't be able to keep it going. His equipment had been breaking down recently, and we didn't know how to fix it. I never told him Demonica had been coming in to work on the stuff, to patch it together, that she'd been the one that had kept it going as long as it had. Better to stop now than to let it deteriorate and have to tell him why we couldn't fix it any more.

"But—but... What am I going to do? You've got to tell me, Marty. You've got to!"

"Oh come on, Ben. You've had a good run. You made plenty of money and you had your time in the spotlight. It's not like you're out on the street. You own your own home and you've got plenty of capital. Buy a restaurant. Take a trip. Go back to school. The world is your oyster, pal, and you're on vacation. Savor it."

"But—"

"Oh, for Christ's sake! Wake up and smell the coffee, Ben. It's over. Real life is back. Cope, already." I hung up, then took the receiver off the hook in case he called back.

I reached for my Rolodex; this was important. Once the news broke—and it would break; no use hiding it—it'd be the biggest nine-day wonder this town ever saw. But the story would fade. King faded. Lennon faded. Everything fades but Chappaquiddick.

So I had to move fast. The first guy I wanted to talk to worked for *Newsweek*, the second for the *Times*, and after that there were a few other good possibilities. Once this story faded, there'd be a lot of reporters leaving town. If I acted now, while I was the only guy who knew, maybe I could get the inside line on a decent place to live.

I ended up in a roomy walk-through near Gramercy Park, and I've been there almost a year now. We came up with a new campaign—the one with the fish—and we pretty much put the old stuff behind us, like we always do. I hadn't realized how much everything changed until I heard about him committing suicide in Miami or somewhere, and it got me thinking about it again. It was pretty wild, I guess, looking at it in retrospect.

But, damn, this used to be a fun town, didn't it?

THE SUPER MAN AND THE BUGOUT
CORY DOCTOROW

In this wry satire, the ubiquitous Cory Doctorow reminds us that Superman was co-created by a Canadian Jew...

"**M**ama, I'm *not* a supervillain," Hershie said for the millionth time. He chased the last of the gravy on his plate with a hunk of dark rye, skirting the shriveled derma left behind from his kishka. Ever since the bugouts had inducted Earth into their Galactic Federation, promising to end war, crime, and corruption, he'd found himself at loose ends. His adoptive Earth-mother, who'd named him Hershie Abromowicz, had talked him into meeting her at her favorite restaurant in the heart of Toronto's Gaza Strip.

"Not a supervillain, he says. Listen to him: mister big-stuff. Well, smarty-pants, if you're not a supervillain, what was that mess on the television last night then?"

A busboy refilled their water, and Hershie took a long sip, staring off into the middle distance. Lately, he'd taken to avoiding looking at his mother: her infrared signature was like a landing-strip for a coronary, and she wouldn't let him take her to one of the bugout clinics for nanosurgery.

Mrs. Abromowicz leaned across the table and whacked him upside the head with one hand, her big rings clicking against the temple of his half-rim specs. Had it been anyone else, he would have caught her hand mid-slap, or at least dodged in a superfast blur, quicker than any human eye. But his mama had let him know what she thought of *that* sass before his third birthday. Raising super-infants requires strict, *loving* discipline. "Hey, wake up! Hey! I'm talking to you! What was that mess on television last night?"

"It was a demonstration, Mama. We were protesting. We want to dismantle the machines of war—it's in the Torah, Mama. Isaiah: they shall beat their swords into ploughshares and their spears into pruning hooks. Tot would have approved."

Mrs. Abromowicz sucked air between her teeth. "Your father never would have approved of *that*."

That was the Action last night. It had been his idea, and he'd tossed it around with the Movement people who'd planned the demo: they'd gone to an army-surplus store and purchased hundreds of decommissioned rifles, their bores filled with lead, their firing pins defanged. He'd flown above and ahead of the demonstration, in his traditional tights and cape, dragging a cargo net full of rifles from his belt. He pulled them out one at a time, and bent them into balloon-animals—fanciful giraffes, wiener-dogs, bumble-bees, poodles—and passed them out to the crowds lining Yonge Street. It had been a boffo smash hit. And it made great TV.

Hershie Abromowicz, Man from the Stars, took his mother's hands between his own and looked into her eyes. "Mama, I'm a grown man. I have a job to do. It's like...like a calling. The world's still a big place, bugouts or no bugouts, and there's lots of people here who are crazy, wicked, with their fingers on the triggers. I care about this planet, and I can't sit by when it's in danger."

"But why all of a sudden do you have to be off with these *meshuggenahs*? How come you didn't *need* to be with the crazy people until now?"

"Because there's a *chance* now. The world is ready to rethink itself. Because—" The waiter saved him by appearing with the cheque. His mother started to open her purse, but he had his debitcard on the table faster than the eye could follow. "It's on me, Ma."

"Don't be silly. I'll pay."

"I *want* to. Let me. A son should take his mother out to lunch once in a while."

She smiled, for the first time that whole afternoon, and patted his cheek with one manicured hand. "You're a good boy, Hershie, I know that. I only want that you should be happy, and have what's best for you."

Hershie, in tights and cape, was chilling in his fortress of solitude when his comm rang. He checked the callerid and winced: Thomas was calling, from Toronto. Hershie's long-distance bills were killing him, ever since the Department of Defense had cut off his freebie account.

Not to mention that talking to Thomas inevitably led to more trouble with his mother.

He got up off of his crystalline recliner and flipped the comm open, floating up a couple of metres. "Thomas, what's up?"

"Supe, didja see the reviews? The critics *love* us!"

Hersh held the comm away from his head and sighed the ancient, put-upon Hebraic sigh of his departed stepfather. Thomas Aquino Rusk liked to play at being a sleazy Broadway producer, his "plays" the eye-catching demonstrations he and his band of merry shit-disturbers hijacked.

"Yeah, it made pretty good vid, all right." He didn't ask why Thomas was calling. There was only one reason he *ever* called: he'd had another idea.

"You'll never guess why I called."

"You've had an idea."

"I've had an idea!"

"Really."

"You'll love it."

Hershie reached out and stroked the diamond-faceted coffins that his birth parents lay in, hoping for guidance. His warm fingers slicked with melted hoarfrost, and as they skated over the crypt, it sang a pure, high crystal note like a crippled flying saucer plummeting to the earth. "I'm sure I will, Thomas."

As usual, Thomas chose not to hear the sarcasm in his voice. "Check this out— DefenseFest 33 is being held in Toronto in March. And the new keynote speaker is the Patron Ik'Spir Pat! The fricken head fricken bugout! His address is 'Galactic History and Military Tactics: a Strategic Overview.'"

"And this is a good thing?"

"Ohfuckno. It's terrible, terrible, of course. The bugouts are selling us out. Going over to the Other Side. Just awful. But think of the possibilities!"

"But think of the possibilities? Oy." Despite himself, Hershie was smiling. Thomas always made him smile.

"You're smiling, aren't you?"

"Shut up, Thomas."

"Can you make a meeting at the Belquees for 18h?"

Hershie checked his comm. It was 1702h. "I can make it."

"See you there, buddy." Thomas rang off.

Hershie folded his comm, wedged it in his belt, and stroked his parents' crypt, once more, for luck.

Hershie loved the commute home. Starting at the Arctic Circle, he flew up and up and up above the highest clouds, then flattened out his body and rode the currents home, eeling around the wet frozen cloudmasses, slaloming through thunderheads, his critical faculties switched off, flying at speed on blind instinct alone.

He usually made visual contact with the surface around Barrie, just outside of Toronto, and he wasn't such a goodiegoodie that he didn't feel a thrill of superiority as he flew over the cottage-country commuters stuck in the end-of-weekend traffic, skis and snowmobiles strapped to their roofs.

The Belquees had the best Ethiopian food and the worst Ethiopian decor in town. Successive generations of managers had added their own touches—tiki-lanterns, textured wallpaper, framed photos of Haile Selassie, tribal spears and grass dolls—and they'd accreted in layers, until the net effect was of an African rummage sale. But man, the food was good.

Downstairs was a banquet room whose decor consisted of material too ugly to be shown upstairs, with a stage and a disco ball. It had been a regular meeting place for Toronto's radicals for more than fifty years, the chairs worn smooth by generations of left-wing buttocks.

Tonight, it was packed. At least fifty people were crammed around the tables, tearing off hunks of tangy rice-pancake and scooping up vegetarian curry with them. Even before he saw Thomas, his super-hearing had already picked his voice out of the din and located it. Hershie made a beeline for Thomas's table, not making eye-contact with the others—old-guard activists who still saw him as a tool of the war-machine.

Thomas licked his fingers clean and shook his hand. "Supe! Glad you could make it! Sit, sit." There was a general shuffling of coats and chairs as the other people at the table cleared a space for him. Thomas was already pouring him a beer out of one of the pitchers on the table.

"Geez, how many people did you invite?"

Tina, a tiny Chinese woman who could rhyme "Hey hey, ho ho" and "One, two, three, four" with amazing facility said, "Everyone's here. The Quakers, the commies, a couple of councilors, the vets, anyone we could think of. This is gonna be *huge.*"

The food was hot, and the different curries and salads were a symphony of flavours and textures. "This is terrific," he said.

"Best Ethiopian outside of Addis Ababa," said Thomas.

Better than Addis Ababa, Hershie thought, but didn't say it. He'd been in Addis Ababa as the secret weapon behind Canada's third and most ill-fated peacekeeping mission there. There hadn't been a lot of restaurants open then, just block after block of bombed-out buildings, and tribal warlords driving around in tacticals, firing randomly at anything that moved. The ground CO sent him off to scatter bands of marauders while the bullets spanged off his chest. He'd never understood the tactical significance of those actions—still didn't—but at the time, he'd been willing to trust those in authority.

"Good food," he said.

An hour later, the pretty waitress had cleared away the platters and brought fresh pitchers, and Hershie's tights felt a little tighter. One of the Quakers, an ancient, skinny man with thin grey hair and sharp, clever features stood up and tapped his beer-mug. Gradually, conversation subsided.

"Thank you," he said. "My name is Stewart Pocock, and I'm here from the Circle of Friends. I'd like us all to take a moment to say a silent thanks for the wonderful food we've all enjoyed."

There was a nervous shuffling, and then a general bowing of heads and mostly silence, broken by low whispers.

"Thomas, I thought *you* called this meeting," Hershie whispered.

"I did. These guys always do this. Control freaks. Don't worry about it," he whispered back.

"Thank you all. We took the liberty of drawing up an agenda for this meeting."

"They *always* do this," Thomas said.

The Quakers led them in a round of introductions, which came around to Hershie. "I'm, uh, the Super Man. I guess most of you know that, right?" Silence. "I'm really looking forward to working on this with you all." A moment of silence followed, before the next table started in on its own introductions.

"Time," Louise Pocock said. Blissfully. At last. The agenda had ticks next to INTRODUCTION, BACKGROUND, STRATEGY, THE DAY, SUPPORT AND ORGANISING and PUBLICITY. Thomas had hardly spoken a word through the course of the meeting. Even Hershie's alien buttocks were numb from sitting.

"It's time for the closing circle. Please, everybody, stand up and hold hands." Many of the assembled didn't bother to stifle their groans. Awkwardly, around the tables and the knapsacks, they formed a rough circle and took hands. They held it for a long, painful moment, then gratefully let go.

They worked their way upstairs and outside. The wind had picked up, and it blew Hershie's cape out on a crackling vertical behind him, so that it caught many of the others in the face as they cycled or walked away.

"Supe, let's you and me grab a coffee, huh?" Thomas said, without any spin on it at all, so that Hershie knew that it wasn't a casual request.

"Yeah, sure."

The café Thomas chose was in a renovated bank, and there was a private room in the old vault, and they sat down there, away from prying eyes and autograph hounds.

"So, you pumped?" Thomas said, after they ordered coffees.

"After *that* meeting? Yeah, sure."

Thomas laughed, a slightly patronising but friendly laugh. "That was a *great* meeting. Look, if those guys had their way, we'd have about a march a month, and we'd walk slowly down a route that we had a permit for, politely asking people to see our point of view. And in between, we'd have a million meetings like this, where we come up with brilliant ideas like, 'Let's hand out fliers next time.'

"So what we do is, go along with them. Give them enough rope to hang themselves. Let 'em have four or five of those, until everyone who shows up is so bored, they'll do *anything*, as long as it's not that.

"So, these guys want to stage a sit-in in front of the convention centre. Boring! We wait until they're ready to sit down, then we start playing music and turn it into a *dance-in*. Start playing movies on the side of the building. Bring in a hundred secret agents in costume to add to it. They'll never know what hit 'em."

Hershie squirmed. These kinds of Machiavellian shenanigans came slowly to him. "That seems kind of, well, disingenuous, Thomas. Why don't we just hold our own march?"

"And split the movement? No, this is much better. These guys do all the postering and phoning, they get a good crowd out, this is their natural role. Our natural role, my son," he placed a friendly hand on Hershie's caped shoulder, "is to see to it that their efforts aren't defeated by their own poverty of imagination. They're the feet of the movement, but we're its *laugh*." Thomas pulled out his comm and scribbled on its surface. "*They're the feet of the movement, but we're its laugh*, that's great, that's one for the memoirs."

Hershie decided he needed to patrol a little to clear his head. He scooped trash and syringes from Grenadier Pond. He flew silently through High Park, ears cocked for any muggings.

Nothing.

He patrolled the Gardner Expressway next and used his heat vision to melt some black ice.

Feeling useless, he headed for home.

He was most of the way up Yonge Street when he heard the siren. A cop car, driving fast, down Jarvis. He sighed his father's sigh and rolled east, heading into Regent Park, locating the dopplering siren. He touched down lightly on top of one of the ugly, squat tenements, and skipped from roof to roof, until he spotted the cop. He was beefy, with the traditional moustache and the flak vest that they all wore on downtown patrol. He was leaning against the hood of his cruiser, panting, his breath clouding around him.

A kid rolled on the ground, clutching his groin, gasping for breath. His infrared signature throbbed painfully between his legs. Clearly, he'd been kicked in the nuts.

The cop leaned into his cruiser and lowered the volume on his radio, then, without warning, kicked the kid in the small of the back. The kid rolled on the ice, thrashing painfully.

Before Hershie knew what he was doing, he was hovering over the ice, between the cop and the kid. The cateyes embedded in the emblem on his chest glowed in the streetlamps. The cop's eyes widened so that Hershie could see the whites around his pupils.

Hershie stared. "What do you think you're doing?" he said, after a measured silence.

The cop took a step back and slipped a little on the ice before catching himself on his cruiser.

"Since when do you kick unarmed civilians in the back?"

"He—he ran away. I had to catch him. I wanted to teach him not to run."

"By inspiring his trust in the evenhandedness of Toronto's Finest?" Hershie could see the cooling tracks of the cruiser, skidding and weaving through the projects. The kid had put up a good chase. Behind him, he heard the kid regain his feet and start running. The cop started forward, but Hershie stopped him with one finger, dead centre in the flak jacket.

"You can't let him get away!"

"I can catch him. Trust me. But first, we're going to wait for your backup to arrive, and I'm going to file a report."

A *Sun* reporter arrived before the backup unit. Hershie maintained stony silence in the face of his questions, but he couldn't stop the man from listening in on his conversation with the old constable who showed up a few minutes later, as he filed his report. He found the kid a few blocks away, huddled in an alley, hand pressed to the small of his back. He took him to Mount Sinai's emerg and turned him over to a uniformed cop.

The hysterical *Sun* headlines that vilified Hershie for interfering with the cop sparked a round of recriminating voicemails from his mother, filled with promises to give him such a *zetz* in the head when she next saw him. He folded his tights and cape and stuffed them in the back of his closet and spent a lot of time in the park for the next few weeks. He liked to watch the kids playing, a United Nations in miniature, parents looking on amiably, stymied by the language barrier that their kids hurdled with ease.

On March first, he took his tights out of the overstuffed hall closet and flew to Ottawa to collect his pension.

He touched down on the Parliament Hill and was instantly surrounded by high-booted RCMP constables, looking slightly panicky. He held his hands up, startled. "What gives, guys?"

"Sorry, sir," one said. "High security today. One of Them is speaking in Parliament."

"Them?"

"The bugouts. Came down to have a chat about neighbourly relations. Authorised personnel only today."

"Well, that's me," Hershie said, and started past him.

The constable, looking extremely unhappy, moved to block him. "I'm sorry, sir, but that's not you. Only people on the list. My orders, I'm afraid."

Hershie looked into the man's face and thought about hurtling skywards and flying straight into the building. The man was only doing his job, though. "Look, it's payday. I have to go see the Minister of Defense. I've been doing it every month for *years*."

"I know that, sir, but today is a special day. Perhaps you could return tomorrow?"

"Tomorrow? My rent is due *today*, Sergeant. Look, what if I comm his office?"

"Please, sir, that would be fine." The Sergeant looked relieved.

Hershie hit a speed dial and waited. A recorded voice told him that the office was closed, the Minister at a special session.

"He's in session. Look, it's probably on his desk—I've been coming here for years; really, this is ridiculous."

"I'm sorry. I have my orders."

"I don't think you could stop me, Sergeant."

The Sergeant and his troops shuffled their feet. "You're probably right, sir. But orders are orders."

"You know, Sergeant, I retired a full colonel from the Armed Forces. I *could* order you to let me past."

"Sorry sir, no. Different chain of command."

Hershie controlled his frustration with an effort of will. "Fine then. I'll be back tomorrow."

The building super wasn't pleased about the late rent. He threatened Hershie with eviction, told him he was in violation of the lease, quoted the relevant sections of the Tenant Protection Act from memory, then grudgingly gave in to Hershie's pleas. Hershie had half a mind to put his costume on and let the man see what a *real* super was like.

But his secret identity was sacrosanct. Even in the era of Pax Aliena, the Super Man had lots of enemies, all of whom had figured out, long before, that even the invulnerable have weaknesses: their friends and families. It terrified him to think of what a bitter, obsolete, grudge-bearing terrorist might do to his mother, to Thomas, or even his old high-school girlfriends.

For his part, Thomas refused to acknowledge the risk; he was more worried about the Powers That Be than mythical terrorists.

The papers the next day were full of the overnight cabinet shuffle in Ottawa. More than half the cabinet had been relegated to the back-benches, and many of their portfolios had been eliminated or amalgamated into the new "superportfolios": Domestic Affairs, Trade, and Extraterrestrial Affairs.

The old Minister of Defense, who'd once had Hershie over for Thanksgiving dinner, was banished to the lowest hell of the back-bench. His portfolio had been subsumed into Extraterrestrial Affairs, and the new Minister, a young up-and-comer named Woolley, wasn't taking Hershie's calls. Hershie called Thomas to see if he could loan him rent money.

Thomas laughed. "Chickens coming home to roost, huh?" he said.

"What's that supposed to mean?" Hershie said, hotly.

"Well, there's only so much shit-disturbing you can do before someone sits up and takes notice. The Belquees is probably bugged, or maybe one of the commies is an informer. Either way, you're screwed. Especially with Woolley."

"Why, what's wrong with Woolley?" Hershie had met him in passing at Prime Minister's Office affairs, a well-dressed twenty-nine-year-old. He'd seemed like a nice enough guy.

"What's *wrong* with him?" Thomas nearly screamed. "He's the fricken antichrist! He was the one that came up with the idea of selling advertising on squeegee kids' T-shirts! He's heavily supported by private security outfits— he makes Darth Vader look like a swell guy. That slicked-down, blow-dried asshole—"

Hershie cut him off. "Okay, okay, I get the idea."

"No you don't, Supe! You don't get the half of it. This guy isn't your average Liberal—those guys're usually basic opportunists. He's a *zealot*! He'd like to beat us with *truncheons*! I went to one of his debates, and he showed up with a *baseball bat*! He tried to *hit me* with it!"

"What were you doing at the time?"

"What does it matter? Violence is never an acceptable response. I've thrown pies at better men than him—"

Hershie grinned. Thomas hadn't invented pieing, but his contributions to the art were seminal. "Thomas, the man is a federal Minister, with obligations. He can't just write me off—he'll have to pay me."

"Sure, sure," Thomas crooned. "Of *course* he will—who ever heard of a politician abusing his office to advance his agenda? I don't know what I was thinking. I apologise."

Hershie touched down on Parliament Hill, heart racing. Thomas's warning echoed in his head. His memories of Woolley were already morphing, so that the slick, neat kid became feral, predatory. The Hill was marshy and cold and grey, and as he squelched up to the main security desk, he felt a cold ooze of mud infiltrate its way into his super-bootie. There was a new RCMP constable on duty, a turbaned Sikh. Normally, he felt awkward around the Sikhs in the Mounties. He imagined that their lack of cultural context made his tights and emblem seem absurd, that they evoked grins beneath the Sikhs' fierce moustaches. But today, he was glad the man was a Sikh, another foreigner with an uneasy berth in the Canadian military-industrial complex. The Sikh was expressionless as Hershie squirted his clearances from his comm to the security desk's transceiver. Imperturbably, the Sikh squirted back directions to Woolley's new office, just a short jaunt from the exalted heights of the Prime Minister's Office.

The Minister's office was guarded by: a dignified antique door that had the rich finish of wood that has been buffed daily for two centuries; an RCMP constable in plainclothes; a young, handsome receptionist in a silk navy power-suit; a slightly older office manager whose heart-stopping beauty was only barely restrained by her chaste blouse and skirt; and, finally, a pair of boardroom doors with spotless brass handles and a retinal scanner.

Each obstacle took more time to weather than the last, so it was nearly an hour before the office manager stared fixedly into the scanner until the locks opened with a soft clack. Hershie squelched in, leaving a slushy dribble on the muted industrial-grade brown carpet.

Woolley knelt on the stool of an ergonomic work-cart, enveloped in an articulated nest of displays, comms, keyboards, datagloves, immersive headsets, stylii, sticky notes and cup-holders. His posture, hair and expression rivaled one-another for flawlessness.

"Hello, hello," he said, giving Hershie's hand a dry, firm pump. He smelled of expensive talc and leather car interiors.

He led Hershie to a pair of stark Scandinavian chairs whose polished lead undersides bristled with user-interface knobs. The old Minister's tastes had run to imposing oak desks and horsehair club-chairs, and Hershie felt a moment's disorientation as he sank into the brilliantly functional sitting-machine. It chittered like a roulette wheel and shifted to firmly support him.

"Thanks for seeing me," Hershie said. He caught his reflection in the bulletproof glass windows that faced out over the Rideau Canal, and felt a flush of embarrassment when he saw how clownish his costume looked in the practical environs.

Woolley favoured him with half a smile and stared sincerely with eyes that were widely spaced, clever and hazel, surrounded by smile lines. The man fairly oozed charisma. "I should be thanking you. I was just about to call you to set up a meeting."

Then why haven't you been taking my calls? Hershie thought. Lamely, he said, "You were?"

"I was. I wanted to touch base with you, clarify the way that we were going to operate from now on."

Hershie felt his gorge rise. "From now on?"

"I phrased that badly. What I mean to say is, this is a new Cabinet, a new Ministry. It has its own modus operandi."

"How can it have its own modus operandi when it was only created last night?" Hershie said, hating the petulance in his voice.

"Oh, I like to keep lots of contingency plans on hand—the time to plan for major changes is far in advance. Otherwise, you end up running around trying to get office furniture and telephones installed when you need to be seizing opportunity."

It struck Hershie how *finished* the office was—the staff, the systems, the security. He imagined Woolley hearing the news of his appointment and calling up files containing schematics, purchase orders, staff requisitions. It wasn't exactly devious, but it certainly teetered on the meridian separating *planning* and *plotting*.

"Well, you certainly seem to have everything in order."

"I've been giving some thought to your payment arrangement. Did you know that there's a whole body of policy relating to your pension?"

Hershie nodded, not liking where this was going.

"Well, that's just not sensible," Woolley said, sensibly. "The Canadian government already has its own pension apparatus: we make millions of direct-deposits every day, for welfare, pensions, employment insurance, mothers' allowance. We're up to our armpits in payment infrastructure. And having you fly up to Ottawa every month, well, it's ridiculous. This is the twenty-first century—we have better ways of moving money around.

"I've been giving it some thought, and I've come up with a solution that should make everything easier for everyone. I'm going to transfer your pension to the Canada Pension Plan offices; they'll make a monthly deposit directly to your account. I've got the paperwork all filled out here; all you need to do is fill in your banking information and your Social Insurance Number."

"But I don't have a Social Insurance Number or a bank account," Hershie said. Of course, Hershie Abromowicz had both, but the Super Man didn't.

"How do you pay taxes, then?" Woolley had a dangerous smile.

"Well, I—" Hershie stammered. "I don't! I'm tax-exempt! I've never had to pay taxes or get a bank account—I just take my cheques to the Canadian Union of Public Employees' Credit Union and they cash them for me. It's the *arrangement.*"

Woolley shook his head. "Who told you you were tax-exempt?" he asked, wonderingly. "*No one* is tax-exempt, except Status Indians. As to not having a bank account, well, you can open an account at the CUPE Credit Union and we'll make the deposits there. But not until this tax status matter is cleared up. You'll have to talk to Revenue Canada about getting a SIN, and get that information to Canada Pensions."

"I *pay taxes*! Through my secret identity."

"But does this..." he made quote marks with his fingers, "*secret identity* declare your pension income?"

"Of course I don't! I have to keep my secret identity a *secret!*" His voice was shrill in his own ears. "It's a *secret identity*. I served in the Forces as the Super Man, so I get paid as the Super Man. Tax exempt, no bank accounts, no SIN. Just a cheque, every month."

Woolley leaned back and clasped his hands in his lap. "I know that's how it used to be, but what I'm trying to tell you today is that arrangement, however longstanding, however well-intentioned, wasn't proper—or even *legal*. It had to end sometime. You're retired now—you don't need your *secret identity*," again with the finger-quotes. "If you already have a SIN, you can just give it to me, along with your secret identity's bank information, and we can have your pension processed in a week or two."

"*A week or two?*" Hershie bellowed. "I need to pay my *rent*! That's not how it works!"

Woolley stood, abruptly. "No sir, that *is* how it works. I'm trying to be reasonable. I'm trying to expedite things for you during this time of transition. But you need to meet me halfway. If you could give me your SIN and account information right now, I could speed things up considerably, I'm sure. I'm willing to make that effort, even though things are very busy here."

Hershie toyed with the idea of demolishing the man's office, turning his lovely furniture into molten nacho topping, and finishing up by leaving the man dangling by his suit from the CN Tower's needle. But his mother would kill him. "I can't give you my secret identity," Hershie said, pleadingly. "It's a matter of national security. I just need enough to pay my rent."

Woolley stared at the ceiling for a long, long time. "There is one thing," he said.

"Yes?" Hershie said, hating himself for the note of hope in his voice.

"The people at DefenseFest 33 called my office yesterday, to see if I'd appear as a guest speaker with the Patron Ik'Spir Pat. I had to turn them down, of course—I'm far too busy right now. But I'm sure they'd be happy to have a veteran of your reputation in that slot, and it carries a substantial honorarium. I could call them for you and give them your comm...?"

Hershie thought of Thomas, and of the rent, and of his mother, and of all the people at the Belquees who'd stared mistrustfully at him. "Have them call me," he sighed. "I'll talk to them."

He got to his feet, the toe of his boot squelching out more dirt pudding.

"Hershie?"

"Yes, Mama?" She'd caught him on the way home, flying high over the fleabag motels on the old Highway 2.

"It's Friday," she said.

Right. Friday. He told her he'd come for dinner, and that meant getting there before sunset. "I'll be there," he said.

"Oh, it's not important. It's just me. Don't hurry on my account—after all, you'll have thousands of Shabbas dinners with your mother. I'll live forever."

"I said I'll be there."

"And don't wear that costume," she said. She hated the costume. When the Department of Defense had issued it to him, she'd wanted to know why they were sending her boy into combat wearing red satin panties.

"I'll change."

"That's a good boy," she said. "I'm making brisket."

By the time he touched down on the roof of his building, he knew he'd be late for dinner. He skimmed down the elevator shaft to the tenth floor and ducked out to his apartment, only to find the door padlocked. There was a note from the building super tacked to the peeling green paint. Among other things, it quoted the codicil from the Tenant Protection Act that allowed the super to padlock the door and forbade Hershie, on penalty of law, from doing anything about it.

Hershie's super-hearing picked up the sound of a door opening down the hallway. In a blur, he flew up to the ceiling and hovered there, pressing himself flat on the acoustic tile. One of his neighbours, that guy with the bohemian attitude who always seemed to be laughing at poor, nebbishy Hershie Abromowicz, made his way down the hall. He paused directly below Hershie's still, hovering form, reading the note on the door while he adjusted the collar of his ski-vest. He smirked at the note and got in the elevator.

Hershie let himself float to the ground, his cheeks burning.

Damn it, he didn't have *time* for this. Not for any of it. He considered the padlock for a moment, then snapped the hasp with his thumb and index finger. Moving through the apartment with superhuman speed, he changed into a pair of nice slacks, a cable-knit sweater his mother had given him for his last birthday, a tweedy jacket and a woolen overcoat. Opening a window, he took flight.

"Thomas, I *really* can't talk right now," he said. His mother was angrily drumming her rings on the table's edge. Abruptly, she grabbed the bowl of cooling soup from his place setting and carried it into the kitchen. She hadn't done this since he was a kid, but it still inspired the same panicky dread in him—if he wasn't going to eat his dinner, she wasn't going to leave it.

"Supe, we *have* to talk about this. I mean, DefenseFest is only a week away. We've got things to do!"

"Look, about DefenseFest…"

"Yes?" Thomas had a wary note in his voice.

Hershie's mother reappeared with a plate laden with brisket, tsimmis, and kasha. She set it down in front of him.

"We'll talk later, okay?" Hershie said.

"But what about DefenseFest?"

"It's complicated," Hershie began. His mother scooped up the plate of brisket and headed back to the kitchen. She was muttering furiously. "I have to go," he said, and closed his comm.

Hershie chased his mother and snatched the plate from her as she held it dramatically over the sink disposal. He held up his comm with the other hand and made a show of powering it down.

"It's off, Mama. Please, come and eat."

"I've been thinking of selling the house," she said, as they tucked into slices of lemon pound-cake.

Hershie put down his fork. "Sell the house?" While his father hadn't exactly *built* the house with his own hands, he had sold his guts out at his discount menswear store to pay for it. His mother had decorated it, but his father's essence still haunted the corners. "Why would you sell the house?"

"Oh, it's too big, Hershie. I'm just one old lady, and it's not like there're any grandchildren to come and stay. I could buy a condo in Florida, and there'd be plenty left over for you."

"I don't need any money, Mama. I've got my pension."

She covered his hands with hers. "Of course you do, bubbie. But fixed incomes are for old men. You're young, you need a nest egg, something to start a family with." Her sharp eyes, sunk into motherly pillows of soft flesh, bored into him. He tried to keep his gaze light and carefree. "You've got money problems?" she said, at length.

Hershie scooped up a forkful of pound-cake and shook his head. His mother's powers of perception bordered on clairvoyance, and he didn't trust himself to speak the lie outright. He looked around the dining room, furnished with faux chinoise screens, oriental rugs, angular art-glass chandeliers.

"Tell Mama," she said.

He sighed and finished the cake. "It's the new Minister. He won't give me my pension unless I tell him my secret identity."

"So?" his mother said. "You're so ashamed of your parents, you'd rather starve than tell the world that their bigshot hero is Hershie Abromowicz? I, for one, wouldn't mind—finally, I could speak up when my girlfriends are going on about their sons the lawyers."

"Mom!" he said, feeling all of eight years old. "I'm not ashamed and you know it. But if the world knew who I was, well, who knows what kind of danger you'd be in? I've made some powerful enemies, Mama."

"Enemies, shmenemies," she said, waving her hands. "Don't worry yourself on my account. Don't make me the reason that you end up in the cold. I'm not helpless you know. I have Mace."

Hershie thought of the battles he'd fought: the soldiers, the mercenaries, the terrorists, the crooks and the super-crooks with their insane plots and impractical apparati. His mother was as formidable as an elderly Jewish woman with no grandchildren could be, but she was no match for automatic weapons. "I can't do it, Mama. It wouldn't be responsible. Can we drop it?"

"Fine, we won't talk about it anymore. But a mother *worries*. You're sure you don't need any money?"

He cast about desperately for a way to placate her. "I'm fine. I've got a speaking engagement lined up."

There was a message waiting on his comm when he powered it back up. A message from a relentlessly cheerful woman with a chirpy Texas accent, who identified herself as the programming coordinator for DefenseFest 33. She hoped he would return her call that night.

Hershie hovered in a dark cloud over the lake, the wind blowing his coat straight back, holding the comm in his hand. He squinted through the clouds and distance until he saw his apartment building, a row of windows lit up like teeth, his darkened window a gap in the smile. He didn't mind the cold, it was much colder in his fortress of solitude, but his apartment was more than warmth. It was his own shabby, homey corner of the hideously expensive city. On the flight from his mother's, he'd found an old-style fifty-dollar bill, folded neatly and stuck in the breast pocket of his overcoat.

He returned the phone call.

The super wasn't happy about being roused from his sitcoms, but he grudgingly allowed Hershie to squirt the rent money at his comm. He wanted to come up and take the padlock, but Hershie talked him into turning over the key, promising to return it in the morning.

His apartment was a little one-bedroom with a constant symphony of groaning radiators. Every stick of furniture in it had been rescued from kerbsides while Hershie flew his night patrols, saving chairs, sofas and even a scarred walnut armoire from the trashman.

Hershie sat at the round formica table and commed Thomas.

"It's me," he said.

"What's up?"

He didn't want to beat around the bush. "I'm speaking at DefenseFest. Then I'm going on tour, six months, speaking at military shows. It pays well. Very well." Very, very well—well enough that he wouldn't have to worry about his pension. The US-based promoters had sorted his tax status out with the IRS, who would happily exempt him, totally freeing him from entanglements with Revenue Canada. The cheerful Texan had been *glad* to do it.

He waited for Thomas's trademark stream of vitriol. It didn't come. Very quietly, Thomas said, "I see."

"Thomas," he said, a note of pleading in his voice. "It's not my choice. If I don't do this, I'll have to give Woolley my secret identity—he won't give me my pension without my Social Insurance Number."

"Or you could get a job," Thomas said, the familiar invective snarl creeping back.

"I just told you, I can't give out my SIN!"

"So have your secret identity get a job. Wash dishes!"

"If I took a job," Hershie said, palms sweating, "I'd have to give up flying patrols—I'd have to stop fighting crime."

"*Fighting crime?*" Thomas's voice was remorseless. "What *crime*? The bugouts are taking care of crime—they're making plans to shut down the *police*! Supe, you've been obsoleted."

"I know," Hershie said, self-pitying. "I know. That's why I got involved with you in the first place—I need to have a *purpose*. I'm the Super Man!"

"So your purpose is speaking to military shows? Telling the world that it still needs its arsenals, even if the bugouts have made war obsolete? Great purpose, Supe. Very noble."

He choked on a hopeless sob. "So what can I do, Thomas? I don't want to sell out, but I've got to *eat*."

"Squeeze coal into diamonds?" he said. It was teasing, but not nasty teasing. Hershie felt his tension slip: Thomas didn't hate him.

"Do you have any idea how big a piece of coal you have to start with to get even a one-carat stone? Trust me—someone would notice if entire coalfaces started disappearing."

"Look, Supe, this is surmountable. You don't have to sell out. You said it yourself, you're the Super Man—you have responsibilities. You have duties. You can't just sell out. Let's sleep on it, huh?"

Hershie was so very, very tired. It was always hardest on him when the Earth's yellow sun was hidden; the moon was a paltry substitute for its rejuvenating rays. "Let's do that," he said. "Thanks, Thomas."

DefenseFest 33 opened its doors on one of those incredibly bright March days when the snow on the ground throws back lumens sufficient to shrink your pupils to microdots. Despite the day's brightness, a bitterly cold wind scoured Front Street and the Metro Convention Centre.

From a distance, Hershie watched a demonstration muster out front of the Eaton Centre, a few kilometers north, and march down to Front Street, along their permit-proscribed route. The turnout was good, especially given the weather: about 5,000 showed up with wooly scarves and placards that the wind kept threatening to tear loose from their grasp.

The veterans marched out front, under a banner, in full uniform. Next came the Quakers, who were of the same vintage as the veterans, but dressed like elderly English professors. Next came three different Communist factions, who circulated back and forth, trying to sell each other magazines. Finally, there came the rabble: Thomas's group of harlequin-dressed anarchists; high-school students with packsacks who industriously commed their browbeaten classmates who'd elected to stay at their desks; "civilians" who'd seen a notice and come out, and tried gamely to keep up with the chanting.

The chanting got louder as they neared the security cordon around the Convention Centre. The different groups all mingled as they massed on the opposite side of the barricades. The Quakers and the vets sang "Give Peace a Chance," while Thomas and his cohort prowled around, distributing materiel to various trusted individuals.

The students hollered abuse at the attendees who were trickling into the Convention Centre in expensive overcoats, florid with expense-account breakfasts and immaculately groomed.

Hershie's appearance silenced the crowd. He screamed in over the lake, banked vertically up the side of the CN Tower, and plummeted downward. The demonstrators set up a loud cheer as he skimmed the crowd, then fell silent and aghast as he touched down on the *opposite* side of the barricade, with the convention-goers. A cop in riot-gear held the door for him and he stepped inside. A groan went up from the protestors, and swelled into a wordless, furious howl.

Hershie avoided the show's floor and headed for the green room. En route, he was stopped by a Somali general who'd been acquitted by a War Crimes tribunal, but only barely. The man greeted him like an old comrade and got his aide to snap a photo of the two of them shaking hands.

The green room was crowded with coffee-slurping presenters who pecked furiously at their comms, revising their slides. Hershie drew curious stares when he entered, but by the time he'd gotten his Danish and coffee, everyone around him was once again bent over their work, a field of balding cabbages anointed with high-tech hair-care products.

Hershie's palms were slick, his alien hearts throbbing in counterpoint. His cowlick wilted in the aggressive heat shimmering out of the vent behind his sofa. He tried to keep himself calm, but by the time a gofer commed him and squirted directions to the main ballroom, he was a wreck.

Hershie commed into the feed from the demonstration in time to see the Quakers sit, en masse, along the barricade, hands intertwined, asses soaking in the slush at the kerbside. The cops watched them impassively, and while they were distracted, Thomas gave a signal to his crew, who hastily unreeled a stories-high smartscreen, the gossamer fabric snapping taut in the wind as it unfurled over the Convention Centre's facade.

The cops were suddenly alert, moving, but Thomas was careful to keep the screen on his side of the barricade. Tina led a team of high-school students who spread out a solar collector the size and consistency of a parachute. It glinted in the harsh sun.

Szandor hastily cabled a projector/loudhailer apparatus to the collector. Szandor's dog nipped at his heels as he steadied and focused the apparatus on the screen, and Szandor plugged his comm into it and powered it up.

There was a staticky pop as the speakers came to life, loud enough to be heard over the street noise. The powerful projector beamed its image onto the screen, bright even in the midday glare.

There were hoots from the crowd as they recognised the feed: a live broadcast of the keynote addresses in the Centre. The Patron Ik'Spir Pat's hoverchair prominent. The camera lingered on the Patron's eyes, the only part of him visible from within the chair's masking infrastructure. They were startling, silvery orbs, heavy-lidded and expressionless.

The camera swung to Hershie. Szandor spat dramatically and led a chorus of hisses.

Hershie hastily closed his comm and cleared his throat, adjusted his mic, and addressed the crowd.

"Uh..." he said. His guts somersaulted. Time to go big or go home.

"Hi." That was better. "Thanks. I'm the Super Man. For years, I worked alongside UN Peacekeeping forces around the world. I hoped I was doing good work. Most of the time, I suppose I may have been."

He caught the eye of Brenda, the cheerful Texan who'd booked him in. She looked uneasy.

"There's one thing I'm certain of, though: it's that the preparation for war has never led to anything *but* war. With this show, you ladies and gentlemen are participating in a giant conspiracy to commit murder. Individually, you may not be evil, but collectively, you're the most amoral supervillain I've ever faced."

Brenda was talking frantically into her comm. His mic died. He simply expanded his mighty diaphragm and kept on speaking, his voice filling the ballroom.

"I urge you to put this behind you. We've entered into a new era in human history. The good Patron here offers the entire Universe; you scurry around, arranging the deaths of people you've never met.

"It's a terrible, stupid, mindless pursuit. You ought to be ashamed of yourselves."

With that, Hershie stepped away from the podium and walked out of the ballroom.

The camera tracked him as he made his way back through the Convention Centre, out the doors. He leapt the barricade and settled in front of the screen. The demonstrators gave him a standing ovation, and Thomas gravely shook his hand. The handshake was repeated on the giant screen behind them, courtesy of the cameraman, who had gamely vaulted the barricade as well.

The crowd danced, hugged each other, laughed. Szandor's dog bit him on the ass, and he nearly dropped the projector.

He recovered in time to nearly drop it again, as the Patron Ik'Spir Pat's hoverchair glided out the Centre's doors and made a beeline for Hershie.

Hershie watched the car approach with nauseous dread. The Patron stopped a few centimetres from him, so they were almost eyeball-to-eyeball. The hoverchair's PA popped to life, and the Patron spoke, in the bugouts' thrilling contralto.

"Thank you for your contribution," the bugout said. "It was refreshing to have another perspective presented."

Hershie tried for a heroic nod. "I'm glad you weren't offended."

"On the contrary, it was stimulating. I shall have to speak with the conference's organisers; this format seems a good one for future engagements."

Hershie felt his expression slipping, sliding towards slack-jawed incredulity. He struggled to hold it, then lost it entirely when one of the Patron's silvery eyes drooped closed in an unmistakable wink.

"Hi, Mama."

"Hershie, I just saw it on the television."

He cringed back from his comm as he shrank deeper into the corner of the Belquees that he'd moved to when his comm rang.

"Mama, it's all right. They've signed me for the full six months. I'll be fine—"

"Of course you'll be fine, bubbie. But would it kill you to brush your hair before you go on television in front of the whole world? Do you want everyone to think your mother raised a slob?"

Hershie smiled. "I will, Mama."

"I know you will, bubbie. You're a very good-looking man, you know. But no one wants to marry a man with messy hair."

"I know, Mama."

"Well, I won't keep you. Do you think you could come for dinner on Friday? I know you're busy, but your old mother won't be here forever."

He sighed his father's sigh. "I'll be there, Mama."

GRANDMA

CAROL EMSHWILLER

Move over, Frank Miller and your *The Dark Knight Returns*, with its geriatric Batman, Carol Emshwiller, the Grande Dame of weird fiction, examines the legacy of an aged superwoman.

Grandma used to be a woman of action. She wore tights. She had big boobs, but a teeny-weeny bra. Her waist used to be twenty-four inches. Before she got so hunched over she could do way more than a hundred of everything, pushups, situps, chinning.... She had naturally curly hair. Now it's dry and fine and she's a little bit bald. She wears a babushka all the time and never takes her teeth out when I'm around or lets me see where she keeps them, though of course I know. She won't say how old she is. She says the books about her are all wrong, but, she says, that's her own fault. For a long while she lied about her age and other things, too.

She used to be on every search and rescue team all across these mountains. I think she might still be able to rescue people. Small ones. Her set of weights is in the basement. She has a punching bag. She used to kick it, too, but I don't know if she can still do that. I hear her thumping and grunting around down there—even now when she needs a cane for walking. And talk about getting up off the couch!

I go down to that gym myself sometimes and try to lift those weights. I punch at her punching bag. (I can't reach it except by standing on a box. When I try to kick it, I always fall over.)

Back in the olden days Grandma wasn't as shy as she is now. How could she be and do all she did? But now she doesn't want to be a bother. She says she never wanted to be a bother, just help out is all.

She doesn't expect any of us to follow in her footsteps. She used to, but not anymore. We're a big disappointment. She doesn't say so, but we have to be. By now she's given up on all of us. Everybody has.

It started...we started with the idea of selective breeding. Everybody wanted more like Grandma: Strong, fast-thinking, fast-acting, and with the desire...that's the most important thing...a desire for her kind of life, a life of several hours in the gym every single day. Grandma loved it. She says (and says and says), "I'd turn on some banjo music and make it all into a dance."

Back when Grandma was young, offspring weren't even thought of, since who was there around good enough for her to marry? Besides, everybody thought she'd last forever. How could somebody like her get old? Is what they thought.

She had three..."husbands" they called them (donors, more like it), first a triathlon champion, then a prize fighter, then a ballet dancer.

There's this old wives' tale of skipping generations, so, after nothing good happened with her children, Grandma (and everybody else) thought, surely it would be us grandchildren. But we're a motley crew. Nobody pays any attention to us anymore.

I'm the runt. I'm small for my age, my foot turns in, my teeth stick out, I have a lazy eye... There's lots of work to be done on me. Grandma's paying for all of it though she knows I'll never amount to much of anything. I wear a dozen different kinds of braces, teeth, feet, a patch over my good eye. My grandfather, the ballet dancer!

Sometimes I wonder why Grandma does all this for me, a puny, limping, limp-haired girl. What I think is, I'm her real baby at last. They didn't let her have any time off to look after her own children—not ever until now, when she's too old for rescuing people. She not only was on all the search and rescue teams, she was a dozen search and rescue teams all by herself, and often she had to rescue the search and rescue teams.

Not only that, she also rescued animals. She always said the planet would die without its creatures. You'd see her leaping over mountains with a deer under each arm. She moved bears from campgrounds to where they wouldn't cause trouble. You'd see her with handfuls of rattlesnakes gathered from golf courses and carports, flying them off to places where people would be safe from them and they'd be safe from people.

She even tried to rescue the climate, pulling and pushing at the clouds. Holding back floods. Re-raveling the ozone. She carried huge sacks of water to the trees of one great dying forest. In the long run there was only failure. Even after all those rescues, always only failure. The bears came back. The rattlesnakes came back.

Grandma gets to thinking all her good deeds went wrong. Lots of times she had to let go and save...maybe five babies and drop three. I mean even Grandma only had two arms. She expected more of herself. I always say, "You did save lots of people. You kept that forest alive ten years longer than expected. And me. I'm saved." That always makes her laugh, and I am saved. She says, "I guess my one good eye can see well enough to look after you, you rapscallion."

She took me in after my parents died. (She couldn't save them. There are some things you just can't do anything about no matter who you are, like drunken drivers. Besides, you can't be everywhere.)

When she took me to care for, she was already feeble. We needed each other. She'd never be able to get along without me. I'm the saver of the saver.

How did we end up this way, way out here in the country with me her only helper? Did she scare everybody else off with her neediness? Or maybe people couldn't stand to see how far down she's come from what she used to be. And I suppose she had gotten difficult, but I'm used to her. I hardly notice. But she's so busy trying not to be a bother, she's a bother. I have to read her mind. When she holds her arms around herself, I get her old red sweatshirt with her emblem on the front. When she says, "Oh dear," I get her a cup of green tea. When she's on the couch and struggles and leans forward on her cane, trembling, I pull her up. She likes quiet. She likes for me to sit by her, lean against her, and listen to the birds along with her. Or listen to her stories. We don't have a radio or TV set. They conked out a long time ago, and no one thought to get us new ones, but we don't need them. We never wanted them in the first place.

Grandma sits me down beside her, the lettuce planted, the mulberries picked, sometimes a mulberry pie already made (I helped), and we just sit. "I had a grandma," she'll say, "though I know, to look at me, it doesn't seem like I could have. I'm older than more grandmas ever get to be, but we all had grandmas, even me. Picture that: Every single person in the world with a grandma." Then she giggles. She still has her girlish giggle. She says, "Mother didn't know what to make of me. I was opening her jars for her before I was three years old. Mother... Even that was a long time ago."

When she's in a sad mood, she says everything went wrong. People she had just rescued died a week later of something Grandma couldn't have helped. Hanta virus or some such that they got from vacuuming a closed room, though sometimes Grandma had just warned them not to do that. (Grandma believes in prevention as much as rescuing.)

I've rescued things. Lots of them. Nothing went wrong, either. I rescued a junco with a broken wing. After rains I've rescued stranded worms from the wet driveway and put them back in our vegetable garden. I didn't let Grandma cut the suckers off our fruit trees. I rescued mice from sticky traps. I fed a litter of feral kittens and got fleas and worms from them. Maybe this rescuing is the one part of Grandma I inherited.

Who's to say which is more worthwhile, pushing atom bombs far out into space or one of these little things I do? Well, I do know which is more important, but if I were the junco I'd like being rescued.

Sometimes Grandma goes out, though rarely. She gets to feeling it's a necessity. She wears the sunglasses and a big floppy hat and scarves that hide her wrinkled-up face and neck. She still rides a bicycle. She's so wobbly it's scary to see her trying to balance herself down the road. I can't look. She likes to bring back ice cream for me, maybe get me a comic book and a licorice stick to chew on as I read it. I suppose in town they just take her for a crazy lady, which I guess she is.

When visitors come to take a look at her, I always say she isn't home, but where else would a very, very, very old lady be but mostly home? If she knew people had come she'd have hobbled out to see them and probably scared them half to death. And they probably wouldn't have believed it was her, anyway. Only the president of the Town and Country Bank—she rescued him a long time ago—I let him in. He'll sit with her for a while. He's old, but of course not as old as she is. And he likes her for herself. They talked all through his rescue and really got to know each other back then. They talked about tomato plants and wildflowers and birds. When she rescued him they were flying up with the wild geese. (They still talk about all those geese they flew with and how exciting that was with all the honking and the sound of wings flapping right beside them. I get goosebumps—geesebumps?— just hearing them talk about it.) She should have married somebody like him, pot-belly, pock-marked face, and all. Maybe we'd have turned out better.

I guess you could say I'm the one that killed her—caused her death, anyway I don't know what got into me. Lots of times I don't know what gets into me and lots of times I kind of run away for a couple of hours. Grandma knows about it. She doesn't mind. Sometimes she even tells me, "Go on. Get out of here for a while." But this time I put on her old tights and one of the teeny-tiny bras. I don't have breasts yet so I stuffed the cups with Kleenex. I knew I couldn't do any of the things Grandma did, I just thought it would be fun to pretend for a little while.

I started out toward the hill. It's a long walk but you get to go through a batch of piñons. But first you have to go up an arroyo. Grandma's cape dragged over the rocks and sand behind me. It was heavy, too. To look at the satiny red outside you'd think it would be light, but it has a felt lining. "Warm and waterproof," Grandma said. I could hardly walk. How did she ever manage to fly around in it?

I didn't get very far before I found a jackrabbit lying in the middle of the arroyo half-dead (but half-alive, too), all bit and torn. That rabbit was a goner if I didn't rescue it. I was a little afraid because wounded rabbits bite. Grandma's cape was just the right thing to wrap it in so it wouldn't.

Those jackrabbits weigh a lot. And with the added weight of the cape...

Well, all I did was sprain my ankle. I mean I wasn't really hurt. I always have the knife Grandma gave me. I cut some strips off the cape and bound myself up good and tight. It isn't as if Grandma has a lot of capes. This is her only one. I felt bad about cutting it. I put the rabbit across my shoulders. It was slow going, but I wasn't leaving the rabbit for whatever it was to finish eating it. It began to be twilight. Grandma knows I can't see well in twilight. The trouble is, though she used to see like an eagle, Grandma can't see very well anymore either.

She tried to fly as she used to do. She did fly. For my sake. She skimmed along just barely above the sage and bitterbrush, her feet snagging at the taller ones. That was all the lift she could get. I could see, by the way she leaned and flopped like a dolphin, that she was trying to get higher. She was calling, "Sweetheart. Sweetheart. Where are yoouuu?" Her voice was almost as loud as it used to be. It echoed all across the mountains.

"Grandma, go back. I'll be all right." My voice can be loud, too.

She heard me. Her ears are still as sharp as a mule's.

The way she flew was kind of like she rides a bicycle. All wobbly. Veering off from side to side, up and down, too. I knew she would crack up. And she looked funny flying around in her print dress. She only has one costume and I was wearing it.

"Grandma, go back. Please go back."

She wasn't at all like she used to be. A little fall like that from just a few feet up would never have hurt her a couple of years ago. Or even last year. Even if, as she did, she landed on her head.

I covered her with sand and brush as best I could. No doubt whatever was about to eat the rabbit would come gnaw on her. She wouldn't mind. She always said she wanted to give herself back to the land. She used to quote, I don't know from where, "All to the soil, nothing to the grave." Getting eaten is sort of like going to the soil.

I don't dare tell people what happened—that it was all my fault—that I got myself in trouble sort of on purpose, trying to be like her, trying to rescue something.

But I'm not as sad as you might think. I knew she would die pretty soon anyway, and this is a better way than in bed looking at the ceiling, maybe in pain. If that had happened, she wouldn't have complained. She'd not have said a word, trying not to be a bother. Nobody would have known about the pain except me. I would have had to grit my teeth against her pain the whole time.

I haven't told anybody partly because I'm waiting to figure things out. I'm here all by myself, but I'm good at looking after things. There are those who check on us every weekend—people who are paid to do it. I wave at them. "All okay." I mouth it. The president of the Town and Country Bank came out once. I told him Grandma wasn't feeling well. It wasn't exactly a lie. How long can this go on? He'll be the one who finds out first—if anybody does. Maybe they won't.

I'm nursing my jackrabbit. We're friends now. He's getting better fast. Pretty soon I'll let him go off to be a rabbit. But he might rather stay here with me.

I'm wearing Grandma's costume most of the time now. I sleep in it. It makes me feel safe. I'm doing my own little rescues as usual. (The vegetable garden is full of happy weeds. I keep the bird feeder going. I leave scraps out for the skunk.) Those count—almost as much as Grandma's rescues did. Anyway, I know the weeds think so.

THE DYSTOPIANIST, THINKING OF HIS RIVAL, IS INTERRUPTED BY A KNOCK ON THE DOOR

JONATHAN LETHEM

Jonathan Lethem's most famous contribution to the superhero canon is the bestselling novel *The Fortress of Solitude*. The idea of the superhero is a manifestation of the utopian urge; wouldn't the idea of the supervillain then be an expression of the dystopian impulse?

The Dystopianist destroyed the world again that morning, before making any phone calls or checking his mail, before even breakfast. He destroyed it by cabbages. The Dystopianist's scribbling fingers pushed notes onto the page: a protagonist, someone, *a tousle-haired, well-intentioned geneticist,* had designed a new kind of cabbage for use as a safety device—*the "air bag cabbage."* The air bag cabbage mimicked those decorative cabbages planted by the sides of roads to spell names of towns, or arranged by color—red, white, and that eerie, iridescent cabbage indigo—to create American flags. It looked like any other cabbage. But underground was a network of gas-bag roots, *vast inflatable roots,* filled with pressurized air. So, *at the slightest tap,* no, more than a tap, or vandals would set them off for fun, right, *given a serious blow such as only a car traveling at thirty miles or more per hour could deliver,* the heads of the air bag cabbages would instantly inflate, drawing air from the root system, to cushion the impact of the crash, saving lives, *preventing costly property loss.* Only—

The Dystopianist pushed away from his desk, and squinted through the blinds at the sun-splashed street below. School buses lined his block every morning, like vast tipped orange-juice cartons spilling out the human vitamin of youthful lunacy, that chaos of jeering voices and dancing tangled shadows in the long morning light. The Dystopianist was hungry for breakfast. He didn't know yet how the misguided safety cabbages fucked up the world. He couldn't say *what grievous chain of circumstances* led from the *innocuous genetic novelty* to another *crushing totalitarian regime.* He didn't know what light the cabbages shed on the *death urge in human societies.* He'd work it out, though. That was his job. First Monday of each month the Dystopianist came up with his idea, the *green poison fog* or *dehumanizing fractal download* or *alienating architectural fad* which would open the way to another ruined or oppressed reality. Tuesday he began making his extrapolations, and he had the rest of the month to get it right. Today was Monday, so the cabbages were enough.

The Dystopianist moved into the kitchen, poured a second cup of coffee, and pushed slices of bread into the toaster. The *Times* Metro section headline spoke of the capture of a celebrated villain, an addict and killer who'd crushed a pedestrian's skull with a cobblestone. The Dystopianist read his paper while scraping his toast with shreds of ginger marmalade, knife rushing a little surf of butter ahead of the crystalline goo. He read intently to the end of the account, taking pleasure in the story.

The Dystopianist hated bullies. He tried to picture himself standing behind darkened glass, fingering perps in a line-up, couldn't. He tried to picture himself standing in the glare, head flinched in arrogant dejection, waiting to be fingered, but this was even more impossible. He stared at the photo of the apprehended man and unexpectedly the Dystopianist found himself thinking vengefully, hatefully, of his rival.

Once the Dystopianist had had the entire dystopian field to himself. There was just him and the Utopianists. The Dystopianist loved reading the Utopianists' stories, their dim, hopeful scenarios, which were published in magazines like *Expectant* and *Encouraging.* The Dystopianist routinely purchased them newly minted from the newsstands and perverted them the very next day in his own work, plundering the Utopianists' motifs for dark inspiration. Even the garishly sunny illustrated covers of the magazines were fuel. The Dystopianist stripped them from the magazines' spines and pinned them up over his desk, then raised his pen like Death's sickle and plunged those dreamily ineffectual worlds into ruin.

The Utopianists were older men who'd come into the field from the sciences or from academia: Professor this or that, like Dutch burghers from a cigar box. The Dystopianist had appeared in print like a rat among them, a burrowing animal laying turds on their never-to-be-realized blueprints. He liked his role. Every once in a blue moon the Dystopianist agreed to appear in public alongside the Utopianists, on a panel at a university or a conference. They loved to gather, *the fools,* in fluorescent-lit halls behind tables decorated with sweating pitchers of ice water. They were always eager to praise him in public by calling him one of their own. The Dystopianist ignored them, refusing even the water from their pitchers. He played directly to the audience members who'd come to see him, who shared his low opinion of the Utopianists. The Dystopianist could always spot his readers by their black trench coats, their acne, their greasily teased hair, their earphones, resting around their collars, trailing to Walkmans secreted in coat pockets.

The Dystopianist's rival was a Utopianist, but he wasn't like the others.

The Dystopianist had known his rival, the man he privately called *the Dire One,* since they were children like those streaming into the schoolyard below. *Eeny meeny miney moe!* they'd chanted together, each trembling in fear of being permanently "*It,*" of never casting off their permanent case of *cooties.* They weren't quite friends, but the Dystopianist and the Dire One had been bullied together by the older boys, quarantined in their shared nerdishness, forced to pool their resentments. In glum resignation they'd swapped Wacky Packages stickers and algebra homework answers, offered sticks of Juicy Fruit and squares of Now-N-Later, forging a loser's deal of consolation.

Then they were separated after junior high school, and the Dystopianist forgot his uneasy schoolmate.

It was nearly a year now since the Dire Utopianist had first arrived in print. The Dystopianist had trundled home with the latest issue of *Heartening,* expecting the usual laughs, and been blindsided instead by the Dire Utopianist's first story. The Dystopianist didn't recognize his rival by name, but he knew him for a rival instantly.

The Dire Utopianist's trick was to write in a style which was *nominally* utopian. His fantasies were nearly as credible as everyday experience, but bathed in a radiance of glory. They glowed with wishfulness. The other Utopianists' stories were crude candy floss by comparison. The Dire Utopianist's stories weren't blunt or ideological. He'd invented an *aesthetics* of utopia.

Fair enough. If he'd stopped at this burnished, closely observed dream of human life, the Dire Utopianist would be no threat. Sure, heck, let there be one genius among the Utopianists, all the better. It raised the bar. The Dystopianist took the Dire One's mimetic brilliance as a spur of inspiration: Look closer! Make it real!

But the Dire Utopianist didn't play fair. He didn't stop at utopianism, no. He poached on the Dystopianist's turf, he encroached. By limning a world so subtly transformed, so barely *nudged* into the ideal, the Dire One's fictions cast a shadow back onto the everyday. They induced a despair of inadequacy in the real. Turning the last page of one of the Dire Utopianist's stories, the reader felt a mortal pang at slipping back into his own daily life, which had been proved morbid, crushed, unfair.

This was the Dire One's pitiless art: *his utopias wrote reality itself into the most persuasive dystopia imaginable.* At the Dystopianist's weak moments he knew his stories were by comparison contrived and crotchety, their darkness forced.

It was six weeks ago that *Vivifying* had published the Dire One's photograph, and the Dystopianist had recognized his childhood acquaintance.

The Dire Utopianist never appeared in public. There was no clamor for him to appear. In fact, he wasn't even particularly esteemed among the Utopianists, an irony which rankled the Dystopianist. It was as though the Dire One didn't mind seeing his work buried in the insipid utopian magazines. He didn't seem to crave recognition of any kind, let alone the hard-won oppositional stance the Dystopianist treasured. It was almost as though the Dire One's stories, posted in public, were really private messages of reproach from one man to the other. Sometimes the Dystopianist wondered if he were in fact the *only* reader the Dire Utopianist had, and the only one he wanted.

The cabbages were hopeless, the Dystopianist saw now.

Gazing out the window over his coffee's last plume of steam at the humming, pencil-colored school buses, he suddenly understood the gross implausibility: a rapidly inflating cabbage could never have the *stopping power to alter the fatal trajectory of a careening steel egg carton full of young lives.* A cabbage might halt a Hyundai, maybe a Volvo. Never a school bus. Anyway, the cabbages as an image had no implications, no *reach*. They said nothing about mankind. They were, finally, completely stupid and lame. He gulped the last of his coffee, angrily.

He had to go deeper, find something resonant, something to crawl beneath the skin of reality and render it monstrous from within. He paced to the sink, began rinsing his coffee mug. A tiny pod of silt had settled at the bottom and now, under a jet of cold tap water, the grains rose and spread and danced, a model of chaos. The Dystopianist retraced his seed of inspiration: *well-intentioned, bumbling geneticist,* good. Good enough. The geneticist needed to stumble onto something better, though.

One day, when the Dystopianist and the Dire Utopianist had been in the sixth grade at Intermediate School 293, cowering together in a corner of the schoolyard to duck sports and fights and girls in one deft multipurpose cower, they had arrived at a safe island of mutual interest: comic books, Marvel brand, which anyone who read them understood weren't comic at all but deadly, breathtakingly serious. Marvel constructed worlds of splendid complexity, full of chilling, ancient villains and tormented heroes, in richly unfinished story lines. There in the schoolyard, wedged for cover behind the girls' lunch-hour game of hopscotch, the Dystopianist declared his favorite character: Doctor Doom, antagonist of the Fantastic Four. Doctor Doom wore a forest green cloak and hood over a metallic slitted mask and armor. He was a dark king who from his gnarled castle ruled a city of hapless serfs. An imperial, self-righteous monster. The Dire Utopianist murmured his consent. Indeed, Doctor Doom was awesome, an honorable choice. The Dystopianist waited for the Dire Utopianist to declare his favorite.

"Black Bolt," said the Dire Utopianist.

The Dystopianist was confused. Black Bolt wasn't a villain or a hero. Black Bolt was part of an outcast band of mutant characters known as the Inhumans, the noblest among them. He was their leader, but he never spoke. His only *demonstrated* power was flight, but the whole point of Black Bolt was the power he restrained himself from using: speech. The sound of his voice was cataclysmic, an unusable weapon, like an atomic bomb. If Black Bolt ever uttered a syllable the world would crack in two. Black Bolt was leader in absentia much of the time—he had a tendency to exile himself from the scene, to wander distant mountaintops contemplating... What? His curse? The things he would say if he could safely speak?

It was an unsettling choice there, amidst the feral shrieks of the schoolyard. The Dystopianist changed the subject, and never raised the question of Marvel Comics with the Dire Utopianist again. Alone behind the locked door of his bedroom the Dystopianist studied Black Bolt's behavior, seeking hints of the character's appeal to his schoolmate. Perhaps the answer lay in a story line elsewhere in the Marvel universe, one where Black Bolt shucked off his pensiveness to function as an unrestrained hero or villain. If so, the Dystopianist never found the comic book in question.

Suicide, the Dystopianist concluded now. The geneticist should be studying suicide, seeking to isolate it as a factor in the human genome. "The Sylvia Plath Code," that might be the title of the story. The geneticist could be trying to *reproduce it in a nonhuman species.* Right, good. To breed for suicide in animals, to produce a creature with the impulse to take its own life. That had the relevance the Dystopianist was looking for. What animals? Something poignant and pathetic, something pure. Sheep. *The Sylvia Plath Sheep,* that was it.

A variant of sheep had been bred for the study of suicide. The Sylvia Plath Sheep had to be kept on close watch, like a prisoner stripped of sharp implements, shoelaces, and belt. And the Plath Sheep escapes, right, of course, *a Frankenstein creature always escapes,* but the twist is that the Plath Sheep is dangerous only to itself. *So what?* What harm if a single sheep quietly, discreetly offs itself? *But the Plath Sheep,* scribbling fingers racing now, the Dystopianist was on fire, *the Plath Sheep turns out to have the gift of communicating its despair.* Like the monkeys on that island, who learned from one another to wash clams, or break them open with coconuts, whatever it was the monkeys had learned, look into it later, *the*

Plath Sheep evoked suicide in other creatures, all up and down the food chain. Not humans, but anything else that crossed its path. Cats, dogs, cows, beetles, clams. Each creature would spread suicide to another, to five or six others, before *searching out a promontory from which to plunge to its death.* The human species would be powerless to reverse the craze, the epidemic of suicide among the nonhuman species of the planet.

Okay! Right! Let goddamn Black Bolt open his mouth and sing an aria—he couldn't halt the Plath Sheep in its *deadly spiral of despair!*

The Dystopianist suddenly had a vision of the Plath Sheep wandering its way into the background of one of the Dire One's tales. It would go unremarked at first, a bucolic detail. Unwrapping its bleak gift of *global animal suicide* only after it had been taken entirely for granted, just as the Dire One's own little nuggets of despair were smuggled innocuously into his utopias. The Plath Sheep was a bullet of pure dystopian intention. The Dystopianist wanted to fire it in the Dire Utopianist's direction. Maybe he'd send this story to *Encouraging.*

Even better, he'd like it if he could send the Plath Sheep itself to the door of the Dire One's writing room. *Here's your tragic mute Black Bolt, you bastard!* Touch its somber muzzle, dry its moist obsidian eyes, runny with sleep goo. Try to talk it down from the parapet, if you have the courage of your ostensibly rosy convictions. Explain to the Sylvia Plath Sheep why life is worth living. Or, failing that, let the sheep convince you to follow it up to the brink, and go. You and the sheep, pal, take a fall.

There was a knock on the door.

The Dystopianist went to the door and opened it. Standing in the corridor was a sheep. The Dystopianist checked his watch—nine forty-five. He wasn't sure why it mattered to him what time it was, but it did. He found it reassuring. The day still stretched before him; he'd have plenty of time to resume work after this interruption. He still heard the children's voices leaking in through the front window from the street below. The children arriving now were late for school. There were always hundreds who were late. He wondered if the sheep had waited with the children for the crossing guard to wave it on. He wondered if the sheep had crossed at the green, or recklessly dared the traffic to kill it.

He'd persuaded himself that the sheep was voiceless. So it was a shock when it spoke. "May I come in?" said the sheep.

"Yeah, sure," said the Dystopianist, fumbling his words. Should he offer the sheep the couch, or a drink of something? The sheep stepped into the apartment, just far enough to allow the door to be closed behind it, then stood quietly working its nifty little jaw back and forth, and blinking. Its eyes were not watery at all.

"So," said the sheep, nodding its head at the Dystopianist's desk, the mass of yellow legal pads, the sharpened pencils bunched in their holder, the typewriter. "This is where the magic happens." The sheep's tone was wearily sarcastic.

"It isn't usually *magic*," said the Dystopianist, then immediately regretted the remark.

"Oh, I wouldn't say that," said the sheep, apparently unruffled. "You've got a few things to answer for."

"Is that what this is?" said the Dystopianist. "Some kind of reckoning?"

"Reckoning?" The sheep blinked as though confused. "Who said anything about a reckoning?"

"Never mind," said the Dystopianist. He didn't want to put words into the sheep's mouth. Not now. He'd let it represent itself, and try to be patient.

But the sheep didn't speak, only moved in tiny, faltering steps on the carpet, advancing very slightly into the room. The Dystopianist wondered if the sheep might be scouting for sharp corners on the furniture, for chances to do itself harm by butting with great force against his fixtures.

"Are you—very depressed?" asked the Dystopianist.

The sheep considered the question for a moment. "I've had better days, let's put it that way."

Finishing the thought, it stared up at him, eyes still dry. The Dystopianist met its gaze, then broke away. A terrible thought occurred to him: the sheep might be expecting *him* to relieve it of its life.

The silence was ponderous. The Dystopianist considered another possibility. Might his rival have come to him in disguised form?

He cleared his throat before speaking. "You're not, ah, the Dire One, by any chance?" The Dystopianist was going to be awfully embarrassed if the sheep didn't know what he was talking about.

The sheep made a solemn, wheezing sound, like *Hurrrrhh.* Then it said, "I'm *dire* all right. But I'm hardly the only one."

"Who?" blurted the Dystopianist.

"Take a look in the mirror, friend."

"What's your point?" The Dystopianist was sore now. If the sheep thought he was going to be manipulated into suicide it had *another think coming.*

"Just this: How many sheep have to die to assuage your childish resentments?" Now the sheep assumed an odd false tone, bluff like that of a commercial pitchman: *"They laughed when I sat down at the Dystopiano! But when I began to play—"*

"Very funny."

"We try, we try. Look, could you at least offer me a dish of water or something? I had to take the stairs—couldn't reach the button for the elevator."

Silenced, the Dystopianist hurried into the kitchen and filled a shallow bowl with water from the tap. Then, thinking twice, he poured it back into the sink and replaced it with mineral water from the bottle in the door of his refrigerator. When he set it out the sheep lapped gratefully, steadily, seeming to the Dystopianist an animal at last.

"Okay." It licked its lips. "That's it, Doctor Doom. I'm out of here. Sorry for the intrusion, next time I'll call. I just wanted, you know—a look at you."

The Dystopianist couldn't keep from saying, "You don't want to die?"

"Not today," was the sheep's simple reply. The Dystopianist stepped carefully around the sheep to open the door, and the sheep trotted out. The Dystopianist trailed it into the corridor and summoned the elevator. When the cab arrived and the door opened the Dystopianist leaned in and punched the button for the lobby.

"Thanks," said the sheep. "It's the little things that count."

The Dystopianist tried to think of a proper farewell, but couldn't before the elevator door shut. The sheep was facing the rear of the elevator cab, another instance of its poor grasp of etiquette.

Still, the sheep's visit wasn't the worst the Dystopianist could imagine. It could have attacked him, or tried to gore itself on his kitchen knives. The Dystopianist was still proud of the Plath Sheep, and rather glad to have met it, even if the Plath Sheep wasn't proud of him. Besides, the entire episode had only cost the Dystopianist an hour or so of his time. He was back at work, eagerly scribbling out implications, extrapolations, another illustrious downfall, well before the yelping children reoccupied the schoolyard at lunchtime.

SEX DEVIL
JACK PENDARVIS

Absurdist Jack Pendarvis (*The Mysterious Secret of the Valuable Treasure*, etc.) shows us mere mortals how to pitch a superhero comics series to potential publishers.

*G*entlemen:

I would like to give you my idea for one of your comic books. Well it is not one of your comic books yet, but it soon will be! I call my idea Sex Devil.

Sex Devil starts out as a normal high school student. Unfortunately his fellow classmates do not think he is normal. For you see, Sex Devil (real name Randy White) has a cleft palate.

Sex Devil attempts to get his fellow classmates to like him. Unfortunately he pretends that he knows karate, which is a lie. Sex Devil's lies are soon discovered. After that his fellow classmates put a thing on the blackboard. It is a picture of Sex Devil (I mean Randy White) with slanting eyes, which he does not have. Underneath the picture it says Wandy Wite, Kawate Kiwwah. Also there is a bubble coming out of Randy White's mouth. Randy White is saying WAH!

A school janitor sees Randy White's humiliation. After school the janitor who is Asian American pulls Randy White to the side. Randy White is apprehensive yet he follows the school janitor to his creepy shack. Underground beneath the shack there is a training facility for a rare form of karate called Jah-Kwo-Ton. Randy White goes there every day and learns how to fight Jah-Kwo-Ton style which nobody else in America knows except the janitor.

The janitor has vowed not to fight because he accidentally killed a man once. He has also made Randy White swear not to defend the janitor in case anything happens to him. The janitor has learned to accept his fate.

One day the same classmates who pick on Randy White accidentally kill the janitor. Well it is partially on purpose and partially on accident. Randy White attempts to aid the janitor but the janitor tells him to remember his vow. Randy White remembers his vow. Now his classmates assume that Randy White is more cowardly than ever.

Now we go forward into the future. Sex Devil can afford the right kind of medical insurance to where his cleft palate can be surgically fixed. While he is pretending to be Randy White he continues to talk like he has a cleft palate. This is just to conceal his secret identity.

All of the boys of Sex Devil's high school class have grown into manhood to become a criminal organization. They run the city under cover of darkness, plotting fake terrorist plots to keep the city in turmoil while they make their robberies. As a result some innocent Arab Americans get sent to prison.

Sex Devil is the prison psychiatrist for the innocent Arab Americans. They can tell that Sex Devil is their friend. The Arab Americans instruct Sex Devil in the ways of a secret cult to where Sex Devil now has ultimate control over his body. Now Sex Devil is an expert in two different secret cults of ancient lore. He is also a trained psychiatrist with mastery over the human mind. No one can match his prowess based on his unique balance of science, skill and sorcery.

Sex Devil finds out from the Arab Americans that the very same people who framed them are the same people who used to pick on Sex Devil all the time. Sex Devil vows revenge.

One night he goes undercover at the chemical factory of his old enemy, who now goes by the name of Black Friday. In the middle of a fight where Black Friday unfairly uses guns Sex Devil gets chemicals spilled on his genital region. Black Friday uses the opportunity to get away.

Sex Devil retreats to his underground lair, which is located beneath the janitor shack. He examines his genital region and discovers that his genital region now has amazing powers. Combined with the bodily control he has learned from the Arab Americans now Sex Devil realizes he has a unique opportunity.

Sex Devil starts out by dating Black Friday's girlfriend. This is the same girl that used to make fun of Sex Devil but she doesn't know it is the same person because he talks completely different.

First Sex Devil takes Jennifer to a nice restaurant. Jennifer is impressed by Sex Devil's worldly manners. Because of his secret mastery of bodily control he is also the best dancer anyone has ever seen. It is the greatest date ever. Jennifer asks Sex Devil if he wants to come up for some coffee. Sex Devil jokes, who knows where that will lead. Sex Devil leaves politely without taking advantage of Jennifer.

When Sex Devil gets home he has about six or seven phone calls from Jennifer on his answering machine. Please Sex Devil, I need to see you.

Sex Devil goes back over to Jennifer's apartment. On the way he stops and buys some flowers. Then he climbs up a drainpipe and enters Jennifer"s bedroom.

Jennifer thanks Sex Devil for the flowers. They are so beautiful Sex Devil. Black

Friday never buys me flowers. Sex Devil says enough of this talk. Then Sex Devil and Jennifer have intimacy.

Black Friday wonders what is wrong with Jennifer. She seems to be distracted all the time. He does not know she is secretly thinking of her intimacy with Sex Devil. Jennifer refuses to have intimacy with Black Friday. Intimacy with Black Friday has become hollow. Nothing can compare to the amazing powers of Sex Devil's genital region.

Black Friday becomes depressed. Black Friday loses his ability to have intimacy. He must see a psychiatrist. Get me the best psychiatrist in the city! Little does he realize it is Sex Devil.

Black Friday unburdens the problems of his soul to Sex Devil. On the outside Sex Devil is concerned. On the inside Sex Devil is ha ha ha!

Black Friday can no longer do his criminal activities because he has lost all worth of himself as a human being. Black Friday can no longer perform intimacy because of his crippling depression. Every time Black Friday leaves the house Sex Devil comes over and has intimacy with Jennifer. Please Sex Devil I love you, can't we get married? No, Jennifer, I am married to my work.

At the end of the first issue Black Friday falls off a cliff. Now Sex Devil must go to work on the rest of the class. At the end of every issue one of Sex Devil's fellow classmates falls off a cliff or is caught in the gears of a large machine or blows themself up in an explosion or capsizes or a similar disaster. Or they are in a submarine that slowly fills up with water. It is never Sex Devil's fault but he doesn't feel bad about it because they are getting what they deserve. Every time Jennifer is like please won't you spend the whole night Sex Devil? What is with all this wham bam thank you mam. And Sex Devil is like maybe some other time baby. Because Sex Devil has more important things on his mind. And Jennifer is like I am starting to think you are just using me for intimacy like a hor. And Sex Devil is like now you are getting the picture baby.

In conclusion I hope you will start making the comic book Sex Devil because it deals with issues that young people care about today.

THE DEATH TRAP OF DR. NEFARIO

BENJAMIN ROSENBAUM

Short-fiction writer Benjamin Rosenbaum (*The Ant King and Other Stories*) doesn't exactly name names, but we know who he's talking about, don't we?

The phone rang at 3 a.m., and Hannah said, "Oh God!" It rang as if to prove her point: that I was working too hard, allowing my clients to call me at all hours, leaving no space for her. That's why we were up at 3 a.m.: we were fighting.

"I have to take this call, Hannah," I said. "Let's finish talking about this later, maybe tomorrow."

"I don't see the point," she said. "You don't listen. Fine, take it. I'm going to sleep." She walked into the bedroom and slammed the door behind her.

I pressed the GO button on the phone and said, "This is Dr. Goodman."

"Hi, Doc, sorry about the hour, but I'm really upset."

"No problem, Dick," I said. Dick was one of my somewhat unusual clients, a celebrity crimefighter—a very successful and accomplished person, who had made great progress on some difficult memories during the year we'd been working together. "What's on your mind?"

"I'm just feeling all this resentment against Bruce coming up again." I settled onto the leather couch and said, "I'm glad you're telling me."

"I'm so tired of feeling this way."

"Yes," I said. "So what triggered it this time?"

"Well, I'm currently trapped in one of Dr. Nefario's death traps..."

"Really? Are you safe?"

"Well, you know, Doc, safe is a relative thing in my profession, but I have you on the headset, and I'm picking the lock on these handcuffs as we're talking. I think I'll be fine, the piranhas are still five or six feet below me."

"All right, but isn't our conversation going to distract you?" I asked. "I know you're upset, but wouldn't you rather call back at another time?"

"I'd really like to talk about it, Doc. I always find talking to you clears my mind and makes me more effective. I may need to go if the henchmen come back, though."

"All right, as long as you're sure you're acting appropriately in your current environment. I trust you to make that decision. So how did this trigger your feelings of resentment?"

"Well, the thing is, it's kind of funny, but this is the exact same death trap Dr. Nefario had us in—Bruce and me, I mean—God, it must have been eighteen years ago. I was really just a kid. I was scared, frankly, and I suggested that when we got out, we should make a run for it, you know, go back to base and regroup. And he just laughed at me, you know, 'don't worry, little fella, we'll be out of this in a jiffy!' And I clammed right up. I had to run along after him and fight off the lesser henchmen while he captured Dr. Nefario, and I'd just had enough, you know? I was scared and I wanted to go home and curl up with a good book. It was a school night, too, that was also typical. Other guys were going to parties and on dates and I was slugging it out with men in rubber suits."

"And you didn't feel you had any choice in the matter."

"Not really. I mean, it's not like he would have forced me to stay, but it was so important to me to have his approval, and he was so stingy with it."

There was a clanging sound.

"What was that?" I asked. "Do you have to go?"

"No, that was just me crawling into the ventilation system, I got the handcuffs off."

"I'm relieved. Go on."

"That was the only time I felt I got any approval, you know, if I took out several henchmen on my own, then occasionally, and I mean occasionally, I'd hear 'Good hit.' Or that post-combat glow, you know, with groaning, injured criminals lying around us, sometimes then he'd put a hand on my shoulder and grin at me. The rest of the time he was so demanding and repressed."

"I'm glad you're telling me these feelings."

I could hear Hannah in the other room, getting ready for bed. She'd be taking off her stockings now. Thirty years of marriage, and I still wanted to be in there watching her take off her stockings.

"Dick, I find it striking that you're in such a similar situation today as you were then. Did you go out tonight to win Bruce's approval as well?"

"I don't know. No, I don't think so. I do feel like I have to stop Dr. Nefario. I know we've talked about this and maybe my sense of personal obligation is exaggerated, but..." He sighed. "Also, I enjoy my work. So much of law enforcement is bureaucratic drudgery, I feel really privileged to occupy the niche I do."

"When you used to go out crimefighting—is that the right word, crime-fighting?"

"Sure."

"Did anyone else ever come along with you and Bruce?"

"Sometimes. He had some friends, you know, other celebrities. You'd recognize the names."

"What about other helpers? Did anyone ever apply for your job, as it were?"

"Sure, we got tons of letters, some even from gymnasts and prizefighters and so on, but he always laughed them off."

"Dick, I think you know how much I appreciate the difficult aspects of your young adulthood, and the ways it was exceptional, and I want to emphasize that the feelings of resentment you have about it are perfectly appropriate and understandable. At the same time, I want to offer you a different perspective."

"Okay."

"You spoke about how Bruce was stingy with approval. Now, he's a very unusual character, very suited to the job he has, possibly less suited to other jobs—like being an adoptive father. You might want to consider that he had other ways of communicating approval—maybe ways that weren't effective at the time, but if you go back and look at them, approval was there."

"Like what?"

"Well, considering how picky he was with who he took along, didn't those very invitations to come crimefighting on a school night express a lot of approval?"

There was a long silence. I wondered if I'd pushed too far. "Dick?" I asked.

"Sorry, Doc, I just had to reprogram this access lock. I'm at Dr. Nefario's command center, so I'll have to go in a few seconds."

"All right."

"I guess you're right, Doc. I mean, I know Bruce picked me to train, he took me in, he must have been proud of me. But I don't feel it. It's like he was... proud of himself for picking such a great ward. But he didn't..." He sniffed and then stopped. I couldn't even hear him breathing.

"He didn't what?"

"I wonder if Dr. Nefario's goons have glue guns?" he said hoarsely. "I didn't pack any anti-glue tonight."

"Dick, what were you just going to say? He didn't what?"

"I could make some anti-glue out of a gas mask filter and some super solvent..."

"Dick..."

"But I only brought one gas mask."

"Dick, what were you going to say?"

"About what?"

"You said, Bruce was proud of himself for picking such a great ward, but he didn't...what?"

"Oh, that."

"Yes. Please go on."

"That was stupid anyway."

I squeezed my eyes shut and massaged the bridge of my nose with my thumb and forefinger. "Dick, didn't you say you were going to have to go in a few seconds?"

"Yeah. I guess." He sounded like a sullen teenager.

"So do we need to wrap this up?"

I could sense him shrugging. "Whatever. I don't even feel like going in there."

"But Dick...aren't they going to find you?"

"No, they're all busy with the Shrink Ray."

"The Shrink Ray?"

"Yeah, Dr. Nefario is going to shrink the city, put it in a bottle, and auction it off online."

I felt myself squeezing the cell phone tighter. "Well...don't you need to stop him?"

"You were the one who said my personal sense of responsibility is exaggerated. Someone will handle it. There's no shortage of us."

I took a deep breath. Somehow, I was not being effective in this situation. I was finding Dick childish. I wasn't giving him the empathy he needed and deserved. I took another deep breath.

"You okay, Doc? You're breathing heavily."

"Dick, I don't think what you were going to say was stupid. I think it's very important. That's what makes it so hard to say. As long as you can't say what you feel about Bruce, it owns you. Once you say it, you begin to own it."

"He didn't love me," Dick said, and burst out crying.

The door to the bedroom opened and Hannah said, "This is your last chance, Gabe Goodman. I'm turning out the light."

I stabbed the mute button with my thumb. "Hannah, please! I've told you never to interrupt me when I'm on the phone with a client!"

"Oh of course, I forgot, the clients always come first."

"This particular client is in a life-or-death situation!"

Hannah looked tired. "When are they not, Gabe? When are they not?" She went into the bedroom and shut the door softly.

"Doc," Dick said hoarsely, "it sounds like you've got to go."

I looked down at the phone display. It appeared I'd missed the mute button. I lowered my forehead into the palm of my hand. Now I felt like crying. "Never mind, Dick. Please go on."

"No, Doc, you listen to me. That was your wife, right?"

"Yes, that was my wife."

"Well it doesn't sound like she's so happy about your clients calling you in the middle of the night."

"Dick, please, that's between me and Mrs. Goodman. Let's move on."

"No, let's not move on! Why should you let me break up your marriage, Doc? The work always comes first, is that it?"

"Dick—"

"You're just like Bruce!"

"Did the work always come first with Bruce?"

"It sure as hell did! It came before everything! It came first and last, and I just couldn't take that anymore, and that's why I left, Doc! That's why! I wanted a more balanced life!"

To my astonishment, we were getting somewhere. "Do you feel guilty about leaving Bruce?"

He paused. "Yeah." He sounded surprised. "Yeah, I guess I do."

"Let's talk about that."

"No, Doc, let's not talk about that, because in a minute you and your cell phone are going to be really small and then your voice will be really high-pitched and tinny and it'll be hard to take you seriously as a therapist."

I cleared my throat. "All right."

"Doc, do you love your wife?"

I was surprised to find tears in my eyes. "I do, Dick, I really do."

"Then you go do something about that, and I'll handle Dr. Nefario. See you on Friday."

"Goodbye, Dick. Be careful."

I stayed on the line for a minute, listening to the *Bang!* and *Kapow!* sounds, and then I hung up and went into the bedroom. Hannah was reading.

"I'm a stubborn bastard, Hannah," I said.

"Yes, you are." She put her book down. "I'm sorry I interrupted your call. I just don't know how to get through to you anymore."

I sat at the edge of the bed. "Hannah, I love you."

She blinked. Her face softened, but she shook her head. "I love you too, Gabe. But we've got problems."

I took her hands in mine. "What do you say we go away next weekend? Just the two of us. I'll leave my cell phone here, and tell my clients that."

She shrugged. "It's a start."

We were still normal-sized. Our voices weren't high-pitched and tinny. I leaned down and kissed her on the forehead. She smirked at me. "There are people with bigger problems," I said. My intention was to reassure her, or perhaps myself.

She yanked her hands out from mine. "I'm sure there are! But that doesn't change the size of ours! Jesus, Gabe, there you go again!" I started to cry. Despite my recognition of its therapeutic value, I don't in fact cry myself all that often. I put my face in my hands. Hannah pulled me into her embrace. "Oh, come on," she said.

"I don't want to lose you," I sobbed. "I'm a lousy husband."

"Yes, sometimes," she said. "But you're a great therapist."

"No, I'm a lousy therapist too! That was a fiasco. I almost got us all shrunk."

"Cut it out!" Hannah said. "What are you talking about? Look at all the issues these people have—the body image issues, the megalomania, the post-traumatic stress—the childhoods they had, for God's sake! These are hard clients, Gabe. They're all teetering on the border of nuts to begin with, and then they get mind-swapped or kidnapped by robots every month. Half of them can't have sex without worrying about burning or crushing someone to death. They're lonely and scared and everyone expects them to act confident all the time. You hold them together, Gabe, and that means you hold this city together. Listen to me. I'm proud of you. You're my hero."

I cried harder. I cried for a while. Hannah's body was soft and warm against mine. Finally I stopped and Hannah wiped my cheeks and nose with a Kleenex.

"You want my theory?" she asked. Her eyes twinkled. "I think you spend so much time with your clients because their lives are so full of action."

"Maybe," I sniffled.

"So I think you need some more action yourself. Get in bed, Gabe Goodman. And leave the light on."

I was happy to comply.

MAN OH MAN—IT'S MANNA MAN
GEORGE SINGLETON

Although superheroes, or at least proto-superheroes, debuted more than a century ago, the archetype took root with the back-to-back double whammy of the Great Depression and the Second World War. The genre then floundered for a decade or so before being reenergized and given more permanent footing by another back-to-back double whammy: the Space Age and Pop Art. Since then, superheroes have stayed with us always, adapting and evolving along with the larger culture. George Singleton's "Man Oh Man—It's Manna Man," for example, is a product of the Information Age.

Janie Satterfield does not recalculate. She tries to block out the howling dogs and cats. There's enough money for a week of food—two weeks if a Christian Youth Group comes in and adopts half the strays. Sometimes she dreams of this: If every Boy and Girl Scout troop in the country adopted one dog or cat, then the number of strays would decrease somewhat. Not much, but a little. If every elementary school in America adopted a mascot. If every hospital. If every retirement home. Janie keeps a notebook of people and organizations that she thinks might help control the pet population in America. If every contestant on a game show, if every person who worried about getting into Heaven, if every church and synagogue and mosque, if every prison.

The telephone rings. Janie does not answer. It'll be one of her volunteers from the Junior League calling to cancel, she knows. Every day, it seems, one of her volunteers calls, faking a cough, saying that she doesn't want to bring the flu into the kennel area.

The machine beeps. An older woman says, "I hope I got the right number. I'm calling to donate. I can do the five-dollar-a-week program. Just tell me where to send it." The woman leaves her telephone number and address. Janie stares at the answering machine.

The phone rings again and, thinking that it's probably the older woman calling to say she misdialed earlier, Janie answers with "Graywood County Humane Society."

"Yes. I'm calling to offer my donation," a man says. "I'd like to send a hundred dollars to you."

Line two, then line three rings. Janie brightens her voice. She says, "That's so kind of you, sir," and gives him the post office box address.

And it happens and it happens and it happens. For six straight hours Janie Satterfield picks up the phone, takes donations, and at the end of the day she's been promised more than a hundred thousand dollars. And she is amazed to learn that a television evangelist, one Reverend Leroy Jenkins, has directed all of his listeners to donate to the Graywood Humane Society.

"I need to write Reverend Jenkins a thank-you card," she says to herself, still alone without a volunteer. She steps into the kennel area and says to her barking strays, "Maybe we'll take a photograph of us all and send it to Reverend Jenkins."

Janie had never heard of this particular television evangelist.

And she'd never heard of Manna Man, working his powers, redirecting.

Manna Man checks the internet. He glances over the Local sections of over three hundred smalltown weekly newspapers to which he subscribes. He takes notes. He categorizes, and tries not to make assumptions. The mail carrier detests Manna Man. The mail carrier comes home on Thursdays and asks his wife if she'll keep quiet should Ben Culler's house burn down mysteriously one night soon.

The food bank will close in midwinter, right when it needs to be most available. For three years Lloyd Driggers has operated the food bank on Wednesday and Saturday mornings, doling out canned goods, bread, and milk in large paper bags. He does not question anyone in regard to hunger or thirst. He makes no judgments. Unfortunately, the donations have dwindled. Area preachers have hinted, then outright demanded, that their congregants give to their *own* soup kitchens, their *own* food banks. The preachers have said things like, "Why would you give your hard-earned money and canned yams to an organization that doesn't even try to save the unsaved? Lloyd Driggers doesn't offer testimonials. No, he just hands out food. That's not enough!"

The congregants listened, as congregants do.

Lloyd Driggers's shelves soon went empty. He spent his savings. He went into his IRA and bought groceries on a weekly basis—one thousand dollars every Tuesday to help feed the homeless, the unemployed, the working poor. He sold his house and moved into his food bank space—which used to be a two-bay Gulf service station back in the 1960s. His two children—son and daughter—talked between themselves often about how they would need to take their father in soon, how he'd never recovered from their mother's long-term illness and subsequent death.

The electricity would be cut first, then the water. When the electricity went, so would his telephone.

"Food bank," Lloyd says.

"Yessir. Is this Lloyd Driggers?"

"Polk County Food Bank, Lloyd Driggers speaking."

The man on the other end clears his throat. "I can give five dollars a week. I'd like to do more, but you know my medicine's costing me. But I can do five dollars a week." The man asks where to send his money.

And the phone rings again and again until finally Lloyd asks a young girl with a full piggy bank, "How did you get this number?"

"My grandma told me to call. She wants to talk to you next."

"Your grandmother gave you this number?"

"No sir. The preacher man on TV gave out this number. He told us to send you money."

Lloyd thinks, Preacher man? He thinks, Maybe all these preachers have understood their wrong-headed actions of the past.

The grandmother gets on the phone and says, "We was watching one them evangelists like we always do on channel 17 and he says for us to send directly to you. He says it'll get us one more smile from the Lord."

"Which preacher?" Lloyd asks. "From around here?"

"No, no, no. The one out in Oklahoma. The one with the hair."

Lloyd Driggers has never heard of the hairy preacher from Oklahoma.

He has not heard of Manna Man, either.

It's so easily done these days, with high-definition television, Manna Man thinks. This is so much easier than having to attend the tent revivals—feigning a limp, a goiter, a lack of speech, blindness, bad blood, invisible afflictions of the major organs—and finding a reason to touch the evangelist's throat.

Now he doesn't have to invest in cheap polyester suits. Now Manna Man can wear his superhero attire at home in front of a bank of Sonys—six across and three high—all tuned to different TV evangelists' separate networks.

He works in his boxer shorts most days.

He keeps Icy Hot and Ben Gay available to keep his elbows loose, his wrists malleable, his fingers scalding hot.

Herbert Kirby has the paperwork. He's built one prototype and seeks funding. There are only a handful of scientists and dendrologists out there who believe in him—that his machine can turn pine sap into fresh drinking water without killing off the trees. Herbert Kirby's even proven that a strong evergreen grows stronger after being "slightly fondled" by his sap-into-water contraption. He likens the process to blood-letting, to frost hardening.

Of course most people think he's insane. And then there's the bottled-water industry executives who understand the consequences of a mass-produced potable drinking water apparatus.

"Make sure it's in my obituary," Herbert tells his wife and children. "Make sure it reads 'This man could've saved the entire drought-stricken West Coast and southeastern United States, but greedy capitalists kept him from being a savior.'"

His relatives don't believe him. "It's one of the first signs of dementia," his forty-six-year-old son, Herb Junior, says. "Visions of martyrdom. Visions of grandeur. Visions. There should be some kind of law that no one is allowed to have visions past the age of fifty, especially if said person used to be a car mechanic, precomputers."

Herb Junior works as an optician. He works inside a Wal-Mart and pretends to know what he's talking about when customers ask him questions concerning glaucoma, cataracts, and conjunctivitis.

Manna Man understands, though. Manna Man read a human interest story in the weekly *Forty-Five Platter*, and studied up on the molecular structure of tree sap. He gazed at Herbert Kirby Senior standing in front of his machine, which looked more or less like an iron lung, or an old-fashioned sauna.

When Herbert Kirby's telephone rings back in his workshop—and no one ever calls the number, not even his wife—he picks it up and says, "Yeah."

Is it really Donald Trump? And later, is it really Oprah, Bill Gates, Warren Buffet, the director of the Kellogg Foundation? If Herbert Kirby only knew. He gives out his address. He says that most of his backers send cashier's checks. "I'll send you the first case of sap-to-water, free of charge," he says. Up until this point he'd only said those words to his dog.

Manna Man will never know the consequences. He will never ask, What were those people doing watching TV evangelists?

*At night Manna Man dreams of people skipping in fields, down country dirt roads,
down sidewalks, across water. On the horizon, though, there's always a balding man
wearing a checkered coat, his deep-set eyes as hollow and vacant as doughnuts riding
a conveyor belt toward a faulty jelly-filler nipple. In the dreams he knows that it's his
nemesis.*

*He knows it's the exact opposite of Manna Man, from a parallel universe. Or from
an alternate universe. He can never remember if those two terms are synonymous.*

Ben Culler's father suffered from psychosomatic pains that left his right arm
limp and useless. A religious man, he went to a traveling preacher's faith-healing
revival outside of Decatur, Alabama, walked up on the stage, and spoke into the
microphone. He'd said, "I got my arm crushed back at the quarry. It ain't worked
since. *I* ain't worked since, either."

The preacher slayed him in the spirit, right in front of everyone. He shoved
his shirt cuff, doused in ether, right up into Ben Culler's fake-lame father's face.
Mr. Culler went down in a pile. And when he regained consciousness he pushed
himself off of the makeshift wooden stage built of scavenged pallets, lifted both
arms in the air, and said, "Thank you, Jesus, my arms's been reborned!"

The Alabamans danced and gyrated and praised Jesus and spoke in tongues.
They held their arms up high, too. They cried, and begged for mercy, and—if the
scene had been captured on silent film—did not act dissimilarly to Turkish Sufi
dervishes.

That night at home, Ben Culler's father raised his right arm up high to his son
and said, "You been getting away with way too much, and now Jesus has come
to the rescue. I guess God's telling me that I got to make up for lost time." He
struck his son across the face. His second hard blow landed on the boy's solar
plexus. Ben Culler yelled out for his runaway mother. He did not have time to
form tears.

His father's third forceful open-handed blow caught Ben just south of his
thyroid cartilage—this may have been from where Manna Man's powers sprang.

The fourth roundhouse didn't land. Ben Culler caught his father's wrist and
squeezed it with superhuman strength. His father fell to his knees in much the
same manner as when he was slayed in the spirit earlier that day. Before his
father expired on the kitchen floor of their trailer, Ben Culler said, "You will not

strike me. You will not take my lawnmowing money and give it to scam artist preachers. You will not be a vengeful Christian."

Thus spake Manna Man for the first time.

If the scene had been captured on film with sound, someone would've remarked on how his voice sounded like that of a restrained madman. If the scene had been captured on film with digital enhancement, someone would've noticed the aura that surrounded young Ben's palm—an aura that revealed strength, and electricity, and the ability to change wrongs into rights.

Nowadays, if there is a person watching a television evangelist, and the evangelist edges into how his ministry needs money to aid the little half-hearted babies he visited in Haiti, or the lepers in Mongolia, or the heathens of upper Cambodia, or the tendon-lacking children of Zimbabwe, or the green children of Tonga, or the blind babies of Eritrea, or the secular humanists of Lithuania, or the involuntary flinchers of Mali, or the cursed teenagers of Indonesia, then Ben Culler transforms into Manna Man involuntarily and touches the television screen. The preacher will hear his own voice change into a higher octave. The preacher will think he's saying, "God will reward you in Heaven for helping our ministry help the little poor twelve-toed newborns of Paraguay get special-fitted shoes." He'll feel a tingle in his throat just as Manna Man transforms the speech into, "God will reward you in Heaven for helping our ministry help the Springer Mountain Library Association in its need to buy books published after the Civil War," and then offer up the telephone number where desperate Heaven seekers can call.

Afterward, the television evangelist moves onward. He wonders why the phone bank's silent. He thinks, Jesus H. Christ, I need to come up with some better needful ailing people of the world.

Ben Culler knows that, if there were a Hell, he'd be going. He misused his powers once: He got people to donate him money. Can't operate without paying the bills, he thought. Can't get a job at Best Buy and make sure all of the television sets are tuned to different TV evangelists full-time. Can't work forty hours a week doing something to pay the bills, and another 140 hours funneling money to good causes.

But there is no Hell, Manna Man knows. He read all the philosophers for five straight years after his father's death. He's read all the religious texts ever written by man.

He's read all the cookbooks, too, and would one day like to see a world without TV evangelists, so he could settle down with a woman and cook her a nice six-course meal.

There's a new evangelist—a country-looking preacher—dressed in a checkered coat. Manna Man focuses on the far-right television set in his den. He mutes the other channels. There's something about this guy: slick-backed real hair, a face that might've been used by geology professors when they couldn't find a decent example of "alluvial formations." Quiet voice and piercing eyes. It's not the typical studio setup either—it looks as though this might come out of a basement, or bunker: one man and a cameraman.

"God is punishing America for all the homosexuals we got going here. God has chosen me as one of the few elected to Heaven, and he has not chosen the rest of these homos and homo pimps and homo pimp seekers..."

Manna Man wonders if it's parody, if maybe channel 6 has changed ownership and now runs *TVLand*. In his downtime—and that's only an hour at most per day—Manna Man likes to watch reruns of *Mr. Ed*, *The Andy Griffith Show*, *Sanford and Son*, and the rest of those programs that his father wouldn't let him watch back when they were on prime time.

Manna Man waits for this new evangelist to ask for money. Here it comes, he thinks, and sure enough the man says, "That's why I need all you watching out there to send money to..."

Manna Man shoves his palm on the man's televised neck. Manna Man thinks to himself, "...the Women's Shelters of Eastern Tennessee who need money to continue operation."

"...our church here in Topeka so we can continue protesting funerals and bail out our Chosen parishioners who are doing God's work in this here United States of Sodomy."

Manna Man pushes his palm harder onto the set. He reaches for the channel changer and flips the next television over to channel 6 so that this unknown man appears. He shoves his left hand onto the man's face, and concentrates. "Women's Shelters of Eastern Tennessee, Women's Shelters of Eastern Tennessee, Women's Shelters of Eastern Tennessee..."

The TV evangelist pauses. He looks to his left. He clears his throat. Manna Man knows that he's come across an adversary with powers that might, indeed, cause the average person to believe in Satan. The evangelist says, "We will be doomed and cursed forever until our so-called leaders understand that the Nazis might've been..."

"What an asshole," Manna Man, says. He's got his right palm on the top-right television, his left hand on the third level TV beside it. He reaches with his left foot and toes the bottom-floor Sony to channel 6 and shoves his sole across the evangelist's face.

He concentrates. He says, "Women's Shelter of Eastern Tennessee" like a mantra.

The evangelist pauses, then says, "I know you're out there, Manna Man. I know all about you. You can't stop me. I've been ordained by God Hisself. He knows all about you and your wicked ways, funneling money to the soulless homosexuals and perverts and the godless and..."

Manna Man lets loose with his right hand, grabs the channel changer, and flips the television set right in front of his boxer shorts to channel 6. He drops the changer, shoves his right hand back so hard that he fears reaching through straight into the television's innards. Manna Man thinks, This is the nemesis of my dreams. He thinks, This is the heartless enemy I've been training for all of these years: Part mentally deranged attorney, part egomaniacal evangelist—I'm dealing with...the Attornelist!

He leans forward and shoves his penis right onto the Attornelist's mouth. Manna Man focuses. He leans hard, left and right hands touching screens, left foot, penis. There's silence. Then, finally, the Attornelist muffles out, "Please send your much-needed donations to the Women's Shelters of Eastern Tennessee," and gives up the 1-800 number.

Manna Man backs off of his bank of television sets. He looks into the Attornelist's cavernous black eyes and says, "You will never beat me." He slips his penis back inside his boxer shorts.

"Manna Man!" the Attornelist screams out. "Man oh man, I hate you Manna Man. I'll get you one day! I'll get you!"

The four screens turn to snow.

For now.

Manna Man crawls to the refrigerator, reaches up, and touches his magnets. They melt onto the floor. He had a feeling this would happen. He's sapped from the Attornelist.

He opens the refrigerator and pulls out beet juice he'd made earlier in his favorite Viking 12-Cup Food Processor with Commercial-Grade 625-Watt Induction motor.

Replacing the iron, he thinks. Regaining my powers. Refueling.

A man sits in his recliner, the business end of a .45 in his mouth. He's already covered the wall in plastic behind him. He doesn't want to leave a mess for anyone to find. He's always been that way. Maybe that's why he's been named Citizen of the Year twice. Maybe that's why, up until this point, he'd been able to run a hospice service run entirely on local contributions, staffed with two full-time nurses, and caregivers willing to undergo classes, seminars, and biannual evaluations.

But the donations haven't increased, and the number of elderly people in town, most of them laid off years ago from the cotton mill and fighting off lung ailments, has quadrupled. The man needs at least two more nurses, and twice as many qualified caregivers.

He eases back the hammer and almost pulls the trigger when the phone rings.

It might be his daughter calling. It might be one of the nurses. It might be news that someone else has died and the family needs help with funeral arrangements.

On the other end of the telephone, a woman says she'd like to put the hospice service in her will. She says she'll send a hundred thousand dollars immediately, but promises the remainder of her estate once she passes on. "To Heaven," she says. "I'll be going to Heaven for sure, now."

Manna Man's back on the job, revitalized.

THE JACKDAW'S LAST CASE

PAUL DI FILIPPO

In crime fiction, there's a subgenre reimagining historical celebrities as detectives, including Isaac Newton, Arthur Conan Doyle, Jane Austen, Groucho Marx, and countless others. Here, literary trickster Paul Di Filippo (*Ribofunk*, *Lost Pages*, etc.) goes one further: What if a certain Eastern European personage had become a masked crimefighter...?

> "Whatever advantage the future has in size,
> the past compensates for in weight...."
> —*The Diaries of F. K.*

Pale light the color of old straw trodden by uneasy cattle pooled from a lone streetlamp onto the greasy wet cobbles of the empty street. Feelers of fog like the live questing creepers of a hyperactive Amazonian vine twined around standards and down storm drains. The aged, petulant buildings lining the dismal thoroughfare wore the blank brick countenances of industrial castles. Some distance away, the bell of a final trolley sounded. A minute later, as if in delayed querulous counterpoint, a tower clock tolled midnight. A rat dashed in mad claw-clicking flight across the street.

Shortly after the tolling of the clock, a rivet-studded steel door opened in one of the factories, and a trickle of weary workers flowed out in spurts and ebbs, the graveyard shift going home. Without many words, and those few consisting of stale ritual phrases, the laborers apathetically trudged down the hard urban trail toward their shabby homes.

The path of many of the workers took them past the mouth of a dark alley separating two of the factories like a wedge in a log. None of the tired men and women took notice of two ominous figures crouched deep back in the alley's shadows like beasts of prey in the mouth of their burrow.

When it seemed the last worker had definitely passed, one of the gloom-cloistered lurkers whispered to the other. "Are you sure she's still coming?"

"Yeah, yeah, don't sweat it. She's always late for some reason. Maybe tossing the boss a quickie or something."

"You'd better be right, or our goose is cooked. We promised Madame Wu we'd bag her one last dame. And the boat for Shanghai leaves on the dot of two. And we still gotta get the baggage down to the dock."

"Don't get ants in your pants, fer chrissakes! Jesus, you'd think you'd never kidnapped a broad before! Ain't the white slavery racket a lot better'n second-story work?"

"I guess so. But I just got this creepy feeling tonight—"

"Well, keep it to yourself! You got the chloroform ready?"

"Sure, sure, I'm not gonna screw up. But there's something—"

"Quiet! I hear footsteps!"

Closer the lonely click-clack of a woman walking in heels sounded. A bare white arm and a skirted leg swung into the frame of the alley-mouth. Then the assailants were upon the unsuspecting woman, pinioning her arms, slapping an ether-drenched cloth to her face.

"OK, she's out! You get her legs, I'll take her arms. Once we're in the jalopy, we're good as there—"

Suddenly the night was split by an odd cry, half avian, half human, a spine-tingling ululation ripe with sardonic, caustic derision.

The kidnappers dropped their unconscious burden to the pavement and began to tremble.

"Oh, shit, no! Not him!"

"Where the hell is he! Quick!"

"There! I see him! Up on the roof!"

Standing in silhouette on a high parapet loomed the enigmatic and fearsome bane of evildoers everywhere, a heart-stopping icon of justice and fair play.

The Jackdaw.

The figure was tall and cadaverous. On his head perched a wide-brimmed, split-crown felted hat. An ebony feathered cape, fastened around his neck, hung from his outstretched arms like wings. A cruel beaked raptor's mask hid the upper half of his face. From his uncovered mouth now burst again his piercing trademark cry, part caw, part madman's exultant defiance.

"Don't just stand there! Blast him!"

The frightened yeggs drew their pistols, took aim, and snapped off several shots.

But the Jackdaw was no longer there.

Facing outward, the forgotten woman behind their backs, and swiveling nervously about like malfunctioning automata on a Gothic town-square barometer, the kidnappers strained their ears for the slightest sound of movement. Only the drip, drip, drip of condensing fog broke the eerie stillness.

"We did it! We scared off the Jackdaw! He ain't such hot shit after all!"

"OK, quit bragging! We still gotta get this broad to the docks—"

"I think not, gentlemen."

The kidnappers swung violently around, teeth chattering. Bestriding the unconscious woman, the Jackdaw had twin pistols clutched in his yellow-gloved hands and trained on the quaking assailants. Before the thugs could react, the Jackdaw fired, his strange guns emitting not the flash and boom of gunpowder, but only a subtle *phut, phut.*

The kidnappers had time only to slap at the darts embedded in their necks before crumpling to the ground.

Within a trice, the Jackdaw had the men hogtied with stout cord unwrapped from around his waist. Picking up the girl and hoisting her in a fireman's carry over one shoulder, one gloved hand resting not unfamiliarly on her buttocks, the Jackdaw said, "A hospital bed will suit you better than a brothel's doss, *liebchen.* And I should still have time to meet that Shanghai-bound freighter. Altogether, this promises to be a most profitable night."

With this observation the Jackdaw plucked a signature feather from his cape and dropped it between the recumbent men. Then, with a repetition of his fierce cry, he was gone like the phantasm of a fevered brain.

When Mister Frank Kafka reached the office of his employer at 1926 Broadway on the morning of July 3, 1925, he found the entire staff transformed from their normally staid and placid selves into a milling, chattering mass resembling a covey of agitated rooks, or perhaps the inhabitants of an invaded, ax-split termite colony.

Hanging his dapper Homburg on the wooden coatrack that stood outside the door to his private office, Kafka winced at the loud voices before reluctantly approaching the noisy knot formed by his coworkers. The center of their interest and discussion appeared to be that morning's edition of the *Graphic,* a New York tabloid that was the newest addition to the stable of publications owned by the very individual for whom they too labored—that is, under normal conditions. All labor seemed suspended now

The clot of humanity appeared an odd multilimbed organism composed of elements of male and female accoutrements: starched detachable collars, arm garters, ruffled blouses, high-buttoned shoes. Employing his above-average height to peer over the shoulders of the congregation, Kafka attempted to read the large headlines dominating the front page of the newspaper. Failing to discern their import, he turned to address an inquiry to a woman who resolved herself as an individual on the fringes of the group.

"Millie, good morning. What's this uproar about?"

Millie Jensen turned to fix her interlocutor with sparkling, mischievous eyes. A young woman in her early twenties with wavy dark hair parted down the middle, she exhibited a full face creased with deep laugh lines. Today she was clad in a black rayon blouse speckled with white dots and cuffed at the elbows, as well as a long black skirt belted with a wide leather cincture.

"Why, Frank, I swear you live in another world! Haven't you heard yet? The streets are just buzzing with the news! It's that mysterious vigilante, the Jackdaw— he struck again last night!"

Kafka yawned ostentatiously. "Oh, is that all? I'm afraid I can't be bothered keeping current with the doings of every Hans, Ernst, and Adolf who wants to take the law into his own hands. What did he accomplish this time? Perhaps he managed to foil the theft of an apple from a fruit-vendor's cart?"

"Oh, Frank!" Millie pouted prettily. "You're such a cynic! Why can't you show a little idealism now and then? If you really want to know, the Jackdaw broke up a white-slavery ring! Imagine—they were abducting helpless working girls just like me and shipping them to the Orient, where they would addict them to opium and force them into lewd, unnatural acts!"

Kafka smiled in a world-weary manner. "It all seems rather a short-sighted and unnecessary waste of time and effort on the part of these outlaw international entrepreneurs. Surely there are many women in town who would have volunteered for such a position. I counted a dozen on Broadway alone last night as I walked home."

Millie became serious. "You strike this pose all the time, Frank, but I know it's not the real you."

"Indeed, then, Millie, you know more about me than I do myself."

Kafka yawned again, and Millie studied him closely. "Didn't get much sleep last night, did you?"

"I fear not. I was working on my novel."

"*Bohemia,* isn't that the title? How's it going?"

"I draw the words as if out of the empty air. If I manage to capture one, then I have just this one alone and all the toil must begin anew for the next."

"Tough sledding, huh? Well, you can do it, Frank, I know it. Anybody who can write that lonely hearts column the way you do—well, you're just the bee's knees with words, if you get my drift." Millie laid a hand on the sleeve of Kafka's grey suitcoat. "Step aside, a minute, won't you, Frank? I—I've got a little something for you."

"As you wish. Although I can't imagine what it could be."

The pair walked across the large open room to Millie's desk. There, she opened a drawer and took out a small gaily wrapped package.

"Here, Frank. Happy birthday."

Kafka seemed truly touched, his self-composure disturbed for a moment. "Why, Millie, this is very generous. How did you know?"

"Oh, I happened to be rooting around in the personnel files the other day and a certain date and name just caught my eye. It's your forty-first, right?"

"Correct. Although I never imagined myself ever attaining this advanced age." Millie smiled coyly. "You sure don't look that old, Frank."

"Even into my late twenties, I was still being mistaken for a teenager."

"Was that back in Prague?"

Kafka cocked his head alertly. "No. I left my native city in 1902, when I was only nineteen. That was the year my Uncle Lowy in Madrid took me under his wing and secured me a job with his employer, the Spanish railways."

"And that's what led to all those years of traveling the globe as a civil engineer, building railways?"

"Yes." Kafka fixed Millie with a piercing gaze. "Why this sudden inquisition, Miss Jensen? It seems purposeless and unwarranted."

"Oh, I don't know. I like you, I guess. I want to know more about you. Is that so strange? And you're so close-mouthed, it's a challenge. Even after two years of working almost side by side, I feel we hardly know each other. No, don't protest, it's true. Oh, I admit you contribute to the general office conversation, but never anything personal. Getting anything vital out of you is like pulling teeth."

Kafka seemed about to reply with some habitual rebuff, then hesitated as if summoning fresh words. "There is some veracity to your perceptions, Millie. But you must rest assured that the fault lies with me, and not yourself. Due to my early warped upbringing, I have been generally unfitted for regular societal intercourse. Oh, I put up a good facade, but most of the time I feel clad in steel, as if my arm muscles, say, were an infinite distance away from myself. It is only when—well, at certain times I feel truly human. Then, I have a feeling of true happiness inside me. It is really something effervescent that fills me completely with a light, pleasant quiver and that persuades me of the existence of abilities of whose nonexistence I can convince myself with complete certainty at any moment, even now."

Millie stood with jaw agape before saying, "Jiminy, Frank—that's deep! And see, it didn't hurt too much to share that with me, did it?"

Kafka sighed. "I suppose not, for whatever it accomplished. You must acknowledge that if I am not always agreeable, I strive at least to be bearable."

Millie threw her arms around Kafka, who stood rigid as a garden beanpole. "Don't worry, Frank! Everybody feels a little like a caged animal now and then!"

"Not as I do. Inside me is an alien being as distinctly and invisibly hidden as the face formed from elements of the landscape in a child's picture puzzle."

Releasing Kafka, Millie stepped back. "Gee, that is a weird way to feel, Frank. Well, anyhow, aren't you going to open your present?"

"Certainly."

Discarding the colored paper and bow, Kafka delicately opened the box revealed. From within a nest of excelsior, he withdrew a small carving.

"Very nice, Millie. A figurine for my desk, I presume."

"Do you recognize it?"

Kafka twirled the object, showing no emotion. "A bird of some sort, obviously. A crow?"

"A *jackdaw*, actually. How do you say that in Czech?"

"Why, something tells me you already know, Millie. Back home we say, 'kavka.'"

Smiling as if she had just been awarded a trophy, Millie repeated, "'Kavka.'" Then, rather alarmingly, she flapped her arms, crowed softly, and winked.

Closing his office door gently behind him so as not to make a loud report that would disturb his acutely sensitive hearing, Kafka bestowed a long appraisal on his desk, where a Corona Model T typing machine reigned in midblotter like a machine-age deity. Wearily, he shook his head. Nothing good could be done on such a desk. There was so much lying about, it formed a disorder without proportion and without that compatibility of disordered things which otherwise made every disorder bearable.

Kafka set about cleaning up the mess. Soon he had a stack of unopened mail, one of interoffice memos, and another of miscellaneous documents. Finally he could truly work.

However, just as soon as he had positioned himself behind the writing machine, ivory-handled letter opener in one hand and faintly perfumed envelope in another, a male shadow cast itself on the frosted glass of his door, followed by a tentative knock.

Sighing, Kafka urged entrance in a mild voice.

Carl Ross, the office boy, was a freckled youth whose perpetually ink-smeared face bore a constant smile of impish goodwill. "Boss wants you, Mr. Frank."

"Very well. Did he say why?"

"Nope. He seemed a tad steamed though."

"Undoubtedly at me. Well, the fault is probably all mine. I shall not reproach myself, for shouted into this empty day it would have a disgusting echo. And after all, the office has a right to make the most definite and justified demands on me."

"Cripes, Mr. Frank, why do you want to go and beat up on yourself like that for, before you even get called on the carpet? Let the Boss do it if he's going to. Otherwise, you're just going to suffer twice!"

Kafka stood and advanced to lay a hand on Carl's tousled head. "Good advice, Carl. Perhaps we should trade jobs. Well, there's no point putting this off. Let's go."

At the end of a long, blank corridor was a door whose gilt lettering spelled out the name of Kafka's employer: *Bernarr Macfadden.* Kafka knocked and was admitted with a gruff "Come in!"

Bernarr Macfadden—that prolific author, self-promoter, notorious nudist and muscleman, publishing magnate, stager of beauty contests, inventor of Physical Culture and the Macfadden Dietary System—was upside down. His head was firmly ensconced on a thick scarlet pillow with gold-braid trim placed against one wall of his large office, against which vertical surface his inverted body was braced. In his expensive suit and polished shoes, his vibrant handsome mustachioed face suffused with blood, Macfadden reminded Kafka of some modern representation of the Hanged Man Tarot card, an evil omen one would not willingly encounter.

As if to reinforce Kafka's dire whimsy, Macfadden now bellowed, "Have a seat and hang in there, Frank! I'll be done in a couple of seconds!"

Kafka did as ordered. True to his words, in only a moment or two Macfadden broke his swami's pose, coiling forward in a deft somersault that brought him to his feet, breathing noisily.

"There! Now I can think clearly again! Sure wish I could get you to join in with me once in a while, Frank!"

"I appreciate your interest, sir. However, I have a nightly course of exercises of my own devising which keep me fit."

"Well, can't argue with success!" Macfadden snatched up a stoppered vacuum bottle from his desktop and gestured with it at Kafka. "Care for a glass of Cocomalt?"

"No, thank you, sir."

"No matter, I'll have one." Macfadden poured himself a glass of the chilled food-tonic. "Anyhow, I must confess you're looking mighty fit. You're following my diet rules though, aren't you?"

"Indeed."

"Good, good. You were on the road to goddamn ruin when you first applied for a job here. I can't believe you ever fell for Fletcherism! Chew every mouthful a dozen times! Hogwash! As long as you lay off the tobacco and booze, you'll be A-OK! Why, look at me!" Abruptly, Macfadden stripped off his coat, rolled back one sleeve, and flexed the biceps thus exposed. "I'm fifty-seven years young, and at the peak of health! A little grey at the temples, but that's just frost on the roof. The fire inside is still burning bright! You can expect the same, if you just stay the course!"

Kafka coughed in a diversionary manner. "As you say, sir. Uh, I believe you needed to speak to me about a work-related matter...?"

Macfadden grew solemn. He propped one lean buttock on the corner of his expansive desk. "That's right, son. It's about your column."

"So then. I assume that 'Ask Josephine' is losing popularity with the readers of *True Story*. Or perhaps you've had a specific complaint...?"

"No, no, no, nothing like that. Your copy's as popular as ever, and no one's complained. It's just that your advice to the readers is so—so eccentric! Always has been, but I just read the latest issue and, son—you're moving into some strange territory!"

"I'm afraid I don't see—"

"Don't see! Why, how do you justify this? 'Anxious in Akron' asks for your advice on whether she should have more than one child. Here's your reply in its entirety: 'The convulsive starting up of a lizard under our feet on a footpath in Italy delights us greatly, again and again we are moved to bow down, but if we see them at a dealer's by hundreds crawling over one another in confusion in the large bottles in which otherwise pickles are packed, then we don't know what to do.'"

"Very clear, I thought."

"Clear? It's positively lurid!"

Kafka smiled with his typical demure sardonicism. "A charge you yourself have frequently had leveled at your own writings, sir."

"Harumph! Well, yes, true. But hardly the same thing! What about this one? 'Pining in Pittsburgh' wants to know how she can get her reluctant beau to pop the question. Your counsel? 'The messenger is already on his way. A powerful, indefatigable man, now pushing with his right arm, now with his left, he cleaves a way for himself through the throng. If he encounters resistance he points to his breast, where the symbol of the sun glitters. The way is made easier for him than it would be for any other man. But the multitudes between him and you are so vast; their numbers have no end. If he could reach the open fields how fast he would fly, and soon doubtless you would hear the welcome hammering of his fists on your door. But he is still only making his way through the inner courts of a palace infinite in extent. If at last he should burst through the outermost gate—but never, never can that happen—the whole imperial capital would lie before him, the center of the world, crammed to bursting with its own sediment. Nobody could fight his way through there. But you sit at your window when evening falls and dream it to yourself.'"

For a space of time Kafka was silent. Then he said, "It's best, I think, not to raise false hopes...."

Macfadden slammed down the magazine from which he had been reading. "False hopes! My god, boy, that's hardly the issue here! With such mumbo jumbo, who can even tell if you're talking about this planet or another one! I know the motto of our magazine is 'Truth is stranger than fiction,' but this kind of malarkey really beats the band!"

Kafka seemed stung. "The readers appear to take adequate solace from my parables."

"I'll grant you that if someone's heartsick enough they can find comfort in any old gibberish. But that's not what we're about at Macfadden enterprises. The plain truth plainly told! No flinching from hard facts, no mincing or obfuscation. If you can only keep that in mind, Frank!"

Rising to his feet, Kafka said, "I will do my best, sir. Although my nature is not that of other men."

Macfadden got up also, and put an arm around Kafka's shoulders. "That brings me to another point, son. You know I like to keep a fatherly eye on my employees and their home lives. And it has risen to my attention that you're becoming something of a reclusive loner, a regular hermit bachelor type. Now, take this advice of mine to heart, both as a stylistic example and on a personal level. You cannot work for yourself alone, and rest content. You need a satisfying love life, and the home and children with which it is sanctified. It is the stimulus of love that makes service divine. To work for yourself alone is cold, selfish, and meaningless. You need a loved one with whom you can double your joys and divide your sorrows."

During this speech Macfadden had been escorting his subordinate to the exit. Now, opening the door, he slapped Kafka with hearty bonhomie on the back, sending the slighter man staggering forward a step or two.

"Have a yeast pill, son, and get back in the harness!"

Silently, Kafka accepted the offered tablet and departed.

Back in his office, Kafka deposited the yeast pill in a drawer containing scores of others. Then he picked up the envelope the slitting of which had been interrupted by his boss's summons and extracted its contents.

"Dear Josephine," the letter began. "I hardly know where to start! My sick, elderly parents are about to be evicted from our farm because they had a number of bad years and can't pay their loans, and my own job—our last hope of survival—could be in danger itself. It's my boss, you see. He has made improper advances toward me, advances I've modestly refused. Still, I get the impression that he won't respect my virtuous stand much longer, and I'll have to either bend to his will or be fired! I've made myself sick with worry about this, can't sleep, can't eat, etc., until I almost don't care about anything anymore, just wish I could escape from it all somehow. Does this make me a bad daughter? Please help!"

Kafka rolled a sheet of paper into his typing machine. Attempting to keep Macfadden's advice in mind, he moved his fingers delicately over the keys.

"Don't despair, not even over the fact that you don't despair. Just when everything seems over with, new forces come marching up, and precisely that means that you are alive." Kafka paused, then added a codicil. "And if they don't, then everything is over with here, once and for all."

Seated in the study of his Fifth Avenue apartment at a desk that was the tidy twin to its office mate, with the dusk of another evening mantling his shoulders like a moleskin cape, Kafka composed with pen in their native German his weekly letter to his youngest and favorite sister, Ottla, now resident with her husband Joseph David in Berlin.

Dearest Ottla,

I am gratified to hear that you are finally feeling at ease in your new home and environs. The claws of our "little mother" Prague are indeed difficult to disengage from one's skin. Sometimes I envision all of Prague's more sensitive citizens as being metaphorically suspended from the city's towers and steeples on lines and flesh-piercing hooks, like Red Indians engaged in ritual excruciations. Although I myself have been a wandering expatriate for some two decades now, I still recall my initial disorientation, when Uncle Alfred took me under his wing and forcibly launched me on my globe-circling career. I think that my strong memories of Bohemia and my intense feelings for our natal city were what prevented me from settling down until recently. Although, truth be told, I soon came to enjoy my peripatetic mode of existence. The lack of close and enduring ties with other people was not unappealing, neither were the frequent stimulating changes of scenery.

Of course, all that changed after "The Encounter," which I have expatiated about to you in, I fear, far too copious and boring detail. That meeting in the rarefied reaches of the Himalayas with the Master—hidden like a pearl of great worth in his alpine hermitage—and my subsequent revelatory year's tutelage under him has finally resulted in my settling down to pursue a definitive course of action, one calculated to make the best use of my talents. My adopted country, I feel confident in saying, is now Amerika, practically the last country unvisited by me in an official engineering capacity, yet one of which I have often dreamed—right down to spurious details such as a sword-wielding Statue of Liberty! It is here, at the dynamic new center of the century, that I have finally planted sustainable roots.

As for your new role as wife and mother, you must accept my sincerest congratulations. You know that I esteem parenthood most highly—despite having many reasons well known to you for the likely development of exactly the opposite opinion. Once I actually dared dream of such a role for myself. But such a happy circumstance was not to be. For although there have been many women in my life, none seemed equal to my idiosyncratic needs. (Any regrets I may have once had regarding my eternal bachelorhood are long extinguished, of course.) Curiously enough, my employer, Herr Macfadden, saw fit to accost me on this very topic today. Perhaps I shall take his blunt advice to heart and resume courting the fair sex, if only for temporary amusement. Although the rigors of my curious manner of existence have grown, if anything, even more demanding than before....

Fleshing out his letter with another page or two of trivial anecdotes and polite domestic and familial inquiries, Kafka paused at the closing endearment. After some thought, he finally inscribed it: "Give my regards to Mother—and Mother alone." Weighing the sealed letter with a small balance, he affixed the precisely requisite postage to it, then took the elevator down to the lobby of his building, where he left the missive with the concierge.

But then, instead of returning to his apartment or exiting onto the busy Manhattan street, Kafka moved to an innocuous door in a forlorn corner of the lobby.

Looking about to ascertain whether anyone was observing him, he quickly insinuated himself through the portal.

A wanly lit flight of stairs led downward. Soon Kafka was in the basement. Crossing that nighted realm, Kafka reached another set of stairs. Within seconds, he was in a subcellar.

This underground kingdom seemed even darker than the level above, save for a distant flickering glow. Kafka moved toward this partially shielded light source.

Heat mounted. On the far side of a gap-slatted wooden partition, Kafka came face to face with an enormous, Moloch-like furnace. Its door was open, and from an enormous pile of coal a half-naked man shoveled scoop after scoop of black lumps.

For some time Kafka watched the brawny sweating man work. He knew neither the man's name nor his history. Kafka assumed he lived here, within reach of his fiery charge, for no matter when Kafka visited he found the stoker busy tending his demanding master.

The congruence with his own situation did not go unregarded by Kafka.

On the floor stood a pail of cinder-flecked water with a dipper in it. Kafka took up the dipper and raised it to the stoker's lips. Without stopping his shoveling, the laborer greedily drank the warm sooty liquid. After several repetitions of this beneficence, the man signaled by a grunt his satisfaction.

Feeling free now to tend to his own business, Kafka stepped around the bulk of the furnace. Behind this asbestos-clad monster was another door, seemingly placed without sense. Through this door Kafka stepped.

And into the Jackdaw's sanctum.

Strange machines and devices bulked in the shadows not entirely dispelled by several low-wattage bulbs. An exit leading who-knows-where could be vaguely discerned. Near the entrance door on a peg hung the famous feathered cape; on a table sat mask, hat and canary-colored gloves. In a glass case was a gun belt and sundry other portable gadgetry.

With lingering, almost fetishistic pleasure, Kafka donned his disguise. A transformative surge passed through him, rendering him somehow larger than life.

Emitting a mild *sotto voce* version of his shrill cry, the Jackdaw stepped to a ticker-tape device. Picking up the trailing paper, he began to scan its contents.

"Hmmm… The Mousehole Gang suspected in daring daylight bank robbery, but police on the case… Dogface Barton in prison break, but likely hideout believed known… The dirigible *Shenandoah* to make maiden flight… Ku Klux Klan to stage Washington rally… Yes, yes, but nothing here for me—Wait, what's this? 'The Federal Bureau of Investigation under its new director Mr. Hoover is pursuing reports of an extortion attempt upon oil and steel magnate John D. Rockefeller by a hitherto unknown Zionist agent provocateur using the pseudonym of "The Black Beetle...."' Ah, this has the Jackdaw's name writ large upon it!"

The door to Kafka's office opened and Millie Jensen entered, carrying a sheaf of papers. She stood quietly for a moment, regarding the affecting sight before her, which evoked a tender sigh from her sympathetic nature.

Kafka's face rested insensibly on a surface definitely not intended for such a purpose: the uncomfortable keys and platen of his Corona typing machine. Gentle snores issued from the sleeping columnist.

Millie tried awakening him by tapping her foot. When this method produced no effect, she began to cough, at first femininely, then with increasing violence, until her ultimate efforts resembled the paroxysms of a tuberculosis victim.

Her ploy worked at last, for Kafka jolted awake with a start, almost like a caged dangerous beast, taking in his situation with a single wild-eyed glance before his usual mask of calm fell into place.

"Ah, Miss Jensen, please excuse my inattention. I was inspecting the mechanism. Its performance was unsatisfactory—"

"Oh, you don't need to make excuses with me, Frank," said Millie, not unkindly. "I know you're exerting yourself night and day to accomplish—certain things."

"Yes, quite correct. My, um, novel is presenting me with certain intractable difficulties. Important lines of the plot refuse to resolve themselves—"

"Yeah, gotcha, kiddo." Millie regarded Kafka slyly and with a humorous glint in her green eyes. "Say, did you ever think that by relaxing a little, you might find an answer to your problems unconsciously?"

Kafka smiled. "Why, Millie, you sound positively like a disciple of Herr Freud."

"Oh, a girl likes to keep abreast of the latest fads. But I'm serious. You like the movies, don't you?"

"I believe that the cinema represents a valid new sensory experience akin to the exteriorization of one's dreams."

"And their popcorn generally ain't so bad either. Well, it's a Friday, and the new Chaplin is playing downtown. *The Gold Rush*. Wanna catch it with me tonight?"

Kafka deliberated momentarily before brightening and giving a surprisingly hearty and colloquial assent. "Millie, I'm your man!"

Turning to leave—or so that she could regard Kafka coquettishly over one shoulder—Millie replied, "That remains to be seen!"

Streaming out from the doors of the Nature Theater of Oklahoma—a popular begemmed movie palace owned by the most famous and successful son of that prairie state, the comedian Will Rogers—the happy moviegoers soon dispersed into the evening bustle of Manhattan. Left behind were a single man and woman; the pair seemed hesitant or unsure of their next destination, like moths deprived of their phototropism.

After a protracted silence, Millie chirpily asked Kafka, "So, Frank, whadda'd you think? What a riot, huh?"

Millie's date seemed lost in thought, his dark features enrapt in a fugue of consternation. "That scene where Chaplin is starving and forced to eat his own shoe made me feel so strange.... It corresponded exactly to an enervating emotion I myself have had on numerous occasions."

"Really? Gosh, I feel plenty bad for you, Frank. Look at you—you're wound up so tight you're ready to burst to pieces! What you need is a feminine presence in your life, someone to take care of you and nurture you. Don't you think that would be nice?"

"If you speak of marriage, Miss Jensen, I fear that such a normal mortal luxury is forever denied me. A formal union with a woman would result not only in the dissolution of the nothingness that I am, but doom also my poor wife."

"Holy cats, Frank, you've been reading the fake sob stories in our rag too much! Or maybe you've even been dipping into *Weird Tales*! Life just isn't as complex or melodramatic as you or those three-hankie writers make it out to be!" Millie linked her arm through Kafka's and leaned her head on his shoulder. "A man and a woman together—what could be simpler?"

Kafka did not disengage, but instead, seeming to take some small encouragement from the simple human contact, managed to pull himself together with a visible effort.

"I'm sorry to be such a wet blanket, Millie, when all you sought was a gay night out. Truthfully, I have not felt so melancholy for nearly twenty years. This black humor was something I thought I had left behind in the dank and dismal streets of Prague. The cosmopolitan, globe-trotting engineer known as Frank Kafka was a mature, vibrant, self-assured fellow. But it appears now that he was only a paper cutout that quickly withers in the flames of frustration."

Since Kafka was at least communicating again, Millie's natural exuberance reasserted itself. "Oh, bosh and piffle, Frank! Everyone gets a dose of the blues now and then. It'll pass, you'll see! All we have to do is spend an hour or two doing something pleasant. What do you really, really like to do? How about grabbing a coffee and some pastry? The Hotel Occidental has a great coffee shop. I bet their jelly donuts will make you think of Vienna!"

"That sounds fine, Millie. But if you'd really like to know what I enjoy—"

"Yes, yes, Frank—tell me!"

"I like to contemplate the Brooklyn Bridge. Mr. Roebling's masterpiece reminds me of some of the humbler constructions I myself was once responsible for. Sometimes those noble buttresses alone seem endurable and without shame to me, amidst all the city's charade. But I don't suppose—"

"Frank, I'd love bridge-watching with you! Let's go!"

With Millie forcefully tugging on her coworker's arm, the mismatched couple began to move up Broadway. Soon, they were within sight of City Hall and not far from the majestic span across the East River.

As they crossed the small park in front of City Hall, the shrill scream of a hysterical woman brought them to an abrupt halt. This initial call of alarm was quickly followed by a swelling chorus of indignation, fear, confusion, and outrage.

Kafka raced toward the source of the noise, Millie trailing behind.

A growing, growling, agitated crowd lifted its gaze skyward. Atop the very roof of City Hall stood an ominous figure. Diminutive yet powerful, with the warped back and hypertrophied cranium of a Quasimodo, he was clad in a form-fitting black union suit that merged into face-concealing, antennae-topped headgear. From his back sprouted small, wire-stiffened cellophane wings; from his torso, parallel rows of artificial abdominal feelers. The creature could be none other than—

"The Black Beetle!" shouted an onlooker.

"Where're the cops?" yelled someone else.

"Where's the Jackdaw?" yelled another.

Kafka stood quivering beside Millie like a dog on a leash faced with an impudent raccoon or squirrel.

The Black Beetle began to harangue his audience in a slightly accented English, showering them with incomprehensible slogans and demands.

"Down with all anti-Semites! Up with Zionism! Palestine for the Jews! The Mufti of Jerusalem must die! America must support the Zionist cause! If she does not do so willingly, with guns and money, we shall compel her to! Take this as a sign of our seriousness!"

There was nothing equivocal or esoteric about the round bomb which the Black Beetle now produced from somewhere on his person. The sight of its sizzling fuse raised a loud inchoate cry from the crowd, and people began to scatter in all directions.

"Long live the Stern Gang!" shouted the Black Beetle as he hurled his explosive device.

Kafka knocked Millie to the ground and covered her body with his lanky form.

The bomb went off, filling their world with noise and the reek of gunpowder, hurtling shrapnel, flying cement chips, and clumps of sod.

Immediately after the detonation, Kafka leaped to his feet and surveyed the situation. By a miracle of Providence, it appeared that no person had been caught in the blast, the destruction confined to turf, sidewalk, and park benches.

As for the Black Beetle—in the confusion, he had made good his escape.

Kafka slumped in despair, muttering, "Useless, useless, all ambition. And yet what joy, imagining again the pleasure of a knife twisted in my heart...."

Millie had regained her feet and was brushing her clothes clean. "Frank—are you okay?"

Kafka straightened. "Millie, our night together is over. I trust you can find your own way home? I have—I must be going."

"Why, sure, Frank. See you in the office."

Kafka hurriedly departed. Millie hung back until he turned a corner. Then she slipped after him, always keeping a shield of pedestrians between them.

She followed her quarry as far as Times Square. There, in a squalid doorway apart from the more wholesome foot-traffic, as Millie watched from concealment behind a shuttered kiosk, Kafka approached two gaudy women of obvious ill repute, leaving, after a slight dickering, with both of the overpainted floozies, plainly headed toward the entrance of a nearby fleabag hotel.

"Oh, Frank! Why?" Millie exclaimed, and began to weep.

Dearest Ottla,

I write to you today hoping to clarify my own thoughts on one particular matter, that being our shared ancestry and heritage. A disturbing incident of late has unleashed a savage pack of old feelings and recriminations I thought long tamed. I have always admired at a suitable distance your passionate embrace of an ultra-modern synthesis of our old family religion—perhaps strictly for its certitude—although I could never myself feel comfortable in its suffocating clutches. Perhaps your perspective will aid me in seeing my own status afresh.

We are Jews, of course. Jews by birth, an inescapable heritage of the blood. You have affirmed this ancient taint wholeheartedly, passionately enlisting in such causes as the rescue of the *Ostjuden* and the formation of a Jewish homeland in the Palestine protectorate. I, on the other hand, have violently abandoned any such affiliations and attitudes, a decision enforced not solely by my rational intellect and the study of comparative cultures enabled by my extensive travels, but equally by my gut.

How you ever maintained any religious feeling, raised in our household as you were, I cannot imagine. Dragged by *him,* we went to synagogue a bare four times a year, and it was a farce, a joke. No, not even a joke. I've never been so bored in my life, I believe, except later on at dance lessons. I did enjoy the small distractions, such as the opening of the Ark, which always reminded me of a shooting gallery where, when you hit a bull's-eye, a door flips open the same way, except that at the gallery something interesting popped out, while here it was always the same old dolls without heads.

Later, I saw things in a slightly less harsh light and realized what could lead you to believe. You had actually managed to salvage some scraps of Judaism from that small, ghettolike congregation. For me, it was not to be, and I firmly affixed a Solomonic seal to the whole stinking corpse of my incipient, puerile Judaism and buried it deep.

But now, this old specter has arisen again, lashed into an unnatural afterlife by the chance meeting with a Zionist demagogue.

What I humbly request from you, dearest sister, are two things. First, a well-marshalled explanation and defense of your own faith. Second, and perhaps more vitally, some information regarding the chief figures of the European Zionist scene, specifically any particulars concerning a certain crook-backed firebrand…

The door to Kafka's office was thrust open so violently that it swung through a full half-circle of arc to bang against the wall in which it was hung, making the inset glass pane quiver like a shaken quilt.

Kafka clapped his hands to his ears and winced. "Millie, was that strictly necessary?"

Millie snorted, then stomped across the room. "That's 'Miss Jensen' to you, *Mr.* Kafka!" She flung an armful of papers down on Kafka's desk and pivoted to leave.

Kafka stood and moved to her side. "Millie—or if you insist, Miss Jensen. I realize that our date did not end in a particularly satisfying fashion, and that perhaps your nerves are still abuzz from our shared brush with death. And yet, I fancied that until that unforeseen, inaesthetic climax we were enjoying ourselves much like any other couple."

Millie's jade eyes flared with anger. "Oh, sure, right till we nearly got blown up things were hunky-dory. But what came *after* was the real shocker!"

"After? I don't understand—No, surely you couldn't have—"

"But I did, Mr. Barn Veeve-ant, Filly-der-joy Kafka! And let me just tell you this, buster! Any guy who'd pass up some heavy petting with me in favor of two clapped-out, gussied-up old trollops is not someone who's ever going to learn if I wear my stockings rolled!"

And with that obscure assertion, Millie departed as noisily as she had come.

Kafka sat down at his desk and cradled his head in his hands. There came a polite knock, followed by the entrance of officeboy Carl.

Kafka looked up. "The Boss?"

Carl simply nodded, his expression and demeanor conveying the utmost solemn sympathy.

Once more Kafka stood before the forbidding door to Bernarr Macfadden's office. Dispiritedly he knocked, wearily entered when bidden.

Macfadden was employing an apparatus of steel springs and Bakelite grips in exercises intended to strengthen his upper body. Seated behind his massive desk, he stretched and released the resistant springs like a demented candymaker fighting recalcitrant taffy. Sweat dripped from his aggressive mustache as, grunting, he nodded Kafka to a seat.

Watching in horrified fascination, Kafka sought within him for some last untapped resource of strength. A phrase of the Master's came back to him unbidden: "The axe that cleaves the frozen sea within us…" Why could he no longer lay his grip upon that once familiar haft?

Finally Kafka's superior finished his exertions. Dropping the device, he wiped his brow and then poured himself some brown sludge from his flask. That Kafka was not offered any of the drink, the advice columnist considered a bad omen.

Macfadden began to lecture, on a topic of seemingly small relevance.

"I'm not one of your hypocritical, church-going, priest-worshipping, narrow-minded Babbits, Frank. Far from it! Open-minded toleration and clear-sighted experimentation has always been my game plan. I'll endorse any mode of living that honors the body and the mind and the soul. But I draw the line at one thing. Do you know what that is?"

"No, sir. What?"

"Blasphemy!" thundered Macfadden. "Blasphemy of the sort contained in these galleys of yours, which I took the precaution of securing a look at before they reached print! And thank the Lord I did! I can't imagine the magnitude of the hue and cry that would have followed the publication of this corker!"

"Sir, to what are you referring…?"

"This answer of yours to 'Doubting in Denver.' 'If we were possessed by only a single devil, one who had a calm, untroubled view of our whole nature, and freedom to dispose of us at any moment, then that devil would also have enough power to hold us for the length of a human life high above the spirit of God in us, and even swing us to and fro so that we should never get to see a glimmer of it and therefore should not be troubled from that quarter.'"

Weakly, Kafka replied, "You misconstrue my meaning—"

Macfadden crumpled the galleys savagely. "Misconstrue, hell! It's the most blatant decadent Satanism I've ever seen! That poor girl! I hate to imagine how her life could have been ruined by these aberrant Nietzschean gutter-sweepings of yours! No, Frank, you've had your chance. You had a good job, but you threw it away. I want you to clean out your desk right now, collect your last wages, and be off."

Kafka said nothing in his own defense. He knew that all he could say would appear quite incomprehensible to Macfadden, and that whether a good or bad construction was to be put on his actions had all along depended solely on Macfadden's judgmental spirit. And besides, the summed weight of all the misunderstandings he was the center of now sat upon his shoulders like a sack of coal on a stevedore's back, robbing him of speech. A flickering, cool little flame had taken up residence in the left side of his head, and a tension over his left eye had settled down and made itself at home. Coming to his feet, Kafka turned to go.

Now that he had vented his spleen, Macfadden softened somewhat toward his ex-employee, to the point of offering advice. "Maybe you should try something that doesn't involve contact with the public so much, Frank. Go back to the railroads. Or you could always try the insurance industry. Lots of call for analysts and writers there."

Kafka left without a word.

On his way from the building, he was forced to thread an unwelcome, albeit generally friendly gauntlet of his ex-coworkers. Most of them uttered sympathetic farewells and useful advice, all of which pelted Kafka like hailstones.

The ultimate face in the series belonged to Millie. Seemingly genuine tears of sorrow had snailed her cheeks.

"Oh, Frank, I had no idea—"

Kafka came alert, straightening his back. "Millie, I regret anything I have done to cause you distress. For a time, I acted like a lost sheep in the night and in the mountains. Or rather, like a sheep which is running after this sheep. But now my course is clear."

"What's that, Frank?" sniffled Millie.

"To let my own devil fully possess me."

And with that, Kafka walked with what he hoped was a passably erect carriage through the door.

A wrinkled, disintegrating newspaper, half soaking in the wet gutter, half draped over the granite curb, bore large headlines just legible under the wan buttercup-colored glow of a streetlamp:

> JACKDAW TERRORIZES UNDERWORLD!
>
> POLICE HARD PUT TO JAIL ALL MALEFACTORS DELIVERED TO THEIR DOOR!
>
> COURTS CLOGGED!
>
> "WHAT IS HE AFTER?" ASKS PUBLIC
>
> COMMISSIONER O'HALLORAN SPECULATES:
>
> "IT SEEMS HE HAS A GRUDGE AGAINST THE BLACK BEETLE"

A booted foot ground down upon the discarded tabloid, pulping its substance. The foot moved on, followed by its mate, carrying their owner with determined stealth across the sidewalk and up to the very wall of a derelict building. There the boots halted.

The Jackdaw studied the structure before him. His keen eyes caught sight of a line of ornamental carvings above the second-story windows. Deftly the masked avenger uncoiled a grapple and cord from around his waist. In mere seconds he was standing on a ledge some dozen feet above the ground. From there he progressed rapidly up the side of the seemingly abandoned building until he crouched before the lighted panes of a sixth-floor window.

Inside, men clustered around a table on which bomb-making materials were scattered. Consulting a plan and arguing among themselves, they were oblivious to their watcher.

Chuckling softly to himself, the Jackdaw stood. Tugging the rope secured above him to test its stability, he next leaned backward into sheer space at an angle to the wall, supported by his yellow-gloved grip on the rope. With a kick, he propelled himself away from the wall. At the end of his short arc into darkness, he was aimed feet first for the glass and moving at some speed.

As he hit, glass and wood exploding inward, the Jackdaw emitted his nerve-shattering cry.

It was enough. The bombmakers fell cowering to the floor, failing even to reach for their weapons.

"We give up! Don't kill us! Please!"

The Jackdaw picked up one of the spineless hirelings of the Black Beetle with maniacal force. "Where is he! The Black Beetle! Talk!"

"Lower East Side! In the basement of Schnitzler's Market on Delancey Street! That's his headquarters! Honest!"

"Very well! Now, you gentlemen look as if you could use a little nap before your ride in the Black Maria—"

The pick in the lock of the rear door to Schnitzler's Market tickled the tumblers as delicately as a virgin toying with the strap of her camisole in some Weimar brothel. Within seconds, the Jackdaw had gained entrance. Tiptoeing across the shadowy storage room thus revealed the Jackdaw spied what was patently the basement door.

As he twisted its handle, there came a noise from above of rattling chains.

With a tremendous crash a large cage fell, trapping the Jackdaw!

Gas hissed out from hidden nozzles.

Consciousness departed from the Jackdaw like an offended customer offered inferior goods huffily exiting a carriage-trade establishment.

When he awoke, the Jackdaw found himself lying belly down on some kind of padded platform, secured at wrists, waist, and ankles, and stripped of his mask and cape. His chin was cupped in a kind of trough, and a leather strap went around his brow, forcing him to bend his neck at a strained angle. The sole sight before his eyes was a brick wall with flaking grey paint and blooming excrescences of niter.

Into the Jackdaw's view now walked a man.

The Black Beetle, bent of back, bulging of skull.

"So, we meet again after so long, Franz Kafka!"

Even in extremis, his careful deliberation of speech had not deserted Kafka. Far from blurting out a plea for mercy or a useless threat, Kafka now uttered a simple, "Again?"

An ooze of false sincerity and hollow bonhomie dripped from the Black Beetle's voice. "Ah, but of course! I am still masked. How discourteous! Allow me...." The Black Beetle doffed his headgear, so that the attached piece of his suit with its antennae hung down his back like an improperly molted skin. Kafka saw the gnomish face of a stranger his own age, in no way familiar.

"I see you are still puzzled by my identity," continued the Black Beetle. "Naturally, there is no reason for you to remember such a nonentity as Max Brod!"

"Max Brod? Weren't you at the Altstadter Gymnasium with me as a youth? But that was over two decades ago, and we hardly ever spoke a single word to each other even then!"

"Of course we never spoke! Who would bother to seek out conversation with a crippled, graceless overachiever such as I was then? Not the haughty, handsome Franz Kafka, by any means! Oh, no, he never had time to see the pitiful, adoring youngster who idolized him, who hung on the fringes of his precious little circle—Pollack, Pribam, Baum, that whole bunch!—desperately hoping for some little crumb of attention! And then, when you left me behind in Prague, the agonies of severed affection I suffered! The sleepless nights in a sweat-soaked bed, writhing under the lash of your image! The long hikes and swims intended to burn away your memory, but which only succeeded in somewhat alleviating my childhood bodily afflictions. Even your absence became a kind of presence, for the glorious figure of Engineer Kafka and his faraway glorious deeds were forever thrust before my eyes by all and sundry in the small world of Jewish Prague society."

The strain on Kafka's neck was beginning to nauseate him. "And—and have you tracked me down then only to sate your unnatural obsessions and take revenge?"

Brod laughed sourly. "Even now you cast all events with yourself at the center! Far from it, Mr. Vaunted Jackdaw! This victory is merely a sweet lagniappe. You see, the only way I was able to forget about you and recover my wits and energies was to plunge myself into a cause larger than myself. Zionism was the flame that reignited me!

"At first, I allied myself with one of your old buddies, Weltsch, and his journal *Selbstwehr*. But he proved too meek and mild for my tastes, and I soon found more radical companions. Willingly, to spite all those who see the Jew as the cockroach of civilization, I adopted this disguise. Now I and my comrades wage a worldwide campaign of terror and coercion with the aim of establishing a Jewish state in Palestine. You in your foolish crimefighting role stood in the way of my goals here in America, so I simply chose to stomp on you. The wonderful irony of our early connection was merely a token that Yahweh continues to smile on me."

"And now what will you do with me?"

From somewhere on his person, Brod produced a crisp crimson apple. After polishing it on his sleeve, he began to crunch it, chewing avidly, as if to mock his captive. "I shall enlist you in a scientific experiment. You are secured, you see, to the bed of a unique apparatus intended to convince the enemies of Zionism of their folly. Above you is an adjustable clockwork mechanism which can be set to reproduce certain movements in what we call 'the Harrow,' to which it is connected by various subtle motors.

"The Harrow features two kinds of needles arranged in multiple patterns. Each long needle has a short one beside it. The long needle does a kind of inkless tattoo writing directly into your flesh, and the shorter needle sprays a jet of water to wash away the blood and keep the inscription clear. Blood and water are then conducted here through small runnels into this main runnel and down a waste pipe."

"I see. And what text have you chosen to inscribe on my flesh?"

"A portion of the Talmud dealing with traitors to the Jewish race!"

Discarding the core of his apple, Brod moved out of Kafka's view. In the next second, Kafka felt his garments being slit open to expose his back.

"I am sorry you will not survive your reeducation, my dear Franz. But the process, to be effective, must be repeated hundreds of times over many hours!"

Kafka waited tensely for the start of the physical torture. But what came next was the last thing he expected.

"By the way," said Brod with fiendish glee, "your beloved *father* sends his usual sentiments!"

Kafka swooned straight away.

When he regained consciousness, the reeducation machine was already in action.

What felt like a bed of nails now touched Kafka's back, and he was instantly reminded of enduring a similar sensation under the Master's tutelage. Yet even those lessons in self-mastery were bound to disintegrate under repetitive assaults of the Harrow, especially when his psyche was weakened by the Black Beetle's psychological thrust.

Kafka strained against his bonds, to no avail.

"Perhaps you'd care to vent that ridiculous cry of yours once more? No, I thought not. Very well, prepare yourself—"

Suddenly a loud crash sounded from above them, followed by the clamor of urgent gruff voices.

"Damnation! Well, I see I must leave my fun. But not before witnessing the first prick!"

Dozens of dancing needles pierced Kafka as if he were Saint Sebastian, and he swore his skin could interpret the agonizing shapes of the Hebrew letters. It took all his Oriental training not to scream.

Footsteps galloped down a flight of wooden stairs. The needles continued their cruel and arcane tarantella. Shots rang out. Kafka lost his senses.

He swam up out of blackness apparently only moments later, and felt that his bleeding form was freed from the Harrow and cradled in a soft embrace. The tearful face of Millie Jensen regarded him from above.

"Oh, Frank! Tell me you're going to make it!"

Kafka groaned. "The palimpsest of my hide still has room for a few more passages…"

Millie bent to kiss him. "Thank God! I was sure we'd be too late! I've been haunting the police since the day you were fired, trying to convince them I knew who the Jackdaw was, trying to stop you for your own good! When those bombmakers finally came around and the police beat some information out of them, I tagged along! Everything's fine now, Frank!"

A certain lifelong tension inherent in his very sinews and musculature seemed to have been drained from Kafka along with his blood. Momentarily, he thought to ask whether the Black Beetle had escaped, then realized he didn't care. Max Brod's fanaticism would lead to his own undoing sooner or later, much as Kafka's had nearly led to his.

"Millie?"

"Yes, Frank?"

"Have you ever considered what marriage to me might entail?"

Millie kissed him again. "Well, you're nothing to crow about—"

Kafka winced. "Millie, please, my writer's sensibilities have not been extinguished—"

"But you'd be a feather in any girl's cap!"

THE BIGGEST
JAMES PATRICK KELLY

James Patrick Kelly (*Wildlife*, *Think Like a Dinosaur and Other Stories*, etc.) fixes his scholarly, sciencefictional gaze on the dawn of the superheroic era, the Great Depression.

*B*ig, known to his dear departed mother as Filbrick Van Loon, was startled out of his reverie when a heavy in a cheap gabardine suit dropped into the seat in front of him like a piano falling out of a skyscraper. In his drowsy confusion, Big thought the train itself had derailed, but as he gathered his wits he realized that the Empire State Express was pulling out of Union Station, finally headed south to New York City.

"Guess who I just seen?" said the heavy.

"Can't." A woman's voice oozed boredom. "Jimmy Cagney?"

The seatback shuddered as the heavy thrashed disagreement. "What would Cagney be doing in Albany?"

"Babe Ruth?" said his companion.

"Nope."

"Rin Tin Tin? Judge Crater?"

"The Governor."

"Roosevelt?"

Big stopped feeling sorry for himself and leaned forward to eavesdrop, although the heavy had a voice they could probably hear in Buffalo.

"How did you know it was him?"

"Been in the newsreels, hasn't he? Believe me, this is the guy. He could barely walk 'cause of the polio."

Big stood and pulled his suitcase off the overhead rack.

"They say he got better." The woman was still skeptical.

"If that was better, I'd hate to see worse."

Big headed toward the rear of the train. He'd met the Governor a couple of months after his inauguration. Everything had seemed possible in the summer of '29, before Black Friday had crashed the country. Now most folk were rubbing pennies together just to buy beans. Big was so broke that the whole of his sad life rattled around in a cardboard suitcase with a busted snap. But maybe this was a sign, Roosevelt being on the train. Maybe the Governor could make the sun shine again, at least on Big. It wouldn't hurt to ask.

The train's last carriage was an observation car. As the door wheezed shut behind him, Big hesitated, as if he wasn't sure where he was. He announced to no one in particular that he needed some air. Where was the observation porch? A codger in an old-fashioned suit and a collar stiffer than Calvin Coolidge glanced up from the *Albany Times-Union* in annoyance. Nobody else seemed to notice him, although Big spotted his quarry in the parlor at the rear of the carriage. They sat in plush armchairs beneath tall windows that were bright with October sun. There appeared to be three in Roosevelt's party besides the Governor: two men and a woman. The woman was in her thirties, frail, nervous, handsome maybe, but certainly no looker. She wore a checked dress to the ankles that gave away absolutely nothing. Probably the secretary. A florid man with bug eyes was listening to Roosevelt as if he were explaining the meaning of life or giving the winners from the sixth race at Saratoga. A pol. The other man was hard and square and way too alert. He had big hands and a cop's sneer and looked like he would make trouble for anyone who asked.

As Big picked his way toward them, balancing his suitcase and catching himself on seats against the swaying of the train, the cop rose.

"Keep moving, pally. We're busy here."

Big gave him a nod of understanding but then seemed to stumble over the suitcase. He caught himself on the cop's shoulder and peered around.

"Excuse me, Governor," he said.

The pol and the secretary looked up; Roosevelt kept talking. The cop bellied Big toward the front of the carriage. His hand clamped Big's elbow and began to turn him away.

"Filbrick Van Loon." Big dropped the suitcase on the cop's foot. "We met last summer in Utica, sir. You gave me the medal of honor."

Then Roosevelt noticed him. "Did I?" The cop's grip eased and Big stepped around him and extended a hand. "Van Loon?" said Roosevelt. He wasn't sure but accepted Big's hand, gave it one emphatic shake and was done with it. "A fine Dutch name."

That's what he'd said the first time they had met. Big remembered now how big Roosevelt's head was, how his smile went off like a flashbulb, the way the dark pockets sagged under the eyes. "It meant a lot to me, sir. Being recognized by you, I mean. Especially because I voted for you when you ran for Vice President." From the smirk on the secretary's face, Big wondered if he'd overplayed his hand. "I never got the chance to tell you that."

"Son, I believe you voted for Governor Cox for President." Roosevelt spoke with elaborate care, as if to a first grader or an alderman. He bent forward to tug at the knees of his trousers, which had ridden up his legs to show the metal braces. "I was just filling the ticket." Then he straightened and twinkled at Big. "Max, make room for Mr. Van Loon here." He waved the cop off. "He must remind us of his exploits."

The cop glowered from a chair on the other side of the carriage while Big slid next to the secretary. She gave him a limp nod and introduced herself as Missy LeHand. The pol was Senator Somebody—first name Oscar or maybe Arthur.

"So what brings you to the big city, Phil?" said Roosevelt. "May I call you Phil?"

Roosevelt struck him as a man who didn't like to hear the word *no*, so Big shook his head. "Sure, Governor. Phil is just fine." Actually he hated his name; sometimes he thought it was the cause of all his troubles.

"Are you coming to see me dedicate the bridge? Fabulous achievement, isn't it?"

"Bridge?" said Big. The secretary was blocking his view of the Governor, so he tilted forward to look around her.

"The George Washington Bridge," Missy said. "It was in all the papers."

"The longest span in the entire world." Roosevelt glanced up at the fake candles on the chrome wall sconce and began to speechify. "A mile long."

"3,500 feet," said Missy.

"Over half a mile long." He held up a finger to note the correction. "Six lanes of traffic. Completed five months ahead of schedule for less than the original budget." He seemed to be rehearsing his remarks. "Mr. Ammann is the engineer and Mr. Gilbert is the architect. Yes?"

"Yes, Governor." Now Missy leaned forward, once again blocking Big's view. She studied him as if she might need to identify him someday in a police lineup. "I bet this one is going to see the monkey," she said.

"Terrible mess." Senator Somebody was eager to wriggle back into the conversation. "And how are they going to pay for the cleanup?

"That's a matter for Mayor Walker," said Roosevelt. "He called in the planes without consulting us. The state bears no responsibility for what happened and will assume none of the financial burden of sorting things out now."

"Still, Governor," said the Senator, "when New York sneezes, Albany catches cold."

"I will not open the state's coffers to those thieves in Tammany Hall." Roosevelt flashed his smile. "However, should the mayor request a Kleenex, I'll be happy to accommodate him."

Big took the cue to laugh, although he realized his time with the Governor must be running out. "Actually," he said, "I was hoping to see the Mayor about a job."

"There are so few jobs." Roosevelt fitted a Chesterfield into his cigarette holder. "So many jobless."

"It's just that now that the Skyguard and the Science Pirate are gone," Big continued, "I was thinking that maybe...."

"You want to take the Skyguard's place?" The cop's harsh laugh drowned out the train's clatter. The codger glared at them over his paper and then picked up and left the carriage.

"Just because they're gone, Mr. Van Loon," said the Senator, lighting Roosevelt's cigarette, "doesn't mean they'll stay gone."

"Aha! You're *that* Van Loon." Roosevelt pointed the holder at Big. "From Utica. You saved those people in that fire. You have some kind of power—what was it again?" He turned to his secretary for the answer, but she just shrugged. "Ah, Missy, I don't believe you made that trip. I left in the morning, as I recall, and came back before dinner. Terrible crime problem in Utica. Bootlegging. Rackets. Worst corruption in the state."

"The Genesee Street fire," said Big. "There were eighteen people trapped on the fifth floor."

"And you rescued them," said Roosevelt, pleased with himself for remembering.

The Senator frowned. "You have some kind of power?"

Big nudged his suitcase out of the way with his foot and set himself in the middle of the carriage. He checked the curved ceiling. Maybe eight feet, but he could only do what he could do. At least he was wearing his baggy suit. He always started by thinking about his feet, hungry muscles, greedy bone. His toes curled inside his shoes to grip imaginary stuff. He felt it flow into him: first his legs went rigid with new substance and then they grew. Big got taller, slowly at first and then faster, his skin stiffening into a hardened shell to support him. But he was nervous and too eager to impress, so he let the spurt go on too long. He cracked his head against the ceiling, breaking his concentration.

"Oww. *Shit.*" He gazed down at them. He had Missy's attention and could tell the Senator was impressed.

"Are you all right?" Roosevelt seemed more concerned than awestruck.

When he stopped thinking about getting tall, the stuff flowed back into his imagination. He'd never understood how he did what he did; all he knew was that it was difficult to maintain. His muscles always quivered as they returned to normal and now, when the train lurched over some bad track, he staggered. The cop was up immediately to catch him. "Easy there, Stretch."

"I'm fine."

For a moment everyone considered what had just happened. Big slumped beside Missy, embarrassed by his swearing.

"Nice trick," she said. "Maybe you should be in vaudeville."

The Senator found his voice. "What's the biggest you've ever been?"

"I touched the roof of the Adirondack Bank Building once." Big raised a hand over his head. "That's fourteen stories."

"Incredible." The Senator whistled. "How do you do it?"

"I don't really know. I just think real hard and it happens."

"So when you're that tall, you must be able to cover ground in a hurry," said Roosevelt. "Big strides and all."

"Our very own Paul Bunyan," Missy said. Big flushed, but her grin was more flirting than teasing.

"Actually, moving is hard." He shook his head. "My muscles lock and my legs get all stiff and..." His voice trailed off in embarrassment when he remembered that he was talking to a man who needed a cane, leg braces and a helper to go to the john.

"That's all right, son, I understand perfectly." The Governor reset his pince-nez glasses on his nose. "So about this job you're looking for...?"

"I thought maybe I could help the police. You know, fighting crime like the Skyguard."

"That stuffed shirt didn't fight crime!" The cop bolted from his chair again. "Oh sure, maybe him and the Science Pirate busted a few bootleggers. And they chased those jewel thieves. But did they catch them? No. Then robots came and busted into the Metropolitan Museum. Were there robots before these superheroes showed up? No. Next they're fighting each other." He realized that everyone was staring. "We don't need that kind of help." His voice fell and his arm dropped. "Worse than the crooks."

"I heard their last fight put some bystanders in the hospital," said the Senator. "Tore up Park Avenue so bad that they had to close it between 32nd and 36th."

"But think of the people it put to work," said Missy.

Roosevelt smiled. "I'm not sure we can support that kind of jobs program."

"Take your crime fighting upstate, Stretch," said the cop, "where there's nothing but squirrels and trees."

"Oh, pay no attention to him." Missy's stagey whisper was sweet in his ear. "That one's just mad because this is supposed to be his day off."

"Nuts," the cop muttered.

Was he mistaken or was she making eyes at him?

"Max has a point, Phil." Roosevelt tapped ash into a tray set on a chrome pedestal. "There's not much call for that line of work. Do you have any police experience?"

That was not a question he'd been eager to hear. "No, sir."

"What did you do back in Utica?"

"I was unemployed."

A moment passed. Then another. They waited for him to go on, but Big had nowhere to go.

"Unemployed?" prompted the Senator. "Your entire life?"

"I worked for the A&P." Actually he'd lost that job when he was fourteen. "Stocking shelves mostly. I ran the register some." He'd gotten fired when his cash drawer had been light three times in two weeks. After that he'd fallen in with Happy Regan and his gang and had worked his way up from lookout to driver and finally to the bootlegger's main muscle man. When he got really, really tall, deadbeats crapped silver dollars. "It wasn't much of a job, then they laid me off and then my mother got the consumption and I had to stay with her most days. She died just last month."

"I am sorry for your loss." Roosevelt's expression was polite but distracted. Missy, however, was clearly touched.

"Anyway, there was nothing holding me home and after saving those folks from the fire and getting the medal and all, I thought maybe I might try my luck in the big city." He took a deep breath and made his play. "I was wondering if maybe you could help, sir? I'd really appreciate it."

Roosevelt pulled the stub of his cigarette out of its holder. "Well, you must understand that I'm not exactly on the best of terms with the Mayor. And all the jobs worth having come out of Tammany Hall, not City Hall." He snuffed it in the ashtray. "Walker dances when Boss Curry twitches his strings." He tucked the holder into the vest pocket of his jacket. "I've been at odds with Tammany in the past but there's a kind of truce at the moment. We've been doing each other little favors."

"You spoke at the dedication of the new Hall," said Missy.

"And I've invited Curry and Flynn and McCooey to Hyde Park." He considered. "You mustn't bother John Curry though, not that he'd be likely to see you anyway. Missy, do you have one of my cards?" She retrieved a briefcase. "Take yourself down to the new building," said Roosevelt, "it's just off Union Square. See Jimmy

Dooling. I don't know what kind of work you can do, Phil, but show him my card. He may be able to help."

Missy took a gilt fountain pen from her purse and scrawled something on the back of the card. Roosevelt, Missy and the Senator all had the same bland expression, as if they were doing times tables in their heads. Big took the hint; this was how quality got rid of the likes of him.

Big picked up his suitcase. "Thank you, sir." He took the card from Missy.

"Best of luck, Phil. Come to the dedication tomorrow."

Big pushed through the door to the observation car, so excited that he kept walking until he ran out of train. It was only when he sat down again that he saw what Missy LeHand had written on the back of the card.

Waldorf 9:30.

Tammany Hall was half an hour's walk down Park Avenue from Grand Central Station. As he passed 34th Street, Big caught a glimpse of the crowd pressing around the Empire State Building but didn't stop.

Although the bricks of the new Tammany Hall looked like they had just come out of the kiln and the white limestone trim gleamed, the architecture was supposed to be old-fashioned, as if George Washington had slept there, or at least stopped for a sandwich. The lobby boiled with men of every shape and flavor: sweet and sour, rough and smooth, wearing plus-fours or boilersuits, caps or fedoras. Big was directed to the third floor.

At the desk in front of James Dooling's office, a woman sat reading a copy of *Photoplay* with a picture of Joan Crawford on the cover. His mother used to read *Photoplay*—when he could afford the quarter to buy one for her. This woman looked nothing like poor, shriveled Thelma Van Loon. She was wearing a slinky silver dress, her dark hair was cut in a bob and her eyebrows were plucked to the verge of extinction. If she was a secretary, then Big was the Queen of Norway.

"Excuse me," said Big.

She turned a page as if he hadn't spoken.

"I'm looking for James Dooling."

A couple of men in suits were waiting on the bench opposite the desk. One of them leaned forward. The other one chuckled.

"That's funny." The woman kept reading. "So am I."

"Will he be back anytime soon?"

"If he figures out I'm here waiting to kill him?" She shook her head. "No chance."

Big couldn't think what to say to that. "Can I make an appointment?"

"Not with me."

Now both of the men were laughing. Big could feel the back of his neck burn.

"The Governor sent me," he said. "I have his card."

"Do you?" She looked up from her magazine then and winked at the men on the bench. "Let me guess. Is it the deuce of clubs?"

Big thought about telling her off, but for all he knew she might be Dooling's mistress—or his wife. "Okay then. Thanks for nothing."

He was halfway down the stairs when he heard someone call. "Hey, buddy."

The man from the bench was tall and built like a stevedore. He was wearing a silky double-breasted jacket with just the bottom buttons done and straight-legged trousers that were way too wide at the cuff. His tie was bubble gum pink.

"The name isn't Buddy. It's Big."

"Micky McCabe." They shook hands. "Look, I've been waiting on Jimmy for an hour myself and I'm ready to give it up. You have the look of a drinking man, if you don't mind my saying so. How about we drown our sorrows? Any friend of Franklin Roosevelt is a friend I'd like to make."

"You buying?"

"You bet, Big." He grinned. "I buy *and* sell."

The Old Town Bar was near the corner of 18th and Park. "Boss Curry watches over this place," McCabe said as he held the glass door. "So you can get served, if you know how to ask."

Behind the storefront windows was a long room with a tin-tiled ceiling, black from smoke. To the right were booths; to the left were plate glass mirrors behind a mahogany bar that stretched the entire length of the room. "Fifty-five feet." McCabe knocked on the bar's marble top as they walked toward the back; he and the barkeep exchanged nods. The further into the room they went the darker it was, despite the green tulip-shaped lamps. They slid into a booth and a waiter appeared out of the gloom.

"Afternoon, Mr. McCabe."

"Afternoon, Pete. We'll have a couple of ham sandwiches." He nodded at Big. "You're hungry, yes?"

Big nodded. There was something familiar about McCabe, even though he was certain that he'd never met the man.

"And a round," said his new friend, and the waiter evaporated. "So Big, what brings you to the city?"

"Looking for a job."

He nodded. "What's your line of work?'

Big surveyed the bar—there were maybe twenty customers. "How high would you say the ceiling here is?"

"Dunno. McCabe cocked his head and squinted. "Fifteen feet? Twenty?"

Big slid out of the booth, raised an arm over his head and extended his index finger. He grinned at McCabe.

Then he got tall.

He concentrated on keeping most of the stuff below his knees so as not to split his pants. When his finger touched the ceiling, he wrote *T...H...E...S...T...I...L...T* in the soot and shrank back to normal.

As he'd strolled through the bar minutes before, Big had caught snatches of a dozen conversations, some hushed, some raucous, more than a few profane. Now there was only reverent silence, as if Pope Pius himself had bought a round for the house. Then the bartender started clapping and then everyone was cheering and McCabe pulled him back into the booth.

"How the hell do you do that?"

Big explained, or tried to, and then the drinks came. He and McCabe touched glasses and knocked back a couple shots of something that was clear as water and deadly as sin. He felt it knife down his throat and then take a slice off the back of his skull.

"What's this supposed to be?" He tried not to sputter. "Gin?"

"My dear old Da called it poteen." McCabe thumped his empty glass on the table. "Me, I like to think of it as flavored fire. So let me get this straight. You can grow a hundred feet tall..."

"No, no. More."

"...but you can't move much." He settled back on his bench. "What happens to your clothes when you get that big?"

Big unsnapped his suitcase. "I had this costume made, kind of like the Skyguard's." He pulled the suit out and held it up by the shoulders. "Knit elastic, so it stretches." He admired The Stilt's royal blue fabric with yellow piping, the stylized yellow ladder on the chest. He'd thought about adding a cape, but just this much had cost him his last dollar.

McCabe was dubious. "*That* stretches a hundred feet?"

"No." Big flushed. "I only get really tall in emergencies."

He considered, then his face lit up. "You bust out of your suit?" He had a good laugh. "God damn! Big as the Statue of Liberty and butt naked."

Big stared at a gouge in the tabletop. The problem with the clothes was what had kept him in Utica all these years.

"Don't look so glum, pal." McCabe reached across to punch his shoulder. "That'll get your picture in the paper for certain." He chuckled. "But I don't get the ladder."

"It's my symbol." Big folded the costume and slipped it back in the suitcase.

"Okay."

"Goes with my crime-fighting name." He nodded at what he'd written on the ceiling. "The Stilt. Like it?"

"What's a ladder got to do with stilts?"

The food arrived: a thick slice of ham, Swiss cheese and brown mustard on seeded rye with a half pickle on the side. The waiter asked if they wanted anything else and McCabe slid both empty glasses toward him for refills.

"So why work for the law? Percentage is on the other side, if you ask me."

Big understood then what he'd recognized in McCabe. His familiarity with the speakeasy wasn't just because he was a regular customer. "This is your place."

"I own a piece of it, sure. Try the pickle." McCabe bit into his sandwich.

"Been on the other side," said Big. "It got kind of hot."

"Thought so." He spoke around a mouthful, then swallowed. "I can tell these things, Big. It's a gift. But look, your problem is that nobody is going to hire you to fight crime in this town. I mean, look at what the law is against. A drink to take your mind off your troubles. A woman to remind you why you're alive. A friendly game to change your luck. We're grown men, Big. What are we supposed to do on a Saturday night? Play tiddlywinks?"

"The Skyguard and the Science Pirate went after bank robbers."

"Bank robbers?" He wiped his mouth on the back of his hand. "You sat through too many matinees, pal. Look, those two costumed slickers weren't on anybody's payroll. Self-employed all the way. Upper class and in it for themselves." He tapped the side of his nose. "Now just between us, I could find work for a guy with your talents, but it sure wouldn't be fighting crime. No, sir." Seeing the look on Big's face, he held his hands up to surrender. "Okay, just laying out options. You want my advice? Before you try Jimmy Dooling again, do something amazing. Let him open his morning paper and see how big you can be."

They were finishing lunch when the second round arrived. McCabe toasted Big. "To The Stilt. Stand tall, pally!" They drank. "Tell the truth now," he said, eyeing Big over the edge of his glass, "you don't really have Roosevelt's card, do you?"

Big fished it out of his pocket and held it so McCabe could read only the front.

"They say he's going to run for President," McCabe said.

Big shrugged; he didn't have any use for politics.

"He'd be a fool not to." McCabe dropped a quarter on the table for a tip. "Even

I could beat Hoover. Republicans turn everything to shit." He leaned forward. "But that card is no good at Tammany, my friend. Boss Curry hates Roosevelt, even though they're making nice just now. You keep it handy though—it'll really impress the cops."

When they stood to go, McCabe turned from Big to address his customers. "Hey you huckleberries, listen up." The bar went silent. "This here is The Stilt. Next time you hear it, remember you met him here at the Old Town."

Big couldn't see the Empire State Building as he walked uptown because the buildings on Park blocked his view. He knew he was gawking like a hick from Utica; twice he bumped into other pedestrians. The day's ups and downs had left him lightheaded and when he patted the card in his pocket, the thought of Missy LeHand and what might happen at the Waldorf Astoria at 9:30 burned his brain like McCabe's hooch. His mother always used to say that there was no place for the likes of him in the big city. But she was gone now and he was determined to prove her wrong. More had happened to him in eight hours than had happened in Utica in the past eight years. He'd met Roosevelt but missed Dooling. McCabe had tried to pull him back into the nightmare and then pointed toward Big's most cherished dream. It wasn't enough to get tall. Big needed to be as amazing as this city where the windows glowed with promise and every other door opened into a new world. If only he could stumble upon a holdup. Or a fire. Or Garbo, dangling from a skyscraper.

And then he turned down 34th Street.

For the first time since he'd discovered his power, Big felt tiny. If he got as tall as he'd ever been, he might be able to peer into the windows of the first setback of the Empire State Building. But that wouldn't be even one-fifth its height. The Adirondack Bank in Utica was a fire plug compared to this superbuilding. He slowed, in part from awe and in part because of the smell. By the time he reached Madison Avenue, it was like cramming barbed wire up his nose. He tried to untangle all of the stink's evil strands. Rotting meat, yes. Shit straight from hell, okay. But something cooked—no, *burnt*. Like an electrical fire or failing brakes. This last strand of the smell was fresh and sharp.

Just past Madison, the crowd swarmed the street and both sidewalks. Some, like him, pressed ahead to see the spectacle. Others stumbled away from it, faces ashen, eyes bulging and wet. Big had to tiptoe around splashes of vomit on the street. How long had the monster lain sprawled at the base of the Empire State Building? A week? Ten days? He'd read that the first crowds had brought Midtown to a standstill. That had been before the enormous corpse began to putrefy. Still, there were hundreds of people surging around him holding hats against their faces or breathing through scarves. Big buried his nose in the crook of his elbow and eavesdropped.

"...hundred feet tall, at least."

"Yeah, but that don't include...."

"...happy now?"

"...walked across the bridge for this?"

A crew of workers lashed a forty-foot-long arm onto one of the two logging trucks parked in front of the body. Black fingers curled at one end, the exposed flesh at the other was purplish-gray. A fire engine idled nearby; firemen hosed the foul, runny puddles that had oozed from the severed arm into the sewer.

"...a punishment. Giant apes and flying pirates and lightning men."

"...kid sliced that arm right off."

"Punishment for what?"

The body had landed on its back. The head was still on the torso but both legs were gone and the other arm dangled, almost severed. The shaggy black pelt was charred at the shoulders and there were savage burn holes in the chest. Construction equipment lined up beside what was left of the monster. A sling hung from the hook of a waiting crane. Two of the biggest bulldozers he'd ever seen strained against the corpse, their blades riding up its side and treads chewing asphalt as they failed to get purchase.

"...they trying to do?"

"Turn him over maybe? Get that sling under...."

"You saw the lightning guy?"

"Shot down out of the clouds. *Crack*. Maybe half an hour ago."

"Another damn superhero to...."

"Lightning strikes don't come down, Mabel. They shoot up."

"You're crazy."

"Excuse me." Big's heart was pounding. "Did you say something about a superhero?"

Mabel was a short woman in a pillbox hat made of feathers. "Sure. He was just here."

"Seared the arm right off with his lightning. Just like that." Her companion, an older man wearing a trilby and a silk scarf, snapped his fingers. "What did they say his name was?"

"Bobby, was it?"

"Billy Bolt," said another man. "Kid blasted holes in the chest. Looked like he was having fun. Then he took the one arm but couldn't finish the other."

"Turned himself back into lightning," said the older man. "Amazing."

"Just a kid." Mabel blinked up at Big; she was wearing too much mascara. "He'll be back."

"Think so? He looked kind of dazed."

"Probably has to recharge or something."

Big spotted a reporter with his notebook working the crowd. Cameras flashed near the monster, although he couldn't see the shutterbugs. He should have known that he wouldn't be the only one to take advantage of the disappearance of the Skyguard and the Science Pirate. A kid who could change himself into lightning? Big didn't have much time.

He threaded his way to the uptown sidewalk scanning the storefronts. Newsstand, drug store, laundry, bank; he chose Mendy's Deli. Nobody would be eating in this stench.

"Bathrooms for customers only," said a bored counterman.

"Telephone." Big pointed. "Got to make a call."

His suitcase caught on the folding wooden door and Big had to stand it on end in order to squeeze into the phone booth. When he pulled the doors closed, there wasn't room to get the suitcase all the way open. He twisted The Stilt suit out, stripped naked and wriggled into it. Then he took a deep breath. He realized that his life up until that moment had been nothing but a warmup. Now he was putting himself into the game. He struggled out of the phone booth and planted his feet to get tall. He'd practiced this trick back home, sending the stuff so his torso expanded while his legs stayed normal. Only his bare feet hardened with stuff; that way he could run. He winked at the astonished counterman and bent nearly double to fit through the door.

Big had gotten tall in front of people before but never while wearing the costume. The Stilt stood fourteen, maybe fifteen feet; the suit stretched perfectly. When he started for the corpse, the crowd parted for him. He could feel their eyes on him; their astonishment was intoxicating. People called to him, shouted, *shrieked*. A teenaged girl screamed. He jumped the police cordon and strode across the open space between the crowd and the dead monster.

A beat cop came forward to stop him. "You can't come this way." He gestured for The Stilt to turn around. "You just crossed a police line, chum."

"Afternoon, Officer," The Stilt called. "I'm here to help."

"What did I do to deserve this?" The cop placed himself in The Stilt's way. "You with that other freak? The kid?"

"Nope. It's just me." He took smaller steps so as not to alarm the cop but did not stop his approach. "Name is The Stilt." Another cop came running, clamping his hat down on his head. He was maybe thirty yards away. "Just got the call from the firehouse to come down and lend a hand with the cleanup." The way The Stilt had it figured, he might confuse one cop, but two would be trouble. The first cop had his hand on his Colt but the holster's safety strap was still buckled. The Stilt slowed as if he meant to halt and imagined stuff flowing into his legs. He shot up another five feet. The cop's eyes went wide but he did not give way.

"This won't take long," The Stilt said.

"Mister, I...."

He stepped over the cop without breaking stride, clearing the man's head by a good two feet. He let some stuff go from his legs and started running again toward the monster. He did not look back.

He came from behind the two bulldozers, so the operators didn't see him until he stood between them. One wore a gas mask that looked like it might have seen action in the Great War. The other had a red bandana over his mouth and nose and an engineer's cap pulled down low on his forehead, so that only his eyes showed. The Stilt saluted and the engineer goggled, then slammed his machine in neutral. Gas Mask followed suit.

"I'm here to help," shouted The Stilt.

The engineer cupped a hand over his ear and shook his head. The Stilt made a scooping motion and the engineer cut the engine of his machine.

The Stilt leaned into the cab. "Can I try something?"

"Buddy, be my guest. We're just wasting diesel here."

"I'm going to lift it up," said The Stilt.

"You and what army?"

The Stilt smiled. "Can somebody pull the sling under it?"

The engineer considered, clearly full of doubt. Then he shrugged. "Won't be the craziest thing I seen today." He gestured for Gas Mask to shut down. "I'll tell the crane," he said and began to climb off the dozer.

The Stilt let all the stuff flow out of him until he was his natural size. Standing next to the dead monster, he rolled the sleeves of his costume above his elbows. The stink here was strong enough to bring tears to a statue. He could feel something gluey squish between his toes. He turned his head to one side, took a desperate breath and leaned into the corpse with his arms down, palms brushing against the thick hair of the pelt. His toes curled and stuff began to surge into him through the concrete sidewalk, summoned from the granite spine beneath the city. His feet were no longer flesh as they anchored into the city's bedrock. His arms stretched and burrowed beneath the dead weight of the corpse and his skin thickened into an impenetrable shell. Stuff clotted his chest, slowed his heart, reinforced his backbone. Chin pressed hard against the body, he tried not to think about the smell. When he'd saved the people in Utica he hadn't had time to think. He hadn't noticed when his clothes shredded from his grotesque body, he hadn't minded the searing heat of the fire, and it didn't matter whether the crowd swarming like ants below him had been cheering—or laughing at his bare ass. Back then he'd been able to focus on the men and women climbing across his arms, clinging to his neck, weeping with gratitude. But he hadn't been The Stilt in Utica. He'd been Filbrick Van Loon, a thug who didn't earn enough collecting a bootlegger's debts to pay for the doctors his dying mother needed. He'd been a man who could save strangers, but not the only person in the world who loved him. The memory made The Stilt angry; he tapped that anger to pull more and more stuff into himself, getting bigger and stronger. His heart hardened, and now his thoughts grew sluggish and stony as the monster tilted and began to lift off the street. He was The Stilt, *yes*. Stilt got tall. Stilt was...

"Hold it there, pal."

Hold what? Stilt didn't have any pals.

"*Stop*. You hear me? No higher!"

The Stilt couldn't see anything but coarse hair and gray skin. With a groan he turned his head. The engineer and the gas mask and some cops and firemen and construction workers were frantically working the sling down the length of the corpse. The Stilt couldn't smell anything anymore. His nose filled with stuff.

"Okay, let her go."

The Stilt didn't understand. Let who go? His mother? That secretary? He couldn't remember...Missing? Missy?"

"Wake up, Big Guy! Let go!"

"There's something wrong with him."

"Can he hear us?"

"Hit the siren!"

A high-and-low metallic yowling, as of a machine in pain, and the furious clatter of bells penetrated the crust squeezing The Stilt's brain. Stuff begin to flow away; he could think again and his first thought was *he had done it*!

He was amazing.

They took what seemed like hundreds of pictures. He got ten, fifteen, thirty feet tall. He presented arms folded, boxer-at-the-ready and muscle man poses, then filled the five-story entrance to the Empire State Building for them. He spelled his name for reporters from the *Daily Mirror* and *Evening Post*, told how he'd chosen his superhero identity and explained the ladder on his costume. He glossed over his recent past since he didn't want anyone talking to the cops in

Utica. The engineer asked for his autograph—his first ever. He printed it: *The Stilt.* He gave a kid a ride on his shoulders, although the brat held his nose the entire time.

Yet for all that, The Stilt's debut went nothing like Big had imagined it would. This was not a crime he'd foiled, after all—more like garbage he'd collected. His costume was stained and he smelled like hell's own outhouse. Which meant that the crowd, with the exception of the kid, shied away. No pretty girls offered to kiss him and he signed just the one autograph. Then, as he was telling his story all over again to the reporter from the *Times*, there was a flash of light in the no man's land between the monster and the crowd, followed closely by what sounded like an explosion. He turned to see a teenager wearing a white lab coat, white shirt, blue necktie and doughboy helmet painted blue to match. The kid staggered and fell to hands-and-knees in a circle of smoldering asphalt. When he shook himself and got up, Big could see crude white lightning bolts painted on the helmet. The kid glanced from the butchered corpse sprawled on the crippled truck to Big and his face twisted with anger. The *Times* reporter waved but Billy Bolt gave him the finger. Then he began to glitter and turned into a million snowflakes of light which burst into light and sound. He left only a blue-bright afterimage and a ringing in Big's ears. Maybe he was supposed to be insulted or jealous or scared, but Big's only thought was that the kid's costume needed work.

There was a cop in Mendy's Deli taking a statement from the angry clerk. Both turned when Big came through the door.

"You!" The clerk looked like he was ready to leap across his counter to throttle Big. "This is your fault."

"Huh?"

"You saying this is the thief?" The cop glowered, as if sizing Big up for handcuffs.

"I'm saying this is the freak who put on the damn show. And I'm the lunkhead who left to watch."

"You know anything about this, sir?"

"About what?"

"My till is empty! And three Westphalian hams gone!" The counterman was shouting now. "I've been robbed!"

So had Big. The phone booth was empty; the thief must have used the suitcase to carry off his swag. Big had lost everything he owned.

The cop listened to his story but didn't seem much interested. He jotted Big's name in a notebook. "Mister, you can't be leaving valuables in phone booths." He raised the notebook to his face as if to ward off Big's stink. "Not in this town, anyway."

"What am I going to do?" said Big. "I'm new in town and now I'm broke. I've got no place to go."

"Try the poor house." The cop snapped the notebook shut.

It was almost dark by the time Big got in line at 432 East 25ᵗʰ Street. On the way he'd clipped a flannel shirt and bib overalls with a patch on one knee from a clothesline strung across a fourth-story fire escape. He thought they made him look like a rag picker. He wadded his reeking costume and clamped it under his arm as the line moved up the front steps of the Municipal Lodging House. The frayed man at the reception table wanted to send him to the Registration Bureau at South Ferry until he saw that Big was barefooted. So he took Big's particulars: Filbrick Van Loon; age thirty-three; born Oriskany, New York; lived thirty-three years in the United States; lived six hours in New York City; last address 12 Faxton Street, Utica, New York; occupation none; military service none; not married; no relatives to contact in case of emergency. They sent him to the mess hall where he dipped sliced bread into a bowl of beef stew that was mostly carrots and potatoes and onions. After dinner he traded his stolen clothes and his costume for a brass chit embossed with the number 48. His things were taken away to be disinfected; they'd be returned in the morning. They gave him and the other homeless men towels and nightshirts. The shower was lukewarm but Big stood under it scrubbing until his skin stung. Afterwards he climbed into the lower of a double-decked iron bed. He got a folded blanket to sleep on instead of a mattress and another blanket for cover but the dormitory was warm and it didn't matter if his bunkmates snored. Big couldn't sleep anyway.

He lay awake thinking of all the things he'd ever done wrong, the money he'd stolen, the men he'd beaten up. He thought of his mother and what she'd say if she could see him now. He wished he had a drink. Just one tumbler of Happy Regan's phony whiskey or Micky McCabe's poteen would've turned the world right side up. He should never have left the suitcase in the phone booth. The Skyguard would never have done anything that stupid. And he would never have seen the inside of a poor house, probably lived in one of those mansions facing Central Park. If only Big still had Roosevelt's card. He imagined Missy LeHand waiting for him in the lobby of the Waldorf Astoria, and the more he thought about her the more glamorous and beautiful and distant she became. She would be wearing an evening dress. It would be silvery and show her shoulders. She'd be sipping champagne. A nobody like him would be crazy to chase a girl like her.

Except she had chased him.

He left right after breakfast because he had a lot of ground to cover. It was almost ten miles to Washington Heights. They had found him a pair of brown wingtip shoes that were almost the right size. He wore his costume under his clothes. On the way uptown, he stole a copy of the *Times* from a newsstand and found a *Daily Mirror* in the trash at a bus stop. He was disappointed to see that the *Times* didn't have photographs; at least they spelled his name right on page two. He made the front page of the *Mirror* under a caption "Stiltman Dumps Ape."

It took him most of the morning to hike to the new bridge and as he climbed the ramp he discovered that half of Manhattan had turned out for the dedication. He threaded through several marching bands that were forming up into a parade on the entrance ramp. Big strode down the center lane, scanning the temporary bleachers on either side of the bridge for Missy or Roosevelt. He hadn't worked out much of a plan besides showing up. They must have read about him in the papers; that would give him something to talk about. Maybe he could have his picture taken with the Governor, meet some of the other swells. At the least he could ask Roosevelt for another card. And Missy for another chance.

Evergreen garlands and American flags draped the dignitaries' podium. Roosevelt wore a formal three-piece suit and a top hat. A white carnation glowed on his lapel; his smile was even brighter. Big paused and started to unbutton the stolen shirt. He was planning on getting tall before he made his final approach as The Stilt, but Missy came out of nowhere and caught his arm.

"Button yourself right now, Mr. Van Loon."

"Missy, I can explain."

"Walk with me." She threw all of her weight into marching him past the podium toward New Jersey.

"It wasn't my fault."

She seemed not to hear.

"Did you see I made the papers?"

She picked up the pace.

Finally, when they were past the bleachers and onto the central span, she stopped. "You went to see the monkey instead of me." She was cool as a cloudy Saturday in October. "Why am I not surprised?"

"It wasn't that way at all."

"No?"

He told her everything, more than he intended to. He told her about McCabe and picking up the monster and the smell and the missing suitcase and the stolen

THE BIGGEST | 295

clothes and iron bed at the Municipal Lodging House. He said he'd spent most of the night thinking about her waiting for him.

"I didn't wait," she said. "I was back in my room by 9:35."

"That's good," he said, although he knew it wasn't. "But you asked me to come and I wanted to be there. That's why I'm here now. I thought that maybe you and I...."

"There is no you and I."

"But you wrote on the card...."

"We read the papers this morning. I had to remind Franklin that we'd just met you. He has a lot on his mind. Real problems, not your foolishness." She looked back at the podium. "He's going to run for president, you know. I'm his secretary and his wife doesn't live with him. There's nothing between us romantically..." the word seemed to stick in her throat, "...but people talk. It helps if I'm seen in public with other men."

Big felt as empty as he'd ever been. He thought if he didn't get tall soon he might blow away. "Do you think," he said, "he might give me another card?"

She never got the chance to answer. Big didn't see the flash but the thunder-clap made him jump. He looked up at the tower of exposed steel on the New York side and saw a figure in white bounce and land on one of the two downstream suspension cables. He could hear an ugly sizzling. The fluffy clouds above them twisted and darkened, as if stained by sin. The sky turned green. What was the kid trying to do? Land in front of Roosevelt's podium and introduce himself? Too much steel for that. Had the kid even seen the bridge before? There was a lightning strike on the tower that seemed to skitter down the cable to the writh-ing figure of Billy Bolt. His helmet flew off and he caught fire. The next flash cut a suspender cable directly beneath him; it tipped over the edge of the bridge. People poured out of the stands, shouting and screaming. One last lightning bolt skewered the burning boy, knocking him off the bridge and severing one of the two main cables. Big could feel the deck of the bridge shudder.

They were doomed unless The Stilt did something amazing.

He climbed onto a support truss at the edge of the bridge. The river was impossibly far beneath him. He'd have to get as tall as he'd ever been.

"What are you doing?" Missy was behind him.

"I'll try to jump, but if I can't, you'll have to push me." It was hard to imagine the stuff with her there. "I think I can hold the bridge up."

"What? No."

"You want him to be president?" His feet burst out of the wingtips and the overalls split at the crotch.

"No, I mean you're already too big. How am I supposed to push you?"

The Stilt was twenty feet tall and growing. "Get help then."

He concentrated on his legs. He thought if he was bottom heavy, he would sink upright to the bottom of the river.

He never knew how he came off the bridge. Maybe he stepped off, even though his legs were stone. He fell forever, all the while losing stuff. He thought he saw the top of the Empire State Building. Were there really roller coasters all along the Palisades? Then came a giant slap as he hit the water, followed by a nightmare of darkness, cold, silence and no air. The bottom was the cruelest shock of all because he believed he was already dead. Then his head broke the surface of the river.

In a panic The Stilt got very tall, very fast. Faster than he had ever grown, taller than was possible. Still he had to raise his arms over his head to reach the bottom of the bridge.

But he did it.

And then he was naked in front of all of New York and New Jersey and Missy LeHand and maybe the future President of the United States but The Stilt was beyond embarrassment. The stuff filled his head, squeezing his imagination flat, turning his brain to stone.

His last thought was that his mother had been wrong. *He...was...amazing.*

From Wikipedia, the free encyclopedia:

Filbrick Van Loon (1898–1931), also known as "Stiltman," was an American superhero who had the ability to grow to enormous heights. Scientists at the Carson Institute theorize that he was able to accomplish this by manipulating his molecular structure.

Born in Utica, New York, little is known of his life before his arrival in New York City in October 1931. In one twenty-four-hour period he managed to remove the body of the King Kong from where it had fallen from the Empire State Building and to attempt to hold up the George Washington Bridge after it was damaged in a freak electrical storm. Othmar Ammann, chief engineer of the bridge, has stated that its structure was never compromised, and that Van Loon's sacrifice, while well-intentioned, was unnecessary. For undetermined reasons, Van Loon was unable to recover from his final transformation. His solidified body stands today, two hundred and forty-seven feet from the bed of the Hudson River to the bottom deck of the bridge.

This <u>superhero</u>-related article is a <u>stub</u>. You can help Wikipedia by <u>expanding it</u>.

PHILIP JOSÉ FARMER'S *TARZAN ALIVE:* A DEFINITIVE BIOGRAPHY OF LORD GREYSTOKE
WIN SCOTT ECKERT

The Wold Newton universe is a conceit created by Philip José Farmer—a shared universe where all the heroes and villains of popular culture and adventure fiction are somehow related. Farmer explored this idea in fiction and also, as in this piece by Win Scott Eckert, in works that played with the boundaries between fiction and nonfiction. Eckert has been keeping the PJF flame alive through many projects, including as editor of *Myths for the Modern Age: Philip José Farmer's Wold Newton Universe*, a hefty and delightful anthology of such reality-bending articles by various hands.

"This is a biography of a living person."

So states Philip José Farmer in his foreword to *Tarzan Alive* and in so doing follows the Sherlockian tradition in which the object of the fictional biography is treated as a real person. Sherlockian biographical scholarship (commonly called the "Game") arose as a response to a myriad of discrepancies in Watson's writings of the master detective Sherlock Holmes. In the Sherlockian Game Holmes's amanuensis, Dr. Watson, is also treated as a real person. As Dr. Watson narrates the cases, Arthur Conan Doyle is relegated to the status of Watson's "editor."

Game players then write critical essays that resolve the chronology of the Sherlock Holmes canon and otherwise provide explanations for inconsistencies in Watson's work. Sometimes the inconsistencies are explained as resulting from Watson's carelessness, whereas in other instances we are told that Watson *deliberately* changed certain details, times, and names to protect innocent parties and prevent delicate information from being uncovered through his writings.

Occasionally Game players go so far as to research and write complete biographies of their subjects. Some of the better-known examples are William S.

Baring-Gould's *Sherlock Holmes of Baker Street* and *Nero Wolfe of West Thirty-Fifth Street*, C. Northcote Parkinson's *The Life and Times of Horatio Hornblower* and *Jeeves: A Gentleman's Personal Gentleman*, John Pearson's *James Bond: The Authorized Biography of 007* and *Biggles: The Authorized Biography*, Anne Hart's *The Life and Times of Hercule Poirot* and *The Life and Times of Miss Jane Marple*, and Philip José Farmer's *Doc Savage: His Apocalyptic Life*, which serves as a companion piece to *Tarzan Alive*.

Lesser-known instances of the genre include *The Life and Exploits of the Scarlet Pimpernel* by John Blakeney, *The Flying Spy: A History of G-8* by Nick Carr, *The Wimsey Family* by C. W. Scott-Giles, *Radio's Captain Midnight: The Wartime Biography* by Stephen A. Kallis, Jr., and *John Steed: An Authorized Biography, Volume 1: Jealous in Honour* by Tim Heald.

These fictional biographies, to varying degrees, share the same characteristics; they all:

- discuss and resolve inconsistencies in the canon of the character's novels, stories, or adventures
- provide a timeline of the character's life (either as a formal chronology, or merely through a discussion of the timing of certain events)
- provide information on the character's family tree and forebears
- treat their subject as a real person.

What, then, sets *Tarzan Alive* apart from other fictional biographies? *Tarzan Alive* is patterned on Baring-Gould's biographies of Sherlock Holmes and Nero Wolfe. Edgar Rice Burroughs is cast as a writer who became privy to the real-life Tarzan's adventures but altered certain details and names in order to protect the real Lord Greystoke's identity and family. Farmer provides a chapter-by-chapter breakdown of Burroughs's Tarzan novels, as well as an addendum with a summary timeline of key events in Tarzan's life. He explains discrepancies in the Tarzan canon, such as the mystery of how Korak aged, seemingly overnight, between *The Beasts of Tarzan* and *The Son of Tarzan*. *Tarzan Alive* also offers information on Tarzan's forebears.

What distinguishes *Tarzan Alive* from other fictional biographies is the level of detail with which Farmer imbues his subject and with which he dares us to disbelieve. Farmer has not simply studied Tarzan's—Lord Greystoke's—life; he has actually met and interviewed Greystoke. Farmer has not only identified a few of Tarzan's forebears; he has spent uncounted hours poring over Burke's *Peerage* in an effort to uncover his real name, titles, and arms. Farmer has not merely discovered other real-life personages who are distantly related to Tarzan (such as Lord Byron); he has uncovered a plethora of other ostensibly "fictional" characters to whom Tarzan is related in a massive and complex family tree— *and* provided a cosmic explanation for the almost superhuman nature of these characters' adventures and abilities: the ionized radiation of the Wold Newton meteorite, resulting in the Wold Newton family.

The roster of Farmer's Wold Newton family is nothing if not bold. In addition to Tarzan and Doc Savage, other members include Solomon Kane (a pre-meteor strike ancestor); Captain Blood (a pre-meteor strike ancestor); Sherlock Holmes and his nemesis Professor Moriarty (AKA Captain Nemo); Phileas Fogg; the Time Traveler; Allan Quatermain; Rudolf Rassendyll; A. J. Raffles; Wolf Larsen; Professor Challenger; Arsène Lupin; Richard Hannay; Bulldog Drummond; Doctor Fu Manchu and Sir Denis Nayland Smith; G-8; Joseph Jorkens; the Shadow; Sam Spade; the Spider; Nero Wolfe; Mr. Moto; the Avenger; Philip Marlowe; James Bond; Lew Archer; Kilgore Trout; Travis McGee; and many more. In a dazzling display of non-canonical revisionism, Farmer even goes so far as to place Fitzwilliam Darcy and Elizabeth Bennet (from Jane Austen's *Pride and Prejudice*) and Sir Percy Blakeney (from Baroness Emmuska Orczy's *The Scarlet Pimpernel*) at the actual Wold Newton meteor strike in 1795.

Farmer's creation of the Wold Newton family elevated the fictional biography genre to a whole new level. Instead of focusing on one particular character, Game players following in Farmer's literary archaeological footsteps now determine how to extend and build upon Farmer's original family tree in an ongoing series of essays, timelines, and crossovers.

One of the first such forays into post-Farmerian Creative Mythography (as Farmer termed the Wold Newton Game in *Doc Savage: His Apocalyptic Life*) was The Wold Newton Meteoritics Society's *Wold Atlas* fanzine (1977–78). The *Wold Atlas* included genealogical essays, a serialized novel, and original illustrations and ran for five issues. A few essays inspired by Farmer's Wold Newton concept appeared in the 1980s and 1990s in various pulp-oriented publications such as *The Bronze Gazette*, *Nemesis Incorporated*, and *Pulp Vault*.

However, it took the Internet to coalesce a second wave of Creative Mythography with the 1997 publication of the first Wold Newton Web site, *An Expansion of Philip José Farmer's Wold Newton Universe*, or *The Wold Newton Universe* (http://www.pjfarmer.com/woldnewton/Pulp2.htm). By last count there are fourteen sites that have at least some Wold Newton material on them. Of these, about seven or eight are focused exclusively on the Wold Newton universe. The revived interest in Wold Newton studies has even spawned a new anthology of essays devoted entirely to the concept, *Myths for the Modern Age: Philip José*

Farmer's Wold Newton Universe (MonkeyBrain Books, 2005), with contributions by Farmer himself and several other scholars, writers, and pop culture historians.

Though readers may come to *Tarzan Alive* through a love of Edgar Rice Burroughs's Tarzan—a love deeply shared by Farmer—in finishing the story of Tarzan's life, they gain something more than a mere retelling of the Jungle Lord's adventures. *Tarzan Alive* shines brightly in the unusual subgenre of fictional biographies because it creates a whole world of interacting super-characters outside our window. Farmer makes you believe not only that Tarzan is real but that all the other characters are as well, because he inextricably weaves their history and Lord Greystoke's together.

Which brings us full circle. "This is a biography of a living person."

When Farmer interviewed Tarzan on September 1, 1970, the Lord of the Jungle was in his mid-eighties but looked about thirty-five. There's no reason to doubt that Tarzan is still alive today. Indeed, in the intervening thirty-plus years several more of the ape-man's adventures have been revealed. In various comic book adventures the Jungle Lord has been crossed-over with the rest of Edgar Rice Burroughs's major creations. He has traveled to Barsoom and met John Carter; visited Burroughs's Amtor (Venus) via astral projection; fought Burroughs's Moon Men in the twenty-fourth century; journeyed to the Land That Time Forgot, Caspak; and returned to Pellucidar again and again (once he even fought the Predators there). Tarzan has also encountered Frankenstein's Creature, Dr. Jekyll and Mr. Hyde, and perhaps most remarkably, the Golden Age Batman!

In the mid-1970s, western writer J. T. Edson played on Farmer's background for Lord Greystoke from *Tarzan Alive*, giving Tarzan another adopted son named Bunduki and sending the rest of the Greystoke clan to live in Pellucidar. However, yet another comic book revival saw Tarzan and Jane living back on the surface world in the late 1980s and early 1990s. Joe R. Lansdale completed a Burroughs manuscript, returning the Jungle Lord to the 1940s in *Tarzan: The Lost Adventure*. But readers of *Tarzan Alive* will likely be more intrigued by yet another contribution from Philip José Farmer. In 1999 he finally realized his dream of writing an authorized Tarzan novel with the publication of *The Dark Heart of Time*. True to form, Farmer took a barely hinted-at incident and fleshed it out into a complete "lost adventure" taking place between the events of Burroughs's novels *Tarzan the Untamed* and *Tarzan the Terrible*.

Perhaps most fascinating of all is Farmer's time-travel novel, *Time's Last Gift*. The main character, John Gribardsun, travels back in time from the year 2070 to 14,000 BCE. Inexplicably immortal, he lives a full life for 14,000 years until the year 2140 when he and his wife—*Jane*—depart Earth in a cryogenic sleeper spacecraft bound for the star Capella and new adventures. If Gribardsun is who we think he is (readers have speculated that the abbreviation of *Time's Last Gift*, TLG, provides a significant clue to Gribardsun's identity), then the Jungle Lord's motto—"I still live!"—takes on new meaning.

In *Tarzan Alive* Farmer convincingly demonstrated that there is a real pulp fiction universe just waiting to be explored. His boundless imagination keeps Tarzan alive forever, both figuratively and literally, and, in so doing, Philip José Farmer will also always *still live*.

THE ZEPPELIN PULPS
JESS NEVINS

The best way to make a lie convincing is to pepper it with truth. In this ingenious piece, created as supplemental material to the brilliant superhero/pulp/noir comics series *Incognito* by Ed Brubaker & Sean Phillips, annotator of note Jess Nevins (*Heroes & Monsters: The Unofficial Companion to The League of Extraordinary Gentlemen*, *The Encyclopedia of Fantastic Victoriana*, etc.) details the history of hero pulp magazines that may be very hard to find, indeed.

*P*osterity is cruel to popular culture. Successful series, in any medium, find themselves quickly forgotten. Sexton Blake was the second-most imitated character in the world in the 1930s, after Sherlock Holmes, and today Blake is virtually unknown. The radio serial *Fibber McGee and Molly* was famous internationally in the 1930s and 1940s and is now almost forgotten. This was true of the pulps, as well. One of the best examples of the forgotten pulps is the genre of zeppelin pulps and the most famous of them, *Complete Zeppelin Stories*.

During the late 1920s Frank Armer (1895–1965) was the man behind Ramer Reviews, a publisher of four minor pulps, including *Zeppelin Stories*, which was best known for Gil Brewer's lost apes-and-zeppelins classic, "The Gorilla of the Gasbags." Ramer Reviews failed in late 1929 and afterward Armer became an editor for Harry and Irwin Donenfeld on their "spicy" line of pulps, including *Spicy Detective Stories*. In 1935, for reasons not known, the Donenfelds and Armer had a falling out, and Armer left the Donenfelds' Culture Publications.

On February 12, 1935, the U.S. Navy Zeppelin *Macon*, pride of the Navy's aerial fleet and hoped for model for future U.S. military zeppelins, crashed off the coast of California. The *Macon* disaster, two years before the more famous wreck of the *Hindenburg*, cast doubt on the viability of zeppelins as military vessels. But the zeppelin boosters within the U.S. Army and Navy were unwilling to let a freak accident spoil their plans for a fleet of armed zeppelins, and sought for a way to redeem the image of the zeppelins in the eyes of the public.

This was not the Navy's first public relations problem. In 1934 the Navy was faced with nonexistent enlistment from Americans from non-coastal states. In response, Frank Martinek, a Navy lieutenant, created the comic strip *Don Winslow of the Navy*. Martinek's Don Winslow is an agent of Naval Intelligence who has thrilling adventures fighting against various international supercriminals. *Don Winslow of the Navy* succeeded in boosting enlistment, and a year later, the Navy decided to use the lesson of *Don Winslow* on zeppelins.

They hired Frank Armer, who founded a new publishing company, Stars and Stripes Publishing, and promptly resurrected *Zeppelin Stories* as *Complete Zeppelin Stories*. The lead story in the first issue, in September 1935, was "Death at 30,000 Feet," starring John Paul Jones, Commander of the Naval Zeppelin *Saratoga*. Jones was clearly intended to be the poster child for the series and to act as a recruiting tool, but something unexpected happened: fan interest skewed away from Jones (who, to modern eyes, is colorless and one-dimensional) and toward Professor Zeppelin, the protagonist of the back-up story, "The Sargasso of the Skies."

Modern readers dismiss Zeppelin as a Doc Savage rip-off—and, indeed, he is. Zeppelin is the "Sky Scientist." Zeppelin is reputed to be "the smartest man in the world" and is an expert in every field. Zeppelin is assisted by a team of men, all experts in their fields, including Auberon "The Brigadier" Cooper, the world's foremost expert on aeronautics, and Hammond "Piggy" Higgins, America's leading test pilot. Zeppelin has a floating base, the Zeppelin of Silence, stocked with technologically advanced aircraft. The Zeppelin of Silence also has a medical laboratory in which Zeppelin performs operations to remove the "sickness of evil" from the brains of criminals. And Zeppelin's skin is deeply tanned from months spent in the open cockpit of his zeppelin.

The similarities to Doc Savage are pronounced. But it was these similarities which were the cause of Professor Zeppelin's popularity. *Doc Savage* was at this time hitting its peak, both in quality and popularity, and the demand for more Doc Savage stories was greater than the supply, so Doc Savage imitations—like Jim Anthony and Captain Hazzard—were popular with readers. So, too, with Professor Zeppelin.

That a vigilante like Zeppelin should be more popular than a square-jawed, heroic Naval commander like John Paul Jones was undoubtedly embarrassing to the Navy, but Armer was a wily veteran of publishing and knew to play to his strengths, so in the next few issues he relegated Jones to the back-up features and made Professor Zeppelin the pulp's lead. Over the next nine issues— *Complete Zeppelin Stories*, like many other pulps, was bimonthly—Zeppelin fought an increasingly colorful set of foes: the Nazi aviator Pontius Pilot; the Black Death, the "living disease;" Wu Fang, the Helium Mandarin; Dr. Okayuma, who vivisected spies in his zeppelin laboratory; Amenhotep, the simian Pharaoh of the Congo; and Baron Nosferatu, the Flying Vampire.

Complete Zeppelin Stories was an instant success, and Armer responded by increasing the size of the pulp and including other series characters, most modeled on other popular heroes, in an obvious attempt to further increase sales and perhaps create spin-off pulps. The January 1936 issue introduced Lazarus, the Returned Man, a two-gun-wielding lift of the Shadow. The March issue introduced Agent 1776, who differed from Operator #5 only in the use of a red, white, and blue zeppelin. The May issue introduced the Scorpion, a more obvious-than-usual lift of the Spider. And the July issue introduced both Swift Stevens, a Flash Gordon lift, and Jack Blake, the Zeppelin Vigilante, a combination of the Phantom Detective and Secret Agent X.

By the summer of 1936 the sales of *Complete Zeppelin Stories* approached those of *Doc Savage*, *Love Story Magazine*, and *Western Story Magazine*. As was common in pulp publishing, other publishers rushed to imitate success and churned out a number of zeppelin pulps, including Ace Magazine's *Zeppelins*, Popular's *Dime Zeppelin Magazine*, Red Circle's *Complete Zeppelin Detective Stories*, Columbia Publications' *Flying Cowboy Stories*, and, most absurdly, Culture Publications' semi-pornographic *Spicy Zeppelin Stories*. Few of these pulps lasted long—*Spicy Zeppelin Stories* was such a failure it was cancelled after a single issue—but some had staying power. Street & Smith's *Zeppelin Story Magazine* proved to be a minor hit, and its most popular characters, the humorous, tall-tale-telling cowboy "Gasbag" Gallagher and the Texas Ranger "Dirigible" Adams, made appearances in other Street & Smith pulps into the 1940s. And Popular Publications, who in 1933 created the "weird menace" genre by turning the mediocre detective pulp *Dime Mystery Book* into the best-selling occult horror pulp *Dime Mystery Magazine*, made more money with another weird menace pulp: *Strange Tales of the Black Zeppelin*. *Strange Tales* featured a variety of unusual characters and stories, two of which outlived *Strange Tales* itself. The serial "The Passenger in Berth 12," written by Cornell Woolrich under the pseudonym of "K. Hite," became the famous lost film noir *The Passenger* (1938), which starred Paul Muni and Ann Savage in her first lead role. And the series "Doctor Weird," about an occult detective, was picked up by Chicago radio station WENR and turned into the horror drama *Doctor of Destinies*. Aided by its position following the notorious *Lights Out*, *Doctor of Destinies* was a hit for several years, and its opening was once as famous as *The Shadow*'s: a sepulchral voice intoning the phrase, "Do you dare step aboard the floating mansion of Anton Weird, Doctor of Destinies?"

In May 1937, the zeppelin genre of pulps seemed poised to become as significant and established a pulp genre as sports, romance, and detective pulps were. Hollywood was preparing to capitalize on the genre's popularity. Several zeppelin films were in pre-production, including the Willis O'Brien-directed *War Eagles* (in which Lost Race Vikings, riding pterodactyls, battle German zeppelins in the skies over New York), the Republic Pictures serial *The City in the Sky* (in which Ray "Crash" Corrigan would reprise his role from *Undersea Kingdom* and fight against a floating city of Yellow Perils), and the Universal Pictures serial *Smilin' Jack vs the Mad Baron* (which would have been the first serial for comic strip aviator Smilin' Jack). But on May 6 the *Hindenburg* burned. The *Hindenburg* disaster was the death knell for the use of zeppelins internationally and was equally fatal to the zeppelin films and the zeppelin pulp genre. So powerful was the image of the burning *Hindenburg* etched in the public's mind that pulp publishers didn't wait for sales to kill the zeppelin pulps, but pre-emptively cancelled them or folded them into other, safer pulps, as Street & Smith did, turning *Zeppelin Story Magazine* into *Air Trails*. Frank Armer was the lone holdout, keeping *Complete Zeppelin Stories* going as a Professor Zeppelin vehicle. Zeppelin became land-bound and rode a motorcycle, although his enemies, like the Baron von Mörder, the Future Fuhrer, remained imaginative.

But sales of *Complete Zeppelin Stories* never recovered, and in late 1937 Armer cancelled the pulp, folded Stars and Stripes Publishing, and agreed to sell Stars and Stripes' inventory to Martin Goodman, who was having success as a publisher of pulps like *Best Sports Magazine* and *Detective Short Stories*. Goodman apparently intended to use the *Zeppelin Story Magazine* inventory of stories in a new pulp, *Sky Devils*. But a quarrel between Armer and Goodman over the rights to several of the stories—Armer might have been thinking of the example of *The Passenger*, whose filming reportedly didn't earn Armer anything—led Armer to threaten legal action if Goodman used any of Stars and Stripes' pre-existing characters, like Professor Zeppelin, Lazarus, and The Eagle. Goodman, who already had a stable of characters like Ka-Zar (who appeared in an eponymous pulp in 1936 and 1937) and the Masked Raider, decided the legal battle wouldn't be worth the money and effort. Armer went back to the Donenfelds and Culture Publishing, and Professor Zeppelin, Lazarus, and the rest of the Stars and Stripes crew disappeared, never to reappear.

As a side note, this appears to be the beginning of the Marvel/DC feud. Goodman never forgot or forgave Armer. In 1938 the Donenfelds' National Publications became part of Detective Comics, Inc., or "DC." In 1939 Goodman created Timely Comics and published *Marvel Comics* #1. Reportedly, Goodman's comment, on seeing the first issue of *Marvel Comics*, was, "I hope this sinks those sonsabitches," referring to the Donenfelds and Armer.

WILD CARDS: PROLOGUE & INTERLUDES
GEORGE R. R. MARTIN

In 1987, George R. R. Martin initiated the *Wild Cards* series of superhero anthologies and mosaic novels, a shared-world universe for top science-fiction writers to play around in. The series is still going, with more than twenty volumes and counting. In this virtuoso mosaic of interstitial material created for the first volume, Martin wryly chronicles and deftly constructs the alternate history of the Wild Cards universe.

PROLOGUE

From *Wild Times: An Oral History of the Postwar Years,* by Studs Terkel (Pantheon, 1979)

HERBERT L. CRANSTON

*Y*ears later, when I saw Michael Rennie come out of that flying saucer in *The Day the Earth Stood Still*, I leaned over to the wife and said, "Now that's the way an alien emissary ought to look." I've always suspected that it was Tachyon's arrival that gave them the idea for that picture, but you know how Hollywood changes things around. I was there, so I know how it really was. For starts, he came down in White Sands, not in Washington. He didn't have a robot, and we didn't shoot him. Considering what happened, maybe we should have, eh?

His ship, well, it certainly wasn't a flying saucer, and it didn't look a damn thing like our captured V-2s or even the moon rockets on Werner's drawing boards. It violated every known law of aerodynamics and Einstein's special relativity too.

He came down at night, his ship all covered with lights, the prettiest thing I ever saw. It set down plunk in the middle of the proving range, without rockets, propellers, rotors, or any visible means of propulsion whatsoever. The outer skin looked like it was coral or some kind of porous rock, covered with whorls and spurs, like something you'd find in a limestone cavern or spot while deep-sea diving.

I was in the first jeep to reach it. By the time we got there, Tach was already outside. Michael Rennie, now, he looked right in that silvery-blue spacesuit of his, but Tachyon looked like a cross between one of the Three Musketeers and some kind of circus performer. I don't mind telling you, all of us were pretty scared driving out, the rocketry boys and eggheads just as much as the GIs. I remembered that Mercury Theater broadcast back in '39, when Orson Welles fooled everybody into thinking that the Martians were invading New Jersey, and I couldn't help thinking maybe this time it was happening for real. But once the spotlights hit him, standing there in front of his ship, we all relaxed. He just wasn't scary.

He was short, maybe five three, five four, and to tell the truth, he looked more scared than us. He was wearing these green tights with the boots built right into them, and this orangy shirt with lace sissy ruffles at the wrists and collar, and some kind of silvery brocade vest, real tight. His coat was a lemon-yellow number, with a green cloak snapping around in the wind behind him and catching about his ankles. On top of his head he had this wide-brimmed hat, with a long red feather sticking out of it, except when I got closer, I saw it was really some weird spiky quill. His hair covered his shoulders; at first glance, I thought he was a girl. It was a peculiar sort of hair too, red and shiny, like thin copper wire.

I didn't know what to make of him, but I remember one of our Germans saying that he looked like a Frenchman.

No sooner had we arrived than he came slogging right over to the jeep, bold as you please, trudging through the sand with a big bag stuck up under one arm. He started telling us his name, and he was still telling it to us while four other jeeps pulled up. He spoke better English than most of our Germans, despite having this weird accent, but it was hard to be sure at first when he spent ten minutes telling us his name.

I was the first human being to speak to him. That's God's truth, I don't care what anybody else tells you, it was me. I got out of the jeep and stuck out my hand and said, "Welcome to America." I started to introduce myself, but he interrupted me before I could get the words out.

"Herb Cranston of Cape May, New Jersey," he said. "A rocket scientist. Excellent. I am a scientist myself."

He didn't look like any scientist I'd ever known, but I made allowances, since he came from outer space. I was more concerned about how he'd known my name. I asked him.

He waved his ruffles in the air, impatient. "I read your mind. That's unimportant. Time is short, Cranston. Their ship broke up." I thought he looked more than a little sick when he said that; sad, you know, hurting, but scared too. And tired, very tired. Then he started talking about this globe. That was the globe with the wild card virus, of course, everyone knows that now, but back then I didn't know what the hell he was going on about. It was lost, he said, he needed to get it back, and he hoped for all our sakes it was still intact. He wanted to talk to our top leaders. He must have read their names in my mind, because he named Werner, and Einstein, and the President, except he called him "this President Harry S. Truman of yours." Then he climbed right into the back of the jeep and sat down. "Take me to them," he said. "At once."

PROFESSOR LYLE CRAWFORD KENT

In a certain sense, it was I who coined his name. His real name, of course, his alien patronymic, was impossibly long. Several of us tried to shorten it, I recall, using this or that piece of it during our conferences, but evidently this was some sort of breach of etiquette on his home world, Takis. He continually corrected us, rather arrogantly I might say, like an elderly pedant lecturing a pack of schoolboys. Well, we needed to call him something. The title came first. We might have called him "Your Majesty" or some such, since he claimed to be a prince, but Americans are not comfortable with that sort of bowing and scraping. He also said he was a physician, although not in our sense of the word, and it must be admitted that he did seem to know a good deal of genetics and biochemistry, which seemed to be his area of expertise. Most of our team held advanced degrees, and we addressed each other accordingly, and so it was only natural that we fell to calling him "Doctor" as well.

The rocket scientists were obsessed with our visitor's ship, particularly with the theory of his faster-than-light propulsion system. Unfortunately, our Takisian friend had burned out his ship's interstellar drive in his haste to arrive here before those relatives of his, and in any case he adamantly refused to let any of us, civilian or military, inspect the inside of his craft. Werner and his Germans were reduced to questioning the alien about the drive, rather compulsively I thought. As I understood it, theoretical physics and the technology of space travel were not disciplines in which our visitor was especially expert, so the answers he gave them were not very clear, but we did grasp that the drive made use of a hitherto-unknown particle that traveled faster than light.

The alien had a term for the particle, as unpronounceable as his name. Well, I had a certain grounding in classical Greek, like all educated men, and a flair for nomenclature if I do say so myself. I was the one who devised the coinage "tachyon." Somehow the GIs got things confused, and began referring to our visitor as "that tachyon fellow." The phrase caught on, and from there it was only a short step to Doctor Tachyon, the name by which he became generally known in the press.

COLONEL EDWARD REID, U.S. ARMY INTELLIGENCE (RET.)

You want me to say it, right? Every damned reporter I've ever talked to wants me to say it. All right, here it is. We made a mistake. And we paid for it too. Do you know that afterwards they came within a hair of court-martialing all of us, the whole interrogation team? That's a fact.

The hell of it is, I don't know how we could have been expected to do things any differently than we did. I was in charge of his interrogation. I ought to know.

What did we really know about him? Nothing except what he told us himself. The eggheads were treating him like Baby Jesus, but military men have to be a little more cautious. If you want to understand, you have to put yourself in our shoes and remember how it was back then. His story was utterly preposterous, and he couldn't prove a single damned thing.

Okay, he landed in this funny-looking rocket plane, except it didn't have rockets. That was impressive. Maybe that plane of his *did* come from outer space, like he said. But maybe it didn't. Maybe it was one of those secret projects the Nazis had been working on, left over from the war. They'd had jets at the end, you know, and those V-2s, and they were even working on the atomic bomb. Maybe it was Russian. I don't know. If Tachyon had only let us examine his ship, our boys would have been able to figure out where it came from, I'm sure. But he wouldn't let anyone inside the damned thing, which struck me as more than a little suspicious. What was he trying to hide?

He said he came from the planet Takis. Well, I never heard of no goddamned planet Takis. Mars, Venus, Jupiter, sure. Even Mongo and Barsoom. But Takis? I called up a dozen top astronomers all around the country, even one guy over in England. Where's the planet Takis? I asked them. There is no planet Takis, they told me.

He was supposed to be an alien, right? We examined him. A complete physical, X rays, a battery of psychological tests, the works. He tested human. Every which way we turned him, he came up human. No extra organs, no green blood, five fingers, five toes, two balls, and one cock. The fucker was no different from you and me. He spoke *English*, for crissakes. But get this—he also spoke *German*. And Russian and French and a few other languages I've forgotten. I made wire recordings of a couple of my sessions with him, and played them for a linguist, who said the accent was Central European.

And the headshrinkers, whoa, you should have heard their reports. Classic paranoid, they said. Megalomania, they said. Schitzo, they said. All kinds of stuff. I mean, look, this guy claimed to be a *prince* from *outer space* with magic fucking *powers* who'd come here *all alone* to save our whole damned planet. Does that sound sane to you?

And let me say something about those damned magic powers of his. I'll admit it, that was the thing that bothered me the most. I mean, not only could Tachyon tell you what you were thinking, he could look at you funny and make you jump up on your desk and drop your pants, whether you wanted to or not. I spent hours with him every day, and he convinced *me*. The thing was, my reports didn't convince the brass back east. Some kind of trick, they thought, he was hypnotizing us, he was reading our body posture, using psychology to make us think he read minds. They were going to send out a stage hypnotist to figure out how he did it, but the shit hit the fan before they got around to it.

He didn't ask much. All he wanted was a meeting with the President so he could mobilize the entire American military to search for some crashed rocket ship. Tachyon would be in command, of course, no one else was qualified. Our top scientists could be his assistants. He wanted radar and jets and submarines and bloodhounds and weird machines nobody had ever heard of. You name it, he wanted it. And he did not want to have to consult with anybody, either. This guy dressed like a fag hair-dresser, if you want the truth, but the way he gave orders you would've thought he had three stars at least.

And why? Oh, yeah, his story, that sure was great. On this planet Takis, he said, a couple dozen big families ran the whole show, like royalty, except they all had magic powers, and they lorded it over everybody else who didn't have magic powers. These families spent most of their time feuding like the Hatfields and McCoys. His particular bunch had a secret weapon they'd been working on for a couple of centuries. A tailored artificial virus designed to interact with the genetic makeup of the host organism, he said. He'd been part of the research team.

Well, I was humoring him. What did this germ do? I asked him. Now get this— it did *everything*.

What it was *supposed* to do, according to Tachyon, was goose up these mind powers of theirs, maybe even give them some new powers, evolve 'em almost into gods, which would sure as hell give his kin the edge over the others. But it didn't always do that. Sometimes, yeah. Most often it killed the test subjects. He went on and on about how deadly this stuff was, and managed to give me the creeps. What were the symptoms? I asked. We knew about germ weapons back in '46; just in case he was telling the truth, I wanted us to know what to look for.

He couldn't tell me the symptoms. There were all kinds of symptoms. Everybody had different symptoms, every single person. You ever hear of a germ worked like that? Not me.

Then Tachyon said that sometimes it turned people into freaks instead of killing them. What kind of freaks? I asked. All kinds, he said. I admitted that it sounded pretty nasty, and asked him why his folks hadn't used this stuff on the other families. Because sometimes the virus worked, he said; it remade its victims, gave them powers. What kinds of powers? All kinds of powers, naturally.

So they had this stuff. They didn't want to use it on their enemies, and maybe give them powers. They didn't want to use it on themselves, and kill off half the family. They weren't about to forget about it. They decided to test it on us. Why us? Because we were genetically identical to Takisians, he said, the only such race they knew of, and the bug was designed to work on the Takisian genotype. So why were we so lucky? Some of his people thought it was parallel evolution, others believed that Earth was a lost Takisian colony—he didn't know and didn't care.

He did care about the experiment. Thought it was "ignoble." He protested, he said, but they ignored him. The ship left. And Tachyon decided to stop them all by himself. He came after them in a smaller ship, burned out his damned tachyon drive getting here ahead of them. When he intercepted them, they told him to fuck off, even though he was family, and they had some kind of space battle. His ship was damaged, theirs was crippled, and they crashed. Somewhere back east, he said. He lost them, on account of the damage to his ship. So he landed at White Sands, where he thought he could get help.

I got down the whole story on my wire recorder. Afterwards, Army Intelligence contacted all sorts of experts: biochemists and doctors and germ-warfare guys, you name it. An alien virus, we told them, symptoms completely random and unpredictable. Impossible, they said. Utterly absurd. One of them gave me a whole lecture about how Earth germs could never affect Martians like in that H. G. Wells book, and Martian germs couldn't affect us, either. Everybody agreed that this random-symptom bit was a laugh. So what were we supposed to do? We all cracked jokes about the Martian flu and spaceman's fever. Somebody, I don't know who, called it the wild card virus in a report, and the rest of us picked up on the name, but nobody believed it for a second.

It was a bad situation, and Tachyon just made it worse when he tried to escape. He almost pulled it off, but like my old man always told me, "almost" only counts in horseshoes and grenades. The Pentagon had sent out their own man to question him, a bird colonel named Wayne, and Tachyon finally got fed up, I guess. He took control of Colonel Wayne, and together they just marched out of the building. Whenever they were challenged, Wayne snapped off the orders to let them pass, and rank does have its privileges. The cover story was that Wayne had orders to escort Tachyon back to Washington. They commandeered a jeep and got all the way back to the spaceship, but by then one of the sentries had checked with me, and my men were waiting for them, with direct orders to ignore anything Colonel Wayne might say. We took him back into custody and kept him there, under heavy guard. For all his magic powers, there wasn't much he could do about it. He could make one person do what he wanted, maybe three or four if he tried real hard, but not all of us, and by then we were wise to his tricks.

Maybe it was a bonehead maneuver, but his escape attempt did get him the date with Einstein he'd been badgering us for. The Pentagon kept telling us he was the world's greatest hypnotist, but I wasn't buying that anymore, and you should have heard what Colonel Wayne thought of the theory. The eggheads were getting agitated too. Anyway, together Wayne and I managed to wrangle authorization to fly the prisoner to Princeton. I figured a talk with Einstein couldn't do any harm, and might do some good. His ship was impounded, and we'd gotten all we were going to get from the man himself. Einstein was supposed to be the world's greatest brain, maybe he could figure the guy out, right?

There are still those who say that the military is to blame for everything that happened, but it's just not true. It's easy to be wise in hindsight, but I was there, and I'll maintain to my dying day that the steps we took were reasonable and prudent.

The thing that really burns me is when they talk about how we did nothing to track down that damned globe with the wild card spores. Maybe we made a mistake, yeah, but we weren't stupid, we were covering our asses. Every damned military installation in the country got a directive to be on the lookout for a crashed spaceship that looked something like a seashell with running lights. Is it my fucking fault that none of them took it seriously?

Give me credit for one thing, at least. When all hell broke loose, I had Tachyon jetting back toward New York within two hours. I was in the seat behind him. The redheaded wimp cried half the fucking way across the country. Me, I prayed for Jetboy.

INTERLUDE ONE

From "Red Aces, Black Years," by Elizabeth H. Crofton, New Republic, May 1977

From the moment in 1950 when he declared in his famous Wheeling, West Virginia, speech that "I have here in my hand a list of fifty-seven wild cards known to be living and working secretly in the United States today," there was little doubt that Senator Joseph R. McCarthy had replaced the faceless members of HUAC as the leader of the anti-wild card hysteria that swept across the nation in the early '50s.

Certainly, HUAC could claim credit for discrediting and destroying Archibald Holmes's Exotics for Democracy, the "Four Aces" of the halcyon postwar years and the most visible living symbols of the havoc the wild card virus had wrought upon the nation (to be sure, there were ten jokers for every ace, but like blacks, homosexuals, and freaks, the jokers were invisible men throughout this period, steadfastly ignored by a society that would have preferred they not exist). When the Four Aces fell, many felt the circus had ended. They were wrong. It was just beginning, and Joe McCarthy was its ringmaster.

The hunt for "Red Aces" that McCarthy instigated and fronted produced no single, spectacular victory to rival HUAC's, but ultimately McCarthy's work affected many more people, and proved lasting where HUAC's triumph had been ephemeral. The Senate Committee on Ace Resources and Endeavors (SCARE) was birthed in 1952 as the forum for McCarthy's ace-hunts, but ultimately became a permanent part of the Senate's committee structure. In time SCARE, like HUAC, would become a mere ghost of its former self, and decades later, under the chairmanship of men like Hubert Humphrey, Joseph Montoya, and Gregg Hartmann, it would evolve into an entirely different sort of legislative animal, but McCarthy's SCARE was everything its acronym implied. Between 1952 and 1956, more than two hundred men and women were served with subpoenas by SCARE, often on no more substantial grounds than reports by anonymous informants that they had on some occasion displayed wild card powers.

It was a true modern witch-hunt, and like their spiritual ancestors at Salem, those hauled before Tail-Gunner Joe for the non-crime of being an ace had a hard time proving their innocence. How do you prove that you *can't* fly? None of SCARE's victims ever answered that question satisfactorily. And the blacklist was always waiting for those whose testimony was considered unsatisfactory.

The most tragic fates were suffered by those who actually *were* wild card victims, and admitted their ace powers openly before the committee. Of those cases, none was more poignant than that of Timothy Wiggins, or "Mr. Rainbow," as he was billed when performing. "If I'm an ace, I'd hate to see a deuce," Wiggins told McCarthy when summoned in 1953, and from that moment onward "deuce" entered the language as the term for an ace whose wild card powers are trivial or useless. Such was certainly the case with Wiggins, a plump, nearsighted, forty-eight-year-old entertainer whose wild card power, the ability to change the color of his skin, had propelled him to the dizzy heights of second billing in the smaller Catskill resort hotels, where his act consisted of strumming a ukulele and singing wobbly falsetto versions of songs like "Red, Red Robin," "Yellow Rose of Texas," and "Wild Card Blues," accompanying each rendition with appropriate color changes. Ace or deuce, Mr. Rainbow received no mercy from McCarthy or SCARE. Blacklisted and unable to secure bookings, Wiggins hanged himself in his daughter's Bronx apartment less than fourteen months after his testimony.

Other victims saw their lives blighted and destroyed in only slightly less dramatic ways: they lost jobs and careers to the blacklist, lost friends and spouses, inevitably lost custody of their children in the all-too-frequent divorces. At least twenty-two aces were uncovered during SCARE's investigatory heyday (McCarthy himself often claimed credit for having "exposed" twice that many, but included in his totals numerous cases where the accused's "powers" were established only by hearsay and circumstantial evidence, without a shred of actual documentation), including such dangerous criminals as a Queens housewife who levitated when asleep, a longshoreman who could plunge his hand into a bathtub and bring the water to a boil in just under seven minutes, an amphibious Philadelphia schoolteacher (she kept her gills concealed beneath her clothing, until the day she unwisely gave herself away by saving a drowning child), and even a potbellied Italian greengrocer who displayed an astonishing ability to grow hair at will.

Shuffling through so many wild cards, SCARE inevitably turned up some genuine aces among the deuces, including Lawrence Hague, the telepathic stockbroker whose confession triggered a panic on Wall Street, and the so-called "panther woman" of Weehawken whose metamorphosis before the newsreel cameras horrified theatergoers from coast to coast. Even that paled beside the case of the mystery man apprehended while looting New York's diamond center, his pockets bulging with gemstones and amphetamines. This unknown ace displayed reflexes four times as fast as those of a normal man, as well as astonishing strength and a seeming immunity to handgun fire. After flinging a police car the length of the block and hospitalizing a dozen policemen, he was finally subdued with tear gas. SCARE immediately issued a subpoena, but the unidentified man lapsed into a deep, comalike sleep before he could take the stand. To McCarthy's disgust, the man could not be roused—until the day, eight months later, when his specially reinforced maximum-security cell was suddenly and mysteriously found empty. A startled trusty swore that he had seen the man walk through the wall, but the description he gave did not match that of the vanished prisoner.

McCarthy's most lasting achievement, if it may be termed an achievement, came with the passage of the so-called "Wild Card Acts." The Exotic Powers Control Act, enacted in 1954, was the first. It required any person exhibiting wild card powers to register immediately with the federal government; failure to register was punishable by prison terms of up to ten years. This was followed by the Special Conscription Act, granting the Selective Service Bureau the power to induct registered aces into government service for indefinite terms of service. Rumors persist that a number of aces, complying with the new laws, were indeed inducted into (variously) the Army, the FBI, and the Secret Service during the late fifties, but if true the agencies employing their services kept the names, powers, and very existence of these operatives a closely held secret.

In fact, only two men were ever openly drafted under the Special Conscription Act during the entire twenty-two years that the statute remained on the books: Lawrence Hague, who vanished into government service after the stock manipulation charges against him were dropped, and an even more celebrated ace whose case made headlines all over the nation. David "Envoy" Harstein, the charismatic negotiator of the Four Aces, was slapped with an induction notice less than a year after his release from prison, where HUAC had confined him for contempt of Congress. Harstein never reported for conscription. Instead he vanished totally from public life in early 1955, and even the FBI's nationwide manhunt failed to turn up any trace of the man whom McCarthy himself dubbed "the most dangerous pink in America."

The Wild Card Acts were McCarthy's greatest triumph, but ironically enough their passage sowed the seed of his undoing. When those widely publicized statutes were finally signed into law, the mood of the nation seemed to change. Over and over again McCarthy had told the public that the laws were needed to deal with hidden aces undermining the nation. Well, the nation now replied, the laws are passed, the problem is solved, and we've had enough of all this.

The next year, McCarthy introduced the Alien Disease Containment Bill, which would have mandated compulsory sterilization for all wild card victims, jokers as well as aces. That was too much for even his staunchest supporters. The bill went down to crashing defeat in both House and Senate. In an effort to recoup and recapture the headlines, McCarthy launched an ill-advised SCARE investigation of the Army, determined to ferret out the "aces in the hole" that rumor insisted had been secretly recruited years before the Special Conscription Act. But public opinion swung dramatically against him during the Army-McCarthy hearings, which culminated in his censure by the Senate.

In early 1955, many had thought McCarthy might be strong enough to wrest the 1956 Republican presidential nomination from Eisenhower, but by the time of the 1956 election, the political climate had changed so markedly that he was hardly a factor.

On April 28, 1957, he was admitted to the Naval Medical Center at Bethesda, Maryland, a broken man who talked incessantly about those who he felt had betrayed him. In his last days, he insisted that his fall was all Harstein's fault, that the Envoy was out there somewhere, crisscrossing the country, poisoning the people against McCarthy with sinister alien mind control.

Joe McCarthy died on May 2, and the nation shrugged. Yet his legacy survived him: SCARE, the Wild Card Acts, an atmosphere of fear. If Harstein was out there, he did not come forward to gloat. Like many other aces of his time, he remained in hiding.

INTERLUDE TWO

From *The New York Times*, September 1, 1966

JOKERTOWN CLINIC TO OPEN ON WILD CARD DAY

The opening of a privately funded research hospital specializing in the treatment of the Takisian wild card virus was announced yesterday by Dr. Tachyon, the alien scientist who helped to develop the virus. Dr. Tachyon will serve as chief of staff at the new institution, to be located on South Street, overlooking the East River.

The facility will be known as the Blythe van Renssaeler Memorial Clinic in honor of the late Mrs. Blythe Stanhope van Renssaeler. Mrs. van Renssaeler, a member of the Exotics for Democracy from 1947 to 1950, died in 1953 in Wittier Sanatorium. She was better known as "Brain Trust."

The Van Renssaeler Clinic will open its doors to the public on September 15th, the twentieth anniversary of the release of the wild card virus over Manhattan. Emergency room service and outpatient psychological care will be provided by the 196-bed hospital. "We're here to serve the neighborhood and the city," Dr. Tachyon said in an afternoon press conference on the steps of Jetboy's Tomb, "but our first priority is going to be the treatment of those who have too long gone untreated, the jokers whose unique and often desperate medical needs have been largely ignored by existing hospitals. The wild card was played twenty years ago, and this continued willful ignorance about the virus is criminal and inexcusable." Dr. Tachyon said that he hoped the Van Renssaeler Clinic might become the world's leading center for wild card research, and spearhead efforts to perfect the cure for wild card, the so-called "trump" virus.

The clinic will be housed in a historic waterfront building originally constructed in 1874. The building was a hotel, known as the Seaman's Haven, from 1888 through 1913. From 1913 through 1942 it was the Sacred Heart Home for Wayward Girls, after which it served as an inexpensive lodging house.

Dr. Tachyon announced that the purchase of the building and a complete interior renovation had been funded by a grant from the Stanhope Foundation of Boston, headed by Mr. George C. Stanhope. Mr. Stanhope is the father of Mrs. van Renssaeler. "If Blythe were alive today, I know she'd want nothing more than to work at Dr. Tachyon's side," Mr. Stanhope said.

Initially the work at the clinic will be funded by fees and private donations, but Dr. Tachyon admitted that he had recently returned from Washington, where he conferred with Vice President Hubert H. Humphrey. Sources close to the Vice President indicate that the administration is considering partial funding of the Jokertown clinic through the offices of the Senate Committee on Ace Resources and Endeavors (SCARE).

A crowd of approximately five hundred, many of them obvious victims of the wild card virus, greeted Dr. Tachyon's announcement with enthusiastic applause.

INTERLUDE THREE
From "Wild Card Chic," by Tom Wolfe, *New York*, June 1971

Mmmmmmmmmmmmmmmm. These are nice. Little egg rolls, filled with crabmeat and shrimp. Very tasty. A bit greasy, though. Wonder what the aces do to get the grease spots off the fingers of their gloves? Maybe they prefer the stuffed mushrooms, or the little Roquefort cheese morsels rolled in crushed nuts, all of which are at this very moment being offered them on silver platters by tall, smiling waiters in Aces High livery…. These are the questions to ponder on these Wild Card Chic evenings. For example, that black man there by the window, the one shaking hands with Hiram Worchester himself, the one with the black silk shirt and the black leather coat and that absolutely unbelievable swollen forehead, that *dangerous*-looking black man with the cocoa-colored skin and almond-shaped eyes, who came off the elevator with three of the most ravishing women any of them have ever seen, even here in this room full of beautiful people—is he, an ace, a palpable ace, going to pick up a little egg roll stuffed with shrimp and crabmeat when the waiter drifts by, and just pop it down the gullet without so much as missing a syllable of Hiram's cultured geniality, or is he more of a stuffed mushroom man at that...

Hiram is splendid. A large man, a *formidable* man, six foot two and broad all over, in a bad light he might pass for Orson Welles. His black, spade-shaped beard is immaculately groomed, and when he smiles his teeth are very white. He smiles often. He is a warm man, a gracious man, and he greets the aces with the same quick firm handshake, the same pat on the shoulder, the same familiar exhortation with which he greets Lillian, and Felicia and Lenny, and Mayor Hartmann, and Jason, John, and D.D.

How much do you think I weigh? he asks them jovially, and presses them for a guess, three hundred pounds, three fifty, four hundred. He chuckles at their guesses, a deep chuckle, a resonant chuckle, because this huge man weighs only thirty pounds and he's set up a scale right here in the middle of Aces High, his lavish new restaurant high atop the Empire State Building, amid the crystal and silver and crisp white tablecloths, a scale like you might find in a gym, just so he can prove his point. He hops on and off nimbly whenever he's challenged. Thirty pounds, and Hiram does enjoy his little joke. But don't call him Fatman anymore. This ace has come out of the deck now, he's a new kind of ace, who knows all the right people and all the right wines, who looks absolutely correct in his tuxedo, and owns the highest, *chic*est restaurant in town.

What an evening! The tables are set all around, the silver gleaming, the tremulous little flames of the candles reflected in the encircling windows, a bottomless blackness with a thousand stars, and it is that moment Hiram loves. There seem to be a thousand stars inside and a thousand stars outside, a Manhattan tower full of stars, the highest grandest tower of all, with marvelous people drifting through the heavens, Jason Robards, John and D. D. Ryan, Mike Nichols, Willie Joe Namath, John Lindsay, Richard Avedon, Woody Allen, Aaron Copland, Lillian Hellman, Steve Sondheim, Josh Davidson, Leonard Bernstein, Otto Preminger, Julie Belafonte, Barbara Walters, the Penns, the Greens, the O'Neals...and now, in this season of Wild Card Chic, the aces.

That knot of people there, that cluster of enthralled, adoring, *excited* people with the tall, thin champagne glasses in their hands and the rapt expressions on their faces, in their midst, the object of all their attention, is a little man in a crushed-velvet tuxedo, an *orange* crushed-velvet tuxedo, with tails, and a ruffled lemon-yellow shirt, and long shiny red hair. Tisianne brant Ts'ara sek Halima sek

Ragnar sek Omian is holding court again, the way he must have done once on Takis, and some of the marvelous people about him are even calling him "Prince" and "Prince Tisianne," though they don't often pronounce it right, and to most of them, now and forever, he will remain Dr. Tachyon. He's *real*, this prince from another planet, and the very *idea* of him—an exile, a hero, imprisoned by the Army and persecuted by HUAC, a man who has lived two human lifetimes and seen things none of them can imagine, who labors selflessly among the wretched of Jokertown, well, the excitement runs through Aces High like a rogue hormone, and Tachyon seems excited too, you can tell by the way his lilac-colored eyes keep slipping over to linger on the slender Oriental woman who arrived with that other ace, that dangerous-looking Fortunato fellow.

"I've never met an ace before," the refrain goes. "This is a first for me." The thrill vibrates through the air of Aces High, until the whole eighty-sixth floor is *thrumming* to it, a first for me, never known anyone like you, a first for me, always wanted to meet you, a first for me, and somewhere in the damp soil of Wisconsin, Joseph McCarthy spins in his coffin with a high, thin whirring sound, and all his worms have come home to roost now. These are no Hollywood poseurs, no dreary politicians, no faded literary flowers, no pathetic jokers begging for help, these are *real nobility*, these aces, these enchanting electric aces.

So beautiful. Aurora, sitting on Hiram's bar, showing the long, long legs that have made her the toast of Broadway, the men clustered around her, laughing at her every joke. Remarkable, that red-gold hair of hers, curled and perfumed, tumbling down across her bare shoulders, and those bruised, pouting lips, and when she laughs, the northern lights flicker around her and the men burst into applause. She's signed to make her first feature film next year, playing opposite Redford, and Mike Nichols will direct. The first ace to star in a major motion picture since—no, we wouldn't want to mention *him*, would we? Not when we're having so much fun.

So astonishing. The things they can *do*, these aces. A dapper little man dressed all in green produces an acorn and a pocketful of potting soil, borrows a brandy snifter from the bartender, and grows a small oak tree right there in the center of Aces High. A dark woman with sharply sculpted features arrives in jeans and a denim shirt, but when Hiram threatens to turn her away, she claps her hands together and suddenly she is armored head to toe in black metal that gleams like ebony. Another clap, and she's wearing an evening gown, green velvet, off the shoulder, perfect for her, and even Fortunato looks twice. When the ice for the champagne buckets runs low, a burly rock-hard black man steps forward, takes the Dom Pérignon in hand, and grins boyishly as frost rimes the outside of the bottle. "Just right," he says when he gives the bottle to Hiram. "Any longer and I'd freeze it solid." Hiram laughs and congratulates him, though he doesn't believe he has the honor. The black man smiles enigmatically. "Croyd," is all he says.

So romantic, so tragic. Down there by the end of the bar, in gray leather, that's Tom Douglas, isn't it? It is, it *is*, the Lizard King himself, I hear they just dropped the charges, but what *courage* that took, what commitment, and say, whatever happened to that Radical fellow who helped him out? Douglas looks terrible, though. Wasted, haunted. They crowd close around him, and his eyes snap up and briefly the specter of a great black cobra looms above him, dark counterpoint to Aurora's shimmering colors, and silence ripples across Aces High until they leave the Lizard King alone again.

So dashing, so flamboyant. Cyclone knows how to make an entrance, doesn't he? But that's why Hiram insisted on the Sunset Balcony, after all, not just for drinks out under the summer stars and the glorious view of the sun going down across the Hudson, but to give his aces a place to land, and it's only natural that Cyclone would be the first. Why ride the elevator when you can ride the winds? And the way he dresses—all in blue and white, the jumpsuit makes him look so *lithe* and *rakish*, and that cape, the way it hangs from his wrists and ankles, and then balloons out in flight when he whips up his winds. Once he's inside, shaking Hiram's hand, he takes off his aviator's helmet. He's a fashion leader, Cyclone, the first ace to wear an honest-to-god *costume*, and he started back in '65, long before these other aces-come-lately, wore his colors even through those two dreary years in 'Nam, but just because a man wears a mask doesn't mean he has to make a fetish of hiding his identity, does it? Those days are past, Cyclone is Vernon Henry Carlysle of San Francisco, the whole world knows, the fear is dead, this is the age of Wild Card Chic when *everyone* wants to be an ace. Cyclone came a long way for this party, but the gathering wouldn't be complete without the West Coast's premier ace, would it?

Although—taboo thought that it is, with stars and aces glittering all around on a night when you can see fifty miles in every direction—really, the gathering isn't *quite* complete, is it? Earl Sanderson is still in France, though he did send a brief, but sincere, note of apology in reply to Hiram's invitation. A great man, that one, a great man greatly wronged. And David Harstein, the lost Envoy; Hiram even ran an ad in the *Times*, David won't you please come home? But he's not here either. And the Turtle, where is the Great and Powerful Turtle? There were rumors that on this special magical night, this halcyon time for Wild Card Chic, the Turtle would come out of his shell and shake Hiram's hand and announce his name to the world, but no, he doesn't seem to be here, you don't think...god, no... you don't think those old stories are *true* and the Turtle is a joker after all?

Cyclone is telling Hiram that he thinks his three-year-old daughter has inherited his wind powers, and Hiram beams and shakes his hand and congratulates the doting daddy and proposes a toast. Even his powerful, cultivated voice cannot cut through the din of the moment, so Hiram makes a small fist and does that thing he does to the gravity waves and makes himself even lighter than thirty pounds, until he drifts up toward the ceiling. Aces High goes silent as Hiram floats beside his huge art-deco chandelier, raises his Pimm's Cup, and proposes his toast. Lenny Bernstein and John Lindsay drink to little Mistral Helen Carlysle, second generation ace-to-be. The O'Neals and the Ryans lift their glasses to Black Eagle, the Envoy, and the memory of Blythe Stanhope van Renssaeler. Lillian Hellman, Jason Robards, and Broadway Joe toast the Turtle and Tachyon, and everyone drinks to Jetboy, father of us all.

And after the toasting come the causes. The Wild Card Acts are still on the books, and in this day and age that's a disgrace, something must be done. Dr. Tachyon needs help, help for his Jokertown Clinic, help with his lawsuit, how long has *that* been dragging on now, his suit to win custody of his spaceship back from the government that wrongly impounded it in 1946—the shame of it, to take his *ship* after he came all that way to help, it makes them angry, all of them, and *of course* they pledge their help, their money, their lawyers, their influence. A beautiful woman on either side of him, Tachyon speaks of his ship. It's alive, he tells them, and by now it's certainly lonely, and as he talks he begins to weep, and when he tells them that the ship's name is *Baby*, there's a tear behind many a contact lens, threatening the artfully applied mascara below. And of course something must be done about the Joker Brigade, that's little better than genocide, and...

But that's when dinner is served. The guests drift to their assigned seats, Hiram's seating chart is a masterpiece, measured and spiced as precisely as his gourmet food, everywhere just the right balance of wealth and wisdom and wit and beauty and bravura and celebrity, with an ace at every table of course, of *course*, otherwise someone might go away feeling cheated, in this year and month and hour of Wild Card Chic...

INTERLUDE FOUR

From "Fear and Loathing in Jokertown," by Dr. Hunter S. Thompson, *Rolling Stone*, August 23, 1974

Dawn is coming up in Jokertown now. I can hear the rumble of the garbage trucks under my window at the South Street Inn, out here by the docks. This is the end of the line, for garbage and everything else, the asshole of America, and I'm feeling close to the end of my line too, after a week of cruising the most vile and poisonous streets in New York...when I look up, a clawed hand heaves itself over the sill, and a minute later it's followed by a face. I'm six stories above the street and this speed-crazed shithead comes climbing in the window like it's nothing. Maybe he's right; this is Jokertown, and life runs fast & mean here. It's like wandering through a Nazi death camp during a bad trip; you don't understand half of what you see, but it scares the piss out of you just the same.

The thing coming in my window is seven fucking feet tall, with triple-jointed daddy-long-legs arms that dangle so low his claws cut gouges in the hardwood floor, a complexion like Count Dracula, and a snout on him like the Big Bad Wolf. When he grins, the whole damn thing opens on a foot of pointed green teeth. The fucker even spits venom, which is a good talent to have if you're going to wander around Jokertown at night. "Got any speed?" he asks as he climbs down from the window. He spies the bottle of tequila on the nightstand, snares it with one of those ridiculous arms of his, and helps himself to a big swallow.

"Do I look like the kind of man who'd do crank?" I say.

"Guess we'll have to do mine then," Croyd says, and pulls a fistful of blacks from his pocket. He takes four of them and washes them down with more of my Cuervo Gold...

...imagine if Hubert Humphrey had drawn a joker, picture the Hube with a trunk stuck in the middle of his face, like a flaccid pink worm where his nose ought to be, and you've got a good fix on Xavier Desmond. His hair is thin or gone, and his eyes are gray and baggy as his suit. He's been at it for ten years now, and you can tell it's wearing him out. The local columnists call him the mayor of Jokertown and the voice of the jokers; that's about as much as he's accomplished in ten years, him and his sorry hack Jockers' Anti-Defamation League—a couple of bogus titles, a certain status as Tammany's best-loved joker pet, invitations to a few nice Village parties when the hostess can't get an ace on such short notice.

He stands on the platform in his three-piece suit, holding his fucking hat in his trunk for Christ's sake, talking about joker solidarity, and voting drives, and joker cops for Jokertown, doing the old soft-shoe like it really meant something. Behind him, under a sagging JADL banner, is the sorriest lineup of pathetic losers you'd ever want to see. If they were blacks they'd be Uncle Toms, but the jokers haven't come up with a name for them yet...but they will, you can bet your mask on that. The JADL faithful are heavy into masks, like good jokers everywhere. Not just ski masks and dominoes either. Walk down the Bowery or Chrystie Street, or linger for a while in front of Tachyon's clinic, and you see facial wear out of some acidhead's nightmare: feathered birdmasks & deathsheads & leather ratfaces & monks' cowls & shiny sequined individualized "fashion masks" that go for a hundred bucks a throw. The masks are part of the color of Jokertown, and the tourists from Boise and Duluth and Muskogee all make sure and buy a plastic mask or two to take home as souvenirs, and every half-blind-drunk hack reporter who decides to do another brainless write-up on the poor fucked-up jokers notices the masks right off. They stare so hard at the masks that they don't notice the shiny-thin Salvation Army suits and faded-print housedresses the masked jokers are wearing, they don't notice how *old* some of those masks are getting, and they sure as shit don't pick up on the younger jokers, the ones in leather & Levi's, who aren't wearing any masks at all. "This is what I look like," a girl with a face like a jar of smashed assholes told me that afternoon outside a rancid Jokertown porn house. "I could give a shit if the nats like it or not. I'm supposed to wear a mask so some nat bitch from Queens won't get sick to her stomach when she looks at me? Fuck that."

Maybe a third of the crowd listening to Xavier Desmond are wearing masks. Maybe less. Whenever he stops for applause, the people in the masks slap their hands together, but you can tell it's an effort, even for them. The rest of them are just listening, waiting, and they've got eyes as ugly as their deformities. It's a mean young bunch out there, and a lot of them are wearing gang colors, with names like DEMON PRINCES & KILLER GEEKS & WEREWOLVES. I'm standing off to the side, wondering if the Tack is going to show up as advertised, and I don't see who starts it, but suddenly Desmond just shuts up, right in the middle of a boring declaration about how aces & jokers & nats is all god's chillums under the skin, and when I look back over they're booing him and throwing peanuts, they're pelting him with salted peanuts still in the shell, bouncing them right off his head and his chest and his fucking trunk, tossing them into his hat, and Desmond is just standing there gaping. He's supposed to be the voice of these people, he read it in the *Daily News* and the *Jokertown Cry*, and the sorry old fucker doesn't have the least little turd of an idea of what's going down...

...just past midnight when I walk outside of Freakers to piss casually into the gutter, figuring it's a safer bet than the men's room, and the odds against a cop cruising through Jokertown at this time of night are so remote that they're laughable. The streetlight is busted, and for a moment I think it's Wilt Chamberlain standing there, but then he comes closer and I notice the arms & claws & snout. Skin like old ivory. I ask him what the fuck his problem is, and he asks me if I'm not the guy wrote the book about the Angels, and a half-hour later we're sitting in a booth in the back of an all-night place on Broome Street, while the waitress pours gallons of black coffee for him. She has long blond hair and nice legs, and on the breast of her pink uniform it says *Sally*, and she's good to look at until you notice her face. I discover that I'm looking down at my plate whenever she comes near, which makes me sick & sad & pissed off. The Snout is saying something about how he never learned algebra, and there's nothing wrong with me that about four fingers of king-hell crank wouldn't cure, and after I mention that the Snout shows me his teeth and mentions that while there's a definite scarcity of real high-voltage crank around these days, it just so happens that he knows where he can put his hands on some...

...."We're talking *wounds* here, we're talking real deep-bleeding poisonous *wounds*, the kind that can't be treated with a fucking Band-Aid, and that's all Desmond's got up his trunk, just a fucking lot of Band-Aids," the dwarf told me, after he gave me his Revolutionary Drug Brothers handshake, or whatever the fuck the goddamned thing is supposed to be. As jokers go, he got a pretty decent draw—there were dwarfs long before the wild card—but he's still damned pissed-off about it.

"He's been holding that hat in his trunk for ten years now, and all that ever happens is the nats shit in it. Well, that's *over*. We're not asking anymore, we're telling them, the JJS is *telling* them, and we'll stick it right in their pretty pearllike ears if we have to." The JJS is the Jokers for a Just Society, and it's got about as much in common with the JADL as a piranha has with one of those giant pop-eyed white goldfish you see waddling around in decorative pools outside of dentists' offices. The JJS doesn't have Captain Tacky or Jimmy Roosevelt or Rev. Ralph Abernathy helping out on its board of directors—in fact it doesn't have a board of directors, and it doesn't sell memberships to concerned citizens and sympathetic aces either. The Hube would feel damned uncomfortable at a JJS meeting, whether he had a trunk on his face or not...

...even at four in the morning, the Village isn't Jokertown, and that's part of the problem, but mostly it's just that Croyd is hotwired & crazy on meanass crank, and as far as I can tell he hasn't slept for a week. Somewhere in the Village is the guy we set out to find, a half-black all-ace pimp who's supposed to have the sweetest girls in the city, but we can't find him, and Croyd keeps insisting that the streets are all changing around, like they're alive & treacherous & out to get him. Cars slow down when they see Croyd swinging down the pavement with those long triple-jointed daddy-long-legs strides of his, and speed up fast again when he looks over at them and snarls. We're in front of a deli when he forgets all about the pimp we're supposed to find and decides he's thirsty instead. He wraps his claws around the steel shutters, gives a little grunt, and just *yanks* the whole thing out of the brick storefront and uses it to smash in the window glass... halfway through the case of Mexican beer we hear the sirens. Croyd opens his snout and spits at the door, and the poison shit hits the glass and starts burning right through it. "They're after me again," he says in a voice full of doom & hate & speedfreak rage & paranoia. "They're all after me." And then he looks at me and that's all it takes, I know I'm in deep shit. "You led them here," he says, and I tell him no, I like him, some of my best fucking friends are jokers, and the red & blue flashers are out front as he jumps to his feet, grabs me, and *screams*, "I'm not a joker, you *fuck*, I'm a goddamned *ace*," and throws me right through the window, the *other* window, the one where the plate glass was still intact. But not for long...while I'm lying in the gutter, bleeding, he makes his own exit, right out the front door with a six-pack of Dos Equis under his arm, and the cops pump a couple rounds into him, but he just laughs at them, and starts to climb...His claws leave deep holes in the brick. When he reaches the roof, he howls at the moon, unzips his pants, and pisses down on all of us before he vanishes...

INTERLUDE FIVE
From "Thirty-Five Years of Wild Cards, a Retrospective," *Aces!* magazine, September 15, 1981

"I can't die yet, I haven't seen *The Jolson Story.*"

—Robert Tomlin

"They are an abomination unto the Lord, and on their faces they bear the mark of the beast, and their number in the land is six hundred and sixty-six."

—anonymous anti-joker leaflet, 1946

"They call it quarantine, not discrimination. We are not a race, they tell us, we are not a religion, we are *diseased* and so it is right that they set us apart, though they know full well that the wild card is not contagious. Ours is a sickness of the body, theirs a contagion of the soul."

—Xavier Desmond

"Let them say what they will. I can still fly."

—Earl Sanderson, Jr.

"Is it my fault that everyone likes me, and no one likes you?"

—David Harstein (to Richard Nixon)

"I like the taste of joker blood."

—graffiti, NYC subway

"I don't care what they look like, they bleed red just like anybody else...most of them, anyway."

—Lt. Col. John Garrick, Joker Brigade

"If I'm an ace, I'd hate to see a deuce."

—Timothy Wiggins

"You want to know if I'm an ace or a joker? The answer is yes."

—The Turtle

I'm a joker, I'm insane,
And you cannot say my name
Coiled in the streets
Waiting only for night
I am the serpent who gnaws
the roots of the world

—"Serpent Time,"
Thomas Marion Douglas

"I'm delighted to have *Baby* returned to me, but I have no intention of leaving Earth. This planet is my home now, and those touched by the wild card are my children."

—Dr. Tachyon,
on the occasion of the return of his spaceship

"They are the demon children of the Great Satan, America."

—Ayatollah Khomeini

"In hindsight, the decision to use aces to secure the safe return of the hostages was probably a mistake, and I take full responsibility for the failure of the mission."

—President Jimmy Carter

"Think like an ace, and you can win like an ace. Think like a joker, and the joke's on you."

—*Think like an Ace!*
(Ballantine, 1981)

"The parents of America are deeply concerned about the excessive coverage of aces and their exploits in the media. They are bad role models for our children, and thousands are injured or killed each year while attempting to imitate their freak powers."

—Naomi Weathers,
American Parents League

"Even their kids want to be like us. These are the '80s. A new decade, man, and we're the new people. We can fly, and we don't need no bogus airplane like that nat Jetboy. The nats don't know it yet, but they're obsolete. This is a time for aces."
—anonymous letter in *Jokertown Cry*,
January 1, 1981

WILD CARDS: JUST CAUSE

CARRIE VAUGHN

Carrie Vaughn, author of the bestselling Kitty Norville series and of the superhero novel *After the Golden Age*, contributes a globetrotting adventure culled from the nineteenth Wild Cards volume.

ECUADOR

The hillside had melted, engulfing the street. Mud was moving, swallowing structures. The rain poured, and the slough of mud had turned into a soupy flood, drawn down by its own weight. There had been a town here: the edges of tin roofs emerged from mounds of gray earth, mangled fences stuck up at angles, cars tipped on their sides were mostly buried. And the rain still fell.

Before the jeep even stopped, Ana jumped out and ran into the thick of it.

"Ana!" Kate called.

"Curveball, we got other problems," Tinker said. He gestured to a crowd shoving its way along the road. Some of the people saw Ana and called out to her, "*¡La Bruja! ¡La Bruja de la Tierra!*" Earth Witch. They recognized her, and knew she'd come to help. The refugees needed to get to higher ground, up the next hill, to escape the flood. Ana could handle the mud. Kate and Tinker needed to get those people to safety.

Not every rescue depended on ace powers, she'd learned over the last year. Sometimes you just needed to offer a hand. Provide a working vehicle for people who couldn't make the hike.

Kate's jacket wasn't doing anything to keep her dry, but she wore it for warmth. This was supposed to be the tropics, but they were in the mountains, and it was cold. Didn't seem fair. Water dripped in streams off the brim of her baseball cap, a blue one with the UN logo John had given her. The poor thing was starting to look ragged, like it had been through a war zone or three. Which it had.

She helped Tinker with the evacuation, but she always kept an eye on Ana.

Now, Ana knelt on the muddy slough covering one of the houses. She looked feral, kneeling in mud which had splashed her legs, shorts, and T-shirt. Her black hair was coming loose from its braid and sticking to her round face. Hands on the mud, she glared at it with a knotted expression, setting her will. She called to someone in Spanish, and someone shouted back. People were digging, scooping and flinging away buckets of dirt in the search for survivors.

A sound rumbled, like distant ocean waves. A couple of the guys on the roof cried out and jumped to the road. The dirt under them started moving, particles slipping, falling in waves, dirt pouring out of windows, slumping away from the house. In moments, Ana knelt on a sheet of mud-streaked corrugated tin.

Bodies broke free.

A woman and a child rode the swell of earth that came out the windows. They were limp, their limbs pushed to odd angles by the dirt's movement, their clothing tangled around their bodies. Another child remained hung up on the window sill. Shouting erupted, and people surged toward the victims.

Kate fought her way to the woman. She was still warm, still had color. Still had a pulse. Her hair and skin were caked with mud. Kate cleaned the mud out of her mouth. *Please, let us have gotten here in time.*

The woman choked, sputtering back to life. Other rescuers revived the children. People wearing Red Cross jackets appeared. The convoy must have caught up with them. Kate, Ana, and Tinker had pushed ahead in the hopes that Ana's power could save lives.

Ana didn't stop after freeing the house. She scrambled off the roof and set her hands on the road, which cleared before her. Buildings emerged, and still the wall retreated, groaning, reluctant. Ana crept forward, always keeping one hand on the ground, and pushed the earth back. Rescuers searched the other houses and found more victims who'd been swallowed up, and now spit back out. Not all of them lived, but many did.

When Ana reached the end of the street, a wall rose at the edge of the town, a barren mound of churned-up mud, a tumor against the backdrop of the green jungle. The wall of mud served as a dike, diverting the flood of water around the village, buying them time.

Kate approached her, hesitating, not wanting to break her concentration. Ana, head bowed, was breathing hard, her back heaving.

"Ana?" Kate touched her shoulder.

Ana said something in Spanish. Then her eyes focused, and she smiled. "Wasn't that something?"

"Will it hold?"

She shook her head. "Not with this rain. They're still going to have to evacuate."

"What about you? You holding up?"

"Same as always." She took a deep breath and briefly touched the quarter-sized medallion she wore. Kate offered her a hand up and was startled at how heavily Ana leaned on her. She held her side, at the place where a bullet had struck her a year before. The wound still hurt her sometimes. "I'm going to go help clear the rest of those houses."

Kate knew better than to try to argue, however hurt or tired Ana seemed. She went back to Tinker and the jeep.

The Red Cross had set up a tent and was distributing blankets and coffee. Hypothermia was an issue in the rain and cold. Tinker—Hal Anderson, a burly Australian ace with a beach-bum tan and weight-lifter muscles—had let the jeep stall out, which meant he was now burrowed under the open hood, doing who-knew-what to the engine. He'd rigged the thing to run on tap water—great publicity, not using any of the local fuel supplies during a global oil shortage. If he could mass produce his modification, he'd be rich. But the device needed adjusting every time the engine shut off.

They'd been at this for three days, driving from village to village, staving off mudslides and evacuating towns. They needed a chance to catch their breaths. That was all she wanted.

Someone screamed and cried out a panicked stream of Spanish.

A river was pouring off the mountain. Water lapped the top of the wall Ana had made to hold back the flood. The edges crumbled. Suddenly, the whole thing disintegrated. It was just gone, turned to soup by the rain, and the flood roared through the village. Ana was in the middle of it. Holding a little girl's hand, she knelt in the street, hand on the ground, looking up at the wave pouring toward her. This wasn't the slow, creeping wall that Ana had pushed back earlier. This was a mass of water so powerful it had picked up tons of debris—rocks, trees, a mountain's worth of topsoil—and carried it barreling down.

Too fast for Earth Witch to hold it back. More water than mud, she couldn't control it.

"Ana!" Horrified, helpless, Kate watched.

Ana reacted instinctively. She held the child close to her body and hunkered over, protecting her. Then, both of them disappeared in the torrent.

Kate started to run to her, but Tinker held her back, hugging her to him.

"I can break them out, I can blow through the mud!"

"No, you can't!"

She struggled anyway, trying to break free, but he held her trapped.

Then someone yelled, "¡Mira!" Look.

The river of mud flowed in a steady stream, but something in the middle of it moved, turning like a whirlpool. Then, a shape broke the surface. A platform of stone rose, carrying two figures clear of the flow, which frothed around the interruption. The tower of bedrock stopped some six feet above the surface. It was only a few feet in diameter, but it was enough. Ana crouched there, the child safe in her arms. Both were drenched in dripping mud. Even from where she stood, Kate could see Ana gasping for breath.

"Christ," Tinker breathed.

Kate cheered, laughing with relief.

The little girl shifted in Ana's arms and clung to the woman. Ana cleared the mud from both their faces. She looked up, raised her hand. Kate waved enthusiastically.

Ana touched the ground, and a faint rumble sounded, even over the sound of the flood. More ground broke free, a line forming a narrow bridge from the platform to the hillside. Soon, Ana was able to walk to safety, carrying the girl.

One of the refugees, a young woman, broke from the crowd and cried out. The girl in Ana's arms struggled. "Mama!"

Ana let her go, and she ran to the woman, who swept her up, sobbing. Holding her child, she went to Ana, touching her reverently, crying, "*Gracias*." The ace bore it with a smile.

Kate ran to meet her and pulled her into a hug, mud and all. Like she would notice a little more mud after this week. "Are you okay? Come on, you have to get warmed up, get something hot to drink."

Smiling vaguely, Ana hugged her back. "I'm okay. It's nice to be saving people for a change."

And it was.

The next morning, back in their hotel room at Quito, Ana was asleep. She'd been asleep for ten hours. She didn't even look relaxed, curled up in a ball, hugging the blankets tightly over her shoulders, like she was trying to protect herself from something.

They all needed a break. They'd been running all over the world for a year now. Ana, Michelle, Lilith, and a couple of others had been asked to use their powers almost nonstop. What did that do to a person?

Kate pulled a chair close to the window, took out her cell phone, dialed. John answered on the first ring.

"Hey, Kate. You okay?"

"Hi, John," she said, smiling. That was always his first question: You're okay, you're not hurt, you're coming home? "I'm fine. We're all fine. We saved a lot of people."

"I know, the networks have been carrying the story. What a mess."

"Yeah, half an hour in the shower and I still haven't gotten all the mud off."

"Maybe I can help you with that when you get back." She could hear the suggestive grin in his voice and blushed gleefully. "Speaking of which, aren't you supposed to be on a plane back?"

She sighed. "I made an executive decision to stay an extra day and give Ana a chance to sleep. She's really wiped out, John. I've never seen her this bad, not since Egypt." Egypt, when she was shot in the gut, after she'd cracked open the earth wide enough to swallow an army.

"Is she going to be okay?"

"I think so, eventually. But she could use a break. We need her too much to let her burn herself out."

"I know. She's not the only one." He sounded as tired as she felt.

"Promise me you'll give her a break after this. She hasn't seen her family in months. I think a trip home would do her good. You've brought in half a dozen new aces, more people from *American Hero*—surely you won't need her for a few weeks."

"Okay. Yeah. That should work." Then he sighed, reminding Kate that Ana wasn't the only one who was wiped out. "I'll figure this out."

There he went, taking it all on himself again. I, not we. This was the Committee, not a dictatorship. But Secretary General Jayewardene had named him the chairman, and John took that position seriously.

She was too tired to argue about it right now.

Then John said, "How about I send Lilith to come get you—"

Ah yes, Lilith, who could wave her magic cloak and whisk them around the world in a heartbeat. But only at night, which was somehow appropriate, considering what seemed to be Lilith's other favorite activity. She'd turned the Committee into a soap opera all by herself.

"It's daylight here, John."

"Oh. Right. Maybe later, then."

Or not. "We'll be home tomorrow anyway."

"Fine, okay. But there's something else I wanted to talk about."

"Oh?"

"I was watching news footage. You weren't wearing your vest."

She wrinkled her face, confused for a moment, then remembered: the Kevlar vest that had spent the trip stuffed in her duffel bag.

"That's because no one was shooting at us," she answered. "There weren't even any soldiers. It was the Red Cross and us."

"They don't have to be soldiers to have guns, and you never know when someone might take a shot at you."

"It wasn't a Kevlar situation," she said.

"Is it really that big a deal to wear the vest?"

"It is when you're in a humid tropical country and need to move fast. The thing makes it harder to throw."

"And you couldn't throw at all if anything happened to you."

"And a Kevlar vest is not going to save me from drowning in mud. Or from getting hit by some lunatic jeep driver."

"Now you're making shit up just to argue with me."

Funny how he got all worked up over her not wearing Kevlar, but didn't seem to notice that Ana had been in shorts and a T-shirt. This wasn't supposed to be about *her*, it was supposed to be about the team.

She opened her mouth, ready to snap back at him, her pleasant flush at hearing his voice turning to frustration. These were stupid arguments. Didn't stop them from happening.

Sitting back, she made herself relax and said, "This is when I'd kiss you to break your concentration."

Saying so had about the same effect. She could imagine the nonplussed look on his face. Then he laughed, and the knot in her gut faded.

"I worry about you. I don't know what I'd do if something happened to you."

This, too, was an old conversation. She should have been pleased at how much he wanted to protect her, and she was. But it also felt like being put in a box.

"I'm sorry you were worried," she said. "But the only way you can really keep me safe is to not send me out here at all. And that would just piss me off."

"I know, and you can get killed crossing the street at home. Doesn't mean I'm going to stop worrying."

She smiled. "I love you too, John. I miss you."

"I miss you, too. Get some sleep, okay?"

"Yes, sir."

NEW YORK CITY

Kate and Ana shared an apartment on the Lower East Side. They went home from the airport, and Ana crawled into bed for another round of sleep. Kate checked in on her, then went to see John.

While she and Ana had gone for austere college chic in a close-quarters studio, John lived in his mother's penthouse overlooking Central Park. Peregrine was in Los Angeles for the second season of *American Hero* and had given her son the run of the place.

Kate felt the disconnect every time she went there. She'd grown up with Peregrine on TV and all over the covers of magazines. She was an icon, probably the most visible and famous wild carder ever, with her stunning presence and spectacular wings. And here was Kate, dating her son.

The penthouse was beyond posh. It wasn't opulent or over the top—that was just it. Everything was tasteful and perfect, from the clean lines of the gray leather sofa set and glass coffee table, to the giant arrangement of hyacinths on the twelve-seater dining room table. Real flowers, not silk, changed every week by the housekeeper. Last week had been orchids.

John grew up with this. He walked in here, and it was home. Kate still felt like she'd landed in a photo spread in *Vogue*. She was getting used to it—it was definitely easy to get used to. But sometimes she wondered if she'd fallen down a rabbit hole.

She set her bag by the wall of the living room and took a deep breath, happy to be anywhere that didn't smell like a third world country.

"Hello?" she called. Her voice echoed.

"Hey!" John appeared from the kitchen, a bottle of wine in one hand and a corkscrew in the other. She was on him in a heartbeat, arms over his shoulders, pulling herself into a kiss. Awkwardly, hands full, he hugged her back. Their kiss was warm and long.

"Hi," she said, when they managed to separate.

"Hey," he said, his smile bright. "Let me put this down so we can do this right."

John set the bottle on the coffee table, where two glasses were waiting. Kate pulled him down to the sofa next to her.

The light from the other room glinted off the jewel in his forehead. Sekhmet. A scarab-like joker living in John's head. She gave him his power—he wasn't an ace on his own, not anymore. But Kate didn't like to think about it, that she and John were never really alone. Right now, moments like these, John was all hers.

"Are you sure you're okay?" John said. "You still look beat."

"I'm just starting to wake up."

She pulled her leg across his lap, half-straddling him, and kissed him again. She rested her hand on his cheek, ran it across his curly hair. His lips moved with hers while his hands crept under her shirt, pressing against her back. She drew on his warmth, and the tension faded. They sighed together.

"Welcome home," he said.

"Thanks. It's really, really good to be here." She could curl up in his arms and never leave.

"Yeah. I worry less when you're with me." He ducked his gaze, hiding a smile. "If it weren't for you, I don't think I'd have lasted this long."

So serious. Of course he was, this wasn't a game. The pundits sometimes joked: What, you kids think you can save the world? But they could. They did. Little parts of it at a time.

Not wanting the anxiety to creep back, she joked. "And if it weren't for you, I'd have a million dollars and be the designated ace guardian of San Jose."

He laughed, and she laughed with him, their heads bowed together. He said, "You really want to be the designated ace guardian of San Jose? Showing up for your guest appearance on *Dancing with the Stars*?"

"Oh my God, no. Poor Stuntman. No wonder he went to work for the government after his contract was up."

John's eyes held uncertainty again. Still worrying.

"John, I wouldn't change anything. I don't want to be anywhere but right here."

Their next kiss was slow, studious almost, like neither one of them wanted to miss a single sensation. He worked her shirt off, and she helped, raising her arms, leaning into his touch as his hands slid up her back. He dropped her shirt on the floor, then tipped her back onto the sofa, and it was some time before they actually made it to bed.

Kate heard a voice. She thought she was dreaming, some kind of weird, lucid dream, because her eyes were closed, but she felt awake. Familiarity intruded. John's voice, muttering. But it wasn't John. He wasn't speaking English. She opened her eyes.

He was looking at her, but it wasn't him. Part of him belonged to Sekhmet, and sometimes she took over. The look in his eyes became older, harder, more experienced. That other gaze was looking at her now, with an expression that was both sad and annoyed. The situation was complicated: Isra the joker had been waiting for a great ace with whom she could join her powers and become Sekhmet, the handmaiden of Ra. But John didn't become Ra. He'd been cured of the wild card virus. Isra might call herself Sekhmet, but she never got the power she'd longed for. There was no Ra, now. Her frustration with John, and with those around him, was plain, whenever she came to the fore.

The voice whispered in Egyptian. Kate wished she knew what she was saying. She was afraid the joker was saying, "This won't last."

Self-consciously, Kate pulled up the sheet to cover her chest. "I wish you'd leave us alone," she whispered.

Isra heard her. "You're children. Just children. You don't understand."

Kate frowned. "That's not fair. After what we've been through, after what you've put John through—"

"It wasn't supposed to be like this. He's such a boy."

"No. You ask too much of him." But how could she argue with something that was so much a part of him?

"*You* are just a child."

Angry, Kate started to sit up, ready to yell another retort. But John closed his eyes, sighed, and seemed to sleep again.

She touched John's arm. "John? John, wake up." She kissed his bare shoulder, then again, until he stirred.

"Hm? What's wrong? Is it the phone?" He thought Jayewardene was calling with a new disaster. He started to sit up, but she held him back. It was John this time, looking out of his own eyes.

"Nothing's wrong. I'm sorry, I shouldn't have woken you up."

Only half-awake, he stroked her cheek absently. "You okay?"

She thought about telling him he'd been talking in his sleep—or that Sekhmet had been talking in his sleep. She'd told him on other nights when it had happened. This time, she didn't. "I had a nightmare or something. It's nothing."

Then John's phone *did* ring. They both lurched at the noise. Reflexively, he grabbed it and listened. His frown deepened. Jayewardene. Had to be.

"Got it. Okay. We'll send someone down," he said, then hung up.

"What is it?" she asked

"There's been an explosion in West Texas. Feds are saying a grain elevator went up, but that's not what the people on the ground are saying."

"What are they saying?"

"Terrorists. Sabotaging the oil."

"Oh my God. And we're going?" She pushed the covers back. But John shook his head.

"Lilith and Bugsy can go. They can check things out and report back before we've even gotten to the airport."

"But I want to go—they'll need people, there's got to be some kind of rescue operation—"

"We don't know the story yet, so you're not going."

"John, I want to go. If you're trying to keep me safe—"

He smirked at her. "Are you ever going to stop arguing with me?"

"You ought to be used to it by now." She tried on a smile. Hoped he knew she was teasing.

He ignored the phone for the moment, wrapped his arms around her and kissed her. Which was just what she needed. She leaned into him and kissed back.

And for a moment, everything was just fine.

NEW YORK CITY

Kate and Ana rushed to catch the subway. Dinner at Stellar, the posh restaurant at the top of the Empire State Building, was one thing, but a cab ride during a fuel shortage was too much of an extravagance. They rode standing, holding onto one of the bars, talking in hushed voices about this and that, phone calls home, how Ana's brother was applying to the University of New Mexico and how Kate's parents were still upset that she'd dropped out of college. They got stares. They always got stares, and a few whispers, "Is that really them? It couldn't be... They look so much like..."

Street level was quiet. Perpetually gridlocked traffic had vanished. A few government vehicles, a few cabs, and very few private cars were active. Fifth Avenue might have been a street in any small town. The air actually smelled decent.

As soon as they turned the corner, shouted questions began from the group of reporters waiting outside the Empire State Building. Kate and Ana stood shoulder to shoulder and prepared to run the gauntlet.

"Curveball! Earth Witch! Who's your pick on the new season of *American Hero*?"

Be nice, Kate reminded herself. Keep the press on your side. Those were the rules from *American Hero*, and they still worked. She shrugged and smiled her sweetheart smile. Cameras flashed. "I don't know, I'm not really watching."

"We've been a little busy," Ana added.

More questions. Kate couldn't make them all out.

"Earth Witch! Reports say you collapsed from exhaustion in Ecuador. Is it true? How's your health?"

Ana's face was a mask, the smile frozen in place. "I'm fine," she said.

Someone pushed her way to the front and stuck a digital recorder out. "Is the Committee going to intervene to stop the genocide in Nigeria?"

Amid the way too personal questions about romances, diets, and clothes, the political ones struck like bolts of lightning.

Kate's sweetheart smile turned apologetic. "No comment. I'm sorry."

With the doorman helping to clear the way, they slipped inside, leaving the reporters crowded on the sidewalk.

Ana let out a sigh.

"You okay?" Kate asked.

"I'm sick of people asking me that," Ana said.

"We're just worried—"

"I'm fine," Ana said, her smile tight. It was what they all said. They were all so tough.

They took the express elevator to the restaurant. They were nearly the last to arrive.

John turned to the elevator when it opened; his face brightened. "Kate! Wow, you look great!" She beamed back at him. She'd been hoping for that reaction. She wore a silky, floral halter dress with heels, and her hair was up. That alone made her look about five years older and a ton more sophisticated.

"You don't look too shabby yourself." He wore a suit with a band collar shirt, giving him sophisticated polish. Definitely his mother's son. She reached for him, and they joined hands to pull each other into a kiss.

"You two are, as ever, awfully cute," Bugsy said. "But I'd like to point out that Ana looks *fabulous*."

Ana wore a black wrap-around dress with a low-cut neck and flowing, knee-length skirt that clung and flattered in all the right places. Add her long black hair, dangly gold earrings, and ever-present St. Barbara medallion, and she looked exotic. And now, she was blushing. But smiling, too.

"We went shopping today," Kate said.

"It called to me from the store window," Ana said. The two of them giggled.

Bugsy said, "What a surprise, we all clean up pretty good."

"Maybe someday *People* will stop picking on how I dress," Kate said.

"They named you best dressed at that UNICEF fundraiser last month," Ana argued.

"Only because John's mother picked out the dress."

John got a dreamy look in his eyes. "That was a great dress."

It had been a great dress, with enough architecture to give even Kate cleavage. A picture of the two of them from that night ended up on the cover of *Aces!* They were arm in arm, looking at something off to the side, smiling. They'd looked like royalty.

The Committee: Rusty, wearing a big grin, waved from the far corner, where he was talking with Bubbles and Holy Roller; Gardener was pointing out something on a potted fern to Toad Man and Brave Hawk; the Lama (from Nepal, who was able to turn insubstantial) and the Llama (from Bolivia, who was almost a joker, with a foot-long neck and fuzzy gray hair, and who could spit a gooey venom incredible distances) were glaring at each other across the foyer. Both had refused to change their ace name to avoid confusion. And Lilith, the

British teleporter, standing with Lohengrin and surveying the room critically, like this was all beneath her. She wore an amazing gown, V-neck coming to a point between her breasts, slit in the skirt climbing to her waist, the diaphanous black material deceptively translucent. All the guys were stealing glances—and Lilith knew it.

Being America's ace sweetheart didn't count for a whole lot sometimes, thought Kate, in her cute and completely boring dress.

The absent member was obvious: at seven feet, DB dominated any room he was in.

"Where's Michael?" she asked.

John frowned. "In Chicago wrapping up his concert tour I think. Let's make the introductions," he said, turning their attention to the two women Kate didn't know. Even more new members. "From Canada, this is Simone Duplaix, AKA Snowblind, and Barbara Baden, the Translator, from Israel."

Simone had dyed magenta hair that screamed *look at me*. She wore a black miniskirt, crop top, and a nose stud, and glared like she expected someone to challenge her on the dress code. Also in her twenties, Barbara was a little more upscale, with a clingy, midnight blue cocktail dress. She kept her hands folded in front of her and was a picture of calm.

"Simone, Barbara, this is Kate Brandt and Ana Cortez." Handshakes all around.

"There's hardly a need for introductions," Barbara said. "Everyone knows who you are."

"Introductions are more polite," Kate said.

Tinker came in from the next room, holding one of his gadgets, a gunmetal gray box that looked like a cross between a TV remote and an eggbeater.

"What's that?" Ana asked.

"Bug detector," he said cheerfully in his thick Aussie accent. "John wanted the place swept. Can't have spies now, right?"

"How do you know it even works?" Kate said.

He pointed it at Bugsy, and the device let out a high-pitched squeal that left them all wincing.

"Well," Bugsy said, glaring at the thing. "My confidence is truly won over."

Tinker huffed. "I built it to track down covert listening devices. I think you got a few of those on you, eh mate?"

For the punchline, a small green wasp crawled out of the pocket of Tinker's suit jacket.

"Hey!" Tinker swatted at the bug, and it crunched. Bugsy winced. "Don't you ever get tired of that trick?"

"I have another one, but you wouldn't like it any better."

The center of the next room had been cleared to make way for a long table draped in white linen. The arrangement leant a somber weight to the evening. This felt like a state dinner. And here, in this luxurious setting, on the eighty-sixth floor, Kate really felt on top of the world.

In keeping with its location, Stellar had a neo/retro art deco motif, with muted colors, pale grays, soft blues, streamlined chrome fixtures with inset lighting, ferns pouring from silver planters. The chairs and tables were mahogany and modernist. 1930s movie stars in tuxedos and ballgowns might come sweeping past at any moment. It was romantic, especially the balcony overlooking the Manhattan skyline.

"This place is amazing," she said, taking a chair between John and Ana near the head of the table.

John gazed around, smiling. "This used to be a different restaurant. Aces High. All the big aces used to hang out here, and the owner did this aces-only dinner every year on Wild Card Day. Mom met my father there. My real father, I mean. She says it's the only reason she comes here, since Hiram retired. I guess I thought it'd be cool to come back. Start some new traditions now that aces are heroes again."

He wore a wistful look, like he gazed through a window into that bygone time when everything was bigger, flashier, better. The woman he knew as his mother had been a different person then. And his father was dead.

Dinner first, meeting after. The staff brought out course after course of gourmet dishes, perfect breads, exotic pâtés, oysters with caviar, salmon, quail, and more. Maybe not more food than Kate had ever seen in one place, but certainly more different kinds of food. No holds barred. John ordered champagne, and they drank a toast to friends old and new, to jobs well done. And, as had become tradition, a toast to the friends who were missing. They'd lost people. They wanted to remember.

They relaxed into conversation and gossip.

"Guess who called me yesterday," Kate said.

People threw out names, movie stars and pop singers, and she shook her head for each one. "Apparently, Michael Berman is looking for someone for the rogue ace challenge on *American Hero*."

Groans greeted the name of the network executive who rode herd on the show. Rusty said, "You actually talked to him?"

"God no. He left like five messages. But I'm warning you—you all may be next."

Ana said, "Depends on how desperate he gets."

Kate wanted to argue, but she was probably right. Berman wouldn't be calling her. Ana wasn't considered as photogenic as the more conventionally sexy women who'd been on the show. Didn't matter, because she could still kick all their asses with her power.

Kate rolled her eyes. "The guy's an ass. I mean, have you seen who they picked for this season? Space Cadette? What's up with that?"

"I thought you weren't watching," John said. Kate huffed.

They were finishing the main course when the restaurant doors slammed open. Drummer Boy appeared, lining all six hands on his hips.

"Hey," he called in a booming voice. "Am I too late? No? Good."

He had to duck to enter the room. He was bald, shirtless, showing off not only his impressive canvas of tattoos, but the tympanic membranes on his torso—his namesake.

John frowned, and Kate tensed. "Aren't you supposed to be in Chicago?" John said.

"Not tonight. Had a little extra time so I thought I'd drop by. This meeting is for the whole Committee, right?"

Bugsy tried to divert the tension, opening a space by the table near him. "DB, pull up a chair. Meet the newbies. Simone, Barbara, DB."

DB didn't cooperate. "Ladies," he said, nodding a minimum polite greeting, then grabbing a spare chair from another table and pulling it next to Kate. He couldn't squeeze himself between her and Ana, so he remained behind them. Turning the chair backward to sit on it, he leaned one set of arms on the backs of Kate and Ana's chairs, crossed another set, and Kate lost track of the third. Now, Kate had John on her left, DB on her right, and the two of them were glaring at each other over her head.

Ana, thank God, distracted him. "How's the tour going?"

"It's been fucking amazing. We're playing stadiums. Hell, we're not a stadium band! We started out punk in two-bit bars. Now here we are." That third set of arms spread in a gesture of offering.

"I still haven't seen the show," Ana said.

"You should. When the next tour starts. I'll get you the VIP treatment, front row seats, the works."

"Cool," Ana said.

"Bring earplugs," Bugsy said. "I *have* seen the show."

Lilith, sitting on the other side of the table, licked a bit of sauce off her fork. "Michael, dear, you look so uncomfortable hunched in over there. Why don't you come sit here with me? There's plenty of room at this end."

In fact, there wasn't, except for a sliver of space at the corner. And Lohengrin, already sitting by Lilith, straightened and puffed up his chest, as if he could fill the space by himself.

Kate half hoped DB would move. Except that would involve making Lilith happy.

DB smirked. "That's okay. I wouldn't want to upset Prince Valiant there."

"Oh, Klaus here? He won't be upset. He's a big puppy." She gazed up at the German ace through slitted, silver eyes.

What an amazing bitch, Kate marveled.

A clink of metal on glass rang out. A goblet tipped and splashed water over part of the table cloth, plates, and people.

"Awe, cripes, would you look at that?" Rusty was half on his feet, reaching uselessly after the mess. "Sorry. I'm pretty clumsy, don't you know." His iron jaw creased into a bashful smile.

The tension broke. At least for the next half a second or so.

John made a production of digging in an attaché case for a set of manila folders, which he distributed. Moving on, then.

"Time for business, I'm afraid," John said, standing at the head of the table. "A lot's landed on us all at once, but I think we have the resources to handle it. At least, I'd like to prove that we do." He flashed a smile, almost shy. "We're still keeping an eye on the situation in Texas. We know there was an explosion. Lilith and Bugsy concluded that it was nuclear. We still don't know what caused it, but the feds think it was terrorists. For the moment, there isn't much we can do until we hear further developments. But here's what we *can* do."

Secretary General Jayewardene had given the Committee three separate missions, all of them deemed urgent.

First: A brutal hurricane season appeared to be developing in the Gulf, and Jayewardene had a hunch. The Secretary General had a track record of accurate hunches. If he wanted a team there to help, the Committee would go.

Second: The UN had received reports of genocide in Africa, in the region between Nigeria and the People's Paradise of Africa, a newish, self-declared nation that was either the latest in a long line of corrupt, despotic regimes or the beginning of a new, empowered Africa free of colonial influences. It depended on who you talked to. A Committee team would investigate the genocide claims and make recommendations.

And third: The current oil shortage was artificially induced. Prince Siraj of the Caliphate had manipulated production and forced prices to their current, stratospheric level of three hundred dollars a barrel. In the opinion of the Secretary General, this was nothing short of economic terrorism that was impacting the entire world and causing widespread hardship and depression. A team would go to Middle East to open oil production again, and UN troops were assembling in anticipation of direct intervention.

"I don't think I have to tell you that this last objective is top secret," John said. "We don't want any leaks to the press clowns downstairs. No blogging," he pointed at Bugsy, who held up his hands in a show of innocence.

This was a new development, and Kate was surprised that the Secretary General had decided on such direct action. They'd almost be causing an international crisis rather than fixing one.

John read from his notes.

"Earth Witch, Gardener, Bubbles, and Holy Roller. You'll head to New Orleans tomorrow. See what you can do about reinforcing the levy system and aiding in the evacuation, if that becomes necessary. DB, you'll be leading the team going to the PPA. You'll have Brave Hawk, Snowblind, Toad Man, and the Lama—Han, not Juan—with you. Curveball, Lohengrin, the Translator, Rustbelt, Tinker, and I will be going to Arabia. Bugsy, you and Juan will hold down the fort here, and Lilith will keep us all in communication, and provide emergency transport if needed—"

DB was shaking his head, chuckling quietly.

John regarded him a moment. "Do you have something to add?"

"I see what you're doing," DB said. "Pretty slick, actually." He tapped a couple of beats on the edge of the table.

"And what is that?" John said tiredly.

DB seemed happy to explain. "Here it is. You're taking all the hotshots to Arabia to be the saviors of the western world. And you're sending me and the second stringers to some shithole in Africa—to do what? Observe? Investigate? To do *jack shit* is what."

"Hey, who are you calling second string?" said Buford, glaring at DB with bulging eyes.

Bugsy smirked. "Turning into a giant toad is not exactly A-list."

"Got me further on *American Hero* than you."

Ouch. A year later, people were still throwing that at each other.

"DB," John said. "I'm just trying to put people where their powers will be most useful. I don't know what you think—"

The joker's sarcastic smile fell. "I'll tell you what I think. I think you're a glory hound, I think you're—"

John dropped a folder on the table with a slap. "Who's the glory hound between us, Mr. Rock Star? Really?"

DB didn't slow down. "You're setting me up to fail, maybe even get me killed..."

Kate closed her eyes. Counted to ten. So help her, if either one of them brought her up as an excuse...

"...and I think you'll do anything you can to keep me away from Kate!"

That was it.

John actually laughed. "Geez, would you let it go? This isn't about Kate!"

Kate stood. Picked up a steak knife. Hefted it in her hand, testing its weight. Felt a warmth flow like flames through her arm. Eventually, everyone was staring at the knife in her hand. Things got real quiet.

She looked at John on one side of her, DB on the other. They stared back, stricken.

"Finished?" she asked. "Can we all sit down and play nice?"

DB muttered, "Tell Captain Cruller to stop rigging the missions in his favor."

"You're being paranoid," she said. He had to realize how monumentally bad this looked. Halfway down the table, Snowblind and the Translator stared in fascination.

"Kate, maybe you should put that down." Ana nodded at the knife in her hand. Kate was gripping it white-knuckled. In her mind's eye she could almost see the glow, the build-up of power. In a temper, she'd let it fly and not even realize it. Ka-boom and fireworks. Wouldn't that impress the newbies? But Ana recognized the mood. And Ana was about the only person who could say anything and not piss Kate off.

Carefully, she set the knife on the table and shook the tingle out of her arm.

John shuffled the folders in front of him, a mindless gesture. "Fine. We'll switch. DB, you're on the Arabia team. I'll go to Africa. It's not a big deal." He pulled his chair back and sank into it. Catching her gaze, he was trying to tell her something. Maybe: *See? I can play nice.* But his solution left her feeling a little sick. She hated to think that a squabble like this might damage a mission, any mission.

Mostly, she hated that they were fighting over her. As if her own choice hadn't had anything to do with which of them she'd ended up with.

Seemingly mollified, DB sat, flexing his arms and running a quick riff on his torso.

John was talking again. "You have your assignments. The New Orleans team will leave first thing—"

A commotion sounded from the restaurant's foyer: heavy footsteps, voices arguing. Just what they needed—more excitement. So much for a nice dinner.

A waiter spoke. "I'm sorry, we're—"

"We have a warrant."

Bugsy stared at the entrance and said, "I have a bad feeling—"

Three men and a woman, all wearing suits and an air of government-backed smugness, came through the door. The guy in front, above average in height and notably fit, filled his expensive pale suit well. He had a buzz cut and a face that was hard to describe. Not ugly exactly, but definitely not right. Crooked nose, uneven eyes—broken bones that had knitted a little off, and laugh lines that had developed oddly because of that.

That disconcerting face twisted in a smile that suggested he was enjoying the situation.

"If you'll all remain seated and quiet we'll get this over with as quickly and painlessly as possible," he said in a decisive, cop-in-charge voice.

John didn't stay seated and quiet. "Billy, what—"

"That's *Director* Ray to you, Mr. Fortune. Now please sit down." That was possibly the shit-eatingest grin Kate had ever seen. John sat.

Director Billy Ray drew a folded pack of papers from the inside pocket of his jacket.

"Mr. Jonathan Tipton-Clarke?" He scanned the group like he was looking for someone, but Ray knew exactly where Bugsy was. His gaze fell on him in a second. "I have here a warrant for your arrest."

"What?" John demanded. "What for?"

"For disseminating classified information in a public venue and potentially damaging national security—" Ray said.

Bugsy smirked. "I blogged about Texas."

"Geez, don't admit anything," John said. "He's an affiliate of the United Nations, there are proper channels for this."

It was a valiant effort, but Ray wasn't interested in proper channels, obviously. He was probably *very* interested in parading a handcuffed member of the Committee past the paparazzi downstairs. "Mr. Tipton-Clarke, if you'd stand, please."

Bugsy did. Ray gestured, and one of the agents produced handcuffs.

"You can't do this, mate," Tinker said. Murmurs around the table agreed with him.

"An American citizen engaging in activities damaging to the safety of the American government and people? I certainly can."

Kate glanced around the table. Eighteen aces and jokers, all—most—with formidable powers. All of whom were tense, glaring at Ray and his goons with unhappy expressions. In one of New York City's poshest restaurants. This could end badly.

Obligingly, Bugsy turned his back to the agent and put his hands behind him, letting them cuff him without complaint. That meant Kate saw him smile and wink, right before he disintegrated.

Thousands of green wasps buzzed as clothing and handcuffs fell. Ray lunged with what had to be ace-fueled reflexes. All he managed to do was snatch the shirt before it reached the floor.

"Shit!" Ray said, ripping the shirt and tossing it aside. "I *hate* when that happens!"

The agent who'd been trying to cuff Bugsy yelped and jumped back, reaching inside his jacket for a gun. The other agents did the same.

All around the table, aces and jokers braced for battle.

Kate had hoped her teammates weren't stupid enough to start something against Ray and his goons. So much for that.

John shouted, "Stand down! Back off!"

The bugs swarmed the four federal agents, clouds of them fogging around their heads. The agents slapped and swatted, hissing as they were stung. Ray swore, snarling as he slapped at himself, crushing wasps when he found them, and scratching at new welts.

With a whoosh and crash, a giant toad bounded onto the table, knocking aside water glasses and tea lights. His mouth was already open, the hideous tongue lolling, before Kate could stop him. A few drops of mucus hit her as the tongue whipped out and grabbed a gun out of the nearest agent's hand. Stunned, the guy regarded his slime-covered hands with a look of horror.

The Llama—the Bolivian one—was the second to jump on the table. His long neck stretched forward, his fists clenched at his side, and he puckered his lips.

"Michael, grab him!" Kate yelled at DB, who was closer.

The big joker reached behind the Llama and took hold of various parts—arms, shoulders, back, legs—with all six arms and yanked him backward, off the table and onto the floor, but not before he got off a shot of spit.

Fortunately, the spit bomb went wide. Only part of it landed on the sleeve of Billy Ray's suit jacket.

The federal ace regarded the spot for a moment. Then, with a sigh, he drew a handkerchief out of his pocket and wiped off the glob. He seemed resigned as he tossed the handkerchief aside.

Buzzing, the bugs formed a loose cloud, circling the room and occasionally dropping to take another sting at one of the agents.

"Stand *down*!" Kate shouted. Facing her team, Kate planted herself between them and the agents. Buford had opened his mouth for another go with his tongue, the Llama was unsuccessfully wrestling with DB, the other Lama had his eyes closed and seemed to be meditating, Brave Hawk had sprouted his wings and gripped a steak knife but hadn't actually done anything yet. Lohengrin had donned his armor and looked like he wanted to march forward—but John planted a hand on his chest. The others seemed caught between decisions to stay put and take action. Lilith stood at the end of the table, arms crossed, regarding the scene with an aggravating lilt to her brow.

A sudden breeze ruffled Kate's bangs—the door to the balcony had opened.

Bugsy's swarm banked around the room, stretching into a streamlined shape, shot out the balcony door like an arrow, and disappeared into the New York sky.

Scratching at a swollen spot on his nose, Billy Ray glared at the balcony, and at the Amazing Bubbles, who knelt by the open door with her hand on the latch.

"I thought we needed a little air," Michelle said, shrugging with an air of innocence that wasn't entirely genuine.

The room was quiet, finally. Lohengrin's armor faded. Buford, human now, climbed off the table.

Billy Ray stood at Kate's shoulder. Literally breathing down her neck.

"I am this close to dragging all of your asses to jail," he said to her, holding his thumb and forefinger so they barely touched. "But because you're cute, and I like blondes, I'll give you a break. Today."

Kate rolled her eyes.

Ray wasn't finished with them. As he regarded them, his gaze sweeping from one end of the table to the other, his frown deepened. For a moment, the ace almost looked tired. He muttered, "You kids are going to get yourselves killed. And I'm probably going to be the one who has to scrape your guts off the pavement."

He stalked out, gesturing at his underlings, who fell into step with him. They were all scratching at angry, swollen bug bites. Kate ran a hand through her hair and sighed. When was her life going to stop feeling like reality TV?

A woman giggled. Snowblind, stifling the laugh with a hand over her mouth. The hand was trembling, just a little. "I knew joining the Committee would be exciting, but I had no idea."

Nervous chatter dispelled some of the tension as people straightened chairs and returned to their seats. Some of the wait staff crept out of hiding.

Kate pulled out a chair and sat. John brought over another chair and sat with her.

"So. Bugsy's wanted by the feds," he said. "I guess that's another line on the to-do list."

"What are we going to do about it?"

"Normally I would call the Director of SCARE to clear this up. But Billy Ray *is* the Director of SCARE." He winced. "And how the hell did that happen?"

It never ended. Always another mission. Three more missions, in this case.

Kate leaned close to John and spoke softly. "You promised Ana would get a break. But you're sending her out again tomorrow?"

John had the grace to look chagrined. "I know. But we need her. No one else can do what she does. This isn't going to get fixed by...by a giant toad."

She couldn't argue, because he was right. Ana herself wouldn't want to be left out of this. Even now, the ace was helping the staff pick up scattered glassware and table settings, like she could never sit back and let someone else do the work.

"I'll make it up to her," he said, earnest. "I promise."

"Hey John," Tinker called. "What do you want to do with these?" He held up Bugsy's discarded clothing.

Someone said, "Whoa. I never would have pegged Bugsy as a boxers guy."

John just shook his head in long-suffering bemusement. Smiling, Kate wrapped her arm around his and rested her head on his shoulder. "You sure know how to show a girl a good time."

ARABIA

Hot, exhausted, sweating rivers inside her Kevlar vest—this, she had decided, was a Kevlar situation—Kate looked out the helicopter window at the desert sliding past below her. In a few minutes, they'd reach the pumping station in Kuwait, twenty miles from the coast of the Persian Gulf.

This was their second stop of the day. At the first, they'd spent six hours keeping a crowd of sullen locals at bay while technicians started the wells pumping.

Not a single person on either side had been happy to be there. This wasn't like Ecuador, where the lives they saved stood right in front of them. Hard to see the lives they were saving here.

Her phone beeped—incoming text message.

One word: FUBAR. From Michael.

"What's wrong?" Lohengrin said. Somehow, even in the heat and sand, with everyone around him boiling, he managed to maintain his cool, almost arrogant demeanor.

She showed him the screen. The German ace raised an eyebrow.

"From DB? He wanted to come here," he said. "He shouldn't complain now."

This wasn't complaining. Complaining was bitching about the heat and the food, pouring sand out of your shoe and yelling at your teammates for nothing at all. This was different.

It wouldn't do any good to argue with Lohengrin. He'd just look down his nose at her with the sort of condescending pity people used on children with skinned knees.

The helicopter landed on a concrete pad outside the station in a whirlwind of grit. Ana had called from New Orleans to tell her about the weird ace who showed up channeling the girl's ghost. Kate was happy enough to not be there dealing with that particular mess. She shook the thought of the fallen ace away. She and Lohengrin piled outside first. Despite his confidence, he wasn't taking any chances—he already wore his armor.

They were in a dusty valley, a bowl of sand ringed by rocky outcrops. Some grasses clung to the wasteland, tossing in a constant breeze. The station itself was an industrial complex covering acres. Dozens of wells were marked by steel trees thrusting up from the ground, attached to angled collections of pipes and valves. More pipes, a twisting maze of them, connected various stations of hunched machinery of arcane purpose. It was a sci-fi landscape from some depressing post-apocalyptic future. The air smelled thickly of oil, sulfur, and waste. Kate sneezed.

Sun glared off everything. Even with sunglasses, Kate's face felt like it had frozen in a squint.

A control building and a collection of prefab barracks lay off to one side. But nobody was here. No workers had gathered to block the gate in the chain-link fence surrounding the site. No crowd milled around the barracks. She should have been relieved. The whole place was quiet, still.

Throwing a pebble, she blew the padlock and chain securing the gate. Still nothing. Maybe the place had been abandoned. She waved back at the helicopter, and the team of technicians, with their bright blue UN vests and helmets, ran to meet them.

"Keep your eyes open," she said to Lohengrin.

"You think I would let down my guard?" He sounded offended.

You're sleeping with Lilith, aren't you? "Of course not," she said.

They followed the team to the main building. Their attention was out, looking for trouble. The helicopter's motor was still running, just in case. A trio of UN soldiers stood near it, also keeping watch.

"Curveball!" one of the techs called from the door. He was middle-aged, British, and had a weathered look to him. "It's locked. Care to do the honors?"

She kept looking at the barracks, waiting for someone to lob a grenade from there. "Yeah. Sure." She pulled a pebble from the pouch over her shoulder.

"I could cut the lock off," Lohengrin said.

"Yeah, but people like it when things go boom." She smiled. The techs chuckled. "Stand back, guys."

She almost didn't look at the door before making her pitch, but she lowered her arm at the same time Lohengrin said, "Wait a moment."

They both approached, their attention drawn by a thin line of discoloration at the top of the frame. Like a bad paint job, or a place where someone had tried to patch a crack. It looked almost like caulking.

"Bill?" she said to the British tech. "What's this look like to you?"

He joined them at the door and studied where she pointed. It only took a second for his expression to turn slack, his eyes growing wide.

"Bloody hell," he murmured. "I think it's plastique."

"Set to detonate when the door opens? A booby trap?"

"Probably."

They all backed away.

"What do we do?" Lohengrin said.

"We call it in," Curveball said. "Go back to HQ. This isn't worth blowing ourselves up over."

The technicians trotted back toward the helicopter without argument. She and Lohengrin brought up the rear as they'd initially led the way—watchfully, looking over their shoulders.

They heard the machine gun fire before they saw the gunman.

Instinctively, Kate dropped as squibs of sand burst around her. Then a weight fell on her. Lohengrin, in full armor, including bucket helmet with decorative wings, playing human shield. She couldn't move to reach her pouch.

"Get up!" she hissed, elbowing him. He did, just enough for her to slip out, take shelter, and take stock.

The firing continued. Bullets pinged off Lohengrin's armor.

There was only one of them. A basic model automatic rifle. It was coming from the corner of the control building. She was actually getting experienced enough with this to discern that much from a noisy burst of gunfire.

Golf ball in hand this time, she cocked back and threw over Lohengrin's shoulder. Didn't have to aim, because she steered the projectile, sent it rocketing around the corner. She hoped that would silence the weapon.

It impacted with all the power of her surprise at the turn of events. People shooting at her brought this out. This *anger*. It translated well, and that side of the prefab building went up in a crack of thunder, a burst of dust and debris.

But he'd already run. Lohengrin pointed, and she caught a glimpse of someone peering out around the corner of the other side of the building.

Still just one of them. No army bearing down.

A second explosion blew out the front of the building. Fire ringed the door—the booby trap. Her detonation rattled the door and set the bomb off. Shit.

Billowing flames swallowed the building. She ducked, Lohengrin hunched over her, and debris pummeled them. Pieces of siding, of corrugated roofing, furniture even. Sheltered by Lohengrin's body, she felt the impacts against him.

She didn't see what struck his head, hard enough to whip it back, too fast, too hard. He slumped, boneless—and his armor vanished. She found herself holding a 200-plus pound unconscious German in her lap. The armor couldn't protect against everything—like getting knocked out inside the helmet.

In a panic, Kate felt for a pulse, looked for injuries. She didn't see blood, no obvious marks. She shook his shoulders. "Lohengrin? Lohengrin! *Klaus!*"

They were in the open, totally exposed, and that guy was still out there with a gun. But the rain of fire didn't come. She threw another stone.

And at that moment the gunman emerged and revealed what he was doing. He'd set down his gun and was pulling the pin from a grenade. But he wasn't facing toward them. He'd turned to the tangle of pipelines, the wells, the pumps that held back the pressure of oil and natural gas.

He threw. The grenade sailed up.

She turned her missile toward the grenade. Didn't know if this would work. Was she good enough, fast enough, clever enough. Had to believe she was. Good enough to get this far, couldn't hesitate now.

She wondered what would happen the time she wasn't good enough. It would only take once.

Her missile, glowing red-hot, sailed in a straight line toward the grenade, which was falling toward the pipes.

Squinting, she could barely see her target. But she could see it in her mind, follow the arc. She reached toward her missile, her arm taut and trembling, guiding it faster, still faster. She let out a cry of rage.

It sped up, then slammed into the grenade from the side, carried it forward some twenty yards, and exploded. Both projectiles vaporized. Nothing else happened. Nothing broke, nothing ignited. These oil fields wouldn't burn.

The gunman—young, wearing plain trousers and a T-shirt—screamed in his own fit of rage and ran toward her, waving a handgun, a weapon of last resort. He fired at her again and again in an obvious suicide run. She picked up something—stone, a piece of plastic from the destroyed control room. Didn't matter, because it was solid in her hand, and her arm burned. She pitched.

The missile went through him, all the way, just like a bullet, complete with the spray of blood, a splatter raining from the front, a gory mess spilling from his back. He exploded from the inside and fell like a stone.

She stared, almost smiling with satisfaction.

Lohengrin tried sitting up, shaking his head, blinking until he managed to focus on her. "My lady! I am in your debt."

She pursed her lips.

Blue helmets ran toward them. The UN team, with machine guns. They were shouting.

"Curveball!" one of them called. French accent. She couldn't remember his name.

"Help me get him to the chopper!" she shouted, trying to lever Klaus to his feet. He tried to pull away.

Everything moved quickly. Two soldiers were suddenly there, taking Lohengrin's arms, pulling the big ace away from her. She scrambled after him. "He's hurt, we have to—"

"Curveball!" the French peacekeeper said again. He pulled her to the helicopter. In moments, they were airborne and getting the hell out. But the soldier wouldn't let go, and she started to get angry, especially when another soldier started tugging at her left arm. What the hell were they doing? Between the two of them, they pinned her to the seat.

"What—"

Lohengrin was the one who said, "Kate, your arm!"

She stared at him, blank faced, confused. Then she looked at herself.

Her left arm was covered with blood. Her own blood. The soldier was swabbing at her with an alcohol wipe, searching for the wound. She hadn't even felt it. Why couldn't she feel it?

"Just grazed. You'll be fine," the medic said, poking at her bicep.

He did something—and every nerve lit with pain. She clenched her teeth and pressed her head back while he wrapped a bandage around the arm.

She thought, despairing—what if it had been her right arm?

A few long, terrifying moments of shock passed. After sunset, they arrived back at the tent city that served as their local base of operations. Kate ended up in the infirmary, on a lot of painkillers, sitting on a chair and looking away as a medic stitched the wound in her arm. Eight stitches. She'd have a scar to show for this.

Lilith, still managing to look suave and stylish in black fatigues, regarded her.

"Don't tell John about this," Kate said. She didn't want him to worry. But God, she wanted to see him. Wanted to fall into bed with him and sob about the close call. But he'd try to send her back to New York. "I'll call him later. I don't want him to get distracted because of me."

"You're loopy on drugs," she said. "You're not thinking clearly."

Kate grit her teeth. "Lilith, I know we don't get along. But please don't tell him just to spite me."

Lilith stepped close and glared down at her. "After everything we've been through together, you don't think I'd go out of my way to spite you, do you?"

Of course she would. Spite was her bread and butter. "Bitch," Kate muttered.

She tsked. "Dear, don't aggravate yourself. And you really shouldn't call me names when you want me to do you a favor."

Kate closed her eyes and tried to settle herself. She didn't have anything on hand to throw.

"What are you going to tell John?" she said softly.

Lilith shrugged. "What I have to." She swirled her cape and vanished with a hiss of air.

"Funny. The guys all seem to get along with her just fine." DB pushed through the tent flap.

She wasn't sure she wanted to see him just now. At the same time, she was relieved to see a friendly face. He pulled a chair over with one hand, tapped a patter with another. After sitting, he just looked at her for a long moment. His face was a picture, a conflict of emotions. Shadows darkened his eyes. A multicolored bruise melded with the ink of tattoos on his ribcage. He hadn't slept since his own disaster. Hadn't smiled, either. Together, the two of them must have looked war-ravaged.

"Christ, Kate, when I heard you'd been hurt—"

"I'm fine—"

"Would you listen to me? After everything that's happened, all the shit that's come down, I don't know what I'd do if anything happened to you."

"Michael. I'm not sure I can handle that sort of thing from two sides."

"Is it so fucking wrong that I care?"

"No. Of course not. But—"

"But you've got John. I know."

Incredibly, she felt her lips turn in a smile. He stared at her. "What? What'd I do?"

"You didn't call him Captain Cruller. Or Beetle Boy."

For a moment he looked like he might spout obscenities. Then he ducked his gaze and chuckled. She reached for his nearest hand and squeezed. Friends in a tight spot. She didn't want to lose that. He wrapped three of his hands around hers. All she had to do was say the word, and he'd wrap his whole, immense body around her like that, smothering her with warmth and affection. She didn't say the word.

Sighing, he said, "This mission is completely fucked up."

She pressed her lips in a line. "I know."

That evening, Kate found a TV that picked up CNN and watched John's mission go to hell even worse than this one was. The footage of Sekhmet the lion shrugging off gunfire and tearing the treads off tanks left her nauseous. That was John in there, she kept telling herself. The Committee hadn't stopped a genocide. They'd ignited a war. Reports of injured Committee members were sketchy—all anyone knew was that there were injuries. Calls to John weren't getting through.

When Ana called, Kate left the crowd gathered around the TV to get some privacy.

"How are you?" Ana asked, her voice scratching over the cell connection.

I've been shot. "I'm okay," Kate said instead.

"You're lying," Ana said, a little too flatly for it to be a joke.

"Well, so are you." Both women sighed, unable to explain how much they were really hurting. "Have you been watching the news at all?"

"Haven't had time," Ana said. "Not sure I want to. I take it things aren't going well."

"They could be worse. We haven't lost anyone yet." Then Kate wished she hadn't said it. It was such a close thing.

"Same here. We got through Harriet, but there's a second hurricane on the way. Category five this time."

When it rained it poured. And that was a *really* bad joke.

"Are you getting any rest at all?" Kate said.

Ana sighed. "I'm doing okay."

"No, Ana, you're not. I'm ten thousand miles away and I can hear that you aren't."

"I swear, you're as bad as John with the overprotective thing," Ana said, as frustrated as Kate had ever heard her. Kate didn't know what to say to that. "I'm a big girl, Kate. You worry about your own skin, okay?"

Her own skin, with its gunshot wound and eight stitches.

"Okay," she said weakly.

"I have to get going," Ana said with new urgency. "Chopper's here to take me across the lake." It must have been mid-morning in New Orleans. Ana was just getting started.

"Be careful."

"You too. See you later." She clicked off.

Kate tried not to worry about what was happening on the other side of the world. Too much worry, in too many places. She returned to her room, sitting in the dark, on her cot, in sweat pants and sports bra, curling her left arm protectively to her body.

She didn't know what to do. What the fuck were they going to do?

A brief breeze, maybe a second of whooshing air, passed through the room, like a draft through an open tent flap.

Lilith swept back her arm, flourishing her cape. Beside her stood John.

Her first thought: she didn't want John to see her like this, hurt and defeated. Her second: Lilith told him. The bitch. But she forgot all that when John knelt by her cot and pulled her into his arms. He didn't look a whole lot better than she felt. His face was ashen, almost sickly, his eyes bloodshot. She could smell soot and gunpowder ground into his clothing.

"Are you okay?" they asked each other at the same time.

She hugged him as tight as she could with one arm. "I'm okay, John."

He pulled away to look at her, cupping her face in his hands, smoothing back her hair. "Kate. You were *shot*."

"Grazed. Just a few stitches. Left arm, even. I can still throw."

"Kate—" His look darkened, and Kate braced. Here it came, he was going to try to yank her from the mission.

She tried to beat him to it. "John, we're done here. We're cooked. We need to pull out before something ridiculous happens."

"Lilith says this was an isolated incident. One guy. A disgruntled worker lashing out."

She almost laughed. "You can actually say that with a straight face? After what happened to Michael and Rusty? John, we've seen what's happening here. These people don't want us here. This is an invasion. Michael will tell you the same thing—"

"You're siding with him now?"

She huffed. "God, what is it with you two?"

"It should have been me here. I shouldn't have let him talk me into switching."

"John, would you listen to me? It wouldn't matter if you'd been here. It isn't about you or him or me or who's doing what. It's this place. The situation here is totally fucked up and Jayewardene's crazy if he thinks us being here is going to help anything. The UN needs trained diplomats on the ground here, not...not...a bunch of reality show rejects!"

John looked over his shoulder. Lohengrin was standing in the doorway.

"You lack faith," the German ace said. He'd recovered from his bout of unconsciousness with no ill-effects. Hard-headed, that one. "We're symbols. Powerful symbols. Have faith."

This wasn't a game, she wanted to scream. This wasn't a divine calling. And there wasn't always going to be someone around to save your ass.

"Kate," John said, somber. "We're pulling out of Africa. The mission there's a bust. Tom Weathers—he's psychotic. Insane." He shook his head, as if still trying to understand. "There's nothing we can do there. Which makes it even more important that we do some good here."

Recalling the spray of blood from the man she'd killed, she almost laughed at him. *That* was doing good?

Lilith cleared her throat. "Let's leave these two to their little conversation, shall we?"

Predictably, Lohengrin seemed all too happy to leave with the British ace.

When they were gone, Kate touched John's face and kissed him.

He looked surprised. His brow—his marred, gem-embedded brow—furrowed. "You're hurt."

And if that was going to stop him, he lacked serious imagination.

"Sit with me," she said, scooting back to give him room.

He did, shifting onto the cot. When he was settled, she curled up against him, pulling his arm around her shoulders, resting her head on his chest. Cocooned herself with him. He held her tightly, stroking her hair.

In spite of her plans, the painkillers and exhaustion conspired against her. Feeling safe for the first time in days, she slept.

LIMBO

Kate sat curled up in a chair by John's hospital bed. She'd come here to explain to him in person. She hadn't known he would be in the hospital. The timing of all this was shitty.

He'd have a scar, the doctors said. They'd stitched the wound as well as they could, but Sekhmet had done a lot of damage when she tore out of his head. He was lucky he hadn't bled to death.

Sekhmet had done a lot of damage to him, period.

His forehead was bandaged, so she couldn't see the wound. Probably for the best. John seemed to be sleeping soundly for the first time in... For the first time since she'd started sleeping with him. His expression was slack rather than tense with unconscious anxiety.

She thought she might try to find some soda or coffee or something. Straightening, she winced—her arm was still sore. She'd stopped taking the pain pills. They made her fuzzy. She wanted to stay sharp, for just a little while longer.

Then she could collapse into a sobbing puddle of tears, when no one was looking.

As she stood, John opened his eyes.

"Hey," she said, moving to his side.

He gave a tired smile. He might not be able to do much more than that for now. Maybe they ought to enjoy this time, this moment in limbo, before they had to make any decisions.

"You're here." He even managed to sound surprised. "I thought you were pissed off at me."

"I am," she said. "I was. We can talk about that later."

He shook his head, annoyed, and tried to sit up. Winced, slumped back, and picked at the IV line, which had become tangled with his hand. She helped straighten it.

"This changes everything. It's all different now," he said.

"What are you talking about?"

His weak smile turned bitter. "I'm right back where I started. No powers. Nothing. I'll be resigning from the Committee. Then...I don't know."

If ever there was a moment she wanted to throw something at him, this was it. "Is that what this is about? You feeling sorry for yourself because you don't have a beetle woman living in your head anymore?"

He frowned. "She wasn't that bad."

"Not that bad? She—"

"She left me," he said. "She chose me, and then she left me, and it's like I'm...I'm *empty*. I feel empty."

Kate felt the expression of horror on her face, and she couldn't erase it. John actually sounded sad that he had his own life back.

And for the first time Kate realized that, with their telepathic and emotional link, he'd been closer to Isra than he'd ever be to her.

Kate closed her eyes and took a breath. Probably shouldn't be yelling in a hospital room. But she wanted to.

"John. It's so nice to be talking to just *you* for a change."

"Even if I'm just a nat."

"I liked you before Sekhmet ever came along. It has nothing to do with anybody's powers."

"You liked Drummer Boy, too."

"Wait a minute. Do you think I only hooked up with you because you suddenly got powers? It couldn't possibly be because you were the nicest guy on the set? Because I had such a good time just hanging out with you?" Not to mention John hadn't fucked almost every other girl on the set like DB had. Those days on *American Hero* seemed like such a long time ago now. "You were the only one who saw *me*, not Curveball the ace or the hot chick."

He still wouldn't look at her. "You said you were coming here to talk to me."

He had to know what she wanted to talk to him about. Couldn't put it off any longer.

"I can't do this anymore. It's changed from when we started. I feel like someone else's tool. And I don't like it. So I'm going to take some time off."

"Leaving. With DB," he said. Like a dog worrying a bone.

"Just leaving," she said.

He smirked. Like he didn't believe her. With sudden clarity, she realized the Committee wasn't the only thing she couldn't stay with anymore. She had thought—hoped—she could leave one and not the other. But maybe that was wishful thinking.

She didn't want to have to say this to him. Not like this. But pity was a trap she didn't want to fall into. Feeling sorry for him would make them both unhappy. More unhappy, rather.

"You don't trust me, do you?" And he didn't say anything. She wanted him to deny it. To grip her hand, however weakly, and reassure her. Plead with her. But he didn't say anything. "You're always going to be worried that I'm going to leave you for him. Or the next flashy ace that comes along."

"DB was right. Maybe I was trying to keep you two apart. Because I was right, too. That if you two were together, you'd end up with him—"

Enough of this. Enough of being batted back and forth between them like a tennis ball. They all needed a time out.

"I don't think you even see me anymore," she said. "I think I'm just...just this *thing* to you. Some kind of validation."

"Kate—"

"So I'm going to take some time off."

"Wait a minute—"

"I'm sorry, John." She kissed him. Lingered. Met his gaze for a moment, and didn't like the misery she saw there. But staying wouldn't change it. They'd hash this argument out again, and again—and sooner or later, she'd walk out just the same.

She left the room. Her steps came faster as she traveled down the hallway, looking for the front door. When she reached it, she left the hospital at a run and kept going.

BLUEBEARD AND THE WHITE BUFFALO: A RANGERGIRL YARN

TIM PRATT

Tim Pratt returns to the world of his imaginative and moving debut novel, *The Strange Adventures of Rangergirl*.

Rangergirl rode her multi-legged magnetic steed across the dusty ground, toward a line of smoke rising against the darkening blue sky. Her mount's whirring legs stirred up a steady cloud behind her, so whoever had the campfire going would see her approach, but since she wasn't tracking a bounty, she didn't worry over being seen. Half a mile from the campfire she ran into a knot of fragile dust-and-starshine ghost-children, which whipped into nothing before the softly humming approach of her steed. Rangergirl smiled. The ghosts meant Gilles de Rais was ahead, and she hadn't seen him in a year. She'd been out here in the bleak middle of the West on long patrol for ages, and an evening's company would be welcome, ghosts and all.

Gilles stood in silhouette, his back to the fire, a long rifle in his hands. The ghosts must have murmured direful warnings of her approach—they didn't like it when Gilles made friends. "Gilles, it's me! R.G.!"

Gilles lowered the rifle and raised a hand in greeting. Rangergirl twisted a knob to power down her steed, let it whir to a stop, and dismounted.

"Ma chérie," Gilles said, arms outstretched. Rangergirl embraced him. His ghosts shifted and muttered beyond the edge of the fire, pale dirty faces mournful, teeth bared. They were unhappy, but lacked the substance to interfere with their fellowship.

After initial greetings, the two sat together by the fire, Rangergirl cooking beans over the flame, Gilles smoking one of his noxious handrolled cigarettes. He said the pungent smoke kept the ghosts at bay, and since he'd lost his own senses of smell and taste centuries before, when he first died, the odor didn't bother him.

"Funny our paths should cross again," Rangergirl said. "Maybe it'll be more peaceful than last time."

"We can only hope," Gilles said. They'd first met years before, and fought together against a common enemy: the ancient Aaron Burr, self-proclaimed Emperor of the West and Oppressor of Mexico. Burr had orchestrated a dark plot for conquest from his stronghold in the desert, and Gilles and Rangergirl had thwarted him, bringing his heavily armed war zeppelin down in flames. Burr was Rangergirl's biggest problem these days, since she'd long since defeated most of her other enemies, including Cosmocrator, the Outlaw, and Kentucky Tom Granger.

"You still working for Prelati?" Rangergirl said. Gilles's master was a wily old sorcerer, wicked and ambitious, and she dreaded the day she'd have to fight him. She didn't relish the thought of facing off against Gilles.

"I serve Prelati as the priests of Death Valley serve the dark god Martu," Gilles said. "Because such service is the only alternative to horrible punishments in the afterlife."

"Right," Rangergirl said. "I knew that. I was just...wondering if maybe he'd given you some time off."

Gilles sighed. "Prelati does not believe in time off. He brought me back from the dead, so my every hour belongs to him."

Rangergirl nodded. "My offer's still open. I can hunt Prelati down for you. This thrall he has over you is neither right nor lawful. You've told me before, all you want is peace."

Gilles shook his head. "Killing Prelati would free me from his spell, and let me die. But in death, I would face judgment for my crimes." He glanced at the ghost-children in their peasant rags, dark-eyed waifs, mostly boys. Each was a victim of Gilles's reign of terror in the early 1400s, when he was a French lord, in the years after he fought alongside Joan of Arc. In those days, Prelati was a conjuror who promised Gilles eternal life in exchange for the blood of children. Gilles's crimes were discovered, and he was tried and found guilty of sodomy, heresy, and the murder of 140 children. Prelati even testified against him at the trial. Gilles was hanged and burned...but days after his death, Prelati restored Gilles to life and health, fulfilling his promise of eternal life, and demanding service in exchange.

Rangergirl looked at the ghosts, too. "I can't believe..." she said, but trailed off. She'd studied up some on Gilles's history after they first met, and the records were contradictory, some calling Gilles a monster who'd killed as many as 600 children, others saying he'd killed one or two at most, others insisting he was innocent, victim of a frame-up job by the Church, out to seize his lands.

"I cannot recall my crimes," Gilles said. "Death ruined my memories. I remember my last years in pieces—Prelati, the courtroom, the gallows." He waved his hand vaguely, disturbing a nearby ghost. "Still, what more proof do I need, besides these spirits? But I am not the man I was, and would not commit such crimes again."

Rangergirl stirred the fire with a stick. 400 years had passed since Gilles's death, five long lifetimes, and that was time enough to change someone. But Gilles still served an evil man. "What if Prelati ordered you to harm a child?"

Gilles shook his head. "That was the single point I won. I told him I would rather face the fires of Hell than harm another boy, and he believed me. He may ask me for any other service, and I will give it, but never that. In truth, though he protested, I do not think he minded the concession—children are seldom a threat to a man like Prelati."

Rangergirl leaned back on her elbows. "So if you're not on vacation, what're you doing out here?"

Gilles flicked his cigarette toward the ghosts, who shied away. "You are no friend to my master, but I cannot think of a reason you would care to stop me, so... I have been sent to watch over the birth of a buffalo."

"A buffalo?" Gilles had achieved notoriety as a buffalo hunter years before, as part of Prelati's ongoing vendetta against the mysterious and ponderous buffalo spirits that dwelled on the plains.

"I find it a strange task, too. But this is a special buffalo, a she-calf, all white."

Rangergirl leaned forward. "The white buffalo? I've heard of that, from some of the buffalo people. It's a prophecy, Gilles. What do you know about it?"

"About the prophecy? Nothing. I am to meet a contingent of hired soldiers, and guides, who will take me to the birthing place. I am to protect the white buffalo against any who seek to destroy it. I do not know why. My master does not share his motivations with me. What is the prophecy?"

Rangergirl stared into the fire, trying to recall the words the shaman of the buffalo people had used to tell her about the white buffalo. "When the white calf is born, it will herald the rebirth of the West. The great buffalo herds will return, and the braves fallen in battle with the white man will be restored to life. The poisoned waters will run clear again, and the monsters will retreat back into their lairs underground. The white man's grip on the West will loosen, and the land will be returned to those who lived here before. The shaman told me that some white people—explorers, trappers, guides—would be allowed to remain. But the empire-builders, the ones who want to kill whole tribes and build cities and mine mountains and dam rivers, they'll be driven away." She frowned. "Why in the hell would Prelati want to help something like that? This is a prophecy of the buffalo people, and he hates the buffalo people, right?"

"I think... If the broken nations were reformed, and the white man driven from the West, then Aaron Burr would be cast out, yes?"

Rangergirl nodded.

"That explains my master's support. Burr is his greatest rival here. Prelati would rather fight with the natives than with Burr's army."

"I guess," she said. "These range wars make strange allies. Do you mind if I come, Gilles, to help you protect the buffalo?"

"It would be an honor to stand beside you again," Gilles said.

Rangergirl wrapped herself in a blanket to sleep, some distance from Gilles and the soughing of his ghosts. Gilles hadn't slept since his death. He just sat up all night listening to the ghosts murmur about their misery and his guilt. Rangergirl stared up at the stars, her eyes naturally drifting to the great buffalo constellation. If this was truly the time of prophecy, then everything would change. The idea disturbed her for reasons too numerous to count, but it excited her, too.

Rangergirl stopped her mount and swore. "Raiders!"

Gilles stopped his steam-sled and shaded his eyes against the midday sun, looking where she pointed. "No. They are flying the pale banner. Those are the men we are supposed to meet." He gestured to a bleached white skin dangling from the handle of his sled, and Rangergirl saw the similar banners displayed on the approaching mounts. "My master hired the mercenaries, and the rest of them are guides."

"I recognize some of them," Rangergirl said grimly. Prelati's taste in soldiers apparently tended toward the vicious and the villainous, but she supposed these rogues could be good protectors, if they were well-paid and well-supervised. But they wouldn't be happy to see her.

"Call me...Joanie," Rangergirl said, tying a bandana around the lower half of her face and pulling her hat down low over her eyes. "I don't want them to know who I am. I've been on the wrong side of a few shootouts with some of these 'soldiers.'"

"Understood," Gilles said. "I'll tell them you are Prelati's new protégé, and that the mask hides some magical disfigurement."

The mercenaries arrived on a variety of mounts, most mechanical, one a giant scorpion with its claws wired closed and its tail docked. The riders were familiar to Rangergirl from wanted posters and close encounters, a rogue's cohort of the most vicious guns for hire in the West. Rangergirl nodded to Hart and Boot, the sorceress robber-queen and her eerie tulpa henchman, a man created from

Pearl Hart's need; to the necromancer Ayres, with the mummified hands of Isaac "Hanging Judge" Parker dangling around his neck like a gruesome necklace; the half-crazy rainmaker Charles Hatfield, his undertaker's suit steaming with water vapor, static electricity crackling in his gray hair; and the nameless night sheriff, a silent shadow-doppelganger of Wyatt Earp. Three tall, pale men draped in buffalo skins sat some distance apart on articulated metal arachnid steeds, a dull green light seeping from the domed power sources behind the saddles. Those must be the guides, though they didn't look like native Indians, unless they were one of the albino tribes from the deep caves. But if that were the case, why were they involved with the birth of the white buffalo? The pale tribes didn't follow the buffalo spirits. Rumor had it they worshipped a strange, fungal intelligence in the deep caverns.

"You the trail boss?" Pearl Hart asked.

"I am Gilles de Rais," he said.

Boot lifted his head and turned his sad eyes on Gilles. While Pearl Hart rode astride a hobbled giant scorpion, John Boot traveled on foot beside her. Rangergirl supposed that, since he wasn't truly human, Boot had more endurance than normal men. "You're Gilles de Rais?" Boot said, voice betraying nothing stronger than mild curiosity. "The inspiration for the story of Bluebeard? A captain in Joan of Arc's army? Child murderer, devil-worshipper, heretic?"

Gilles only nodded.

"I reckon you're fit to lead us, then," Pearl said, and everyone relaxed, some laughing. Introductions were made casually after that, and they accepted "Joanie" at face value. Only Boot looked at her strangely, but she couldn't read his expression the way she could a normal man's. The pale tribesmen didn't speak until Gilles rode over to them, and then they all conferred quietly while the others smoked, drank water, and chatted.

Pearl Hart ambled to Rangergirl's side. She was dressed in almost-theatrical cowgirl garb, like a lady sharpshooter in a traveling show. "You're Prelati's new apprentice, huh?" she asked. "Did he take you on 'cause of your vast magical potential, or just for general fuckin' and whatnot?" Pearl was reputed to have the foulest mouth and the basest manners of any woman in the West. Rangergirl just stared at her over her mask, not speaking. Pearl had heard Rangergirl's voice before, during a nasty run-in outside a town called Tolerance, and speaking now wasn't worth the risk.

Pearl sniffed. "No need to get tetchy. Us ladies of the trail should look out for each other."

Gilles, walking toward them, said, "Take no offense, Miss Hart. Joanie does not speak, for reasons best left undiscussed."

"Ah," Pearl said. "Prelati thinks women should be seen and not heard, is that it?" She spat, shrugged, and headed toward Boot, loudly berating him for everything from the dry weather to the sorry state of his hat.

Gilles beckoned the mercenaries together. "The guides will lead us to the birthing place, in a canyon half a day's ride from here. We should arrive shortly after nightfall, and the ritual will begin at midnight. Be on your guard—there may be attacks on the way. Those who oppose this birth are looking for us." Gilles barked out assignments, and if his cohort responded with something less than military efficiency, it was only because they were such a contrary lot. Gilles and "Joanie" would ride in front of the guards, taking directions from them; Hart and Boot would ride to the left of the guides, the night sheriff to the right, protecting their flanks; and Ayres and Hatfield would ride in back. The guides were to be protected at all costs, and failing that, everyone was to guard Ayres, who could make even dead guides speak well enough to give directions, if the need arose. The pale tribesmen seemed untroubled by the straightforward talk of their possible deaths; Rangergirl supposed they had the true religion, a dedication to cause that outweighed concerns for their personal safety. Rangergirl had always wanted to believe in something that strongly. She'd tried to dedicate herself to justice with that level of devotion, but something—perhaps the abstractness and slippery boundaries of the concept, perhaps the inevitable failures of justice she'd seen—kept her from fully experiencing the serenity of unshakeable faith.

The group set off across the plains, and Rangergirl reflected that she'd never before had quite so many villains at her back. One stick of dynamite would get rid of the whole lot, and make the West a better place by far. But they were her allies of circumstance, and if this course would bring the birth of the white buffalo and the restoration of the West's natural splendor and bounty, surely that was worth riding at the head of such a rogue's procession.

Rangergirl almost raised her hand to greet the Wild Rangers as friends, until they started shooting. The five Wild Rangers appeared over the top of a ridge, riding goatish unicorns with their horns filed down; the mounts had been imported from the Fayre Islands long ago, after the sorcerer known as the Outlaw unleashed a plague that killed all the true horses in the West. The Wild Rangers were lawmen led by Texas Jack Slaughter, a private militia formed after the whole state of Texas was rendered uninhabitable by the rampaging Things that rose from the gulf four years earlier. Rangergirl had fought alongside Texas

Jack and his men many times, and so at first, she was pleased to see the Rangers, but after a moment of looking at her group in surprise, they started shooting.

Hatfield raised his arms and shrieked, white crackles of electricity wreathing him, and lightning split the clear sky, striking one of the Wild Rangers dead. The night sheriff shot one of the men off his mount. Then Boot suddenly had a pistol in each hand, and with three calmly aimed shots he killed the other Rangers. Rangergirl stared at their bodies, fallen among the scrub brush and dust. How had she come to this, aligned with villains who murdered lawmen? She wondered if she knew any of the dead men personally, if any of them had ever watched her back or saved her life. Was ousting Burr and bringing back the buffalo worth this?

Pearl Hart spat toward the corpses and took potshots at the unicorns, who fled when the deaths of their riders broke their holding spells. "If that's all we have to contend with, this buffalo-birthin' detail will be the easiest money I ever made," she said.

Gilles shook his head. "Those men were scouts. When they do not return, the other Wild Rangers will know they found something." He sighed. "We should move on."

"I gotta piss," Pearl said.

"All right," Gilles said, over the murmured protestations of the guides. "We'll take a break."

Rangergirl dismounted and beckoned Gilles, who joined her, some distance away from the others. She whispered, fiercely, "Those were good men, Gilles— why were they trying to stop us from protecting the white buffalo?"

Gilles rubbed his forehead. "Ah, chérie, with you it is always 'good' and 'bad'— Jeanne was the same way. You told me the buffalo's birth heralds the return of the Indian nations, the return of the wilderness, yes? But the Wild Rangers want to civilize the West. They are among the very white men the Indians wish to drive away. This is not between good and bad—this is between white and red, water and steel, trails and railroads. I know when you think of marauding white men you think of Aaron Burr, ageless in his fort, but the buffalo spirits will not see much difference between Burr and the Rangers. They both want to build towns and cities and armies and laws."

Rangergirl took off her hat and mopped her forehead. In her heart, Rangergirl loved the West that once was, not the West that could be. The wilderness suited her nature. The coming of the white buffalo would change everything, if the prophecies were true—cleanse the taint on the demon-haunted Comanche, drive the Things back into the gulf, close the fumaroles from which hell-beasts sometimes emerged, strike the giant vultures out of the sky. She had to support that, even if it meant fighting her old allies, much as it pained her. Burr and the

Rangers could retreat back to the East, where their kind had already changed the face of the world to suit them. "All right," she said. "I'm still with you."

"I'm glad," Gilles said. "I would not want you for an enemy."

The villains were a superstitious lot, mostly, and when Gilles's ghosts began to precipitate from the air as night fell, they swore and shied away, except for the necromancer Ayres, who just sniffed.

"Do not fear them," Gilles said. "They are my burden, and will not harm you." The villains were not much reassured, so Gilles took the rearguard, his ghosts trailing behind him, leaving Rangergirl to follow the whispered directions of their pale guides.

Ayres rode up beside Rangergirl, tipping the broad brim of his black hat. His clothes were shabby-genteel, a dusty black suit that had once been fine, and he smelled of juniper berries and the musty fleshlessness of the mummified hands that hung around his neck. "Ma'am," he said, and Rangergirl nodded. She'd never fought against Ayres, had only heard of him, and his reputation was more for self-interest and cowardice than true villainy. "You're Prelati's new protégé, then? Did he take your voice?"

Rangergirl nodded.

"Ah, Prelati's a cruel old bastard," Ayres said. "That business with Gilles and his ghosts—it's a nasty trick, but I admire the showmanship."

Rangergirl raised an eyebrow.

"Didn't you know?" Ayres said, and Rangergirl realized he was showing off—maybe even flirting. "Those sad little boy-ghosts, they're not real. I've heard the stories, about how when Prelati brought Gilles back from the dead, the souls of all the children he'd killed followed him out of Hell. It's a good story, no mistake, but those aren't ghosts. I know ghosts, hungry desperate lost things, I can feel their presence and speak their languages. But those things...they're just a magic lantern show, shadow puppets on a wall."

Rangergirl stared at him. Prelati was just tricking Gilles with these ghosts? That was monstrous.

"Of course," Ayres went on, "that doesn't mean Gilles was innocent, mind you, maybe he did kill 100 or 300 or 600 children, whatever story you believe. But maybe not, maybe it was a frame-up, a way to seize riches from a nobleman without heirs. It wouldn't be the first time something like that happened. I once spent a long night swapping stories with the bones in a catacomb under Paris, and the stories I heard..."

Ayres rattled on, but Rangergirl wasn't listening. What if Gilles was innocent of the horrible crimes he'd been charged with? If so, he didn't need to fear the judgement of the afterlife. As long as he believed in his own guilt, he was a willing tool for Prelati, because serving the wizard was better than the alternative, burning in whatever Hell awaited. That explained why Prelati had conjured false ghosts, and scrambled Gilles's memory—after all, if Gilles didn't fear damnation, he might refuse to serve Prelati. Rangergirl had to tell Gilles about this, to let him know that things might not be as they seemed, to—

"Over this hill," one of the pale guides said. "The canyon mouth."

Rangergirl beckoned to Gilles, who raced forward on his steam sled, ghosts trailing. "Men!" he shouted. "You will treat those in this canyon with respect. Now that we have arrived, your duty is to guard the canyon. Hatfield, you go up on that side and keep a lookout. Hart and Boot, you take the other side. Night sheriff, you watch the entrance. No one else is expected, so if anyone approaches, stop them. Ayres, you—"

"The necromancer must come inside," one of the guides said. "He will be our midwife."

"Gentlemen," Ayres said. "With all respect, I don't know much about birthing calves. My specialty is more the end of life than the beginning."

"You will come," the guide said, and the pale tribesmen all rode into the canyon. Ayres shrugged.

"You and Joanie, follow me," Gilles said, and they passed through the canyon's mouth. The going was narrow and rocky at first, boulders strewn about, but the canyon gradually opened into a dim clearing lit by small fires, the rock walls receding into sky and darkness on all sides. A score of the pale tribesmen milled around, and a shaggy she-buffalo stood at the center of their movement and attention, chained to five wooden posts pounded deep into the soil. The buffalo lowed mournfully. This was not what Rangergirl had envisioned. Shouldn't the mother of the white buffalo be treated with reverence, venerated rather than bound?

"Gods, this place reeks of death," Ayres said, holding a handkerchief over his face. Rangergirl smelled nothing but dust and buffalo, but when it came to death, Ayres could sense things she couldn't.

"Of course," said a new voice, and one of the pale natives approached. He wore a shirt of clattering bone-mail, innumerable knuckle- and toe-bones woven together, and a headdress of slick green moss. He was taller than the rest of his tribe, nearly seven feet, and he moved with the easy grace of a cave fish in a stream. "I am the priest of my people, and this is Blanchard's Canyon, where the last untainted Comanche made their stand against Aaron Burr's army. The Comanche were cut down by the hundreds, and the ground swallowed their corpses rather than let Burr's men take trophies. This place is a temple to death, and to even scuff the soil with your heel is enough to reveal the bones."

"Blanchard's Canyon," Gilles said. "I've heard of it, but—"

"As a buffalo graveyard," Ayres said. He still held his handkerchief over his face, and his words were muffled. "The Outlaw's buffalo hunters drove a whole herd into this canyon, blocked the opening, and then killed the animals with shots from the canyon walls. But when they came down to harvest their pelts, the earth opened in great rifts and swallowed the buffalo. This is a sacred canyon, home to an ancient death-god that died itself centuries ago. But enough power lingers to make this place devour corpses and leave only bones in the dirt."

"Until tonight," the priest said. "Tonight, with the coming of the pale buffalo, the canyon will give up its dead, and the slain buffalo and murdered braves will return. From this place, the pale buffalo's power will spread like a ripple in a lake, and all the dead will rise again."

Pale buffalo? Rangergirl wondered about the phrase—she'd always heard the buffalo people refer to their totemic savior as the white buffalo. But then, these weren't the buffalo people, so maybe their legends used different words to refer to the same prophecy. Still, it felt all wrong—this strange underground tribe, the chained buffalo, the reverence with which the priest spoke the word "death."

Pearl Hart approached. "I told you to stand guard," Gilles snapped.

"Sorry, Frenchie, but we got word from a higher power," Pearl said. "Prelati's out front, and he sent us in to fetch you."

"And her," Boot said, materializing—perhaps literally—from the shadows behind Rangergirl, and clamping his arm around her throat. She stomped down on his instep hard enough to splinter bone, but he only sighed and pressed a knifeblade against her belly. "Please," he said. "Pearl wants me to gut you, but I'll go easy if you let me."

Rangergirl relaxed her body, but her mind worked furiously. Prelati was here, in the flesh, and if she could kill him, Gilles would finally be able to die—and since Rangergirl knew his ghosts were fraudulent, there was probably no harm in letting Gilles go to face his judgement.

Of course, her first priority was to keep Prelati from killing her.

The four of them left the canyon, Boot holding a gun to her back. Outside, Prelati stood leaning on a walking stick, his small form draped in a long brown coat, his face hidden by a battered hat. "Ah, Gilles," he said, voice like the scuttling of spider, like the hissing of black rain. "You've always had a weakness for a woman with a mission. But this woman does not have my interests at heart."

"Master, she wants the buffalo to be born, she offered her help. I only concealed her identity to avoid conflict with the others."

Prelati stood before Rangergirl, and said, "Would you make common cause with me, woman? You want to bring back the dead buffalo and the dead tribes of warriors?"

Rangergirl nodded, though most of all she wanted to knock Prelati out and then string him up.

"You think you understand," Prelati said. "I haven't laughed in a decade, but this almost makes me want to take up the habit again. No, Ranger, we cannot be allies."

"I will not serve if you kill her," Gilles said. "I have committed atrocities in your service, but I will not stand by if you do her harm."

"Only I preserve you from damnation, Gilles," Prelati said.

"That's a lie!" Rangergirl shouted into Prelati's face. "Ask—"

Prelati gestured, and Rangergirl's jaw clamped shut, closed by his nasty magic.

"I will not betray her," Gilles said stubbornly. "The deepest place in Hell is reserved for traitors."

"Due respect," Boot said. "They say you murdered hundreds of children. I suspect that earns you a spot in the deepest Hell they've got." Pearl laughed.

Prelati thumped his walking stick on the ground. The ghost children clustered around him, murmuring, and Prelati shook his head. "No, little ones, not death, not for Gilles. He is still useful. I will spare the life of his friend, then. Aren't I merciful, Gilles?"

"Even my service has limits," Gilles said.

"You stop at betrayal, yes, of course. Unless it's me you're betraying, the man who granted you eternal life."

"I wish I'd never invited you into my house," Gilles said. "That was the greatest mistake of my first life. My friends said you were a charlatan, but I had faith."

"You had no friends, Gilles, only lickspittles and sycophants. And I wasn't a fraud—your faith was justified. I promised you dark rites and eternal life, and I delivered. And now I've promised to let your friend live, and I will, for now." He drew a circle in the dirt with his walking stick, and Boot shoved Rangergirl into its circumference. A flash brightened the air around her, and she shouted, the spell of silence suddenly lifted. Purple spots floated in her vision, and she found herself surrounded by iron bars, a round, floorless, woman-sized cage sprung up around her.

"I'll set her free when the birth is over," Prelati said. "It really doesn't make any difference if she survives until then, as long as she's kept out of the way. Boot, watch her. The rest of you, to your places. There are Wild Rangers and shamans of the buffalo people en route, and they mustn't interrupt the birth." Prelati walked into the canyon, Gilles following, Pearl Hart returning to her place on the canyon wall.

Boot had taken her pistols, but Rangergirl reached down for the Derringer in her boot and had it aimed at his chest in an instant. "Get me out of this thing, or I'll shoot you," she said.

Boot shook his head. "The cage has no door, and while I suppose I could lift it off you, I prefer not to."

"I will shoot. I can put the bullet someplace that will hurt."

"Save your ammunition. You might be able to harm Prelati, if you catch him unawares, and you can certainly kill my beloved Pearl, but not me. Pain is my lot, not death." As if to demonstrate, he stuck his knife into his own throat, wiggled it meditatively, and withdrew it, leaving only a bloodless slit. "See?"

Rangergirl leaned against the cage in hopes of tipping it over. No such luck—it weighed hundreds of pounds. She was well and truly trapped. "Let me out, Boot, and I'll help you. I'll kill Pearl, and let you go back to nothingness."

"Ah. You make the mistake of assuming that just because I despise every moment of consciousness, I would betray Pearl for my freedom. But, no. Our relationship is more complicated than that. She is my lover and my maker, as well as my captor. Do you hate your mother?"

Rangergirl frowned. "Well, not hate exactly, but—"

"Yes. It's complicated." Boot squatted on his heels. "Take your ease. In all likelihood, we'll all be dead soon, once that thing in there is born."

"Thing? You mean the white buffalo?"

"I mean the pale buffalo. The difference is more than semantic. The white buffalo is the bringer of rebirth and renewal, sacred to the buffalo people of the plains. The pale buffalo is something different, sacred to the underground tribes. They hate those of us who dwell above the earth, and after centuries of inbreeding with refugees from various hells and underworlds, their sympathies lay more with the dead than the living. The pale buffalo's birth will not usher in an age of peace and plenty."

"How do you know all this?"

"Because I listen. I comprehend all human languages, and I can be in two places at once."

"What?"

"Bodily bilocation," he said from behind her, though he was still in front of her, too. "I can be in more than one place at once, as long as I'm not all the way in either place."

Now that Rangergirl looked, she could see he'd gone almost translucent, parts of him shimmering. "Good trick."

"It's easy when you're a sorcerer's imaginary friend," he said. "When the pale buffalo is born, that's it, probably. You'll die, Hatfield, Ayres, maybe Pearl, possibly the night sheriff, probably not Prelati, therefore not Gilles, certainly those three Wild Rangers creeping up on Pearl—ah, no, they're dead already, she turned their blood to molten lead. You know, she's been trying for years to tweak that spell so the blood turns to gold instead of lead, but she can't manage it." His tone never altered from its flat, uninflected baseline. "Prelati doesn't care if his mercenaries die, and I'm the only one of the bunch who listened and understood when the pale tribesmen spoke among themselves."

"You could warn them! And there must be other Wild Rangers nearby, you could—"

"Oh, but I don't *care*," he said. "Shall we look in on the delivery room?" His expression became more abstracted. "Prelati is arguing with the priest. He knows the Wild Rangers are coming, and the shamans of the buffalo people will be here soon. Prelati wants to speed things up. He's telling the priest that a midnight birth is just idiot superstition. Apparently Ayres could induce labor early—ah, I see, first they'll slay the mother, then Ayres can animate her corpse in order to make her give birth to the buffalo calf. Gods, you begotten things enter the world in a disgusting way."

All Rangergirl's hopes of convincing Boot to help her evaporated. He was a fundamentally alien being, and she could not fathom his fears or desires well enough to threaten or bribe him.

Boot said, "The priest is agreeing, reluctantly—"

Lightning flashed and crackled, and a unicorn screamed.

"The Wild Rangers are upon us," Boot said. "Hatfield is hurling thunderbolts. It's your cavalry, but they can't ride charging into the canyon, not with Prelati in there, and all the boulders in the way besides. I'd better go check on Pearl." Boot faded, not so much vanishing as sinking into the dark.

"Wild Rangers! To me!" Rangergirl shouted, and banged one of her rings against the iron bars to make a clatter.

Three men appeared, their faces dusty black, and one of them was Texas Jack Slaughter, head of the Wild Rangers, her old friend and more. "Let's get this cage off her, boys," he said.

"Good to see you, Jack."

"Always a pleasure," he said, smiling beneath his vast bristling mustache. He helped his men lift and tilt the cage enough for Rangergirl to scramble out from underneath.

She picked up her gunbelt—Boot had left her weapons in the dirt as if they were worthless—and buckled it on. "What's the plan?"

"You tell me," Texas Jack said. "You've tussled with these folks already. What's the lay of the land?"

"You know about the buffalo?"

"All we know is what the buffalo shamans told us, that some of the mushroom-suckers from the caves hired a bunch of shadow riders to protect them while they worked some wicked magic bullshit, and that's the sort of thing I'm opposed to on principle. But I assume you're here to catch the bad men and collect the bounties?"

"Not exactly." She described the layout of the canyon, and the forces arrayed against them. "I thought the white buffalo was a good thing," she said. "I can't believe I was so stupid."

"Hush," Texas Jack said. "Having faith ain't stupid. If I didn't think I'd get Texas back one of these days, I wouldn't be able to get up in the morning. As for the plan, well, we already caught Hatfield, got him tied up with rubber straps. Now...shit. Maybe we should hang back until the buffalo shamans show up. They move slow, but they're tough, and they can fight Prelati better than we can. Guns are no match for wizardry, even if the wizard is a damn Frenchman."

"There's no time," Rangergirl said. "They're speeding up the birth. I'm going in. If you can cover me."

Jack sighed. "Boys, get the rest of the fellas together. We're storming the goddamned canyon on goddamned foot." He put a hand on her shoulder. "I can't resist you when you start advocating rash acts of violence. If we survive this, you should come back and play the next hand of our poker game. It's been a year since I called your raise."

"We'll see." They'd been playing a game of Texas hold 'em for years, one round at a time, with both their futures in the pot. If Jack won, she'd quit the bounty-hunting life and join up with the Wild Rangers. If she won, he'd quit trying to take Texas back from the Things that came from the Gulf, and help her clean up the rest of the West. She had a feeling on the next round of betting he'd want her hand in marriage, and she hadn't decided yet whether to call, raise, or fold on that bet. "Let's tend to business first."

A dozen rangers made a charge, guns barking, as Rangergirl buttonhooked around to approach the canyon obliquely. She paused to take aim at the night sheriff, who was drawing a bead on the Wild Rangers. He moved, and her intended killshot only wounded him in the leg, but that was enough for the Rangers to capture him. Other Rangers were keeping Hart and Boot busy, so she slipped into the canyon unnoticed.

Until she walked into the barrel of Gilles's rifle. He grabbed her arm and pulled her behind a heap of rubble. "Shh," he said. "Prelati might not see you if you stay down." The child-ghosts were agitated, bursting from among the rocks like frightened doves, settling onto boulders, twisting and muttering.

"Gilles, the buffalo is a monster."

"I am not surprised."

"I have to kill it," she said, and darted from her place behind the rocks, toward the chained buffalo, the nervous pale priest, and Ayres, who knelt by the pregnant beast. Prelati was nowhere in sight. The priest and Ayres hadn't noticed her, and if she could just circle around, find a position to get a clear shot, she could kill the pale buffalo as soon as it slid out of its mother.

She didn't make it very far before something swept her legs out from under her. She fell, sprawling on her belly, and a great weight came down on her back, pressing her flat. Gilles spoke in her ear, regretful but firm. "I can't let you interfere, chérie." His knees pinned her down, and she gasped for breath, her face inches from the dirt. If she could only fill her lungs, she could tell him that his ghosts were fraudulent, that he didn't need to fear the afterlife, he could betray Prelati—

—but as his weight pressed the air slowly from her lungs, she realized how foolish she'd been. Even if Gilles hadn't murdered those children, he was hardly an innocent. He'd committed horrible acts in Prelati's service. The false ghosts might have been a goad at first, a way to ensure Gilles's loyalty, but now they were just habit, something Prelati did to keep up appearances. Even if the ghosts were dispelled, Gilles would still rightfully fear death, and the settling of his life's accounts.

"Can't...breathe..." she gasped, and Gilles eased up a little, enough for her to draw breath.

"I will let you escape if I can," he said. "After everything is done here."

Gunfire and screams erupted from outside the canyon. Hart and Boot, and possibly Prelati himself, were fighting with the Wild Rangers.

Boot materialized beside Rangergirl and Gilles, only half-here while his other half was doubtless occupied murdering Texas Jack's men with bored efficiency. "Look," Boot said, and Rangergirl turned her head to see the pale priest slit the buffalo's throat with a knife almost as big as a machete. The buffalo bucked, heaved, and sagged, but the chains held its dying body upright. Rangergirl had a good view of the buffalo's side, and Ayres knelt behind, murmuring, gesturing with his hands as the dying buffalo's flesh rippled. She watched, fascinated and horrified, as did Boot and Gilles; even the child-ghosts seemed rapt.

Something pale and wet slid from the she-buffalo's hindquarters, and the priest shoved Ayres aside, kneeling to catch the newborn beast himself.

"Gilles," Rangergirl gasped, "you have to kill it, shoot it, please, this is important—"

"It's the apocalypse of the West," Boot said. "The way the West was wasted."

"I serve my master," Gilles said, still pressing her down. "It is too late for me to change that."

The pale buffalo lifted its oversized head from the priest's lap and made a sound between a bleat and a cry. Its eyes were milky and blind, and its skin was discolored by fungal patches of a different whiteness than its skin. A wind rose in the canyon, smelling of dust and buffalo blood, and then the earth trembled, not as in an earthquake, but in a more localized upheaval. Bones were rising from the soil, assembling themselves into their former living shapes.

"What is this?" Gilles said, voice low and troubled. The pressure on Rangergirl's body eased further as he shifted his weight back. Rangergirl realized that Gilles still didn't know exactly what the birth of the pale buffalo portended.

"The dead buffalo are rising," Boot said. He sat down cross-legged to watch. "Forming a skeletal herd. And that's just the beginning."

"The dead men will come next, Gilles," Rangergirl said, now that she had all the breath she needed. "The dead braves will come to life, shambling things risen to serve the pale tribes and Prelati. This magic will spread through the West, dead tribes climbing up out of the dirt to serve your master."

"No," Gilles said, but Rangergirl could not tell if it was disbelief, denial, or outrage. The pale tribespeople were shouting with joy, the newborn buffalo whined piteously in the priest's arms, and the herd of skeletal buffalo grew, first five of them, then a dozen, then a score, spines and ribs and limbs rising and joining, the resurrection an eerily quiet event, just clacking bones and the low howl of the wind. The sounds from outside the canyon were diminished but ongoing, occasional screams and gunshots testament to the fact that the Wild Rangers were still fighting.

"Oh, it's true," Boot said. "It won't be just the tribes, either—everyone who's died violently in the West, from murdered settlers to defeated gunfighters, will return from the dead to serve the tribes—and every person they kill will rise again to join his army. The underground tribes and Prelati are still dickering over how to divide up their new empire."

"No dead man will ever rest in the West again," Rangergirl said. "They'll all become monsters. They'll all become—" she hesitated, but had to say it—"just like you."

For a moment, she thought Gilles was unswayed, but then the pressure of his knees on her back let up. "Yes, yes," he said. "Your point is well-taken."

Rangergirl sat up in time to see Gilles walk to the center of the canyon, where the skeletal buffalo stood, surrounding the priest and the mewling calf. Gilles stepped up onto a boulder to reach a better vantage point, towering over the silent white herd, and aimed his rifle with the ease of long practice. He fired. The boom of the shot echoed in the canyon, and the pale buffalo's bleats ceased as its head snapped back. The strange wind ceased instantly. The priest, pierced by the same bullet, fell as well. Gilles lowered his rifle, and for a moment, all was silence. Then the child-ghosts began to shriek, and Gilles dropped his rifle to the ground, covering his ears with both hands.

"That was surprising," Boot said, barely audible over the shrieking, and faded from view.

Rangergirl had expected the skeletal buffalo to collapse when the pale calf died, but the resurrective magic was more durable than that, for they remained standing, every pair of eye sockets fixed on Gilles. As the pale tribespeople cried out in rage and dismay, their voices joining the wails of the ghosts, the skeletal herd surged forward, stampeding toward Gilles, who did not try to escape.

The white stampede knocked Gilles from his boulder to the ground, and the dead things trampled him with their sharp hooves, churning his body into the ground. Rangergirl started forward, drawing her useless pistols, but Ayres—of all people—held her back. "Let the dead bury the dead," he said, and Rangergirl stood still. Throwing herself into that herd would only kill her, and wouldn't help Gilles. Besides, in a way, this was the best thing—he'd committed an act of courage and sacrifice, and now he would die. If there was any redemption to be had, Gilles had earned it.

The screaming of the child-ghosts faded as they disappeared, wisping away to the nothingness they'd been drawn from.

The herd of skeletal buffalo bolted en masse for the canyon's entrance, raising a great cloud of dust in their wake. When the dust settled, there was almost no sign of Gilles left, just his broken rifle and fragments of clothing and bone. As she watched, the earth rumbled, split, and gaped, swallowing Gilles's remains into the darkness below. When Gilles's body was wholly consumed, the earth closed again. Similar cracks opened to swallow the priest, the dead buffalo calf, and its mother, until the canyon seemed strangely empty, with only the living left behind.

While the remaining Wild Rangers rounded up the people from the underground tribes, Texas Jack touched Rangergirl on the shoulder. "You stopped something bad from happening," he said.

"Not me. It was Gilles."

"Yeah. I'm sorry, darlin'. I know he was your friend. But at least he's at peace now."

"Oh, Gilles isn't dead," Ayres said, as one of the Wild Rangers tied his hands behind him. "He's been ground into bone meal, yes, but he's still alive—as alive as he has been for the past 400 years, anyway. Only Prelati can grant Gilles release, and he hasn't bothered to do that yet." Ayres shook his head. "Gilles might even still be conscious. He's certainly suffering. I guess leaving him alive in little pieces is Prelati's punishment for his betrayal. I told you that old wizard was a cruel son of a bitch."

"Rangergirl," Texas Jack said. "Don't listen to that old fraud, he's just messing with your head. I don't like that look in your eyes. Just settle down, help me catch Hart and Boot, and round up those bony buffalo, and then we can go finish that card game—"

"No," Rangergirl said. She couldn't remember the last time she'd been so exhausted, but she couldn't stop, not now. Gilles had done the right thing, even though it was hard, and he hadn't had a night's sleep in over 400 years. "Ayres is telling the truth. I know Prelati." She scuffed at the dirt with her heel, over the spot where Gilles had been trampled. Not knowing if he could hear, she said, "Remember that offer I made you, Gilles? To hunt down Prelati and set you free? I'm going to make good on that."

"I can help you," Texas Jack said.

She put her hand on his shoulder. "You've got enough to do. You have your mission, and I have mine. Don't worry about me."

"Don't get killed," he said. "We've got a game to finish."

"There's worse things than getting killed," Rangergirl said, and both Ayres and Texas Jack nodded in glum agreement, looking at the place where Gilles had fallen.

Hitching up her gunbelt, Rangergirl walked out of the canyon, into the night, toward the oncoming sunrise.

THE PENTECOSTAL HOME FOR FLYING CHILDREN

WILL CLARKE

The idea of a school or institution for superpowered children has been popularized by Marvel's X-Men, with Professor Xavier's School for Gifted Youngsters, which serves both as haven from the fears and hatred of the mundane world and as training academy for fledgling mutant superheroes. Will Clarke presents his own wry, fabulist twist on that enduring trope of the superhero genre.

"Baby oil and iodine works way better than Crisco," Tamara Cooksey admonished her fellow cheerleaders. Then to prove her point, she hiked up her cheerleading skirt, pulled down the left side of her bright yellow bloomers, and revealed a stripe of fluorescent white skin on her otherwise mahogany hip. "See, look at that tan line."

Tamara Cooksey was Shreveport's version of Christy Brinkley. She was blonde and famous. Tamara's double-decker smile and her savage tan were sure signs of hope for our hard-luck town. After all, she had sprung up from all the chaos and shame brought upon us in the seventies, just as pure and radiant as a lotus bloom growing from a pile of dung. She was one of the best things that Shreveport had going for it in an otherwise very grim time in our history.

Tamara Cooksey had dedicated her life to tanning and cheerleading. When she wasn't practicing her pom-pom routines, she was lying out, making sure that she was the darkest girl with the blondest hair in all of Shreveport.

You could always tell when she was sunbathing because there, high above the Cookseys' ranch-style house, would be a flock of circling buzzards. However, upon closer inspection, you'd see that those weren't buzzards at all; they were a flock of flying teenage boys—the abandoned sons of the Redbird. The boys would fly over Tamara Cooksey, as she lay there all greased up and glistening in her string bikini. They would shout stupid teenage-boy things like, "Look-see, look-see, it's sexy Tamara Cooksey!"

Some days the boys would hoot and holler. Other days, they'd just fly in circles, with one or two diving to take a closer look. Sometimes they would shout things that were profound if not a little odd, like, "The seed of God is within all of us!"

Other times, they'd shout profane and disturbing things, like, "Hey, Tamara Cooksey! Suck it!"

Some of the flying boys, the gentler ones, tried to shower Tamara with rose petals. They were crestfallen when the wind carried the flurry of velvet-red petals into the backyard of Tamara's neighbors instead of bathing her in their beauty.

One petal, however, did drift down to her, and it landed on her belly button. This made Tamara laugh. So the next day, in an effort to thrill Tamara Cooksey even more, the boys stole thousands of Hershey's kisses and poured them on her as she lay out. The silver kisses pelted her, bringing huge, red welts to her perfect tan skin. Tamara had to cover her head with her beach towel and run inside to escape the chocolate hailstorm.

Afraid that they might have hurt their earthbound crush, the boys never showered her with anything ever again. Instead, they settled on circling high above, as she lay there, glistening and sweating, in the midst of her father's tomato garden.

It was Mr. Cooksey's tomato plants that kept the Redbird brothers far away from Tamara. The flying boys knew that all Redbird children were deathly allergic to any plant in the nightshade family—tomatoes, bell peppers, eggplants, even potatoes. The mere fumes given off by the leaves and stalks of a nightshade could drop a Redbird child from the sky and kill him. So the boys flew high above Mr. Cooksey's tomato garden and rode the thermals as they spied on his sylphy daughter with stolen binoculars and deer rifle scopes. Like the rest of Shreveport, the Redbirds had to admire Tamara Cooksey from afar.

In 1984, Shreveport, Louisiana, was experiencing a woeful lack of economic growth, turbulent race relations, and a rash of flying teenagers. The airborne bastards were the offspring of the Redbird—a handsome alien half-breed who had once graced the cover of *Life* magazine for rescuing Chicago from The Stalinizer—a radioactive cosmonaut who could shoot lasers from his mouth.

Unfortunately, the Redbird didn't possess the necessary might to be a major-league superhero. In the world of superpowers, flight was pretty much table stakes. Who couldn't fly? Flying was just the delivery method, a mode of transportation for real superpowers like invincibility, colossal strength, or energy blasts. You couldn't very well *fly* a supervillain to death. Without invincibility and superstrength, how could you ever stop a nuclear missile? Sure, the Redbird looked pretty up there doing loopty-loops in the sky wearing those bright red tights, but other than marshalling Fourth of July parades, he really wasn't much use in America's fight against super evil. So the Redbird was relegated to working in the superhero farm leagues. He was banished from New York and assigned to Shreveport.

Our town welcomed the Redbird with more than open arms. Everyone loved the idea that we had our very own superhero to look after us. We didn't care if all he could do was fly. That was more than any of us could do.

In fact, the Redbird united our city with hope. We loved this alien half-breed with his magic red hair and his black mask, and this love we had for him overflowed from our hearts and spread to one another. Redbird-mania transcended racial lines and mended our violent histories with one another. The Redbird allowed us to see the good in everyone—black, white, rich or poor. The Redbird's reign ushered in a golden age for Shreveport. We became a city known for our brotherly love and dreamlike prosperity.

However, as the years passed, it became apparent that the Redbird had moved to Shreveport for less-than-savory reasons. Turns out the Redbird came to our town not just for the easy work, but for our chronically bored housewives, our prodigal daughters, and our all-too-easily seduced Baptist Ladies Prayer Circle.

By the time we figured out that the Redbird was turning us all into pillars of salt, he up and flew away—leaving his lovers' hearts ragged, his red-headed babies abandoned, and our city unprotected.

The Pentecostal Home for Flying Children was founded by Pauline Pritchard, a barren Pentecostal woman with long gray hair that hung to her ankles when she took it down at night. One day while eating a dipped cone at the Dairy Queen, Pauline Pritchard heard a terrible mewling sound coming from the restaurant's dumpsters. So she walked over to the trash, still licking her ice cream, thinking it was perhaps the screams of feral cats mating, but the sounds were loud enough and human enough to press her concern.

When Pauline opened the dumpster lid, she dropped her ice-cream cone and screamed. There among the greasy wrappers and the industrial-sized mayonnaise jars was a naked baby boy with red locks that danced and shone like the fire of the Pentecost.

The baby was crying just as loud as Pauline was now screaming. Then something happened that took Pauline's screams away: the wailing infant began to float like a soap bubble out of the trash bin, drifting into the air above Pauline's considerable mound of gray hair. Pauline quickly removed the pale brown cardigan that she had just bought at TG&Y.

Pauline jumped, jumped, jumped—swatting at the infant with her sweater before finally netting him out of the air. She then swaddled the child in her sweater and ran as fast as her ankle-length skirt would let her.

"The good Lord has answered my prayers just like He answered Sarah and Abraham's." Pauline pulled her makeshift blanket away from the baby's face to show her husband the redhead she had just found.

"We should call the police." Jeffery Pritchard put his finger into the baby's tender fist and shook it ever so gently. "Someone's probably missing this little fella."

"They left him in the dumpster, Jeffery."

"It's the right thing to do."

"Jesus gave him to me."

"All I'm saying is that you can't just up and take a baby."

"I didn't take him."

"Then what do you call it?

"I found him like Pharaoh's daughter found Moses in the basket."

If you had ever dared to ask Pauline Pritchard if she was submissive to her husband as it says to be in Ephesians, she would have been wildly indignant that you would have even asked such a question.

"My husband is my master," Pauline would have said without a whiff of irony. And Jeffery would have agreed.

"I wear the pants around here!" he would have barked.

While Jeffery Pritchard may have worn the well-starched pants in that marriage, it was Pauline who brandished the fiery iron. In short, Jeffery Pritchard never called the police and Pauline named the boy Zaccheus.

One night when Pauline was washing Zaccheus in the kitchen sink, she was given a word of faith—a message straight from the Holy Ghost. Pauline hosed off the baby with the vegetable sprayer, and ran into the garage where her husband Jeffery was repairing the lawnmower.

"The Lord! He spoke to me!" Pauline held the dripping baby to her chest.

"Calm down, woman. You'll drop the baby."

"He said we should open our home to all the Redbird's babies!"

"Well." Jeffery looked into the engine filter and shook it. "Then I guess we better get busy."

Being a man of exuberant faith, Jeffery Pritchard painted a sign and hung it on his front porch that very night. The sign alerted the brokenhearted harlots of Shreveport that the Pentecostal Home for Flying Children was now open for business and ready to receive their newborn sins.

From that point on, the Pritchards' doorbell rang at all hours of the night and day. Every time they unfastened the seven locks and seven bolts on their big blue front door, there stood a shorn-haired Baptist woman, a painted Methodist, a pants-wearing Presbyterian, a cleavage-baring Catholic, an ankle-flaunting Lutheran, a drunk Episcopalian, a teenage Pentecostal, a divorced Jewess, a lock-jawed Seventh-Day Adventist, a black-eyed Mormon—all holding crying babies or struggling toddlers in their arms.

Sister Pauline gathered up the flying babies from their mothers. Despite Pauline's warmth and grace, there was often very little said in the exchange. Sometimes the women would tell Pauline the child's name. Sometimes they would be weeping so hard that Pauline had to pry the child from the mother's arms, and then politely shut the door. Each handoff was painful both for the mother and for Pauline. Because now that Pauline's heart was full of babies, she could feel the sting of these women's tears as if they were her own.

Pauline's husband and master, Jeffery, had wanted to splash the weeping mothers with holy water and cleanse them with prayer, but Pauline broke with her code of wifely obedience.

"Don't you say a word to them, Jeffery."

"They brought it on themselves, fornicating and carrying on like that." He mixed a flask of holy water imported all the way from Galilee with a bucket of tap water.

"Maybe so. But that's between them and the Lord and their husbands."

"A little splash would do them good."

"Don't, Jeffery. I'm asking you, don't."

As the flying babies filled the Pritchard house, Pauline rejoiced in the squalling, the feeding, and the diapers. Her house was blessed with chubby redheaded babies everywhere just as the Lord had promised. As the Redbird babies grew, they learned how to walk and talk, and of course, fly. This made keeping them out of harm's way almost impossible, but somehow the Pritchards managed to do it.

Their biggest problem was when the children slept. The babies would float out of their beds while dreaming and sometimes fall to the floor in a start. Once a red-haired babe drifted out of an open second-story window, but luckily for him, he landed on the bows of the Pritchards' magnolia tree, where Jeffery found him sleeping the next morning.

Flying babies were a much bigger problem to take care of than any of us would have ever imagined. And soon the babies were all over the place, bumping their noggins, busting their lips, knocking out their teeth, and breaking every little delicate thing that Pauline had ever loved. But Pauline Pritchard was a faithful and industrious woman who loved the Lord and those wayward children. She would sit in her rocker on the front porch of her enormous old home, speaking in tongues and crocheting for the babies. She would pour her prayers into pink and baby blue tethers that she fastened to the children's ankles and bedposts to keep them from floating away in the night. During the day Pauline would gather up the babies by their tethers and carry them around like a bunch of squirming balloons. It was a site to behold, and eventually a now-famous photo of Pauline and her tethered babies made the cover of the *Shreveport Times*.

To remedy the bumps and bruises of the babies' midair collisions, Pauline had Jeffery staple-gun goosedown pillows to the ceilings of their house. She also used donated quilts as wallpaper and she glued down bushels of disregarded stuffed animals to cushion the floors. Pauline Pritchard amazed us with her maternal ingenuity, and there was a time there that we almost admired her for it.

The real mystery for most of us was how Pauline got all those flying babies potty trained. We can all remember a time when the Pentecostal Home reeked of piss and poo. The stains were everywhere: on the pillowed ceilings, the stuffed-animal floors, the padded walls, and the tattered yarn restraints. Bits of who-knows-what were forever caught in Pauline's hair, and the stains were eternally splattered all over Jeffery's coveralls. How Pauline and Jeffery Pritchard took care of all those crying, pooping, suckling, slobbering, flying babies was surely a miracle of God's own hand—at least that's what Pauline told everyone.

Apparently, she had made some kind of blood covenant with God, and that's why she was able to take care of all those flying babies like she did. It's also why she rechristened the children with biblical names of famous sinners like Cane, Bathsheba, and Lot. Pauline gave the children the most unwanted names in the Bible to forever remind them that they, too, had been born unwanted, and that the only way to make their lives right with God was by washing away the sins of their parents.

While it was disconcerting for most of us to call a three-year-old girl in pigtails Jezebel, and her adorable baby brother Onan, we did appreciate Pauline and Jeffery Pritchard's hard work. By taking in the Redbird bastards, the Pritchards allowed our families to heal. The Pentecostal Home for Flying Children offered so many of us a certain kind of grace. So we all pulled together and everyone did what they could to help out. Some of us made cash donations to the cause, while others donated canned foods and clothes. It wasn't cheap keeping all those flying children clothed and fed. Eventually we had to resort to sending our own kids out to sell popcorn and candy bars door-to-door while our churches raised money with weekly bingo nights, cakewalks, and carwashes. We did what we had to do to keep the lights on at the Home. We did it because we had to, because we had to keep our mistakes in a place where we could live with them.

From the moment that Pauline had wrapped Zaccheus Redbird in her sweater, he had clung very closely to her heart. Though Pauline would have denied it, everyone knew that this child was her favorite. She was often heard around town telling the boy that one day he "would bring the devil to his knees." Pauline Pritchard saw something special in Zaccheus, something that the other Redbirds didn't have, and that was why she named the boy for a redeemed tax collector instead of a whoremaster or a sodomite. It's also why she kept all his baby teeth in the jingle-jangledy lockets that she wore on her wrists despite her religion's strict rules against jewelry.

Now that Zaccheus, or Zac, as his classmates called him, had entered high school, he was living proof that Pentecostalism could redeem even the most wretched among us. Zac, though he was quite obviously the Redbird's son, refused to fly. Which, to Pauline, proved that Zac had somehow conquered his father's wicked ways.

Zac refused to indulge in any sort of pride that would put him above the rest of us or do anything that might seem cruel. Instead he did as he was told: He sold Gideon Bibles in front of K&B Drugs to raise money for the Home, he took care of Sister Pauline when she lost her leg to the diabetes, he troubled over scripture and his schoolwork in equal measure. He wasn't just respectful of everyone he met, he was kind—effortlessly kind in the way that one would imagine that Jesus must have been to lepers and whores and the like. And because of this, we all thought that Zaccheus Redbird was the biggest weirdo we had ever met.

"Why don't you ever fly?"
"I don't want to talk about it."
"Your brothers landed on my roof today."

"I'm sorry. They shouldn't do that."

"Don't apologize. I think they're funny."

Why and how Tamara Cooksey fell so hard for Zaccheus Redbird was not public knowledge. Tamara, for once in her life, was keeping her mouth shut, which was odd, because usually Tamara was a one-girl power station broadcasting Tamara Cooksey's ever-fascinating, always-scintillating life twenty-four hours a day.

Typically, Tamara Cooksey held court in the cafeteria where she would report on the most intimate and minute details of her teenage life: the brutal frequency of her menstrual cramps, the adorable iced cookies that she made for the JV football team, her need to make herself throw up after her mother made her eat meat loaf, the kind of toilet paper she used to vandalize Lacey Monroe's house, the number of lipsticks she had filched from Selber's Department Store.

But when Tamara's friends would ask her about Zac, she would only wink and say, "Nunya."

Eventually her friends grew weary of this response, and they mounted a full-fledged interrogation with Tamara's best friend, Holly Peterson, leading the charge.

"Oh, come on, Tam. Don't be a whore. Tell us about you and Zac." Holly said one day in the locker room after a pep rally.

"I already told you. Nunya. Nunya business."

"What's the matter? Are you embarrassed to be dating one of those Pentecostal flying retards or something?"

"Embarrassed?"

"Yeah, embarrassed."

"Holly, I'm not the one stomping around out there with my big white thunder thighs and cellulite. So, no, I'm not embarrassed."

There are words that can never be taken back or forgiven. For Holly Ferguson, "thunder thighs" and "cellulite" were three of those words. From that day forward, she never spoke to Tamara Cooksey again.

So that left the rest of Shreveport to pry where we shouldn't be prying, to figure out how someone like Tamara Cooksey ended up with someone like Zaccheus Redbird. Ten thousand notes were passed back and forth in civics and algebra classes. Two hundred forty-two malicious theories were whispered by concerned mothers at PTA meetings. Seven hundred seventy-seven phone calls were placed by the cheerleaders alone. Zac and Tamara's secret romance became the impolite topic to broach at potluck suppers and church picnics all over town.

"I. Love. You."

"Shhh, my dad will hear you."

"I don't care."

"You'll care when he comes in here and shoots your pecker off."

The now-famous phrase "beat you like a redheaded stepchild" was actually coined in Shreveport. It referred, of course, to the Redbird children, and Jeffery and Pauline's tough-love efforts to set them on the straight and narrow. Jeffery never spared the rod to spoil the child. He'd take his belt off and whip their little hides as red as their hair if he had to. And not a day went by that Pauline Pritchard wasn't seen chasing one of the flying children down the street with a flyswatter, and when she finally caught the offending brat, she would beat the devil out of the child. Some hippies actually protested the Pritchards' public whippings of the flying children. The hippies made signs and picketed the Pentecostal Home. They sang folk songs and shouted, "Free the Baby Birds!" Nobody paid them much attention, though, so the hippies eventually took their free-loving, no-deodorant-wearing ways down to New Orleans.

Now history has proven that those hippies were bigger idiots than we initially thought. In fact, the Pritchards were perhaps not strict enough with their Redbird charges as Jeffery Pritchard met a dubious end in June 1985 when he supposedly fell from the roof of the Pentecostal Home and broke his thick neck.

The Pritchards had dedicated their lives to putting the fear of God into those Redbird bastards, but foster parents can only do so much. Once most of the Redbirds reached their teenage years, their alien blood somehow trumped their strict upbringing—the lone exception being good-hearted Zaccheus.

The problem with most of the flying children was that you never knew what one of them would do. They were constantly pulling pranks. The boys' favorite stunt was to fly up behind people, grabbing their victims underneath the armpits and taking them fast and high into the sky. All the while their victims would be kicking and screaming, terrified that they would fall to their death. The Redbirds would then drop their victims into a swimming pool or a shallow lake. The little bastards laughed maniacally, as if this life-threatening attack was just one big joke. Many of their victims reported that their flying attackers smelled of Pabst Blue Ribbon and marijuana.

The Redbird girls were actually worse than their brothers. They had no shame. They would strip down naked and fly all over town, through grocery stores, church services, weddings, even funerals. With their long, red Pentecostal hair, they thought of themselves as flying Lady Godivas, but they were no better than common strippers and prostitutes to most of us.

The Redbird girls were notorious for floating in front of our teenage sons' windows, knocking at the glass and giggling. When the boys unlatched the windows to let them in, the Redbird girls would fly away. This kind of teasing was meant to drive our sons crazy, and it did. Oh, how it did.

It was during one of these stunts that Bobby Tyler discovered the full power of the nightshades. One night, Salome Redbird was hovering by his teenage son's window, pressing her breasts up against the glass, torturing his son like the devil's own succubus. Bobby grabbed the closest thing he could find to throw at the tramp. He grabbed a rotting tomato.

"Get!" He hummed the tomato at the girl, hitting her square in the chest. The tomato exploded into a fury of seeds and juice, killing the girl and crashing her into his wife's pink azaleas below.

Our town had run out of patience for those flying freaks, and now that Pauline had the diabetes and Jeffery was dead, something had to be done. Those scurrilous Redbirds were using the Pentecostal Home for Flying Children as a haven for their misdeeds and their liquor-sloshing parties. Meanwhile, crazy old Pauline Pritchard, with her one good leg, stayed locked away in her room, watching Oral Roberts and Pat Robertson, ignoring her duties to us and her promises to God.

It was finally time to rid our city of this scourge. So we planted gardens full of red, yellow, and green peppers. We grew tomatoes of every variety: Big Boys, Yellow Brandywines, Cherokee Purples—you name it. There were over fifty varieties of eggplants growing all over our fair city. Our ladyfolk kept tomato sandwiches in their purses, and we all kept handfuls of new potatoes in the glove compartments of our cars, just in case.

Eventually, the Redbirds got the message, and interestingly enough, none of them thought it was very funny to fly naked through the funerals for their own brothers and sisters. We, the mere mortals of Shreveport, had finally taught the Redbird bastards a lesson: Don't mess with good people.

"I wanna run away."

"Tamara."

"I'm serious."

"I can't."

"They're going to kill you.

"Trust me, they won't."

The Nightshade Retaliation Program was the city-sponsored initiative for "growing and throwing" nightshade vegetables at Redbird delinquents. State laws were even amended to clear any citizen of murder charges if they had to resort to throwing a nightshade in self-defense. This program was hugely successful. It only took five nightshade throwings for all the Redbirds to pick up and fly away from Shreveport—well, all except for one, Zaccheus, who was so kind and mannerly that most of us forgot that he even was a Redbird.

However, the terror that the Redbirds had raged over our town for all those years had obviously affected the tender minds of our own teenagers, and many of our kids had a hard time turning the other cheek here, which would explain why they had such a hard time with the last Redbird dating Captain Shreve's head cheerleader, no matter how nice he was or how much he refused to fly—which would also explain why our otherwise very Christian kids left eggplants and death threats in Zaccheus Redbird's locker.

On August 13, 1986, Zaccheus Redbird was with Tamara Cooksey, holding hands at the Circle K on Youree Drive. They were both drinking Icees and smiling when Holly "Thunder-Thighs" Ferguson snuck up behind them.

Holly Ferguson held her breath and lobbed a Hazel Mae yellow tomato at Zaccheus Redbird's head. The golden fruit splattered against Zac's skull and ran down his neck in yellow gobs of seed and slime.

That's when the holy kindness of Zaccheus Redbird must have curdled into biblical vengeance because he exploded into hundreds of redbirds—cardinals, to be exact. Tamara screamed and covered her face, while Holly Ferguson dropped to the ground, scared that the birds would scratch out her eyes for what she had just done, but the screeching flock of cardinals flew past her. They flew high into the sky, multiplying with each flap of their wings until the flock was in the millions.

The skies turned red and our blood turned white. Millions upon millions of redbirds pecked and ravaged our tomatoes, peppers, and eggplants. They even pulled up our potato plants and flew away with them. It was like a plague of the Old Testament kind.

After tearing our gardens and yards apart, the waves of cardinals once again darkened our skies, but this time they blanketed our homes, our parks, and our cars in oceans of horrible splatters. By nightfall, they had nearly destroyed our town.

Now that there wasn't a single nightshade vegetable left in Shreveport, we waited under our beds with our guns loaded and our doors bolted. We waited for the Redbird Children to return and take their revenge on us. We waited for weeks, but they never came.

Some people say that they saw the cardinals swarm together that night and reform into Zaccheus Redbird, and it was a reborn Zaccheus who stole Tamara Cooksey from us. Others say that the cardinals landed on the Cookseys' front lawn, and when Tamara went outside to see them, to say goodbye to what was left of Zac, the birds tore her to pieces and flew away with her remains in their tiny yellow talons. Some people swear that Holly Ferguson, a half-eaten box of Ding-Dongs, and a piano wire were somehow involved in Tamara Cooksey's disappearance. Somewhere between the gossip, the legends, and the lies is the truth, but we won't go looking for it now. It flew away with the redbirds.

PINKTASTIC AND THE END OF THE WORLD
CAMILLE ALEXA

Camille Alexa, author of the collection *Push of the Sky*, is co-editor (I am the other editor) of the anthology of all-new superhero fiction *Masked Mosaic: Canadian Super Stories*. Here, she explores the complex relationship between hero and villain, the thin line between heroism and villainy.

Gretchen waited while the random old guy locked the community garden gate and packed his hoe and spades into the trunk of his car, pressing herself against the chain-link fence near the riotous green tangle standing vivid and lush beside the neighboring plots' scraggly broccolini and limp arugula. The car growled to life, backfiring once, sending Gretchen hunching lower into the shrubbery. If she'd paid attention to exactly which of the dozens of long narrow plots had been that old dude's she could've sent a little zap in there, wiped out some snap peas or something for making her wait an hour for him to leave, maybe flooded a couple rows of his strawberries, washed them all into the gutter.

But it wasn't worth it. Wasn't worth the risk of getting caught. Wasn't worth missing her chance to water Pinktastic's tomatoes.

The old guy and his jalopy's rumble faded into the evening quiet. Gretchen stood, brushed leaves off her rear and shot a cursory glance up and down the darkening street. Lights were winking on in houses along the lane, warm gold squares behind which, Gretchen imagined, people were probably sliding steaming dishes onto polished wood tables covered with shiny silverware and surrounded by smiling family or friends or spouses and whatnot. Whatever.

Wedging her boot in the fence, Gretchen hauled one leg up over the spiky top. Stupid city bureaucracy, to put some dinky little barrier around a place if they didn't want people to climb right over it. Fence like this practically begged to be climbed. Who wanted a few lousy old turnips and raspberries and squash anyway? Who even *ate* turnips on purpose?

Well, Pinktastic apparently did, or at least sold them at her organic vegetable stand at the market. Gretchen heaved her other leg over the fence and dropped onto the rich soil. The sky was clear, starting to dot with pinprick stars, the air crisper than it had been in weeks. Gretchen breathed deep, letting the humidity, the slight salinity, the ions in the air tingle through her body. Nobody else would be able to practically taste the cool front rolling in, though there might be a couple other weather Supers along the coast. Apparently some joker in Cleveland could draw down lightning nearly as well as she could, but only if it was already occurring naturally.

Whatever. Any idiot with a little zing in his fingers and a goddamn cape could call himself Thunderpunk and whip up a freaking light show. Let him try to get the exact balance in moisture and temperature and sunlight for a two-hundred-square-foot garden plot for an entire summer—a whole freaking summer!—and see how well he did then. That stuff took finesse, yo.

Saturday market. Stalls crammed with shoppers and lookie-loos, yupster couples with stroller tanks, suburban indie kids sporting dreadlocks and tattoos loading up on free samples of kombucha and vegan baked goods. Gretchen crouched between a Victorian baby carriage and an enormous wrought-iron bird cage, trying to get a clear line of sight to the other end of the market where Pinktastic's vegetable stall shone with rainbowed greenery plumpness. Pinktastic herself was radiant, all apple cheeks and rose-tinted hair and smiles for everyone. Gretchen couldn't quite make out details from her lurking spot, but she'd come so often to watch the girl from afar she could picture the whiteness of her teeth as she smiled, practically smell her honey shampoo.

"Destructova! Haven't seen you in, like, forever!"

Gretchen cringed, scanning the aisles past the rack of vintage aprons and the shelf of scuffed antique cowboy boots to see if anybody had heard. Smash Chick clapped her shoulder and Gretchen reluctantly turned. "It's Gretchen," she said, keeping her voice down, hoping the other girl would get the hint. "Destructova's lying low at the moment."

Smash Chick nodded slowly. "Oh yeah...you guys disbanded after that whole public transit fiasco. Wow. Epic fail there, huh?" She laughed, a big crunching sound that made Gretchen cringe again. "Whose brilliant idea was it for the Dastards to destroy every bus in town? Got yourselves on the feds' domestic terrorist list for that one, eh?"

Stupid Franco. That bus thing had been his idea; his dad held the Metro fleet contract with the city. But Gretchen only shrugged, shoving aside a moulting feather boa tickling her where it dangled from a rickety hat stand. "Seemed like an okay idea at the time," she said. "Seemed like something to do."

With a sympathetic moue, Smash Chick patted her shoulder, her hand the size of Gretchen's skull. "And I was sorry to hear about you and Powerpunch—"

"Franco."

"Yeah, Franco. You guys were a cute couple. And he's *gorgeous*! His unauthorized headshots sell like hotcakes at my friend Loki's stall." She waved vaguely in the same direction as Pinktastic's vegetable stand. "I help Loki out sometimes. He's kind of hard up since the Chromatic League shut down the Deadly Pranksters."

Gretchen nodded, distracted, half-turning so she could watch Pinktastic slide zucchinis into a customer's bag. Huge shiny bright green zucchinis the size of baguettes, plump and flawless from Gretchen's secret ministrations.

Smash Chick gave up squinting across the market trying to figure out what Gretchen was looking at. "Well, whatever. You're between gigs, and that's cool, but when you're ready to pick a new band, call me. I'll put in a good word with the Hacktacious Seven. We've got some *serious* income potential."

"But if you took another member," Gretchen murmured, still watching Pinktastic, "wouldn't you be the Hacktacious Eight?"

"Who cares? The band has like, twelve already. Number manipulation is our racket, baby!"

"Thanks, Smash," Gretchen said, forcing her attention back to the other girl. "I appreciate the thought. Not sure hacking's my thing, but I'll keep you guys in mind."

Smash was pretty, in a hard, rough sort of way. Her forearms were solid as tree trunks, and she had these big grey eyes that kind of melted you if you looked at them for long. Not melted you like The Scorcherizer from the Dastards, where your skin started sloughing off and your organs cooked on the inside, but melted you like you could tell she was way too nice for hardcore villain work. Seriously, the Hacktacious Seven? Not much street cred on the baddie circuit for a bunch of computer geeks siphoning a third of a cent per transaction off millions of ATMs around the world. International Super villains. Sheesh.

Smash Chick smiled, kind of sad. "You action types, it's in your blood, huh? Along with your powers. Like, my band built me this special keyboard for these big mitts..." she held up fists like two raw tofurkeys, "...and I was filled with this sense of *rightness*, you know? Like, I could do evil every day in my pajamas, from the comfort of my own apartment. The best of all possible worlds." She let her hands drop in an almost-shrug. "Anyways, you have my number. See you around."

The big Super turned to squeeze from the cramped stall between two boxy sofas standing on their sides like giant button-tufted bookends, but Gretchen called out, "Hey, Smash." The girl looked back, something like hope flaring in her big grey eyes. "Smash, don't you ever...don't you ever miss it? The hardcore action stuff you did before you got recruited by the Seven? Don't you miss that rush when, like, you're all out there in the flesh, evaporating the city's water supply, or mass-kidnapping the entire season's cast of *Dancing with the Stars*, or whatever? You got your gauntlets on, or your cape or your mask or your infrajet powerboots. And you know the Chromatic League is on their way to stop you, and your vision's all blazing and your heart's up in your throat and your blood feels like pumping lava and you know you and your band could crush anything, *anything* standing between you and your evil deed...."

The hopeful glimmer had faded from Smash Chick's face. She smiled again, that same sad little quirk to the lips. "Nah," she said. "I'm no action junkie. I get the urge to smash something these days, I go out to the woods and find some dead tree stumps or a couple boulders. I love long-distance evil. Don't miss all that blood-pumping stuff at all...guess I'm just not wired like you are."

Long after Smash Chick had disappeared past used furniture and rehabbed power tools and an acre of fresh fruit and mountains of gluten-free baked goods and vegetarian dog biscuits, Gretchen thought about what she'd said. She tried to picture not craving the excitement, the thrill of action when it was *on*, when things got dire and on fire and you had those incandescent moments of perfect glory between one live-or-die second and the next, when you felt more powerful than anything no matter whether you got defeated this time, or came out on top or barely escaped or made a million or lost your shirt. In those moments, everything was right even if it was all going wrong, and you wanted to laugh out loud at the incredible beauty of everything, because it was *all* beautiful: even your fellow villains with their unsavory appetites and unfortunate costume choices; even your victims, with their mewling cries for mercy or their impotent blustery threats or offers of cash to let them go. Even your nemesis, with her white, white teeth and her shiny pink hair that smelled of honey and green garden-y stuff, like flowers and clover.

She thought about all these things, hunkered between the bird cage big enough to hold the Police Commissioner's husband and the wheeled baby buggy straight out of *Masterpiece Theatre*, and watched Pinktastic gently place little green cardboard pints of strawberries and raspberries into her customers' eco-friendly market bags. Pints of strawberries and raspberries Gretchen could practically taste on her tongue past market dust and the loose-feathery tickle of the old boa. Taste them from the hundred times she'd illicitly tasted them in Pinktastic's garden, crouched in darkness between towering tomato vines as small gentle rainclouds formed directly overhead, obscured by twilight and silence.

The racetrack-wide aisles at the MegaHome Mart were packed. Gretchen shoved her cart along in front of her, cursing under her breath when the defective fourth wheel seized up and sent her careening into a stack of three-for-one sod squares where she collided with a dull thump. So many Supers in this city, the store might as well've made a sign in those hot-orange bubble letters they liked so much: *Backyard Secret Hideaway Camouflage at half the price!*

"Destructova. Haven't seen you around much lately."

Gretchen blinked up from the floor where she wrestled with her cart's wheel. Franco, of course. With The Succubus hanging on his arm like he was a million-dollar ransom victim.

After a last wrap of her knuckles against the unyielding rubber as though that fixed the balky wheel, Gretchen stood. "Hi, Powerpunch. Didn't think the MegaHome was your scene." Franco preferred Super titles in public. Always said it was *kowtowing to the Man* to lurk around under civilian names.

Franco peered off into the distance, looking cool, kind of a specialty of his. "Sale this big," he said, "every Super in town's snapping up bargain hideaway and lair stuff. Stupid recession."

The Succubus nodded, sending her trademark pigtails bobbing. "You're *so right*, Powerpunch; I knew I'd bump into you here."

Sheesh. Only Succubus would wear her Super suit to the flipping MegaHome. Shiny plaid skirt, skintight blazer with nothing underneath and straining at the buttons, glossy white knee-highs.... She looked like a life-sized Catholic Schoolgirl Barbie dipped in vinyl.

"Hi, Succubus. Kind of thought you and Franco had already bumped into each other. More than once, in fact," Gretchen said. "Back when he and I were together."

"Hi, Destructova. Glad you're still out here representing the forces of villainy in your own special way, dressed like a goth librarian. You sure you want her to join our new band, Powerpunch? She doesn't exactly exude the right vibe."

Franco studied Gretchen. "She's good in a fight," he said.

Watching him watch her, Gretchen remembered some of the good things about being with him. She remembered how she felt when he lifted her in his toned arms up into the sky with his Superflight, his trademark black split cape flapping around her like protective wings while she plunged her fists into clouds to send lightning down to crisp entire cornfields, to rattle the earth below with her terrible thunder and scorch it with her searing winds.

Going solo was lonely. Even though the International Antivillainy Coalition had placed them on the watch list—Franco, Gretchen, Dan and Mike and Lisa and all the other ex-Dastards and their cohorts and minions; even though the Chromatic League was watching for any sign the Dastards might be reforming under a new name or in a new part of town; even though Pinktastic had taken the Hero Pledge along with the rest of her band at the Police Commissioner's public ceremony last week: even though all that, Gretchen missed the real action. God, did she miss it.

She took a deep breath. "Franco, maybe...."

But she forgot what she was going to say. Straight ahead, about the length of three getaway cars and an unconscious sidekick, Pinktastic was standing in the checkout line. Her cart was full of painting junk: rollers, dropcloths, brushes, a small bank vault's worth of paint cans—okay, maybe only a credit union vault's worth—piled in a neat pyramid, each with a rosy smear on the metal lid to show the color inside. And she was looking right at Gretchen. And she was smiling.

Gretchen's knees went watery and her throat got tight. Pinktastic's smile was gorgeous. She was gorgeous. And now she was wheeling her cart out of line. And now she was coming this way.

"Okay," said Gretchen. "Right then. Great to see you, Powerpunch. Later, Succubus." Gretchen wrenched her cart sideways, dragging the stupid locked wheel across the polished concrete MegaHome floor with a spine-raking squeal. But then the thing seized up again and she was stuck in the middle of the aisle, frozen like she'd been hit with one of Icebergatron's freeze rays.

"You're Gretchen, right?" And Pinktastic was there, *right flipping there*, looking straight at Gretchen. And she knew her motherflipping name and everything. Oh god. Oh crap. Oh holy flipping hell.

One good thing, at least: Gretchen's ex and his new girl had made themselves scarce. No villain in town willingly stood around for close scrutiny by a member of the Chromatic League. Not after the Commissioner's nifty little speech. Not after the Dastards, one of the most dastardly bands on the coast, had had their asses kicked halfway to Sunday and handed back on a plate, forcing them to disband and lay low, not even go to all the regular baddie bars and baddie parties. Hardly seemed worth following the path of villainy if you never even got to go to the best parties.

Pinktastic thrust out her hand. Gretchen stared like it was one of Medusaman's infamous pet monsters instead of a slender-fingered bit of ordinary human flesh with pale pink polish on the nails.

When Gretchen didn't move, Pinktastic reached for her hand and shook it. "I'm Alice," she said. "I have a stall at the Saturday market? I see you there practically every week."

Saw her there? But Gretchen had been so careful! She never got close enough to activate Pinktastic's famous Chromasense, which gave her the ability to see villainy in the air like an aura of darkness. Oh god. Oh crap. She must look like a big old grey smudge right now. Charcoal mist must be clinging all over her, baring her dark heart like it had been ripped from her chest.

Maybe alarmed by the way Gretchen's face was turning blue from holding her breath, Pinktastic let go of her hand. "Anyway, I asked around, and Loki's friend Lucy told me your name. Thought I'd introduce myself so we'd be even."

Lucy. Smash Chick. Gretchen thought she might vomit right there in the MegaHome garden aisle, she was so freaked.

Pinktastic's smile faltered. Probably because she could tell Gretchen was about to throw up on her shoes. That, or she'd finally noticed the scent of villainy clinging to Gretchen like Pigpen's dustcloud in the old *Peanuts* cartoons. "Okay... well, nice to meet you, Gretchen. See you around?"

Gretchen barely managed to nod, a stilted motion reminiscent of the Grim Puppeteer's automated minions. As soon as Pinktastic wheeled around, Gretchen bolted, abandoning her traitorous shopping cart near the mountain of bargain sod still filled with stuff she could no longer remember wanting or needing. As she ran, she imagined her villainous aura trailing after her, a tattletale streak of black fog in the clean clear air.

The old warehouse door rammed shut with a bang and Gretchen sank to the floor, sobbing. After a while her legs started hurting where they'd fallen asleep under her. She managed a clumsy stagger across the room, her feet lumps of pins and needles where circulation tried to return, her cheeks tight and sticky from dried tears. She flopped on the couch, sending a flurry of dustmotes into the air to be caught in rays of light slanting past the enormous casement windows taking up one crumbling brick wall.

Lying on the couch, Gretchen pictured her life as it should be. She imagined her leaky rundown warehouse as a genuine lair, brick walls painted a deep smoldering purple, no water stains or ancient tarred patches, no looming cracks past which you could see daylight. She imagined her back-alley sofa replaced with something sleek and modern, black crushed velvet maybe, or textured vinyl: some cool fabric that didn't need old blankets to hide where someone else's cat had used the arms as scratching posts. She imagined her hotplate and microwave replaced with the latest brushed steel appliances, and maybe a kitchen island of black Italian marble like she'd seen in that magazine at the dentist's.

And in the middle of this sleek modern wonderland of ultimate villainy, Gretchen imagined Gretchen. This imaginary Gretchen had the hair she'd always wanted: long and loose and darker than midnight. Her clothes were just the right clothes, her Super suit a dream of sophistication, her waist and hips and thighs worthy of a Parisian catwalk and of the sleek lines demanded by the latest in villain fashion.

The rest of the afternoon passed as so many had passed in recent weeks: with Gretchen fading in and out of sleep, arm thrown over her eyes to block out daylight filtering though the grimy cracked windows, dream mingling with fantasy mingling with memory, until Destructova and Pinktastic jetted through the air via the latest Super technology, zapping each other with forked lightning and chromatic rays...*biff!...bam!...pow!...boom....*

Wasn't it dark enough yet for the random old guy to bugger off and get out of here? Who gardens after dark? Gretchen stifled a curse and hunkered lower in the ancient rosemary bush. It wasn't the same random old dude who'd been in the community garden last time; a small truck was parked at the curb rather than the jalopy. And this dude listened to the radio as he weeded—the freaking *radio*! Who listened to a motherflipping radio anymore? Random old dudes hoeing cabbage at the community garden, that's who.

Trying not to resort to her old nail-biting habit, Gretchen, from sheer boredom, began listening to the old dude's radio. Geezer music played awhile, kind of peppy and orchestral. Then an interview with some hero Gretchen had never heard of, who'd written a memoir about discovering his Super powers as a smalltown boy in the middle of Noplace, Nowhere. Seemed they were making it into a movie. Sheesh.

And then the regular programming was interrupted by that sound. It was a buzz, a howl, a screech or a hum or a combination of all those. Whatever, it was designed to get your attention, and it did. It was an alert from the Emergency Broadcast System.

"*Regional Alert! After forcing what would have been a passing meteoric cluster into a collision course with Earth, powerful archvillain Tectonic Shifter has perished in the upper stratosphere. Minutes earlier, the International Antivillainy*

Coalition received his demand for an undisclosed amount in gold bullion. But before negotiations began, Tectonic Shifter was killed by one of the first meteors diverted toward Earth. Repeat: Tectonic Shifter is dead. The Coalition is calling all Super heroes in the region to instant action. Non-Supers are urged to begin immediate emergency evacuation...."

At some point without realizing, Gretchen had emerged from the rosemary bush. The old dude had gone ramrod straight, hoe poised midair as he listened. Gretchen made one scrambling leap at the fence and vaulted over, scarcely noticing the rip in her tights when her leg didn't quite clear. In a few strides she was at the old guy's side.

"Did they say where the Supers are supposed to meet?" Gretchen swooped the small radio off the ground from between two modest pumpkins barely starting to show. The man shied away, shaking his head, even older up close than she'd thought, all skinny and weak. She could break his back with a powerful gust of wind if she wanted, or ram rainwater up his nose until he drowned on moisture materialized from the very air he breathed.

"Well," said Gretchen, "you heard the alert: go!" He cowered, half lifting his hoe as though it afforded some small protection. Gretchen kicked it from his hand so it went spinning off into the dusk. "Evacuate, motherflipper! Don't you know what emergency means?"

He nodded and backed away toward his truck.

"And I'm keeping this freaking radio, though if you're not gone by the count of three I'll ram it down your non-evacuating throat. One. Two."

As the old dude's taillights disappeared around the corner, Gretchen fumbled with the dial, trying to tune into a station not preprogrammed with rush-hour talk shows or insipid pop music. Any station. Any station at all. Stupid antique piece of crap.

With an offhand flip of the wrist she sent a small rainshower scooting across Pinktastic's end of the gardens. The neighboring plots would benefit from Destructova's attentions, just this once. Couldn't be helped. Destructova had someplace else to be tonight.

The city was a mess. Cars idled bumper to bumper, belching invisible poisons for miles along every possible route out of the urban core. Destructova congratulated herself for the millionth time on never learning to drive as she sprinted along the empty sidewalks, radio clutched to her ear like an icepack to a bruise after a Super training session.

According to the radio, heroes from all over were gathering at City Hall. The first tiny meteors—practically pebbles compared to the largest—had already crashed in the suburbs. Thousands were reported missing or dead, while wildfires sparked by the blazing missiles devastated farmlands to the east. Every station had either ceased broadcasting or was playing repeated emergency alerts urging the locals to flee. Gretchen finally settled on a station with moment-by-moment analysis of the situation.

Only Tectonic Shifter, it was believed, had possessed Super powers capable of rerouting solid masses the size of the biggest meteors headed for Earth. Ironic that he'd been killed by the smallest of them, a rock so tiny it probably would've burned to nothing before hitting the planet. The largest mass, the one Supers around the world were preparing to meet, was capable of unspeakable destruction. Dinosaurs were mentioned, followed by long smarty-pantsy sounding discussions about the effects of smoke and dust in the atmosphere. Stupid brainiacs might as well have been yelling, *Duck! We're all going to die!*

After her summer of lying low, Gretchen was more out of shape than she'd realized. The many weeks since the Dastards' disbandment had left her flabby and soft. Okay; the many weeks of lying on the couch all day sobbing her guts out and eating coconut chocolate ice-cream with peanut butter swirls had left her flabby and soft. Whatever. All she knew was, she was totally huffing when she sprinted the last block.

City Hall was blazing, lit like a white stone beacon with wide marble steps and fifty-foot columns. And the heroes! Gretchen had never seen so many Supers gathered in one place at the same time, not even when the Commissioner had held her big party honoring the Chromatic League for driving baddies like the Dastards underground, keeping the citizenry safe to guzzle their Big Gulps and drive their sucktacious SUVs back and forth from the suburbs, strewing pollutants and poisoning the air.

The Chromatic League. Gretchen could see them from the street, a rainbow of Supercolors and self-righteousness. Leader Roy Gebiv stood at the top of the steps under the brightest spotlight, his shifting multihued cape with its patented bulletproof coating a fitting backdrop for his square jaw and smug weatherman's grin. Flanking him were his personal sidekicks, Rain and Bow—like either of them were even worthy of kissing a real rainbow's feet. In a semicircle behind Roy—the Chromatic League liked a good cover-shot pose and always snagged tons of media footage—stood the rest of his band: Indigo Avenger and Green Axe and Violetina and Orange Alert and, at the very end, Pinktastic. She looked small compared to the rest, but glorious, radiating goodness like a perfume.

The Commissioner finished her rousing speech to a flurry of flash photography and a smattering of halfhearted applause, and was whisked away in an armored car. Probably to an underground bunker, or a waiting helicopter. The airspace above City Hall was conspicuously empty, cleared for the Supers to take off en masse and try to save the planet from what the radio commentator Gretchen had ceased listening to the minute she'd seen Pinktastic up on the steps—little pink flats and pink headband and thin matching mask making her hair look more strawberry than rose—called *impending destruction on a scale unprecedented in human history*.

Gretchen pushed past a crowd of gawkers. Hundreds of non-Supers stood watching, smoking, crying, laughing. Either these people had decided it was useless to try to get the hell out of the city deemed ground zero for the biggest asteroid Earth had seen since the brontosaurus, or they had way too much faith in their heroes. Heroes were only people, after all. People with problems. People with leaky apartments and overdue bills and jerkoff ex-boyfriends.

"Here," Gretchen thrust the little radio at the nearest onlooker, a patchouli-scented private school girl reeking of a future English degree. "You might want to listen to this. Something about an emergency evacuation of the region."

Without waiting for the girl's reaction Gretchen bounded up the enormous steps, dodging Super heroes she'd seen on the news, heroes she'd defeated in minor skirmishes with the Dastards, heroes who'd defeated her, sent her and her fellow villains running from thwarted heinous acts like cockroaches from a bare bulb at midnight. Heroes, heroes everywhere, and she wasn't even nervous. They were all going to die anyway; nobody living had enough power to divert a mass the size of Jamaica from plowing into the Earth.

Abruptly Gretchen was at the top with no more stairs to climb, and it was just her and the Chromatic League up there under the bright lights between soaring stone columns. Her and Pinktastic.

All Gretchen's forward momentum drained away. All the purpose and impetus, gone. "Hi, Alice," she said.

Pinktastic smiled. It was a strained smile, the smile of someone about to try to save the world, pretty sure she's going to fail. "Hi, Gretchen. You shouldn't be here. Emergency evacuation in progress, you know."

"I know."

Roy Gebiv and his sidekicks were powering their infrajet boots, which were way noisier than Gretchen remembered. Alice gave Gretchen an apologetic look. "That's my cue," she said, shouting over the jets, reaching to flip the toggles on her boots.

Gretchen nodded and stepped back to give the Chromatic League room for their fancy signature group takeoff. But Pinktastic called to her, shouting even louder above the drone of dozens of powerboots warming up under Supers without natural flight ability: "Destructova!"

Gretchen looked up. Pinktastic was holding out her hand.

"Destructova! Gretchen...."

Gretchen leapt over the top couple steps in a single bound and grasped Pinktastic's hand. Alice pulled her close, shouting into her ear.

Want to come? she was saying. *Want to come with me to save the world?*

And Gretchen nodded and stepped behind Pinktastic and wrapped her arms around the other girl's slim capeless shoulders. The Chromatic League could afford the very best Super technology, their boots able to lift two people, or three— handy for saving the hapless from rising floods or oncoming trains or stampeding rhinos. Handy for taking your nemesis with you into the stratosphere to meet almost certain death in the process of great heroic sacrifice.

Roy Gebiv gave the signal and they rose in a flurry of capes and jets and air, Destructova and Pinktastic and all the Chromatic League and other Supers. A sense of rightness settled in the core of Gretchen's middle, and she finally understood what Smash Chick had meant: *The best of all possible worlds.* She felt that rightness sing through her blood, surging along with her power, and hugged Pinktastic tight as they zoomed up, up, up into the stratosphere, together.

THE DETECTIVE OF DREAMS

GENE WOLFE

We end with a dream by Gene Wolfe, whose many classic works of science fiction
and fantasy include canny, powerful, and mysterious investigations into the nature
of heroism, most especially in *The Book of the New Sun*, *The Urth of the New Sun*, *The
Knight*, and the *Soldier* novels.

I was writing in my office in the rue Madeleine when Andrée, my secretary,
announced the arrival of Herr D_____. I rose, put away my correspondence,
and offered him my hand. He was, I should say, just short of fifty, had the high,
clear complexion characteristic of those who in youth (now unhappily past for
both of us) have found more pleasure in the company of horses and dogs and
the excitement of the chase than in the bottles and bordels of city life, and wore a
beard and mustache of the style popularized by the late emperor. Accepting my
invitation to a chair, he showed me his papers.

"You see," he said, "I am accustomed to acting as the representative of my
government. In this matter I hold no such position, and it is possible that I feel a
trifle lost."

"Many people who come here feel lost," I said. "But it is my boast that I find
most of them again. Your problem, I take it, is purely a private matter?"

"Not at all. It is a public matter in the truest sense of the words."

"Yet none of the documents before me—admirably stamped, sealed, and
beribboned though they are—indicates that you are other than a private gentleman
traveling abroad. And you say you do not represent your government. What am I
to think? What is the matter?"

"I act in the public interest," Herr D_____ told me. "My fortune is not great,
but I can assure you that in the event of your success you will be well recompensed;
although you are to take it that I alone am your principal, yet there are substantial
resources available to me."

"Perhaps it would be best if you described the problems to me?"

"You are not averse to travel?"

"No."

"Very well then," he said, and so saying launched into one of the most astonishing relations—no, *the* most astonishing relation—I have ever been privileged to hear. Even I, who had at first hand the account of the man who found Paulette Renan with the quince seed still lodged in her throat; who had received Captain Brotte's testimony concerning his finds amid the Antarctic ice; who had heard the history of the woman called Joan O'Neal, who lived for two years behind a painting of herself in the Louvre, from her own lips—even I sat like a child while this man spoke.

When he fell silent, I said, "Herr D_____, after all you have told me, I would accept this mission though there were not a *sou* to be made from it. Perhaps once in a lifetime one comes across a case that must be pursued for its own sake; I think I have found mine."

He leaned forward and grasped my hand with a warmth of feeling that was, I believe, very foreign to his usual nature. "Find and destroy the Dream-Master," he said, "and you shall sit upon a chair of gold, if that is your wish, and eat from a table of gold as well. When will you come to our country?"

"Tomorrow morning," I said. "There are one or two arrangements I must make here before I go."

"I am returning tonight. You may call upon me at any time, and I will apprise you of new developments." He handed me a card. "I am always to be found at this address—if not I, then one who is to be trusted, acting in my behalf."

"I understand."

"This should be sufficient for your initial expenses. You may call me should you require more." The cheque he gave me as he turned to leave represented a comfortable fortune.

I waited until he was nearly out the door before saying, "I thank you, Herr Baron." To his credit, he did not turn; but I had the satisfaction of seeing a red flush rising above the precise white line of his collar before the door closed.

Andrée entered as soon as he had left. "Who was that man? When you spoke to him—just as he was stepping out of your office—he looked as if you had struck him with a whip."

"He will recover," I told her. "He is the Baron H_____, of the secret police of K_____. D_____ was his mother's name. He assumed that because his own desk is a few hundred kilometers from mine, and because he does not permit his likeness to appear in the daily papers, I would not know him; but it was necessary, both for the sake of his opinion of me and my own of myself, that he should discover that I am not so easily deceived. When he recovers from his initial irritation, he will retire tonight with greater confidence in the abilities I will devote to the mission he has entrusted to me."

"It is typical of you, monsieur," Andrée said kindly, "that you are concerned that your clients sleep well."

Her pretty cheek tempted me, and I pinched it. "I am concerned," I replied; "but the Baron will not sleep well."

My train roared out of Paris through meadows sweet with wildflowers, to penetrate mountain passes in which the danger of avalanches was only just past. The glitter of rushing water, sprung from on high, was everywhere; and when the express slowed to climb a grade, the song of water was everywhere too, water running and shouting down the gray rocks of the Alps. I fell asleep that night with the descant of that icy purity sounding through the plainsong of the rails, and I woke in the station of I_____, the old capital of J_____, now a province of K_____.

I engaged a porter to convey my trunk to the hotel where I had made reservations by telegraph the day before, and amused myself for a few hours by strolling about the city. Here I found the Middle Ages might almost be said to have remained rather than lingered. The city wall was complete on three sides, with its merloned towers in repair; and the cobbled streets surely dated from a period when wheeled traffic of any kind was scarce. As for the buildings—Puss in Boots and his friends must have loved them dearly: there were bulging walls and little panes of bull's-eye glass, and overhanging upper floors one above another until the structures seemed unbalanced as tops. Upon one gray old pile with narrow windows and massive doors, I found a plaque informing me that though it had been first built as a church, it had been successively a prison, a customhouse, a private home, and a school. I investigated further, and discovered it was now an arcade, having been divided, I should think at about the time of the first Louis, into a multitude of dank little stalls. Since it was, as it happened, one of the addresses mentioned by Baron H_____, I went in.

Gas flared everywhere, yet the interior could not have been said to be well lit—each jet was sullen and secretive, as if the proprietor in whose cubicle it was located wished it to light none but his own wares. These cubicles were in no order; nor could I find any directory or guide to lead me to the one I sought. A few customers, who seemed to have visited the place for years, so that they understood where everything was, drifted from one display to the next. When they arrived at each, the proprietor came out, silent (so it seemed to me) as a specter, ready to answer questions or accept a payment; but I never heard a question asked, or saw any money tendered—the customer would finger the edge of a kitchen knife, or hold a garment up to her own shoulders, or turn the pages of some moldering book; and then put the thing down again, and go away.

At last, when I had tired of peeping into alcoves lined with booths still gloomier than the ones on the main concourse outside, I stopped at a leather merchant's and asked the man to direct me to Fräulein A_____.

"I do not know her," he said.

"I am told on good authority that her business is conducted in this building, and that she buys and sells antiques."

"We have several antique dealers here, Herr M_____—"

"I am searching for a young woman. Has your Herr M_____ a niece or a cousin?"

"—handles chairs and chests, largely. Herr O_____, near the guildhall—"

"It is within this building."

"—stocks pictures, mostly. A few mirrors. What is it you wish to buy?"

At this point we were interrupted, mercifully, by a woman from the next booth. "He wants Fräulein A_____. Out of here, and to your left; past the wigmaker's, then right to the stationer's, then left again. She sells old lace."

I found the place at last, and sitting at the very back of her booth Fräulein A_____ herself, a pretty, slender, timid-looking young woman. Her merchandise was spread on two tables; I pretended to examine it and found that it was not old lace she sold but old clothing, much of it trimmed with lace. After a few moments she rose and came out to talk to me, saying, "If you could tell me what you require?..." She was taller than I had anticipated, and her flaxen hair would have been very attractive if it were ever released from the tight braids coiled round her head.

"I am only looking. Many of these are beautiful—are they expensive?"

"Not for what you get. The one you are holding is only fifty marks."

"That seems like a great deal."

"They are the fine dresses of long ago—for visiting, or going to the ball. The dresses of wealthy women of aristocratic taste. All are like new; I will not handle anything else. Look at the seams in the one you hold, the tiny stitches all done by hand. Those were the work of dressmakers who created only four or five in a year, and worked twelve and fourteen hours a day, sewing at the first light, and continuing under the lamp, past midnight."

I said, "I see that you have been crying, Fräulein. Their lives were indeed miserable, though no doubt there are people today who suffer equally."

"No doubt there are," the young woman said. "I, however, am not one of them." And she turned away so that I should not see her tears.

"I was informed otherwise."

She whirled about to face me. "You know him? Oh, tell him I am not a wealthy woman, but I will pay whatever I can. Do you really know him?"

"No." I shook my head. "I was informed by your own police."

She stared at me. "But you are an outlander. So is he, I think."

"Ah, we progress. Is there another chair in the rear of your booth? Your police are not above going outside your own country for help, you see, and we should have a little talk."

"They are not our police," the young woman said bitterly, "but I will talk to you. The truth is that I would sooner talk to you, though you are French. You will not tell them that?"

I assured her I would not; we borrowed a chair from the flower stall across the corridor, and she poured forth her story.

"My father died when I was very small. My mother opened this booth to earn our living—old dresses that had belonged to her own mother were the core of her original stock. She died two years ago, and since that time I have taken charge of our business and used it to support myself. Most of my sales are to collectors and theatrical companies. I do not make a great deal of money, but I do not require a great deal, and I have managed to save some. I live alone at Number 877 _____strasse; it is an old house divided into six apartments, and mine is the gable apartment."

"You are young and charming," I said, "and you tell me you have a little money saved. I am surprised you are not married."

"Many others have said the same thing."

"And what did you tell them, Fräulein?"

"To take care of their own affairs. They have called me a manhater—Frau G_____, who has the confections in the next corridor but two, called me that because I would not receive her son. The truth is that I do not care for people of either sex, young or old. If I want to live by myself and keep my own things to myself, is it not my right to do so?"

"I am sure it is; but undoubtedly it has occurred to you that this person you fear so much may be a rejected suitor who is taking revenge on you."

"But how could he enter and control my dreams?"

"I do not know, Fräulein. It is you who say that he does these things."

"I should remember him, I think, if he had ever called on me. As it is, I am quite certain I have seen him somewhere, but I cannot recall where. Still..."

"Perhaps you had better describe your dream to me. You have the same one again and again, as I understand it?"

"Yes. It is like this. I am walking down a dark road. I am both frightened and pleasurably excited, if you know what I mean. Sometimes I walk for a long time, sometimes for what seems to be only a few moments. I think there is moonlight, and once or twice I have noticed stars. Anyway, there is a high, dark hedge, or perhaps a wall, on my right. There are fields to the left, I believe. Eventually I reach a gate of iron bars, standing open—it's not a large gate for wagons or carriages, but a small one, so narrow I can hardly get through. Have you read the writings of Dr. Freud of Vienna? One of the women here mentioned once that he had written concerning dreams, and so I got them from the library, and if I were a man I am sure he would say that entering that gate meant sexual commerce. Do you think I might have unnatural leanings?" Her voice dropped to a whisper.

"Have you ever felt such desires?"

"Oh, no. Quite the reverse."

"Then I doubt it very much," I said. "Go on with your dream. How do you feel as you pass through the gate?"

"As I did when walking down the road, but more so—more frightened, and yet happy and excited. Triumphant, in a way."

"Go on."

"I am in the garden now. There are fountains playing, and nightingales singing in the willows. The air smells of lilies, and a cherry tree in blossom looks like a giantess in her bridal gown. I walk on a straight, smooth path; I think it must be paved with marble chips, because it is white in the moonlight. Ahead of me is the *Schloss*—a great building. There is music coming from inside."

"What sort of music?"

"Magnificent—joyous, if you know what I am trying to say, but not the tinklings of a theater orchestra. A great symphony. I have never been to the opera at Bayreuth; but I think it must be like that—yet a happy, quick tune."

She paused, and for an instant her smile recovered the remembered music. "There are pillars, and a grand entrance, with broad steps. I run up—I am so happy to be there—and throw open the door. It is brightly lit inside; a wave of golden light, almost like a wave from the ocean, strikes me. The room is a great hall, with a high ceiling. A long table is set in the middle and there are hundreds of people seated at it, but one place, the one nearest me, is empty. I cross to it and sit down; there are beautiful loaves on the table, and bowls of honey with roses floating at their centers, and crystal carafes of wine, and many other good things I cannot remember when I awake. Everyone is eating and drinking and talking, and I begin to eat too."

I said, "It is only a dream, Fräulein. There is no reason to weep."

"I dream this each night—I have dreamed so every night for months."

"Go on."

"Then he comes. I am sure he is the one who is causing me to dream like this because I can see his face clearly, and remember it when the dream is over. Sometimes it is very vivid for an hour or more after I wake—so vivid that I have only to close my eyes to see it before me."

"I will ask you to describe him in detail later. For the present, continue with your dream."

"He is tall, and robed like a king, and there is a strange crown on his head. He stands beside me, and though he says nothing, I know that the etiquette of the place demands that I rise and face him. I do this. Sometimes I am sucking my fingers as I get up from his table."

"He owns the dream palace, then."

"Yes, I am sure of that. It is his castle, his home; he is my host. I stand and face him, and I am conscious of wanting very much to please him, but not knowing what it is I should do."

"That must be painful."

"It is. But as I stand there, I become aware of how I am clothed and—"

"How are you clothed?"

"As you see me now. In a plain, dark dress—the dress I wear here in the arcade. But the others—all up and down the hall, all up and down the table—are wearing the dresses I sell here. These dresses." She held one up for me to see, a beautiful creation of many layers of lace, with buttons of polished jet. "I know then that I cannot remain; but the king signals to the others, and they seize me and push me toward the door."

"You are humiliated then?"

"Yes, but the worst thing is that I am aware that he knows that I could never drive myself to leave, and he wishes to spare me the struggle. But outside—some terrible beast has entered the garden. I smell it—like the hyena cage at the *Tiergarten*—as the door opens. And then I wake up."

"It is a harrowing dream."

"You have seen the dresses I sell. Would you credit it that for weeks I slept in one, and then another, and then another of them?"

"You reaped no benefit from that?"

"No. In the dream I was clad as now. For a time I wore the dresses always—even here to the stall, and when I bought food at the market. But it did no good."

"Have you tried sleeping somewhere else?"

"With my cousin who lives on the other side of the city. That made no difference. I am certain that this man I see is a real man. He is in my dream, and the cause of it; but he is not sleeping."

"Yet you have never seen him when you are awake?"

She paused, and I saw her bite at her full lower lip. "I am certain I have."

"Ah!"

"But I cannot remember when. Yet I am sure I have seen him—that I have passed him in the street."

"Think! Does his face associate itself in your mind with some particular section of the city?"

She shook her head.

When I left her at last, it was with a description of the Dream-Master less precise than I had hoped, though still detailed. It tallied in almost all respects with the one given me by Baron H_____; but that proved nothing, since the Baron's description might have been based largely on Fräulein A_____'s.

The bank of Herr R_____ was a private one, as all the greatest banks in Europe are. It was located in what had once been the town house of some noble family (their arms, overgrown now with ivy, were still visible above the door), and bore no identification other than a small brass plate engraved with the names of Herr R_____ and his partners. Within, the atmosphere was more dignified—even if, perhaps, less tasteful—than it could possibly have been in the noble family's time. Dark pictures in gilded frames lined the walls, and the clerks sat at inlaid tables upon chairs upholstered in tapestry. When I asked for Herr R_____, I was told that it would be impossible to see him that afternoon; I sent in a note with a sidelong allusion to "unquiet dreams," and within five minutes I was ushered into a luxurious office that must once have been the bedroom of the head of the household.

Herr R_____ was a large man—tall, and heavier (I thought) than his physician was likely to have approved. He appeared to be about fifty; there was strength in his wide, fleshy face; his high forehead and capacious cranium suggested intellect; and his small, dark eyes, forever flickering as they took in the appearance of my person, the expression of my face, and the position of my hands and feet, ingenuity.

No pretense was apt to be of service with such a man, and I told him flatly that I had come as the emissary of Baron H_____, that I knew what troubled him, and that if he would cooperate with me I would help him if I could.

"I know you, monsieur," he said, "by reputation. A business with which I am associated employed you three years ago in the matter of a certain mummy." He named the firm. "I should have thought of you myself."

"I did not know that you were connected with them."

"I am not, when you leave this room. I do not know what reward Baron

H_____ has offered you should you apprehend the man who is oppressing me, but I will give you, in addition to that, a sum equal to that you were paid for the mummy. You should be able to retire to the south then, should you choose, with the rent of a dozen villas."

"I do not choose," I told him, "and I could have retired long before. But what you just said interests me. You are certain that your persecutor is a living man?"

"I know men." Herr R_____ leaned back in his chair and stared at the painted ceiling. "As a boy I sold stuffed cabbage-leaf rolls in the street—did you know that? My mother cooked them over wood she collected herself where buildings were being demolished, and I sold them from a little cart for her. I lived to see her with half a score of footmen and the finest house in Lindau. I never went to school; I learned to add and subtract in the streets—when I must multiply and divide I have my clerk do it. But I learned men. Do you think that now, after forty years of practice, I could be deceived by a phantom? No, he is a man—let me confess it, a stronger man than I—a man of flesh and blood and brain, a man I have seen somewhere, sometime, here in this city—and more than once."

"Describe him."

"As tall as I. Younger—perhaps thirty or thirty-five. A brown, forked beard, so long." (He held his hand about fifteen centimeters beneath his chin.) "Brown hair. His hair is not yet gray, but I think it may be thinning a little at the temples."

"Don't you remember?"

"In my dreams he wears a garland of roses—I cannot be sure."

"Is there anything else? Any scars or identifying marks?"

Herr R_____ nodded. "He has hurt his hand. In my dream, when he holds out his hand for the money, I see blood in it—it is his own, you understand, as though a recent injury had reopened and was beginning to bleed again. His hands are long and slender—like a pianist's."

"Perhaps you had better tell me your dream."

"Of course." He paused, and his face clouded, as though to recount the dream were to return to it. "I am in a great house. I am a person of importance there, almost as though I were the owner; yet I am not the owner—"

"Wait," I interrupted. "Does this house have a banquet hall? Has it a pillared portico, and is it set in a garden?"

For a moment Herr R_____'s eyes widened. "Have you also had such dreams?"

"No," I said. "It is only that I think I have heard of this house before. Please continue."

"There are many servants—some work in the fields beyond the garden. I give instructions to them—the details differ each night, you understand. Sometimes I am concerned with the kitchen, sometimes with livestock, sometimes with the draining of a field. We grow wheat, principally, it seems; but there is a vineyard too, and a kitchen garden. And of course the house must be cleaned and swept and kept in repair. There is no wife; the owner's mother lives with us, I think, but she does not much concern herself with the housekeeping—that is up to me. To tell the truth, I have never actually seen her, though I have the feeling that she is there."

"Does this house resemble the one you bought for your mother in Lindau?"

"Only as one large house must resemble another."

"I see. Proceed."

"For a long time each night I continue like that, giving orders, and sometimes going over the accounts. Then a servant, usually it is a maid, arrives to tell me that the owner wishes to speak to me. I stand before a mirror—I can see myself there as plainly as I see you now—and arrange my clothing. The maid brings rose-scented water and a cloth, and I wipe my face; then I go in to him.

"He is always in one of the upper rooms, seated at a table with his own account book spread before him. There is an open window behind him, and through it I can see the top of a cherry tree in bloom. For a long time—oh, I suppose ten minutes—I stand before him while he turns over the pages of his ledger."

"You appear somewhat at a loss, Herr R_____—not a common condition for you, I believe. What happens then?"

"He says, 'You owe...'" Herr R_____ paused. "That is the problem, monsieur, I can never recall the amount. But it is a large sum. He says, 'And I must require that you make payment at once.'

"I do not have the amount, and I tell him so. He says, 'Then you must leave my employment.' I fall to my knees at this and beg that he will retain me, pointing out that if he dismisses me I will have lost my source of income, and will never be able to make payment. I do not enjoy telling you this, but I weep. Sometimes I beat the floor with my fists."

"Continue. Is the Dream-Master moved by your pleading?"

"No. He again demands that I pay the entire sum. Several times I have told him that I am a wealthy man in this world, and that if only he would permit me to make payment in its currency, I would do so immediately."

"That is interesting—most of us lack your presence of mind in our nightmares. What does he say then?"

"Usually he tells me not to be a fool. But once he said, 'That is a dream—you must know it by now. You cannot expect to pay a real debt with the currency of sleep.' He holds out his hand for the money as he speaks to me. It is then that I see the blood in his palm."

"You are afraid of him?"

"Oh, very much so. I understand that he has the most complete power over me. I weep, and at last I throw myself at his feet—with my head under the table, if you can credit it, crying like an infant.

"Then he stands and pulls me erect and says, 'You would never be able to pay all you owe, and you are a false and dishonest servant. But your debt is forgiven, forever.' And as I watch, he tears a leaf from his account book and hands it to me."

"Your dream has a happy conclusion, then."

"No. It is not yet over. I thrust the paper into the front of my shirt and go out, wiping my face on my sleeve. I am conscious that if any of the other servants should see me, they will know at once what has happened. I hurry to reach my own counting room; there is a brazier there, and I wish to burn the page from the owner's book."

"I see."

"But just outside the door of my own room, I meet another servant—an upper-servant like myself, I think, since he is well dressed. As it happens, this man owes me a considerable sum of money, and to conceal from him what I have just endured, I demand that he pay at once." Herr R_____ rose from his chair and began to pace the room, looking sometimes at the painted scenes on the walls, sometimes at the Turkish carpet at his feet. "I have had reason to demand money like that often, you understand. Here in this room.

"The man falls to his knees, weeping and begging for additional time; but I reach down, like this, and seize him by the throat."

"And then?"

"And then the door of my counting room opens. But it is not my counting room with my desk and the charcoal brazier, but the owner's own room. He is standing in the doorway, and behind him I can see the open window, and the blossoms of the cherry tree."

"What does he say to you?"

"Nothing. He says nothing to me. I release the other man's throat, and he slinks away."

"You awaken then?"

"How can I explain it? Yes, I wake up. But first we stand there; and while we do I am conscious of...certain sounds."

"If it is too painful for you, you need not say more."

Herr R_____ drew a silk handkerchief from his pocket, and wiped his face. "How can I explain?" he said again. "When I hear those sounds, I am aware that the owner possesses certain other servants, who have never been under my direction. It is as though I have always known this, but had no reason to think of it before."

"I understand."

"They are quartered in another part of the house—in the vaults beneath the wine cellar, I think sometimes. I have never seen them, but I know—then—that they are hideous, vile and cruel; I know too that he thinks me but little better than they, and that as he permits me to serve him, so he allows them to serve him also. I stand—we stand—and listen to them coming through the house. At last a door at the end of the hall begins to swing open. There is a hand like the paw of some filthy reptile on the latch."

"Is that the end of the dream?"

"Yes." Herr R_____ threw himself into his chair again, mopping his face.

"You have this experience each night?"

"It differs," he said slowly, "in some details."

"You have told me that the orders you give the under-servants vary."

"There is another difference. When the dreams began, I woke when the hinges of the door at the passage end creaked. Each night now the dream endures a moment longer. Perhaps a tenth of a second. Now I see the arm of the creature who opens that door, nearly to the elbow."

I took the address of his home, which he was glad enough to give me, and leaving the bank made my way to my hotel.

When I had eaten my roll and drunk my coffee the next morning, I went to the place indicated by the card given me by Baron H_____, and in a few minutes was sitting with him in a room as bare as those tents from which armies in the field are cast into battle. "You are ready to begin the case this morning?" he asked.

"On the contrary. I have already begun; indeed, I am about to enter a new phase of my investigation. You would not have come to me if your Dream-Master were not torturing someone other than the people whose names you gave me. I wish to know the identity of that person, and to interrogate him."

"I told you that there were many other reports. I—"

"Provided me with a list. They are all of the petite bourgeoisie, when they are not persons still less important. I believed at first that it might be because of the urgings of Herr R_____ that you engaged me; but when I had time to reflect on what I know of your methods, I realized that you would have demanded that he provide my fee had that been the case. So you are sheltering someone of greater importance, and I wish to speak to him."

"The Countess—" Baron H_____ began.

"Ah!"

"The Countess herself has expressed some desire that you should be presented to her. The Count opposes it."

"We are speaking, I take it, of the governor of this province?"

The Baron nodded. "Of Count von V_____. He is responsible, you understand, only to the Queen Regent herself."

"Very well. I wish to hear the Countess, and she wishes to talk with me. I assure you, Baron, that we will meet; the only question is whether it will be under your auspices."

The Countess, to whom I was introduced that afternoon, was a woman in her early twenties, deep-breasted and somber-haired, with skin like milk, and great dark eyes welling with fear and (I thought) pity, set in a perfect oval face.

"I am glad you have come, monsieur. For seven weeks now our good Baron H_____ has sought this man for me, but he has not found him."

"If I had known my presence here would please you, Countess, I would have come long ago, whatever the obstacles. You then, like the others, are certain it is a real man we seek?"

"I seldom go out, monsieur. My husband feels we are in constant danger of assassination."

"I believe he is correct."

"But on state occasions we sometimes ride in a glass coach to the *Rathaus.* There are uhlans all around us to protect us then. I am certain that—before the dreams began—I saw the face of this man in the crowd."

"Very well. Now tell me your dream."

"I am here, at home—"

"In this palace, where we sit now?"

She nodded.

"That is a new feature, then. Continue, please."

"There is to be an execution. In the garden." A fleeting smile crossed the Countess's lovely face. "I need not tell you that that is not where the executions are held; but it does not seem strange to me when I dream.

"I have been away, I think, and have only just heard of what is to take place. I rush into the garden. The man Baron H_____ calls the Dream-Master is there, tied to the trunk of the big cherry tree; a squad of soldiers faces him, holding their rifles; their officer stands beside them with his saber drawn, and my husband is watching from a pace or two away. I call out for them to stop, and my husband turns to look at me. I say: 'You must not do it, Karl. You must not kill this man.' But I see by his expression that he believes that I am only a foolish, tenderhearted child. Karl is...several years older than I."

"I am aware of it."

"The Dream-Master turns his head to look at me. People tell me that my eyes are large—do you think them large, monsieur?"

"Very large, and very beautiful."

"In my dream, quite suddenly, his eyes seem far, far larger than mine, and far more beautiful; and in them I see reflected the figure of my husband. Please listen carefully now, because what I am going to say is very important, though it makes very little sense, I am afraid."

"Anything may happen in a dream, Countess."

"When I see my husband reflected in this man's eyes, I know—I cannot say how—that it is this reflection, and not the man who stands near me, who is the real Karl. The man I have thought real is only a reflection of that reflection. Do you follow what I say?"

I nodded. "I believe so."

"I plead again: 'Do not kill him. Nothing good can come of it...' My husband nods to the officer, the soldiers raise their rifles, and...and..."

"You wake. Would you like my handkerchief, Countess? It is of coarse weave; but it is clean, and much larger than your own."

"Karl is right—I am only a foolish little girl. No, monsieur, I do not wake—not yet. The soldiers fire. The Dream-Master falls forward, though his bonds hold him to the tree. And Karl flies to bloody rags beside me."

On my way back to the hotel I purchased a map of the city; and when I reached my room I laid it flat on the table there. There could be no question of the route of the Countess's glass coach—straight down the Hauptstrasse, the only street in the city wide enough to take a carriage surrounded by cavalrymen. The most probable route by which Herr R_____ might go from his house to his bank coincided with the Hauptstrasse for several blocks. The path Fräulein A_____ would travel from her flat to the arcade crossed the Hauptstrasse at a point contained by that interval. I need to know no more.

Very early the next morning I took up my post at the intersection. If my man were still alive after the fusillade Count von V_____ fired at him each night, it seemed certain that he would appear at this spot within a few days, and I am hardened to waiting. I smoked cigarettes while I watched the citizens of I_____ walk up and down before me. When an hour had passed, I bought a newspaper from a vendor, and stole a few glances at its pages when foot traffic was light.

Gradually I became aware that I was watched—we boast of reason, but there are senses over which reason holds no authority. I did not know where my watcher was, yet I felt his gaze on me, whichever way I turned. So, I thought, you know me, my friend. Will I too dream now? What has attracted your attention to a mere foreigner, a stranger, waiting for who-knows-what at this corner? Have you been talking to Fräulein A_____? Or to someone who has spoken to her?

Without appearing to do so, I looked up and down both streets in search of another lounger like myself. There was no one—not a drowsing grandfather, not a woman or a child, not even a dog. Certainly no tall man with a forked beard and piercing eyes. The windows then—I studied them all, looking for some movement in a dark room behind a seemingly innocent opening. Nothing.

Only the buildings behind me remained. I crossed to the opposite side of the Hauptstrasse and looked once more. Then I laughed.

They must have thought me mad, all those dour burghers, for I fairly doubled over, spitting my cigarette to the sidewalk and clasping my hands to my waist for fear my belt would burst. The presumption, the impudence, the brazen insolence of the fellow! The stupidity, the wonderful stupidity of myself, who had not recognized his old stories! For the remainder of my life now, I could accept any case with pleasure, pursue the most inept criminal with zest, knowing that there was always a chance he might outwit such an idiot as I.

For the Dream-Master had set up His own picture, and full-length, and in the most gorgeous colors, in His window. Choking and sputtering I saluted it, and then, still filled with laughter, I crossed the street once more and went inside, where I knew I would find Him. A man awaited me there—not the one I sought, but one who understood Whom it was I had come for, and knew as well as I that His capture was beyond any thief-taker's power. I knelt, and there, though not to the satisfaction I suppose of Baron H_____, Fräulein A_____, Herr R_____, and the Count and the Countess von V_____, I destroyed the Dream-Master as He has been sacrificed so often, devouring His white, wheaten flesh that we might all possess life without end.

Dear people, dream on.

ACKNOWLEDGMENTS

Many thanks to fellow super-storytellers Camille Alexa, Paul Di Filippo, Jim Kelly, Joe Lansdale, James Lowder, Dick Lupoff, John McNally, and Chris Roberson. Thanks also to Christopher Yates for allowing me to consult his superhero fiction index.

ABOUT THE EDITOR

Claude Lalumière (lostmyths.net/claude) is the author of several superhero stories, including "Hochelaga and Sons," "Spiderkid," and "Destroyer of Worlds," which were gathered in his debut collection *Objects of Worship* (ChiZine Publications 2009); "Let Evil Beware!" which served as chapter two of his mosaic novella *The Door to Lost Pages* (ChiZine Publications 2011); and "The Weirdo Adventures of Steve Rand" in the anthology *Tesseracts 15: A Case of Quite Curious Tales* (Edge 2011).

He has edited or co-edited eleven previous anthologies, including, with Camille Alexa, the all-Canadian, all-original superhero anthology *Masked Mosaic: Canadian Super Stories* (Tyche Books 2013).

With Rupert Bottenberg, Claude is the co-creator of the multimedia cryptomythology project, Lost Myths (lostmyths.net).

Originally from Montreal, Claude now enjoys a nomadic life.